<WATCH, RIGAT. WATCH AND LISTEN.>

The familiar predawn hush had settled over the forest. Although the sky overhead had lightened to charcoal, the shaft of moonlight in which the fox stood was as brilliant as ever. The fox's brush lashed again, and the moonlight rippled like someone drawing a finger across the still surface of a pool. As Rigat rose to his knees, the shaft of moonlight split open. But instead of the trunks of pines, he found himself staring at the back of a man in a long robe.

Again, the thick brush moved, more lazily this time. The gap widened, as if two unseen hands had grasped the edges of the white light and were slowly pulling them apart. There were dozens of people, he realized, gathered in a circle. Peering between their bodies, he spied a dark, gaping pit.

A red-robed priest in a feathered cloak raised his staff. Although the man had to be forty paces away, Rigat could clearly see the black markings zigzagging down its sinuous length, the painted red eyes that stared skyward, even the grain of the wood. His eyesight had always been keen, but this was impossible. It took him a moment to realize that the staff looked like a giant adder.

<VERY GOOD, RIGAT.>

As one, the people began to chant. The language was unfamiliar, but Rigat was certain the meaning of the words lay just beneath the surface of his consciousness. Determined to see more, he pushed himself to his feet and took a cautious step forward.

A man's head jerked toward him. He shouted something unintelligible. The chanting faltered. More heads turned. People gaped at him, some frozen in shock, others pointing. Fingers flew as they made signs across their chests, all the while jabbering in their tongue.

Guards converged around a black-haired girl on the far side of the circle. Another spun toward him, spear upraised. Before Rigat could do more than open his mouth, the spear arced toward him.

BARBARA CAMPBELL'S
Trickster's Game Series:

HEARTWOOD (Book One)
BLOODSTONE (Book Two)
FOXFIRE (Book Three)

FOXFIRE

Trickster's Game #3

BARBARA CAMPBELL

DAW BOOKS, INC.

DONALD A. WOLLHEIM, FOUNDER

375 Hudson Street, New York, NY 10014

ELIZABETH R. WOLLHEIM
SHEILA E. GILBERT
PUBLISHERS

http://www.dawbooks.com

First Printing, February 2009
1 2 3 4 5 6 7 8 9

DAW TRADEMARK REGISTERED
U.S. PAT. AND TM. OFF. AND FOREIGN COUNTRIES
—MARCA REGISTRADA
HECHO EN U.S.A.

PRINTED IN THE USA

Acknowledgments

The gang at The Never-Ending Odyssey 2006 for critiquing the opening chapters, with special thanks to Jennifer Brinn, Geoffrey Jacoby, and Susan Winston.

Robin Fitzsimmons Meng, L.M. Prieto, and Michael Samerdyke for wading through the first draft and providing terrific feedback.

Rita Oakes and Jason Ridler for pointing me to resources on ancient battle tactics.

Susan Herner, my friend and loyal agent.

Sheila Gilbert, the best editor a writer could ever have. Her questions, comments, and suggestions were invaluable and helped make *Foxfire* a much stronger story.

And finally, my husband David Lofink. He's been living with these characters for seven years—and with me for twenty-five. He read countless drafts, offered vital input on characters and plot, and even kept a straight face when I bought a gift for my protagonist at a craft fair. His love and faith and support sustain me—in writing and in life—and I dedicate the final book of *Trickster's Game* to him.

To learn more about the *Trickster's Game* trilogy, visit my Web site: www.barbara-campbell.com.

PART ONE

He is the fox that stalks its prey on silent paws.
The weasel that sheds its summer coat for winter white.
He is the jackdaw that scolds in the treetops
And the snake that slithers through the grass.
No man shall see his true form.
No woman shall know his heart.
Honor him.
Praise him.
And pray that your paths never cross.

—Song of the Trickster

Chapter 1

THE SUDDEN STAB of fear stole Keirith's breath.

He told himself that his father's head might be bowed in prayer, that the splayed legs simply meant he was dozing. But when his father failed to respond to his call, fear swamped him.

He scrambled up the hillside. Clumsy in his haste, he tripped. Pebbles skittered through the grass, clicking against each other like bones. When he straightened and found his father watching him, he breathed a shaky prayer of thanks and continued climbing.

A gust of wind tugged at his woolen mantle, and he shivered. As a boy, cold had never bothered him, but Xevhan had grown up in the sun-baked plains of Zheros, and his body still seemed to resent the brisk springs of the north.

Not his body. Mine.

Even after fourteen years, he sometimes slipped.

He clambered onto the ledge and sat beside his father. The hill blocked the worst of the wind, but even with the warm slab of rock at his back, he hugged his knees to his chest.

"Did your mam send you?"

"Nay. I just thought I'd enjoy this fine afternoon with you."

His father smiled and closed his eyes. "You're a terrible liar."

"And you're stubborn as a rock."

His father's smile widened. Keirith smiled, too. Then he remembered his duty. "It's a steep climb. You know Mam worries."

"Your mam's a born worrier. Like you. Besides, I like it up here."

"Surveying your kingdom, mighty chief?"

Without opening his eyes, his father smacked him on the knee. "Disrespectful pup."

"Cantankerous old man."

His father shrugged, unrepentant.

They sat in companionable silence. Only here—away from the hill fort, alone with his father—was Keirith truly content. Although the tribe seemed to accept his appearance and his power, the gulf would always exist. He was a fisherman with a shaman's gift of touching spirits. A child of the Oak and Holly who had taken the body of a Zherosi priest. The man who had been cast out of his tribe for his crime against nature.

In the last two years, he'd learned to expect the reactions when newcomers learned this tawny-skinned, dark-eyed man was the eldest son of the great Darak Spirit-Hunter: confusion or surprise from the refugees who hadn't heard the story, suspicion or fear from those who had. All received the traditional night of hospitality, but only those who accepted him were permitted to stay longer.

His father's hand came down on his knee again, this time in a silent question.

"You're right," Keirith said. "Mam is a worrier."

His father accepted the half-truth with a nod. He didn't need to press. Their spirits had dwelled together in one body. They had shared each other's deepest fears and darkest thoughts. And the bond created during that perilous time had only grown stronger in the intervening years.

Keirith shot him a sour look. "You know it's a pure pain in the arse sometimes."

His father laughed. "It's not like I always know what you're thinking."

"But you always know when I'm . . . troubled."

"I've only to look at your face to know that." His father hesitated, then asked, "Is it your mam? Or . . . Rigat?"

"Rigat? Why? Has something happened?"

"Not today."

Observing his father's grimace, Keirith quickly changed the subject. "How was the council meeting?"

His father shrugged and traced a sparkling vein of quartz with his thumb. So now it was Fa's turn to elude and his to pursue.

Suppressing a grin, Keirith pulled off his mantle and draped it around his father. "No wonder you look so tired," he said, his voice oozing solicitude. "Now you just rest a bit and—"

His father cursed genially and flung the mantle back. "Can't an old man have any fun?"

"Nay. Tell me."

"Well. The elders agreed that we needed to clear more land."

Keirith curbed his impatience. Even before Temet brought the last group of refugees to their valley, they could barely grow enough barley to sustain them. One bad harvest meant the difference between starvation and survival.

"And," his father continued, drawing out the tale, "they agreed that the lower slope of the eastern hill was the best place."

Again, a foregone conclusion. On every side of the valley, hills plunged down to the lake. The few strips of arable land were already under cultivation, and the hilltops were too exposed.

Try as he might, his father couldn't hide his satisfaction. In fact, he looked so smug that Keirith knew the council had approved their plan.

He had gotten the idea from the Zherosi holy city. If the Zherosi could build low walls of rubble to keep the earth from sliding into the sea, why couldn't their tribe construct terraces to keep the rain from washing away the newly sprouted barley?

"It'll be brutal work hauling the rocks," his father said. "I'd give the rest of my fingers for a couple of bullocks."

Bullocks—like level ground for planting—were a thing of the past. Breaking the rocky soil with foot plows was arduous enough; leveraging the boulders would test the strength and willpower of the strongest men.

"It'll work, Fa. I know it will."

"I told them it was your idea."

"And they still voted for it?"

Although he had kept his voice light, his father gave him a sharp look. "There was the usual discussion. But not half so bad as the business about the name."

With their village comprised of refugees from many different tribes, dissension was inevitable. It had taken a full year to agree on the name Alder Tribe. But a new name could not change old allegiances; Keirith still considered himself a member of the Oak Tribe that had cast him out.

Hircha and his family had chosen to share his exile from Eagles Mount. It had taken two moons to reach this remote upland valley, their progress slowed by six-year-old Callum and the three sheep. It was a welcome haven after their long journey, but the only trees for miles were the alders that lined both banks of the stream.

Still, there was a stark beauty to the rolling moors. At Midsummer, the fragrance of gorse sweetened the air. In autumn, the hills blazed with the scarlet fire of bracken. If the tiny lake froze solid in the winter, it provided amusement for the children who greased their shoes with tallow and slid across it, squealing and laughing. If the stream was small enough to jump across, its pools were rich with trout, and the cheerful splash of its water soothed the spirit during the harsh winters.

His father's gaze shifted south to the distant blue-green blur of pine-covered hills. Longing softened the lines on his face carved by age and worry and years of squinting against sunlight and bitter winds.

"Who'd have thought I'd end my days so far from the forest," he mused. Before Keirith could reply, he added, "Do you miss the old days? When it was just us?"

Relieved to abandon thoughts of his father's mortality, Keirith said, "Oh, aye. I'd love to live in a damp cave again. With three sheep. And a screaming babe."

"That was only the first winter. And I'll not have you say anything against the sheep."

Keirith noticed he didn't include Rigat in his protest.

"Old Dugan served us well," his father said. "Nearly broke my heart when we lost him."

Callie had named the irascible ram after their mam's uncle. He had wept when Dugan died and refused to eat a bite of the meat. Not that he'd missed much, tough and stringy as it was.

"Young Dugan's a fine breeder," Keirith said.

"But he just doesn't have the same spirit. It seems more an obligation to him than a pleasure. When Old Dugan chased after a ewe, his eyes would roll and his tongue would hang out and those great black ballocks of his would swing back and forth like waterskins."

The wistfulness in his father's voice made Keirith laugh. "And all these years I thought it was your heroic deeds that won Mam's heart. When really you were chasing her through the First Forest with your tongue hanging out."

His father's hand shot out to cuff him. Keirith accepted it with good grace, but his mood darkened as he considered the question again. "I do miss when it was just us. And the village at Eagles Mount."

Before I tore it apart.

"That's an old battle," his father said, responding to the thought rather than the words. "Let it go."

"Like you have?"

That stubborn look came over his father's face. He and Conn called it The Obstinate Scowl, a tribute to the gestures and expressions they had named when they returned from their vision quests and were desperately trying to mimic what they considered manly behavior.

Conn. Another painful subject.

"For years, you accused Gortin of holding a grudge," Keirith said. "But you're doing the same with Elasoth."

"It's different."

"Because Gortin was wrong and you're right."

"Aye! Besides, Gortin never thought I caused Struath's death. He just couldn't bear to hear me criticize him. Elasoth voted to cast you out of the tribe."

"Fourteen years ago! If I've forgiven him, why can't you?"

"Aye. Well. I'm stubborn as a rock." His father's expression softened. "And you're a better man than I am."

"Oh, Fa . . ."

"I could forgive him for voting against me. But not my child."

No point in reminding him that he was a grown man now. His father would always look upon him as his child, to be protected against any threat. "This is our place," he had told the thirty-five survivors from their old village when they straggled into the valley two years ago. "It was our sweat, our hands, our bodies that made a home here. Those who stay, stay on my terms."

And the terms were clear: to accept him as chief, his daughter as a hunter, and his firstborn son's gift of touching spirits.

Although Keirith knew some people still feared his power, others had benefited from it: Duba whom he had brought back from years of silence after the death of her son; little Luimi whose silent cries of terror sent him racing to the deep pool into which she had stumbled. In truth, he used his gift so infrequently that most would have forgotten it were it not for his swarthy skin and dark eyes. But his father was always watching, always listening, fearful that someone would turn on him again.

Observing his anxious gaze, Keirith said, "You're right. These are old battles. And we need to save our strength for new ones."

"You've Seen something?"

"Not since the last vision. But I'm sure she's safe."

His father's mouth tightened. He rarely spoke of Faelia, but Keirith often found him at this spot, gazing south as if he expected to see her striding over the hills. Hoping to ease his fears, Keirith had used his power more often this last moon, calling on Natha, the adder who was his spirit guide and vision mate. But even with Natha's help, he had found Faelia only once, sitting in a forest clearing with Temet and his band of rebels.

His visions gave him glimpses of the world beyond their valley, fleeting images of villages abandoned, forests razed, men dragging logs onto the great ships that carried them south to Zheros. He had hoped his visions would show him Hua, but the boy whose spirit he had healed so many years ago seemed as lost to him now as the dream of creating a spirit-linked network of communication among the tribes.

Gazing over their valley, the disturbing visions seemed unreal. Children raced to greet a returning band of hunters. Girls carried bulging waterskins up from the lake. Only the hill fort that crowned the highest promontory testified to the danger that lurked beyond.

"Will it last?" his father asked quietly.

The westering sun bathed the hill fort in warm, golden light. Clumps of greening moor grass studded the earthworks. If not for the thin curls of smoke drifting up from the huts, no one would guess that a village lay behind that carefully constructed wall of earth.

"We're more than one hundred strong," he finally said, "but half are children and old folk. If the Zherosi come in force—"

"I know we can't stand against them. I'm asking if they *will* come."

It was the first time his father had ever admitted the possibility. Lacking the oaks and pines the Zherosi coveted and navigable waterways to float the logs to the sea, there was little here to tempt them. But Keirith's gaze lingered on the hills to the west where the two peaks they had named The Twins protected the pass. Sentinels stood silhouetted against clouds striped rose and gold from Bel's dying rays. Day and night, they kept watch, every man and woman between the ages of thirteen and fifty taking a turn.

"Urkiat once compared them to a lightning strike," his father said. His voice was just a little too casual; even after fourteen years, it was hard for either of them to discuss Urkiat.

"Lightning strikes just happen," Keirith reminded him. "The Zherosi plan everything." Including the rape of a land and the annihilation of a people.

"He also said it would take every man, woman, and child in the tribes to stand against them."

The same words Temet repeated each time he came to the village to beg Fa to join the rebellion.

His father sighed. "I just keep going round and round and coming up with the same answers. If we attack their fortresses, we'll provoke reprisals. If we wait . . ."

For twelve years, they had lived in total isolation. Since then, each new wave of refugees brought news of the outside world and each time, the news was grimmer. The Zherosi were pushing east. The twice-yearly tribal Gatherings had been suspended. Some tribes bought peace with a tribute of pelts. Others even countenanced the destruction of the forests. A few fought back, most in scattered bands like Temet's, but the tribes were as likely to betray the rebels as aid them, for their villages paid the price in steeper tribute or summary executions.

Keirith eyed the thumbs drumming an agitated tattoo on his father's thighs. "I'm sorry, Fa. I wish I had the answers you need."

"And I wish . . ."

"What?"

"Nothing."

"Tell me."

For a long moment, his father studied him. "I was remembering how you flew with the eagle all those years ago. And wishing you could do that now. Fly over the mountains and spy out the land for us."

Fourteen years and still he could recall every moment of that brief flight and the welter of emotions that had accompanied it. The exultation of finally overcoming the eagle's wariness. The terror of those first giddy moments when they soared, spirit-linked, over Eagles Mount. And the wonder of seeing the world in a way he had only dreamed.

With an effort, Keirith kept his voice calm. "I gave Gortin my oath."

"I know."

"I promised I would never—"

"I know!"

Then why bring it up? Why remind me of what I can never have?

"I'm sorry, Son. I shouldn't have said anything."

"It's all right. It was a long time ago."

He fought the urge to keep talking, to share the memories. Like picking at an unhealed scab. He had always thought the ache was akin to the dull throb his father sometimes complained of in the stumps of his severed fingers. Or the twinges his mam got when the joint-ill stiffened her hands and made it hard for her to mix her healing brews.

Everyone had wounds—of the body and the spirit. Some were just slower to heal than others.

And some never heal.

Because concern etched deeper lines in his father's face and because he trusted him more than anyone in the world, Keirith said, "It's hard. Harder than I expected. To give it up. The way you felt, I suppose, when you stopped being a hunter."

"Then talk to Gortin. Get him to release you from your oath."

"What I did was forbidden. Have you forgotten that?"

"Nay. Nor have I forgotten that I lost fifteen years of my life trying to be something I wasn't. Gortin knows you would never use the power to hurt any creature."

He thought of Xevhan whom he had killed. And Urkiat whose death he had caused, even if it had been his father's hand that drove the dagger home. Flying with the eagle was a pleasure he didn't deserve.

Faint shouts from the village saved him from answering. With a muttered curse, his father pushed himself to his feet, ignoring the hand Keirith thrust out to help him.

As they started down the slope, Keirith said, "It can't be strangers. The sentinels would have blown their horns. . . ."

He glanced over his shoulder and found his father standing perfectly still, one fist pressed against his chest and a distant expression on his face, as if he were listening to voices only he could hear.

"Fa?"

"I just got up too quickly." His father took a careful breath, then smiled. "You can let go of my arm now. Before you twist it off."

Keirith relaxed his fingers, but kept a grip on his father's arm as they made their way down the slope. As they started up the rise to the hill fort, his father's breathing grew labored, but when they neared the top, he fell into the long, loose-limbed stride his mam liked to compare to a wolf on the prowl. Keirith thought of it as his "chief's gait"—purposeful and calm. Combined with his height, it gave him an air of authority few would contest. At another moment, he might have teased his father, but now he simply doubled his pace to keep up.

"Don't tell your mother," his father said quietly. Without waiting for him to agree, he strode through the narrow break in the earthworks and into the village.

The crowd was already drifting away, old folk shaking their heads and muttering, mothers shooing children into their huts for supper. When Keirith saw his brother's bright red hair, he suppressed a groan.

Clearly, the dispute had something to do with the doe lying on the ground before Gortin and Nemek. Two arrows protruded from her side. Their owners glared at each other. Mam dabbed Rigat's nose with a blood-spattered cloth, while Madig, Rothisar, and Jadan stood behind Seg, shoulder to broad shoulder. The three hunters were so inseparable that Faelia had once speculated sourly that they probably pissed in unison.

His father surveyed the scene dispassionately. "What happened here?"

Although he had addressed his question to Gortin, Madig stepped forward to stand at Seg's side. "Just a quarrel over which of them has the right to claim the kill. Nothing to concern yourself with. Alder-Chief."

The hesitation was just long enough to be noticeable. Madig had been chief of his tribe, and although he served on the council of elders, it still stung him that the title belonged to another.

Keirith's father eyed the two arrows. "Neither shot would have been a clean kill. But you don't need me to tell you that."

"Nay."

"So why was there a quarrel?"

"We were hunting together," Rothisar said, then glanced quickly at Madig who gave an almost imperceptible nod. "Except Rigat, that is. Seg spotted the doe and signaled us. We let him draw first. 'Twas his right. And then . . ."

"Rigat pushed me!" Seg exclaimed.

"I was twenty paces away," Rigat retorted.

His father regarded Rigat for a long moment before his gaze swung back to Seg.

"I felt it, Alder-Chief. I know it sounds crazy, but . . ." Seg spat. "Who else would have done it?"

"He still got off a shot as the doe bolted," Madig said, clearly proud of his son's achievement. "And 'twas that shot brought her down."

Keirith silently willed his brother to look at him. When Rigat gave a small, cool shrug, Keirith quelled the urge to walk over and shake him. Perhaps his frustration showed, for Rigat's cockiness vanished, replaced by the same pleading expression their mam wore.

After a few more questions, Keirith's father said. "I'm not denying what you felt, Seg. Nor can I explain it. A hunt . . .

well, it's always a mystery, isn't it? Every sense pitched so keen you think you'll snap in two. I've always imagined it must be similar to a shaman having a vision, but I'm a man with no magic, so you'll forgive me, Tree-Father."

A quick smile for Gortin, a self-deprecating shrug. Around the circle, heads nodded. Even Madig smiled, for like all the hunters, he understood the mystery, too. Poor Gortin merely looked confused. These days, his old mentor often was.

"Whatever happened, the credit for the kill belongs to both of you." He waited long enough to receive nods from all the men before adding, "Rigat. Seg. Clasp hands."

"Nay!"

Keirith's stomach churned as his father turned slowly toward Rigat.

"He had no right to accuse me. He's just jealous because I'm a better hunter."

With a bellow of outrage, Seg launched himself at Rigat, only to be yanked back by his father. "You see how it is?" Madig demanded.

Fa nodded without taking his eyes off Rigat. "A good hunter doesn't need to boast about his skills. Or belittle the abilities of others."

Rigat opened his mouth to reply, but closed it again when Mam tugged on his arm.

"Clasp hands. Now."

Keirith winced. Some men shouted when they were angry. His father became very cold and very quiet.

Madig shoved Seg forward. Mam pushed Rigat. Their fingers met in a fleeting touch. Both boys were turning away when his father said, "You can put your energy to better use than fighting. Go to the lake and fetch water for every family. And at every hut, you will apologize for disturbing the peace of this village."

Seg glanced at Madig, who gave him a sour nod. Rigat glowered, but even he knew better than to defy Fa twice. Without a word, he strode toward their hut.

"Tree-Father. Memory-Keeper." His father acknowledged Gortin and Nemek with a small, formal bow before turning back to Seg. "You're going to be as fine a hunter as your father."

A rare smile lit Seg's face. "Thank you, Alder-Chief."

Madig punched him lightly on the arm as Rothisar and Jadan hefted the doe onto his shoulders. Seg staggered a little, but bore the doe proudly through the earthworks.

Nemek offered his father a sympathetic smile as he walked away. Gortin just stood there, muttering to himself. Then Othak stepped forward and touched him lightly on the shoulder. Still muttering, Gortin let Othak lead him toward the hut they shared, one hand clutching his blackthorn staff, the other clinging to Othak's arm.

Mam was gnawing her upper lip, a sure sign of distress. Her mouth went still as Rigat emerged from their hut with two waterskins slung over his shoulder. After a quick glance at Fa, he strode off, red head high, pointed chin thrust out.

"I'll talk to him," Keirith said.

His father nodded once as he walked toward Mam. The chief's confident gait was gone. Now he moved like a tired old man.

Of all the gifts Rigat possessed, the greatest seemed to be the power to destroy their parents' happiness.

Keirith loitered at the lake, helping Elasoth and Adinn repair the fishing nets. While his fingers tied on new stone sinkers and replaced broken strands of nettle-rope, his eyes followed Rigat, who scampered back and forth to the hill fort with a zeal that belied his earlier defiance. His moods had always been as changeable as the weather in spring, but he seemed positively cheerful now, reveling in his ability to complete his task before Seg.

The sun had dipped behind The Twins when Rigat made his way back to the lake yet again. But instead of refilling his waterskins, he veered west, following the shoreline to the stream. With a sigh, Keirith rose and followed him.

For years, he had been aware of Rigat's power, but he had yet to determine its full extent. He had forced himself to talk about his gift, hoping it would encourage his brother to confide in him. But even as a child, Rigat had evaded his questions, offering either plausible explanations or wide-eyed looks of confusion. After the refugees arrived, he'd warned Rigat about careless displays of power. Until today, his brother had obeyed.

He pushed through the tangle of alders, cursing as low-hanging branches snagged his mantle. The swollen stream cascaded over the rocks, obscuring all sounds except his undignified crashing through the underbrush. Pale shafts of light filtered through the leafless branches, but he still missed Rigat at first. Then he spotted the faint gleam of his hair and discovered him sitting on a rock. He picked his way along the muddy bank until he stood over him.

Without looking up, Rigat asked, "Is Mam very upset?"

"What do you think?"

Even in the dim light, he could see Rigat wince. "And Fa?"

"He's . . . disappointed."

When Rigat winced again, Keirith felt a pang of sympathy. Fa had smacked Faelia's bottom as a child, and once—only once—taken his belt to Rigat. Keirith wondered if he realized that all of them would have preferred physical punishment to his silent disapproval.

Fastidious as always, his brother had cleaned the last traces of blood from his face. Thankfully, his nose was only a little swollen. Keirith tweaked it gently and squatted beside him, staring up into the face that could be so expressive one moment and the next, a mask.

"I didn't mean to cause so much trouble."

Keirith had rarely heard such misery in his brother's voice. He offered an encouraging nod, recalling that moment of anger so many years ago when he had "pushed" Fa. He hadn't meant to do that either. Or invade his spirit. The power had just poured out of him, as wild as the stream after the spring thaw. He shuddered, recalling his father's inarticulate terror echoing inside of him, then pulled his mantle closer, pretending it was just a chill.

"Was it like the time you pushed Faelia?" he asked.

Rigat's eyes widened, just as they had all those years ago. Before he could deny it, Keirith said, "Tell me how you do it."

Rigat hesitated. "I don't know. I just . . . push. With my mind. And it happens."

"How long have you been able to do this?"

"As long as I can remember."

He must have failed to hide his dismay. For the first time, Rigat looked frightened. "Is that bad?"

"Nay." When he had told Gortin about flying with the eagle, the Tree-Father's horror had terrified him. He refused to scare Rigat that way.

"You've had your power since you were little," Rigat said.

"Aye."

"But mine's . . . different. Isn't it?"

"I don't know. Tell me what else you can do."

After another hesitation, Rigat said, "I used to talk to Old Dugan. That was fun. At first. Sheep are pretty boring."

"You . . . talked to him?"

"Not like we're talking now. It was more like seeing things. And feeling things. The way he could see and feel them. Like if I wanted to talk about how noisy the stream is, I'd picture the water and hear the different parts of the song and—"

"The song?"

"You know. The roaring where the water pours over the boulders and the foamy hiss when it reaches the pool and the little gurgle when it tumbles between the rocks."

Rigat spoke impatiently, as if anyone with ears should be able to hear the stream's song. His description reminded Keirith of how he had communicated with the adders in Zheros. But he had needed Natha's help for that; Rigat simply concentrated.

"So you touched Dugan's spirit," Keirith said.

"What's wrong with that? Tree-Father Gortin touches spirits. So do you."

"People's spirits. Animals can't give us permission. They'd be frightened if we invaded them."

"Dugan wasn't frightened. And I wasn't invading him."

Unwilling to argue, Keirith asked, "What else can you do?"

Rigat looked away. "Feel people's spirits. Without touching them," he added quickly. "It's like there's this little flame around them. And each one's different. I think that's why I never got lost when I was little and went exploring. I'd just concentrate on Mam and I'd feel her and I could always find my way home." Rigat hesitated and shot him a quick glance.

"And?"

"And . . . I can shape things."

"What kind of things? How?"

Rigat just stared at the stream. The intensity of his expression pulled Keirith's gaze toward the water as well.

Small enough to hold in his hand, the stag was perfectly formed from the tines of its antlers to the water dripping off its hooves. It bounded toward them and froze in midair. Then it dissolved into the foam, spraying them with a fine mist.

Keirith could feel Rigat's gaze, but the magic left him speechless.

"Earth's easiest to work with," Rigat explained, "but water's not too bad. Fire's harder. I can't do much of anything with air."

"Why didn't you tell us? Before?"

Rigat blew out his breath in exasperation. "I'm not stupid. I saw the way Mam and Fa looked at me when I did something. Like they were scared."

The same way they had looked at him when they learned about his powers. Only then, their anxiety was leavened by anger because he had kept his gift a secret.

"You hid your gift, too," Rigat reminded him.

Keirith frowned. He expected to have moments of unspoken communication with his father, but sometimes Rigat seemed to possess that same ability of knowing what people were thinking. Was that another aspect of his power or was he simply as skilled at reading a person's expression as he was at conjuring animals out of water?

"Aye, I hid my gift," Keirith finally said. "But that was a mistake. If I'd told Gortin—"

"They'd have cast you out that much quicker. People are scared of things they don't understand. And they don't like people who are different. That's why they hate me."

"Seg's a bully. And he *is* jealous of—"

"Not just Seg. All of them."

"They don't—"

"I try!" Rigat blurted. "I hide my power, and I'm polite to the old folk, and I do my share of the work. More than my share. I even tried to be friends with Seg in the beginning. But nothing helps. They all know something's wrong with me. They just can't figure out what."

Keirith seized Rigat's shoulders. "There is nothing wrong with you. You can't help it if you have a gift. But you *can* learn to use it wisely. And to control your temper. What were you thinking? Defying Fa in front of the whole tribe."

"I didn't mean to. The 'nay' just popped out. I couldn't back down after that or everyone would have thought I was a coward."

"So it's better to have them think you're a willful child?"

Rigat's head jerked up, blue eyes blazing. This time, though, he bit back the retort. As Keirith watched, the fire slowly died.

"I wished they'd never come," Rigat muttered. "It was better when it was just us."

"In some ways. But remember how many winters we came close to starving? How Mam worried every time Fa or Faelia went hunting?"

"I know we need them. I just wish we didn't." Before Keirith could reply, he asked, "Doesn't it ever bother you? That you should be Tree-Father after Gortin instead of Othak?"

"You know I can't—"

"Your casting out happened ages ago."

Keirith almost smiled; to a boy of thirteen, the events that occurred before his birth must seem like ancient history.

"What matters," Rigat continued, "is the power. Everybody knows you have it. And you use it. Sometimes. So why—?"

"I cannot be Tree-Father."

Rigat studied him for a long moment. "Why are you afraid of it? Because it's . . . bad?"

"Magic isn't good or bad. It's how people use it." He felt like a child reciting his lessons.

"But if someone has power, there must be a reason."

He'd wondered about that so often over the years, desperately seeking an explanation for his kidnap and rape and casting out. To destroy the Zherosi? The earthquake had done more damage than he had. To discover his path as a healer of spirits? But he'd helped only a few people. To save his father's life? Aye, perhaps that was the reason. Who else could help the children of the Oak and Holly withstand the Zherosi?

Perhaps anyone with determination and sensitivity could tap into magic. Or perhaps burdening some mortals with power was simply a cruel joke of the gods.

"I think we're like Fa and Tinnean," Rigat said, jolting him out of his thoughts. "We're brothers, too. I'm a hunter like Fa. And you wanted to be a shaman like Tinnean. It took both of them to save the world. So maybe it'll take both of us to do . . . something."

"Like what?"

Rigat eyed him suspiciously, seeking the hidden barb. Apparently satisfied none existed, he said, "I don't know. But it can't be an accident that we both have power. It must mean we're supposed to do something important."

"Like pushing Seg?"

"All right. That was stupid."

"And selfish."

"I know, I know."

"You don't know!"

Keirith rose and stalked away. Talking about his power always made him uneasy, but he had to put aside his discomfort and help his brother understand.

"I loved the power, too. I could do things no other boy in the village could. Maybe things no other boy in the world could. I felt . . ."

"Like a god."

At his sharp look, Rigat's eager expression became uncertain. "Aye," Keirith admitted. "But I'm not a god. And neither are you. Our power should be used for helping people, not for stupid pranks. Suppose when you pushed Seg he'd loosed his arrow and hit one of the other hunters. Did you think of that?"

Rigat hung his head. "I won't do it again. I promise." Then he grinned. "But you should have seen his face. He whirled around like there was a demon behind him."

"Instead of one behind the gorse." But Keirith had to

smile, too. It was hard to stay angry with Rigat for long. Then his smile faded. "You've got to tell Mam and Fa."

Even before he finished speaking, Rigat was on his feet. "Nay!"

"It'll be worse if something happens and they find out that way."

"Nothing will happen. I'll . . . I'll never use the power again."

Keirith just shook his head wearily. "Do you want me to talk to them?"

Rigat looked even more horrified. "Nay, I'll tell them. But not tonight. Not when they're already mad at me."

"Then when?"

"Soon."

"Rigat . . ."

"After my vision quest. And until then, I won't do anything bad. Please, Keirith."

He hesitated, torn between his desire to keep Rigat's trust and the memory of his parents' anger after Gortin revealed the truth about his powers. But Rigat's vision quest was only a few days away. Then everything would be out in the open. At least within the family.

Reluctantly, Keirith nodded. Rigat threw his arms around his neck and hugged him. It unnerved him that his baby brother was almost the same height as he.

As they walked back to the village, Rigat's analogy nagged at him. They did seem to be reliving the past, but instead of emulating the heroic deeds of their father and uncle, they were repeating the pattern of secrecy that had pitted their family against the rest of the tribe.

As Gheala rose over the hills to the east, Keirith silently entreated the moon goddess to illuminate his path—and Rigat's—in the days to come.

Chapter 2

G RIANE GRIMLY STABBED her needle through the doeskin patch on Callie's mantle.

"It'll be all right, Mam." Callie's anxious smile belied his words. "Rigat blows up fast, but he's always sorry later. In a few days, everyone will have forgotten what happened."

Except me. And Darak.

She looked up as pale light flooded the hut, but it was only Hircha, a withy basket over her arm. Those cool blue eyes assessed her, but all she said was, "Callie, can you take Conn's supper to him?"

Callie nodded and mumbled something unintelligible through a mouthful of stew.

Thank the gods the lambing would be over soon. Then Callie could return to his studies with Nemek and spend his evenings at home instead of shivering on the moors. With Ennit still recovering from the Freshening cough, the responsibility of minding the flock rested with Callie and Conn. Young Lorthan was still too inexperienced to be much help.

"I made extra nutcakes," Griane said.

Callie gingerly plucked one off the baking stone and tossed it back and forth between his fingers to cool it. "Remember that first batch Faelia made?" he asked with a grin.

"I remember you were supposed to make sure there weren't any shells," Hircha said very sweetly.

"I was only seven," Callie protested.

"And Darak's tooth doesn't bother him at all now," Hircha replied in the same sweet tone. "Unless he drinks something cold. Or chews on that side. Or—"

Laughing, Callie hurled the nutcake at Hircha, who batted it away. Griane's hand darted out to snag it. Every autumn, the young folk ventured south to scavenge nuts and berries, and to cut tree limbs for crafting weapons. For them, it was a pleasant change—very pleasant, judging from the crop of babies born the following summer. But it was their mothers who had the chore of grinding the acorns and pine nuts into flour; she wasn't about to lose a single cake in the bracken strewn on the dirt floor.

A stern glance made Callie lower a second nutcake. "Wrap them up," she told him. "Unless you want to bring crumbs to poor Conn. And don't forget the heather tea."

From autumn to spring, she kept a stone bowl simmering on the peat. The other brew she mixed once a sennight for Darak. Tonight, with the addition of the baking stone and the large pot containing the stew, the fire pit was so crowded it was a wonder anything was hot.

Again, the deerskin swung back. This time, Darak's large form blocked the faint rectangle of light.

"They're coming."

The momentary cheer vanished. Callie silently wrapped the nutcakes in nettle-cloth. Hircha shoved the pebble stopper into the flask of tea. Griane snatched up the discarded dipper to ladle Darak's warmed wine into a cup.

The bracken crackled as Darak sat beside the fire pit. From long experience, she watched his hands, which rested quietly on his thighs. Perhaps they would have a pleasant meal, after all.

She handed him the tonic of quickthorn berries and broom blossoms, then drew back with a startled exclamation. "Your fingers are freezing."

He gave her a tired smile. "Stop fussing."

Quelling the urge to do just the opposite, Griane lowered her head over her mending. Faelia's departure had aged him. Sometimes Griane had resented their closeness, but now that her daughter was gone, she missed her energy and fire, even—occasionally—her sharp tongue.

Maker, keep her safe.

If only Temet had agreed to remain in the village. But of course, he would never give up his cause. His passionate defense of the rebellion had drawn Faelia to him, despite the fact that he was closer to her father's age than hers.

Or perhaps, given Faelia's devotion to Darak, Temet's age only enhanced his allure.

A pity he had never gotten her with child. Clearly, the gods had other plans for Faelia.

Griane's bone needle fell still. She eyed the bunches of wildflowers hanging from the heather thatch, wondering if they had more to do with Faelia's inability to conceive than the gods. In her head, she heard Mother Netal's voice, tunelessly chanting the rhyme: *"Yarrow, tansy, ground-runner—three. Call the moon flow painlessly. Lacha, Gheala. Water and moon. Pluck the child from out the womb."*

Her strangled moan silenced the murmur of conversation. Muttering something about her clumsiness, she sucked the drop of blood from her thumb. With trembling fingers, she knotted the deer gut and cut the dangling thread of sinew. Then she handed the mantle to Callie, avoiding Hircha's gaze. In matters of healing, Griane always welcomed her assistant's keen perception and attentiveness; in matters of the heart, those same qualities were unnerving.

Hircha followed Callie out of the hut. Even after all these years, she favored her right leg. Xevhan had maimed her as surely as Morgath had maimed Darak. During their first moons of exile, Griane had feared that she was too scarred by her ordeals to make a new life with them. She had told her that no one could wipe out the past, only acknowledge it—for better or worse—and move on. She hadn't known then what long shadows the past could throw or how frightening the consequences could be.

It was just a foolish prank. It doesn't mean anything.

Griane heard Callie greet his brothers with his usual affection, then lower his voice, probably to warn Rigat about what he might expect inside. Hircha's greeting was cooler, but it was hard to tell much from that; she was always self-possessed. Keirith's reply was so stiff that Griane sighed.

They'll have to sort it out themselves. I can't worry about that, too.

Keirith held up the deerskin to allow Rigat to duck inside. As always, Rigat's gaze went first to her. She gave him an encouraging smile and received a halfhearted one in return. It fled as he faced Darak.

"I fetched water for every hut. As I was told." Water

sloshed in the skins as he held them up. "And I ask your forgiveness for disturbing the peace of the village."

Darak stared into his cup and nodded.

Say something. Don't make him beg.

"Give them to your mother."

Silently, Rigat picked his way around the fire pit and dropped the skins beside her. She touched his ankle, so vulnerable and white against the ruddy hide of his breeches. Again, their eyes met. Her heart clenched into a tight fist at the misery on his face. She reached for his hand, but he was already walking back to Darak.

"I'm sorry, Fa."

Darak nodded, still staring into his cup.

"I'll try to do better."

When Darak simply nodded again, Rigat reached for his leather belt. Impatiently, he yanked it from his waist and held it out.

"Beat me."

Darak's head jerked up. Griane pressed her lips together to stifle a cry.

Rigat was the only one of the children Darak had ever whipped. Darak had warned him more than once that he must never leave the valley alone, but that morning, he had wandered off again. When he finally returned, breathless with the excitement of having climbed one of The Twins, Darak ordered him out of the hut.

Four years ago now. It had been spring then, too. She could still recall the faint but discordant honking of geese between the rhythmic slap of leather on flesh. Ten blows, and she had flinched at each, her breath hissing in and out with her son's. Rigat was pale when they returned, but Darak had seemed more shaken.

As he did now.

Rigat finally broke the tense silence. "I don't mind. Well, I do," he added, wincing. "But I'd rather eat supper standing up than have you angry with me."

She caught her breath as Darak pushed himself to his feet and held out his hand. Swallowing hard, Rigat gave him the belt. Darak caressed the leather, but his eyes were on Rigat, who watched the slow movement of Darak's thumb as if mesmerized.

Abruptly, Darak thrust the belt at Rigat. "It won't make

me feel better. And it won't have any effect on you. So we might as well save my arm and your arse."

"Fa . . ."

"Take it."

For once, Rigat's hands were clumsy. It took several attempts before he managed to knot the belt around his waist.

"Look at me."

Reluctantly, Rigat met Darak's gaze.

"What am I to do with you?" Despite the frown creasing his forehead, Darak's voice was soft, almost musing.

"I'm sorry, Fa."

Darak was turning away when Rigat flung himself forward. His arms went around Darak's waist, fingers clenching the doeskin.

Darak's eyes closed. Slowly, his hands came up. He hugged Rigat so hard Griane could hear the breath wheeze out of him. And then Darak pulled free and backed away.

"Supper's getting cold."

For a moment, Rigat stood there, arms still outstretched, face still shining from his father's rare display of affection. Then the smile faded and his arms fell to his sides.

Rigat kept up a desperate stream of chatter during supper about where the blackcocks were displaying this season, the number of geese he'd seen flying north, the plan to build terraces—anything to avoid talking about what had happened with Seg.

After the meal was finished, he poured cold water into their bowls, dropped hot pebbles from the fire pit into each one, and vigorously scoured them with the heather brush, all the while plying Keirith with endless questions about fishing. Keirith—Maker bless him—tried to lighten the mood by telling stories of his first awkward attempts to spear a fish. Darak just hunched over his pile of flints, grimly chipping away at them with his hammerstone.

Seeing him squinting in the feeble light, Griane threw a handful of gorse twigs on the fire. A brief smile curved his mouth, but it faded as he studied Rigat.

Conscious of Darak's stare, Rigat's voice ran down. It

was Keirith who turned the conversation to Rigat's upcoming vision quest, Keirith who relived the dawn his adder had come to him. And Keirith who finally drew Darak into the conversation by asking him to tell the tale of his vision quest.

Darak's voice took on the dreamy cadence of the Memory-Keeper as he described the cold night the she-wolf howled his name. Rigat listened as intently as if it were the first time he'd heard the story.

"What animal do you think I'll find, Fa?"

"Hard to say. It's the animal that does the choosing."

"I hope I find a wolf like you."

"A wildcat would suit your temper better." Keirith's smile took any sting from the words. "Or a fox."

"Nay!" Griane exclaimed before she could help herself.

"What's wrong with a fox?" Rigat asked. "They're good hunters. Loyal to their mates. And clever."

Darak rose. "It's getting late. Time we were all in bed."

Keirith laid down the fishing spear he was sharpening and rubbed his neck. Rigat just stared at Darak.

"I'll make you proud, Fa."

Keirith saved Darak from answering. "You'll make us all proud. But you heard Fa. It's late. And you'll need to be up before dawn if you're going hunting."

As Keirith guided him firmly to the pallet they shared with Callie, Griane banked the fire, softly singing the old chant as she heaped ashes over the glowing peat bricks.

> Sleep, my babe,
> Safe and warm as the peat.
> Wind, do not chill us.
> Rain, do not dampen us.
> Night dwellers, do not seek us.
> Sleep, my babe,
> Safe until dawn.

Her voice mingled with the soft slide of leather as clothing was shed, the louder rustle of bedstraw as her family crawled onto their pallets. She rose to find Darak propped up on one elbow, watching her. It had been years since she'd sung the night prayer.

She removed her shoes and skirt, but left her tunic on for added protection against the chill that seeped in through the chinks in the wall. She slid under the wolfskins, grateful for Darak's warmth. Except in the dead of winter, he always slept naked, heedless of the cold—as if a small fire smoldered inside him.

The rabbitskins spread over the bedstraw were soft against her bare legs, a startling contrast to the wiry hairs of Darak's thigh. Although he lay perfectly still, his leg was rigid with tension. She groped for his hand and squeezed it, thumb tracing the seamed scars on the stumps of the two fingers Morgath had severed.

After a moment, his hand moved in hers so he could massage her swollen knuckles. The joint-ill had grown more troubling this winter. Willow bark tea helped relieve the pain and swelling, but she always hoarded her precious supply for those with fevers.

Her body provided a daily reminder that she was growing old, but her mind—and her heart—simply refused to accept it. When she was fourteen, she'd looked at the life stretching ahead of her and known what it would hold. Marriage. Children. Healer to her tribe. She had expected age to bring wisdom and peace as well, but those continued to elude her.

The movement of Darak's thumb slowed as he drifted into sleep. Griane remained awake, staring into the darkness. Her prayer might banish the creatures of the night—the wolves and wildcats of this world, the restless spirits of the other—but the fears that dwelled in memory were harder to rout. Better to face them boldly than wait for them to pounce.

She summoned the sharp tang of tansy, the minty aroma of ground-runner, the dry, faintly bitter scent of yarrow. The heat in the hut as she crouched beside Mother Netal. The prickle of sweat on her forehead as she stared down at the neat piles of herbs. Two pairs of hands—one blotched with the brown spots of age, the other with freckles. Two identical frowns of concentration.

"You want three small handfuls of ground-runner," Mother Netal had instructed. "Two of yarrow and tansy. Double the amounts if you're using fresh herbs. Speak the words twenty-seven times while the brew steeps."

"Twenty-seven?" she had asked.

"Three times three times three. It's a powerful medicine you're brewing, and it needs a powerful charm to contain it. And you must walk in a circle while you say it. Against the sun. This is a spell for banishing, after all."

That was the first time she had heard the chant to scour away an unborn child.

"Six cups," Mother Netal had told her. "Day and night until the moon blood comes."

"What if it doesn't?"

"It will."

It was years before she had cause to test Mother Netal's recipe—the morning after her return from the Summerlands with Fellgair.

Unwilling to dwell on the memory of the painful cramping, Griane chose to recall the autumn that followed when she realized she was pregnant. The prospect of giving birth with only Hircha to help worried her, but joy outweighed the fear, for she knew the child was Darak's, conceived the night he had returned with Keirith. They'd had no time— or energy—for lovemaking during the long journey.

"Are you sure?"

Darak's voice, too casual. Darak's eyes, carefully averted. Not questioning that she was pregnant, but seeking reassurance that he was the father.

"I'm sure."

That was the only time since he'd learned of her bargain with Fellgair that he ventured close to the forbidden topic of whether she had lain with the Trickster.

Neither of them was disturbed when Rigat arrived half a moon early; given their harsh living conditions, they were simply grateful that she hadn't lost the babe. The labor was brief and far easier than any of the others. Hircha had little to do other than catch the babe as he slid between her legs, tie off the cord, and cut it. At midday, Griane presented Darak with his son.

Did he hesitate before taking Rigat in his arms or was it the events that came later that made her think so now? He peered down at the babe, as if searching for some feature that resembled his, but Rigat looked like all her other children: red-faced and squalling, damp hair plastered against his skull, blue eyes screwed shut as he protested his arrival.

She named him for the child she had lost so many years earlier. He, too, had been born before his time. Although the laws of the tribe prohibited a couple from naming a child for a moon after its birth, it had comforted her to name him in her heart. Just as it comforted her to bestow that secret name upon her newborn son.

The doubts came later. Although Rigat was a fretful infant, he was never sick. As a child, he never broke a bone. Even ordinary cuts and scrapes healed quickly. And then there was the wordless communion they seemed to share, his gift of knowing what she thought and felt. At first, she had imagined it proof of their special bond. From the moment she knew she was carrying him, she had sworn she would never make the mistakes with him that she had made with the other children. She would never hurt him as she had Keirith. She would be the perfect mother.

But there were other things: his sensitivity to birds and beasts; the sudden tantrums and the easy charm; the morning he "pushed" Faelia without ever touching her; the afternoon Darak discovered him by the stream, sitting in a pile of fallen leaves, laughing as they swirled around him in a wild dance while those on the trees hung motionless.

She conjured every memory and faced it. The memories of what happened after each incident were harder to face: the silent exchange of looks with Darak, her fierce struggle to find explanations. It was her imagination. It was guilt. Rigat was different. Rigat was special. If Keirith possessed power, why shouldn't he?

The fear pounced, and she stifled a moan. She had taken every precaution a woman could, but what human precautions could defeat the power of a god?

The bracken crunched softly. She felt more than saw the shadowy figure creeping toward her. Careful not to disturb Darak, she rolled over.

Rigat crouched beside her. One hand sought hers, lacing their fingers together in a strong, warm grip. The fingertips of the other brushed her face, feather-light. His thumb traced the bone of her cheek, the curve of her nose, then moved lower to circle her chin.

How many times had she played this game with him when he was a babe? A hundred? A thousand? Delighting in the incredible softness of his skin, his hiccuping gurgle of pleasure. And when he was older, repeating the name for each part she touched, laughing with him as he mastered the words.

Hot moisture burned her eyes. She squeezed them shut, but one tear oozed down her cheek. Rigat brushed it away. She heard a soft, wet noise and shuddered when she realized he was sucking the tear from his thumb.

"Is anything so delicious as the taste of human tears?"

"I'm cold," he whispered.

"You're too big now." But her hand was already lifting the furs.

She rolled onto her back as he slid in beside her. His cheek rested against her breast, his arm curved around her waist. She breathed in the mingled scents of peat smoke and tanned leather, the sharper tang of male sweat, and the faintest hint of a sweet fragrance she prayed was not honeysuckle.

"I love you, Mam. More than anything in the world."

Her arms tightened around him, feeling the strong bones and the tight cords of muscle. Nearly a man, now, but still—always—her little boy.

"And I love you," she whispered.

Beside her, Darak stirred. His fingers closed on her thigh. With a contented grunt, he drifted back into sleep.

If only she could preserve this moment forever: the warmth of their bodies, the comfort of their hands—one scarred by life and veined with age, the other smooth and taut and covered with downy hairs. A moment of perfect peace, perfect balance, in which she could hold them both, possess them both, love them both equally. But beyond this safe cocoon, the fear lurked like the night dwellers she had sought to banish with her prayer—the fear that one day, she would have to choose between them just as the Trickster had forced her to choose between Keirith and Darak.

Why, Fellgair? Why did you do this?

But it was Fellgair's son who answered. "Sleep, Mam. Just sleep."

Chapter 3

FAELIA WINCED AS A LOW-HANGING branch slapped her wounded arm. Winced again as she tripped over a root and slammed into something hard.

A tree. Only a tree. Her palms scraped bark sticky with pine resin. Something sticky in her shoe as well. Blood? Or just a blister?

No matter. Keep moving.

The old woman ahead of her moved in and out of the shafts of moonlight like a spirit, but Faelia could hear the hoarse rasp of her breath and her footsteps crunching unevenly on the dead pine needles.

An ominous creak made her freeze. Her fingers gripped the hilt of her sword, then relaxed as she realized it was branches rubbing together in the wind.

She had taken only a single step when someone careened into her. As she spun around, hands gripped her arms and a voice whispered, "Sorry." She clasped bony elbows, steadying the boy. For a moment they clung to each other, two strangers taking comfort in the fleeting touch of hands. Then she released him and quickened her pace before she lost sight of the old woman.

She forced herself to concentrate on the next step and the next and the next after that. If she thought about the Zherosi warriors who were trailing them or the unexpected hazards that might lie ahead, the panic would rise like bile.

"It's a lost cause."

She mustn't think about her father's words either. The cause wasn't lost. It couldn't be. Too many lives had been sacrificed.

She'd had no chance to talk with Temet since the slaughter in the village. And what words would assuage his guilt and grief? She'd watched him send three of their mortally wounded comrades to the Forever Isles, his dagger driving up and under each breastbone. They knew the risks. They all took the oath. Better to die under a friend's blade than face torture and death at the hands of their enemies. But there had been no time to ease the way for all. If even one had been taken alive, their hiding places would be known. So now they must run.

It shouldn't have ended this way. They had planned so carefully. Temet had left scouts around Gath's village, others watching the Zherosi fortress at The Bluff. Outnumbered three to one, the ambush was still successful, the entire Zherosi force wiped out. She could still hear the whoops of victory, still see Temet's face, shining with exultation under the film of sweat and dirt and blood. And then the runner staggered toward them with the news of a second Zherosi war party converging on the village.

They had probably sent for reinforcements days ago. The river was too shallow and rocky for their great ships to reach The Bluff. They must have come overland from the fortress at Little Falls. Kept to the hills. Traveled by night. Else Temet's scouts would have seen them.

One mistake. That's all it took.

Perhaps their early victories had made them careless. Within days of joining Temet's band, she'd been blooded. The Zherosi never expected an ambush so early in the spring. Their second and third attacks had been equally successful. By then, she'd grown less squeamish about the torture. It wasn't as if Temet enjoyed it. He'd learned that a man broke much faster when he had to watch a dagger pierce a comrade's eye or listen to his finger bones crack. Temet always chose an older man to torture and a young one to witness it. A battle-scarred veteran would endure more pain than a recruit. The young ones were usually in tears when they were released. And their terror gave added weight to the message they carried back to their fortresses. "Your warriors are dead. You will all die if you continue to rape our land."

Temet had picked up a few Zherosi phrases during his

captivity in their holy city. Some of the other men—those whose tribes had capitulated without a fight—knew more. They were the most bloodthirsty for they had known the shame of appeasement. And they still dreamed of driving the Zherosi to the sea. Temet only hoped to stop them from encroaching any deeper into tribal lands.

Until two days ago, Faelia had believed it was possible. But images of the battle kept flashing through her mind. A man whose legs still carried him forward—three steps? four?—while his head flopped uselessly on his neck. A small mangled form that had once been a child. The white-rimmed eyes of a girl watching a sword slashing through the air. And the screaming that disturbed even the brief moments of sleep she managed to snatch.

Don't think. Just keep moving.

Belatedly, she realized the pace had slowed. Shadows moved among shadows. A voice whispered, "Stream."

She was suddenly aware of her overwhelming thirst and rumbling belly. She couldn't remember when she had eaten last; the few supplies they had managed to salvage went to the old folk and children.

Hearing the water below her, she moved up to help the old woman. Slowly, carefully, they sidestepped down the slope. The old woman clung to her good arm, grunting a little with the effort of keeping her balance.

"Thank you, child. After all I've lived through, I'd hate to break my neck now."

Unexpected moisture stung Faelia's eyes. This nameless old woman had lost her family and her home, but her spirit was still strong.

This is why we fight. For people like her.

She helped the old woman kneel beside the stream, then flung herself on the muddy bank. The icy water burned and the faint taste of peat carried memories of home. She choked down another mouthful and forced herself to stop.

The boy showed no such restraint. Hearing his frantic gulps, she grabbed the back of his tunic and yanked him away from the water.

"No more. Or you'll be sick."

Already, whispered commands urged them to move on. She paused long enough to fill her waterskin, then offered her arm to the old woman. Together, they picked their way across the stream. By the time they reached the other side, her right foot was numb from the water seeping between the seams of her shoe. Careless. She should have repaired it before the battle.

One step. Then another.

Crawling up the opposite slope. Weaving along the trail. Peering into the darkness in search of obstacles: tree roots that trapped a foot, vines that ensnared an ankle. Always she had thought of the forest as a friend. Tonight, it had turned against her.

The night was waning when the line slowed again. Her gaze sought Temet, but he was lost among the dark figures in the clearing. He would be giving orders, sending some to guard the trail behind them, posting others as sentries around their makeshift camp.

When no one approached her to stand watch, relief quickly gave way to guilt. To assuage it, she forced herself to walk among the villagers, offering water to those who were still awake, pulling mantles around those who had fallen into exhausted sleep.

Behind her, footsteps crunched on dead pine needles. She turned, automatically reaching for the hilt of her sword, and recognized Temet. Gheala's uncertain light leached the color from his fair hair and reduced his eyes to hollow, black pools. He gripped her shoulder briefly—a comrade's touch rather than a lover's—and carefully lowered himself to the ground.

Stronger than the sharp tang of his sweat was the smell of fresh blood. Ignoring his whispered, "Leave it," her fingers sought his thigh and came away damp. Only since joining the rebels had she learned that blood looked black in the moonlight.

She cut a strip of doeskin from her tunic and offered a silent apology to her mam. As a child, she had complained endlessly about the tedium of sewing. If she'd known then that she would be stitching bodies instead of tunics, she would have kept her mouth shut.

The bag with the medicinal supplies her mam had so carefully packed was lost. She still had her bone needle and sinew in her belt pack, but Gheala's waning light was too feeble to allow her to stitch the wound now. She could only wad the old bandage over the gash and bind it with the strip of doeskin.

Temet was as silent and unmoving as a boulder as she tied the makeshift bandage. After their victories, he would come to her, hot and fierce. Lovemaking offered a welcome release after the chaos of battle—for them and all those with partners—and a triumphant declaration of life. But there would be no passion tonight. The lucky ones would huddle with their lovers, grateful to be alive and to share each other's warmth. The rest could only hope for sleep to banish despair.

She leaned her cheek against his shoulder. He shifted slightly so he could put his arm around her, careful of her wounded arm and bruised ribs. Were all big men so gentle? Perhaps that's what had drawn her to him—that same combination of strength and gentleness that her father possessed.

"How long do we have?" she whispered.

"Dawn." The subtle shift of his body told her he was scanning the sky. "The rest of the rear guard will have joined us by then."

"The rest?"

"Mikal caught up with us at the stream."

She'd been too grateful for the water to notice.

"They're still following us," he said.

Panic surged, but she fought it back.

"Mikal said they'd camped for the night, but they'll be back on our trail at daybreak."

"They might give up."

"Not this time."

The Zherosi had never pursued them so relentlessly. Temet claimed they were afraid of the shadowy forest. From his description of their arid, treeless homeland, it might be true. Perhaps these warriors had lived in the north long enough to vanquish their fear. More likely, the hunger for revenge outweighed it.

"What will you do?" she asked.

"Take most of the band with me. Try to draw them off."

"Draw them off?"

He pulled away to cup her cheeks. "I need you to lead the villagers to your home."

"What?"

"A mile from here, the trail splits. Take the north fork. Follow it past the waterfall. Then look for the black circle."

"The place where the lightning struck." Temet had made her memorize all the landmarks on the journey south. Then, it had seemed like a game to pass the time.

"Aye. You'll come to another stream."

"The one with the boulder like an arrowhead in the middle."

He squeezed her hand in approval. "The forest will start to thin after that. You'll reach the moors in two days. I'll send a few men with you, but I need to keep the bulk of the force intact. What's left of it."

She gripped his uninjured arm. "It wasn't your fault."

"I'm their commander."

"Aye. But getting yourself killed won't bring back the others."

"Your father's the hero. I'm just going to keep running. The Zherosi will tire of this chase eventually."

"Then why not stay together? If we keep moving—"

"Look at them." Temet jerked his head toward the sleeping villagers.

He was right. They could never sustain this pace. She'd be lucky to get them all home.

Fa would welcome them as he had the other refugees Temet had brought. He'd even welcomed Temet after the Freshening, when the Zherosi ceased their logging operations and his band dispersed until spring. Throughout the moon that followed, the two had debated, her father claiming the rebel forces were too scattered to offer any effective resistance and Temet insisting that was why Fa had to join them.

"There's no one else—no one!—who can unite us. Only then can we drive them out."

"You've been to Zheros," her father had replied. "You've seen them. If they bring the might of their empire to bear in the north, we'll be the ones driven out."

"That's why we have to act now. While they reckon us too weak to be a threat."

"It's a lost cause."

"Why, Fa?" she had asked. "Why won't you support this fight?"

"Because it will destroy our people."

"Our people are being destroyed now."

"Not the ones in my village."

And there it was. For all her impassioned words about the rape of their land and the destruction of their Tree-Brothers, her father still clung to the illusory safety of their isolated valley.

"The fight will continue," he had insisted, "whether or not I join it."

"But we'll lose. There are too many timid folk who would rather sit by their fires and pay their tribute and remember the old days."

"Aye. Well. Perhaps I'm one of them."

She had denied that fiercely. Her father might be reluctant to fight, but he was no coward. She could still remember him the day Keirith was stolen—ax in one hand, Zherosi sword in the other, an arrow sticking out of his arm and blood spattering him from his face to his bare feet. There was a warrior. There was a man who could inspire hundreds—thousands—to follow him. But only if someone could convince him to fight.

Her heart thudded when she realized that a victory might still be salvaged from this terrible defeat. She opened her mouth to share her idea, then closed it again. Temet had given Fa his oath to tell no one the village's location lest he jeopardize the tribe's safety. If she was going to put her plan into action, she must do it without his knowledge.

Praying she was making the right decision, Faelia lay back in her lover's arms and waited for dawn.

Chapter 4

THIS WAS THE TIME—before day leached the darkness from the sky, before the birds stirred in their roosts—the time when the whole world held its breath. Even the breeze died, as if it, too, awaited the dawn. Whether lying under his wolfskins or crouching on a windswept moor, Darak could feel that hushed expectancy, potent as a prayer. But here in the forest, where every sense was more alive, it resonated in flesh and blood, in bone and spirit. A few moments—a dozen beats of the heart—when day and night hung in perfect balance and a man had to wonder if dawn would come or if time would remain suspended forever.

The first time he had taken Callie hunting, he'd had to hush the boy's excited chatter so he could experience this moment. Keirith had looked guilty for failing to notice it. Even Faelia, whose senses were so attuned to the natural world, simply thought he had glimpsed a deer.

Darak glanced at Rigat. He was standing utterly still, his head cocked.

Only Rigat understood. Only Rigat had truly shared this moment with him, requiring no warning of its coming or explanation after to appreciate its perfection, to understand the anxiety that warred with the anticipation, the melancholy that tinged the joy.

Love swelled and with it, the familiar pain. Darak waited for the pain to wash over him and drain away, determined that nothing would spoil this day.

A wood pigeon coughed. Another answered. And the moment passed.

Beyond the hill, the stream babbled, as oblivious to the wonder as Callie had been. Darak let out his breath, his gaze locked with Rigat's. He nodded in the direction of the stream. Rigat nodded back. Together, they padded up the slope.

In the early years, it had been ridiculously easy to bring down a deer; they had never seen a human before and simply did not recognize them as predators. That had changed with the influx of refugees. None of the other hunters could be bothered with the half-day's journey to the forest when deer were plentiful on the moors, but Darak still preferred to hunt here. He loved the chinks of sky peeping through the pine boughs, the ever-shifting pattern of color and light, the carpet of pine needles cushioning his feet, the tang of resin filling his nostrils.

Although Rigat had grown up on the moors, he understood the forest's magic, too. Darak was grateful for that—and grateful that they could share these two days.

He'd hesitated before suggesting this journey. The work on the terraces had just begun and some would view the trip as an indulgence. His doubts had fled when Rigat's face lit up, making him all the more ashamed of his coldness the night before.

They reached the pinewoods just before the light went. A storm made it impossible to start a fire, but even that failed to dampen their spirits. They took shelter in the lee of a hill where the boughs of two partially uprooted pines protected them from the squalls that swept through the valley. Wrapped in their mantles, they shared a cold meal of smoked trout and suetcakes, talking only of safe topics like hunting. Darak slept soundly, too tired to dream, and awakened Rigat before dawn so they could rub acorn oil on the soles of their shoes before walking the short distance to the spot he had discovered more than ten years earlier.

Rigat halted at the top of the rise. Darak drew up beside him, panting. The roar of the stream was loud enough to drown out the chorus of birdsong. Through the trees, he glimpsed the gray-green water gushing over the banks, leaping from rock to rock as if delighted that winter had finally ceded its hold on the land.

There was one spot where the stream had eaten away

the bank and a pine had fallen, creating a little pool. Here, the stags would drink before heading north to spend the day browsing on the moors.

It had been more than a year since they had hunted together. Darak had tried to convince himself that Rigat no longer needed his guidance, that both of them preferred to hunt alone. But the excuses simply allowed him to avoid the darker truth.

Let it go. Just for today.

Without a word, Rigat started downhill. Yesterday's rain had left the thick mulch of pine needles slick and treacherous, and Darak had to pick his way carefully to the outcropping of rock. Squinting in the gloom, he could just make out Rigat's figure, crouched behind the tumble of boulders. In all the years of hunting together, Rigat had always hit his target. Once, Darak had taken pride in that, believing Rigat had inherited his skills as a hunter.

Shaking off the traitorous thought, he strung his bow and nocked an arrow. The waist-high shelf of rock partially screened him from the stream. From this distance, he would appear as innocuous as a spar wedged between a crack in the rocks.

He waited, relaxed but alert, seeking the inner stillness and peace the forest always gave him. Today, his thoughts were as wild as the stream. Always the same thoughts, and never any answers.

Rigat could be temperamental and selfish, but Faelia was the same. He could be as broody as Keirith or as sweet-natured as Callie. But Darak had loved him.

I still love him.

And never more than now. Separate yet linked in the hunt—the patient waiting, the carefully banked eagerness, the knowledge that their quarry was coming and that they were ready.

The subtle tension in Rigat's shoulders alerted him.

Without turning his head, Darak watched the stag move out of the trees. It scented the air and scanned the underbrush for predators. Six others emerged behind it. Most were two-year-old spikers, their short tines soft and rounded with the spring growth of stag-moss. The leader was older, three or four years judging from the branching antlers.

Rigat ignored the spikers, his arrow aimed at the older stag. If anything spooked the herd before it came within range, they would all be gone before he got a shot off. A hunter had to be supremely confident of his skills to risk it.

Two spikers lifted their dripping snouts and trotted through the shallow pool. Rigat remained utterly still as they bounded past his hiding place. Another followed, picking its way carefully over the rocks. And still Rigat waited.

Only when the last spikers raised their heads did the stag approach. It paused at the edge of the stream. Its brown eyes seemed to stare directly at Rigat. Then it lowered its head to drink.

Rigat drew the bowstring back. As the arrow hissed past, the spikers bolted. The stag's head came up and it swung toward the trees, but after a single bound, it crumpled. Rigat leaped up, his triumphant shout mingling with Darak's.

He had been sixteen before he'd brought down a deer with one shot through the heart. Rigat had bested him by three years. Darak acknowledged his wistfulness with a rueful grin. Then a darker speculation intruded: could an ordinary boy have done it?

Rigat knelt beside the fallen stag and gently stroked the ruddy hide. As Darak waded toward him, his hand stilled.

"Do you mind very much?"

"Of course I do." But he smiled, and the tension left Rigat's body.

"It was like a dream, Fa. At the end, I mean. I was concentrating so hard and I was scared my hands would start shaking and I was praying every prayer I could think of. But when he lowered his head and I drew . . ." Rigat sighed happily.

"Aye."

That feeling of being in the moment and standing apart, hushed and expectant as the world at dawn.

"There's nothing better, is there?" Rigat asked.

Darak thought of telling him that making love to a woman—the right woman—could be better. Or holding your newborn child for the first time. Instead, he simply said, "It'll always be one of the best moments of your life."

Rigat's expression clouded. "But it won't be as good. The next time."

"It won't be the same. But you'll have the pride of knowing you've done it twice. And the third time, you'll have bested me for good and all. So be kind to an old man and wait a few years."

Rigat's grin became a grimace as he braced himself against the stag's haunch and tugged the arrow free. He looked up, panting a little. "You could have taken one of the spikers, Fa."

"Well, thank you very much," he said so dryly that Rigat laughed. "But we'll have our work cut out for us carrying this one home."

Rigat meticulously cleaned the arrowhead and shaft before slipping the arrow into his quiver. Then he removed his dagger, sliced off the stag's tongue, and laid it on a flat slab of rock.

Darak closed his eyes. During his life, he must have made a thousand such offerings to the Forest-Lord, the rite more ancient than any the priests conducted: kneeling beside a kill; whispering a prayer of thanks to the animal he had slain; breathing in the salty-sweet aroma of blood; savoring the triumph and gratitude and contentment of knowing that this was where he belonged.

These days, such moments were rare. There were always council meetings to attend and disputes to settle, new refugees who needed homes, new ground to be cleared for planting. He had taken on the role of chief to protect his family and he had never regretted that decision, but hunting had become a luxury.

Soon he would be too old to enjoy it. When he was young, he'd taken his keen eyes and strong arms and tireless legs for granted. He could spend all day traipsing through the forest or plowing a field or hauling stones to build a hut and still make love to Griane afterward. Twice. It never mattered how tired he was. A look, a smile—gods, just watching her tie up a bundle of herbs—and the next thing he knew . . .

Aye. Well. It wasn't only a man's eyes and arms and legs that betrayed him as he got older. He should thank the gods that part of his anatomy still worked reliably. More or less. If they made love less often, it was sweeter than ever. And only now did he truly appreciate the pleasure of a good piss in the morning.

He had a horror of dying from some lingering illness as his father had. If not for Griane, he'd pray that his fluttering heart would simply stop beating while he was hunting—right at that moment before dawn. A quick, clean death with the smell of the forest around him and the cool earth beneath him. And the Forest-Lord smiling down at him in blessing.

Fingers brushed his shoulder, and he started. It was Rigat, of course, not Hernan. When he saw the stout branch at Rigat's feet, he realized he'd been drifting for some time, like an old graybeard dreaming in the sun.

He pulled a length of nettle-rope from his hunting bag and sliced off two sections. As Rigat lashed the stag's hooves together, Darak said, "I'm glad I was with you today. To see it."

"That's why I waited."

The rope slipped from Darak's hands. Rigat jumped up to finish the job. Darak watched his fingers—quick and clever like Griane's—deftly truss the stag's rear legs.

"Waited?" he finally asked.

Rigat tugged on the rope, testing the knots. "For the stag."

The tension drained out of him, replaced by shame. Lately, he was always reading into what Rigat said, looking for a reason to doubt his intentions.

"I was showing off, I guess. But I . . . I wanted you to be proud."

"I was. I am."

Rigat studied him, as if to peer into the most secret parts of his spirit—or dare him to look away. Darak met that unblinking gaze, but it required an act of will.

"I didn't use magic."

For a moment, he thought the noisy stream had distorted Rigat's words or that his mind had conjured them.

"Keirith said I should tell you. That I have powers. Like his. I wanted to wait. Until after my vision quest. But I couldn't bear it if you thought I'd cheated."

The shock of hearing him admit to possessing magic was lost in the relief that flooded him. Powers like Keirith's. Hard enough to accept that, but—oh, gods!—nothing as bad as the nightmarish doubts that had plagued him for so many years.

"I know you knew," Rigat whispered. "But it seemed to scare you so much—"

He pulled his son into his arms. Rigat was shaking as if he had a fever. Or maybe that was him.

All his life, he'd distrusted and feared magic. Tinnean's fascination with it had drawn him to the shaman's path and then to that fateful Midwinter battle. Keirith's gift had saved their lives, but it had cost him his body and his home. Young as he was, Rigat was already paying the price—too wise for his years, too impatient with those of lesser ability, a clever boy but a lonely one. And paying the worst price of all: having a father who couldn't hide his suspicion that his youngest child wasn't his.

He drew back to stare into his son's face. "It's my fault. I should have said something, helped you. Gods, you'd think I'd know better. After what Keirith went through as a lad." He squeezed Rigat's shoulders. "It'll be different now. You'll see."

"But it'll never be like it is with Callie or Keirith."

Worse than the words was Rigat's smile—so knowing, so sad, so forgiving.

"Aye. Well. You're all different people." But that was an evasion. Rigat had already turned away when he added, "Callie was always easy. Keirith . . . it was harder with him. He was the first. You always make mistakes with the first."

Rigat nodded cautiously.

"What happened in Zheros changed things. We shared a body. Our spirits were linked. It's hard—sharing yourself like that. But it brought us closer."

Closer than a father and son ought to be, he sometimes thought. But he couldn't tell Rigat that.

"I forget sometimes. What it's like to be your age. I was a loner like you. Never had any friends to speak of. Only happy in the forest. Always pushing myself—to provide for the tribe, to take care of my mother and brother, to be better than everyone else. Especially my father."

"And you were."

"A better hunter, maybe. But not half so wise."

"Well, he *was* dead. When you found him in Chaos, I mean. That probably helped."

Rigat's earnest expression made him smile. "Maybe we're all wise after we die."

"That doesn't help much now."

"Nay. But we have to keep trying."

Rigat's gaze fell. "I do try, Fa."

"I know you do. And so do I."

"I know."

Darak winced. Had his doubts been so plain, his efforts to be a loving father so forced?

"I make mistakes, Rigat. All the time. I try to learn from them, but . . ." He shook his head. "You're my son. As much as Callie or Keirith. If I can't understand your gift, I can share this with you." His hand swept out to encompass the forest. "Not only the hunt or even today's kill, as wonderful as that was. You and I . . . we're children of the forest. It's in our blood and our bones and our spirits. It's the home we always long for, the dream we always seek."

He stopped, embarrassed by his poetic outpouring. He was talking like a Memory-Keeper, not a father. Rigat's thoughtful nod told him he understood, but the moment called for something more powerful than words.

He drew his dagger and scored his wrist before holding out the blade. Rigat's hand shook as he made the cut, the blood welling in a string of tiny bright beads.

Darak took Rigat's hand and pressed their wrists together. "You are the son of my blood. The child of my spirit. And today, we start anew." He flicked his wrist four times, once in each direction, and Rigat did the same.

They smiled awkwardly at each other. A shaman understood how to bring his people back to the everyday world from the rarified one of the spirit. Even a Memory-Keeper knew how to end a tale. Darak just stood at the edge of the stream, the blood warm on his fingers.

Finally, he said, "Aye. Well. At this rate, we'll both bleed to death before we get home."

Rigat's laugh was as pure and refreshing as the crisp air. Using strips cut from the bottom of their tunics, they bandaged their wrists. Together, they slid the branch under the stag's bound hooves. Even Darak staggered when he hefted the branch onto his shoulder; the deer weighed more than a full-grown man. It would be a long walk home.

As Rigat led the way across the stream, Darak saw his head jerk toward a pine spar.

"What is it?" he called. "Did you see something?"

Rigat glanced back over his shoulder. "Just a fox." His forehead creased in sudden concern. "You're shivering, Fa. Do you want my mantle?"

"Nay, I'll warm up soon as we start moving."

Darak kept his smile in place until Rigat turned away.

Chapter 5

T HE TRIUMPH OF THE HUNT convinced Rigat to return to the forest for his vision quest. It was a risky choice—Seg would probably venture only a mile from the village—but the kill had been too clear a sign to ignore.

Even before darkness fell, he grew impatient. He shifted restlessly on the mound of pine needles and toyed with the charms he had collected over the last moon: the feather of a blackcock; a fire-blackened heather twig; the scaly fin of a trout; and a mossy tine from the antler of the stag he had brought down—his most precious and powerful charm.

He returned them to the small doeskin bag he wore around his neck and shoved back his sleeve to examine his right forearm. The Tree-Father should have created the tattoo, but Gortin's eyesight was so poor that Othak had to do it. Rigat had borne the pain stoically, too thrilled by the sight of the branching antlers slowly taking shape above his bandaged wrist to mind the repeated stab of the bone needle. Almost as wonderful as the hunter's tattoo was the quiet pride on Fa's face—and the envy on Seg's.

When he completed his vision quest first, his rival would have another reason to be envious. Rigat was certain his vision mate would come before moonrise. If he left for home immediately, he would arrive just as the sun was cresting the hills. He smiled as he pictured himself striding past the lake, sunlight framing his body and turning his hair to fire. And while Seg squatted in the bracken, he would stand before the Tree-Father and hear the words he'd awaited so eagerly: "Today, a man walks among us."

As the night waned and Gheala's swollen body sailed west, his confidence ebbed. Perhaps the gods were punishing him for being too cocky. Certainly, Gheala peeped between the pines, as if teasing him with his vision mate's tardiness. Swaying branches created shadowy forms that danced through the patches of moonlight. The stream danced, too, and gurgled with laughter as the moon goddess coaxed tiny sparks of light from its surface.

The whole forest seemed to be singing tonight: dead needles rustling as a small animal crept over them; pine boughs sighing in the breeze; dead branches rattling like the dice Keirith had carved from an antler. The snort of a deer. The hoot of an owl. A rush of wings and the terrified squeak of a mouse, suddenly silenced.

He yawned and shifted position again. His arse was getting sore from sitting so long. And his empty belly growled after a day of fasting. To distract himself, he crafted figures from the tumbling water, calling forth the silhouette of a hawk, the lithe body of a stalking fox. He shaped the foam into a mound of snow. The fox stepped onto it, leaving a trail of tiny prints.

Too late, Rigat remembered his promise to Keirith. The fox melted into the freshet with a barely perceptible splash.

He was glad he'd confided in his brother—and in Fa. He hadn't told them everything, of course, but at least he'd laid their worst fears to rest. Fa's, he could understand; in spite of all he had done, he knew little of magic. But Keirith's ambivalence baffled him.

Only once had he managed to wheedle his brother into talking about the battle to cast out the spirit of the Zherosi priest. Of course, a child of the Oak and Holly wasn't supposed to do such things, but the man was an enemy. Keirith should be proud that he'd used his power to destroy him and save Fa's life. That's the kind of thing heroes did. Except Keirith never acted like a hero. He seemed almost . . . ashamed.

Rigat frowned and searched for something more pleasant

to occupy his mind. He settled on his favorite game: When I Become Chief. The best part was deciding which of his tribe mates to cast out. Elasoth would have to go. Hard to imagine the meek little man had ever possessed the courage to defy Fa and cast Keirith out of the tribe. Harder still to believe that Keirith was actually friends with him. He never would have forgiven such a betrayal.

He felt a fleeting regret for Elasoth's daughters, but allowing them to remain was a risk. For all he knew, an aptitude for treachery could be handed down from one generation to the next.

Which made the issue of Nemek so tricky. True, his father had been the chief who had voted to cast out Keirith, but he liked Nemek. Everyone did. Besides, the tribe needed two Memory-Keepers to ensure that the bloodlines and legends were preserved, and Callie was still completing his training. But such difficult choices made the game more challenging.

He went hut by hut, disposing of some tribe mates quickly, lingering over others. He was proud of his leniency toward Faelia; if he were vindictive, he would toss her out with the rest. She had ignored him when he was little and as he got older, had directed more than her usual share of caustic comments at him. He wasn't sure if she was jealous of his hunting prowess or if she just disliked him. But blood was blood. And history had proved how important it was for family to stick together.

One day, he would play the game in earnest, but only after his father's spirit had flown to the Forever Isles. The thought cast a shadow over his pleasure. Fa always shrugged off their concerns about his heart, but they all worried about him. Especially Mam.

Maybe after his vision quest, though, he and Fa could come back here. Just for a few days. They could hunt during the day and at night, Fa could tell him the story of his quest to find Tinnean and the Oak-Lord. As many times as he'd heard it, he still found it thrilling. Especially the part where Fa bargained with the Trickster.

He was trying to imagine what he would say to a god when something about the wavering moonlight made him sit up straighter.

The fox rose out of the stream, just like the one he had conjured with his magic. Although its ruddy fur and white ruff looked real enough, he could see right through its body to the foaming water beyond.

It stood utterly still on a flat rock in the middle of the stream, watching him. He waited in an agony of impatience, praying that the moment had finally arrived. And then, in a high-pitched, rasping voice that Rigat heard only in his mind, the fox called his name.

He thought his heart would burst, it was pounding so hard. He opened his mouth to thank his vision mate, but before he could, it melted back into the water.

Rigat leaped to his feet with a triumphant whoop. Then, abashed, he knelt and offered a prayer to the Maker. Only then did he remember his mam's outburst when Keirith predicted he would a find a fox during his vision quest. Her reaction still puzzled him, but he refused to allow it to lessen his joy.

Too excited to sleep, he returned to his bed of pine needles and relived the brief encounter again and again. Every few moments, he paused to scan the sky, as if that would hurry the dawn. Finally, he decided to return to his game. At least that would keep his mind busy.

He had no particular grudge against Othak, although the Tree-Brother always looked like he'd eaten something that disagreed with him. But he had to leave the tribe so that Keirith—in spite of his silly objections—could become Tree-Father after Gortin died.

Conn presented a bigger problem. He was Keirith's best friend, but he was married to Hircha. And Hircha belonged with Keirith. They had shared all that wonderful danger in Zheros, had practically slept side by side in the years that followed. He didn't understand why it hadn't worked out. He'd dropped any number of casual hints about marriage, yet when Conn arrived, Keirith had just stood aside and let him woo and wed the woman who should have been his.

Clearly, Keirith needed *someone*. Over the years, Rigat had been jolted out of sleep many times by his brother's thrashing. Until recently, he had assumed it was just one of his nightmares. But this past year, he had discovered for himself that another sort of dream could pull a man from sleep. The first time he'd experienced one, Keirith eased his embarrassment with the whispered reassurance that all boys had such dreams. Less comforting was the knowledge that his body—always prone to arousal at the most inopportune moments—was sneaky enough to betray him while he was asleep.

His parents still made love. He tried not to listen, but it was a small hut, after all. He was glad they still wanted each other. Proud, too, that such old folk had the stamina for it. Faelia had Temet—he wasn't around much, but when he was, they were always doing it—and Callie would surely marry Ela at the Fall Balancing. But Keirith had no outlet at all—save for his fist.

Did he sneak off to watch the young women bathing in the reeds at the eastern edge of the lake? Or spy on the courting couples as they made love in the bracken? Rigat prided himself on knowing the best spots for observation, but it was a little disturbing to think of his brother crouching in them, too. A man shouldn't have to do that. *He* certainly wouldn't, once he was old enough to take a wife.

He realized he was stroking himself through his breeches and quickly snatched his hand away. Then he shrugged. He had to do something to pass the time. And this was even more enjoyable than When I Become Chief.

He closed his eyes, fingers moving with delicious slowness over the laces of his breeches as he considered various candidates. Callie's courtship had put a definite crimp on his fantasies; it just felt wrong to be lusting after Ela now. Her older sister, on the other hand . . .

During more than one rite, his gaze had drifted to Nedia, enjoying the outline of her firm thighs beneath her robe, the sway of her full breasts as she circled the worshipers. She'd make a far better Grain-Mother than Barasa who was tall and stately, but awfully skinny. No wonder the barley crop was always so meager.

He blew into his fist to warm it before reaching inside his breeches. With a contented sigh, he settled back and allowed his mind to conjure Nedia's soft hands, Nedia's generous mouth, and Nedia's welcoming thighs.

He was rapidly approaching the climax of that welcome when something intruded on his concentration. He shrugged off the distraction and found the rhythm again, but still something felt . . . not wrong so much as out of place. Frowning a little, he redoubled his efforts. Nay, there it was again. Barely discernible over the sighing of the breeze and the moaning of the branches and the gurgling song of the stream.

Laughter.

Rigat opened his eyes. His hand tightened reflexively, and he bit back a yelp.

The fox sat between his splayed legs, observing him down the length of its narrow muzzle. There was only one reason why his vision mate could have returned. He had failed to preserve the holiness of his quest and now he was going to be punished. Oh, gods, why hadn't he forced himself to sleep? Why hadn't he prayed until his knees ached?

<Don't mind me. Sleep. Pray. Finish what you were doing. I'll wait.>

Once again, the voice spoke only in his mind. The teasing tone was even more astonishing than the words themselves. Keirith's vision mate had no sense of humor, but what could you expect from an adder? Callie claimed his Starling was good-natured, though, and Fa's Wolf was often playful. Perhaps it depended upon the animal.

Oddly, though, his vision mate's voice sounded deeper and less raspy. And its—nay, the voice was definitely masculine—*his* body seemed more substantial, too.

The shaft of moonlight in which he sat leached the ruddiness from the fur on his shoulders and back, but the white of his neck, chest, and belly seemed to glow in Gheala's light. It took Rigat a moment to realize that the moonlight couldn't possibly be so bright. Nor could it be streaming through the branches from the east when Gheala was barely visible in the west.

<Very observant, Rigat.>

Of course, his vision mate could look and sound any way he chose. If it really was his vision mate and not simply a vision. Maybe he *had* fallen asleep. Maybe this was just a dream.

The large, triangular ears pricked forward. *<Oh, I'm real. As real as the hand still clutching your manly member.>*

A hot flush suffused him. He yanked his hand free and

hastily adjusted his clothes. This was not at all what he had expected from his vision quest.

<*But a lot more interesting, don't you think?*>

He had to grin, although he knew the poor Tree-Father would die of embarrassment when he touched his spirit during the testing.

The fox's black whiskers twitched. <*Then it would be wise to shield him from this particular aspect of your vision quest.*>

"How?" His voice cracked, and he cleared his throat.

<*Picture the images you wish him to share. The fox's sleek body poised on the rock. The commanding voice calling your name. Your rush of excitement . . .*>

The fox directed a pointed glance at his lap, and Rigat's face grew warmer.

<*. . . and your boundless gratitude to be chosen by such a hunter. Gortin will be suitably impressed, and your tribe will rush to congratulate you.*>

Well, his family would. He wasn't so sure about the others.

<*Does their approval matter so much?*>

He shook his head, but his vision mate was too wise to be fooled.

<*You've spent your childhood trying to fit in. Now you're a man. Whether or not the tribe can accept your gifts, you must.*>

The wave of relief surprised him. Even Keirith couldn't understand—not completely. But his vision mate did.

When the fox rose, he failed to suppress a cry of dismay. The thick brush lashed once and he winced, fearing he'd angered his vision mate.

<*Do you feel any anger?*>

The voice was calm, but there was an undercurrent of . . . something. Anticipation? Eagerness?

<*Clever boy. You and I are going to get along, I think. Now watch, Rigat. Watch and listen.*>

The familiar predawn hush had settled over the forest. Although the sky overhead had lightened to charcoal, the shaft of moonlight in which the fox stood was as brilliant as ever. Rigat waited, sharing his vision mate's eagerness.

The fox's brush lashed again, and the moonlight rippled

like someone drawing a finger across the still surface of a pool. As Rigat rose to his knees, the shaft of moonlight split open. But instead of the trunks of pines, he found himself staring at the back of a man in a long robe.

Again, the thick brush moved, more lazily this time. The gap widened, as if two unseen hands had grasped the edges of the white light and were slowly pulling them apart. There were dozens of people, he realized, gathered in a circle. Peering between their bodies, he spied a dark, gaping pit.

A red-robed priest in a feathered cloak raised his staff. Although the man had to be forty paces away, Rigat could clearly see the black markings zigzagging down its sinuous length, the painted red eyes that stared skyward, even the grain of the wood. His eyesight had always been keen, but this was impossible. It took him a moment to realize that the staff looked like a giant adder.

<Very good, Rigat.>

As one, the people began to chant. The language was unfamiliar, but Rigat was certain the meaning of the words lay just beneath the surface of his consciousness.

The chant grew louder as the sky lightened. Perhaps it was some kind of prayer to welcome the dawn. But the gaze of every person remained fixed on the pit as if fascinated by whatever was happening in it. Determined to see more, he pushed himself to his feet and took a cautious step forward.

A man's head jerked toward him. He shouted something unintelligible. The chanting faltered. More heads turned. People gaped at him, some frozen in shock, others pointing, still others peering uncertainly as if they could not quite make him out. Fingers flew as they made signs across their chests, all the while jabbering in their tongue.

Guards converged around a black-haired girl on the far side of the circle. Another spun toward him, spear upraised. Before Rigat could do more than open his mouth, the spear arced toward him.

Panic ignited his smoldering power. It penetrated flesh and muscle and bone. It warmed his belly and stiffened his cock. It surged through his legs and down his arms until his toes and fingertips tingled.

The spear slowed as if the air around it had grown thick.

Tiny details impressed themselves on his mind: the sweet-smoky scent of the torches, a tiny scratch on the surface of the bronze spear point, the fox's eyes—golden as honey.

He controlled the power, feeding on it and allowing it to feed on him. And all the while, he watched the point of the spear coming closer. Now ten paces away. Now five. Only when he felt his body would burst with the power, only when he could smell the metal, cold and bitter as a winter morning, did he whisper, "Stop."

The spear hung in the air, the point a mere handsbreadth from his chest. Rigat reached up and wrapped his fingers around the shaft. Only then did he accept that it was real. Distantly, he heard shouts and screams, but when he raised his head, the portal snapped shut.

His arm fell to his side, suddenly heavy. The spear slipped from his grasp. Then his shaking legs folded.

The pungent odor of male fox vied with something sweet—honeysuckle? But that only bloomed in the summer.

The slide of a wet tongue against his cheek startled him. Opening his eyes, he found his vision mate staring down at him.

<You did well, Rigat. I'm proud of you.>

A small part of him registered happiness, but body, mind, and spirit were numb. Never before had the use of his gift left him so drained.

<It will get easier. In time. For now, just sleep.>

He summoned enough strength to ask, "Why did you show me that?"

<There will be time to talk later.>

Stubbornly, he fought the overwhelming lethargy. "When?"

<Soon. But now you must sleep. Sleep and grow strong, my beautiful boy.>

This time, Rigat succumbed to the soothing voice. As he drifted off, he smiled. My beautiful boy. His mam used to call him that when he was little.

He woke to a chorus of birdsong, the chirps and twitters of sparrows and starlings vying with the throbbing purr of wood pigeons. The chorus melted into the raw air of dawn and coaxed the watery sun into the sky. Rigat wasn't sure if a few moments had passed or an entire day and night. He certainly felt strong and rested. Perhaps it was only the lingering exhilaration of his vision quest, but his legs carried him effortlessly over the hills; even the wind blew from the south as if to speed him homeward.

Only when he reached their valley did he hesitate. He circled west and, discovering no one at the stream, paused long enough to hide the spear between two boulders, carefully mounding a shallow layer of dirt over it. If his vision mate wanted him to conceal their second encounter from the Tree-Father, he couldn't very well walk into the village clutching a spear. Later, perhaps, he would show it to Keirith. His brother could confirm his growing suspicion that he had witnessed some strange Zherosi rite. Besides, the truth was too exciting to hide from everyone.

As he hurried toward the lake, anticipation gave way to puzzlement. There was no one in sight, not even any children playing along the shore. If not for the threads of smoke rising from the hill fort, he would have thought the village deserted.

Suddenly scared that something had happened to Fa, he raced up the slope and skidded to a halt just inside the entrance. The wall of backs confronting him was eerily reminiscent of the scene he had glimpsed through the portal. Instead of chanting, the Tree-Father's quavering voice broke the silence: "Today, a man walks among us. That man is Seg, son of Madig and Anetha. And his vision mate is the wolf."

The roar of acclamation made his stomach churn, but he could not help craning his neck for a glimpse of Seg. There he was, standing between Gortin and Othak, grinning like a fool. Rigat shrank back against the earthworks, but Seg had already spotted him. His grin widened. He raised both hands, commanding silence, then called out a greeting.

Head high, Rigat marched forward. Gortin smiled and handed his blackthorn staff to Othak. The white film that dimmed Gortin's right eye made it look like the sky on a misty autumn morning, while the scars around his empty eye socket appeared to be bleeding.

Rigat flicked his forefinger against his thumb, then resolutely stilled his fingers. The poor Tree-Father couldn't help the way he looked or how the sunlight struck his face. He mustn't allow his overactive imagination to conjure an evil omen out of such ordinary things.

Gortin's hands groped for his shoulders. In a halting voice, he recited the ancient words. Finally, he closed his eye. Quelling the urge to stroke his bag of charms for luck, Rigat took a deep breath and willed himself to be calm.

When Callie had returned from his vision quest, Keirith had performed the rite with him. Rigat could still remember sitting beside the fire pit, watching Callie's eyes widen and his mouth become a round O of surprise when Keirith touched his spirit. Fa had described Tree-Father Struath's touch as feather-light. Keirith had warned him that Gortin was less skilled than his predecessor, but Rigat was still shocked by the sudden, brutal assault.

Like a bear blundering through the underbrush, Gortin shoved deep into his spirit. The relentless battering made Rigat gasp, each agonizing jolt resonating throughout his spirit until he thought he would scream.

Desperately, he concentrated on what he wanted the Tree-Father to find: the fox poised on a rock in the middle of the stream, the shadowy trunks of the pines visible through its body. But other memories kept spilling through: his vision mate's mocking laughter, the warmth of that teasing voice, the dispassionate golden eyes watching as the spear hurtled toward him.

With a strangled cry, Rigat jerked free of Gortin's hands, breaking the connection between them.

Gortin swayed. Othak rushed forward to support him, but Gortin shook his head. He raised a trembling hand, silencing the worried murmurs of the onlookers.

Rigat lowered his head, trying to still his frantic heartbeat.

Gods, don't let him denounce me.

Labored breathing filled the awful silence. Gortin's fingers tightened on his shoulders. He looked up and saw a tear oozing down the deep crease beside the Tree-Father's nose.

"Forgive me," Rigat whispered.

The Tree-Father's hands cupped his cheeks, the palms as

dry as birch bark. "So young," he murmured. "But so powerful. Like your brother."

Gortin turned him to face the tribe. "Today, a man walks among us. That man is Rigat, son of Darak and Griane. And his vision mate is the fox."

Somewhere in the crowd, Rigat heard Callie give a great whoop, provoking laughter and cheers. Dazed, Rigat listened to the unexpected acclaim. Fa's hug made his ribs ache. Keirith and Callie thumped him on the back so hard he nearly fell over. Hircha pressed a quick kiss to his cheek, then ran her palm over the soft whiskers that his brothers called fuzz. Mam's mouth trembled as she smiled. So did the arms that came up to embrace him. Was she just relieved that he had passed his testing or worried because he'd found a fox?

He let himself be swept up by his family and marched to their hut where Fa retrieved a leather flask of elderberry wine and poured a cup for everyone. Rigat's grimace drew a laugh from his brothers, but the wine left a pleasant afterglow that made up for its tartness.

One by one, his family presented him with their gifts: a new doeskin tunic from his mam, arrowheads from Fa, a flask of elderberry wine from Hircha, a scrap of fleece Callie had lovingly preserved from Old Dugan—"because you and he were such good friends." Even Faelia had left him a gift: six new arrow shafts fletched with owl feathers. He was surprised and touched at her thoughtfulness, but he lingered longest over Keirith's gift.

He had seen the dagger only once. He had come upon Keirith, sitting alone by the stream, staring at it. When he had admired the delicate spirals incised on the bronze blade, Keirith had replied, "Aye. It's beautiful to look at." But he refused to say more about it, and when they returned to the hut, he put it away. Although his brother had never said as much, Rigat had always wondered if it was the same dagger the priest had driven into Keirith's heart.

There was no time to question him now. He had to change into his new tunic, drag a bone comb through his tangled hair, and scrape the whiskers from his cheeks—not an easy task with his father and brothers speculating about whether he would cut his throat, and Mam alternating between scolding them and cautioning him about how sharp the flint was.

The afternoon was waning when they all trooped down to the lake for the feast. When the Grain-Mother sliced off the first piece of mutton and offered it to Seg, it was all Rigat could do not to snatch it out of her hands. Instead, he waited his turn and accepted his slice with a polite bow. After a quick exchange of glances, he and Seg fell on the meat, drawing laughter from the rest of the tribe and a shouted observation from someone that Seg might have found a wolf, but they both ate like one.

After that, the day only got better. When his name was shouted—along with Seg's—he responded with the obligatory swig of wine and won roars of approval from the men—especially those who had been hefting their flasks a little too often. Sour or not, the wine helped ease the headache that lingered from Gortin's testing.

"Go easy," Callie warned him. "It has a way of sneaking up on you."

Rigat laughed, recalling the aftermath of Callie's celebration of manhood. "Don't worry," he boasted. "Fa won't have to carry me to bed."

He wandered through the crowd, shrugging modestly when the men congratulated him, smiling at the women who tweaked his braids and called him "Fox Cub." Unlike Seg who pointedly ignored the younger boys, Rigat answered all their stammered questions about his vision quest, thrilled by their awestruck expressions. He was prouder still when some of the men asked him to speculate about his father's reasons for refusing to lend his support to the rebellion, and gladly offered his opinion on the matter.

He was a man now—a full member of the tribe. He could drink, he could venture an opinion, he could even choose a wife if he wanted, although, of course, he would wait. No sense rushing into anything. The son of Darak Spirit-Hunter was a catch. No wonder so many of the older girls smiled when he strolled past.

Nedia's smile warmed him even more than the wine. A priestess could choose any lover she wished. Why not him? If only Seg would leave her alone. Every time he circled back, Seg was there, touching her hand, nudging her shoulder, leaning close to whisper something but obviously just trying to brush up against her breast. Even more infuriating was the way Nedia smiled at his boasts and laughed when he threw back his head and howled like a wolf. If that kind of behavior appealed to her, perhaps she wasn't the one for him, regardless of her flashing dimples and full breasts and lovely, round bottom.

Still, you'd think Ennit and Lisula would do something. Or Conn. But Nedia's parents just walked away. Conn—as always—had eyes for no one but Hircha, and Hircha—as always—observed everything and said nothing.

Well, he was a man. And no one was going to show him up. Ignoring Hircha's cool blue gaze, he squeezed past her to stand at Nedia's shoulder.

"Well, if it isn't the Fox Cub," Seg boomed. When Nedia patted the ground beside her, he shook his head. "Nay. Foxes and wolves don't get along."

Nedia frowned. "Today they do."

Seg staggered to his feet and hooked his thumbs in his belt. "Wolves drive intruders from the pack."

"Just because you found a wolf doesn't mean you are one," Rigat replied, injecting the perfect note of bored indulgence into his voice.

Nedia giggled. Seg's head snapped toward her, then jerked back up. "At least my vision mate is noble. You won't catch a wolf stealing eggs from a plover's nest."

Heads had begun to turn in their direction. Pitching his voice to carry, Rigat replied, "With all you've had to drink, you couldn't catch an egg, never mind a fox." Savoring the chuckles from those around him, he sketched an elaborate bow and swaggered off.

He had reached the edge of the crowd when a hand seized his arm.

Seg glared at him through narrowed eyes. "You can't fool me. I know you pushed me the other day. It's just the kind of sneaky thing you'd do. No wonder you found a fox."

"Let me go."

Seg's fingers bit deeper into his arm. "If not for you, I'd have brought down that doe myself."

"But you didn't. And I'm the one with the antler tattoo." Rigat shoved back his sleeve, enjoying Seg's scowl.

"Aye. But I finished my vision quest first."

It was Rigat's turn to scowl. "I was in the forest and—"

"If you were stupid enough to go that far away, it serves you right to be second."

"I still would have beaten you. But my fox came back to show me . . ."

Rigat's voice trailed off. Cold sweat bathed his body.

"Show you what? A vision? So now you're a shaman?" Seg leaned so close that Rigat averted his face to escape the wine fumes. "Or just an abomination like your brother?"

Slowly, Rigat's head turned. Whatever Seg saw on Rigat's face made him release Rigat's arm and take an uncertain step back.

The power swelled, more potent than any wine. Rigat trembled with the desire to release it. He would scour the evil words about Keirith from Seg's mouth. He would sear those lips, rip out that tongue, shatter every tooth in his head until Seg was on his knees, begging for forgiveness.

It took all his control to contain the power, to force it deep inside him. The effort left him gasping and evoked a scornful smile from Seg.

What choice did he have but to fling the words into that sneering face?

"You want proof? Come with me."

Chapter 6

D ARAK NODDED TO ENNIT AND Lisula, but his gaze remained fixed on Rigat and Seg.

Please, gods, don't let them get into another fight.

Lisula sighed as she sat down beside him. "They're sweet, aren't they?"

His frown of incomprehension turned to a smile when

he realized she was watching Callie and Ela wander along the lakeshore, hand in hand.

"We used to do that," Lisula said with a fond glance at Ennit.

"Ennit was always romantic." Griane's glance was as pointed as the elbow she poked into Darak's side.

"And he would whisper the most wonderful, wicked things to see if he could make me blush."

"Mostly, she giggled." Ennit placed his hand over his heart and batted his eyelashes at Lisula, who—predictably—giggled. Despite the streaks of silver in her dark hair and the wrinkles that seamed the skin around her eyes, she still seemed like the plump little Grain-Sister of Darak's youth.

"He once told me my breasts were like goose down."

"Goose down?" Darak grimaced. "Good gods. Now I'm going to picture you with feathers sprouting on your bosoms."

"Because they were very white," Ennit explained.

"So I gathered."

"And so soft that—"

"Thank you, Ennit." Darak gave his best friend a quelling glare.

"Now it's my hair that's white." Lisula heaved a mournful sigh.

Griane paused in her examination of a nutcake to frown at her braid. "Darak once said my hair was so bright it was like I carried the sun on my shoulders."

"Aye. Well."

"But you never compared my breasts to anything."

Ennit patted Griane's knee. "Darak was never the poet I was."

Darak snorted. "Breasts like goose down?"

"He was a man of action. Fighting his way through Chaos, romping in the First Forest . . ."

"I have never romped."

"Making his wife yowl like a wildcat." Ennit snatched his hand back before Griane could smack it. "If I have one regret in my long and happy life, it's that my wife has never yowled when we've made love. A moan, now and then, but nothing like Griane. Why, you could hear her clear across—ow!" He rubbed his shoulder and shot Griane a reproachful glance.

Griane's frown deepened. "Stop looking so smug, Darak, or you'll get the same."

"I'm just sitting here," he protested.

"Looking smug."

Before he could ask how she knew he looked smug when she was peering at the nutcake in her hand, Griane gave a triumphant cry. She brandished a fragment of shell, then flicked it away. "Duba makes the best nutcakes in the village—"

"But she always misses the shells," the rest of them chorused.

Gods, it was good to sit with friends and forget his worries. He rolled his shoulders to ease the knots of tension that had been there ever since Rigat returned. Although he'd acted cheerful, Darak knew he hated being bested by Seg. Still, his testing had gone well. Well enough. Gortin seemed to have recovered now and was talking with Keirith. As usual, Othak hung on every word.

"I wish Othak would leave him be."

"Gortin would be lost without him," Lisula replied.

"Not much risk of that," Ennit muttered. "I'm lucky if Othak lets me into the hut to visit. And Gortin my brother!" A rare scowl darkened Ennit's face. "If Othak hadn't become a priest, I could have used him to guard the flock."

"You just don't like him," Lisula said.

"Neither do you."

Lisula pursed her lips primly, then sighed. "Poor boy. Jurl ruined him."

"He's not a boy," Ennit said. "And he's had years to get over Jurl's beatings."

Darak massaged the stumps of his first two fingers thoughtfully. "Some things linger in a man's mind long after the bruises fade." He looked up to find them all watching him. When he realized they thought he was brooding about Morgath, he quickly added, "My father blistered my arse any number of times, but I can't remember those whippings half as well as the one I gave Tinnean."

Or the one I gave Rigat.

"Where did he go?"

The others exchanged glances. "Darak," Griane said, "you know where Tinnean is."

"I wasn't . . . good gods, woman, I haven't lost my senses. I went from Tinnean to Rigat."

"And I'm supposed to read your mind?"

"He and Seg were pestering Nedia," Ennit said. "She's a flirt. Like her mother." He caught Lisula's hand and pressed it to his lips.

"I would never have looked at a boy three years my junior. No matter how manly he was." Lisula giggled. "Remember Conn and Keirith after their vision quests?"

"The way they strutted around," Ennit said. "Like they'd grown an extra set of ballocks."

"Or Griane had shoved bear grease up their arses to loosen their bowels," Darak said.

"And now they hardly talk."

Griane's words made Ennit shift uncomfortably. "It'll work itself out. In time."

"They've had time," Griane retorted. "Conn and Hircha have been married since the Fall Balancing."

"Interfering won't help matters." Ennit's voice was equally sharp.

Before Griane could reply, Darak took her hand. "It's Rigat's day. Let's enjoy it."

As the talk turned to birthings and deaths and illnesses, Darak rose and pretended to stretch, all the while scanning the crowd. Still no sign of Rigat. Or Seg. He spotted Keirith easily enough, though. He was talking with Hircha now. As he watched, Keirith strode off. Judging by the determined way Hircha followed, she was not about to let him escape.

It was past time for Keirith and Conn to sort things out. But he doubted even Hircha—strong-willed as she was— could reconcile them if Keirith wasn't ready.

"Why can't you let it go?" Keirith demanded.

"Because this nonsense has gone on long enough. You never visit us. You hardly even talk to Conn. Or me. We used to be best friends."

Keirith turned away from Hircha's piercing gaze to stare

at the lake. The Twins shadowed the western half, but to the east, the water sparkled with red-gold flashes that reminded him of the coins the Zherosi called serpents.

Together, he and Hircha had survived Zheros—and Xevhan. In time, she had learned to look past the body he wore and see him, not the man who had abused her. But although they had grown close, it was friendship, not passion that had evolved.

When Conn's family first arrived in the valley, his milkbrother had been jealous of that friendship, but soon realized he could share it. For nearly a year, things had been perfect.

"Why does everything have to change?" he whispered.

"Conn hasn't changed. Neither have I."

"So it's my fault."

Hircha just regarded him silently.

"Things are different now," he said.

"How?"

"I've another body, for one thing."

"You had that before we left Eagles Mount."

"And we're both older. We have responsibilities."

"And I'm Conn's wife."

"Aye."

"What difference does that make?" she demanded.

"Because I'm the one who's alone!"

Appalled at having blurted it out, he turned on his heel. Hircha caught his arm. "You idiot. We're right here. Every day."

"And every night, you lie together under your furs. While I lie next to my little brother and wake with my seed spurting onto my belly like a boy!"

"Then take a wife," she snapped. "If you think marriage is just a warm body under the furs and a warm sheath for your cock!"

"Thank you, but I'd prefer to sleep alone than with someone I don't love."

Her head snapped back.

"I didn't mean that." But he had and she knew it. "I'm sorry."

It was Hircha's turn to stare at the glistening lake. "Not everyone is like Darak and Griane. Not everyone wants that . . . closeness."

Hircha might not, but he suspected Conn did. Still, they

seemed happy enough. Conn clearly adored her. And Hircha had found a way to fit in.

"I'm sorry," he repeated. "I'm just . . . there are times I hate my body and my powers and everyone around me who's . . . normal. And that makes me feel like the worst brother and the worst son and the worst friend in the world."

"You're never happy unless you're miserable."

"That's not true."

"Instead of taking it out on me or Conn, go beat your head against a rock. That ought to cheer you up."

"It's not funny."

"And it's not always your fault."

"You just said I was the one who pulled away."

"All right. That *was* your fault. Happy now?"

Keirith could feel a smile twitching the corner of his mouth up. "I'm pathetic, aren't I?"

"Aye. And the worst brother, the worst son, the worst friend . . . did I miss anything?"

Hircha smiled. She was not a person who smiled often or easily, so it was always a sort of gift when she did. When he'd first seen her—the morning of his interrogation by Malaq and Xevhan—he'd been struck by her physical beauty: the moon-gold hair, the slender, graceful body. But her face was as cold as stone. Stolen as a child by the Zherosi, she'd learned very early to hide her feelings and thoughts. She might give Conn affection and loyalty and kindness, but Keirith believed that she only opened her heart to him. Or maybe he just wanted to believe he possessed something of her that Conn did not.

"Sometimes, I feel so . . . separate from everyone," he said.

Her smile vanished. "Sometimes I feel that way, too." She surprised him by resting her palm against his cheek. "Talk to Conn."

"I will. Soon."

Her gaze shifted. "Sooner than you expected."

He turned to find Conn running toward them. At first, he wondered if Hircha had arranged this, but the expression on Conn's broad face made it clear something was wrong. Only then did he become aware of a commotion around the fire pit.

"What is it?" he asked Conn.

"Seg claims Rigat found a Zherosi spear."

Hircha was the first to recover. "I'll fetch Darak."

Stupid, stupid, stupid!

Why had he insisted on showing off? He should have known Seg wouldn't keep his mouth shut. Already men were shouting that the Zherosi must be on the move, that an attack was imminent. Claiming he had found the spear in the forest would only feed the panic. But how could he possibly reveal the truth?

Think, Rigat, think!

His vision mate had called him clever, but he'd behaved like a fool. Too much wine, too much boasting. And now he was trapped.

When he saw his father pushing through the crowd, relief made his legs tremble.

"All right," Fa said. So calm, that voice, so steady. "What's all this about a spear?"

Madig thrust it out. "Rigat claims he found it on his vision quest."

"Not found it," Seg corrected. "He said . . . something about his vision mate."

It was his word against Seg's. Just like before. Only this time Seg was drunk. No one would believe him. But that still didn't explain the presence of a Zherosi spear in the wilderness.

A hand came down on his shoulder. "Rigat is afraid to tell you what happened," Gortin said. "But I know."

The fear was a live thing, clawing at his belly.

"After Rigat's vision quest, a portal opened before him. A portal to Chaos. And a Zherosi warrior hurled this spear at him."

Chaos was the only word to describe the uproar that ensued. But Gortin just stood there, utterly composed and utterly convinced of what he had Seen.

"A Zherosi warrior?" Rothisar snorted. "In Chaos?"

"They call it the Abyss," Keirith said.

"Chaos or the Abyss," Madig shouted, "a spirit cannot hurl a real spear through a portal!"

"Did not our own chief enter Chaos as a living man?" Gortin demanded. "Armed with a real dagger?"

The shouting was dying down now. Feeble as Gortin was, he was still Tree-Father.

"I've witnessed the opening of a portal. At that Midwinter battle when the spirit of the Oak-Lord was lost and Morgath returned to this world."

The silence was absolute now. Even Rigat was caught by the passion in Gortin's voice.

"I can still remember the terror of that night. As Darak must recall the terror of plummeting through a portal into the Unmaker's realm. Is it any wonder Rigat was too frightened to speak of it? And if he had, how many would have dismissed his tale as the imaginings of a young man caught in the glory of his vision quest?"

Dear gods, I'm going to get away with it.

"Rigat?"

His father's expression was as calm as his voice. But was there a warning in those gray eyes?

The silence stretched, the breathless anticipation of the crowd as real as Gortin's hand on his shoulder. Rigat wished he could draw out the moment, savor it like wine, but his boastfulness had gotten him into too much trouble already.

"I should have known the Tree-Father would See what really happened. But I was too scared to tell."

Everyone would believe fear made his voice shake, but it was simply relief. He would offer a sacrifice to the Maker in thanks for his reprieve. Or perhaps he should offer one to the Trickster; it was just the sort of irony the god would appreciate.

Madig tossed the spear to the ground as if it were contaminated. The crowd began to drift away. Keirith was still eyeing him though, and Rigat had no desire to talk with his brother. He snatched up the spear, intent on slipping away, when a firm hand grasped his arm.

"We need to talk," his father said.

"Now?"

"Aye. The three of us."

That's when Rigat noticed his mam hovering a few paces away, her face pinched and worried.

He wanted to tell her that it was all right. That nothing bad had happened. That his power was a good thing. More than anything though, he just wanted to run away.

"We can't talk here," he said, desperate to postpone the discussion.

"Nay. At home. It's time, Rigat," his father added in a gentler voice.

Rigat nodded and numbly followed them toward the hill fort. Then he heard a renewed commotion behind him and froze. Had the Tree-Father realized his error? Or had Seg said something else to turn the tribe against him?

Darak spun around, frowning. "Bel's blazing ballocks. What now?" Then he saw Nemek's younger boy, Arun, tottering toward him. Sweat streaked his face and his chest heaved, but it was the terror in his white-rimmed eyes that held Darak's gaze.

Arun reeled and Darak lunged forward to catch him. The boy's fingers dug into his forearms as he struggled to form words. Darak steadied him, then went down on one knee.

"Are you hurt?"

Arun shook his head.

"Take a deep breath."

The breath wheezed out in a soft whimper. Darak heard an echoing whimper from Catha. Her left hand reached for Arun, while her right cradled her belly as if to protect her unborn child as well. Nemek's hand descended on her shoulder, stilling her, but her body trembled with the need to comfort her son.

"Arun." Darak kept his voice soft. "Tell me what's wrong."

"I was on the hill. Taking food to Jadan. He's on watch today and—"

"What happened, Arun?"

"We saw people. Running across the moor."

Darak frowned. Jadan should have sounded the ram's horn when he sighted the strangers.

"And there were other people. Chasing them."

Darak silenced the frenzied babble with a peremptory shout.

"Arun. Tell me everything. Quickly."

The boy closed his eyes, as if picturing the scene. "Twenty or so people running. Trying to run. The ones chasing them—they were in a square. Once they stopped and shot arrows. But they were out of range. So they started moving again." Arun's eyes popped open. "There was a man in front. With a metal helmet. I saw the sun glinting off it."

"It's the Zherosi!"

"An attack!"

"We'll all be killed!"

Arun burst into tears. A woman screamed.

Before the outcry could escalate, Darak jumped to his feet. "By the gods, I will not have panic!" He glared at Catha who happened to be closest; her hand flew to her mouth, stifling her sobs. "Arun. How many warriors did you see?"

"They were all bunched together—"

"How many do you think?"

"I . . . a hundred?"

"How far?"

"A mile. Maybe."

"In what direction?"

Arun pointed south, then swallowed hard. "The people who were running? I think the one in the lead was a woman. Her hair . . . it looked too long to be a man's." Arun bit his lip. "It was red, Alder-Chief. Her hair. Bright red."

Darak closed his eyes.

Fear is the enemy.

Stealing his breath. Constricting his heart.

Control the fear.

He could taste it, cold and bitter as bronze.

Control yourself.

He took a deep breath. Then another. Swallowed the bile that filled his mouth. And opened his eyes.

His gaze found Griane. Rigat. Keirith. Where was Callie? He couldn't find Callie. Wait, there he was, with his arm around Ela.

"All right." He raised his voice to ensure that those in the back could hear. "We have prayed this day would not come, but it has. Douse that fire. Smother it," he corrected. "And those in the village."

Jadan had wisely realized that this war party was unaware of their existence and refused to sound the ram's horn. They must use the element of surprise to their advantage.

Every member of the tribe knew the plan; the children recited their roles at Nemek's knee along with the tribal legends. Still, he took a few moments to review it; in a crisis, it was too easy to forget details.

As he spoke, he scanned the faces of the leaders: Madig's, cold and determined—as irritating as a thorn in the foot, but he could be counted on to do his part; old Trath's, seamed and tanned as leather—he would defend the hill fort to the death; Mirili's, creased with concern as she calmed Catha—a survivor of many attacks, her presence would steady the younger women; Rothisar's, eyes blazing with excitement—best keep him close or he'd charge across the moor alone to attack the invaders.

Othak looked like he was going to be sick, but Gortin stood straight as an oak. Even after all these years, the man continued to surprise him. Barasa was trembling visibly, while Lisula—whose head barely reached the Grain-Mother's shoulder—patted Barasa's clenched fists. Lisula and Gortin—one still brimming with energy, the other whose life was draining away. Like The Twins that guarded the eastern pass, they were the spiritual strength of the tribe.

Griane would never let him down. Already she'd be tallying her supplies and mentally ticking off which women could be relied upon to help with the wounded. But Hircha's fist was clenched over her heart, and her eyes were fixed on him as if his mere presence could ward off the attack. This was the first time since their escape from Zheros that the enemy had threatened her. She had to be recalling her capture as a child and the long years of slavery that followed. But as he watched, she slowly lowered her fist and nodded once.

Keirith's gaze met his. We have fought them before, his

expression said. Fought them and won. But his fingers ceaselessly rubbed his left forearm where the black tattoo of the Zherosi's sacred adder twisted from wrist to elbow.

So many thoughts chasing after each other in his mind while his voice calmly laid out the strategy. So many frightened faces turned to his, but he could only see those terrified people on the moor, running for their lives. He pictured the leader desperately herding them toward the gap in the hills. Saw the tangled red hair streaming behind her, heard her shouted exhortations to hurry, felt his heart pounding in rhythm to hers.

"If we can save these strangers, we will. But our first priority is to protect our folk. I want no heroics. No needless sacrifices."

Faelia, my only daughter. My brave hunter. Forgive me.

"Let's go. And may the gods keep us safe."

Chapter 7

THE OLD WOMAN STUMBLED. The boy seized one arm and Faelia grabbed the other. Between them, they hauled her to her feet again.

"Go on," the old woman wheezed. "Braden will help me. You see to them." She jerked her head toward the cluster of villagers who had simply halted at the bottom of the slope.

"Keep moving!" Faelia shouted. "Toward that gap in the hills."

One or two turned to follow the direction of her finger, but most just stood there, dazed.

The old woman—why had she never thought to ask her name?—and Braden set off in a shambling trot. Faelia hurried toward the others, exhorting the faltering, helping the slow. But they were all slow. The burst of speed they had found when they first spied the Zherosi had long since faded. She tugged on arms, on tunics, herding them like a shepherd.

I am their shepherd. And unless I get them moving, they'll all be slaughtered.

She dared a quick glance over her shoulder. Still no sign of the rear guard, but they had to retreat soon. At best, the six men would only slow the enemy. If their shots got past the Zherosi shields. If they weren't cut down first.

They were willing to sacrifice their lives for the people of Gath's village. It was up to her to ensure their sacrifice was not in vain.

She bent over a fair-haired girl who had fallen to her knees. "It's only a little farther."

"I can't," the girl muttered, her eyes glazed with exhaustion and hopelessness.

"You must."

"I'm so tired."

With an oath, Faelia drew back her hand and slapped her. "Get on your feet. Now!"

The girl gasped, but allowed Faelia to pull her to her feet. Flinging an arm around her waist, Faelia forced her into a trot.

Half a mile. Maybe less. But the survivors were spread out across the moor, lurching across the uneven terrain, clinging to boulders or each other as they crawled up the gentlest slope. She had to keep them moving. She had to get them home.

With her eyes on the beckoning hills, she failed to notice the rabbit hole until her ankle twisted. She staggered, dragging the girl down with her. Pain lanced through her ankle as she pushed herself to her feet again. "Go," she told the girl. "Keep running."

One careless mistake.

Limping badly, she crested the rise. A short distance ahead, she glimpsed the old woman, her white hair bright as a signal fire among the greening grass. And there, at last, was the shadowed gap between the two sunlit hills.

She shouted to the others and pointed. Light returned to a few of the weary faces, but in others, she saw the flash of fear that so often accompanied hope. *Is it real or just my imagination? Can I reach it or will the Zherosi catch me first?*

The old man ahead of her reeled, and Faelia flung out a hand to steady him. He seemed unaware of her, muttering incessantly as he plodded on. Only when she caught a phrase did she realize he was repeating the traveler's prayer.

She had heard it last on the morning she and Temet left the village. Grain-Mother Barasa had sketched the signs of protection on her forehead and over her heart while reciting the ancient blessing: "May the wind be at your back and the sun upon your shoulders. May the moon chase away the darkness and the stars guide your feet. May your path be smooth, your journey swift, and your homecoming joyous."

Although the path was far from smooth and the journey agonizingly slow, the wind gusted from the south and the last rays of the sun beat warmly on her shoulders. Surely, those were good signs.

The thin wail cut through her hopeful thoughts like a dagger. Whirling around, she spied two men racing across the moor. Atop the hill behind them stood a line of warriors.

Over the terrified wheezing of the old man, Faelia heard the screams of the women and the higher, shriller shrieks of the children. She told herself to move, but her legs refused to obey. She could only stand and watch the Zherosi commander lift his hand.

The archers raised their bows. Her hand automatically reached for an arrow before she remembered that she had none. No bow, no arrows, only the sword hanging uselessly at her side and the dagger sheathed at her waist.

Helplessly, she watched her comrades dodge between clumps of heather in a desperate, hopeless attempt to outrun the arrows arcing toward them. Only when they flung out their arms and tumbled onto the grass did her mind reassume command.

She fell into an awkward, lurching trot, afraid to put too much weight on her right foot lest it buckle. As she passed the old man, she grabbed his arm, dragging him after her.

Ahead of her, the old woman staggered into the pass. "Stay to the right and the left!" Faelia shouted. She had told them about the pits, but in their frantic attempt to escape, they were bound to forget. Abandoning the old man, she quickened her pace. She had not brought these people so far to lose them now.

Another glance over her shoulder revealed the Zherosi trotting down the hill. A perfect square of warriors, every foot moving in unison. It was inhuman, that precision.

She scanned the hills before her, hoping to see movement among the sprouting bracken or heads peering out from behind the rocks and boulders. When she didn't, she fought the nauseating panic and told herself that her folk were simply well-hidden. That they were waiting for the Zherosi to come within bowshot. That they would take them by surprise and turn that perfect square of warriors into a disorganized mass of men fleeing for their lives.

As she reached the gap, she saw Braden shoving people to the right and left. She squeezed his shoulder and turned back to help the stragglers. A hoarse moan escaped her when she saw how quickly the Zherosi were closing in.

She tugged at a boy's tunic. Pulled a weeping woman's arm. Bent over a sobbing child, wincing at the stab of pain in her wounded arm as she lifted him. The child's breath warmed her left cheek. Something soft brushed the other. She heard a dull thunk off to her right and turned to find an arrow quivering in the turf.

Why weren't her folk shooting? The Zherosi had to be within range now. If they waited to catch them in the narrow confines of the pass, it would be too late.

She thrust the child into the arms of a passing woman and turned toward the tortured gasping behind her. A tremulous smile lit the old man's face.

"We're almost home," she assured him.

His smile froze. Between one step and the next, his legs faltered. He was still reaching for her when he fell facedown in the dirt. Only then did she see the arrow in his back.

"Fa!" she screamed to the hills. "Where are you?"

"Fa . . ." Callie whispered.

"Hold."

Darak knew Callie would obey. He was less sure about Rothisar. He could sense his eagerness for the kill as surely as he could smell Callie's sweat. The very air was alive with that eagerness. Dread mingled with urgency, it danced over his exposed skin like a lover's caress.

Ruthlessly, he tamped down the surge of bloodlust. Just as ruthlessly, he forced his gaze away from Faelia to assess the Zherosi once again. Ten rows of ten—more than twice their number. And all warriors, skilled in hand-to-hand combat. Against that, he had hunters who could bring down a doe at a hundred paces. Fishermen who had only used their spears to kill salmon. And boys armed with slings.

Only if they lured them into the pass did they have a chance. And only if he used his daughter as bait might the Zherosi fall into the trap.

No seasoned commander would enter the pass without knowing what lay beyond. But no seasoned commander would have followed these few survivors so far. Temet must be dead, the rest of his warriors scattered. From what he could see, these were refugees—women, children, old folk—weaponless and exhausted, counting on Faelia to lead them to safety.

They would have to kill at least half of the invaders with their arrows before risking a close fight. Temet—may his spirit live on in the Forever Isles—had told him they wore padded leather vests to protect their chests and loins, but squinting against the brilliance of the setting sun, he could swear several wore bronze armor. Those must be the commanders. Kill them and the others might panic.

But not yet.

His fingers stroked the haft of the ax that lay at his feet. During the raid in which Keirith had been stolen, he'd had to have his son tie it to his wrist. Age had curled the stumps of the missing fingers into claws. If they were unsightly, they gave him a better grip.

The bow first. Then the ax.

Again, the bronze-helmeted leader raised his hand. Again, the formidable square halted. The archers took aim. His gaze snapped to Faelia who had gone back to help the stragglers.

Get down, child. Get down!

She yanked a woman behind a boulder. They huddled together as the arrows hissed past them. Three more stragglers toppled. As the Zherosi resumed their march, Faelia pulled the woman to her feet. Shouting encouragement to the others, they struggled on.

"She won't leave them." Keirith's voice, off to his right, strained but calm.

"Hold."

He tore his gaze from his daughter to glance down into the pass. The first of the refugees had reached the far end. Already, Arun was herding them toward the hill fort. He spied Nemek among the boulders, readying the net. The boy at the entrance to the pass continued to direct the stragglers. He couldn't be much older than Rigat, but apart from frequent glances to monitor the progress of his pursuers, he seemed as steady as the rocks that studded the hillsides.

The six stragglers shambled toward the pass with an agonizing slowness that made his heart pound. As if in response, the Zherosi quickened their pace. Out of the corner of his eye, he saw Rigat shift slightly. His bow lay across his upraised knee, the nocked arrow held loosely between his fingers. Only the quick rise and fall of his chest betrayed his nervousness.

The wind carried the shouted command to him. The Zherosi broke into a trot, like a pack of wolves closing in for the kill. But still they maintained that tight formation. Gods, the commanders must train them for moons to instill that kind of discipline.

The stragglers stumbled into the pass. Faelia and the woman lagged behind. From this height, they looked as small as children. Strands of hair hung across Faelia's face. She never took the time to braid her hair properly. Griane always scolded her about that.

Another shouted command and the Zherosi began to sprint.

They can taste it now. They're hungry for it. The screams. The crunch of bone under their swords. The blood spattering their faces. They can smell the fear and its stink is sweeter than honeysuckle. Even their commander couldn't stop them from charging into the pass now.

"Fa . . ." Callie's voice trembled with urgency.

"Hold."

"She won't make it."

"She will."

The two women lumbered awkwardly through the pass. The boy rushed forward to help, seizing the woman's free arm and draping it around his shoulders. But for every step they took, their pursuers took three.

Leave her, Faelia! Save yourself!

The sun slipped behind the southernmost Twin. Without its blinding glare, Darak could see the huge swell of the woman's belly—and knew Faelia would never leave her behind.

As the Zherosi entered the pass, their perfect formation heaved and broke apart. The archers in the front were squeezed back. The warriors on the sides scrambled over the sharply rising ground. Then the commander shouted an order, and the seething mass reformed, marching five abreast behind him.

Only fifty paces separated them from Faelia and her companions. The three were practically crawling through the pass, clinging to boulders and clumps of grass, slipping on the loose scree of pebbles and dirt.

"Fa!"

It was too soon. Only half of the Zherosi force was inside the pass. But dear gods, he couldn't just crouch here and watch them cut down his daughter.

Faelia stopped. She said something to the boy who made a violent gesture of negation.

Good gods, there's no time for this!

As the boy took the woman's arm and led her away, Faelia turned to face the advancing Zherosi.

"Please!" Callie implored.

Faelia tucked an errant lock of hair behind her ear. With her right hand, she drew her sword. With her left, she unsheathed her dagger. She scanned the ground for a long moment, then limped slowly into the center of the pass. She planted her feet. And waited.

My clever girl. My brave, clever, foolish girl.

Through the film of tears, Darak saw the commander throw up his hand. As the Zherosi came to a halt, he called out something to Faelia that made his warriors laugh. Faelia's only response was to shift her weight. Again, the commander taunted her and again, she refused to rise to the bait. He made an impatient gesture and one of the archers stepped forward.

Darak raised his bow and silently cursed his shaking hands.

"I can take him, Fa."

He studied Rigat for a moment, then nodded. "On my signal."

And if you possess the magic to make arrows fly true, use it now.

Faelia threw back her head and laughed, hoarse and raucous as a raven. "Is this Zherosi courage?" she shouted. "Are you afraid to fight a woman?" And she spat.

Even if the commander didn't understand the words, the tone and the gesture were clear. He drew his sword and strode forward. The warriors in the front ranks lowered their shields, exchanging grins and remarks. Those in the back scrambled up the sides of the hills to get a better view.

Darak waited, counting each step the commander took. Over the jeers of the warriors, he imagined he could hear the pebbles crunching under the man's feet and the rasp of Faelia's breath.

Just ten more steps.

His heart was pounding so hard that he thought the entire Zherosi force must hear it.

Five.

He took aim on a warrior in the front line.

Two.

It was like that moment before dawn, when time seemed to stutter to a halt and the world held its breath.

One.

The commander's foot came down. The thin layer of turf gave way. His head whipped back. His free hand clawed at the air. His startled cry became a scream as his body hit the sharpened stakes at the bottom of the pit.

"Now, Rigat!"

A moment later, an archer was clutching the shaft of the arrow embedded in his throat. A dozen more went down in the rain of arrows that followed. Men reeled as stones slammed into their foreheads. Shields went up, protecting heads and chests. Slowly, they began to retreat.

"Aim for the men in the back. Go for their legs!"

Darak drew another arrow from his quiver, nocked it, chose his target, and let fly. His right hand moved ceaselessly, from bowstring to quiver and back again. Nock. Aim. Draw. Release.

Caught in the deadly crossfire from his men and Madig's, the Zherosi stumbled over the fallen and clawed their way up the hillsides, seeking escape. A few bolted for the far end of pass, only to be cut down, easy targets in the open.

One archer paused. Too late, Darak realized the man's quarry. He drew the bowstring back to his ear and released, but the archer's arrow was already flying toward the limping figure.

Faelia's hair swirled around her head as the impact spun her sideways. Before she hit the ground, Darak was charging down the slope.

As Keirith raced after Fa, Callie sprang up. Rigat lunged for him and grabbed his arm. "You can't fight them with a dagger!"

"I have to do something!"

"Then stay here and use your sling. That'll help the most. Please, Callie!"

Conn stepped forward and squeezed Callie's shoulder. "I'll go."

Before Rigat could urge him to stay, Conn charged down the hill after Keirith.

He waited in an agony of fear until Callie crouched beside him again. Only then did he draw on the simmering power. Just enough to ensure that each arrow flew true, piercing the legs driving closer to Faelia, the unprotected throats bellowing with rage and fear. Like a hawk stooping on a pigeon, each arrow sliced through the air, screaming a shrill song of defiance, of blood, of death. As one song ebbed, another rose, feeding the power, feeding him.

His tribe mates raced down from the hills. Those at the far end of the pass abandoned their net to converge around

Fa and Faelia, Keirith and Conn. He might be able to guide his arrows through that milling mass of people, but he had never used his magic that way and didn't dare test it now.

Madig's men were engaging the retreating Zherosi, but they would never be able to penetrate their defenses or keep the tight wedge of warriors from breaking through to freedom.

There must be a way.

Atop the opposite hill, he spied a group of men straining to leverage a boulder free. A shiver of excitement rippled down his spine, sparking a sympathetic flash of power.

Not yet.

He closed his eyes, drawing strength from the earth beneath his feet and the cool breeze caressing his face. From the sweat rolling down his forehead and the last rays of the setting sun. Feeding his power with that of earth and air, water and fire. He called on Halam, the earth goddess, and Lacha, goddess of lakes and rivers. On Bel, the sun god, and Hernan, god of the forest. He whispered the Maker's name and the Trickster's. Finally, he invoked the name of the Unmaker, the Lord of Chaos, for chaos was what he must wreak if his people were to survive.

Slowly, patiently, Rigat fed the power and smiled as the fire within him crackled with anticipation.

They hesitated. They saw his swarthy skin, his black hair, his dark eyes—and they hesitated, trying to understand why their comrade was dressed like one of the Tree People. By the time they realized their mistake it was too late.

Keirith had long since discarded his fishing spear and snatched up a sword from a dead Zheroso. He ripped through leather and flesh, feeling the warm spatter of blood against his cheeks, tasting the salty tang of it on his lips. The screams of the wounded and the dying filled his ears and echoed with sickening intensity through his spirit.

He was dimly aware that others had joined them: Rothisar, bellowing like a stag in rut; shy Adinn, slashing with mindless ferocity; and Conn, who had abandoned the safety of the hilltop to charge after him, Conn, who guarded his weak side with a captured shield and his formidable club.

Behind him, Faelia grunted with every blow she landed.

When Keirith dared a glance over his shoulder, he discovered his father swinging an ax with his right hand and a Zherosi sword with his left, snarling like the wolf that was his vision mate. He half expected him to dash into the thick of the fighting as he had during that long-ago raid on their village at Eagles Mount.

Memories of that battle clashed with this one. Each warrior who lunged at him was the Big One, eager to drag him away from his home, creep into the dark hole in the belly of the ship, and force him to his knees. Each jab of the sword was one of his captors thrusting into him. Each scream was his, a raw cry of shock and protest.

Keirith stumbled backward to avoid a thrust. Conn pivoted, club crashing down on Keirith's attacker. Pulled off balance by the blow, Conn staggered, trapping his stolen shield beneath his knee. A backhanded swing of his club caught a charging Zheroso on the leg and sent him reeling, but another stepped into the breach. Blocked by Conn's body, Keirith could only watch as the man raised his sword for the killing blow.

Unbidden, the power flared. As it slammed into the Zheroso's unprotected spirit, the man's shock reverberated through Keirith. More shocking was the wave of savage joy that filled him, the same joy he had felt the day he had attacked Xevhan.

For a heartbeat, they stared at each other, more intimately joined than lovers. A shadow crossed the man's face. And then the side of his head caved in, crushed by Conn's club.

The Zheroso fell to his knees. The sword slid from his grasp. Blobs of gray-red brain matter oozed out from beneath the leather helmet. His mouth gaped, desperately sucking air. And all the while, the dark eyes stared up at him. Then they glazed over and he slid to the ground.

He was only a little older than Rigat.

<Keirith.>

For one horrifying moment, he thought it was the fallen Zheroso. Then he recognized his brother's voice. He had not even felt Rigat's presence, had never suspected that he possessed the power to enter another man's spirit unnoticed. Instinctively, he fled deeper into himself.

<Keirith, stop! Listen to me!>

With a supreme effort of will, he obeyed.

<You've got to get them out of the pass.>

We're trying!

The wave of impatience jolted him. *<Our men, not theirs!>*

But . . .

<Just do it. Now! I don't know how well I can control it.>

He could feel the effort behind the brusque words, and the simmering power, barely contained. Dear gods, such power. Far stronger than Xevhan's. How would Rigat control it? He'd be destroyed—they would all be destroyed— if he unleashed it.

<Please, Keirith. Go. Now!>

His father and sister were in the middle of the group pursuing the retreating wedge of Zherosi. Everyone was too intent on the chase to listen to his shouts. He finally fought his way past the others and seized his father's arm.

With a feral snarl, Fa spun around. Keirith leaped back to avoid his slashing sword. A wave of cold sweat broke out over his body. His legs shook uncontrollably. Then he realized it wasn't his legs shaking, but the ground.

For a moment, he was back in Pilozhat, crouching on the steps of the temple of Zhe, holding Malaq in his arms, watching his smile fade as death claimed him. But instead of Malaq's dark eyes, his father's gray ones locked with his.

The sounds of battle faded in the anguish of shared memory. The thrust of Xevhan's blade. The initial burst of agony. His spirit soaring higher and higher, flying as it once had with the eagle, seeking peace and calm and escape, only to be summoned by his father's beseeching voice: "Come into me!"

The earth shuddered, forcing them back to the moment. They were alone, surrounded by the bodies of the dead and dying. A dozen paces ahead, Faelia and the others pressed their attack.

"We have to retreat!" Keirith shouted. "We have to get out of the pass."

The gray eyes searched his face, then scanned the hillsides. Rigat and Callie stood atop the eastern hill, bathed in the red-gold light of sunset. As they watched, Callie raised something in his hands. Even above the tumult of battle, the mournful bleat of the ram's horn was clear.

Together, he and Fa raced toward the others, shouting at them to retreat, grabbing arms, shoulders, the backs of tunics in their urgency. The ram's horn sounded again. Anger changed to confusion as their shouts penetrated minds numbed by violence. Impelled by the passion in his father's voice and the desperation in his face, they began to fall back.

A third time, the ram's horn sounded.

"Get them out of here!" Keirith shouted.

As he searched in vain for Conn, a bronze-helmeted warrior stepped forward. Seeing his comrades rallying around him, Keirith summoned the grim, unforgiving face of the Son of Zhe and the resonant voice of the god-made-flesh that had brought men and women to their knees. He recalled words in a language unspoken for years. And just as he had in Pilozhat, he called down doom upon the Zherosi.

"Womb of Earth speaks. Tremble before her anger."

Here and there, a hand made a furtive gesture to avert evil. Most simply stared at him. Slowly, he backed away; to turn and run would shatter the illusion. He felt a hand clasp his elbow. Fourteen years ago, half of Pilozhat had followed him through the predawn gloom, chanting and praying and shouting his name. The light was just as dim in the shadowy depths of the pass, but today, his father was his acolyte, guiding him over the blood-slick earth, past the bodies, around the pit.

Pebbles skittered down the hillsides. Rock cracked against rock. The hills themselves began to creak and groan.

In the tribal tongue, he shouted to those on the hilltops to run. Then he cried, "Womb of Earth screams! Even in the land of the Tree People. And she brings death to those who rape her!"

With a sound louder than a hundred cracks of thunder, boulders ripped away from the earth, uprooting gorse bushes and clumps of moor grass as they careened downhill. Rocks caromed off them and hurtled through the air. But only in the middle of the pass where the Zherosi were trampling each other in a vain attempt to escape.

Boulders crashed into the tightly packed mass of men, throwing up a shower of dust and debris, obscuring the crushed bodies, the shattered limbs. But neither the incessant rumble of the rockslide nor the louder thud of boulders hitting earth could drown out the screams.

The ground shuddered, throwing him against his father whose face bore a look of stunned shock. On the hilltops, men scattered like rabbits. Where Callie and Rigat had stood, there was only a lone figure, silhouetted against the darkening blue of the sky.

He spotted Conn bending over a fallen Zheroso. When he shouted his milk-brother's name, Conn straightened. A huge grin split his face. Keirith started toward him, but Conn waved him back.

"Go on! I'll be right behind you."

Fa tugged his arm. They raced off, raising their arms to protect their heads from the stones that rained down, choking on the wave of dust that engulfed them. By the time they reached safety, the ground had fallen still.

As the dust settled, he made out Faelia's tall figure among a knot of boys. Their slings hung forgotten at their sides as they stared into the pass. It took him a moment to recognize the stranger as the boy who had helped Faelia lead the stragglers to safety. He'd thought him younger because he was so short, but judging from the fair stubble that sprouted on his hollow cheeks, he was probably fifteen.

"Braden," Faelia said, nodding to him. But her eyes were on Fa who slumped onto a boulder, one fist pressed against his chest.

As Keirith fell to his knees, his father's head came up. "I'm fine, son." Leaning heavily on Keirith's shoulder, he pushed himself to his feet and reached for Faelia. He cradled her face between his hands, their foreheads touching in a wordless moment of thanksgiving. Then Fa drew himself up and glanced around, frowning.

"Nemek? And the others?"

"I sent them to reinforce Madig," Faelia replied. As Fa turned to follow, she plucked at his sleeve. "It'll be over before you get there. One way or another."

After a moment, he nodded. His frown deepened as he gazed at the broken shaft of the arrow still protruding from Faelia's shoulder.

"Mam'll take care of it." Despite her obvious pain, Faelia managed a smile.

Fa's breathing was less labored now, but his face was still strained. Suddenly, the tension left his body. Keirith heard him mutter, "Thank you, Maker," and saw Callie stumbling toward them, panting like a winded deer.

"You're all right?" Fa demanded.

Callie nodded, his gaze lingering on Faelia. "I was so scared for you . . ."

"And Rigat?"

A shudder racked Callie's thin frame. "Rigat's . . . fine. And there are more men coming."

"Dear gods . . ."

"Not Zherosi! Our people. Twenty or thirty. I saw them from the hill."

"Temet," Faelia whispered.

"He's alive?" Fa asked. "But I thought—"

"He tried to draw them off. The Zherosi. But they followed us instead."

His father nodded and slumped against the boulder again. "Are you hurt, son?"

Keirith shook his head. He had shallow sword cuts on both arms and he ached all over—especially his ribs where the edge of a shield had buffeted him—but such minor wounds weren't even worth mentioning. He was surprised when Fa pulled him down beside him and leaned close to kiss his cheek.

"Did you cause it?" his father whispered. "The rockslide?"

"Nay." He scanned the eastern hilltop, but Rigat was gone. As he searched the clusters of exhausted men stumbling through the pass, he frowned. "Where did Conn go?"

A tumble of rocks and debris marked the place where he had been standing.

"Maybe he's looking for Ennit," Fa said.

Slowly, Keirith got to his feet. He took one step, then another. Then he started running, slipping on the shifting stones, dodging the larger boulders and the helmeted corpses, veering toward each bare-headed figure, only to hurry past, shock at spying a fallen tribe mate warring with the guilty relief that it was not Conn.

Please, Maker, let him be all right.

He saw a dark-haired figure, belly down and half-buried

under the debris. A hand, flung out as if beseeching his help. And his milk-brother's face, deathly pale beneath the dust and grime.

"I'll be right behind you."

Keirith fell to his knees and seized the limp hand. Conn's pulse fluttered under his fingertips, faint and erratic.

He clawed at the stones, cursing and praying as he fought to free him. The stones were too small to crush his legs. The blood matting the hair on the back of his head worried Keirith more. And Conn's right arm, wedged under his body. He could easily have broken it in the fall. But Mam could take care of that. And the bruises. Even a concussion. Conn was alive. That was all that mattered.

His breath caught when he saw the blood. Pooling on the stones between Conn's legs, soaking his breeches from hip to knee. Frantically, he grabbed Conn's arm and rolled him onto his back. Only then did he see the broken sword gripped in his fist and the blood spurting from the jagged rent in his breeches.

He ripped off his belt and tied it around Conn's leg. Then he yanked his tunic over his head and used his dagger to slice through the seams at one shoulder. Even before he finished knotting the makeshift bandage, the blood had soaked through it.

He cut off the other sleeve. Bound Conn's leg again, knowing it would not stop the relentless spurt of blood, but unable to sit there and watch his life leak away.

Cursing, he pried the sword from Conn's fingers and flung it aside. He could imagine him bending over a fallen Zheroso, pausing for just a moment to snatch up the coveted bronze blade, never imagining that such a small delay would matter.

Chance. Ill-luck. The will of the gods. The same gods who allowed a stone to smash into Conn's head. Who watched his knees buckle and his body slump. Who stood by—uncaring, unfeeling—and allowed him to fall in just such a way that the blade would rip open his leg.

He pulled Conn's unresisting body into his arms and called his name. Conn's eyes fluttered open. An uncertain smile blossomed on his dirty face.

"Keir?"

"Aye."

"My head . . . it hurts."

"A stone hit you."

Conn's chest heaved as he gasped. "My legs, too? Can't feel them."

"I . . . I think maybe you broke something."

"Damn. Can't do . . . The Dignified Walk. Maybe . . . A Lugubrious Lurch."

Conn's wheezing laugh turned into a frantic gasp for air. As Keirith reached for the flailing hand, he spied the familiar scar at the base of Conn's right thumb, the scar from the blood oath they had twice sworn: to be friends in this life and brothers in the next.

"Keir?"

"I'm right here. I've got you."

"Hope . . . I didn't tear . . . my breeches. Hircha . . . will . . . scold me. Clumsy . . ."

Conn wheezed again. Then his back suddenly arched and his heels dug into the ground.

As if his senses were failing with Conn's, the shouts and screams around him faded until he heard only his milk-brother's tortured gasps and his own voice, hoarse and broken, murmuring ceaseless, useless words of comfort and promises that could never be fulfilled—that everything would be different now, that their bond would be stronger than ever, that they would be friends in this life and brothers in the next.

All the while, he searched for the stillness and emptiness of trance, hoping to ease the convulsions, to stop the pain, to help Conn's spirit slip free. Rigat could have done it—he might even have been able to save Conn—but Keirith could only hold him and pray for his release.

Yet when that strong, solid body finally relaxed, it brought no relief, only a heavy weight squeezing his chest, denying him the breath to weep or protest or scream curses at the gods. As if the burden of breathing had passed from Conn to him, he gasped, rocking his milk-brother in his arms, burying his face in the soft hair that still smelled faintly of grass and sheep, squeezing the limp hand that was always so soft from the grease in the wool.

And then he felt arms around him, rocking them both,

and his father's voice, murmuring his name. But he found no comfort in those sheltering arms or that soft voice.

"It was Rigat," he blurted. "He did it."

He knew it wasn't Rigat's fault. If not for him, many more would have been lost today. But that knowledge couldn't ease his grief. Conn was dead. And the boy Keirith had once been—who had suckled at the same breasts as his milk-brother, played with him on the slopes of Eagles Mount, and always believed they would grow old together— today, that boy had died as well.

Chapter 8

"PUSH!" MOTHER NARTHI COMMANDED.

Wila just crouched on the birthing stones, sobbing. Griane blew a hank of hair off her face and exchanged an impatient glance with the old healer.

Within moments of stumbling into the hill fort, Mother Narthi had volunteered to help with Wila's birthing. Blessing her good fortune, Griane had accepted, knowing it would ease the girl to see a friendly face.

Since the birthing hut was outside the hill fort, they had brought Wila to the hut the three priestesses shared, leaving Hircha to tend to the other survivors. Most were simply exhausted and hungry and terrified, but soon enough, the longhut would be filled with the wounded.

Please gods, let it be over.

She wasn't sure if she prayed for the end of Wila's labor or the end of the battle. After the ram's horn had sounded, she'd heard that awful noise—louder than any clap of thunder—but all they could see from the entrance to the hill fort was a cloud of dust. Since then, she had been too busy to learn more.

Crouched between Wila's feet, Narthi looked like a large, white-haired frog. When she frowned up at the straining girl, the resemblance grew stronger.

"Push!"

The poor girl was little more than a child herself. She'd seen her village destroyed, her family murdered, and now—among strangers—she was giving birth half a moon before her time. Small wonder she wept. But weeping wouldn't help the child in her belly.

"Lift her higher," Griane told Barasa, and won an approving nod from Narthi; if Wila crouched too low, she risked crushing the newborn.

Together, they heaved her up, arms bracing her back, shoulders propped in her armpits. Wila hung there like an overstuffed bag of barley and seemed to weigh twice as much.

Narthi brushed back the filthy hair. "I know you're tired, child. But I need you to help me. To help your babe. Do you understand?"

Panting fiercely, Wila managed to nod.

"Good. When the next pain comes, push with it."

Wila grunted as another contraction seized her. As her grunt grew to a bellow, Griane shared a satisfied smile with Narthi. Not long now, thank the gods. Her arms ached and Barasa looked like she was going to faint. Merciful gods, the woman was Grain-Mother to the tribe, the symbol of fertility. And she had brought two children into the world—may their spirits live on in the Forever Isles. How could she be so squeamish?

"Hah! There's the top of the head. One more push ought to do it."

Wila pushed, crying out with the effort. This time, a new voice joined hers. With a crow of triumph, Narthi slipped the babe from between Wila's legs and lifted it.

"A girl! A beautiful girl."

As Griane and Barasa eased Wila onto the rabbitskins, Narthi cleaned the babe with a soft scrap of lamb's wool. Half laughing, half sobbing, Wila whispered, "Let me hold her."

Griane took the babe from Narthi and laid her in Wila's arms where she began rooting at Wila's breast. Narthi looked up from tying a second knot of twine around the cord connecting mother and child.

"Impatient. A good sign."

Griane fetched the brew of feverfew and Maker's mantle sweetened with honey, then held Wila's head as she sipped. As always, the brew did its work. Soon, Wila was obeying Mother Narthi's instructions to push again. The old healer used her needle-sharp dagger to cut the cord, then frowned at the afterbirth until Griane held out a bowl.

"When we relight the fires, we can throw it in and count the pops."

"I hope there's lots," Wila said dreamily. "We want lots of babes." Then her face screwed up and she began to weep.

Griane looked down at the tiny scrap of humanity suckling fiercely at the girl's breast. Homeless, fatherless, thrust into the world too soon—still, this child was strong, a survivor like her mother.

She kneaded the ache in the small of her back and ducked out of the hut. Drawn by the newborn's cries, Lisula and Nedia hurried toward her. They would join Barasa in the ritual blessing. Mother Narthi would look after Wila. But the man who should have held out his arms in recognition of his firstborn child lay miles away, a feast for maggots.

Please, gods, let Darak be safe. And my boys. And Faelia.

"Someone's coming!"

Arun's voice made her heart thud. Boys scrambled up the uneven stones pounded into the earthworks to join him on the narrow shelf, all of them standing on tiptoe to peer over the top. Old men clutching spears and axes shouted up to the boys, demanding to know what they saw. The women's anxious voices only added to the confusion.

Trath elbowed his way through the crowd, shouting for quiet. The noise abated to nervous muttering, and finally to a silence filled with anticipation and dread. Then Griane heard a young voice hailing the hill fort. Relief made her legs tremble.

"It's Rigat!" Arun called, confirming what she already knew.

She swiped at her eyes and wormed her way to the front of the crowd.

"I said . . . oh, it's you." Frowning, Trath nudged Donncha, allowing Griane to squeeze in between them.

In the deepening gloom of twilight, she could just make out Rigat's figure pelting up the hill, but the renewed babble of the women drowned out his words.

"It must be all right," Donncha said. "They must have driven them away."

"Woman, would you hush?" Trath bellowed.

But nothing could silence the speculation and prayers. Trath had to be content with shooing everyone back so that Rigat could enter the hill fort. Even before he spoke, his shining face told her they had won.

"They're running away! We've driven them out!"

In the burst of weeping and exclamations, he spared her a quick, hard hug. "Fa's safe. And Keirith and Callie. Faelia's hurt, but not too bad."

Rigat sketched out the details of the attack, including the devastating rockslide that had buried at least half of the Zherosi force, but when the women began inundating him with questions about their sons and husbands, Trath silenced them with another bellow.

"We'll find out soon enough. For now, no one is to leave the hill fort. There may still be some gods-cursed Zherosi in the valley. Light your fires. Get these new folk settled. And help Mother Griane and Hircha with our wounded."

From somewhere in the crowd, Griane heard Gortin's quavering voice, raised in the song of thanksgiving. They all joined in, a ragged chorus broken by outbursts of weeping. Even Trath's eyes looked suspiciously moist.

This was the hardest time. She remembered that all too well from the raid on Eagles Mount. Every woman around her stared at the pass, each filled with the same desperate hope.

My man is alive. My son is safe. Soon, I'll see them walking toward the hill fort. Soon, I'll hold them in my arms.

Then came the reasoning.

It's all right if they're hurt. Torn flesh can be stitched. Broken limbs can be set. Just let them be alive.

And finally, the bargaining.

Merciful Maker, I'll offer a sacrifice every day for the rest of my life if you bring them home safe.

Did any of them, in the secret recesses of their hearts, ever offer up one of their men for another?

If you must take one, take my husband. He's lived a full life. But not my boy. Please, Maker, don't take my son.

Griane closed her eyes. Her heart squeezed into a tight fist. She could hear Mirili's voice, quiet and competent as always, as she gathered the group of women in whose homes the newcomers would shelter. The longhut had already been prepared for the wounded, but food must be cooked, clothes found to replace the rags the survivors wore. Protecting and nourishing life—the task of women through the ages.

She felt Rigat's arm around her waist and opened her eyes. As she wiped a smudge of dirt from his cheek, he whispered, "It was me, Mam. I did it."

Ever since he was a child, he had always come to her first, the words tumbling out of him as he shared his latest triumph.

Griane smiled. "What did you do, love?"

In the same excited whisper, he told her.

Darak left Callie with Keirith while he went in search of Ennit. He found him atop the eastern hill where Conn had been positioned.

Ennit's worried expression brightened as he approached. "Have you seen Conn? I can't find him anywhere."

He had planned how he would break the news, chosen the words with care. But now, he simply stammered, "Ennit. Conn's . . . I'm sorry. Gods. Conn is dead."

Ennit just stared at him.

"Come. I'll take you to him."

With every step, Ennit seemed to age, growing smaller and weaker before his eyes. But he only broke down when he saw his boy. Darak held him as he had held Keirith. He had no words of comfort to offer Ennit either. What words could console a father who had lost his only son? Or a man who had lost his best friend? As he watched them carry Conn home, he could only be grateful that his sons were safe, that his best friend was alive, that—perhaps—Keirith and Ennit could comfort each other.

Reluctantly, he assumed the mantle of chief again. He sent the younger boys back to the hill fort for mullein stalks to use for torches, fishing nets to carry the dead and

wounded. He sent two groups of men to scour the hills for
the fallen. Faelia stubbornly refused to go to the hill fort
until she knew Temet's fate, but finally Darak convinced
her that she would only injure her ankle further by clam-
bering over fallen rocks. He watched her hobble away, then
walked into the pass to dispatch the dying Zherosi.

Callie insisted on accompanying him. After the third killing, his son took the dagger from his trembling fingers. He
knelt beside the next man and gently tilted his head. Then
he thrust the tip of the dagger into the spot behind the ear
and, with swift, brutal efficiency, sliced downward through
the jugular. Sweet, softhearted Callie, who could never
bring himself to help Conn and Ennit with the autumn
slaughtering.

Only when they had completed their grisly mission did
Callie give way. Darak knelt beside him while he retched.
As he stroked his son's hair, he recalled the savagery of
the battle and the burning, gut-deep joy that had filled him.
Was that why he was so reluctant to join Temet's rebellion?
Because, despite all his talk of keeping his people safe, he
simply feared he would enjoy the killing too much?

He thrust the thought aside; he had more immediate concerns now.

When he and Callie reached the southern end of the
pass, they found dozens of Zherosi sprawled on the blood-
slick grass. The tribe's dead had already been laid out,
hands folded over their bellies. In the gathering dusk, he
had to bend close to identify them.

Jadan and Easad lay side by side. Easad was only twelve;
his father must have given in to his pleas to fight with the
men. Kithean, Trath's only grandson. Ifan, the last of Ifrenn's
line. Usok, the youngest member of the council. Elasoth,
whom he had never forgiven for turning against Keirith.

In a subdued voice, Sion told him Madig and Nemek had
just been carried away, both unconscious and bleeding from
multiple wounds. Then he jerked his head toward a still
figure, slumped against a pile of rocks.

Darak caught Temet as he tried to stand and eased him
back down. A filthy bandage, stained with fresh blood,
bound his left leg. Another, equally filthy, was wrapped
around his head.

"Faelia?" Temet demanded in a hoarse voice.

"She took an arrow in her shoulder. And twisted her ankle. But she's safe."

Temet let his breath out in a shuddering sigh and turned his face away. "My warriors . . ."

"We'll get them to the hill fort."

"I sent the rest—the ones who could still march—after the Zherosi." His fingers dug into Darak's bicep. "We won't let any get away."

But night was coming on and Temet's men were exhausted. It would be all too easy to lose the trail. And if even one Zheroso managed to escape . . .

Let it go. Just for tonight.

Darak squeezed the hand still gripping his arm. It was ice cold. Shock. And exhaustion.

"Come on, man. Let's go home."

Torches flickered on the hillsides and across the moors as men searched for the missing. They carried the body of young Nionik down from the western hill. Born to Catha the day he and Keirith had returned to the village—the symbol of hope for them all—he still clutched his sling in his grimy fist.

Seg lay in the pass. He must have been trapped in the rockslide, for his body was crushed, the back of his skull shattered. If Madig's wounds didn't kill him, the loss of his only son might.

No one had seen Rigat.

With Gheala and the torches lighting the way, they carried their dead home. The curving stars of the Sickle were just visible in the southeast. "Sickle in the sky at night, blackbirds singing at first light." The old rhyme that celebrated the first signs of spring. But the only song his tribe would sing was the death chant.

As he trudged up the hill, he could hear lamentations, punctuated by a keening wail as another woman learned the fate of her son or husband. Darak wished he could simply give way to grief, but while his body was heavy with exhaustion, his mind kept ticking off the plans that must be made.

The priestesses will clean the bodies. Gods. Poor Lisula. Too many to lay out in the Death Hut. We'll have to cut gorse for a pyre.

Strip the Zherosi dead on the morrow. Then dump the bodies in the pits. Pit. The one's buried under the rockslide. We'll have to dig another. Or bury them out on the moors.

But first, tally our folk. Tonight. Make sure they're all accounted for. And post sentries on the hills. In groups. In case there are any Zherosi stragglers. I'll have Trath— Nay, he'll be grieving. We're all grieving. We've all lost someone. Except my family. How did we escape?

What did Rigat do?

A shrill scream jolted him from his thoughts. He hurried into the hill fort and discovered a cluster of women and children: Alada with her arms around Madig's little girls, Mirili and Arun hushing Catha. She had lost her firstborn son and her brother Elasoth today. Darak prayed she would not lose her husband, too.

As Catha struggled in Mirili's arms, Darak seized her shoulders and forced her to look at him. "Nemek's still alive. And so is your father," he quickly added, nodding to Madig's girls.

Alada knelt before the trembling children. "Mother Griane and Hircha will take care of your father. The Grain-Mother and Tree-Father will sit with Seg all night so he won't be alone. And you two can stay with me and Duba."

It was the best place for them now. Alada and Duba had already adopted four orphans. Both women understood sorrow. Alada had lost her beloved father, his old mentor Sanok. Duba, her husband and son. Neither had sought a husband after their losses, finding strength in each other and love from the little ones in their care.

"Just until your father is well enough to come home," Alada was saying. She shot him a warning glance, but he knew enough not to caution them that Madig might never come home.

As Alada led the girls away, Darak turned to Arun. "Take your mam home. Try and get her to rest."

Arun's thin frame trembled, but he nodded. Only eleven, but the man of his family for now.

Just as I was at that age.

As Arun led his mother away, Darak said, "Nemek is strong, Mirili. In body and spirit."

She nodded, white-faced but calm. "I'll sit with him."

"Why not let Griane see to him first?"

A grim smile twisted her lips. "I'm no stranger to blood, Darak. Or death. I've felt Ardal's breath upon my neck before. Felt him brush past me to choose another. If he comes for Nemek, I want to be there. I may not be able to defeat the Dark Hunter, but at least I can fight him." After a moment, she added, "These are the battles women wage." Without waiting for his reply, she followed the men carrying Nemek to the longhut.

Someone had already strewn hides and furs in the center of the village and laid the bodies atop them. Lisula and Nedia knelt on either side of Conn. Tears coursed down Nedia's cheeks as she washed the dirt from Conn's face, but she continued to chant with her mother and Barasa.

Darak crouched beside Lisula, uncertain whether he should touch her or speak. Her soft chanting ceased, but her hands continued cleaning Conn's ghastly wound.

"I know there are many calls on you tonight, Darak. But if you can spare the time, would you go to Ennit? Nedia and I must stay here, and Ela . . . she just weeps."

"Of course I'll go to him. Hircha knows?"

"Aye. She's with Griane. That's the best place for her right now. But Ennit . . ." For the first time, the calm voice faltered. "He's not . . . strong like you."

Only death could have wrung such an admission from Lisula. He touched her shoulder gently as he rose, feeling anything but strong.

As he walked toward Ennit's hut, a slender figure slipped out of the shadows. Gheala's light and that of the flickering torches revealed the tension in Rigat's body and the wariness of his expression.

For a long moment, they regarded each other. Finally, Darak forced himself to ask, "You're not hurt?"

Rigat shook his head.

He had to say something, but he could not voice the questions that filled his mind. Instead, he asked, "Can you stand a watch tonight?"

Rigat's shoulders seemed to sag, but perhaps that was only a trick of the uncertain light. With a brusque nod, he strode toward the entrance of the hill fort. Torn between the desire to call him back and the need to put as much distance between them as possible, Darak watched him go.

Abruptly, he turned toward the longhut. He had only one thought now, only one desire.

The deerskin had been drawn up to let in the cool night air, but even from the doorway, the stench of blood and piss and tallow-soaked torches overwhelmed the comforting smell of peat smoke. An old woman—the one he had seen in the pass—dabbed at a bloody shoulder. Hircha was very pale, her expression frozen, but her needle rose and fell as she stitched another man's arm.

He heard doeskin rip and found Griane parting the flaps of a ruined tunic. She bent closer to inspect the wounds, then glanced toward the doorway. Perhaps she had caught the inadvertent movement of his hand. Or perhaps, after so many years, she was simply aware of his presence.

He wanted so much to touch her, to feel the curve of her neck, the bony ridge of her shoulder. To reassure himself that she was real and alive and his.

In an instant, tenderness transformed to a more urgent need. To take her, here on the filthy bracken. To bury himself inside of her and reaffirm his existence in the midst of so much death. To forget grief and pain and the fear of what the morrow might hold and lose himself in her warmth. And then to lay his head against her breast and sleep, cradled in her skinny arms.

He lifted his hand, palm out. She did the same. His fingertips tingled, as if feeling her touch. Then she turned back to the wounded man who needed her, and he walked away to resume the burdens of chief.

Chapter 9

THE WIND SWIRLED AROUND the hilltop, tugging at robes and skirts. Rain slid like tears down the faces of the dead. As Darak eyed Gortin's guttering torch, he offered a silent prayer to Taran and Nul to restrain the storm until the bodies were consumed.

They had built the pyre at first light. Sacrificed a ewe in thanks for their deliverance. Struggled up the hill with their dead slung in mantles and carefully placed the bodies on the gorse branches. They lay shoulder to shoulder—his folk and Gath's and Temet's—awaiting the flames.

Rigat plucked at his sleeve. "Don't worry," he whispered. "The fire will burn."

Darak nodded automatically, his troubled gaze fixed on Keirith. At least, he'd managed to break through Ennit's stunned silence last night; all his efforts to draw Keirith out had failed.

Gortin intoned the final words of the rite and lifted the mullein torch. For a long moment, he stared at the bodies, shaking his head. Suddenly, his despairing expression grew fierce.

"Too many times we have performed this rite. Too many times we have carried our loved ones to the Death Hut or consigned their bodies to fire. Merciful Maker, can you not see our grief? Can you not hear our cries?"

Ennit's face twisted in anguish. Keirith's might have been carved from stone.

"Oak and Holly, we may be far from your forests, but we are still your children, descendants of the rowan and the alder who pulled their roots from the soil of the First

Forest and crossed the boundary between their world and ours to become the first woman, the first man. How can you let these invaders destroy us? Destroy our tree-brothers?"

He could feel Faelia's burning gaze. Despite Griane's protests, she had insisted on hobbling up the hill. It was her duty, she claimed, and her right.

"Gods of our people. Welcome these new spirits to the sunlit shores of the Forever Isles. And remember those who are left behind. Show us the path of deliverance. Comfort us in our time of need. Give us a sign of your love and your protection."

Gortin thrust the torch into the base of the pyre. The gorse ignited with a whoosh of air that made him stagger backward. Orange flames leaped up, licking eagerly at the resinous wood and the tallow-smeared garments of the dead.

Clutching his blackthorn staff for support, Gortin cried, "A sign! No rain can quench the flames. Just as no enemy can destroy our people."

A roar rose up from the men. Women screamed their defiance, clutching their hair, beating their breasts, swaying and swirling and stamping the earth in the ecstasy of grief.

The shiver that crawled down Darak's spine owed little to the cold wind or the driving rain.

"Don't worry. The fire will burn."

By the time they returned to the village, the storm had passed and the sun peeked through a break in the clouds. Another good omen, some said.

They shared a paltry feast—whatever the women could throw together. Later, there would be time to honor the dead. Now, there was too much to do for the living.

Rothisar led a party back to the pass to strip the Zherosi dead and dispose of the bodies. Alada and Duba carried furs and spare mantles to the cave. Temet's warriors were still in the longhut with the rest of the wounded, but when they recovered, they would need somewhere to sleep; the huts were already crowded with the folk from Gath's village.

Darak convened the council meeting in his hut. With Usok and Elasoth dead, and Madig and Nemek fighting for their lives, only five members remained: the Tree-Father and Grain-Mother, him and Lisula, and old Trath.

He wished he could nominate Ennit to replace one of the fallen elders, but with only Callie and young Lorthan to help, his friend would be busy enough tending the flocks. Instead, after waiting impatiently while Gortin and Barasa offered the ritual prayers, he proposed Sion, a reticent hunter and a bit of a loner, but a man of common sense and wisdom.

Everyone agreed that Callie should join them until Nemek recovered. Trath suggested two fishermen—Adinn and Hakiath. When Barasa put forward Rothisar's name, Darak suppressed a grimace; the last person he wanted on the council was Jurl's belligerent nephew.

The elders might take a year to decide upon a name for their tribe, but in a crisis, they were far more decisive. With little discussion, Sion and Adinn were elected as permanent members, with Callie and Hakiath serving until Nemek and Madig recovered.

If Rothisar bristles at the slight, I'll just tell him we need his hunting skills. With so many of our hunters dead or wounded, it won't even be a lie.

They waited for the new members to join them before summoning Faelia and Temet. Their accounts were brief and grim. When Temet finished speaking, Darak said, "It's early in the season for the Zherosi to be on the move."

With obvious reluctance, Temet said, "We struck first. Ambushed a couple of their scouting parties."

All winter, they had wrangled, Temet arguing that they had to attack the Zherosi whenever and wherever they could, Darak claiming that those tactics only provoked reprisals. This time, Gath's village had paid the price.

Temet shifted his wounded leg, grimacing. "They'd never come in such numbers before. I don't know how many there were. Two hundred? Three? The villagers fought like wolves. Old men with axes. Women with clubs. Boys younger than your Rigat . . ."

"How many did you lose?" Darak asked quietly.

"Seventy-three. Including those who fell yesterday."

And likely, there would be more: the badly wounded ones in the longhut, perhaps even some of those Temet had sent after the Zherosi.

"It was chaos after the battle," Faelia said. "Temet tried to rally us, but—"

"We scattered," Temet interrupted. "As soon as I'm able to travel, I'll round up the survivors. If there are any. Those who are still recovering from their wounds can stay behind to help defend the village."

Of course, Temet would have to leave the wounded behind. But volunteering them to defend the village told Darak that he had little hope that all the Zherosi would be caught.

Helpless anger made him want to reject the offer, but common sense prevailed. They would need those extra men and women—to hunt, to teach his folk to fight with swords, to improve their defenses. Gods, they needed their strong arms and backs to help build the terraces so they could get the barley into the ground.

And if the Zherosi come back in force? Who will be left alive to harvest it?

After a brief discussion of the immediate steps that must be taken, Darak called the meeting to a halt. It would be days before Temet could travel. Time enough to craft more detailed plans later.

As the elders filed out of the hut, Darak eyed Temet, considering the deep grooves pain and grief had carved around his mouth, the hollowness under his cheekbones, and his slow, careful movements. But this was one confrontation he refused to postpone.

"A word with you, Temet. If I may."

Faelia hesitated in the doorway, then reluctantly allowed the deerskin to fall behind her.

Temet took a deep breath and straightened his shoulders, as if preparing for a blow.

Careful to keep his voice soft, Darak said, "You gave me your oath."

"And I kept it."

"Oh, aye. *You* didn't lead them here. You let Faelia do that."

"I tried to draw them off. That was the plan."

"You expect me to believe that?"

"Believe what you want and be damned!"

Darak started toward him, then drew up short as Temet gripped the hilt of his dagger. Temet stared down at his hand, frowning, as if he couldn't quite believe what he had done. Then he slumped wearily against the wall of the hut.

"Forgive me. I never used to be such a hothead."

"I remember."

"Do you? I wonder sometimes."

Although Temet's voice was quiet, the words stung. "I remember you went singing to your death. And bought me the chance to save my son. It's not your fault I failed."

"You didn't fail. Keirith lives. You'll never know if you could have saved his body, too. And blaming yourself for what you did or didn't do won't change that."

The blunt words might have been cruel if another man had spoken them. But Temet knew more about loss and blame than he did. He had lost his home, his wife, his child. Seen his comrades slaughtered. Yet he was not too hardened to grieve—or to love.

For his daughter's sake, Darak kept his voice gentle. "Keirith's life is a debt I can never repay."

"I didn't bring up the past to win your trust. Or perhaps I did. I don't know." Temet ground the heels of his palms into his eyes. "As bad as things were, it was easier in the slave compound."

"Aye. Well. We were drugged."

Temet's short exhalation might have been a chuckle or an exasperated sigh. "We acted together. In that moment, we were men again. In control of our lives, our fate."

"Then you should know how I feel now. When you've taken that control away from me."

"You can stay here."

"Can I? All it takes is for one man to escape—one!—and the Zherosi will know where this place is. The place I chose because it was a safe haven."

Temet shook his head wearily. "There is no such thing."

"There was! Until you came. Sooner or later, they're bound to seek revenge. The only way to keep my people safe is to join your damn rebellion." Darak's mouth twisted in a bitter smile. "So it looks like you've won the Spirit-Hunter's support, after all."

"I didn't want it this way. I hope you believe that."

"Does it matter?"

Before Temet could answer, a freckled hand flung back the deerskin. Faelia limped into the hut.

"Don't blame Temet. It was me."

"What are you talking about?" Darak asked.

"I led the Zherosi here. I made sure they followed my group. Temet knew nothing."

Darak stared at her, too stunned to speak. The hope that she was lying to protect her man vanished when Temet seized her good arm and spun her toward him.

"You little fool! You could have been killed. And everyone with you."

"It was a risk."

"That cost the lives of every man I sent with you. And what? Eight of the villagers who were counting on you to get them to safety."

"We all discussed it. And we all agreed. But it was my plan. So if you want to whip anyone for disobeying orders, whip me."

Her words were directed to Temet, but her gaze remained fastened on her father, begging forgiveness and understanding. When Darak shook his head, her expression grew fierce.

"They'd given up. All of them. But I told them we would be luring their enemies to the village of Darak Spirit-Hunter. That you'd give meaning to their suffering and avenge the deaths of their loved ones and help our people reclaim this land. And I watched mothers bind the bleeding feet of their children and old men's eyes gleam with hope."

He looked at this tall stranger in men's clothing, this warrior he had helped create, whose voice shook with passion and whose eyes brimmed with tears she refused to shed. The woman blurred with the memories of the child who used to ride through the village on his shoulders, small hands reaching up as if to snatch a cloud from the sky. Who disdained needle and thread for sling and stone. Who would crawl into his lap after supper, idly playing with a braid, freckled face raised to his as if she couldn't bear to let him out of her sight for a moment.

He squeezed his eyes shut. When he opened them again, he had a firm grip on his emotions.

"More than thirty people died yesterday. Others will be

maimed for life. This village will be crippled because we've lost most of our hunters. All this to secure the allegiance of one man. Tell me, Faelia. Was it worth it?"

"It will be. If Darak Spirit-Hunter joins us."

Her hand came up as if to touch him. Furious, he batted it aside. The savage gesture made her press her clenched fist against her mouth. The old gesture—one that she'd made ever since she was a child—made him catch his breath, but his voice was cold when he spoke.

"Let me pass."

"Fa . . ."

"I cannot do this! Not with the ashes of our dead filling the air and the stink of their roasting bodies tainting every breath."

Temet took Faelia's arm and eased her away from the doorway. Without looking at either of them, Darak stalked outside.

He visited the homes of the bereaved and sat with grief-stricken widows and frightened children. He went to the longhut to check on the wounded. He told Rothisar to organize combat training, asked Trath to assign watches—and realized he was beginning the transformation from chief of the Alder Tribe to spiritual leader of a rebellion.

Already, he could feel the forest calling, urging him to leave the treeless moors and the wrangling of the elders and the dozens of petty concerns that filled his days. Leave it all behind. Walk again among the oaks and ashes, the rowans and pines. Carry the tale to every village. Remind every listener of the sacred bond between the land and its people.

But he could not commit to that path until he had spoken with Griane.

It was late afternoon before he had time to seek her out. By then, the hopeful sun had lost its battle with the clouds and the skies were as dark as his mood. Rain pelted down as he ducked into the longhut, but in the end, he found her at home with all three of the boys. Their guilty looks and quick exchange of glances made it clear they had been discussing him.

"Where's Faelia?" Callie asked.

"I don't know."

"She should be here."

"Nay!" His vehemence drew puzzled frowns and another furtive exchange of glances. They waited for him to say more, but he simply repeated, "Nay."

As he slumped beside the fire pit, Griane glanced at him, then quickly resumed stirring the stew. When had anyone had time to snare rabbits? Rigat, perhaps. He could keep a fire blazing through the morning and bring home a brace of rabbits in the afternoon.

Rigat cleared his throat. "You wanted to talk to me. The other night. At the feast."

Aye, but not now. I cannot hear it now.

Ignoring his frown, Rigat began speaking in a low, clear voice. He spoke of pushing Seg, of the portal, of the rock-slide. Darak's fists clenched and unclenched in his lap as he fought the growing wave of nausea. He couldn't look at the boy. Or at Griane.

When Rigat's voice finally ran down, Darak rubbed his damp palms against his thighs, knowing he had to speak, to reassure Rigat, to reassure all his boys. And if he could not reassure Griane, he must, at least, hide his fear that the moment had finally arrived—the moment he had dreaded for so many years.

"You spend your life trying to be strong for those you love. Not wanting them to see your uncertainty lest they be afraid, too."

He wished his father could be here, guiding him. He wished he could close his eyes and pretend that the bad thing would go away as he used to do when he was a child and heard unfamiliar sounds in the dark. He wished he could succumb to the frightened voice inside him that kept screaming, "Nay, nay, nay!" Or just run away and lose himself in the comforting depths of the forest.

But he was no longer a child and he was far from the forest. Faelia wanted him to be the Spirit-Hunter and Rigat needed him to be his father.

He forced himself to smile. "Forgive me. I'm . . . tired. The last two days . . ."

"It'll be all right." Oddly, it was Callie who offered the comfort, not Keirith as he would have expected, the new sad-eyed Callie whose smile was bittersweet, as if he realized how untrue his words were but couldn't help speaking them. Keirith was still so numbed by Conn's death that he could only give him a bleak nod.

Griane refused to look at him.

"We're family," he said. "We stand together. Nothing can change that."

Griane's knuckles grew white as she clenched the spoon. "Thank you for telling me, Rigat. It's past time we talked. Nay, it's not your fault. We were all afraid to face the truth."

He stopped himself before he said more. He felt thin, strained, his body taut with nervous energy, but heavy, so very heavy.

"I'm tired," he repeated. "I think . . . if you don't mind . . . I'll rest before supper."

Rigat leaped up to pull the wet mantle from his shoulders. Callie ladled a cup of his tonic. Keirith finally stopped their fussing and shooed his brothers toward the doorway.

"But it's raining," Rigat protested.

"Then make yourselves useful," Griane said. "Take fresh bandages to the longhut. Fill the waterskins. The wounded are always thirsty. Take the two wolfskins by the doorway to Alada. Tell her we can't spare more. The stew will be ready by the time you're back."

Keirith and Callie ducked outside, but Rigat hesitated in the doorway. "You're not mad, are you, Fa?"

"Nay."

"Or . . . disappointed?"

Gods, he was so young. And it wasn't his fault.

"Nay," he managed.

"But you wish I was like the other boys."

Please, Maker, don't let me weep.

His legs shook as he pushed himself to his feet and walked toward the son who was and wasn't his. "Aye. I do. Magic . . . scares me. Always has. Tinnean . . . he saw the wonder in it."

"It *is* wonderful, Fa. And it'll never hurt us. I won't let it." Rigat's grave smile was so like Fellgair's that Darak caught his breath.

After Rigat left, he just stood there, listening to the pat-

ter of rain on the thatch and the sizzles from the fire pit
when errant drops fell through the vent hole. When he
finally turned to Griane, he found her staring down at her
clasped hands.

Her gaze finally rose to meet his. And still he couldn't
move. Then his legs responded to his mind's command. He
walked back to the fire pit and sat down opposite her. He
tried to still the fluttering of his heart, but hearts were more
difficult to control than legs.

Neither of them wanted to be the first to say it. Because
he loved her and because he thought it might be easier
somehow if he was the one to speak the words aloud, he
took a deep breath and said, "He's Fellgair's son."

Even though he knew what her answer would be, her
small nod made his heart clench. As if Fellgair were squeezing it between his fingers as he had that afternoon in
Zheros. The afternoon he had demanded that Darak open
his spirit as the price for saving Keirith—and hinted at the
bargain with Griane.

He felt his head nodding, as if she had confirmed something ordinary—that there were wild onions in the stew or
that she would be out on the moor gathering plants on the
morrow. He heard her say something about a brew that
would rid a woman of a child, of her moon flow coming
after she took it, but he needed all his concentration simply
to breathe. He took shallow, careful breaths to ease the
pressure in his chest. When it did, he became aware of the
ache in his hands.

He looked down to discover them balled into fists.
Slowly, he relaxed his fingers. There were two freckles near
the puckered white scar left by Morgath's dagger. So long
ago now. Half a lifetime. More. He had been young and
strong and whole then. He had believed that losing Tinnean
was the worst thing that could ever happen to him.

Not freckles. Age spots. Of course.

Griane's voice seemed to come from a great distance. "I
was sure he was yours. Even after the . . . incidents began.
Keirith had power, too."

But how could the power of a mortal ever compare to
that of a god? A god never grew old. He was always young
and strong and whole. He could bind a child in a woman's

womb. Beguile you with a glance. Choose any form he pleased.

Had he worn the body of the fox-man that day in the Summerlands?

Don't.

But Darak could no more stop the thoughts than he could control his shaking hands. Griane burying her face in the soft, spiky fur of Fellgair's chest. Griane digging her fingers into his hips to pull him deeper inside of her. Griane crying out his name at the end.

Don't!

Did she still dream of that summer day? Remember the tickle of his fur on her thighs and the rasp of his tongue on her cheek? Had she pretended all these years that it was Fellgair's hands, Fellgair's mouth, Fellgair's body loving her?

Fingers grasped his arm. Griane's fingers. When had she moved to his side? He looked up and saw tears in her eyes.

"Don't."

She snatched her hand away as if she had burned it. When he realized why, his throat closed in silent protest. That she should think that he hated her touch, that he could hate her because of what she had done, that she could imagine he could ever stop loving her no matter how much the visions tormented him, no matter how much the truth scalded his spirit . . . somehow that was worse than everything else.

He tried to say, "Don't cry," but the words emerged as a strangled croak. He staggered to his feet, reeling like a drunken man. And suddenly she was there, steadying him, holding him. His girl, his fierce, strong girl.

Darak pulled her close, but when he buried his face in the crook of her neck, she went rigid. Suddenly unsure, he drew back. Her face was so white, the freckles stood out like plague spots. But it was her eyes that caught him. Wide with shock, they stared at something over his shoulder.

Even before he turned, he knew what he would see.

Rigat stood in the open doorway. Rain plastered his hair against his head and streamed in rivulets down his cheeks. His eyes were as wide and disbelieving as his mother's.

Griane cried out his name, but he had already spun away. With a low moan, she tottered toward the doorway. Darak caught her as she collapsed.

Chapter 10

RIGAT RAN ACROSS THE moor, heedless of the pelting rain. He didn't know where he was going. He didn't care. He just had to get away from Mam and Fa.

He's not my father.

All his life, he had tried to win Darak's love. Now he understood why he had failed. Seeing him standing there, staring at him with horror . . . that was bad enough. But his mam . . .

Blinded by tears and rain, he stumbled and quickly regained his balance.

Anyone else would have fallen.

But he wasn't "anyone else." He was the Trickster's son. That was why he could hear the song of the stream and the speech of animals. Why he could stop a spear in midair. Why Darak had always watched him and his mam had tried to kill him before he was born.

Did his brothers and sister know? Was that why Faelia had always disliked him? Why even Keirith was so distant sometimes?

He swiped his palms across his eyes and raced on. Faster than any man. Fast enough to outrace the truth.

The moor melted into a blur of gray and brown and green. He leaped over stones, dodged sprawling gorse bushes, all without thought, without effort. He could fly if he put his mind to it. Just spread his arms and will his body into the air. He didn't need an eagle like Keirith. He could do it alone. Soar over the trees and the mountains and never come back again. Then they'd be sorry.

His steps slowed. The world fell back into place. Each breath tore at his chest. His throat felt like he had swallowed fire. And his legs shook, muscles hot and aching from the frantic race.

Just like a normal person.

Over the roaring in his ears, he heard the sound of water tumbling over rocks. Through the tangle of underbrush at the bottom of the slope, he caught a flash of gray-green. Slowly, he made his way down the hill and slid to his knees on the muddy bank.

The icy water burned his throat. He forced himself to stop after a few mouthfuls, lest he make himself sick, but continued to splash water on his cheeks. How could they be so hot when he was shivering?

He collapsed on a slab of rock and drew his sodden mantle closer. He had no weapons save his dagger. No spare clothes or food. No place to hide.

I am the Trickster's son.

There was water aplenty. Alder branches that could be carved into fishing spears, vines that could be twisted into snares. A small hollow in the hill where he could shelter for the night.

I am the Trickster's son.

Why rely on the skills of ordinary men? If he could hear the song of the stream, he could sing trout into his waiting fingers. If he could make leaves dance on a windless day, he could weave vines and branches into a shelter.

But not here. Darak would come after him. And he couldn't face him. He would rest here tonight, but at dawn, he must leave. Head south to the forest. The only home he had now.

I am the Trickster's son.

Darak wouldn't come after him. He would make up some excuse, convince everyone that he'd run away. Keirith would believe him. And Callie. Faelia had never liked him. His mam might grieve for a while, but even she didn't want him.

It was better to be on his own. Keirith had been banished for casting out a man's spirit. What would the tribe do to him—the half-breed whelp of an unpredictable god? They might demand his death. Cut his heart out. Like Morgath. But they wouldn't succeed. It took more than a mere dagger to kill the son of a god. Didn't it?

They ought to be grateful. They ought to go down on their knees and thank him. He had saved them with the rockslide, kept the fire burning during the rite. He had used his power to help. It wasn't his fault if Seg had been too stupid or slow to save himself.

Why had he shown Seg the spear? That's when it all started to go wrong. But he was so sick of his taunts and boasting. As if a wolf were a better vision mate than a fox.

Rigat wiped his nose and called, "Fox!"

Nothing happened. He had to swallow several times before the lump in his throat eased. Even his vision mate had deserted him.

"Don't be so impatient."

His head snapped toward the familiar voice, but there was no sign of his vision mate. Then he caught a flash of red among the greens and grays of the underbrush. His greeting died unspoken. Dry-mouthed, he watched the tall figure walk down to the stream.

Keirith had only known him as the black-haired Suppli-cant of the Zherosi. This was the god Darak had bargained with. The god his mam had lain with. The god—only now did he realize it—who had come to him during his vision quest and called him "my beautiful boy."

In spite of the ruddy hair that covered his body like a garment, he looked far more human than Rigat had imag-ined. The white beard gave an illusion of fullness to the narrow face. The ears were large and distinctly triangular, but the long nose was human enough. So were the fingers—except for the curving, black claws.

From the opposite bank of the stream, the Trickster stud-ied him. Had the god observed him for years? Did he see every action? Know every thought? If so, the Trickster must feel his trembling, must sense both his fear and his determination to meet that inscrutable stare no matter how much he wanted to look away.

What if he doesn't like me?

He searched for something intelligent to say, something that would show the Trickster that his son was worthy. And heard himself blurting out, "What happened to your brush?"

Heat flooded his face. The Trickster could take whatever

shape appealed to him: Zherosi priestess or mortal man or fox—or any strange amalgam in between.

The Trickster smiled. "I got tired of it."

Rigat's answering smile faded as the Trickster splashed through the stream. He tried to force himself to his feet, but his legs wouldn't obey. He could only sit there, watching the approach of the god who had created him.

The potent scent of male fox nearly overwhelmed the delicate aroma of honeysuckle. He should have remembered that from the tale. Golden eyes stared down at him, the slitted pupils darker than any shadow.

The Trickster crouched in front of him. A black-clawed hand rose, and Rigat fought hard to keep from flinching. The palm rested against his cheek. "Spongy as a dog's pads," according to the tale Nemek told, but to Rigat, it merely felt warm and slightly callused. Like Darak's hand.

The Trickster's eyes blurred into a smear of gold and black. Rigat wanted to duck his head—dear gods, to be weeping like a child—but those eyes held him.

"Hush."

The Trickster brushed away the tear. His long red tongue flicked out to lick his thumb. Then he caught another tear on his forefinger. He held it out. After a moment's hesitation, Rigat licked it.

He had tasted his tears before and never noticed they were anything but salty and warm. Now he tasted the fear of hiding his true self for so long. The loneliness of possessing gifts he could never share. The guilt of not being the son Darak wanted. And the bitterness of learning that his mam had tried to kill him.

"Taste again."

As if obeying the Trickster's command, a tear slid into the corner of Rigat's mouth. Salty like the last one with an underlying hint of bitterness, but—impossibly—sweet.

She hadn't known he'd existed when she had cleansed her womb. She would never have done it if she had realized then how much they would love each other. His earliest memories were of his mother's arms holding him, his mother's voice singing to him, his mother's scent—herbs and milk and soap-scoured flesh—filling his nostrils. Fear had made her hide the truth, but her love had cradled him and kept him safe, preparing him for this meeting that had been destined from the day of his conception.

Tears and rain slipped down his cheeks unheeded. His mam had given him love. The Trickster had given him power. And now—with the gift of a tear—knowledge that reminded him of who—and what—he was.

He had never imagined a tear could be so powerful—or so delicious.

"What . . . what should I call you?"

"Call me Fellgair. Your mother does."

Fellgair rose and held out his hand. Rigat took it, restraining the impulse to fling his arms around him. But Fellgair must have felt his need, for he opened his arms without hesitation. So strong, those arms, stronger even than Darak's. Yet just as gentle as his mam's.

"It's all right," his father said. "We're together now."

Chapter 11

"GONE?" KEIRITH ECHOED. "Where?"

"I don't know." His father shot a quick look at Mam who sat in white-faced silence.

"Did you argue? After Callie and I left?"

"Just leave it, Keirith."

"But why would he—?"

"Leave it!"

After a moment of shocked silence, Callie ventured, "Perhaps someone said something. About the portal. Or Seg. But he'll come home. After he's calmed down."

"Which way did he go?" Keirith demanded.

His father hesitated.

"You didn't track him? You just let him go?"

"This is not your concern."

"He's my brother!"

"And he'll be safe."

"Of course he will," Callie said. "He knows the moors as well as he knows this village."

"He could trip. Twist an ankle. Or—"

"He'll be safe," Fa repeated. "And he'll come back." He squeezed Mam's hand, but she continued staring at the glowing peat. "Please, boys. Just . . . trust us."

The misery in his face made Keirith soften his voice. "We do, Fa. What's harder to understand is why *you* won't trust us."

A third time, Fa turned to her, as if awaiting some sign. When none was forthcoming, he said, "Later. Please."

Unable to bear the tension, Keirith shoved back the deerskin and ducked outside. Yanking his mantle over his head, he stalked through the village.

It had taken all his willpower to watch the flames devour Conn's body. Now, he feared he would shatter like clay heated too long in the fire.

He slumped against the wall of a hut, recalling the night that he had "pushed" Fa and fled the village. His father had scoured the hills with Conn. His mam had begged Gortin to use his vision to seek him. Although his parents were clearly upset by Rigat's disappearance, they seemed content to let him go.

Two confrontations. Two sons fleeing. And two attacks by the Zherosi. Hard to believe that was merely coincidence; harder still, to accept it as fate.

A racking cough from inside the hut interrupted his thoughts. Only then did he realize where he was. He wondered if this had been his destination all along.

He reached for the doeskin, then hesitated. Ennit and Lisula had enough worries. And he had not spoken to Hircha since he had carried Conn into the village.

While he continued to hesitate, the doeskin was flung up. Hircha drew back with a startled exclamation. "Keirith? Good gods, you're soaked. Come inside."

Ennit was huddled beside the fire pit, flanked by Ela and Lisula. Lisula managed a tired smile. "It's good of you to come, Keirith. Sit down. Ela, take his mantle."

"What's wrong?" Hircha demanded.

He shook his head.

"Something's happened," she persisted.

By now, even Ennit was looking at him with concern.

"It's Rigat. He's . . . run off."

Ela's cry of dismay was so like Callie's that he almost smiled.

"Sit down," Hircha ordered. "Tell us what happened."

Ennit and Lisula were his parents' best friends. Ela was as good as promised to Callie. Whatever his concerns, he could share them here.

"They're not speaking to each other?" Lisula asked when he finished.

"It's more like they know something they're not telling us."

Ennit's curse brought on another coughing fit. When Lisula dipped a cup into the sweet-smelling brew simmering in the fire pit, he shook his head and hawked a gob of phlegm onto the peat bricks. For a few painful moments, there was only the sound of his wheezing and the sizzle of the peat. Then Ennit exchanged a brief glance with Lisula and nodded.

"Darak and Griane may not talk to us either, but we'll go to them."

"That's not why I came," Keirith protested.

"But that's what friends do," Lisula said.

She pulled her mantle off the bone hook by the doorway. Ela held out Ennit's. Once, he would have protested that he was only walking a dozen paces; tonight, he simply drew the mantle around his shoulders.

"Is Callie all right?" Ela asked.

Before Keirith could respond, Ennit jabbed a blunt forefinger at her. "Tell him to check on the sheep. Or take you for a walk."

"In the rain?"

"Just get him out of the hut! And take your mantle," he added, shoving it into her arms as she darted past. With a weary sigh, he held back the doeskin for Lisula. "You'd think the gods could grant us one day of peace. Just one."

"If the gods cared about us," Keirith said, "they wouldn't have let Conn die."

Lisula flinched. As Keirith mumbled an apology, she shook her head. "I used to believe that the gods had a purpose for all that happened. Including death. But I was younger then. It's hard to understand why Conn was taken. I'd like to believe he was simply too good for this world. That he was so perfect that the gods wanted to bless the Forever Isles with that loving spirit. But I suppose every mother believes that about her child."

"He *was* good," Keirith said. "And kind and loving. And a better friend to me than I ever was to him."

"Don't!" Lisula's fingertips pressed against his lips. "It doesn't help. And it won't bring Conn back. He knew you loved him. And he'd rather have you honor his life and his memory than blame yourself for his death."

Her lips brushed his cheek. Then she led Ennit from the hut.

"Does Faelia know?" Hircha asked.

Keirith shrugged helplessly. That was another mystery. Why had Fa been so adamant about excluding Faelia during Rigat's revelations?

"Perhaps that's what she was upset about," Hircha said.

"Faelia was upset?"

"I saw her after the council meeting. She wouldn't talk either." Hircha took a deep breath and slowly let it out. "If she doesn't know, there's no sense worrying her tonight. And if she does . . . well, she has Temet." The keen gaze locked with his. "You don't have to stay with me."

"Do you want me to go?"

"I didn't say that. But you needn't sit with the grieving widow if it makes you so uncomfortable."

"It doesn't—"

"Ennit's the one who needs a hand to hold. Lisula needs to believe Conn died for a reason, that his death was more than just a senseless accident."

"And what do you need?"

"Not your bottomless guilt. So spare me that, Keirith. Just for tonight."

He winced. If he blamed himself for failing Conn, Hircha was surely blaming herself for failing to love him as he deserved—and desired—to be loved.

"If Conn were here," he said quietly, "he'd knock us both senseless."

Hircha pressed her lips together tightly. "Nay," she finally whispered. "He'd hit the wall. Or the stones of the fire pit. He'd break his hand before he'd lift it to either of us. And then he'd apologize for making me bind it." She took a deep breath. "I still have a flask of elderberry wine. I was saving it. For a special occasion."

"Then let's drink to Conn."

Unwilling to dwell on his death or their recent estrangement, Keirith shared memories of their childhood. At first, his words were slow and faltering, the memories only feeding his grief. But after he won a smile from Hircha by confessing how they used to spy on the girls bathing in the lake, the words flowed more easily and the constriction in his chest eased. Then Ennit and Lisula returned, grim-faced, and the comfort evoked by his stories leached away.

He rose and left them. Although the rain had stopped, the wind chilled him. Somewhere on the moors, Rigat huddled under a clump of heather or in the lee of a boulder. At home, his parents maintained their silent vigil. And Keirith could think of no way to help any of them.

His steps slowed when he saw the figure leaning against the wall of their hut, staring up at the night sky.

His father's head turned toward him, then tilted skyward again. "Do you think we look as small to the stars as they appear to us?"

Unprepared for such a question, Keirith just stared at him.

"Like ants, I'd think. Or beetles. Scurrying about. Gathering food. Living. Dying. With so many of us to watch, we must seem insignificant."

"But that doesn't mean we are."

"True. We have our loves, our hates, our fears. Our choices." His father took a long, shuddering breath. "Fellgair once told me each man's life was a web of possibilities. A pattern woven by chance and luck, the choices of others and the choices he makes. Strands woven and broken and rewoven hundreds of times. Thousands. Shaping and reshaping a life.

"Who knows what might befall us on the morrow because we lingered here instead of crawling under our furs? I might be weary from lack of sleep and snap at a man leaving for the hunt. Perhaps he shrugs it off and returns with a deer. Or perhaps he broods and cannot concentrate. He comes home empty-handed. Every pot has less meat. Every child goes to bed hungry. All because I'm standing here, gazing at the sky. And if such a small act carries such weighty consequences, what of the more important choices we make?"

"Please, Fa. Won't you let me help?"

His father just stared at the tiny, unblinking stars.

"No matter what's happened—no matter how bad it seems—you can trust me."

"I do," his father assured him. "More than anyone in the world." And then he winced.

It took Keirith a moment to understand. It wasn't just Rigat. It was something to do with Mam, too. Suddenly, he was as terrified as that spring morning when he heard the wood pigeon's scream echoing through his spirit.

Chapter 12

GRIANE PAUSED NEXT TO THE boulder to trace the cluster of acorns and the jagged holly leaf Darak had carved during their first moon in the valley. Rain and snow and ice had worn away all but the faintest marks of his dagger, but at the full moon, the priestesses daubed fresh dye on the stone. Today, the holly berries looked like tiny drops of blood.

Despite the disturbing thought, she wished she could linger here; although the boulder would never hold the same power as the ancient heart-oak, this was still a sacred place. But she knew she had to move on; she was far too close to the village.

She headed east, the direction Darak claimed Rigat had

taken. She felt naked and exposed on the empty moor, trapped between the vast sky and the endless expanse of rolling hills. Still, she pushed on until she spied the line of alders. The fishermen never ventured this far upstream— and it comforted her to have these few scraggly trees as allies.

She had brought no gift for Fellgair. She knew he would come; he'd promised her that when they returned from the Summerlands. Whether he would allow her to see Rigat was another matter.

Anger swelled, swamping the despair. She clasped her hands together to keep from pounding the slender trunk of an alder, but the rage still simmered.

Let him feel it. He's stolen my son. Nothing worse could happen.

The first time she called his name, her voice cracked. The second time, it rang out clearly, startling a raven that took flight with a loud croak of annoyance. She wanted to believe that was a good omen—hadn't Struath's spirit guide been a raven?—but she could only remember the carrion eaters circling over the bodies of her kinfolk the morning the raiders stole Keirith.

Was that when it all began? Or was it earlier still—at her first encounter with the Trickster? Or when Tinnean defended the One Tree? In the tribal legends, the gods always seemed so wise, so helpful. Few of the tales hinted at the dire consequences that could ensue when a mortal attracted their attention.

She called his name a third time. As she waited, anger slowly gave way to fear. Was he just playing with her? Or punishing her?

A dipperbird flew past, a gleam of chestnut and white. The branches of a shrub swayed. Ruddy fur gleamed in a shaft of sunlight as the Trickster emerged from the under-brush.

Usually he liked to startle her, appearing without a sound or transforming from fox to man before her eyes. Today, he simply splashed across the stream like an ordinary mortal and, instead of offering a clever quip, regarded her gravely.

What did he see when he looked at her? Not the girl

who had boldly kissed him in the First Forest or the woman
who had lain beneath him on the warm grass of the Summerlands. An old woman, shrunken and small, knuckles
swollen with the joint-ill, breasts sagging beneath her tunic.
Her hair was probably as untidy as ever, but now it was as
white as his beard.

"You'll always be beautiful to me."

She had long since grown used to his compliments, but
even now, his voice could still send a shiver of delight down
her back. For some reason, he had chosen to look more
like a man than a fox today, but she had more pressing
concerns than Fellgair's appearance.

"Is he safe?"

"Yes."

"Will you bring him back?"

"If he wishes to come."

What if Rigat refused? What if he never wanted to see
her again?

"He loves you, Griane."

"You weren't there. You didn't see his face. He
looked . . ."

Scared. Angry. Horrified.

"He loves you."

She pressed her hand against her mouth to hold back the
sob, but the tears came anyway. The storm was brief; perhaps she had shed so many tears in her life that she had
only a few left.

"Will you take him away again?"

"If he chooses to remain with me—"

"He's not ready."

"Is that my fault?" When she didn't reply, he added,
"You've had him for thirteen years, Griane. You could
have told him anytime."

"How do you tell a child such a thing?"

"By accepting that he is not simply a child, but the son
of a god." The golden eyes narrowed. "You've known the
truth for years. You should have trusted his ability to accept it."

"How dare you lecture me! After what you've done."

"I've offered my son acceptance and understanding."

"That's not what I meant. You always claim that you

don't—you can't!—interfere in human affairs. Yet you gave me a child."

"Some women would have considered it a gift."

"He is a gift, but—"

"Should I take him back? I have the power to—"

"Nay! Nay," she repeated more quietly. "You knew when we parted that I carried a child. You could have taken him then. Or let my brew do its work. Before I knew him. Before I loved him." When Fellgair simply continued to study her, she asked the question that had haunted her for years. "Why? Why did you do it?"

He was silent so long that she feared he would refuse to answer. Finally, he said, "Our son has the potential to change the world, Griane."

"He's just a boy. He shouldn't have to. When may I see him?"

Fellgair hesitated, as if he meant to pursue the topic further. Then he shrugged. "Meet me here at midday tomorrow." As she turned to go, he added, "And bring Darak."

Slowly, she faced him. "Why?"

"I wish to see him."

"Why?"

"I'm fond of him."

"That's not—"

"And this might be the last time we shall ever see each other."

Her mouth opened, but no words emerged.

"I'm not foretelling his death, Griane. He may live for years. But one day, that great heart will fail him."

She was the one who made up the tonic. Who worried every time he walked up a steep hill. Who counted each day, each night like a squirrel hoarding nuts before a long winter. She knew she could not ward off death forever, but hearing the words spoken aloud was unbearable.

As always, Fellgair sensed her feelings. When he put his arms around her, she was angry and grateful for their strength. Every encounter with him left her more confused, more uncertain of the future. She hated him for giving her a child—and she loved the child he had given her. She wanted to scream at him for possessing such arrogance, such willful blindness that he could imagine a child was just another playing piece on some immortal game board—and she wanted to cling to him and pretend that everything would be all right.

"I don't regret giving you Rigat," he said. "But I do regret making you unhappy."

She freed herself from his embrace. "I don't regret him either. And I can bear my unhappiness. But if you hurt my boy—or Darak—I shall find a way to make you suffer."

Chapter 13

LIKE THE REST OF THE FAMILY, Keirith maintained the fiction that Rigat was keeping watch in the hills. They all tried to behave normally. His father supervised the construction of the terraces. His mother cared for the wounded. Faelia conducted daily trainings in swordplay, and Callie alternated between tending the flocks and teaching the children.

Keirith resumed his duties with the other fishermen. Twice, he sought a vision to help him find Rigat, but he could not even manage to contact Natha. So when Duba asked him to use his gift to help Elasoth's younger daughter, he hesitated, fearing he would only fail again.

"You helped Luimi before," Duba reminded him. "And she trusts you. You must try, Keirith. She's just . . . drifting away."

As Duba had after her son died. Until he reclaimed her shattered spirit, she'd lived a kind of half-life, silent and unresponsive. He could not allow that to happen to Luimi.

He followed Duba to the hut she shared with Alada and their orphans. Dirna glanced up before returning her bleak gaze to her sister. Luimi lay on the rabbitskins, staring up at the thatch. He sat beside her and explained that he wanted to touch her spirit, but if his words reached her, she gave no indication.

He took her unresisting hand. Closed his eyes. Tried to shut out the crackle of dead twigs in the fire, the scent of salmon simmering in its nest of damp leaves, the weight of the hopeful eyes watching him. Relinquished his fear that he would fail this little girl. Concentrated only on the slow tattoo of his heart, the rhythm of his breathing, and the small hand clasped in his. Sought stillness and emptiness— and Natha.

Later, he was shocked that it was so easy. At the time, he felt only relief when Natha's sinuous warmth flooded his spirit. He let the energy pass from his hand to Luimi's. It seeped through flesh and bone, pulsed through her blood, flowed into her spirit.

He calmed the instinctive jolt of panic, but resisted the urge to probe deeper. Like Hua and Duba, Luimi had erected barriers to shield herself from the painful memories. Hers were still fragile and uncertain, the work of days rather than moons or years. But breaking through them would only force her to flee—or shatter her spirit completely.

Instead, he offered memories of her father: Elasoth guiding Luimi's fingers as she tied sinkers onto his net; Elasoth supporting her belly as he taught her to swim; Elasoth cradling her in his lap as he sang a lullaby.

The violent outpouring of pain ripped through Keirith's spirit. New images flashed before him: Elasoth surrounded by bronze-helmeted Zherosi; Elasoth desperately parrying the swords that slashed toward him; Elasoth's scream as one ripped open his belly; Elasoth's fingers fumbling helplessly at the entrails that spilled out of his body like a tangle of worms.

Abruptly, the images vanished, leaving only the wail of Luimi's spirit.

<Don't make me look, Keirith!>

The words—so like Hua's. And the agony of loss. One, a little boy who had seen his mother and father cut down before his eyes. The other, a little girl who had conjured her father's last moments from her memories of the raids she had survived, the men she had seen die, the whispered comments she had overheard.

Keirith trembled with the effort to absorb the pain and the loss and the terror that threatened to shatter Luimi's fragile spirit. Natha coiled around him, cradling him, cradling Luimi, enfolding them both with his warmth, flowing through them like a calming stream. He drew on Natha's strength to find images to comfort Luimi and coax her back from the darkness: Dirna playing hop-frog with her by the lake; Dirna teaching her to weave the nettle fibers into rope; Dirna's body cuddled close on a winter night; Dirna's voice whispering, "Don't leave me"; Dirna's arms flung wide to welcome her home.

For a moment, Luimi hesitated, caught between the father she longed to follow and the sister who urged her to stay. Elasoth's gentle smile released her. As she fled the darkness, Natha dissipated like autumn mist before the sun. Keirith touched Luimi's spirit once more—in acknowledgment and farewell—and gently withdrew.

She gazed at him uncertainly. At his nod, she turned her head and found her sister sitting at her side, hands clenched in her lap.

"Dirna? I'm home."

Dirna's arms locked around her sister, pulling her into a fierce embrace. As they clung together, rocking and laughing and weeping, Keirith felt a light touch on his shoulder. He looked up to find Duba smiling at him.

He always forgot how exhausted he was after such healings, remembering only the deep peace that filled him. Watching the two sisters, it filled him again, as warm and comforting as Natha's presence.

Afterward, Duba insisted that he seek out others who were willing to allow his healing touch. But as he left her hut, he spied his parents slipping out of the hill fort together. Before he could heal others, he had to heal his own family.

Although his body cried out for rest, he followed them across the moor. As they approached the alders, he flung himself down in the bracken. Only when they disappeared into the trees did he trot down the hill after them. He slowed as he reached the tangle of alders; his father's eyesight had grown weaker, but his hearing was as sharp as ever.

Squatting in the underbrush, he realized they were both too preoccupied with their thoughts to detect his presence. His mam stared at the ground, chewing her upper lip. His father stalked back and forth along the stream bank, his gaze shifting from her to the sky. Clearly, they were waiting for something—or someone. Had Rigat arranged to meet them here?

He crawled closer, grateful that the splashing water drowned out the cracking of twigs. Then he heard the hoarse croak of a raven and a loud flapping of wings. He froze, but his father's head had already jerked toward him.

"Come out!"

Feeling like a complete idiot, Keirith rose from his hiding place. Expecting anger, their horrified expressions shocked him.

"What are you doing here?" his father demanded.

"I was worried."

"There's nothing to worry about. Go home."

He shoved through the underbrush. "I'm not a child. Or a fool. You've found Rigat, haven't you? You're meeting him here."

"Would you do what I—?"

"Enough!" His mam's voice cut through their wrangling. "He'll find out eventually, Darak. Better he should hear it from us."

All sorts of dire possibilities flitted through his mind: Rigat was dead; Rigat was injured; Rigat had run off to fight the Zherosi. Nothing prepared him for his mother's words.

"Rigat is Fellgair's son."

Even as he whispered, "That's impossible," his mind said, "Of course." He kept shaking his head, unwilling, unable to accept the truth, although everything he knew of Rigat's power and personality confirmed it. But if Rigat was the Trickster's son . . .

His mam flinched.

His parents' love had been one of the few constants in his life, as certain as the sun rising in the east. How could she have betrayed that love? And how long had the knowledge of her betrayal been eating away at Fa?

"It's not your mother's fault. She did it to protect you."

"Don't, Darak."

"To protect both of us. She went to the Trickster. When we were in Zheros. And the price he wanted . . . he would only help her if . . ."

"If I agreed to lie with him."

Keirith closed his eyes. He felt his father's arm around his shoulders. Heard his father's voice, low and urgent, telling him that Gortin had had some sort of terrible vision, that his mam had been alone and frightened, that she had taken every precaution afterward to prevent a child. That they had both been certain that Rigat was theirs.

He heard the words. He understood their meaning. But still the bile rose up in his throat.

Bad enough that his kidnapping had driven her to this unholy bargain. But to have believed for a moment that she would ever betray Fa out of loneliness or anger or lust . . .

He heard his mother walking toward him, but he couldn't bring himself to look at her. "Forgive me," he whispered.

She seized his shoulders and shook him hard. "You will not take this upon yourself. Do you hear me? This is not your fault. The raiders kidnapped you. Your father went after you. And I went to the Trickster." Her hands came up to cup his face. "Every day since you returned to me . . . in this body . . . every day for fourteen years, I've blamed myself for . . . not doing more."

"You did everything you could."

"I did . . . what I did. And I have to live with the consequences of my choices and go on."

He nodded. Later, he would find some way to help her bear this and make amends for his lapse of faith. What mattered now was Rigat. Gods, it must have crushed him to learn that the man he had loved and admired all his life was not his real father.

"He went to Fellgair, didn't he?"

His mam nodded. The fierceness had left her. She looked tired and old and unbearably frail.

"And they're coming here today."

Again, she nodded.

"Will he come home?"

"I don't know."

Rigat was the son of her heart. It would kill her to lose him.

"Do you still want me to go?" he asked her.

"Go? When the drama is just beginning?"

The voice was deeper than he remembered, but the mocking tone was just the same.

Ever since Zheros, he had pictured the Trickster in the guise he had worn then—a tall, black-haired priestess with eyes as dark as a Midwinter night. This was the fox-man of his father's tales, but the eyes—while golden—held the same unblinking intensity.

The Trickster's claws rested lightly on Rigat's shoulder. Seeing them standing side by side—the intent gazes, the preternatural stillness—his last doubts about Rigat's parentage vanished. Then Rigat gave him a nervous half smile and the Trickster's son transformed into his little brother, silently pleading for understanding and support.

Mam was blinking back tears. Fa was still as stone, but there was murder in his eyes. As Keirith tensed, the rage vanished. Only the muscle twitching in his jaw betrayed his emotions.

"I told you we'd meet again, Keirith." Despite the greeting, the Trickster was watching Fa, too.

"Rigat." His mam breathed the name like a prayer. "Are you all right?"

"Aye, Mam."

"Hello, Darak," the Trickster said.

"You're sure?" Fa asked Rigat, ignoring the Trickster.

"Aye."

Not "Aye, Fa." Just "Aye." His father's wince told Keirith he had noticed, too.

"I'm sorry I ran away."

"You were upset," Keirith said. Nervous sweat prickled his forehead. The Trickster's nostrils flared as if he could smell it. "It was a shock. Naturally. Gods, I can't imagine . . ." He was babbling and he knew it, but the tension was thick, the air as heavy and unsettled as if a thunderstorm approached.

"We should have told you," Mam said. "Long ago."

"You were scared. I was, too. But only at first."

His manner was unnaturally calm, his smile so like Fellgair's that Keirith shuddered.

"We kept waiting," Fa said. "For the right time. But—"

"You thought I was your son," Rigat interrupted. "In the beginning."

"I . . . you are my son."

"I don't remember how old I was when I realized things were different," Keirith said. "That *you* were different. With me. But I was little. Five, maybe. Or six."

"Six." The single word was heavy with grief.

"When I made the leaves dance." Rigat nodded as if satisfied, then turned that thoughtful gaze on him. "When did they tell you, Keirith?"

"Just now."

"And you never suspected?"

"Nay."

"And now you'll blame Mam, too."

"Nay! At first, I . . . but that was before I understood she was only trying to protect me."

"Protect *you?*" The Trickster's gaze shifted briefly to Mam before settling back on Fa. "I see."

Fa's hands clenched and relaxed. "I'm sorry you had to find out this way, Rigat. We never meant . . ." He shook his head impatiently. "Aye. Well. It's done now. And words won't change it. The important thing is for you to come home."

"Rigat doesn't belong there," the Trickster said.

"You cannot stay with him. You know that."

"He's a man now. Let him choose his own path."

Fa's head jerked toward the Trickster. "How can he choose when he's dazzled by you?"

With a visible effort, he calmed himself, but it was Mam who said, "You don't know him, Rigat. Or what your power might lead to."

"I'll get to know him. And I'm not afraid of my power."

"You should be," Keirith said. "It can turn a man's head."

"But I'm not a man. I'm the son of a god."

"Even gods make mistakes."

"Is that what I am?" Rigat asked in a soft voice. "A mistake?"

"Nay! But no man should possess such power. It's dangerous."

"Only if he wields it unwisely. Isn't that what you told me?"

"You saw what happened in the rockslide. You killed people, Rigat!"

"So did you, Keirith! Only you used a sword. I know my power is strong. But only one person can show me how to use it. And that's my father. My real father."

Keirith winced at Fa's sharp intake of breath. But again, it was his mam who spoke. "Fellgair might have begotten you, but he is not your father. Did Fellgair hold your hand when you took your first steps? Or teach you to wield a sling or read the stars?"

"Nay. But now it's time I had a new teacher."

"He can teach you things I can't," Fa said, "but he can never love you."

"Neither can you."

His father's head snapped back. Keirith waited for him to vehemently deny Rigat's words, but he hesitated. Only for a moment. A heartbeat, perhaps. Then he said, "Of course I love you."

But Keirith knew it was already too late.

Mam hurried forward and pressed Rigat's hand to her heart. "Please, Rigat."

She was the only one who might sway him, the only one whose power over Rigat matched Fellgair's. Mam offered love and Fellgair, knowledge. Mam was home and safety, Fellgair, the lure of adventure and unknown worlds. But if she forced Rigat to choose between them, she would taint their love forever.

Let him go, Mam. And trust that he'll come back in the end.

"I love you," Rigat whispered. "More than anything in the world." And very gently, eased his hand free.

Mam moaned. Fa strode toward her, but in his haste, he stumbled. Keirith lunged for him, but the Trickster was quicker. His father gripped the arms that steadied him. Then he straightened.

Surely, even a god must quail before the fury in those cold, gray eyes. Fellgair simply studied Fa's face, as if memorizing every feature.

Suddenly, Fa recoiled, his forehead creasing in pain. Keirith heard him whisper, "It's too late." And realized the Trickster was touching his spirit.

Even now, Keirith could recall that touch—infinitely powerful, infinitely gentle. No man could shield himself from that. And for his father, nothing would be a greater violation.

"Let him go!" he shouted at the same time that Rigat cried, "Don't! Please!"

Fellgair ignored them both, staring at Fa with an expression that could only be described as tender. The face of a father scanning the features of a beloved son. Or a man gazing upon the face of his lover.

"Get out!" his father demanded.

The Trickster let his hands fall. Fa backed away unsteadily, but this time, Fellgair made no move to help him. "It appears Rigat has made his choice."

"He never had a choice," Fa replied. "Not after he met you."

"You seem to think my influence will be wholly bad. You should know better. In me—"

"Order and chaos combine. Aye. And that's fine for a god. But Rigat doesn't deserve to be the battleground for order and chaos. He's just a boy."

"He was never 'just a boy.' "

"You used my wife to gratify your lust. You gave her a child. And now, you're stealing him away from her. From all of us. But I suppose we've only ourselves to blame. For trusting you. For believing you would ever leave us in peace."

"Spare me your self-righteous indignation. You're hardly a paragon of unflinching honesty, Darak. You've lied to yourself for years, not for Rigat's sake, but because you couldn't bear to picture your wife in my arms. You've lied to Rigat. You're still lying to him, clinging to the pretense that you love him. Oh, you try. It's a measure of your decency that you try so very hard. It's just a pity the effort is so obvious. Every time you look at him or force yourself to touch him or avoid calling him son."

"Enough!" Keirith cut through the mesmerizing flow of words only to have that pitiless golden gaze turned on him.

"And then there's Keirith. And the lies you've told him."

"Nay!" His mam blazed with the ferocity he had seen earlier. "You will not hurt him!"

"But we all must live with the consequences of our choices. Isn't that what you said?"

Fa seized his arm. "Go, Keirith. Please. Go now."

Keirith's gaze darted from face to face, trying to understand how he had become the focus of contention.

Fellgair's eyes gleamed. "Such a small family to have so many secrets."

<It wasn't Mam's fault.>

Keirith started when he felt Rigat's presence inside his spirit.

<Fellgair made her choose. Between you.>

Dimly, Keirith was aware of his parents shouting at Fellgair, but their voices were drowned out by those clamoring in his mind. His father's, insistent: *"She did it to protect you."* Fellgair's, surprised and skeptical: *"Protect you?"* His mam's, trembling with sorrow: *"Every day for fourteen years, I've blamed myself . . ."*

Fellgair made her choose. And she had chosen Fa.

He stumbled away, flinging out a hand to ward his father off. Ignoring the warning, Fa pulled him into an embrace. Keirith just stood there, arms hanging at his sides.

"She went to Fellgair for you, Keirith. She didn't mean to say my name. It just happened. Your mam loves you. You know that."

He turned his head to escape the suffocating protection of his father's shoulder. Rigat had his arm around Mam's waist and was speaking urgently, but for once, she ignored her beloved child to stare at him, her eyes huge in her stark, white face.

Fa claimed it had just happened. But he was wrong. Or lying. She had chosen Fa because she loved him more. And although a part of him had always recognized that—had even accepted it—the truth knifed through him with the remembered agony of Xevhan's dagger. Only this agony would go on and on, dimming a little in the course of time, but always present, a wound that would never completely heal.

Poor Mam. No wonder she had refused to force Rigat to choose. She knew from experience how that felt. And poor Fa. He had endured the mutilation of his body, the rape of his spirit, and now this damning revelation by the god who had seduced his wife and splintered their family.

He made himself look up. The anxious lines of his father's face collapsed into each other and for a moment, Keirith was afraid he would weep.

"Don't," he said. "I couldn't bear that."

His father nodded, but continued watching him, silently pleading. He knew what Fa wanted, but he couldn't face her, not yet. Later, perhaps, when he could banish the bitterness from his voice and the pain from his face and trust himself to say the right things. Later, he could tell her that he understood, that these things "just happened."

All he could do now was glance her way and mutter, "It's all right. I'm all right." As he turned away, fingers clutched his shoulder, spinning him around.

"Please, Keir. Give it time," Rigat pleaded. "I know it's hard. But don't walk away."

"Take care of yourself," Keirith replied. "And don't stay away long. Mam needs you."

"She needs you, too."

Keirith nodded, but he was desperate to put this place and everything that had happened here behind him. He had nearly reached the safety of the underbrush when he heard his mother's voice.

"I curse you, Trickster. Not for what you did to me all those years ago, but for the pain you caused Keirith today and the harm I know you will do Rigat. Every morning when I wake and every night before I sleep, I will curse your name. And pray that the gods who created you will make you suffer for what you've done."

Fellgair opened his mouth to reply. Then he shrugged and held out his hand to Rigat. Instead of taking it, Rigat flung himself into their mother's arms.

"I love you. All of you. And I'll make you proud."

His brother's eyes met his. Then Rigat hurried toward the Trickster, and Keirith fled, pursued by his mother's anguished voice, calling his name.

Chapter 14

GRIANE MOVED THROUGH THE subsequent days like a dream-walker. Outwardly, life in the village settled into a kind of routine. The men filled what little free time they had with lessons on defensive strategy with Temet and the construction of the new terraces with Darak. The women gathered stones and cut turf to build homes for the newcomers. The children lost their pinched expressions of anxiety and no longer froze in fear when they heard an unexpected shout.

Darak flung himself into every activity with a single-minded intensity that left him exhausted at day's end. But every night, he turned to her as they lay under their wolf-skins, offering the strength of his arms and the comfort of his body. Every night, she squeezed his arm and rolled away, unable—unwilling—to be comforted.

They explained Rigat's continued absence by saying that he had gone south to search for Temet's warriors. Callie and Faelia knew it was a lie, but they never voiced their questions and seemed to attribute her withdrawal to grief.

Keirith avoided her. When forced to share her company in the evenings, he was invariably polite, but kept his eyes averted, as if the very sight of her sickened him. Yet despite their estrangement, she was still shocked when he announced his intention to accompany Darak and Faelia when they left the village.

"We've discussed the matter," he said, nodding to Temet.

Darak's expression made it clear that Keirith had not discussed it with him, but it was Callie who said, "Surely, you can do more good here. With your gift of vision—"

"That can be used anywhere. And my . . . appearance . . . could be useful."

"As a spy, you mean?" Callie shook his head. "It's been years since you've spoken the language. If you're caught—"

"I'll claim I was captured. And managed to escape."

"It's too risky. If you really want to help—"

"I've made up my mind."

"You're no more a warrior than I am."

"He can learn," Faelia said. "I did."

"But he hates killing!" In desperation, Callie turned to Darak who just said, "Keirith's a man. It's his choice."

Griane winced; the words were too reminiscent of Fell-gair's. Only then, of course, it had been her youngest son she was losing, not her firstborn.

"When will you go?" she asked Temet.

"Two days," he said. "Three at the most."

She had not expected it would be so soon. When she discovered her fist was pressed against her breastbone, she lowered her hand.

"Those who are badly wounded will need another half a moon to recover," Temet continued. "We can't wait that long."

At that moment, she hated Temet: his kind voice, his sympathetic expression. First, he had stolen her daughter. Now her husband and son. Silently, she corrected herself. Temet might have maneuvered Darak into leaving, but Gri-ane knew she alone was responsible for Keirith's decision.

She felt her head nodding. Heard her voice asking what supplies they would need. But inside she was screaming, "Just go! Now! Fight your stupid battles. But leave my husband and children out of it."

"Well," she said. "I think the stew's finally hot. I hope you're hungry, Temet."

Her hand was steady as she held out the bowl and her cheeks ached with the effort of smiling.

The next morning, Darak went to the longhut to ask Madig to serve as chief during his absence. Although he didn't like the man, he respected him. And having served as chief of his own tribe, Madig was the best choice to guide theirs through the moons to come.

The fierce light that filled Madig's eyes told Darak he had made the right choice. Until today, Madig had been listless and withdrawn. His grief over Seg might rage as strong as ever, but his desire to prove himself would give him the will to recover.

Darak ducked out of the hut, gratefully gulping in lungfuls of clean air. To his surprise, Hircha followed him outside and regarded him with a thoughtful frown.

"What?" he finally asked.

"You need to speak with Faelia. Nay, she's said nothing to me. But anyone with eyes can see something has happened."

"It doesn't . . ." With an effort, Darak bit back the words. Although he had never regarded Hircha as a daughter, she was a member of his family and their troubles *did* concern her.

He leaned against the side of the longhut, staring up at the sky. He had planned to settle things with Faelia after they left the village, but he realized now that Hircha was right. How could he urge Keirith to make peace with Griane if he was unwilling to do the same with Faelia?

In a low voice, he asked, "Has Keirith said anything to you?"

Hircha's frown deepened. "He told me he was leaving. But not why."

"He thinks his appearance—"

Impatiently, Hircha batted the air as if his words were a cloud of midges. "I know all that. But he didn't tell me the rest." Her mouth quirked in a bitter frown. "We're a great family for secrets."

He grimaced, recalling Fellgair's words. "Too many secrets."

And then he told her everything: the truth about Rigat, the encounter with Fellgair. Once he started speaking, he couldn't seem to stop. His lack of control surprised him less than the overwhelming relief he felt in confessing the truth to someone.

Hircha listened in utter silence, although her breath caught when he told her about the choice Fellgair had forced upon Griane. When the flow of words finally ebbed, he simply stood there, relief giving way to anxiety. It was Griane's secret to reveal, not his.

"I knew the Trickster was dangerous," Hircha said. "But I never understood why he took such an interest in your family."

"It's a game," Darak replied.

"At first, perhaps. But even a god can get caught up in his own game." She studied him for a long moment before adding, "He never expected to fall in love with you."

Darak felt the heat burning his face. As he struggled to find the words to deny it, Hircha said, "You and Griane." Her voice was gentle, like a mother explaining something to a very young child. "He had you both, didn't he? He forced you to offer him your spirit and Griane to offer her body."

"And got a son on my wife. What more does he want?"

"Perhaps he simply wants to be loved."

"He wants to possess. That's different."

"Maybe that's the closest he can manage. And since he couldn't possess you or Griane—not forever, not completely—he took Rigat."

"But why hurt Keirith? Why go out of his way—?"

"To hurt you. And Griane. Always, in the past, you've acknowledged his power and forgiven him for the pain he caused. This time, you refused. If he can't have your love, at least he can earn your hatred. Any passion is better than simply being . . . ignored."

Unwillingly, Darak recalled the words Fellgair had whispered: *"I know you feel angry. And betrayed. But if you would trust me—this one, last time . . ."*

Hircha shrugged helplessly. "I might be wrong. I don't know him as you do. What he feels—or doesn't feel—matters less than what he's done." She clasped her hands around her arms as if suddenly chilled. "Giving a woman a child . . . no god has ever done such a thing."

"The spirits of the Oak and Holly had never left the One Tree. But in the end, balance was restored."

"Aye. But at what cost?" After a moment of gloomy silence, she gave him a brittle smile. "Well. We can't worry about the whims of the gods. I have wounded men to care for—and you have to talk to Faelia."

"Thank you. For listening. And for talking."

"I just gave you more to worry about."

"Nay. It eases my mind to know Griane will have you. That you'll be able to help her. I can't."

Her fingertips brushed his sleeve. "She's lost Rigat. She's losing you and Keirith and Faelia. If she gives way, even to you—especially to you—she'll shatter." Again, that brief, bitter smile. "I speak from experience."

He squeezed her hand. "Maybe that's why you see so much—while I always seem to be groping about in the dark."

She pulled her hand free. "Don't be silly. And stop groping for compliments."

"The day I get a compliment from you, I'll probably drop dead from surprise," he said with a rueful smile.

She smiled back at him, a trace of the old mischief on her face. "Why do you think I never offer them?"

"Aye. Well. I guess that means I'll live forever."

Still smiling, she ducked back into the longhut. He stared after her a moment, then strode toward the lake, where he knew his daughter would be drilling the men.

Faelia first. Then Keirith.

Ever since that afternoon on the moor, Keirith had spent his days at the stream. His few attempts to soothe the spirits of troubled children had failed miserably. He should have known better than to try; his emotions were far too turbulent to allow him to find the stillness and emptiness of trance. At least here, he was useful.

With the spring salmon run at its peak, the fishermen had enlisted a few of the older boys and girls to help. Willow rods driven into the stream bottom created a barrier that made spearing the salmon easier. Those that leaped over the barrier elicited screams and squeals from the watching children, but only a few escaped the fishermen waiting upstream or the traps they placed in the riffles between pools.

It was cold, wet work and by the end of each day, his arms ached from hefting the heavy willow traps and lifting his spear with its wriggling bounty. But it gave him an excuse to avoid his parents.

He regretted leaving Adinn and Hakiath to supervise the fishing, but Dirna would help. She had appeared at the stream the day after Luimi's healing. If Faelia was permitted to hunt with the men, how could they deny Elasoth's daughter the right to fish? At fourteen, she was skilled in constructing traps and mending nets. And perhaps his absence would give Adinn an opportunity to ask Dirna to marry him. More likely, though, she would do the asking; her brisk, efficient manner reminded Keirith of his mam.

Painfully so, right now. He was glad when she herded the children back to the village for the midday meal, leaving him and Adinn to set the willow traps back in the shallows. Their task completed, they lurched up the steep bank, staggering a bit from the weight of the salmon strung on long lines of deer gut.

As they emerged from the alders, Keirith spied his father striding toward them. He felt like a rabbit helplessly watching a wolf close in for the kill. Shamed, he nodded brusquely.

"I need to speak with you, Keirith."

"Later, Fa. I've got to—"

"Now. Please. Adinn, you'll excuse us?"

Adinn's brows drew together in puzzlement, but he simply nodded and moved on. As soon as he was out of earshot, Fa said, "This is our last night at home."

"I know that."

"Talk with her."

"I have talked to her."

"*To* her. Not *with* her. For fourteen years, she's carried this guilt. And now she thinks you're leaving just to avoid her."

"She said that?"

"She didn't have to. Son, the gods only know when we'll come home again. Or if . . ." He stopped before he could ill-wish them, little finger flicking against his thumb in the sign to avert evil. "Don't leave like this. For your sake as well as hers. She's hurting, Keirith."

"So am I!"

"I know."

"You don't know! You can't. She chose you."

The words lay between them, painful and ugly.

His father's shoulders sagged. "Maybe you're right. Maybe I can't understand. Not completely. But your mother can. Because long ago, Fellgair forced me to choose between her and Tinnean. And I chose him."

"That was . . . it's not the same! You weren't even married to Mam then. You didn't love her."

"Maybe not. But she left everything behind to join me on that quest. And I abandoned her. She knows how that feels, Keirith. And she loved me, in spite of it."

His father walked away, then stopped. Without turning, he said, "If you can't forgive her, just tell her that you love her. You do, you know. And sometimes, a man needs to say those words. Especially if he doesn't know when he'll get the chance again."

The day passed far too quickly for Griane. She filled it with the mundane tasks of mending torn breeches, shelling her dwindling supply of nuts, preparing suetcakes. Hircha had already gathered the few bandages, herbs, and ointments still remaining after the attack. Griane began filling a doeskin pouch with quickthorn berries and broom blossoms for Darak's tonic. This supply had to last until autumn when the berries ripened.

Five moons. Surely they couldn't be gone longer than that.

The berries spilled from her palm. She got down on her hands and knees to dig them out of the bracken and remained there, huddled like a wounded animal, until the nausea ebbed.

Five moons. Never knowing if they were alive or dead. At least Fellgair would keep Rigat safe. Temet would protect Darak—he was too valuable to lose. But Keirith was no warrior. And if he was captured . . .

She beat her fists against her temples, as if that could drive away the thoughts. All it did was give her a headache.

She shoved a hank of hair out of her face and proceeded to gut the salmon for tonight's supper. As long as she had a task to occupy her, it was harder for her thoughts to stray. It was the night she feared, when she would lie beside Darak for the last time.

The last time for several moons, she silently corrected.

As afternoon faded to evening, they began to straggle in. Callie looked tired, but at least tonight Ennit and young Lorthan would mind the flocks so he could spend time with his family. Faelia seemed calmer; she and Darak must have made their peace. Even Temet looked relaxed—or perhaps merely relieved to be leaving on the morrow.

She had invited Hircha to join them for supper, as well as Ennit, Lisula, and Ela. The hut was so crowded they could scarcely squeeze around the fire pit. When Darak arrived, he quickly scanned all the faces. His expression darkened when he saw Keirith was missing.

They had started eating when he finally ducked into the hut. Darak made a space for him, but he chose to squat beside Faelia.

After supper, Callie pulled out Tinnean's old flute and began to play. Temet rose and excused himself, claiming he wanted to spend this night with his warriors. Faelia let him go, moving around the fire pit to sit next to Darak. Ennit left soon after, accompanied by Lisula's admonishment to let Lorthan chase after any wandering sheep. All too soon, she rose as well.

"The Grain-Mother will bless you all on the morrow, but I'll do so now."

She waved Keirith over and gestured for Darak and Faelia to stand before her. All three bowed their heads as she sketched the signs of protection on their foreheads and over their hearts. Then she stood on tiptoe to kiss Darak softly on the cheek.

"Be safe, old friend. And hurry home to us."

As Lisula shooed a sniffling Ela out of the hut, Keirith took Hircha's arm. "I'll be back soon," he said as he led her to the doorway.

For one dreadful moment, Griane feared Darak would insist that he stay, but after a silent contest of wills, he simply said, "Don't be long."

"He won't be," Hircha said.

But the night was waning before he finally returned. Lying sleepless on her pallet, Griane felt Darak tense and dug her fingers into his thigh. They lay there, neither moving nor speaking until they heard the rustle of Keirith's bedding. Then Darak rolled toward her and rested his head against her breast. His hand slid under her tunic to caress her naked thigh. His head came up. Even in the darkness, she could sense his question.

When they had lost Keirith that first time, she had been the one to comfort him. Now, he wished to do the same for her. Although his touch could not dispel the misery of her heart, she rolled toward him, breathing in his breath, tasting the faint bitterness of the wine on his lips.

He was slow and tender, wanting to please her. But it was not tenderness she desired. She wanted him inside her, marking her as his, driving out every other thought, every other need.

He tried to hold back, but she urged him on, digging her fingers into his buttocks, thrusting her hips against his, until he obeyed her silent commands and became as wild and fierce as a young lover.

Later, as he drifted into sleep, she held him, relishing the hard solidity of his head on her breast, the pressure of his leg flung over hers, and the tickle of his pubic hair against her thigh. The smell of him, salty and sweet. The callused palm resting on her bare hip. The stickiness of his seed and the faint sheen of sweat already drying on his shoulders and back. After so many years, his body was as familiar as her own, yet she had never lost her delight in it—even tonight, when her spirit felt so heavy.

Long after he had fallen asleep, she stared into the darkness. But she must have slept at some point, because she woke at dawn as he rolled away from her and reached for his clothes.

She lingered over the meal, but of course, the moment of parting still came too soon. One moment, Callie was making them smile as he pretended to inspect his nutcake for fragments of shell, and the next, everyone was scrambling for their supplies: spare clothes rolled in wolfskins; belt pouches stuffed with flints and tinder, bone needles and sinew; the bag of food, bowls, and turtle shells; another with firesticks and fishing line, bone fish hooks and flint arrowheads, braids of ropes, and a dozen other things that Griane was certain they would need, including nettle-cloth bandages, pouches of herbs, and tiny stone jars of ointments and creams, each carefully stoppered with a pebble and sealed with suet.

By the time they ventured outside, the entire tribe had gathered in the center of the village, along with Temet and the few warriors who were fit enough to travel. Griane took her place in the circle with Callie, while the travelers received the ritual blessing.

Gortin's hand shook as he sketched the signs of protection in the air, but his voice was strong as he intoned the final words. "The blessing of the gods upon you. The blessing of the Oak and the Holly upon you. And the blessing of your Tree-Father and Grain-Mother."

He thrust his staff at Othak and clutched Darak's hands. "Twice before, you have left us: once to save the spirit of the Oak-Lord and once to save your son. This time, you go to save our land from those who would destroy it. The gods smile upon your quest, Darak, and bring you—and all who go with you—back to us soon."

She watched them walk toward her—her husband, her daughter, her son. Faelia flung herself into her arms and whispered, "I'll watch over him, Mam. I promise."

Darak hugged Hircha and Callie before taking her in his arms. She clung to him, telling herself to remember the heat of his body against hers, the feel of those broad shoulders under her fingertips.

After Keirith hugged his brother, he turned to her. He hesitated only a moment, but the hurt sliced through her like a dagger. Then his arms went around her in a bruising hug. Her hands had barely closed on his shoulders when he pulled free.

As he walked away, Darak bent and kissed her cheek. "I'll bring him back," he whispered. "I'll bring them both back."

She bit her lip and nodded, determined not to weep.

It was Lisula who saved her, raising her voice in the song of farewell, just as she had all those years ago when their family left the village after Keirith's casting out.

> *However far we must travel,*
> *However long the journey,*
> *The Oak and the Holly are with us.*
> *Always, forever, the Oak and the Holly are with us.*

The rest of the tribe joined in the song their ancestors had sung when they left their homeland, driven out by the Zherosi who once again sought to steal their land.

> *In the heart of the First Forest,*
> *In the hearts of our people,*
> *The Oak and the Holly are there.*
> *Always, forever, the Oak and the Holly are there.*

Slowly, the tribe dispersed. Lisula and Ennit paused beside her. Griane let out her breath when they moved on; even the smallest gesture of kindness would have broken her. Callie lingered, though, and when she walked out of the hill fort to catch a final glimpse of her husband and children, she heard his footsteps behind her.

Early morning mist still shrouded the lake. Along the shore, it had dissipated into wispy skeins that drifted around the travelers and transformed them into strange, otherworldly beings. Like the restless spirits Darak had encountered in Chaos.

Callie's arm stole around her shoulders, a bleak reminder that only one of her children remained with her. Rigat had always been hers. Faelia had always belonged to Darak. After Zheros, so did Keirith. Callie was the only one they had shared, the only one who had never caused them a sleepless night. And because of it, he had gotten so much less of them—their attention, their worry, and possibly their love.

"We should have given you more," she said, and felt him start.

"You gave me everything I needed. You and Fa both."

He drew her closer, and she leaned against him, surprised at the strength of his arm. Together, they watched the figures crest the rise. The tallest among them paused at the top. Darak's hand rose. Then Faelia's. But Keirith simply stood there.

Darak turned away first. That surprised her; she would have expected it to be Faelia. Instead, she lingered a moment, still waving, then slowly followed her father down the hill.

Griane lowered her head, unable to look at that solitary

figure. Then she heard Hircha insistently repeating her name. She looked up and discovered her pointing at the hilltop.

Keirith's right hand was raised in farewell. Frantically, she waved back. Through the hot wash of tears, she watched him turn away, visible from the knees up, then the waist, then the shoulders, until—between one step and the next—he was gone.

Merciful Maker, you wept when death came into the world. You must be able to understand a mother's grief, to hear a mother's prayer.

My life for his, Maker. My life for my boy.

PART TWO

Three things you can never trust:
A rusted blade,
A traitor's oath,
And the smile of a deceitful woman.

—Zherosi proverb

Chapter 15

IN HIS THIRTEEN YEARS OF LIFE, Rigat had never ventured more than a half-day's journey from home. During his first moon with Fellgair, he discovered how vast the world truly was.

He explored deserts where golden sand rippled like the waves of an endless sea, and forests so dense and humid that water dripped ceaselessly from giant leaves. Glimpsed stone temples that towered over sprawling cities, and tiny villages guarded by tall wooden columns carved with animal faces. Observed fur-clad shamans pouring blood over sizzling stones, and naked priestesses tossing garlands of flowers into bubbling springs.

He was surprised that they never visited Zheros, for he knew Fellgair was worshiped there as the God with Two Faces. Nor did they enter the First Forest. But Fellgair did take him to the Summerlands.

Rigat stared in wonder at the enormous tree that would shelter the spirit of the Oak-Lord after his defeat at Midsummer. He gaped at the tree-folk his mam had met and shivered with delight when Rowan's leafy fingers touched his hair. Then Fellgair took him to a pretty little waterfall.

"This is where I brought your mother after I rescued her from Morgath."

Rigat nodded. Although Darak and his mam rarely spoke of Fellgair, he knew that much from the tale Nemek told.

"This is also where you were conceived."

This time, the shiver that raced down his spine was far less pleasant. It was one thing to know he was the Trickster's son and another to picture Fellgair and Mam lying together in the thick grass.

Fellgair allowed him to walk openly through the Summerlands, but during the rest of their travels, they remained hidden by the strange mist Fellgair conjured to shield them from observation. At first, Rigat feared his father was disappointed with him. Fellgair just shook his head, smiling, and explained that he must master his power before showing it off to strangers.

Under Fellgair's tutelage, Rigat learned to control his power so he could call upon it at will. To open portals and travel from one place to another. To understand languages that at first seemed like gibberish.

Although he was still too much in awe of his father to feel completely comfortable, it was a relief to talk openly about his power and get answers to the questions that had plagued him for years. Fellgair was an ideal teacher—patient, amusing, and wise. If he never hugged him after he mastered a new skill, his smile assured Rigat that he was proud. If he sometimes vanished for a day, he always returned, eager to see what Rigat had accomplished in his absence.

Left on his own, Rigat dutifully practiced his magic and hunted for food. But hunting lost some of its allure once he learned to guide an arrow straight to his quarry's heart, and it always conjured bittersweet memories of that day with Darak, just as visits to the Summerlands reminded him of his mam. Alone at night, he recalled the noisy meals around the fire pit and the warmth of his brothers' bodies flanking his. But he reminded himself that the knowledge he was gaining was worth any sacrifice.

During one of Fellgair's absences, he rose before dawn, determined to visit the First Forest. Guided by Darak's description of the One Tree, he pictured it in his mind, then raised his hand and jabbed the air with his forefinger. The air shuddered, as if in protest, then reluctantly gave way. He inserted his fingers into the long rent and peeled it back. After a moon of practice, it was as easy as skinning a rabbit, but it still unnerved him to see another forest through the gap.

He stepped through and carefully sealed the portal behind him. "Never leave a portal open," Fellgair had warned, "lest some unwary creature stumble through it."

He had heard the tale of the ancient tree that had stood since the world's first spring, its trunk so massive that twenty men with their arms outstretched could not encircle it. And the tale of the second tree that had sprouted from Tinnean's body after Morgath destroyed the first. But mere words failed to capture the beauty of the grove.

Although sunlight had yet to penetrate the canopy of leaves, the One Tree seemed to glow. Its pale bark was the only reminder that it had once been the body of a man. Compared to the giants around it, the Tree was small and slender. It might almost be mistaken for a birch, if not for the leaves of holly and oak that grew from its branches.

The Oak's heavy boughs nearly obscured the Holly, a single branch that sprouted from the notch where the trunk split in two. Yet like the Oak, its leaves seemed to shimmer, imbued with the spirit of the god who gave it life.

Darak and his mam had stood in this very place. Had Darak wept as he watched his brother's transformation? Had Mam chewed her upper lip, torn between wonder at the miracle unfolding before her and concern for the man beside her?

She might be chewing her lip now, wondering if I'm safe, if she'll ever see me again.

A Watcher flitted past him, a welcome distraction from such painful thoughts. Darak had described them as a shadowy flash of movement, but Rigat saw them clearly, some with the pale, mottled coloration of birches, others darker and thick-trunked as the oaks they once had been. Their agitation increased as he stepped toward the One Tree, then stilled as if recognizing that he represented no threat. Tentatively, Rigat raised his hands.

As a child, he had made leaves dance. Fellgair had taught him to see inside a leaf, to feel the movement of water through its tiny veins. Where once he could only hear water singing in a stream, his power now allowed him to detect the graceful sigh of waterweed swaying beneath the surface, the chatter of pebbles in the rapids, the trill of darting minnows and the deeper hum of a fat trout.

Would he be able to hear the voices of the gods? Or Tinnean? That would be something—to give Darak a message from the brother he had lost. But it was more than pride or a desire to prove himself to Darak that made him rest his palms against the trunk. Tinnean was the only being in the world who was both human and "other"—like him.

At first, all he could feel was the same thrum of life that emanated from an ordinary tree. As he drew more deeply on his power, it grew stronger, washing over him like water, but through him—into him—as well. As the thrum swelled, so did his power, as if fed by the life-stream of the Tree's energy.

Not a single stream, he realized, but two. One roared through his spirit like a river swollen with the spring runoff. That must be the Oak, whose power grew stronger as Midsummer approached. The other—a mere trickle—must be the Holly-Lord, so weak that it seemed impossible that he could defeat his brother and rival during the Midsummer battle.

Underlying both was a faint vibration, steady and rhythmic as a heartbeat. He could feel his heart slowing to match it, his chest rising and falling with the inexorable rhythm. A wave of warmth engulfed him, and then another. His body flushed with heat as it did when he climaxed, but this pleasure filled the mind as well as the body, spirit as well as flesh.

This must be the song Darak had heard in that dream-cavern in Chaos—the song of the World Tree, created by the Maker at the beginning of time, linking the realm of the gods who dwelled among its silver branches to the world of men who existed within its trunk to the sunlit Forever Isles that floated among its roots.

The song filled him, flooding him with awareness. He knew the ant that marched around his shoe and the robin that sang in the branch above his head. He knew the Watchers that circled the grove and the tree-folk who wandered the Summerlands. He knew the whisper of the wind and the call of the distant sea and the ceaseless flow of time, spiraling through him as slow and certain as sap rising in the spring.

His legs were trembling so much he had to lean his forearms against the Tree to support himself. Like a leaf caught in a current, he drifted, carried by the song and the twin streams of energy that were the Tree-Lords. His helplessness should have frightened him, but instead, he felt a peace and a contentment he had never known.

Was this what Tinnean had experienced—was experiencing? Did his spirit still live within the World Tree or had his essence been absorbed into it after so many years?

Something brushed against his consciousness, so fleeting a touch that he thought he had imagined it. But there it was again, a soft patter like rain hitting thatch. Only when he brought all his power to bear upon it did he realize the pulse was as regular as the rhythm of the World Tree's song.

When he whispered Tinnean's name, the pulse swelled. He touched excitement and joy and love—radiant, fierce, and utterly human. He gasped, too overcome to do more than absorb the flood of emotion.

Suddenly, the pulse faded. The eternal flow of the World Tree faltered. Crestfallen, he let his hands slide down the smooth bark.

The mingled scents of honeysuckle and wild animal filled his nostrils. Rigat whirled around, blinking hard to clear his vision.

"They didn't want me," he whispered.

"You surprised them," Fellgair replied. "They've never encountered a being like you. There has never *been* a being like you."

"I thought Tinnean would understand."

"He does."

"But he wanted Darak." For the first time, he truly understood how Keirith must have felt when he learned their mam had chosen Darak instead of him.

"Of course he did," Fellgair replied in the same reasonable voice. "Tinnean loves his brother. And he doesn't know you."

"But the Tree-Lords . . ."

"Gods are creatures of habit."

"You're a god."

"But I'm different. They were created by the Maker, the supreme force of order in the world. I am the child of the Maker and the Unmaker. I appreciate . . . disorder."

"That's what I am? Disorder?"

"In a sense."

Rigat hesitated, then blurted out the question he had longed to ask since their first meeting. "Why did you create me?"

Fellgair studied him in silence. "To change things."

"What things? How?"

"That is for you to discover." Fellgair raised a hand, forestalling another question. "I may have given you life, Rigat, but you still have free will. There are many ways you could shape events in the world. For good or ill."

"Is that why they didn't accept me? Because they think I'll use my power for evil?"

"Every man possesses that potential. In you, the potential—for good and evil—is greater." Fellgair frowned, considering. "A person's life is like a spiderweb—an intricate pattern of possibilities. Throughout any life, the web is rewoven a thousand times. In most cases, the reshaping has little effect upon the wider world. But sometimes, a choice alters not one life, but thousands. Millions."

"Like Tinnean's decision to become the One Tree."

"Exactly. During the quest for the Oak-Lord, your world teetered on the brink of extinction. It took many forces—mortal and immortal—to avert that fate." Fellgair scowled. "Some might consider my actions 'interference.' But didn't the Forest-Lord lead Darak back to the grove of the One Tree? Without Hernan's assistance, Darak would likely have died and the spirit of the Oak-Lord would have been lost. What was that but 'interference?'"

Fellgair stared off into space, as if arguing with an unseen presence. Then he smiled. "Your life holds even more possibilities than Tinnean's because you are my son and possess greater power. But power comes at a price. And part of that price is the necessity to wield it responsibly."

"That's what Keirith said. But . . ."

"Go on."

"What if I choose wrong? And make things worse? Or—"

"Hush." Fellgair's claws dug into his shoulders, silencing the rush of words. "I know it seems overwhelming. That's why I was reluctant to speak of this. If Tinnean had known his fate, would he have rushed to defend the One Tree? If Darak had known what he would have to endure to free his brother's spirit, would he have embarked on the quest?"

"Nothing would have stopped Darak."

Fellgair smiled. "Probably not. He's as stubborn as an ox."

"He's the greatest man in the world!" Rigat exclaimed. "He would have given his life for Tinnean. For any of us. Even for me . . ." His throat grew thick and he clamped his lips together.

"Do you miss him so much?"

Rigat stared at the ground, unable—unwilling—to answer.

"You could have asked to see him. Or your mother. I would not have been offended."

"It seemed . . . ungrateful."

"Gratitude for my teaching and love for your family are not mutually exclusive. Far from it. If you had been able to turn your back on them so easily, I would have been disappointed."

He had not even recognized the test, but still, he had failed it.

"So tell me. Honestly. Do you wish to see them?"

"Why bother to ask? You know everything!"

Aghast at his outburst, he started to babble an apology, but Fellgair merely cocked his head, studying him as he might an interesting beetle or an unusual mushroom. "Sometimes I forget how young you are."

Rigat managed not to squirm under that steady gaze, but he cursed himself silently for allowing his frustration to show.

"First," Fellgair said, "I do not know everything. There are many matters in the world that require my attention and I do not constantly monitor your needs. Second, I've made a conscious effort not to pry into your mind and spirit, believing that you deserved some privacy as we became acquainted."

He resented Fellgair's pedantic tone as much as the idea of begging to see his family. Then he remembered that Darak—the proudest man he knew—had gone down on his knees to the god. And—if he was honest—Fellgair hadn't asked him to beg, simply to acknowledge the truth aloud.

What will he think of me? I'm behaving like a child.

He wiped his damp palms against his breeches and took a deep breath. "I miss my family and I'd like to see them. Would you help me?"

"Of course."

At the flick of Fellgair's fingers, the grove vanished. Expecting to see his village, Rigat was surprised when another forest took shape before him. Slender trunks of pines rose skyward. Sunlight slanted through their boughs. Just visible at the bottom of a rise, two men knelt beside a stream, their faces obscured by Fellgair's strange mist. One of the men looked up, water dripping from his cupped hands. Rigat's heart thudded when he recognized Darak.

"The other man is named Sorig. Temet's second-in-command."

Before he could ask, Fellgair told him what had happened since he had left home.

"Faelia?" he demanded in a fierce whisper. Then he remembered the two men could neither see nor hear him. "Faelia led the Zherosi to the village? To trick Fa into joining the rebellion? Gods, it must have killed him."

"Obviously not."

"But he doesn't want to fight. And even if he did, he's too old. What are they doing out here by themselves? Where's Temet? And—"

"Darak and Sorig are going from village to village, seeking recruits. Since they're still alone, it would seem their efforts have been less than successful."

As Darak rose slowly to his feet, Rigat asked, "Is he all right? He looks tired. Don't you think he looks tired?"

"As you pointed out, he's an old man."

"He's not old! He's just . . . not young. And his heart . . ."

His voice trailed off as Darak splashed across the stream. He eyed the steep slope, then shifted his pack grimly and followed Sorig up the hill. When he slipped on a patch of moss, Rigat automatically moved forward to help him.

"If you take another step, he'll see you. Is that what you want?"

Reluctantly, Rigat stepped back. Still, it was hard to watch Darak's progress. His chest was heaving by the time he crested the rise. He bent over, palms splayed on his thighs as he caught his breath. Then he straightened and nodded to Sorig.

He passed so close that Rigat could have touched him.

Then he disappeared from view and there was only the crunch of dry needles, growing steadily fainter.

The forest melted into a smear of brown and green. Then the colors coalesced. Trees took shape, alders and crack willows instead of pines. A trail hugged the base of a rocky outcrop, skirting the waterlogged ground where a stream had overrun its banks. The chorus of birdsong suddenly fell silent, allowing him to hear the rhythmic tramp of feet.

A man appeared around the bend in the trail. And then four more. And four more behind them. A long column of Zherosi, marching shoulder to shoulder. Most carried spears, but those at the front had arrows nocked loosely in their bowstrings. They twisted their heads from side to side, darting nervous glances at the shadowy forest.

The leader raised his hand, and the column halted. As he scanned the terrain, the stillness was broken by a crashing in the underbrush. Rigat started as a man staggered past him and collapsed onto the muddy trail.

Despite his torn and filthy clothes, he was clearly a Zheroso. His empty quiver carved a shallow furrow in the mud, and he wore a battered leather helmet on his head.

"What's he saying?"

"Concentrate. You can understand him."

All he could make out was "Help me" and "Please."

At a signal from the leader, the column started forward again. Rigat heard muttered curses as the warriors on the left sloshed through the ankle-deep mud, while those on the right jostled each other as they were squeezed back by the sheer rock face.

The leader trotted ahead and went down on one knee beside the stranger. Even he seemed unable to make sense of what the man was saying. He held out his waterskin, but instead of reaching for it, the man seized the leader's arm, obviously overcome by his unexpected rescue.

Rigat was turning toward Fellgair to ask why he had brought them here when arrows rained down from the outcrop. The Zherosi archers toppled onto the trail. The warriors behind them whirled to their right, struggling to raise their shields; most only managed to knock their comrades off balance.

Another wave of arrows flew out of the forest, thudding

into unprotected backs. A few men fled into the swampy ground, only to be cut down. Caught in the deadly crossfire, those in the rear retreated, then suddenly drew up short. Only then did Rigat spy the net stretched across the trail, but even with his keen eyes, he couldn't spot the men who must have pulled it taut.

Someone was shouting, trying to restore order, but the screams of the wounded and dying drowned out the words. A group of warriors backed up against the outcrop, shields raised in a protective barrier. Spears hurtled toward them. Some glanced off the rock face with the thunderous crack of giant hailstones, but most found their targets, splintering shields with an ear-piercing screech of wood.

With wild shrieks, the attackers charged out of the trees and fell on the survivors, hacking with axes and swords, or simply clubbing them to death.

It was over in moments. Numbed, Rigat stared at the corpses littering the trail: legs twisted at grotesque angles, arms hanging from a few strands of muscle, pulpy brain matter leaking down shattered faces, steaming loops of intestine spilling through ripped tunics. Men reduced to bloody hunks of meat.

The leader of the Zherosi sprawled near the stranger; in the chaos of battle, Rigat hadn't seen them fall. As he watched, the stranger slowly pushed himself to his feet. Did he intend to fight the rebels alone? The massacre must have shattered his mind.

The rebels surged toward him, whooping and brandishing their weapons. Rigat spied Temet, his fair hair and height betraying his identity. And Faelia who flung her arms around the stranger. But only when the man pulled off his helmet did Rigat recognize his brother.

Keirith's face was utterly expressionless. All around him, the rebels were looting the dead, yanking arrows and spears from corpses, collecting undamaged bows and quivers, pulling off helmets, dagger sheaths, sword belts. In the midst of the frantic activity, Keirith knelt and methodically wiped his dagger clean with a handful of damp leaves.

"Why?" Rigat demanded. "He has a gift. If he wants to fight . . ."

Fellgair shrugged. "Ask Keirith."

Silently, he vowed that he would. But not now. The stench of blood and shit and piss sickened him. As he turned away, he heard a hoarse caw—the first crow arriving to feast.

"Do you want to see her?" Fellgair asked.

Rigat hesitated, then nodded.

At first, all he could make out were green hills and the pale yellow patches of blooming gorse. Then a figure moved out from behind a gorse bush, a withy basket over her arm.

He must have made some sort of sound, for Fellgair's hand descended on his shoulder. Gods, how could she have changed so much in one moon? Her hair was totally white, the last faint streaks of red gone. And her face was so deeply carved with lines of worry that she seemed to be frowning, even when she lifted her head to smile at Hircha.

She stooped to cut a stalk of mullein, then straightened, one hand pressed against the small of her back. Hircha took her arm, only to release it when Mam batted the helpful hand away. The familiar gesture brought tears to his eyes.

She brushed a wisp of hair off her face as she gazed south. Where Darak must be. And Keirith and Faelia. How could they all have left her?

"Callie?" he choked out.

The greens and yellows of the moor transformed into the mottled gray of a stone wall. Callie sat with his back against it, surrounded by a semicircle of children. They repeated his words in a toneless singsong, but now and then, a high voice would interrupt with a question.

"Where's Nemek?" he asked, afraid to learn the answer.

"He died. Half a moon ago. Of the wounds he sustained in the attack."

So Callie was Memory-Keeper now. Just as Darak had once been.

Without asking, Fellgair shifted the scene back to the hilltop.

"We should go back," Hircha said, eyeing the thickening clouds. "Else we'll get caught in the rain."

His mam gave a dismissive snort. "It won't rain till sunset."

Just hearing her voice made the ordinary words seem painfully sweet.

"Well, don't blame me if you catch a chill."

His mam's scowl only deepened the lines around her mouth, but her expression softened as she rested her hand against Hircha's cheek. "You're a good girl. I don't know what I would have done without you this last moon."

Whether it was the words that surprised Hircha or the gesture, she recovered quickly. "Oh, crawled onto your pallet and pulled the wolfskins over your head, I expect."

"Tongue like an adder," Mam replied, turning the caress into a pinch.

Hircha rolled her eyes in her best Faelia imitation. "As opposed to your honey-sweet one?"

They chuckled together and started toward the village. His mam stopped once to gaze south again. Hircha said something that made her raise her chin in the gesture of defiance Rigat had known from childhood.

"Enough," he whispered, closing his eyes. When he opened them again, they were standing on an empty moor.

He told himself that she might have been gathering plants since daybreak, that the walk from the village had tired her. If her legs were a little unsteady, her spirit was still unbowed.

"She's strong. She'll be all right." When Fellgair remained silent, he asked, "She will, won't she?"

Fellgair sighed. "All humans are mortal, Rigat. Even you."

"But if someone was sick or hurt or . . . dying . . . could I use my power to heal her?"

Fellgair's brows contracted, then relaxed. "Give me your hand."

When Rigat obeyed, Fellgair turned his hand palm up and pushed up his sleeve, revealing the bold shape of the branching antlers and the fainter white scar at the base of his wrist where he had made the blood oath with Darak. "Today, we start anew," Darak had said. And they had—but in a way neither of them had expected.

A black claw slashed across his wrist. The shock was greater than the searing pain. Rigat could only gasp and stare at the blood that welled up from the deep gash.

"Heal yourself."

The blood pulsed with the same frantic rhythm of his heart. He told it to stop, commanded it to stop, but unlike the spear that had flown through the portal during his vision quest, it refused to obey.

"I can't!"

"You can. Concentrate."

He closed his eyes, but that only made him more aware of the contrast between the warm blood and his cold, shaking fingers. Deliberately, he blocked out the sensations. He took a deep breath and held it for a count of three before releasing it. Another breath and then another until his heartbeat began to slow and with it, the spurt of his lifeblood.

Don't think about that. Think about the earth beneath your feet. And the cool breeze against your face. The fire of the sun and the song of the stream.

He could feel the blood, flowing out from his heart, down through his limbs, and then up again to return to his heart. An endless circle of energy, moving as inexorably through his body as time unfolded through the roots and trunk and branches of the World Tree.

He could see the blood, as clearly as he had seen the tiny droplets of water inside the leaf. As he traced its path, warmth flowed into his forearm, into his fingers. Like a spider repairing her web, he directed his power to his wrist. And as he wove, the warmth spread, as if molten fire flowed through him.

A great lassitude filled him and an overwhelming desire for sleep. But he continued his weaving, painstakingly sealing the severed arteries and veins before joining the flaps of skin at his wrist the way his mam sewed a rip in his breeches. Over and under and through, the power pricking his flesh like so many tiny needles, until at last he knew the wound was closed.

He opened his eyes and stared down at the raw stripe of flesh. Fellgair's forefinger glided across the wound, so cool after the fire. When he lifted his finger, a new white scar had obliterated the one from his blood oath with Darak.

"You did well, Rigat. Very well."

All he could do was nod.

"You're tired now. That's only natural. Even your power has limits. It will be days before you can use it again. If the wound had been deep, it might have drained you completely."

"And then I'd . . . I'd die?"

"No. You'd simply be a man. Like any other."

Never to hear the song of the stream or the language of the birds. Never to travel between worlds or touch the spirits of the Tree-Lords. To be . . . ordinary.

"And if I healed someone else?"

"An infusion of your power will always strengthen the recipient. But strong as you are, you're not a god. So the power—and the healing—will fade. That's why I sealed your wound. By the time your healing unraveled, your body's natural healing would have begun. But a serious injury would require multiple infusions of power." Fellgair's mouth quirked. "And the more prosaic assistance of a healer."

"Why didn't you just tell me that?"

"Because showing you was more powerful. Come, my son. You need to rest and grow strong again."

Fellgair lifted him as if he weighed nothing at all. Rigat rested his cheek against the furry chest and closed his eyes. Sunlight bathed his face. He breathed in air so sweet and fresh he knew that Fellgair had brought him to the Summerlands.

He would willingly sacrifice some of his power for his mam. Or he could bring her those magical plants she had discovered long ago in the Summerlands. Heart-ease would soothe her troubled spirit and heal-all would help the aches of her body. But news of Darak and Keirith and Faelia would restore her faster than any magic. As soon as he was stronger, he would bring her that gift—and watch the light return to her tired face.

Chapter 16

GERIV DO KHAT SAT CROSS-LEGGED in the pavilion of the warship, scanning the two peaks that guarded the narrows. Either would have made an ideal site for a fortress, but judging from the size of the palisades atop both crags, they were used only as lookout posts.

Another example of a commander taking the easy way out. But why should this one make any effort when the Vanel of the Northern Army—the former Vanel—had spent all his time in his hilltop villa, extorting bribes from the local merchants to purchase marble to pave his floors, tapestries to line his walls, and slave boys to warm his bed?

Geriv permitted himself a small smile. He hadn't been able to do anything about the marble floors, but the tapestries had bought enough grain and arms to fill the holds of the two supply ships that sailed with them. The Vanel—the former Vanel—had squealed like a virgin when they were pulled off the walls, but hadn't dared do more. After his lackluster handling of the rebellion, he was lucky the queen was permitting him to retire to his country estate in Zheros. She should have ordered his execution. But, of course, she couldn't risk alienating his family, one of the richest in the empire.

Politics. The bane of every warrior.

The ear-splitting blast of a kankh horn interrupted his thoughts. Korim clutched his forearm. "That must be the hill the Tree People call the Mountain of Eagles."

"Eagles Mount."

Although he had spoken gently, a dark flush stained his son's cheeks. Geriv suppressed a sigh. At fourteen, he, too, had been stung by every criticism—real or imagined—but he had never been as sensitive as Korim.

Nothing like serving as aide to Vazh do Havi to thicken a man's skin.

The thought of his irascible uncle evoked another smile. After Geriv had lost his left eye in the first Carilian campaign, he had feared he would never see active duty again. Vazh's intercession resulted in a transfer to the lands of the Tree People. A bitter disappointment at the time, for only second-rate officers were posted here, but he had risen faster—and higher—than he could have elsewhere.

Twelve years in the southern provinces of the Tree People, the last three as Vanel. He had hoped his success in subduing those provinces would win him a command in Carilia. Instead, the queen sent him north.

He had cleaned up the mess at his new headquarters at Graywaters in just two moons. Another moon would complete his inspection of the river fortifications. After that, he would deal with the rebels. And then—please, gods—he could leave this barbarous land forever.

He felt less confident about his ability to deal with his son. It might have been different if the other children had lived. Or if he had been home to supervise Korim's upbringing. Instead, the boy had remained in Pilozhat, pampered and petted by his mother and grandmother. After Kezha's death, he had summoned Korim to his command post, determined to toughen him up. He had spent more time with his son in the past year than in the previous thirteen, but they were still strangers.

Korim leaned out from under the awning for a better view of Eagles Mount. Then he flopped back on the cushions with a heavy sigh. "There's not a single eagle," he said, clearly disappointed.

As they entered the channel, the ship rocked, its timbers groaning like a dying man. Geriv reached for his protective amulet, then firmly quelled the desire and contented himself with tracing the spiral of the gold serpent that clasped his cloak. He had insisted on traveling in the warship after all. The tricky currents and easterly wind necessitated the use of rowers. Although the tubby supply ships offered better accommodations, he refused to arrive in a vessel that, under oars, resembled a fat insect trying to fly with small, weak wings.

The drum master quickened the beat and the rowers responded, muscles bunching in their naked backs and arms as they bent over the oars. On the fifth stroke, the ship shot out of the narrow channel onto the broad, placid expanse of a lake.

Korim caught his breath and let it out in a soft exhalation of wonder. "It's beautiful."

Geriv bit back a dismissive retort. True, the gray-green water sparkled in the sunlight, but it couldn't compare with the magnificent blue of the sea at Pilozhat. Instead of white sand, the shore was littered with pebbles. Green reeds testified to a marsh at the far end of the lake. Three smaller warships, suitable for patrolling upriver, were beached on the northern shore. In contrast to their sleek silhouettes, the fishermen's coracles looked like oversized drinking cups.

"I wonder if the fishing's good," Korim mused.

"There will be salmon," Geriv replied without enthusiasm.

"And trout," Korim said, still eyeing the bobbing coracles.

Two moons ago, the only things bobbing on the lake would have been logs, ready to be floated downriver after the spring thaw. And the log-riders with their spiked boots and poles. The first time he had seen them herding the logs downriver, he had been as breathless as Korim.

It was a ritual almost as significant to the people of Zheros as the shedding of the adders. Since both events occurred in the early spring, the priests claimed this was proof that the gods blessed their logging operations.

Blessed or not, it irritated Geriv that his warriors spent so much time felling trees. But that sentiment he shared only with his uncle Vazh, who inevitably responded with a filthy curse and a lament about the old days "when a man could concentrate on chopping off heads instead of branches."

Unfortunately, Zheros needed timber for its ships, so its warriors had to ensure the logs reached the sea. And its Vanel had to answer to the queen if they didn't.

"Imagine how beautiful it must have been before they cut down all the trees."

Frowning at the wistful note in Korim's voice, Geriv scanned the hills that loomed dark green and treacherous in the distance. That's how this place would have looked. Gloomy even at midday, a narrow track—ridiculous to call it a road—meandering through forests so dense that a man could see only a few paces into their depths. Easy to imagine a rebel behind every tree trunk. Easier still for a superstitious man to hear spirits whispering instead of the rustle of leaves.

Realizing he was stroking his amulet, Geriv let his hand drop to his lap and surveyed the southern shore. The usual circle of turf and stone huts. A field of sprouting barley. White blobs among the tree stumps on the hills—the ubiquitous sheep. Figures milling on the beach, attracted by the arrival of the ships.

"The villages are so much smaller in the north," Korim said.

"And more isolated. It's made the conquest difficult. That and the stubbornness of the people. The southern chiefs were wiser, and their villages have prospered under our rule."

"They look peaceful enough. Mostly women and children."

"Women and children can spy for the rebels as easily as men," Geriv reminded him. "But this village hasn't given us any trouble in years. That's why we bring them grain—when our harvests are good. To reward them for their good behavior."

Before he continued upriver, he would have to arrange for someone to row him across the lake so he could personally present the sacks of millet. That would honor the chief, but it would entail making pleasant conversation with the tribal elders and enduring the eye-watering peat smoke, the stench of their unwashed bodies, and an interminable meal.

Dear gods, let it be venison. Any more salmon and I'll grow scales.

"Can we go there today?"

Geriv eyed the opposite shore. He spotted only three company standards. And although the line of warriors extended the length of the beach, the three komakhs were clearly undermanned; a quick estimate indicated barely two hundred men instead of the five hundred that should be posted here.

"No," he finally replied. If the administration was as sloppy as he feared, he might be tied up for days putting things to rights. The chief of the Tree People could wait.

Shouts rang out aboard ship. The steersman leaned on his long oar and the rowers on the starboard side redoubled their efforts. As the ship swung away from the northern shore, he glimpsed the pointed stakes of a large palisade rising above a steep embankment.

Both sets of rowers bent over the oars. At another shout from the captain, the drum fell silent, the oars rose skyward, and the ship drifted toward the unseen shore behind him. Pebbles scraped the hull, and the ship shuddered to a halt.

While the crew ran out the boarding plank, Korim jumped to his feet. He kept smoothing his khirta until Geriv was forced to still him with a glance.

The slap of bare feet on the planks alerted him to Pujh's presence. Geriv raised his arms so the old slave could strap on his sword belt. Pujh gave the buckle a proprietary pat, then stepped back with an appraising frown.

Geriv endured a quick tug on the bottom of his tunic, a flick of the dexterous fingers to remove a speck of lint from his sleeve, but when Pujh licked his fingers and started smoothing the three eagle's feathers, Geriv seized his helmet and thrust it on his head. Pujh bowed and backed away, all the while grumbling about the importance of first impressions and the dignity of their house.

"Be quiet, old man. Or my first act after stepping ashore will be to have you beaten."

"I *should* be beaten if I allow you to appear in public looking like you'd slept in your clothes." Pujh's mouth pursed as he observed two slaves sliding poles into the brackets at the base of the pavilion. "No, no, no! The Vanel will walk." As the slaves touched their foreheads to the deck, he muttered, "Fools. As if my Vanel would arrive at a post in a litter. Like some fat nobleman or rich widow."

Geriv wearily lifted the patch over his left eye and

rubbed the jagged, scarred socket. He abhorred the easy familiarity that sometimes arose between master and slave, but it was hard to be stern with the man who had guided your fingers as you struggled to drape your first khirta around your hips.

"Leave it," he ordered as Pujh's fingers fluttered toward his cloak. Scowling, Pujh contented himself with inspecting Korim, patting, adjusting, and remonstrating until Geriv waved him away.

"You look very nice, Master Korim. Skalel do Khat, that is."

Thankfully, his son did not return Pujh's wink. The honorary rank accorded the personal aide to the Vanel might impress a slave, but it would take more than that—or the new sword proudly slung on Korim's hip—to win the respect of the seasoned warriors lining the shore.

He's a dreamer, like his mother. A scholar, not a soldier.

Geriv thrust the disloyal thought aside. Korim's gift for languages, his knowledge of the Tree People's legends and rituals . . . all had proved useful. He always fulfilled his duties eagerly, but despite the training Geriv had insisted upon, he was more comfortable with a fishing line in his hand than a sword, and preferred playing his flute to dicing.

Observing Korim's anxious expression, Geriv gave him an approving nod. "You'll do fine," he said, as much to reassure himself as his son.

Frowning, he strode across the stern deck to the boarding plank.

After inspecting the troops, Geriv spent the afternoon tramping about the encampment with the acting commander. Despite his limp, the wiry little Komal had no trouble keeping pace with him. His responses were gruff and blunt, but he answered Geriv's questions readily enough. Even without the scars on his hands and the small campaign medallions clasped to his cloak, Geriv would have known him as a veteran, but unlike so many who had been sent north as a demotion, do Nizhi's manner suggested competence.

His inspection bore out that impression. Following the approved protocol for provincial camps, two deep ditches had been dug around the perimeter. A rectangular palisade of sharpened logs, twice a man's height, protected the huts. Earth from the ditch filled the space between the logs and was mounded high enough against the inside to create ramparts for archers.

Inside the walls, fifty huts lined the two stone paths that quartered the camp. Some were clearly the original dwelling places of the Tree People who had once inhabited the village. The newer ones were constructed of logs, each big enough to accommodate the ten men who made up a skalekh.

The officers' residence and headquarters were larger, but hardly luxurious. Workshops, storage huts, and an infirmary occupied one quarter of the grid, along with two small pens for the oxen and donkeys. As a result, the living quarters were packed closely together. Still, the huts were clean, pallets neatly arranged around the central fire pit. And unlike many camps where the men simply squatted over a ditch, night soil jars stood outside each doorway.

The afternoon was waning by the time he completed his inspection. After a brief soak in the bathhouse, he and his staff joined do Nizhi and his officers at headquarters for a plain if hearty meal of roast mutton, flatbread, dried fruit, and wine. The officers gradually relaxed as they responded to Korim's stream of questions. Geriv allowed his son's chatter. Korim's questions conveyed only eager curiosity; his might seem like an interrogation.

At an unseen signal from do Nizhi, the officers rose from their cushions and retired. Geriv nodded to the four members of his staff who followed them. Then he and do Nizhi stepped outside.

Woodsmoke and roasting meat scented the air. He heard laughter and curses from the nearby huts, along with the inevitable rattle of dice. The trill of a flute vied with the occasional bray of a donkey. Silhouetted against the sky, sentries stood watch at the corners of the ramparts and on either side of the wooden gate.

"Nights come on slow this far north," do Nizhi said, eyeing the deep blue of the western sky. "At Midsummer, it's still light when you go to sleep and before you know it, the birds are singing."

"How long have you been posted here?"

"Two and a half years now."

"I take it the previous commander had good reason to place the camp here rather than fortify Eagles Mount."

The Komal's mouth worked, but he refrained from spitting. "Too much work. The village was already here." After a moment's hesitation, he added, "To be fair, we arrived in late autumn. We barely had time to throw up a palisade and build more huts before the snows came. After that, we had to spend all our time logging."

Geriv noted the scorn in his voice, but merely asked, "When did the Remil die?"

"Early this spring. Natives call it the Freshening cough."

Geriv nodded. The malady seemed especially virulent among new recruits unused to the bitter winters. What was odder was that the former Vanel had failed to send a replacement or promote do Nizhi. The acting commander still wore the black tunic of a komal rather than the green one of a regimental commander. When do Nizhi failed to elaborate, Geriv bluntly asked him about it.

"We sent word downriver. Never heard back." This time, do Nizhi did spit. "Since I was the only komal who'd been here from the first, the officers voted me commander." After a long, considering stare, he added, "When we heard the new Vanel was coming, there were some who thought there'd be . . . changes."

"News travels fast," Geriv replied noncommittally, wondering who had sent a bird upriver to alert do Nizhi.

"Well, you know soldiers. Gossipy as old women. Especially when there's no fighting to be done. Or logging," he added as an afterthought.

"Is that why you sent two komakhs upriver after the ambush?"

"Which one?" do Nizhi asked gloomily.

"The first one," Geriv snapped.

A gob of phlegm spattered on the stones. "They insist on sending the new recruits upriver. Begging your pardon, Vanel, but it's madness. Hard enough for veterans to stomach those forests, but the young lads . . . they panic at every shadow. I'll say this for my commander—he was after Headquarters for years to send our men inland and post the new recruits here. But nothing ever changed. And it's that kind of mistake that cost The Bluff dear."

"The former Vanel can hardly be held responsible for a poor command decision in the field."

"No. But look at the officer who made it. A nobleman's son with his first command. Thinking to cover himself with glory by chasing a few miserable rebels. Instead, he walks into an ambush and gets his men killed." The Komal slapped his palm against a rough-hewn log. "It's the inland fortresses that need the men. That's where the fighting is. And the timber. But instead of sending troops out in strength—" With an effort, he choked back his next words.

"Go on."

"Well, it's obvious, isn't it?" His voice grew impassioned again. "Little Falls is the only base of any size. At full strength, it has five hundred fighting men. Same as this one. But Deepford and The Bluff—they're small. Only two komakhs each. You can't log the forests and defend your camp with only two hundred men. The rebels pick 'em off like flies. So why keep so many men stationed here when they're needed upriver?"

"Why, indeed?"

"I'll tell you why," do Nizhi retorted. "Because this was the Spirit-Hunter's village. And there's some think we need to maintain a presence here—a symbol of Zherosi authority. Well, symbols are all well and good, but . . ."

The rest of do Nizhi's fierce but muted tirade washed over him, unheard. It had to be the same man. Fourteen years since that day in the temple of the God with Two Faces and Geriv could still see him, standing head and shoulders above everyone else. Those strange eyes, pale as polished silver. And the voice—deep and soft and terrifying—accusing the Zheron of murdering the Pajhit and cursing him to an eternity in the Abyss.

He interrupted do Nizhi to demand, "Is he alive? The Spirit-Hunter?"

"You know the tale, then."

"Is he alive?"

"Who's to say? He left here years ago. Him and his family.

But there are rumors. Some say he's the leader of the rebellion. Some even claim he's responsible for the recent ambushes." The Komal shrugged. "You can't believe every rumor you hear, Vanel. Especially when they come from the Tree People. Zhe's coils, they believe this Spirit-Hunter single-handedly brought an end to the Long Winter. As if he were a god, not a man."

No, he was definitely a man. A man who had wept when he thought his son was dead. The same son who had cast out the spirit of the Zheron and stolen his body.

Could he ask about Kheridh without implicating Vazh? Or giving away his own involvement in the escape of the Spirit-Hunter and his son from Zheros? Even after so many years, the memory filled Geriv with shame.

"Why would they leave?" he finally asked. "The natives are as rooted in their villages as the trees they worship."

"Banished from the tribe or some such tale. If you're that interested, you might ask old Mardon. He's chief of the village."

Geriv nodded and shifted the conversation to a general discussion of the relations between the Tree People and the Zherosi. But while he nodded thoughtfully at do Nizhi's observations, he was still reeling from the knowledge that the Spirit-Hunter had lived here, had walked this ground, might have stood on this very spot, watching the stars come out.

He was alive. Whether or not he was leading the rebellion, he was a legendary figure among his people. More god than man to the Tree People, according to do Nizhi. How would the rebellion fare if their hero was captured—or killed?

He had advised his uncle to execute both father and son, but Vazh had chosen to honor a promise to a dead friend, leaving Geriv the bitter responsibility of guiding the Spirit-Hunter to freedom.

This time, he vowed, it would be different.

Chapter 17

AFTER LEAVING TEMET'S FORCE, Darak traveled for a half a moon with Sorig as his only companion. They never stayed more than one night in any village, never mentioned where they were heading next. They had to be cautious, Sorig explained. Spies might report their movements to the Zherosi.

The thought that their own people might betray them saddened Darak, but did not surprise him. Nor did his failure to win recruits. The tale of the massacre in Gath's village preceded them, and while they always received food and shelter, the chiefs of the neighboring villages bid them farewell the next morning with obvious relief.

Although he missed his family, the forest soothed him. Each time he'd ventured south to hunt, his joy was marred by the knowledge that he would soon return to the bleak, empty moors. To feel the soft mulch underfoot, to breathe in the musty fragrance of the earth, to fall asleep to the sigh of the breeze and wake to a chorus of birdsong . . . he felt almost guilty for enjoying it.

And the leaves. After years of seeing only alders and evergreens, his eyes were starved for the colors of a deciduous forest—the shimmering greens of young leaves, the soft pinks and golds and reds of the feathery tufts just beginning to unfurl.

He even enjoyed camping under the stars at night. If they were lucky with sling or snare or fishing line, they cooked their catch over a fire. If not, they subsisted on food provided by the last village or Griane's dwindling supply of suetcakes. Inevitably, they shared stories about themselves, which is how Darak learned that Sorig had been born into the Holly Tribe just across the lake from his old village.

"You might remember my fa," Sorig said. "Jorn was his name."

"Jorn? Mardon's boy?"

A rare smile lit Sorig's long face as he nodded.

"You've got the look of him. I see it now. A good hunter. And fast. Gods, that man could run like a deer. Of course, that was a long time ago. He must be . . . what? . . . close to forty now."

Sorig's smile vanished. "He's dead."

"I'm sorry, lad."

"Eight years ago now."

"It's hard to lose a father so young. I was eleven myself."

For a long moment, they both stared into the fire, lost in their memories. Then Darak roused himself to ask, "And your mam?"

"She died before him. Her and the babe."

Darak winced and vowed to ask no more questions.

"I lived with my uncle's family. Until the Zherosi came. Some folk wanted to fight. But my grandfather—" Sorig spat the word out like a curse. "He said there was no point."

Hard to believe Mardon had capitulated without a fight. The chief was always wrangling with the Oak Tribe about fishing rights and hunting territory—and hauling the Maker into every discussion, no matter how trivial. But that was years ago. Even a pious old stick like Mardon could change.

"Is he still chief?"

"Aye. Or was a year ago. That's the last time I was that far west. I hardly recognized the place. Your village is still there, too—only now it's Zherosi sleeping in the huts. Behind a great wall of wood. The trees are gone. Nothing but stumps on the hills now."

Darak winced again, unwillingly picturing the beauty of his birthplace despoiled. "And Mardon permitted it?"

Sorig's expression grew darker. "That's why I left. I went to my mother's people. At Little Falls. Later, I joined up with Temet, along with Mikal and a few others. He's my cousin, you know. Mikal."

Darak nodded. They both had the same wiry builds, the

same long jaws. But Sorig's features were softer and his eyes more hopeful, as if there were some part of him that life's adversities had been unable to touch.

"We're the only ones left now—Mikal and I."

Which explained how such young men could have risen so quickly to become leaders. Darak guessed Sorig was about Urkiat's age. Throughout this journey, he'd found himself drawing parallels between them, both young, both bitterly opposed to the Zherosi occupation. Like Urkiat, Sorig had fought with his family over its collaboration with the Zherosi, but he had chosen to carry his battles away from his village so they would not suffer.

"Will we be going to Eagles Mount?" Darak asked quietly. "To look for recruits?"

"No point," Sorig said, bitterness creeping into his voice. "They'll never join us."

But as they traveled farther west and south, others did. At every village, their numbers swelled until they had fifty young men and three women traveling with them.

"Thanks to you, we'll double that number before Midsummer," Sorig assured him.

Their pace was more leisurely now. Sorig spent part of each afternoon instructing the recruits in battle tactics and close-quarter fighting. Darak used the time to hunt; it was too painful to watch them jab at each other with the fallen branches they had shaped into mock swords, to listen to their boasts and laughter as they compared bruises.

It was still a game to them, an exciting diversion from plowing and planting, hunting and fishing. Too soon, they would have to parry the blows of real swords instead of wooden ones. Darak vowed to remain aloof, unwilling to learn about their families, their hopes, their dreams. It would make it that much harder to bear their deaths.

When they reached the next village, he accepted the welcome of the chief, joined the rest of the tribe at a feast in his honor, and ate his food amid awestruck stares and whispered comments. As always, he revealed his true purpose in coming and, as always, the chief reluctantly allowed him to speak after the feast was over.

As he rose from his place and walked slowly into the center of the circle, a hush fell. He gazed at their expectant faces and began to speak in the deep, melodious cadence old Sim had taught him so many years ago.

Sorig slipped quietly away. Darak couldn't blame him; he'd heard the tale more than a dozen times by now. But the new recruits seemed as bespelled as those hearing it for the first time. A tale that linked his listeners to the earth beneath them and the sky above, to the sacred waters of their lakes and rivers, to the trees and animals that were their brothers and sisters, to the gods who walked in the First Forest, to the spirits of the Oak and the Holly.

He filled them with his words, made the tale resonate like the song of the World Tree. And when the longing reached its pinnacle, he led them into a darker tale. One that told of the blood that must be shed, the lives that must be offered. Of revenge against those who had raped their land and stolen their children and cut down their tree-brothers. Of arrows singing through the air and swords biting into flesh and the sweet screams of dying men.

The eyes of the children grew round, while those of the young men gleamed. Even the old men, who understood the cost . . . even they were swept up in the grandeur of the vision.

But not the women. Here, as in the other villages, he might discover a few like Faelia who were warriors at heart. But the rest?

He watched their faces grow pinched and fearful. Watched their arms tighten around their babes or draw a child close to their skirts. Watched them gaze around their village, as if imagining piles of rubble where their homes now stood.

Each anxious face was Griane's, each pair of haunted eyes. When callused hands clutched the arm of a son, a lover, a husband, he remembered hers: drifting over his body, swaddling a babe's bottom, washing skinned knees and sewing torn tunics, ladling stew into a bowl and grinding herbs for a poultice. Hands that offered pleasure and nourishment and protection. Comforting, capable, life-affirming hands that tried so hard to keep the dangers of the world at bay, and when that was impossible, provided relief from the inevitable pain.

And although he continued to weave the tale, he felt

only a weary disgust at cloaking danger and death in seductive words. All he could offer was the slender hope that they might restore the balance that had been lost and the peace that had been shattered and a world where children could worship at the sacred tree of their tribe and walk in the shadows of a forest that had been old when their ancestors were young.

For this, Faelia had been willing to sacrifice everything—even the love of her father. To preserve his family, he had committed himself to the same path. But even as he smiled at the young men and women who crowded around him at tale's end, the doubts continued to assail him, the bitter self-loathing as lacerating as the thorns of that twisted tree in Chaos.

As the twilight deepened, he excused himself and quietly slipped away from the village. When he reached a small clearing in the forest, he offered a silent prayer for his wife and children. Then he called his vision mate.

She emerged from the deep shadows under the trees and padded toward him. Although she moved more slowly these days, her tail waved its usual exuberant greeting.

He got down on his knees, grunting a little with the effort. Her tongue rasped against his face. He rested his cheek against the fur of her neck and felt her wriggle with pleasure. They had met many times in the years since he had led his family east. Time might have altered her appearance, but she was still—would always be—his Wolf.

"It is good to see you, Little Brother."

"And to see you, Wolf."

She cocked her head. "You are troubled."

"Aye."

Her head came up as she scented the air. "Is it this new pack?"

"They're so . . . young."

"And so many. Why do you need a pack this large?"

He tried to explain, but the concept of war was alien to her.

"What of your old pack? Your mate and your pups?"

"I'll go back to them—when this is over."

"Better to stay with the pack you know. The pack you trust." She shook herself, as if irritated. "You are always

searching for new packs, Little Brother. I do not understand this."

"Only by joining this new pack will I help my old one.'

"This makes no sense. How can a strange pack help you?
It has its own territory to defend."

Darak struggled to find words she would understand, but
could only reply, "It's a strange time, Wolf. Many things
are changing."

"Pack is pack."

"Aye. But now many packs are coming together. This is
something men do in times of trouble. Join with others in
a common cause."

She regarded him intently. In the faint light of Gheala's
newborn crescent, her golden eyes looked as silvery as the
fur on her muzzle. "But it is not your cause, Little
Brother."

He hung his head, unable to deny the truth.

"And this is what troubles you."

"Aye. But I've started down this trail and there's no
turning back now."

"There are many trails through the forest. Many scents
to follow. If you are hunting the stag, you must not be
distracted by the scent of a rabbit."

"I'm not sure what I'm hunting these days."

"Then you must choose your prey, Little Brother. Soon.
Or your pack will grow hungry and weak. And then it will
drive you away." She whined softly. "That is the way with
wolves and men alike."

Chapter 18

BABBLING TEARFUL THANKS IN Zherosi, Keirith tightened his grip on the man's sword arm. He was careful to keep his right hand free, to keep his left arm away from his body so he could draw his dagger and drive it up under the man's chin. During the other ambushes, he'd accomplished the move with ease. So why did his limbs feel so heavy, as if he were moving underwater?

This isn't real.

The man reared back, fingers closing around his wrist. He could feel his hand going numb, the dagger slipping from his grasp.

I'm dreaming.

Helpless, he fell onto his back, the earth hard as stone beneath him. Even in the shadows under the trees, the bronze blade glittered, blinding him with the reflected radiance of the sun. His arms shook as he gripped the man's wrist, desperate to stop the blade's inexorable descent.

I have to wake up.

The tattoos on the man's naked forearms writhed in fear and ecstasy. Two black heads ripped free of the constraining flesh. The man screamed, then screamed again as the serpents slithered down his wrists and over their locked hands. They wriggled up Keirith's arms and burrowed into his skin, leaving a trail of fire behind them and a scent like roasting meat. But no pain, no pain at all, only the hot bloodlust flooding his body and the warm, salty taste of victory in his mouth.

His arms were light again, his hands strong. With practiced ease, he ripped the dagger from the man's fingers, then threw him to the ground and straddled him.

Laughter froze him in mid-thrust. For the first time, Keirith looked into the man's face—and saw himself.

<Kill him.>

Xevhan's voice whispered inside his spirit. Too shocked
to speak, Keirith just shook his head, staring into the face
that was Xevhan's and his.

<You know you want to. I can feel it. I feel everything.>

This isn't . . . it's a nightmare.

Xevhan winked. When he opened his eye, Keirith saw a
figure reflected in it. An auburn-haired boy, his grimy face
streaked with tears. But as he watched, the pale skin deepened to the tawny color of deer hide. Blue eyes darkened
to brown. The hair fell out in clumps, leaving his head
smooth and bald. Then new hair sprouted, black as the
tattoos on their forearms, wriggling like adders, twisting
into a long, neat braid.

*<We have the same body. The same thoughts. The same
spirit.>*

Nay!

*<These rebels will never accept you. Because we are one,
Kheridh. Now and always.>*

With all his strength, Keirith drove the dagger up and
under Xevhan's breastbone. But it was his heart he pierced,
his mouth that opened in a silent scream of agony, his lifeblood that gushed out. The red torrent filled Xevhan's
mouth, but could not choke off the delighted laughter.

<Keirith. Wake up.>

Xevhan's laughter shook him as if he were laughing, too.
Like old friends sharing a good joke.

"Keirith!"

He jerked upright, flailing at the unseen hands that tried
to restrain him. Then he recognized his sister's voice.

Faelia's fingers relaxed. "Are you all right?" she
whispered.

He nodded, then realized she probably couldn't see him
and whispered, "Aye."

"You were moaning in your sleep."

She was crouching so close it took all his control to keep
from scuttling away.

"Lots of men have them after a battle. It's nothing to be
ashamed of. Or . . ." Her fingers groped for his. "Is it the
old nightmare?"

Because Faelia was trying to be kind, he whispered, "Both, I expect."

"Do you want to talk about—?"

"Nay." Afraid he had sounded too abrupt, he added, "I'm all right now. Really. I'm sorry I worried you."

Faelia squeezed his hand. "An ambush . . . it strains everyone's nerves. But you did well. Not just today, but the other times, too. Without you, we could never have achieved so much."

"Our secret weapon," Temet called him. At least in front of the others. Privately, Temet kept pressing him to use his vision to spy on Zherosi troop movements, but so far, he'd only managed to reach his spirit guide once. And that was to help young Eilin, who had been so traumatized by his first battle that he alternated between violent nightmares and apathetic silence.

As with little Luimi, Natha came to him at once. After soothing Eilin's initial panic, he had managed to touch the dark places in the boy's spirit, share his own fears about battle, and ease his lingering doubts about his bravery. Since then, Eilin's nightmares had faded. Now it was the healer who suffered them.

As Faelia crawled back to Temet, Keirith wondered at his continued failure to achieve the kind of visions Temet expected. Was it a sign that he was not meant to use his gift to help the rebels kill their enemies? Or was he simply afraid of what he would See?

He heard Temet's deep whisper and Faelia's lighter one as she lay down beside him. None of the others stirred and the low buzz of conversation around the fire continued unabated. Thank the gods only Faelia had noticed his thrashing.

Unable to sleep, he rose, but instead of escaping into the solitude of the forest, he reluctantly walked toward the fire. Better to let them know where he was going and why. There were still those who eyed him with suspicion because he looked like a Zheroso; slipping off into the night would only feed their doubts.

His eyes had grown accustomed to the darkness, and he saw Faelia's head come up as he passed. He paused long enough to rest his hand on her hair, then continued across the clearing. The group around the fire looked up, but no one invited him to join them.

"Bad dream?" Mikal asked.

Damn. They had heard. "I just need to piss."

"They plague some recruits. Especially those who've never seen a real battle."

"I was blooded at fourteen. When the Zherosi attacked my village."

"That's right. I forgot."

He hadn't forgotten; Mikal was just testing him. Faelia claimed he was tough on all the recruits, but he seemed to take particular enjoyment in goading the son of Darak Spirit-Hunter.

Selima punched Mikal on the arm. "Let the man piss. Before he bursts."

"You'll manage all right on your own?" Pedar asked. "It's dark out there."

Pedar's concern surprised him; it was more in his nature to joke.

"I'll be fine. Thanks."

"Just remember," Pedar said, his face solemn, "it's not a dagger. You'll want to draw it out of your breeches nice and slow."

Clearly, the others had been waiting for it. Keirith managed a smile and backed away, hoping to escape before Pedar capitalized on his joke.

"I've got a strong right hand. If you need help."

"He doesn't want that callused paw groping between his legs. Now these . . ." Selima's fingers waggled in the firelight.

Pedar shook his head in mock despair. "It's not a flute, woman. Didn't I tell you that the other night?"

"Oh, aye. But you were happy enough when I blew on it."

Keirith dutifully laughed with the others and strode off. Some of the rebels used coarse humor to keep their fears at bay, while others sought release in sex. Both made him feel awkward—and reminded him that, at nearly thirty years of age, he had never lain with a woman.

What woman would want a man who looked like the ones who'd slain her family? And woke in the night, thrashing and whimpering like a child?

He ruthlessly suppressed the longing that filled him. He was only indulging in such blatant self-pity because he was

far from home—a stranger among strangers—and because
the nightmare had stirred up all the old feelings.

He leaned against a sapling and took a deep breath. It
had been years since he had dreamed of Xevhan, longer
still since one of his nightmares had awakened the family,
but clearly, Faelia remembered.

Rigat would have remembered, too; they slept side by
side, and unlike Callie, Rigat was a light sleeper. Each time
Keirith had jolted awake, his brother held his hand until
the shaking stopped and mercifully refrained from questioning him later.

Only Fa knew the truth: that shattered fragments of Xevhan's spirit had lodged inside him after their battle. Until
tonight, Keirith had believed that he and Natha had rooted
out the lingering traces.

He stiffened, recalling the final words of his nightmare.
Neither Xevhan nor Faelia had urged him to wake. It had
been Rigat. But that was impossible. His brother was with
Fellgair. His dreaming mind must have conjured Rigat's
voice. And—please, gods—Xevhan's. He couldn't bear the
thought that those tainted fragments were still buried deep
inside his spirit.

He scanned the graying sky with relief. From long experience, he knew the terrors that stalked a man by night
seemed far less formidable in the daylight. He almost welcomed the prospect of another long march. Perhaps it
would leave him too exhausted to dream.

Hearing a man's soft chuckle from the underbrush, his
mouth twisted in a bitter smile. Clearly, one couple had
found another way to banish the night terrors. Although
he doubted his presence would distract them, he had no
desire to eavesdrop on their encounter.

As he turned back to camp, he heard another rustle and
froze. Temet always warned them about making careless
assumptions. Likely, it was just a couple making love or a
sentry exchanging a quick word with a comrade, but there
was always the chance—however remote—that a Zherosi
patrol had found them.

Peering into the darkness, his hand moved to the hilt of
his dagger. A soft voice said, "Make sure your fingers are
wrapped around the right weapon."

Before he could do more than gasp Rigat's name, his
brother emerged from his hiding place and flung his arms
around him. They thumped each other on the back, laughing and whispering, too excited to even answer the questions the other asked.

Finally, Keirith pulled back. "How did you find me?"

"Remember how I could follow the trail of Mam's spirit
when I left our valley? Now, I can follow anyone's. Well,
anyone I know. From hundreds of miles away."

Even in the dark, Keirith could hear the pride in Rigat's
voice and the effort he made to sound matter-of-fact rather
than boastful.

"Are you hungry? There's food. A little. And a fire."

"Nay."

It took Keirith a moment to understand Rigat's reluctance. "Nobody knows. About you. We told everyone you
were scouting the moors."

"And they believed that?"

"If they didn't, no one said anything."

"To your face. Nay, it doesn't matter," Rigat added.
"But you mustn't tell anyone you saw me."

"But—"

"Not even Faelia."

"All right."

"Swear."

"Rigat . . ."

"Swear!"

"All right, all right. I swear."

"Now give me your hand. And hold on tight."

The orange glow of the fire winked out. A sudden blast
of wind made him close his watering eyes. When he opened
them, he discovered they were standing on a moor. Even
in the faint light, he could see Rigat's teeth gleam as he
grinned.

"Where is this?"

"You don't have to whisper. No one's here."

Judging from the cool air and the treeless moor, they
were farther north. Boulders encrusted with yellow lichens
reared up above golden deergrass. Thick carpets of moss
covered the flatter rocks. Small pools of rainwater had collected in the pits that time and the elements had carved,

and small pink and white flowers had sprung up around them. He crouched down for a closer look, then quickly straightened when he found himself wondering if his mam would recognize the flowers.

"I saw her."

He spun around to find Rigat studying him intently.

"And Darak, too."

Keirith slowly lowered himself onto a slab of rock, heedless of the flowers he crushed beneath him. His brother sat beside him, careful to choose a dry place. As Rigat described his encounters, Keirith envisioned his father struggling up the slope, his mother clinging to Hircha's arm. He wasn't aware his fist had clenched until Rigat's fingers curled around it.

"Can't you forgive her?"

"I have." But Keirith knew the shadow of her choice would always lie between them.

"And Darak? Can you forgive him for being the one she chose?"

Since that day by the lake, neither he nor his father had broached the subject. Nor had they dared discuss the implications for their relationship. But that gulf was just as real as the one that separated him from his mother. Trust Rigat to recognize what he had refused to face himself.

Rigat sighed and released his hand. For a long while, they simply sat together, watching the clouds change from violet to pink in anticipation of Bel's dawning. Then Keirith blurted out, "It was you, wasn't it? Speaking in my dream?"

Rigat hesitated, his expression wary. Then he nodded.

"And you've done it before."

When Rigat nodded again, Keirith leaped up and stalked away.

"It was an accident. The first time. But there were so many nights when you were thrashing and moaning, and I couldn't think of any other way to help."

With an effort, Keirith steadied his breathing. "I'm not angry. It's just . . . I thought he was gone. But all the time, it was you driving him away."

Without Rigat, there would be more nights like tonight, filled with Xevhan's taunting laughter and insidious whispers.

"They're just dreams, Keirith."

"Are you sure?"

Rigat opened his mouth and closed it again. Finally, he said, "Nay. My power wasn't as strong then. I couldn't tell if the darkness I felt was just the dream or something real. But if I touched your spirit now—"

"There's no time."

Sharing a link with his father had been difficult enough. For his brother to touch those dark places, to sense all his painful secrets . . .

He forced himself to smile. "Thank you for coming. For . . . easing my dreams all these years. And for telling me about Mam and Fa."

Rigat looked as if he wanted to pursue the subject of Xevhan, but all he said was, "There was another reason I came. I saw you, too. Leading a Zherosi war party into an ambush. Why, Keirith?"

"What do you mean?"

"You have a gift."

"A gift that seems to have deserted me," he replied, unable to disguise his bitterness.

"But you have to try."

"I have tried!" Only a few moons ago, he had been the one giving advice. Even knowing that Rigat was the son of a god, the reversal in their roles galled him. "I might not be able to See, but at least I'm doing something to help my people."

"While I've just been having fun?" Rigat shot back.

"I didn't mean—"

"Do you think it's been easy? Trying to deal with everything that's happened and learn about my powers and not having anyone to talk to or think things through with. Except Fellgair. And he doesn't . . . he's not the same as real family."

"I know. I'm sorry."

The anger drained from Rigat's face. "You know what it's like. To be different. Always trying to find a way to fit in and never really succeeding." A look of intense excitement spread across his features. "Remember how I said it would take the two of us?"

Keirith nodded.

"You're right. I haven't done enough. But I can. I can be your eagle."

"My eagle?"

"You can't keep luring the Zherosi into ambushes. Sooner or later, they'll catch on. But I could open portals. Spy on the Zherosi. And tell you what I've seen."

"I'd have to tell Temet where I got the information."

Rigat frowned. "I don't want them to know about me. Not yet. Just pretend it came to you in a vision. You can do that, can't you?"

Just swallow his pride and take the credit. Surely, the simple lie would hurt no one. So why was he reluctant?

They had been lucky so far, Temet anticipating the Zherosi response to their ambushes, scouts stumbling on a column of reinforcements. But to know troop movements instead of relying on luck? To know the exact number of men in each war party, at each fortress? With that kind of information, there was no limit to what they might do.

He looked at Rigat's expectant face and grinned. Rigat grinned back and pulled him into a fierce embrace.

"Tinnean and Darak changed the world," his brother whispered. "So can we."

He hugged Rigat hard, swept away by his confidence. And then he heard the taunting laughter once more: *These rebels will never accept you. Because we are one, Kheridh. Now and always.*

"You're shivering," Rigat said.

"The wind's cold."

"And the sun's coming up. I must get you back. Look, I'm not sure when I'll be able to come again. So for now, just slip away from camp every night and pretend to seek a vision."

Did Rigat even hear the hint of derision in his voice? Or was he too caught up in his scheme to notice?

Swallowing his resentment, Keirith said, "Be careful."

"Don't worry about me. I'll be fine." A confident grin, a careless shrug. "Now hold on tight. And close your eyes else you'll get dizzy."

Obediently, Keirith closed his eyes, shutting out the bloody curve of the rising sun.

Chapter 19

AT FIRST, RIGAT ENJOYED playing eagle. The most difficult part was learning when and where to open a portal. In the end, Keirith gave him the clue he needed, passing along what he knew of the fortresses and their locations. After that, he was able to move from place to place, observing the activities around the fortresses and the movement of troops upriver.

With Fellgair's help, he finally mastered the trick of hiding his presence by pulling moisture from a nearby body of water or cloaking himself in a mantle of sunbeams. It was harder to maintain the illusion while he spied on the Zherosi. Twice, he became so engrossed that he allowed his shield to dissipate and had to hastily seal the portal before a scouting party attacked. But the danger only added to the excitement.

Using his information, the rebels ambushed a relief column marching from Little Falls to The Bluff, then two hunting parties in the hills around The Bluff. After that, the Zherosi rarely left either fortress. An entire sennight went by in which Rigat did little more than squat on a hilltop, waiting for something—anything—to happen.

Spying, he realized, was mostly dull work—and in his case, thankless. Although he knew the victories would have been impossible without him, it was Keirith who received the accolades, Keirith who was acclaimed a hero.

To relieve his restiveness, he ventured farther downriver. At Eagles Mount, he surveyed the place where his entire family had been born and tried to picture it as it must have been before the Zherosi came. Farther west, he found three smaller fortresses and dutifully reported his estimate of the men in each and the number of ships he spotted on the river. He traveled as far as the great sea itself. Even more impressive than the endless expanse of water was the sprawling city at the mouth of the river.

He stared in fascination at the stone buildings—two, three, even four times the height of a man; the orderly grid of streets; the dozen ships rocking gently beside the long stone walkways that jutted out into the water. And the people—he had never seen so many in one place, Zherosi and tribe folk alike.

In Graywaters, the only battles being fought were over the price of goods in the marketplaces. He wandered freely through the streets, observing Zherosi sailors dicing with fishermen, Zherosi servants haggling with hunters over haunches of venison, Zherosi warriors flirting with the local women filling their waterskins at a well.

Not all was harmony, of course. He witnessed the occasional fistfight, a toothless old woman begging at a corner. At sunset, his people retreated to their village, while the Zherosi closed the massive wooden gates at the four entrances of the city and mounted armed guards around the walls. Not once did he observe any of his people entering the sawmill to the east of the city, but neither did they try to burn it down.

Rigat reported his observations to Keirith, but kept his doubts to himself. Temet had only fifty or sixty in his band. Keirith claimed there were other rebel forces scattered throughout the north, but even if they all joined together, how could they possibly defeat the hundreds—thousands—of Zherosi? Especially when most of their people seemed to have given up the fight.

If Fellgair knew he was spying for the rebels, he said nothing. He saw his father less frequently now, but loneliness was better than Fellgair's unblinking scrutiny.

The Summerlands—beautiful and serene—only made him more restless. He preferred to spend his nights in one of his forest lairs, sleeping on a bed of leaves or pine needles.

After one such night, he rose and washed his face and hands in a pool. He stared down at his wavering reflection: the unkempt hair studded with leaves and twigs, the scruffy cheeks, the collar of grime around his neck. Then he drew his dagger.

He shaved the red fuzz from his cheeks, but despite his care, he had to use his power to seal the nicks. He used it yet again to mend the hole in the elbow of his tunic, but satisfied himself with brushing off the worst of the dirt; although he wanted to look his best, he refused to waste his magic on cleaning his clothes.

He opened a portal south of the village. For a moment, he simply stood there, allowing his anticipation to build. Then he strode over the hill, eagerly noting the changes since Fellgair had brought him here. The newly-sheared ewes looked skinny and frail, the irregular pink patches of skin like giant freckles. Gorse set the hills aflame with brilliant splashes of yellow, and barley stood knee-high on the terraces.

Fishermen shouted greetings when they recognized him. Children, attracted by the noise, raced down the slope from the hill fort, calling his name. He entered the village, heady with excitement, and was immediately surrounded by a crowd.

It's just like I imagined it would be.

He answered their questions absently as he searched for his mam. Instead, he saw Callie coming toward him, a great smile on his face. He flung himself into his brother's arms and clung to him for a moment. Then he realized how unmanly that must seem and pulled away, punching Callie lightly on the shoulder. He glimpsed Madig's frowning face and the Grain-Grandmother's smiling one, but the others faded into a blur when he saw his mam.

She stood at the doorway of their hut, motionless at the back of the restless crowd. Her chin shook as she caught her upper lip between her teeth, but her eyes were huge and shining. He pushed past the others, his heart beating a wild tattoo. But when they stood only a pace apart, they both stopped, shy and awkward as strangers.

Her hand came up. Tentatively, she touched his cheek. "I wasn't sure you were real."

Unwilling to trust his voice, he nodded.

Her arms were as strong as he remembered. The scent of herbs clung to her, and wool-fat soap, and that indefinable something that was simply Mam.

She thrust him away, swiping at her nose and laughing. "You're so tall."

"That's what Keirith said."

"Keirith? You've seen him?"

"And Fa and Faelia. And so much else, Mam. I don't even know where to begin."

Her expression changed, as if some light inside her had been smothered. Rigat turned to find Madig studying him.

"So. You're back."

"For a while."

"Where have you been?"

"Scouting. For Temet."

It was impossible to tell from Madig's grunt whether he believed him or not.

"The council of elders will need to hear what you've learned. And Temet's warriors."

"They're still here?"

"A few. Come to the longhut at midday."

"He's just gotten home," his mam protested. "Surely, it can wait until the morrow."

"Midday," Madig said. "Then you can tell us all about scouting for Temet."

Fingers bit deep into his bicep, and Rigat choked back a retort.

"There are fields to be weeded and huts to repair," Madig reminded the onlookers as he limped away. "Let's waste no more time here."

Only then did Rigat discover that the fingers gripping his arm belonged to Hircha.

"Darak named him chief in his absence," she said in an undertone. "Stay out of his way. He's never forgiven you for Seg's death."

"But that wasn't my—"

"It doesn't matter. And mind what you say in front of Callie. He doesn't know."

"Know what?"

"The truth. About you."

Shocked, he glanced at his mam, who nodded. "Darak told her." As Callie approached, she summoned a quick smile. "Let's go inside and talk. The children's lessons can wait, can't they, Callie? Callie is Memory-Keeper now," she added. "Nemek . . . I lost him."

His mam always grieved when her healing skills failed to save a life, but Nemek's loss must have hit her hard. He had always been a favorite of hers—of everyone in the village.

"You did everything you could," he assured her.

"But it wasn't enough."

He studied her face, wondering if she was thinking of Nemek or Keirith.

In the short time they had together before the council meeting, he told them what he could, assuring them that Darak looked well, that Keirith seemed content, that Faelia was heartened by the victories. If they had doubts, they hid them, each pretending for the others that the glimpses he offered were complete, that their loved ones were safe, that soon, they would all be together again.

The succession of half-truths left him nervous and edgy. Repeating them to the council of elders only increased his frustration. Lisula and Gortin seemed genuinely happy to see him, but Madig interrogated him as if he were the enemy. Worse, the elders had invited two of Temet's warriors to attend, and they pressed him impatiently for specifics about the ambushes, the strength of the Zherosi forces, and Darak's success in recruiting others to the cause.

Faced with the need to hide the true extent of his spying, he had to rely on what he had learned from Keirith. Here, too, his brother was hailed as a hero. Beside Keirith's visionary skills and selfless bravery, his efforts sounded puny. When he tried to elaborate on his scouting expeditions, he received skeptical glances from Madig and the warriors who clearly thought he was boasting. By the time they ran out of questions, he was trembling with the effort to control his temper.

"If there's nothing else, I'd like to spend the rest of the day with my family."

"Run along," Madig said, as if he were a child.

He offered a jerky bow and ducked out of the longhut. Unwilling to speak to anyone until he was calmer, he simply stalked past the group of old women scraping hides.

"Oh, look at him." Donncha didn't bother to lower her voice. "Too big for his breeches to even share a bit of news."

"That's enough." Mirili's voice, quiet but firm.

"Looks like Madig put him in his place," Donncha continued. "About time someone did."

He whirled around to tell the meddling old gossip to mind her tongue, but managed to choke back the words. His face must have betrayed his anger, for Donncha clucked her tongue in disapproval.

"Always had a temper. Got that from Griane."

Rigat slowly advanced on her. "Don't you ever speak ill of my mother. Do you hear me?"

There was a moment of shocked silence. Then Donncha clucked her tongue again. "You ought to be ashamed. Talking so disrespectfully to your elders. Who do you think you are?"

He wanted to shout, "I am the Trickster's son! And if you say another word, I'll cast your miserable bones into Chaos!"

"He's my hot-tempered son." His mam's voice came from somewhere behind him. "Who apparently had words with the council members and is taking his frustration out on the first person he sees. Apologize, Rigat."

Staring at the ground, he mumbled an apology.

"You're right, Donncha," Mam continued. "I was just as hot-tempered at his age. I've learned better manners since. While you still enjoy sniping at people behind their backs."

Donncha's mouth opened and closed like a dying fish. Before she could come up with a suitable reply, his mam's hand descended on the back of his neck, steering him toward the entrance of the hill fort.

She waited until they were out of earshot to say, "I've been wanting to tell her off for forty years. Thank you for giving me the opportunity." Then she cuffed him. "Don't ever talk that way to one of your elders."

"Aye, Mam."

"And wipe that grin off your face."

"I will if you will."

She cuffed him again, but the smile remained until he told her about the council meeting.

"I can't believe Fa—Darak—named Madig chief."

"Oh, he's not a bad chief," she said, surprising him. "He drives the people a little hard, but that's only natural. He couldn't protect his son, so he's made it his mission to protect this village. Against any threat."

"Like me."

Her silence was more eloquent than words.

"Do you think he suspects the truth?"

"Nay!"

The words he had held inside since Hircha's revelation burst out of him. "Why would Darak tell Hircha?"

"It's different. She's not my child."

"Callie would never blame you."

A cloud passed over the sun, shadowing her face. She glanced up and flicked her fingers in the sign to avert evil.

After that, neither of them spoke. His mam needed all her breath for the steep climb up the hill. He extended his hand to help her, but she swatted it away. Only when she lowered herself onto a shelf of rock did he realize she had brought him to Darak's favorite spot. Her gaze drifted south, as if she hoped to see him cresting the hill. Then she faced him and folded her hands in her lap.

"All right. Tell me everything."

All afternoon, they talked. Or rather, he talked and his mam listened. As she had commanded, he told her everything: his experiences with Fellgair, his meetings with Keirith, his hope of turning the tide of the rebellion, and the doubts that had been eating away at him since that visit to Graywaters.

It was like returning to his childhood, when they would spend every day together, his mam sewing or grinding herbs or cooking, while he helped with simple tasks like scrubbing a pot or stacking the peat bricks. Or when he was older and would rush home to share his latest triumph, whether it was snaring a rabbit or bringing down a bird with his sling.

They basked in the sunlight and the love that had always bound them together. But as the shadows of the western hills darkened the waters of the lake, Rigat shivered. Just as the day was waning, so, too, was their time together.

"I have to leave soon, don't I?"

His mam's smile was bleak.

"They'll never accept me."

"They accept you as my son and Darak's."

"But only because of that. If they knew who I really am . . ."

"Is that what you want?"

"I don't know! I just . . ." He gripped his knees, rocking back and forth in frustration. "My rockslide saved this village. My spying helps the rebels. I deserve a little . . ."

"What? Gratitude? Respect? Fear?"

"Aye!"

"Then go back to the council and tell them what you've done. Go to Temet and demand recognition. If their gratitude and respect are so important—"

"You're more important. And so is Keirith."

Her face softened and she patted his knee, sighing. "Sometimes, I think it would be better to have it all out in the open. The longer you wait, the worse it will be when people discover the truth. And they will. Lies always catch up with you."

She was clearly thinking about what had happened between her and Keirith as well as what might happen to him. Desperate to reassure her, he said, "I'd never let anyone hurt you."

"Madig, you mean?" She shot him a scornful look. "I'm not afraid of Madig. Or the elders. What could they do?"

"Cast you out."

"They wouldn't dare. I'd tell them Fellgair would destroy them."

"Would he?"

"I doubt it. Cursing a god to his face doesn't win his affection. It's a fine threat, though. And I'll use it if I must. But the only way Madig—or anyone—could hurt me is to threaten my husband or my children."

Did she even realize that she had put Darak first? Again? Probably not. She would never deliberately hurt him.

"Be careful, Rigat. And don't trust Fellgair. Rely on your instincts, not what he tells you to do."

"He doesn't tell me to do anything. Just talks about the great web of possibilities."

She muttered something under her breath, then sighed again. "I know you're a man now. But you're still . . . very young."

"I'll be all right, Mam. Don't worry."

She hugged him hard, then pulled away. "When will you go?"

He knew he should leave at once. But surely, he deserved one night with his family before he returned to his solitary existence.

"On the morrow."

Later, he blamed himself for that choice and for the other mistakes he made. If he had left the village sooner, ensured that no one was following him, scanned for the energy of another person . . . any of those precautions might have averted the disaster.

But he was distracted by thoughts of his mam. He had promised to find a way for them to meet in secret, just as he met with Keirith. As he strode through the dew-slick moor grass, he made another vow: that soon, he would abandon secrecy and let the whole world know his true identity.

But not until Mam is safe. From Madig and anyone else who might turn on her.

He waited until he was a mile from the village to open the portal. After quickly surveying the terrain behind him, he pictured his forest lair and allowed his power to build. Then he slowly carved the doorway out of the sky and stepped through it. As he turned back to close the portal, he saw the figure slipping out from behind a boulder.

Madig froze, staring past him with openmouthed shock. "What is that?"

"Nothing. Just . . . a portal."

"To Chaos?" Madig's voice cracked with panic.

"Nay! To the forest. See? The pines?"

Madig limped toward him, slow and hesitant as a dream-walker. "You did push Seg. During the hunt."

"That . . . it was a stupid prank. I didn't mean—"

"You always hated him. Because he bested you time and time again."

Only because I let him, Rigat thought. But he bit back the words.

"You hated my boy. You shamed him in front of the tribe. And then you killed him."

"Nay!"

"You caused the rockslide."

"To stop the Zherosi. Seg getting killed—that was an accident."

"He tried to tell me. But I didn't believe him."

Madig's voice was soft, almost a singsong. Like Callie when he soothed a sick ewe or Darak praying over a dying stag.

"How could the son of Darak Spirit-Hunter be evil, I asked?"

"I'm not evil!"

"You're a murderer. An abomination. Just like your brother."

"Leave Keirith out of this!"

Madig's hand rose.

"I know you miss Seg. But I didn't kill him. I swear on my mother's life."

Slowly, he drew an arrow from his quiver.

"Don't be stupid!" Rigat shouted. "If you believe I started the rockslide, you know I can stop you from killing me. Please! Don't make me hurt you."

Madig nocked the arrow in his bowstring, all the while cursing him in that soft, musing tone. Frantically, Rigat tried to seal the portal, but his concentration was shattered and his finger slashed helplessly through the air.

The seamless flow of words stopped as Madig raised his bow.

Rigat's power surged. He was as helpless to control it as the cold sweat that broke out on his forehead and the spasm of terror that clutched his bowels.

Madig stumbled, then quickly recovered. He shook his head, grimacing, and flexed his fingers. With a grunt of pain, he drew the bowstring taut. Rigat flung up his hands, shouting, "Stop!" The power raced down his outstretched arms, a tingling surge of energy that burned his fingertips as it leaped toward his attacker.

Madig lurched sideways. The arrow slipped harmlessly from the bowstring and clattered against a rock. He gasped for breath, his eyes bulging. Then he crumpled to the ground.

Rigat managed to totter back through the portal before his legs folded under him.

You have to get up. You have to see if he's alive.

But his legs wouldn't obey, and he no longer had the power to command them.

"You really must learn to close a portal more quickly." Shaking his head, Fellgair stepped through the portal, which snapped shut behind him.

"I killed him." His tongue felt thick, too large for his mouth.

"No."

Unable to stand, Rigat crawled forward on his hands and knees. Even before he reached Madig, he could see his chest rising and falling. His left eye rolled wildly and his mouth was twisted in a horrible grimace, but his pulse was strong, if very fast.

"You could have killed him, of course. If you had directed the power instead of allowing it to pour out of you."

Like water from a broken jug. That's how he felt— broken and empty.

"I shouldn't have come."

"You shouldn't have let Madig catch you."

"He'll tell."

Fellgair strolled over to Madig and nudged him with his foot. Madig made an awful gobbling sound in his throat. As Fellgair bent closer, the gobbling became a strangled moan, thick with phlegm and fear.

"I doubt Madig will be saying anything for a while."

"I didn't mean for this to happen." He wasn't sure if he was talking to Fellgair or Madig. "I just wanted him to stop."

"And threw your power at him with mindless strength."

Rigat nodded miserably.

"Of course, it may not be your fault at all."

He hoped Fellgair was right. Madig had stumbled even before he threw his power at him. But that didn't change the fact that he had struck with—what had Fellgair said?

Mindless strength.

"What should I do?"

Kill him.

At first, he thought it was Fellgair's cold voice whispering inside of him. With growing horror, he realized the thought was his.

If you finish him now, no will ever know.

But he can't speak. So he'll never tell.

The second voice was equally calm, equally reasonable, but far kinder.

And if he recovers? He'll tell everyone in the village that he saw you open that portal. That you caused the rockslide.

They won't believe him. They'll think grief has driven him mad.

Perhaps. But they'll wonder, won't they? They'll remember the other incidents. Demand explanations. What happens to your mam if they learn the truth? You can't take that risk.

You can't commit murder.

Kinder to kill him than leave him like this.

You could get help. Take him back to the village. Tell them Madig had an attack. The Tree-Father will stand behind you. And the Grain-Grandmother. Even if Madig recovers, it will be your word against his.

And if they believe him? You'll be cast out of the tribe, just like Keirith was. You'll never be able to go home again.

He fought the urge to weep. He wanted his mam to stroke his hair and tell him he was not evil. He wanted Darak's arms around him, that deep voice assuring him that he had simply defended himself. He wanted one of Keirith's lectures and the hug that always followed. He wanted Callie to tell him everything would work out in the end. He would even welcome a tongue-lashing from Hircha who had warned him to stay out of Madig's way, or Faelia's reluctant but defiant defense of his actions.

Fellgair simply stood there, watching and waiting.

"He can teach you things I can't, but he can never love you."

Fellgair crouched beside him. Clawed fingers stroked his hair gently. With a soft moan, Rigat leaned against the furry chest.

"Hircha warned you," Fellgair said. "And your mother. Keirith always told you to use your power wisely. Instead, you panicked." Fellgair's arm tightened around his shoulders. "But who could blame you? You had to defend yourself. That wasn't evil. And neither are you. Don't worry. It will all work out in the end."

Rigat smiled. And then the import of Fellgair's words and actions finally reached him.

"Don't mock me!"

Fury changed to horror at his outburst, and he recoiled, awaiting the lash of his father's anger.

Instead, Fellgair sighed. "I wasn't mocking you. I was giving you the comfort you seemed to require. Obviously, it's less effective when I do it." Waving away his stammered apology, Fellgair added, "I have many gifts. Fatherly affection is not one of them. Darak was right about that."

For a moment, his expression grew wistful. Then the golden eyes flicked back to him. "As for Madig, you know your choices. Kill him. Summon help and devise a story to explain his condition. Or leave and let matters sort themselves out."

"I could try and heal him."

"You're far too weak."

"You could heal him."

"Me?" Fellgair looked astonished. "Why would I want to save the man who just attempted to kill my son? Why, for that matter, would *you* want to save him?"

"He was angry. And upset. About Seg."

"And that gives him the right to try and kill you?"

"He wasn't thinking clearly."

"Neither are you. Do you really believe Madig will simply forget this? That he'll be so grateful to be restored to health that he'll forgive you for Seg's death?"

A soft sound escaped Rigat. The whimper of a frightened animal.

"What about Mam?"

"A woman who can curse a god to his face is quite capable of handling a few suspicious villagers."

"Then she'll be safe?"

"For now? Yes. Next moon? Next year? I cannot say. But even if the truth of today's . . . accident . . . comes out, why would they harm her?"

"The only way Madig—or anyone—could hurt me is to threaten my husband or my children."

"Does that satisfy you?" Fellgair asked.

Rigat nodded.

"Can we go now?"

"I can't just leave him lying here."

Fellgair sighed again. "Rothisar will come looking for him."

"He will?"

"Yes. If it will ease your conscience, I'll send him the uncontrollable urge to search for Madig. Later, he'll marvel at that urge and wonder if it was merely his superb hunter's instinct that led him here or whether he had received a divine message. Knowing Rothisar, he'll doubtless interpret it as his inspiration rather than mine."

"Isn't that interfering?"

"Of course, it's interfering! But the net effect will be to allow Madig to drool in his own hut instead of out on the moor."

Rigat winced. He wiped Madig's chin and squeezed his limp hand. "I didn't kill Seg. And I didn't want to hurt you. I hope you can believe that. And forgive me."

Madig made an inarticulate sound, whether of protest or acceptance, Rigat couldn't tell.

Fellgair rose and held out his hand. As Rigat grasped it, the grassy moor vanished. Sunlight blinded him. He raised a hand, squinting against the brilliance. Slowly, the world came back into focus.

A cloudless sky above them. Rock-strewn earth beneath their feet. Far below, a meandering brown river and fields of golden grain. A fortress of stone on a plateau. And a gleaming white city that spilled down the sides of the hill to a sun-dazzled sea.

Fellgair swept his hand across the vista and smiled. "Welcome to Zheros."

Chapter 20

THE SHOUTS SENT GRIANE'S HEART racing. Callie was already on his feet when Hircha appeared in the doorway.

"It's Madig. They found him."

"Alive?"

"Aye, but . . . something's wrong with him."

Pausing just long enough to seize her healer's bag, Griane hurried outside.

A crowd had already gathered in the center of the village. She pushed her way through, noting that every face bore the same sick expression as Hircha's.

Madig lay in the dirt, wriggling like a worm. She suppressed a grimace at the stink of urine. Judging from the loosened drawstrings of his breeches, Madig had tried—and failed—to open them. His right arm and leg twitched convulsively, as if he was incapable of controlling them. The right side of his face looked frozen, but his good eye glared up at her.

"Where did you find him?" she asked Rothisar.

"On the moor. To the south." Rothisar winced. "He was trying to drag himself home."

"Merciful Maker . . ."

Madig shouted something out of the side of his mouth. She crouched beside him and grabbed his fist before he could pound the earth again. "Stop! You'll only make it worse."

He yanked his fist out of her grasp and bellowed, "Eee ahh!"

Rothisar's fingers moved in the sign to avert evil. Griane heard people muttering, "Possessed . . ." "A demon . . ."

"He's not possessed," Gortin declared. "A man in our old village had a similar attack. What was his name?"

"Dren," Griane replied automatically.

Lisula's nod was vehement, but the hand stroking Madig's hair was as gentle as ever. "And he got better. In time. Just as you will. If you do what Mother Griane tells you."

"Eee ahh!"

It was just a meaningless sound. Rigat would not have attacked Madig. And if he had witnessed the onset of this seizure, he would never have abandoned him on the moor.

She glared at the circle of gawking men. "Don't leave him lying in the dirt! Carry him to his hut."

With obvious reluctance, they obeyed. As she followed them toward his hut, she spied Madig's daughters, huddled between Alada and Duba.

"Is he going to die?" Colla whispered.

"Nay! You heard how strong his voice was."

"But he wasn't making any sense."

"It's a strange sickness. Sometimes, it affects the way a man talks. And leaves half his body . . . asleep."

"When will he wake up?"

To a child of ten, a sennight was a long time. Telling her that his recovery would require moons—perhaps years— was as good as telling her it would take forever.

"Soon. But the other man I knew with this sickness? He was like . . . like a little child at first, who had to learn to walk and talk again."

"But he did learn?"

"Aye. And so will your father. With your help."

For the first time, Colla looked at her. Thirty years as a healer had taught Griane that helplessness could be more debilitating than fear.

"You know how proud your father is."

A slow nod.

"You know it would shame him to have you see him when he's so weak."

Another nod, more reluctant.

"So it might be best for you and Blathi to stay with Alada and Duba. Just until he's stronger. And while you're there, I want you to make something. A little ball stuffed with grain that he can squeeze to strengthen his bad hand. Alada can help you sew the covering—"

"I can do it. I mend all his tunics."

"Good. But first, could you help Hircha make a tea for your father? We don't know what he likes to drink—"

"Mint tea. With honey."

"You'll need to gather some water mint at the stream. I'm not sure I have . . ."

But Colla was already hurrying away.

"Put something in it to help him sleep," Griane told Hircha in an undertone. "His bellowing will disturb the children."

Hircha gave her a long, considering look, but merely nodded.

Griane arrived at Madig's hut to find a crowd of people blocking the doorway. She shooed them out of her way and sidled past Othak.

Madig's bellows had subsided to hoarse muttering and his movements had grown feebler. After a day and night on the moor, it was a wonder he had the strength to speak or move at all. Lisula crouched beside him, dribbling water into his twisted mouth. As Griane approached, Gortin paused in his prayers and glanced up.

"Here's Mother Griane now. She'll take good care of you. Just as she did old Dren. His recovery was remarkable. Of course, his speech was always a bit slurred and he dragged his right foot—"

"Thank you, Tree-Father," Griane interrupted. "And all of you. But Madig needs to rest now."

She marched to the doorway and held up the hide. Lisula flashed a worried smile as she ducked outside. Barasa simply looked relieved.

"I'll pray for him," she assured Griane.

"Thank you, Grain-Mother. I know that will help."

Certainly far more than having her stare at Madig with undisguised horror. Best that Barasa stick to prayer; in an earthly crisis, she was helpless.

"Are you sure he's not possessed?" Rothisar asked.

"For mercy's sake, lower your voice," Griane snapped.

"It's just . . . I don't remember old Dren being like this."

"That's because you were a child. And far more interested in hunting than in a sick old man."

"But what's he trying to say?"

"I don't know! And right now, I don't care. The important thing is to keep him calm so he doesn't have another attack." Impatient with the crowd that continued to linger outside the hut, Griane called, "Please. Go home. Hircha and I will see to Madig."

Instead, Callie stepped forward. And old Trath. In moments, she found herself confronted by all the tribal elders.

"Is his mind affected?" Trath's voice was as brusque as ever, but unlike Rothisar, he had the sense to speak softly.

Griane stepped outside and let the deerskin fall. "I can't tell," she replied just as softly. "It might be moons before he can speak. Or walk."

"We'll have to summon the council," Trath replied. "And choose someone to act as chief until he's recovered."

"You're the one with the most experience," Adinn pointed out. "Callie, Sion, and I are still too new."

"Eight."

They all turned toward Sion, frowning. Lisula was the first to make sense of his terse comment. "Sion's right. We need nine members on the council."

"We could bring Hakiath back on," Trath suggested. "He replaced Madig last time."

"Fine!" Griane retorted in a fierce whisper. "Only have the decency not to choose a new chief within earshot of the current one."

They all looked abashed.

"We have as much sense as a horde of midges," Callie said.

"Less." But she patted his cheek before turning back to the hut.

Othak raised the hide, but continued to block the doorway. "It's strange. Madig being taken so suddenly."

"So was Dren. But you were probably too young to remember."

Othak smiled. "Oh, I remember. I remember everything."

His pale eyes fastened on her face, like a hawk eyeing a rabbit. A shiver rippled down Griane's spine.

It's just his way.

But she shivered again as Othak walked off.

The color of peat smoke, those eyes. Nay, the color of the lake—under a coating of ice. And his smile even colder.

"Mam?"

Startled, she turned to find Callie watching Othak as well.

"What does he know?" he asked in a soft voice.

"I don't know."

"Is Rigat involved?"

She took a deep breath and let it out. "I don't know," she repeated.

Callie nodded. It was not his way to press her. But it was past time for her to tell him the truth. If Othak was speculating about Madig's seizure, others would, too. Sooner or later, someone would remember that Madig had left the village soon after Rigat. And then the questions would start, along with whispered exchanges about past incidents.

She took Callie's arm and drew him away from the hut. "There are things you should know, Callie. About your brother."

Chapter 21

WITH FELLGAIR AS HIS GUIDE, Rigat explored the land he had first glimpsed during his vision quest. He studied it with the eyes of Fellgair's son, but also with those of the child reared by Darak and Griane. Perhaps that was why he found it a place of such terrible contrasts, where beauty existed side by side with ugliness, and squalor festered in the shadow of grandeur.

It was a world of brown rivers and brown earth, of hard blue sky and brilliant blue sea, of snow-colored sand that heated the soles of his shoes, and an unrelenting sun that rose red and angry in the morning, burned hot and yellow at midday, and faded to the color of blood by sunset. After only a few days, his eyes were starved for green, but it seemed to exist only in the clothing and gems of the rich.

At Fellgair's insistence, Rigat summoned the mist-shield, although it more closely resembled a dust cloud in Zheros. Hidden behind it, they stood atop hills denuded of trees. They picked their way across swaying bridges suspended over gorges so steep that the sun only brightened the bottom at midday. They followed roads of hard-packed earth that cleaved the fields like spears, most wide enough for the ox-drawn carts of the farmers to pass two abreast and still leave room for the curtained litters of the nobles.

Outside tidy villages, the flyblown corpses of murderers and thieves dangled from gibbets. In eastern Zheros, makeshift refugee camps and charred fields testified to the ravages of the war with Carilia.

Fellgair told him about the war, about the slave uprising in the spring, and the devastating winter of rains that had left the first harvest of barley and millet rotting in the fields. He described the queen who was hundreds of years old but looked like a girl, the annual rite called The Shedding where her spirit slipped free of her old body and into a new one, and the drug called qiij that she and her priests needed to touch spirits and speak with the gods.

From Fellgair, he also heard the ancient tales. Creation stories about Heart of Sky ravishing Womb of Earth who held him captive in the sacred mountain Kelazhat until the birth of Zhe, the winged serpent. The story of Zhe's betrayal of his parents, first by freeing his father and then, his wings singed and blackened by the sun's heat, devouring him, leaving only Heart of Sky's spirit-self, the moon, to light the darkness. Tales of redemption and rebirth, as the tears of The Changing One of the Clouds swept Zhe out of the Abyss and back to Kelazhat, where he disgorged his father and was reborn by the sun's heat. And the tale that promised the Son of Zhe would come to Zheros one day and usher in a new age.

Rigat listened with avid interest; neither Darak nor Keirith liked to speak of Zheros or what had happened to them here.

In Oexiak, Fellgair allowed them to walk openly through the streets. With so many foreigners thronging the seaport,

Rigat's pale skin and red hair attracted little notice. Fellgair's presence caused far more commotion. Nobles and slaves alike eyed him with mingled fear and awe. Even those who had never seen the Supplicant of the God with Two Faces recognized the priestess from the tales. Half-man, half-woman, it was whispered. And Fellgair's garb and appearance bore out the illusion.

"I can understand wearing a robe that's brown and red," Rigat whispered, as two well-dressed men backed into a wall in their eagerness to clear a path. "And shaving half your head and painting the nails on your left hand. Even having breasts and a penis. But do they have to be so . . . big?"

"You should see me without the robe," Fellgair replied. "They're even more impressive. Ask Darak." And laughed when Rigat blushed.

Fellgair won them passage through the crowded market-places where merchants and vendors shouted at each other and flashed the brightly-colored disks called coins as they haggled over bundles of fur and hides, sacks of grain, child-sized jugs of wine, screeching fowl, and slabs of bloody meat. The merchants snarled at the more obstreperous of the loincloth-clad beggars, but most dropped coins into the bowls of the men who sat on one side of the square. Some had lost limbs, others were blind, but all wore cloaks studded with tiny metal decorations, incongruously bright against the dusty wool. Campaign medallions, Fellgair explained.

Although Rigat reminded himself that these men might have been injured fighting against his people, he still felt a twinge of pity. If Darak had returned from Chaos so badly wounded, his tribe mates would have cared for him all his life, whether or not his quest had been successful.

Just as they would take care of Madig.

The memory of that encounter still haunted him, as did the fear that his mam might believe he was responsible. He had tried to touch her spirit, but either she was too far away or he was too unskilled to reach her.

At first, he thought that Fellgair had brought him to Zheros simply to distract him, but as they wandered the cobbled streets of Oexiak, he wondered if his father had another purpose. Perhaps Fellgair meant to impress him with the strength of the Zherosi and convince him to return home and warn Keirith that the fight was hopeless.

From the few bits of information he had gleaned from his family, he knew Darak had come to Oexiak in search of Keirith. Had his foster-father been as overwhelmed as he was by the press of bodies and the ceaseless, mind-numbing clamor? And the smells . . . dear gods, after only a day, Rigat wanted to flee back to the clean, fresh scents of the forest. Even the tempting odors of roasting meat and fragrant incense were overpowered by the eye-watering reek of poorly tanned hides and rotting fish.

Surely, Darak must have stared openmouthed at the ships in the harbor, naked masts rising like a forest of pine spars. He, too, must have shuddered at the long lines of warriors that marched with perfect precision up those boarding planks, and winced at the equally long lines of slaves that shuffled down them. Rigat couldn't help picturing Keirith among the half-naked men, tethered like an animal, head bowed in defeat.

That image gave him the courage to ask Fellgair to take him to Pilozhat, which he had glimpsed only briefly when the portal opened. His father eyed him for a long, unnerving moment before agreeing. But Fellgair insisted on conjuring the mist-shield this time, no doubt suspecting that Rigat would be too distracted to concentrate.

As they followed the steep streets to the plateau, Rigat wondered if he was retracing the path Keirith had taken to the slave compound. He found little evidence of the earthquake that had ravaged the city, save for the fact that the whitewashed houses on the upper slopes of the hill looked less weathered by sun and time than those closer to the harbor. Glancing down at the lower city, he noticed that none of the flat, thatched roofs had vent holes for smoke. Instead, it seemed to be rising from a patchwork of open squares in the center of the houses.

"Sky-wells," Fellgair explained. "To let in light and air and allow the smoke to escape."

"And those?" Rigat asked, pointing at an enormous clay jar atop one roof. "The Zherosi must drink a lot of wine."

Fellgair smiled and shook his head. "They're for collecting

rainwater." He pointed to a narrow pipe that snaked down from the roof. "The pipes carry the water to underground cisterns that supply the wells around the city. And washing tanks like those." He nodded to a group of young women clustered around a raised stone trough. Although their shapeless flaxcloth gowns marked them as slaves, Rigat couldn't help noticing that they laughed and chattered together as they worked.

Unwilling to be impressed by the ingenuity of the Zherosi architects or the apparent happiness of the house slaves, he followed Fellgair up another steep flight of steps. Zigzagging between litters borne by straining slaves, Rigat caught snatches of conversation—women lamenting the rising cost of something called lilmia, men arguing about whether to stockpile their grain or sell it now. Through the gauzy curtains of the litters, he glimpsed golden bracelets adorning women's arms and gem-encrusted dagger sheaths bouncing against the folds of the billowy half-breeches called khirtas.

He loathed these rich, idle strangers who lived off the misery of slaves and were too lazy to walk. He despised their privileged laughter and the harsh, guttural cadences of their speech. And he hated the fact that they worshiped Fellgair just as his people did.

At the top of the steps, he froze, resentment giving way to awe.

The building atop the plateau looked as large as the walled city of Graywaters. Late afternoon sunlight lent a rosy glow to the towering rubblestone walls. Giant pillars marched beside the stone walkways that branched from it. Beyond the gateway facing him, he spied a courtyard large enough to house his entire village. To the west, a long line of men and animals streamed to and from the building: merchants in ox-drawn carts, others leading floppy-eared donkeys piled with so many bundles that only their legs and heads were visible.

"The palace," Fellgair said.

Rigat managed a casual nod. "And the temple of Zhe?"

Fellgair pointed east, then seized his arm to drag him out of the path of an approaching litter. "But first, let's visit my temple."

They headed west, passing a group of shaven-haired boys in red robes arguing earnestly about whether Zhe's betrayal of his mother was fated from the beginning or the god's choice.

"Zhiisti," Fellgair informed him. "Training to become priests of Zhe." Before Rigat could reply, he pointed to a section of the palace that jutted out. "That used to be the slave compound. Where Darak and Keirith were held."

"Used to be?"

"After the earthquake that claimed the life of their king, the Zherosi priests feared that human sacrifices had angered their earth goddess. So now they only offer human sacrifices twice a year. One man at Midsummer and another at Midwinter. Both Zherosi," Fellgair added pointedly. "The rest of the year, they sustain Zhe with the blood of birds and beasts—the same that nourish his sacred adders. And light a fire at dawn on the altar of the sun god so that he may feed on its flames."

Rigat digested this in silence before asking, "And the God with Two Faces? What sacrifices do the Zherosi offer him?"

"This and that. I'm especially partial to honeysuckle."

Fellgair's temple seemed more appropriate to the earth goddess. Built into the side of the plateau, it resembled a cave. But after Rigat ducked inside the low entrance, he discovered soft, golden light spilling through another doorway. Easing past two priests—whose red-and-brown robes and half-shaven heads mimicked Fellgair's—they entered the main chamber of the temple.

It was as queer as the appearance Fellgair adopted as the Supplicant, one half illuminated by oil lamps hanging from the ceiling, the other shadowy and dark. It was mercifully cool, though, and the rugs underfoot as soft and thick as the mulch of pine needles in the forest. The aroma of honeysuckle filled the chamber. The flower couldn't possibly grow in arid Zheros, but the polished stone altar in the center of the chamber was heaped with bunches of yellow blossoms. As they approached it, three priestesses entered from another chamber, their arms overflowing with more flowers.

Fellgair watched them, smiling. For the first time, Rigat

realized that he cared as much about the Zherosi as the children of the Oak and Holly.

Suddenly, the sweet fragrance of the honeysuckle sickened him. Without a word, he fled. When a priest gaped at him, he realized he had moved beyond Fellgair's shield. Moments later, his father caught up with him. The priest stared in shocked disbelief at the spot where Rigat had vanished and inscribed a spiral over his chest with trembling fingers.

Outside, Fellgair observed him silently as he gulped great lungfuls of the hot, dusty air.

"I'm sorry," Rigat managed. "I just . . . I had to get out of there."

Fellgair merely nodded, his expression more disappointed than angry. Perhaps he had hoped that his son would love his temple as much as he did.

Determined to hide his emotions, Rigat followed Fellgair back to the plateau. They circled north around the palace and paused at the temple of Heart of Sky. Behind it loomed the barren crag where Fellgair had opened the portal.

"Kelazhat," Fellgair informed him.

He'd had no idea that they had been standing atop the sacred mountain, but the parched, rock-strewn earth seemed an appropriate site for rape and betrayal.

Two golden-robed priests flanked the fire that blazed atop the stone altar. A few old men knelt at the bottom of the steps, each clutching a small bundle of sticks or straw.

As Rigat watched, a wispy-haired old man held out his bundle. One of the priests accepted the offering and bent down to catch the words the old man whispered. Then he ascended the steps and approached the pyre. Lifting the sticks skyward, he exclaimed, "Heart of Sky, hear his prayer! Heart of Sky, accept his offering!"

The priest tossed the bundle into the fire. As the flames leaped, the old man's expression brightened. He touched his forehead to the dusty earth and rose, glancing skyward as if in thanks.

As they made their way east, Fellgair said, "It's the custom for old folk to make their petitions to Heart of Sky at this time of day. Like them, the sun god is approaching the end of his journey. A young man—seeking strength in a battle or help with a difficult decision—would bring an offering in the morning."

Rigat frowned. It was customary for his people to ask the sun god for strength and enlightenment, too.

His uneasiness grew when he saw the serpentine pillars at the end of the stone walkway. He surreptitiously wiped his damp palms on his breeches as he approached the temple and took a deep breath to steady himself.

A small dove lay on the altar of Zhe, the pristine whiteness of its breast feathers marred by congealed blood. Fourteen years ago, his brother's blood had stained that greenblack slab of stone. It had been close to Midsummer then, too, but just past dawn. The stone would have been cool beneath Keirith's back, the rising sun warm on his face. As warm as the blood pouring out of his chest.

The tears Rigat refused to shed made his eyes feel hot and dry. His face burned with simmering rage. Sensitive to his mood, his power leaped like the flames on the altar of Heart of Sky. He clenched his fists in an effort to contain it, secretly wishing it were strong enough to make the earth shake again and destroy this temple, to reduce every building in the city to rubble.

"I hope he's suffering."

Only when Fellgair asked, "Xevhan?" did Rigat realize he had spoken aloud.

"Aye. I hope he was terrified before Keirith cast him out. And that his spirit's still suffering. Wherever it is."

"His spirit is in the Abyss," Fellgair said quietly. "What's left of it. And yes, it is suffering."

"Good." Seeing Fellgair's impassive expression, Rigat demanded, "Why shouldn't he suffer? After what he did."

"Perhaps he should," Fellgair said in the same quiet voice. "That doesn't mean I relish the thought of it."

Rigat would have thought the Trickster would enjoy the irony that Xevhan had been killed by the very boy he had tried to murder. The more time he spent with his father, the less he understood him.

"Have you seen enough?" Fellgair asked.

"More than enough."

"Then let's go elsewhere."

Rigat took the proffered hand and grimly watched the

temple blur and vanish. As the world slid into place again, he thought he was back atop Kelazhat, but instead of the palace below them, he spied a cluster of huts in a narrow valley.

"What is this place?"

"Just a village. In the northern mountains of Zheros. Come."

"Should I call up the mist to hide us?"

Fellgair hesitated. Then he shook his head.

They picked their way down a winding trail. As they neared the village, Rigat realized it was even smaller than his. Just a dozen mud-brick huts with an enclosure nearby for animals and a tiny field of golden-brown millet.

His stomach growled when he smelled the aroma of roasting meat. Children crouched beside the communal fire pit, turning long skewers over the flames. In the field, women grubbed up weeds. On the lower slopes of the hills, men watched goats cropping the sparse grass. There must be a spring nearby for a shallow stream trickled through the valley. A few scraggly trees clung to its banks and in their shade, girls were scrubbing clothes.

A shout went up when the villagers spotted them. Rigat froze, but Fellgair walked on calmly. From the field, from the stream, from every hut, people converged on him, then suddenly came to a halt and watched his approach in breathless silence. When Fellgair opened his arms as if to embrace them, the men broke into wild shouting and the women into shrieking ululations. If not for their joyful expressions, Rigat would have thought they intended murder.

Fellgair skimmed his fingers over their bowed heads. Mothers held up squalling babes, hunters proffered quivers of arrows. The herdsmen were even driving their goats down from the hills to receive a blessing.

Rigat hung back, conscious of their surreptitious glances. Perhaps they had heard of Keirith's sojourn in Pilozhat and wondered what the arrival of another flame-haired stranger foretold. Or perhaps the color of his hair was simply so unusual they couldn't help but stare.

Aimlessly, he kicked a stone, wondering why Fellgair had brought him here. Surrounded by the herd of bleating goats, his father seemed to have forgotten him.

He kicked another stone, harder than he meant to. It rolled a good ten paces away and came to rest against a small, bare foot.

The boy couldn't be much older than two. Brown-skinned and naked, he stared down at the stone, sucking his thumb. Then he looked up. His eyes grew even bigger when he saw Rigat watching him. Then they disappeared as he buried his face against his mother's thigh.

Rigat kicked another stone toward him. The tousled head came up. The thumb popped out of the child's mouth and hung there, wet and gleaming. Then he giggled and kicked the stone back.

Or tried to. It rolled a hand's length away. He lurched after it, and, after two misses, kicked it again. Zigzagging back and forth across the cracked earth, he came closer, crowing with delight when the stone rolled toward Rigat.

Rigat drew back his foot, once, twice, as if preparing for a mighty kick, all the while watching the little boy whose mouth had fallen open in anticipation. With a grunt of effort, he kicked, deliberately missing the stone, and staggered about like a drunken man before falling to the ground.

The boy's face went blank with shock until Rigat rose and rubbed his arse. Then he laughed. This time, when Rigat sent the stone toward him, he rushed forward. In his eagerness, he tripped, hands and knees slamming into the ground.

For a moment, he crouched there. Then he started to shriek.

Rigat covered the distance between them in three strides. At first, he thought the boy was merely frightened by his sudden tumble, but when he picked him up, he saw blood streaking his left knee. Spying the bloodstained potshard in the dirt, Rigat crushed it under his foot and sat down, pulling the boy onto his lap.

His screams stopped, choked off in a shocked sob. Then they started again, more piercing than ever.

Rigat tried to wipe the blood away, but the boy was kicking and wriggling, desperate to escape. He murmured the sort of soothing nonsense his mam used to offer when he was little, but the boy continued to wail.

Gods, can't I even play a game with a child without hurting him?

By now, all the villagers had heard the noise. The boy's mother rushed forward, only to halt at Fellgair's command. Her body quivered with the need to come to her child's aid, but she remained where she was, unwilling to disobey the Supplicant.

"Hush," Rigat begged. "Please, hush."

The crowd circled around him. He knew he should simply pick the child up and hand him to his mother, but he couldn't bear to have them believe he had hurt the boy.

The child's screams subsided into hoarse, hiccuping sobs. His thrashing grew weaker, but blood still trickled down his leg. When Rigat placed his hand over the wound, the boy flinched and whimpered. So he started to rock him, softly crooning the lullaby his mam used to sing. He closed his eyes and sensed the power simmering, a banked fire waiting for his will to fuel it.

As many times as he had summoned it, he still marveled at its complexity. Heady as wine, fierce as a sudden jolt of lust, yet as comforting as furs in the wintertime and refreshing as a cool stream in the summer. It was a river flowing through him, the sun's heat penetrating him, the air caressing him, a vine that twined around body and mind and spirit, linking all parts of his being with the eternal power of the elements.

Tamping down the energy, he allowed it to seep slowly from his palm. The boy gave a startled squeak, then slowly relaxed, a limp, heavy weight in his arms.

It was a shallow cut, as easy to mend as a rip in his tunic. As he wove the healing, he forgot the watching crowd. There was only the hard ground beneath him, and the hot sun beating down on his shoulders, and this child, enfolded by his arms and his power.

This was what it was meant for. Not to crush men with boulders or to set up ambushes where they could be slaughtered or to shatter the mind of a man already maddened with grief. His power was meant to heal.

As he wiped the knee clean, he heard shocked gasps and exclamations. The child's mother dropped to her knees beside him and raised his hand to her lips. He shot a silent appeal to Fellgair, who stepped forward and lifted the boy

from his arms. He kissed the child's grimy forehead and
handed him to his mother, who became nearly incoherent
with thankfulness. Then he thrust out his hand and pulled
Rigat to his feet.

"You have quite eclipsed me."

"You're not angry, are you?"

"Every father likes to see his son excel. Whether it's
healing an injured child or bringing down a stag with one
shot to the heart."

"You were there? You saw that?"

"I kept an eye on you over the years."

There was no time to say more. The villagers were too
eager to offer hospitality to their guests. The toothless old
chief insisted on slaughtering a goat in their honor. While
it roasted, he ushered them toward the stream where two
rugs of woven goat hair were ceremoniously laid on the
bare earth. Two women knelt before them and touched
their foreheads to the ground. Rigat thought they were
both wives of the chief, but the little man spoke too fast
to be sure.

The younger woman—whose plump face and shy, sidelong glances reminded Rigat a bit of Callie's Ela—removed
Fellgair's sandals and laid them aside. The older one—as
wrinkled and toothless as her husband—had the honor of
washing and drying Fellgair's feet. When it was Rigat's
turn, their deft fingers became clumsy, and they kept glancing up with anxious smiles.

The other villagers displayed the same awe during the
feast that followed. Each time he reached for his cup of
fermented goat's milk, their eyes followed his hands. Every
polite comment elicited a muted buzz of conversation. By
the time the meal was finished, Rigat was so self-conscious
that he lapsed into silence, leaving Fellgair to converse with
the chief about the prospects for the harvest and the health
of—apparently—every goat in the herd. Having exhausted
those subjects, Fellgair called for a song.

A young boy brought out a bone flute that looked exactly
like Callie's. A man raced back to his hut and returned
with a goatskin drum. Under the spell of the music and the
gathering darkness, the wariness of the villagers leached
away, and Rigat began to relax.

Voices rose and fell with the soft patter of the drum and

the throbbing whisper of the flute. And although the tunes were different, they sang about the same things his people did: the joy of a successful hunt, the sorrow of losing a loved one, the fierce winds that screamed through their valley in the winter, the anxious moon waiting for the grain to sprout in the spring.

Rigat watched a woman lean into the arms of her husband, a babe rooting at its mother's breast. And for the first time since arriving in Zheros, he no longer felt like a stranger.

The fire had died to glowing embers when Fellgair rose. The chief offered them his hut, but Fellgair said they preferred to sleep under the stars. If the chief thought it odd, he didn't question the Supplicant. Instead, he bowed very low and thanked them both for honoring his humble village with their presence.

"Your hospitality honors us," Fellgair replied.

"And your songs," Rigat blurted. "They were very beautiful." Realizing he should compliment the chief as well as the musicians, he added, "Thank you for welcoming me. It was . . . you've been so kind. I'll never forget this night."

As the villagers headed to their huts, Rigat became aware of two still hovering nearby. The mother of the little boy, he realized. The young man beside her must be her husband.

"It is you who are kind," she said softly. "We will always remember you in our prayers." Her glance strayed to her sleeping child, nestled against her husband's bare shoulder. "He is our firstborn. And very precious to us." Once again, she raised his hand to her lips, and then hurried away.

Rigat lay on the rug, listening to the sounds of Fellgair's breathing, the trickling water of the stream, and the drone of night insects drawn to the dying fire. Too much had happened for sleep to come easily: the shock of seeing that formidable palace in Pilozhat; his fury at the temple of Zhe; and then the unexpected peace he had found in this remote mountain village.

These people were supposed to be his enemies. But how could he hate them?

"I'll listen," Fellgair said. "If you want to talk."

Rigat sat up, struggling to find the words. Finally, he

said, "You brought me here to show me that the people in this village are like the ones in mine."

"Yes."

"Did you know . . . did you plan for me to heal that little boy?"

"No."

"It's just . . . it felt so . . . right."

"Did it?"

He strained to detect mockery in Fellgair's voice, to glimpse scorn in his expression, but found neither.

"Go on," Fellgair urged.

"And later . . . sitting with them. Listening to their songs. It made me . . . happy."

"I'm glad."

"And it made me think. About why you created me. To change things, you said."

"Yes."

"I don't think my power should be used just to make me feel good. Or heal a few people. Or even save some lives. Besides, then I'd have to decide who to heal and . . ." Rigat swallowed hard, thinking of Madig.

"Who should die," Fellgair finished quietly. "No matter what I say, you'll always wonder if you could have—or should have—healed Madig. But all you can do now is go forward. And learn from what happened."

"I think I see a way. To go forward. And to change things. Not just by healing one boy, but by healing two peoples."

He spoke slowly, still thinking through his idea, but as the plan solidified in his mind, the words tumbled out. Mercifully, Fellgair refrained from teasing him, only interrupting with an occasional question to clarify what Rigat was saying.

When he was finished, Rigat shot a shy glance at his father. "You're the Trickster and the God with Two Faces. And I'm your son. What better way for me to use my power than to try and bring about a peace between my people and the Zherosi?"

"If your plan is to succeed, you must learn to think of the Zherosi as well as the children of the Oak and Holly as your people."

"And if I do?" he asked eagerly. "Will it work?"

Fellgair sighed. "These are very different cultures, Rigat, with different religions and customs. One, an empire ruled by a queen, the other a fragmented group of tribes, each of which is guided—but not ruled—by a chief."

"But all people want to live in peace."

"In theory. In practice, a great many prefer war. For one thing, it keeps the warriors busy. It's expensive to pay them to loaf about the homeland. And dangerous, as well. War brings new slaves to cultivate the fields, new tribute to enrich the coffers, new goods to trade."

"Like timber," Rigat muttered.

"Indeed. And who requires timber? Shipbuilders. Merchants. Craftsmen. And generals who need ships to carry their warriors."

"To get the slaves and the tribute and the goods to trade."

"A bit simplistic, but you see my point. As for the children of the Oak and Holly, they've always squabbled over hunting grounds and marriage portions. They're equally divided on how to deal with the Zherosi. Some want to fight, some want to collaborate. Most just want to be left alone."

"So it's hopeless."

"On the contrary. It might work."

Rigat's breath left him on a helpless exhalation of excitement.

"Mind you, it could also fail. Horribly."

"But the plan could work. It really could."

Rigat caught the gleam of teeth as Fellgair smiled. "Yes, my son. It really could. If you're patient. Change doesn't come about in a moon. Or a year. And in the web of possibilities—"

Rigat groaned.

"The odds of success are slim. So let's discuss your idea further and see if we can improve them."

Rigat studied his father for a long moment. "This is why you created me. Isn't it?"

Fellgair stared up into the sky as if his great web of possibilities hung suspended among the stars. "It's one of the reasons."

Chapter 22

AS THE KANKH BLARED A THIRD time, Jholianna extended her hand to the Motixa, disguising the brief pang of grief with a well-practiced smile. After fourteen years, she had become accustomed to Jholin's absence, but she still mourned him. Now, instead of her brother beside her, it was the priestess of Womb of Earth.

Fitting, perhaps, for among Jholianna's many titles, her principal one was Earth's Beloved. But since Jholin's death, no ruler had embodied Sky's Light. She had refused to consider her council's tentative suggestion that she take another husband. What ordinary mortal deserved to stand at the side of the queen who had ruled Zheros for more than five centuries?

The shifting of sandals on stone interrupted her thoughts. The Pajhit, of course. She glanced over her shoulder. The priest of Heart of Sky flashed a nervous smile and smoothed his golden robe. The man was as twitchy as a virgin in a pleasure house. An amusing contrast to the stolid Zheron who stood beside him. The rabbit and the bullock.

And then there was her Motixa, whose plump cheeks and prominent front teeth made comparisons to a marmot inevitable. But at least the priestess appreciated the importance of making an entrance. Anticipation among the waiting courtiers would be peaking now, wonder shifting to nervousness with every passing moment.

She turned to the Motixa and nodded. Together, they walked past the blank-faced guards and entered the throne room.

A deafening cheer greeted her appearance. The crowd seethed restlessly, every person craning for a glimpse of her new body. Jholianna kept her smile in place as she mounted the steps to the dais. This year's Shedding had been easy, the Host so eager for the sacrifice that her spirit had required only the smallest push to vacate her body. But the effects of the qiij were wearing off and the effort of mastering this unfamiliar body—so much taller than the last— required all her concentration.

The Motixa's eyebrows rose in a silent question. Jholianna nodded again and received a toothy smile in return. Only then did the priestess join the Pajhit and the Zheron.

Like all rituals, this one was carefully choreographed. The Pajhit and the Motixa flanked the thrones of the king and queen. The Zheron, as earthly representative of Zhe, stood between the thrones, just as the winged serpent linked the incompatible gods who had given him life, forever serving—and betraying—them.

With that example of filial loyalty, perhaps it was a blessing that she and Jholin had never produced a child. A living child. Against her will, she recalled the hideous blob of bloody flesh that had slid from her body after her first miscarriage.

Angry at allowing the memory to tarnish the glory of this moment, she observed the crowd. Every face was turned to her, like flowers seeking the sun. Bedewed flowers, she noted, eyeing the multitude of sweat-sheened foreheads. In the sweltering throne room, her courtiers would soon be wilted.

The metaphor made her laugh; clearly, the qiij had not worn off completely. At this evidence of her delight, the cheering swelled. She allowed it to go on for a moment, then raised her hands. The sooner the ceremony concluded the better; if anyone fainted, it would be considered a bad omen.

In hushed silence, the crowd awaited the ritual greeting.

"Behold Earth's Beloved!" she cried. "Reborn to serve her people."

Amid much shuffling and shifting, her people fell to their knees and touched their foreheads to the tiled floor.

Jholianna caught a flicker of movement and silently cursed

the Pajhit for fidgeting during the ritual prostration. Her frown deepened when she saw his motionless figure. Could it have been one of the guards? Or the guttering of a torch? But how could flames flicker when the air was so heavy and still?

Then she saw it again, a subtle disturbance in the air. It had to be an illusion created by the heat or the qiij. But neither heat nor drug could conjure disembodied fingers.

As she opened her mouth to alert her guards, the groping fingers became a pair of hands. They pushed at the air, as if it were somehow solid. Two slender wrists appeared. Two bare arms. A skinny, muscular leg.

A boy stepped out of the air and onto the dais. Although he wore an immaculate khirta and leather sandals, that flaming hair and pale skin proclaimed him one of the Tree People.

Just like the other one.

But Kheridh was dead. She had seen his body. And this one gazed around the throne room with far more confidence than Kheridh had ever possessed—until those final moments before the earthquake.

The kankh blared, and he started. She was dimly aware of people shuffling to their feet, of the Pajhit's squeak of surprise. A few voices recited the ritual greeting, but they were drowned out by the startled exclamations of those who had noticed the stranger. Ignoring the outcry, he smiled at her and raised his hands, commanding silence just as she had.

"Behold the Son of Zhe, the fire-haired god made flesh. Welcome me with reverence and with dread, for with me comes the new age."

In the shocked silence that followed, he whispered, "Look for my signs." Then he vanished, leaving chaos behind.

At sunset, the earth rumbled in a minor tremor that shattered a clay vase and sent her attendants into hysterics. At midnight, a guard roused her from sleep, babbling about a fire atop the sacred mountain. At dawn, the Zheron arrived at his temple to discover an eagle perched on one of the pillars. It rose into the sky and circled the temple three times before winging north.

For the second time in as many days, Jholianna summoned her council. When she arrived, she found everyone clustered around the wooden bench she had installed for the comfort of the Khonsel. They hastily backed away as she entered, but before they could prostrate themselves, she waved them toward the low stone table at the center of the chamber. One by one, they seated themselves on the cushions. No one showed any interest in the platters of food, but both the Pajhit and the Stuavo held out their goblets for wine.

A rabbity priest and a swinish steward. With these, I am to deal with this crisis.

Thank the gods for Vazh do Havi. He had served her for nearly fifty years, the last fifteen as Khonsel in charge of internal security. Together, they had weathered earthquakes and slave revolts, famine and pestilence—and another red-haired boy who had claimed to be the Son of Zhe.

Less comforting was the presence of the Supplicant, as mercurial—and mysterious—as the god she served. Jholianna permitted her erratic behavior because her advice was always wise and her barbed humor offered much-needed relief from the tedium of council meetings.

As if she had spoken her thoughts aloud, the Supplicant broke off her muted conversation with the Pajhit. Brushing the glossy black hair off her left shoulder, she winked.

Oddly, her insolence steadied Jholianna. If the Supplicant remained undaunted, perhaps the situation was not as grave as she feared.

As she waited for the slaves to present more food that would doubtless go uneaten, she fought to conceal her disquiet. She had seen many false prophets, but none had ever chosen to enter her holy city in such an unorthodox manner.

Could he be the one?

It would be a miracle. And she wasn't sure she believed in miracles. Or in the gods.

Her wandering gaze was caught by the mural on the opposite wall. She should have had it repainted years ago. No one should have to render judgment while looking at a vengeful Zhe devouring his father in one panel and in the other the dying god plummeting into a bloodred sea. How appropriate that the vases in the wall niches flanking the mural contained bitterheart.

At her impatient gesture, the slaves scuttled away. Her guards checked the sky-wells for eavesdroppers then bowed and left. Jholianna took a deep breath and fixed each of the council members with her gaze.

"You all know why we're here. Opinions, please."

The Zheron cleared his throat and began a ponderous recitation of the prophecy, which everyone knew, and the recent signs, which everyone had witnessed. Schooling her expression to patience, she waited for him to finish.

"Thank you, Zheron. But let us set aside prophecy for the moment and consider whether these occurrences could have been caused by natural phenomena rather than the boy who appeared in my throne room."

"Womb of Earth has trembled more times than I can count," the Khonsel said. "Eagles are rare in Pilozhat, but they've been seen before."

"Perched atop the temple of Zhe?" the Zheron demanded. "And let us not forget his earlier appearance. At the mating of the adders."

"You said yourself it was too dark to see anything," the Khonsel said.

"I could see a great hole in the air. And trees. He was watching us even then."

"And your guards threatened him!" the Pajhit exclaimed.

"How were they to know?" the Zheron protested. "How were any of us to know? Then."

Jholianna held up her hand and the two priests fell silent. "What of this fire atop Kelazhat? You found no burn marks, Khonsel. No charred wood. No ashes."

"Which might only mean the instigators removed the evidence."

"Then you still believe this is some sort of plot by the Tree People?"

The Khonsel shrugged. "Like you, Earth's Beloved, I like to exhaust every rational explanation before leaping to the miraculous."

"And his appearance in the throne room?" the Motixa asked. "Can any rational explanation account for that?"

"The priests of the Tree People claim to be able to step between the worlds to witness the battle of their gods. Perhaps he did something similar."

"Or perhaps he truly is the Son of Zhe." The Zheron sketched a spiral over his chest.

The Supplicant favored the others with a gracious smile. "That's the trouble, isn't it? How *does* one prove that someone is the son of a god? Short of killing him and seeing if his father levels the city?"

The other priests made strangled sounds of objection. The Khonsel merely snorted.

"Well, I'll say this." The Stuavo stabbed the table with a thick forefinger. "Son of Zhe or not, the city is in turmoil. People are fleeing. Those who remain are terrified. If word of this gets out, it's only a matter of time before merchants refuse to enter Pilozhat."

"Burn me!" the Khonsel swore. "There are more important issues here than trade."

"But as Stuavo, my first concern is trade. Without it, the empire would collapse. So kindly allow me to offer my point of view."

To forestall an argument, Jholianna asked, "Have there been more disturbances?"

"A few demonstrations," the Khonsel replied, repeating for the council's benefit what he had told her earlier that morning. "Nothing violent. Problem is, between The Shedding and the Midsummer rite, the city's already overcrowded. That means more men drinking and dicing and whoring—begging your pardon, Earth's Beloved. And if word spreads that the Son of Zhe's arrived . . ." The Khonsel shook his head. "I've put extra men on the streets, but it'll take more than that if a mob of pilgrims marches into Pilozhat."

"Has he been seen?" the Motixa asked.

"Plenty of rumors. Nothing that can be verified." The Khonsel massaged his leg and grimaced. "Some old crone's charging a copper frog to look at a loaf of bread that she claims bears the imprint of his face."

"What an enterprising creature." The Supplicant leaned

forward to waggle a reproving finger at the Stuavo. "And you said trade would suffer."

"What more can we do?" the Pajhit whined, nervously rubbing the vial of qiij that hung on his chest. "We've offered sacrifices. We've asked the gods to enlighten us."

"And have the gods answered?" Jholianna asked.

"The gods speak in riddles," the Pajhit replied, "and show us mysteries."

"As always. Just once, it would be nice to get a straight answer."

The Khonsel smiled. The Supplicant laughed out loud. The other council members gasped.

"Earth's Beloved," the Motixa chided.

"Yes, yes. It's a time for supplication, not impiety." Jholianna fixed her gaze on the Supplicant, who was examining the painted nails of her left hand. "Has the God with Two Faces offered any insights about this mysterious boy or told you what he wants from us?"

"The God has offered many insights, most of them as contradictory as his nature. As to what this boy wants . . ." The Supplicant glanced toward the doorway and smiled brightly. "Why don't you ask him?"

Chapter 23

THE FIRST THING RIGAT NOTICED was how cool and shadowy the room was. Like a forest. A forest of stone. He even caught the faint whiff of pine, but perhaps that was the incense.

Seated on the ornately carved throne, the queen seemed more delicate than she had standing on the dais. Her shimmering blue skirt clung to her thighs before cascading into a series of flounces that spilled over her knees and ankles like a waterfall. A strip of the same fabric bound her breasts. Her hair hung loose today, like a young girl's, but there were shadows under the dark doe-eyes, as if she had suffered a sleepless night.

He hoped his exhaustion was less noticeable. Even with Fellgair's help, creating the signs had sapped his energy and his power. Fellgair had been less helpful regarding the strategy for this meeting. He had described the council members and the response Rigat might expect from each, but most of his advice could have come from Mam: "Stand up straight. Don't fidget. And double knot your khirta. You don't want it sliding off." Direct pleas for information were met with a shrug and a stream of questions that forced him to think—and rethink—his plan.

When he had imagined these first moments, he had assumed the council members would fall on their knees or exclaim in wonder. Instead, they just stared at him. Perhaps his appearance had shocked them into immobility. The queen, however, appeared more wary than shocked. Waiting for him to make the first move.

Reminding himself that the son of a god outranked even a queen, Rigat nodded gravely. "Greetings, Earth's Beloved."

The queen rose. "Greetings. And welcome to my holy city."

Her manner was calm, her voice light and pleasing. Less pleasing was her obvious omission of his title. If she refused to acknowledge his claim, the council never would.

Should his manner be conciliatory or arrogant? Should he chide them for failing to prostrate themselves or ignore their lack of manners as beneath his notice? He licked his lips nervously and resisted the urge to glance at Fellgair for support. Of all the tests his father had given him, this was the greatest. And he would succeed or fail on his own.

To give himself time to gather his thoughts, he examined the chamber. He marveled briefly at the intricate design of intertwined flowers and leaves on the rug before him. The colors—red and gold, green and brown—reflected those in the mural behind the two thrones. The mountain must be Kelazhat—perhaps long ago, it had been that lush and green—for surely the scarlet-winged serpent rising above it was Zhe.

All in all, he preferred having a fox for a father, but he studied the mural, hoping his face conveyed reverence. Then he faced the council. Only the Zheron's expression looked remotely worshipful. The red-faced Stuavo was sweating, the Motixa seemed worried, and the little Pajhit looked like he wanted to bolt.

His gaze lingered longest on the Khonsel. The old man leaned heavily on his stick, but his right hand rested on the hilt of his sheathed dagger. Fellgair had described him as the most formidable member of the council and the one closest to the queen. Darak had called him a hard man, loyal to his friends and implacable with his enemies. A good thing, then, that Rigat knew the secret the old man had kept for so many years—that the queen's loyal Khonsel had helped Darak, Keirith, and Hircha escape from Pilozhat.

Buoyed by the knowledge, he sauntered toward the queen. With what he hoped was a godlike wave, he said, "Please. Let us be comfortable." And seated himself on the vacant throne.

Someone gasped. One of the men muttered. The queen hesitated, dark eyes boring into his. Her smile was cold, the recognition of a worthy adversary rather than a gracious acceptance of his right to sit on the king's throne. Without taking her eyes off him, she slowly sat. One by one, the council members followed suit.

"I expected a warmer welcome for the Son of Zhe."

"You must forgive us," the queen replied. "There have been so many who have claimed that title. Including a red-haired boy named Kheridh." She leaned back, idly toying with one of the flounces on her skirt. "Perhaps my memory deceives me, but you look very much like him."

He almost laughed. But of course, she was remembering the auburn-haired boy who had come to Pilozhat, not the tawny-skinned, black-haired Keirith that he had known all his life. Should he claim Keirith was a distant relative or boldly admit the truth? If they somehow discovered it later, it would cast doubt on everything he said. As long as he never revealed that Keirith was still alive, perhaps truth would serve him better.

Praying he was doing the right thing, he said, "Keirith was my half brother."

The queen's eyes widened. The Pajhit gave a little squeak of dismay.

"You might remember my foster-father as well. The children of the Oak and Holly call him Darak Spirit-Hunter."

The Khonsel's face was as smooth and hard as stone, but he gripped his stick so tightly that the tendons on his hand stood out like twigs.

Enjoying himself now, Rigat mimicked the queen's gesture and adjusted the drape of his khirta. "My foster-father managed to escape from Pilozhat. Before he was sacrificed. My half brother was murdered by your Zheron. Your former Zheron," he added with a polite nod to the current one.

Their shocked expressions pleased him. They must be afraid that he wanted vengeance. Except the Khonsel, of course. He'd be wondering if his little secret was about to be revealed.

"I did not come here to exact retribution," he assured them. "Xevhan paid for his crime."

"What crime?" the queen asked. "Kheridh helped your foster-father kill our Pajhit. And when Xevhan came to the Pajhit's defense, Kheridh turned on him."

Rigat eyed the Khonsel. "You told her that, I suppose."

"The Khonsel told me what the Spirit-Hunter claimed," the queen replied. "Was I to believe a stranger?"

"As queen, you're supposed to seek the truth."

"Which is what she is doing now," the Khonsel interjected. "Whatever happened fourteen years ago, one fact is clear: despite his gifts, Kheridh was just another in a long line of impostors."

"My lord," Rigat said.

"What?"

"If you will not give me my proper title, you should at least call me 'my lord.' "

He waited, his eyes locked with the Khonsel's, until the old man finally added, "My lord."

Rigat decided to ignore the grudging tone. "And you believe I'm the latest of these impostors."

At the Khonsel's shrug, the Pajhit squeaked again. "Your miraculous appearance in the throne room—and today, of course—those clearly indicate extraordinary power, my lord."

"And the signs," the Zheron added with a stern look at the Khonsel. "Any man of faith would accept those as proof."

One ally, then.

"If he made them." The Khonsel bared his teeth in a grin. "Meaning no disrespect. My lord."

The Zheron glared. The Pajhit seemed ready to piss himself. But the queen was watching the interplay avidly. "She may appear to be a pretty girl of sixteen," Fellgair had warned him, "but her spirit is hundreds of years old. Never underestimate her."

As he eyed the Khonsel, Rigat tapped one forefinger against his lips. When Fellgair did it, his heart always raced in fearful anticipation, but the Khonsel seemed utterly unmoved.

"So what *would* satisfy you, Khonsel? If I killed you?"

His gaze never wavered. "Well, I'd be dead, wouldn't I? So my satisfaction wouldn't count for much. Might impress the others, though."

Rigat heard the queen's quick intake of breath but kept his eyes on the Khonsel, allowing the silence to stretch until he could smell the stink of fear in the chamber. "Vazh do Havi. You have ballocks the size of boulders."

His comment elicited gasps from the priests and a brief smile from the Khonsel, but the old man's fingers remained firmly clenched around the hilt of his dagger.

"If I may interject," Fellgair said. "Regardless of the size of the Khonsel's testicles, I would be too grief-stricken over his death to feel any satisfaction. Might I suggest another test?"

Rigat pretended to ponder, then signaled his willingness with a gracious wave.

"Perhaps our guest would allow the Khonsel to . . . oh, I don't know . . . cut him?"

Had Fellgair foreseen this moment? Was that why he had slashed his wrist?

The Zheron recovered first. "Sacrilege!"

"*If* he is the Son of Zhe. In which case, I shall implore his forgiveness."

"The Son of Zhe is not immortal," the Motixa noted. "He would bleed like any man."

"True," the Khonsel agreed. "But surely, he could heal the wound."

The gleam in the Khonsel's eyes made Rigat hesitate. He had not yet recovered his full power. If the Khonsel merely pricked his finger or scored his forearm, he could close the wound. But if he slashed his wrist as Fellgair had? Or stabbed him in the chest?

Angry at losing the initiative so quickly, he said, "I'm the Son of Zhe, not a trained dog performing tricks for its master. How many more tests will you demand before you accept that?"

"As many as it takes. My lord."

"Enough, Khonsel." Despite the queen's stern tone, Rigat sensed her pleasure at the Khonsel's daring. He wondered if they had planned it together, playing him as surely as a boy played a trout on a fishing line.

"You must understand our dilemma," she said, turning to him with an apologetic smile. "We must be sure. And only one test will prove beyond doubt that you are the Son of Zhe." She waited, eyebrows raised. When Rigat remained silent, she said, "You must allow me to touch your spirit."

He hadn't even been able to shield himself completely from Gortin. The queen's skills must be far greater. But if he backed down, they would never accept him.

"I shall return at sunset, then. You'll require time for the qiij to take effect." And he needed time to prepare.

The queen surprised him by laughing. Her hand came up to stroke the golden vial hanging at the end of the chain around her throat. "But I've already taken the qiij. While you were sparring with the Khonsel."

He had been so intent on that match that he had failed to notice. Just as he had failed to notice her slitted pupils. How could he when her eyes were so dark? The laughter might be a side effect of the drug; Fellgair had told him many users became euphoric when they first took it. But she could just as easily be taunting him.

The queen smiled. "With your permission, of course."

"Of course."

"I'll need to touch you." Lazily, she held up her hand. Even if he stretched out his arm, he would not be able to reach her fingertips without leaving the throne. He was damned if he would stand before her like one of her subjects. He might not be the Son of Zhe, but he *was* the son of a god.

He mimicked her gesture and waited. When she laughed again and rose, Rigat's triumph faded; her graceful acquiescence made him seem like a petulant child.

She grasped his hand. Her thumb traced the outline of the antler tattoo. "Where did you get this?"

"My tribe's Tree-Brother. After I brought down a stag with one shot to the heart."

Her thumb teased its way across the pale scar. "And this?"

"My father. He tested me, too."

"Did you pass the test?"

"That's what you're about to find out."

The ring on her forefinger bit into his wrist bone. She studied his face, frowning, then closed her eyes.

Like a man beckoning his lover, he called forth his power. Eagerly, it responded, flushing his body with heat. It was his to use in any way he chose. To make the earth tremble or a queen.

He banked the power, awaiting her touch. It brushed against his spirit as lightly as her thumb had skimmed across his flesh. To the Hosts whose spirits she cast out during The Shedding, the touch would have been imperceptible. But he was not a helpless girl.

With a suddenness that made him gasp, she drove deep into his spirit, seeking the hidden places where his secrets lay. An assault as brutal as Gortin's, but launched with cunning deliberation.

Anger bathed his body in renewed heat. A tingling burst of energy raced down his arms. As it leaped from his flesh to hers, her eyes flew open. She tried to pull away, but he seized her hands, dragging her closer.

Her perfume was as sweet as the power singing through him, singing through her, penetrating flesh and blood and bone. He heard cries from the council members, heard Fellgair shout, "Wait!" But he ignored them all, guiding the power to her spirit, piercing it as swiftly and surely as an arrow penetrated flesh.

Shock rippled through her spirit. She fled deeper inside

herself, flinging up barriers. He destroyed them with ease, only to be thrust back by her unexpected assault.

Clever. And strong. But he was stronger.

When he renewed his attack, her knees buckled. He slid off the throne and wrapped his arms around her, both of them swaying like dancers, like lovers. But her narrowed eyes and fierce grimace proved that they were combatants, locked together in the tide of their mutual power.

He touched fear, but beneath it was a strange excitement that only fed his. He was wildly aroused—by the battle, by her strength, by her body pressed hard against his. He wanted to throw her to the floor and take her, thrusting into her body as he thrust into her spirit. And she wanted it, too. He could feel her desire, as potent as the power.

<*But then you would fail the test. The Son of Zhe must be a virgin.*>

Humiliation left him vulnerable. She pressed her advantage, driving past his shields, and the memories poured out of him: the uncertainty of the World Tree when he touched it; Madig's voice, soft and malevolent: "A murderer. An abomination. Just like your brother." And Mam's haunted face as she pressed his hand to her heart and whispered, "Please, Rigat."

Fury lent him renewed strength. He turned the full force of his power upon her, stripping away her defenses to probe the secret places of her spirit with the same ruthlessness that she had attempted to uncover his: scarlet flowers blooming in a small garden; a frail youth with glazed eyes and a sleepy smile; a tiny, blood-spattered face, barely recognizable as human.

Her mouth opened. But it was her spirit that screamed.

Shaken by her rage and terror, his fury died, leaving only shame. He had told Fellgair he wanted to use his power to heal. Instead, stung by her teasing, he had lashed out. And although he might have convinced her that he was the son of a god, he had also demonstrated that he was a cruel and vindictive child.

What would his mam think of him? Or Darak? Unbidden, their faces rose before him, Darak's stern with disapproval, his mam's shocked and grief-stricken. He had failed them as surely as he had failed the queen. Even if she

believed he was the son of Zhe, she would never trust him
again. And there would never be peace between their
peoples.

She moaned as he withdrew from her spirit. Gently, he
lowered her onto her throne and waited for her eyes to
focus. And then, because he wasn't sure his thoughts had
reached her, he whispered, "Forgive me."

The others were all on their feet, their expressions ranging from horror to anger to terrified submission. The Khonsel's
dagger was in his hand; only Fellgair's grip kept him from
charging.

His father's expression was unreadable.

Rigat bowed to them all, but directed his words to Fellgair and the Khonsel. "You were right to doubt me. I don't
deserve to be the son of a god."

He could barely manage to rip open a portal. Perhaps
Fellgair helped him; he was too tired to be certain. But
when he saw the welcoming shadows of the forest, he fled
toward them, desperate to leave shame and failure behind.

Chapter 24

"THAT DAMNED FORTRESS is locked tighter than
a virgin's legs," Pedar grumbled.

"That's the price of success," Temet replied. "And we
have Keirith to thank for it."

Keirith saw Temet's grin reflected on the faces of the
others—Faelia and Selima, Mikal and Pedar—the special
few who planned every attack and discussed every strategy.
Now he was part of that inner circle.

If they knew the truth, they would despise me.

It had been more than a sennight since he'd seen Rigat.

At their last meeting, his brother had seemed distracted.
Perhaps the recent inactivity had left him as restless as
everyone else.

"I'm sorry I've been so useless lately," he said.

"You've been pushing yourself too hard," Faelia replied.
"Healing Eilin. And Idrian and Nuala."

Mikal frowned; he'd made no secret of the fact that he
resented Keirith "squandering" his gift on healing the spirits of the "weak."

"You can't seek a vision every night," Faelia continued.
"I told you—"

"I know, I know."

"You may know, but you don't listen."

"You're supposed to listen to me. You *are* my little
sister."

Pedar made a great show of covering his head with his
arms. "Oh, gods. No bloodshed."

Faelia punched his arm, and he yelped. "It's him you
should be hitting."

"You're closer."

"Temet, control your woman."

"You're on your own, friend. It'd be worth my head
to interfere."

"Not to mention other parts of your anatomy," Faelia
said with a sweet smile.

"Don't take those," Selima protested. "They're the only
parts worth having."

Pressing his hand over his heart as if stricken, Pedar
rolled off the log. Mikal waited for the laughter to ebb
before nudging him with his foot. "Get up, fool. And help
us figure out how to open the virgin's legs."

Pedar glanced from Faelia to Selima, but the looks they
gave him were enough to send him back to his place with
only a meek, "Oh. Right. The fortress."

"They have to come out eventually," Selima said. "Even
if it's only to hunt."

Mikal shook his head. "Not if they're rationing their
supplies."

"Or if our people are hunting for them," Temet added.

His words dispelled the lingering good humor created by
Pedar's silliness. They all knew that the village near The
Bluff traded with the Zherosi.

"We could pressure them . . ."

Mikal's voice trailed off as Temet shook his head. "Then we'd be no better than the Zherosi."

"Well, we're too few to consider an assault on Little Falls," Selima said. "And it would be suicide to attack The Bluff."

Faelia leaned forward. "But the garrison is undermanned. And thanks to our ambushes, the Zherosi haven't been able to reinforce it."

"They'd cut us down before we were halfway up the hill," Selima insisted.

"I still say we could fire the palisade."

Pedar groaned. "We've been over this a dozen times."

"Nay, listen. Say a dozen of us sneak up the hill. With some brush to—"

"There's precious little darkness this close to Midsummer," Pedar interrupted. "They're bound to notice a lot of shrubs creeping up on them."

Selima jabbed him with her elbow. "Let her talk."

"Forget the brush," Faelia said. "If we can get within bowshot, we could use flaming arrows to fire the palisade. All we need is pine resin—or animal fat—"

"Or some of that lovely scented oil the Zherosi commanders use on their hair."

"Shut up, Pedar!"

The first time Keirith had witnessed one of their arguments, he'd feared they would come to blows. Only Temet remained aloof, content to listen and offer a quiet remark when tempers flared. Like a father with a brood of quarrelsome children. When he finally raised his hand, the contentious voices immediately fell silent.

"I still say it's too risky. Unless we have Nial's band with us. They're the closest."

"Nial's a stiff-necked bastard," Mikal said. "Do you really think he'll cooperate?"

"That's the whole point of this Gathering. To find ways we can work together."

"Fa and Sorig will be back by then," Faelia said. "If they've brought recruits—"

"A big 'if,'" Selima interrupted. When Faelia stiffened, she quickly added, "If anyone can convince them to fight, the Spirit-Hunter can. But we can't pin our strategy on that."

"Which is why we'll wait until the Gathering to finalize our plans," Temet said.

"What if we fired the ships?" Keirith asked.

They all stared at him. Until now, he had simply relayed Rigat's information and allowed them to discuss strategy.

Pedar blew out his breath in exasperation. "There are no ships at The Bluff. The river's too shallow—"

"Not The Bluff. Little Falls. We could swim across the river at night—"

"Nial tried that," Mikal interrupted. "The guards heard the splashing and picked them off. Like spearing salmon in a fish trap."

"That was at Deepford," Faelia said. "At Little Falls, the rapids would disguise any noise."

Keirith shot his sister a grateful look. "And they wouldn't expect an attack. Not on their largest fortress."

Pedar shuddered. "Which is a damn good reason not to attack it."

"The ships will be guarded," Mikal said. "And we'd have to avoid the village." His scowl reminded everyone that his tribe willingly cooperated with the Zherosi. "It might work. But . . ."

"What?" Temet asked.

Mikal moved his shoulders as if his tunic had suddenly grown too tight. "There's bound to be changes since Keirith's last vision. I'd just feel better if we could see the fortress firsthand."

An awkward silence fell. With Sorig gone, Mikal was the obvious choice, but everyone knew how much he hated going anywhere near his birthplace.

"It can wait," Temet said. "After Sorig returns, we can—"

"Nay," Mikal interrupted. "If we want to convince Nial to help, we'll need as much information as possible before the Gathering."

"Right." Temet's voice was brisk, but he squeezed Mikal's shoulder briefly. "Choose two or three others to go with you."

"It might be better if I went alone." Mikal grimaced. "I can always say I came back to mend my differences with my father."

Temet nodded. "We'll move camp tonight, but stay close to The Bluff for a sennight in case there's another attempt to relieve it. After that, we head west to the Gathering place."

Keirith knew better than to ask where it was. Temet had probably told Mikal the location, but the rest of them would only learn their exact destination on the final leg of the journey.

The group slowly dispersed for the evening meal. Probably suetcakes and smoked venison again. Although they were half a day's journey from The Bluff, Temet had ordered that no fires were to be lit until after the Gathering, fearing a hunter might spy the smoke and report to the Zherosi.

As Keirith wandered through the clearing, he passed men and women sharpening blades and fletching arrows. A few—less industrious—sprawled on the grass, their bodies striped by the sunlight slanting through the trees. Hard to imagine that less than half a moon ago, these same men and women had slaughtered dozens of Zherosi.

At the edge of the embankment, he spied Eilin at the stream below, picking his way across the rocks. The boy started as two of the bathing men playfully hurled gouts of water at him. Then he smiled and brandished his fishing spear with exaggerated menace.

In the first days after his healing, Eilin had tagged after him like a puppy, afraid to let him out of his sight. But he seemed more confident now—and he'd lost that glaze-eyed look of silent terror.

He'd been less successful with Idrian and Nuala. Temet had sent them both home, overruling Keirith's pleas that they simply needed more time to recover.

"Maybe so," Temet had said. "But they'll have to do that elsewhere. I send the wounded home to keep them from slowing us down. These two may have different wounds, but I can't permit them to endanger the rest of us."

At least he had helped them through the worst of it. And Temet had been kind in his farewell, assuring them that he would need them come winter when the Zherosi began their logging operations.

Keirith's worries faded as he meandered through a pretty little copse of birches. He caressed the slender trunks, delighting in the feathery curls of bark. As the trees gave way to a rocky ledge, he caught his breath.

It was like standing at the edge of the world. Rolling hills spread out beneath him, an endless canopy of green that faded into a soft blue in the distance. Shading his eyes against the setting sun, he made out the occasional glint of water, and, far to the west, a thin haze where smoke rose from a village.

Could the Zherosi really destroy all of this? It seemed impossible. Yet he had seen the sun-baked plains of their homeland where legends claimed forests had once stretched for miles.

Choosing a spot well away from the edge, he sat and rested his back against a sun-warmed boulder. He had always loved sunsets in the north, the soft colors melting together as evening approached, the lingering half-light of the gloaming fading so slowly you could still make out the black outlines of the trees far into the night.

Enjoying the rare solitude, Keirith felt contentment banish his lingering anxiety about Rigat's absence and his concern about his spirit-wounded comrades. He watched the wispy clouds fade from rose to violet, and the sky pale to the subtle blue-gray of a wood pigeon. His breathing grew deep, his limbs heavy, as if his body were surrendering to the inevitable twilight. The birds had surrendered as well, their chirps and squawks and warbles fading with the light. Less than fifty paces away, the camp bustled with activity, but stillness filled his body, his mind, his spirit.

A sinuous cloud, purple as a fresh bruise, drifted past. High above it, an eagle soared in a long, slow spiral. Suddenly, it folded its wings and plummeted earthward. The muscular legs reached out. The deadly talons seemed to pluck the cloud from the sky. As the eagle flew toward him, Keirith realized it *had* snatched up the cloud, which dangled limply in its grasp. Transfixed by the vision, he watched the eagle until it hovered before him, so huge that it blocked out the sky.

The talons relaxed. The cloud drifted slowly to the ground. It was as insubstantial as ever, but he could See the color changing from purple to green as it wriggled toward him, just as he could See the black scales that zigzagged down the adder's back, the dark "X" on the back of its head, and the familiar red-brown eyes, wise and unblinking, that stared up into his.

Waves of warmth flooded him as Natha flowed over his feet, up his thighs, across his chest, and finally curled around his shoulders. His spirit guide's tongue caressed his cheek.

"I've tried so hard to reach you," Keirith whispered.

"You try too hard," Natha replied. "You always have. When all you have to do is let go."

"Why do you put up with me?"

"You are a foolish hatchling, but you are mine. Now and always."

The words, so similar to Xevhan's during his nightmare, made Keirith shudder.

"Why do you cling to him?" Natha demanded.

"I don't! I don't want him inside of me."

"Then let him go."

"But . . ."

Natha's tongue flicked out again, and the weight of his anxiety seemed to melt away. "You make everything difficult. Especially excreting that one. Until you understand why, he will never leave you."

He was still struggling to grasp the implications of that as Natha slid down his body. "You're not leaving?"

"No. There is much for you to See. Come. Fly with us."

"Fly?"

Natha gave an irritated hiss. "Are you deaf as well as foolish? For you, I will endure this. But I will never understand why you enjoy it."

The eagle's wings flapped with otherworldly slowness as it descended to the ledge. The feathered head swung toward him. The hooked beak opened to emit a thin chirrup.

With the ease only possible in vision, Keirith vaulted onto the wing, clinging to the tip of one feather. It kept changing beneath his fingers, one moment soft, the next spiky, the next as solid as wood. He pulled himself up, hand over hand, until the eagle apparently lost patience with his slow progress and raised its wing, tumbling him onto the broad back.

Like the feathers, the eagle's body felt utterly unreal—too resilient to be flesh, too yielding to be bone. He dug his fingers into the feathers of the massive neck, but even with his legs outstretched, he could barely grip the eagle's back with his ankles. As he struggled to find a safe position, its body dwindled until it was little larger than a real eagle. After Natha slithered up his back and curled around his neck, the great wings spread and lifted them off the ground.

He was flying. Not spirit-linked as he had been with the eagle at home, but soaring through the sky, fearless and exultant. His hair whipped across his face, and he threw back his head, his laugh mingling with Natha's exasperated hiss.

From this height, the river looked like a strand of gray wool in a huge green mantle. Here and there, the forest gave way to tiny patches of open fields and a cluster of huts small enough to hold in his hand. But near each Zherosi fortress, ugly brown wounds marred the flow of green where the loggers had chopped down the trees.

He closed his eyes, unwilling to allow reality to mar the joy of the flight. Then, shamed by his selfishness, he opened them again.

In the unnerving way that visions shifted time and place, they were much lower now. Three ships crawled upriver toward Little Falls. He must remember to tell Temet.

As the eagle glided over a low hill, a lake appeared. Villages hugged the northern and southern shores. Two peaks jutted up on either side of a narrow channel. And Keirith forgot the ships and the fortresses as he stared down at the village of his birth.

Oddly, everything looked exactly as it had fourteen years ago. There were the fields he had walked through, the familiar circle of huts. And near the summit of Eagles Mount, the pile of sticks and bracken where the eagles nested. But instead of the awkward fledgling he had spied on his last morning, he saw only a small white form nestled under the female's dark breast feathers.

Again, the vision shifted. At first, he was only aware of being enclosed by softness. Then he realized that he had become the newly hatched chick, peering out from under his mother's feathers, craning his neck to watch his father circle closer, clucking and chattering in his eagerness for food.

A faint tapping caught his attention. It came from the egg. In the three days since his hatching, he had watched his mother turn it with her beak, felt her shifting her body to shelter it from the wind and rain.

As the irregular taps continued, the egg shuddered. A tiny crack appeared. Another tap and the crack widened, branching into tiny fissures that snaked across the dark reddish-brown patches that stained the creamy shell. More insistent tapping and the shell splintered, revealing the tip of a tiny, hooked beak.

He butted his head against his mother's breast, but she refused to be diverted. With infinite gentleness, she nipped at the shell. A small, damp head appeared. It lolled against her until she nudged it with her beak. Then the thing began moving again, unseen wings battering against its shell.

Totally engrossed in the wriggling intruder, his mother ignored his high-pitched bark of resentment. When the chick finally broke free, she plucked away the fragments that clung to its damp, downy feathers.

The tiny head turned. Blue eyes stared up at him. Then it fell back on the sticks, basking in their mother's love and attention.

His beak darted out and stabbed the defenseless neck. A bright spot of blood marred the white down. With mingled horror and triumph, Keirith attacked again. The chick struggled helplessly, but his mother only shifted on the nest. For all the tenderness she had shown, she would not stop him. He was the firstborn. It was his duty—his right—to kill this weakling. There was only food enough for one. Only love enough for one. This was not murder, but a sacrifice, ordained by the gods. And he—not this intruder— was the one chosen to carry out their will.

The blood was warm in his mouth, as delicious as the soft flesh he tore with his beak. Two pairs of eyes watched him from the tangle of sticks—one pair the same blue as Mam's, the other the color of the blotches on the shattered eggshell. His brother's pleading eyes grew wide and empty. Natha's watched impassively.

Keirith's triumph vanished. Desperate to escape the carnage, he struggled to the edge of the nest. But his wings were too small, too weak to carry him skyward. Helplessly, he tumbled toward the rocks. He opened his mouth to cry out to Natha, but it was Rigat's name he screamed.

A shadow drifted over him. Strong wings enfolded him. His father cradled him against his breast feathers and lowered him slowly to the ground.

His legs were so weak he could hardly stand. Fa must be holding him up. But that was impossible; Fa was standing before him. When had he changed from eagle to man?

"Please," he whispered. "No more."

"But there is more to See."

As Natha slithered through the grass, Keirith saw a figure rise up out of the ground. It loomed behind Fa, little more than a shadow under the trees. And although there was nothing overtly menacing about the figure, Keirith shouted at Fa to run, to escape while there was still time. The words emerged as shrill chirrups. He heard Natha hiss, then saw something flying toward Fa, and knew the sound had not come from Natha.

The arrow struck Fa in the shoulder. His legs folded under him and he sank slowly to his knees. Only when he fell facedown in the grass did Keirith see the second arrow in his back.

His scream shattered the vision and sent his spirit hurtling back into his body. The first convulsion made him jerk upright. The next slammed him back down. Rock scraped his elbows and knees as he twisted helplessly. He heard voices calling his name, felt hands trying to hold him. He bit down on wood—someone must have shoved a stick between his teeth—but he shook his head wildly and finally managed to spit it out so he could gasp out his name.

"Three times to seal the spirit's return."

Gortin's voice, calm and patient.

"And after the boundaries of the spirit have been reestablished, those of the body must be as well."

As the convulsions eased, he pushed weakly at the hands that still held him.

"Let him go. Don't touch him." Faelia's voice, shrill with fear.

Too exhausted to sit up, he curled into a ball so he could run his trembling hands over his head, his shoulders, his torso, his legs.

"Dear gods, is it always like this?" Temet this time. The concerned father.

Oh, gods. Fa . . .

A hand grasped his. He opened his eyes and looked up into Faelia's face. "Fa . . . and Rigat . . ."

"Don't talk. Not yet."

"It might be important," Mikal said.

"Then he'll tell us when he's able! Temet, help me lift his head."

He closed his eyes, fighting the wave of nausea. They lowered his head onto something warm and soft. Faelia's lap, he realized.

Her callused fingers stroked his forehead. "Do you want anything? Water?"

Right now, all he wanted to do was sleep—and forget.

Visions were unreliable—chancy, Gortin always called them. They could be reflections of your worst fears or glimpses into the future. They could warn you of genuine danger or a threat that existed only in your mind.

Rigat was his brother. He loved him. Worried about him. And aye, sometimes he resented him, but that didn't mean he wanted to kill him. Xevhan had done that, not him.

"Why do you cling to him?"

He was too spirit-sick and exhausted to think about Natha's words now. More important was the connection between the first part of the vision and the second. He must try to remember details, to discover if it was a real place or an imaginary one. He had to warn Fa of the betrayal that would occur.

Might occur.

Might have occurred already.

He seized Temet's hand. "The Gathering. I have to know where it will be. Not the location, but what the place looks like."

"You saw something that will happen at the Gathering?" Mikal asked.

"I don't know."

"Later." Temet squeezed his hand. "You need to rest now."

If the attack was going to occur at the Gathering, Fa was still safe. But who was that shadowy figure?

Not Rigat. He would never hurt Fa.

Not hurt him. Murder him.

There was some other connection between the two visions, some other explanation. There must be.

Chapter 25

JHOLIANNA'S LADIES FLITTED ABOUT her like a cloud of gaudy butterflies, fussing with the flounces on her skirt, sliding bracelets over her wrists, straightening the serpentine crown that circled her head.

Not butterflies, she decided, listening to their chatter. Birds. Butterflies were blessedly silent.

Although she had insisted that the festivities continue as planned, she shuddered at the thought of yet another feast where she would have to smile and laugh and turn aside the inevitable questions.

"Forgive me, Earth's Beloved. Is it too tight?"

The incessant chatter died. Lady Alikia's fingers hovered uncertainly over the golden sheath of lilmia that bound Jholianna's breasts.

"No. It's fine."

A sigh of relief eased around the circle and conversation resumed. Innocuous comments on the mild weather, speculations about the dishes that would be served tonight, fretful lamentations about the shortcomings of this one's new dressmaker and that one's new slave boy, all spiced with the occasional tidbit of court gossip.

Jholianna had heard it all countless times, but today, she detected a nervous undercurrent to the chatter, a sharper edge to the laughter. Belatedly, she realized her attendants were carefully avoiding all mention of the mysterious boy who claimed to be the Son of Zhe.

"Are you unwell, Earth's Beloved? You're shivering."

"You tickled me, Lady Alikia."

The drooping folds of flesh under Lady Alikia's chin shook as she chuckled. "A thousand pardons, Earth's Beloved."

Jholianna waited while Lady Alikia made the final adjustments to her attire. She knew she would blaze like Heart of Sky at tonight's feast. Knew, too, that her appearance was utterly unimportant. Only the boy mattered.

Rigat.

She had sensed the name while their spirits were linked. The memory of the encounter made her shiver again.

Hail the Son of Zhe, the fire-haired god made flesh. Welcome him with reverence and with dread, for with him comes the new age.

She had welcomed him with dread, but hardly reverence. The qiij had made her reckless. But she knew her failure was due more to pride than to the drug.

As soon as she felt his touch, she realized he was more powerful than any person she had ever encountered. But only when he stripped away her defenses, leaving her spirit naked before his, did she believe he might be the son of a god.

His apology had shocked her. Why would the Son of Zhe apologize to anyone, even the queen of Zheros? He was young, of course. Still uncertain of himself and his power. But his humility raised new doubts in her mind.

Is he truly the one?

The question haunted her, as did her inability to contact him.

And if I could . . . what then?

He would never allow her to touch his spirit again. If their battle had not convinced her, what possible test could? The Supplicant was right: there was no sure way to prove who he was.

Lady Alikia finished anointing her throat and wrists with scented oil, then dabbed a bit more onto the thick coil of hair that crowned her head. "You have never looked more beautiful, Earth's Beloved."

"You always say that."

"And it's always true."

From another, it might be sycophancy, but Lady Alikia had served her with loyalty and discretion for more than thirty years. Jholianna laid her palm against the dry cheek, then glanced up as one of her ladies discreetly cleared her throat.

"The Supplicant is here, Earth's Beloved."

"Show her in."

As Lady Varis retreated, Jholianna seated herself on one of the stone benches that flanked the walls. Her ladies sank into deep curtsies as the Supplicant entered, then scattered like quail to the benches surrounding the two pillars farthest away. Lady Varis retrieved her flute and began to play, the soft music a further deterrent to eavesdropping. The rest returned to distaff and spindle and gossip.

As the Supplicant touched her forehead to the floor, Jholianna mused that only the priestess of the God with Two Faces could make the ritual prostration seem an ironic gesture rather than a humble one.

Jholianna nodded to a slave boy, who hurried forward with a bronze tray. The Supplicant favored him with a brilliant smile that made him shake so badly the goblets rattled. Jholianna forestalled disaster by seizing them and dismissing the boy.

"Pretty," the Supplicant commented as he hurried away. "If nervous."

"You have that effect on people."

"Not on you, Earth's Beloved."

"No," Jholianna said firmly. "Shall I call for food?"

"Thank you, no. I would not like to tempt fate twice."

The Supplicant's gaze traveled slowly around the chamber, taking in the murals of green forests and white-capped mountains, the blue-painted pillars with their tiny, white-spiraled waves, and the mosaic of summer flowers that seem to sprout from the tiles. In all the years the Supplicant had served her, this was the first time Jholianna had ever invited her to her private apartments. The Supplicant was certain to guess the reason, but she simply sipped her wine.

"Carilian late harvest. It must be a special occasion."

"A visit with you is always a special occasion."

The Supplicant laughed. "You're a cool one, Earth's Beloved. I've always admired that about you."

"And you possess great power, Supplicant. I've always admired that about you. If I wanted to contact this boy, how would I go about it?"

Far from being unsettled by the sudden change of subject, the Supplicant merely tapped her goblet with a red nail. "Well, there's always prayer."

Jholianna waited, feigning patience.

"Are you certain you want to contact him?"

"No. But if I did . . . would you help me?"

"I'm your loyal servant, Earth's Beloved."

"You're the servant of the God with Two Faces. Whose wishes may—or may not—coincide with mine."

"True." The Supplicant swirled the wine in her goblet. "I thought you were still undecided about the validity of his claim."

"I am."

"Inviting him back will encourage him to believe that you're ready to acknowledge him."

"I know."

This time, it was the Supplicant who waited, her eyebrows elevated in a silent question. Jholianna chose her words with care; she respected the priestess, but she was wary of her, too.

"He has great power. Power that could be . . . useful."

"He's also young. And unpredictable. As you know. You felt his—how did you describe it?—his desire for peace between the Zherosi and the Tree People. His ties there are deep. If he suspects you're manipulating him in an effort to destroy those ties—or the Tree People—you could lose more than his support."

"That's why I'm hesitating."

"What does your heart tell you?"

"My heart?" The question shocked her. "I rule with my mind, not my heart."

The Supplicant rose. "I will pray to my god for guidance. And if I receive any definitive signs, I will tell you."

Jholianna could not escape the feeling that she had just failed an important test.

"My heart . . . wants to believe. That he's the Son of Zhe. That the gods hear our prayers and—occasionally—answer them. As to a peace between the Zherosi and the Tree People . . ."

The Supplicant watched her as intently as a fox stalking a mouse.

"A boy—however powerful—might believe that such a dream is possible. But I've lived a very long time, Supplicant. And I no longer put much faith in dreams."

"But it is only in our dreams—our visions—that we discover the will of the gods."

Jholianna gave herself the rest of the day to consider the Supplicant's words. The next morning, she sent for Vazh do Havi.

She winced when he entered leaning heavily on his stick, too stubborn and too proud to request a litter. She refused to shame him by choosing a seat near the doorway, but it was difficult to watch his slow, painful progress between the six pillars that marched down the center of the chamber.

Shafts of light from the sky-wells revealed sweat glistening on his forehead. The barrel-like body had lost flesh in recent moons, but the arms were still thick and muscular. And although he must be more than seventy years of age, his spirit was as indomitable as ever.

When he finally reached her, she patted the gaily-colored cushion beside hers. As he carefully lowered himself onto the bench, she signaled the hovering slave and pretended to observe him critically until the Khonsel's breathing eased. Only then did she lift the two goblets from the tray.

He waited for her to sip before draining his. "I didn't think there was any Carilian late harvest left."

"The Stuavo had the foresight to put aside a few crates before our relations with Carilia worsened. I'll send one to your quarters."

She gestured to the boy to refill the goblet. This time, the Khonsel sipped more slowly.

"Some food?" She nodded to the platter held by another

slave. A basket of flatbread, a bowl of jhok, a plate of skewered goat; unlike his preference for expensive wine, the Khonsel's taste in food tended toward the plain but hearty fare of the common soldier.

He nibbled a small piece of flatbread out of politeness, then shook his head. As soon as the slave hurried away, he turned to scrutinize her. His face was as wrinkled as a dried apple, but the brown eyes were still keen.

"So," he said, flexing his leg with a grunt. "The Son of Zhe."

"The Son of Zhe," she echoed. As if they were making a toast.

"The oddsmakers are giving three to one against."

"They didn't touch his spirit."

"But you did. And you're still not convinced."

"How many spirits have I touched during my reign? Hundreds. Thousands. Those of my Hosts, my priests, the false prophets . . . too many to count or remember. My brother's spirit—as ancient as mine—even his was still human. But this boy's . . ." She fumbled for the words. "It was unlike any I have ever encountered."

"Which proves he's different. Not the Son of Zhe." The Khonsel leaned against the wall and studied the ceiling, but she doubted the artistic rendering of a rosy sun peeping through a tangle of vines commanded his attention. "He may be powerful, but he's still mortal."

Their eyes met in perfect accord. No need to state explicitly the best solution to this problem. And no fear of unsettling the other by implying it. One did not rise to power—and remain there—without a certain degree of ruthlessness. But the consequences of choosing the wrong path could be deadly—for them and the empire.

"I'll do it," the Khonsel said. "You can deny any foreknowledge of the act."

"That would appease the public. But the priests?"

"I'm old. My wits are wandering. I mistook him for the boy who killed my best friend."

She caught the faint note of bitterness in his voice. So he still mourned Malaq after all these years. How fortunate for both to have shared such a friendship.

"You may be old, but your wits are firmly in place." She

rested her palm briefly on the back of his hand, conscious of the loose, dry skin and the raised fretwork of veins. "That's why I wanted your counsel."

He stared into his goblet, frowning. "We could wait. See if he comes back. That'll give us time."

"Whether or not he's the Son of Zhe, he's wreaking havoc on the peace of my holy city. The sooner we decide how to deal with him, the better."

"All the choices are risky. If we don't acknowledge his claim, we could alienate him. If we try to . . . eliminate him and fail . . ."

"That would definitely alienate him," Jholianna said dryly.

The Khonsel's grin quickly faded. "Once you proclaim him Son of Zhe, there's no turning back. And if he's a fraud—"

"Does it matter?"

The shaggy eyebrows soared, and she had the rare pleasure of knowing she had surprised him.

"Times are bad," she said. "The rebellion among the Tree People. The slave revolt in the east. The war with Carilia."

"We've faced bad times before."

"The people need the Son of Zhe. They need hope."

"Last time, that hope turned around to bite us in the . . . posterior. Begging your pardon, Earth's Beloved."

"Kheridh was stolen from his home, brought here as a slave. And still Malaq was able to win his trust—and his love."

"And it cost Malaq his life." The Khonsel's voice was flat, but his eyes flashed.

Because Malaq made the mistake of loving him in return, she thought. Unwilling to criticize him to the Khonsel, she merely said, "Perhaps if he'd had more time, he might have won Kheridh to our cause."

"That's what you hope to do? Win this boy to our cause?"

"You disagree?"

"Why would the Son of Zhe want peace between us and the Tree People?"

"Men are dying on both sides. Perhaps he objects to it.

After all, his foster-father is one of the Tree People. And his mother."

She was the real threat. That scrawny, white-haired crone Jholianna had glimpsed. The one who held Rigat's heart and his loyalty.

But she's far away. And I'm here.

"All the more reason to avoid any talk of peace," the Khonsel insisted. "His ties in the north jeopardize our interests."

"He's heard only their side of the story. We'll give him ours—and let him judge the truth for himself."

"And if he orders us to suspend the logging? Or withdraw altogether?"

She swirled the golden wine, considering. "We stall for time. Explain the difficulties. Offer him new experiences to distract him. The respect the Tree People have withheld. The acceptance he craves. The worship of thousands. A heady combination for any man, but for a young one?"

"You talk as if were an ordinary boy."

"In some ways, he is. He's neither all-knowing nor all-wise. I touched doubt and insecurity. A desire for recognition. Pride. He enjoys showing off his powers. Proving himself to others. And he is . . . attracted to me."

The Khonsel gave a sort of growl and shifted awkwardly on his cushion.

"I'm envisioning another sort of seduction, Khonsel." She cut off his protest with an impatient gesture. "I'll avoid official recognition as long as possible, but I cannot risk losing him. Or the power he wields."

The Khonsel muttered something under his breath.

"Yes?"

"I was wondering what the oddsmakers would give this venture."

"What odds would *you* give me?"

"You are Earth's Beloved," he said stiffly. "Even the son of a god would have difficulty resisting your . . . blandishments."

"That's a courtier's speech. From Vazh do Havi, I expect bluntness."

He drained the wine in his goblet. "Two to one. Against."

"It's hardly worth the wager."

"The odds might be low, but the stakes are high. It's a dangerous game, Earth's Beloved."

She sipped her wine, observing him over the rim of the goblet. "That's what makes it interesting."

Chapter 26

RIGAT WAS SHOCKED WHEN Fellgair told him the queen wished to see him. Their encounter must have been less disastrous than he had feared. Perhaps she expected gods—and their progeny—to be cruel. Or perhaps, as Fellgair insisted, she simply wished to harness his power for Zheros.

"If you allow that, she will control the game, not you."

"Is that all this is to you? A game?"

"Ignore my phrasing," Fellgair replied, deftly avoiding an answer. "But not my advice."

Although their meeting was arranged for midday, Rigat decided the best way to control the game was to catch her off guard. So just before dawn, he opened a portal onto the balcony of her bedchamber.

Fellgair had neglected to mention the fountain. He had to sidestep past it in order to ease through the portal. Stone benches flanked the walls; a canopy had been erected against the one to his left. He could picture the queen sitting there, shielded from the heat of the morning sun, listening to the gentle splash of the fountain, breathing in the heavy aroma of the flowers that filled the urns.

The gauzy draperies across the doorway stirred in the faint breeze. He parted them cautiously and stepped inside.

Two sky-wells brightened the right side of the chamber. Between them, golden torchlight filtered through a doorway, illuminating a large stone dais in the far corner of the chamber. A white-garbed figure moved restlessly atop a pile of fleeces. Another snored softly on the pallet at the foot of the bed.

He heard the shuffle of sandaled feet outside the chamber, the whispers of the guards. Abandoning his plan to approach the bed, he summoned his power and gently touched the queen's spirit.

She was dreaming. Wandering through a sort of maze. He could feel her frustration grow as each turn led to another corridor, a blank wall, an empty sky-well.

This way.

Her dream-self turned, seeking the source of the voice.

On the balcony. Wake, my queen. Wake and come to me.

Hidden in the shadows of the balcony, he waited.

The draperies parted. In her flowing nightdress she looked as if she were clothed in a waterfall. Her long black hair only added to the illusion of night-dark water and frothing foam. As she padded toward him, he caught the fragrance of her perfume. Her gaze took in his doeskin tunic and breeches. After a moment's hesitation, her fingers sought his.

Against his will, the warmth of her flesh stirred him. It was easy to see only her beauty, her youth, and forget that she had lived for hundreds of years, ruling over an empire whose warriors had raided his people's villages, enslaved women and children, and kidnapped his brother.

Deliberately, Rigat called up the face of the mother in the mountain village, the weight of the child in his arms, the soft voices singing around the fire. His people. Just like those of the Oak and Holly.

He squeezed the queen's hand and watched her mouth curve in a smile.

"You came back," she whispered.

"The Supplicant told you I would."

"I expected you later. I was going to receive you properly this time. Food and wine . . . I had a new gown . . ." She laughed soundlessly. "Foolishness."

"I thought you'd be angry. Because I hurt you."

"I thought you'd be angry. Because I fought you. And because I doubted."

"And now you believe?"

"I don't know. Forgive me, Rigat."

Somehow, his name became musical when she spoke it, the *R* deep and throaty, the rest a mere exhalation of breath.

"There's something I want to show you," he said. "Will you come with me?"

"Where?"

"To my . . . to the land of the Tree People."

She glanced over her shoulder. "I must tell Lady Alikia. My attendant. If she finds me gone—"

"I'll wait."

He stood in the doorway, listening to their soft voices. Lady Alikia laid something over the queen's shoulders, then knelt before her. When the queen returned, she wore sandals and a cloak.

Lady Alikia followed her onto the balcony, wide-eyed and trembling. Graceful despite her bulk, she prostrated herself at his feet. Then her head came up. "My lord, you'll see that no harm comes to Earth's Beloved?"

The queen gave an annoyed hiss. "You must not speak to him so."

"Forgive me, Earth's Beloved. But if anything should happen . . ." Her jowls trembled and tears filled her soft, brown eyes.

Rigat held out his hands. She hesitated a moment before grasping them, then let out a long breath as if relieved to discover that his fingers were mere flesh and bone.

"I'll bring your queen back soon. And I swear she'll be safe with me."

He started as she suddenly bent and pressed her lips to the back of one hand and then the other. A single tear, warm and wet, slid between his forefinger and thumb.

"You're lucky," he said to the queen, "to inspire such love in those who serve you."

"Yes." The queen kissed Lady Alikia on the cheek. "Tell anyone who inquires that I am in seclusion until mid-morning."

"Yes, Earth's Beloved."

When he opened the portal, Lady Alikia gaped. The queen merely stared at the shadowy silhouettes of the trees.

"Close your eyes," he told her. "It's easier that way."

Just before he sealed the portal behind them, a horn
blared, signaling the dawn sacrifices. Then there was only
the sweeter chorus of birdsong and stream.

Her eyes opened. He heard her quick intake of breath.
Although it was still too dark to see much, she turned in
a slow circle, her gaze traveling up the tree trunks to the
pale blue chinks of sky. She stroked the rough bark of a
pine, a moss-furred boulder. Then she walked down to
the bank of the stream and crouched down to scoop up
a handful of water. A shiver ran through her as she
sipped, as if she were drinking the water of the Summerlands.

He led her to the tumble of boulders where he had
hidden during the hunt with Darak. So long ago, that
seemed now. Kneeling together on his mantle, they
waited.

She was as still and silent as any hunter; only her eyes
moved, ceaselessly scanning the forest. Yet she failed to
spot the herd of does among the trees until he squeezed
her hand. She caught her breath, her eyes wide.

The lead doe cautiously scented the breeze, then moved
toward the stream. The others followed, some accompanied
by fawns, others whose bulging sides showed that they
would calve within days. The spindly legs of the fawns
trembled visibly as they walked down the steep bank. One,
bolder than the others, picked his way across the stream,
endearing in his awkwardness. His mother trotted after
him, nosing him gently when he faltered. Slowly, the rest
of the herd crossed the stream and vanished like spirits into
the pattern of sunlight and shadow.

Still staring after them, the queen slowly rose. "This is
where you live?"

"No. It's my . . . special place. Where my father gave me
my first glimpse of Zheros."

Her expression sharpened. "It was you, then? Who appeared at the adder pit? It was too dark to see clearly."

Not too dark to keep the guard from hurling a spear at
him, he thought. But he merely nodded.

"What did he look like? Your father."

"A fox."

Her head jerked toward him. "A fox?"

"I thought at first he was my vision mate. Until he opened the portal."

"Why would Zhe appear to you as a fox?"

Rigat shrugged. "Gods can take any form they please, I guess. He probably thought a fox would be less frightening than a giant winged serpent."

She laughed, her voice as musical as the stream. "Is your village nearby?"

"Not too far," he replied, unwilling to give away its location.

"In this forest?"

When he shook his head, she sighed, her gaze sweeping the trees again. "A pity. It's so beautiful here. Once Zheros had forests like this. But that was long ago."

"What was it like? When you were young?"

"Plains where the grass grew higher than my waist. Mountains wreathed with clouds. Pretty little streams like this one. And forests where it was always cool, even at Midsummer."

"Did you live in the palace?"

"No. Just a simple house. Everything was simpler, then." A frown creased her forehead. Then she smiled. "There were only forty or fifty families in Pilozhat when I was born. We all lived inside the fortress. In mud-brick houses clustered against the walls." Her expression grew soft. "Ours had a little courtyard in the middle. With a fountain. And a tiny garden where my mother grew herbs and flowers."

"Scarlet flowers?" When she started, he added, "I saw them. When I touched your spirit."

She nodded, but her expression was wary now. Cursing himself for spoiling the pleasant mood, he said, "My mother gathers wildflowers. She ties them into bunches and hangs them from the thatch to dry."

A wave of longing suffused him. For his mam. His family. His home.

"You miss her."

He scuffed at the pine needles with the toe of his shoe. "We were . . . close. But I was always different. No one in my family really knew me."

"She did. You began your life in her body. A mother never forgets that bond. Or so I imagine."

Abruptly, she walked away. He watched her anxiously, uncertain if he had said something else to disturb her or if the weight of her memories oppressed her.

She swung toward him again, her face stark. "That was why we Shed. The first time. Jholin and I. We had no children. No one to rule after us."

Fellgair had offered a theory about why the queen had failed to bear a child, even after hundreds of Sheddings. "She conceived. Several times. But she never managed to carry a child to term. Even I'm not sure why, but I think it must be the qiij."

More likely, the fault was Jholin's. Surely that was the youth he had seen when he touched her spirit. How could that frail, spindly creature father a healthy child? But he could never share that suspicion with her.

"I'm sorry," he said. "I've made you unhappy."

"This is too beautiful a place for such memories. Thank you for bringing me. I understand now why your mother's people worship trees."

Eagerly, he strode toward her. "And can you understand why they would fight to keep your people from cutting them down?"

"My people? Are they not yours as well?"

"Of course." He suppressed a wince at his lapse. "But I know this land—and its people—far better."

"We shall have to remedy that."

"You didn't answer my question."

"I can understand why any people would fight to keep their land."

"It's more than that. We believe the trees are alive. That each has a spirit inside it—just like we do. To us, cutting down a tree is murder."

"And this is why you came to Zheros? To stop the logging?"

"And the fighting."

"Without timber, we cannot build ships. Without ships, we cannot trade. Our empire would die. We would become the little people we once were. Would the Son of Zhe wish that?"

"No," he said slowly. "But there must be a way. One that would satisfy both peoples."

"Compromise never satisfies anyone." Her hand came

up to brush his cheek. "I wish I had your optimism. But after five hundred years, I have little faith in men."

"And the gods? Do you have faith in them?"

"I only know that in all the years I've prayed to them, they have never spoken to me. Or shown their faces."

He wished he could tell her one god had spoken to her for generations. But that was Fellgair's secret to reveal, not his.

"Faith is believing without proof."

She grimaced. "My priests remind me of that all the time. But still, I doubt."

"I don't know how else to convince you of who I am. But I can tell you the gods exist. My foster-father knew the Holly-Lord. And my mother bargained with the Trickster. If the gods of the Tree People are real, those of the Zherosi must be, too."

Rigat took her hands in his. "My father told me I was created to change things. And I think the greatest change I could bring about would be an end to the fighting between the Tree People and the Zherosi. All I'm asking for now is a truce. To give us time to come up with a lasting solution."

She studied him as intently as Fellgair ever had. "The Zherosi will do as I command. Will the Tree People trust you to speak for them?"

They didn't even know who he was. The one man who had witnessed his power had called him an abomination. But there was another they would trust.

"My foster-father. Everyone will listen to him. And he'll listen to me. I know he will. He doesn't want this war. If you order a truce, he'll get the rebels to honor it. We could find him now," he added, his excitement growing.

She shook her head, smiling. "I've abandoned my duties for too long. And tomorrow is the Midsummer rite. You must remain for that."

He hesitated, reluctant to let even a day go by before setting his plan in motion.

She squeezed his hands. "And you must help me plan a fitting celebration to welcome the Son of Zhe."

"Then you . . . you do believe?"

Her thumb caressed his palm. "Perhaps I have faith after all."

Chapter 27

THREE HUNDRED PEOPLE FILLED the royal dining hall for the Midsummer feast. The fortunate ones like the council members had the privilege of sitting on the dais with Rigat and the queen. The rest were squeezed shoulder to shoulder on either side of the low wooden tables that stretched from dais to doorway.

The air was stifling, the din incredible, the smoke from the incense so thick that it obscured the paintings on the ceiling, if not the reek of perfumed oil and sweat. Torches blazed along muraled walls and in standing lamps as tall as a man. Everywhere, the soft gleam of gold and bronze vied with the brighter sparkle of gemstones.

Rich ladies and merchants, city officials and noblemen all craned their necks to watch him eat, just like the poor folk in the mountain village. Instead of two musicians, there were twenty playing on the balcony above him, although no one beyond the dais was likely to hear them. Instead of fermented milk and roasted goat, there were chilled fruit juices and heady wines, dozens of platters of meat and fish, overflowing bowls of fruits and nuts.

Fortunately, the slaves served the queen first so he could mimic her behavior: draping the scrap of flaxcloth across his lap before eating; dipping his fingertips into the bowl of water instead of drinking it as he had intended. As the feast went on, he was relieved to discover that the Zherosi seemed to eat and drink much like the children of the Oak and Holly, although the number of dishes presented by the slaves was staggering.

He recognized the rabbits cooked in a thick cream sauce. And the partridges and woodcocks, although he'd never seen them served with their feathered wings intact. He burned his mouth on the crusted spices coating the slabs of mutton and gaped at the gaudy tail plumes that adorned the roast pheasant.

The queen had to identify the more exotic dishes: seaweed pottage; fried squid; boiled langhosti, whose sweet flesh belied its hard shell and wicked-looking claws; pungent greens and crisp vegetables called kugi, blissfully refreshing after the spicy meats. And tiny smoked eels.

"They look like fingers," he said, eyeing them distrustfully. "And they're probably just as chewy."

"Let's see."

She raised his hand and gently nipped his forefinger, offering a teasing smile and a fleeting flick of her tongue.

He shifted uncomfortably on his cushion, grateful that the bulky folds of his khirta hid his arousal. The queen had chosen the shimmering scarlet fabric herself, as well as the ring that adorned his right hand—a rare bloodstone that was completely red save for a few tiny speckles of black. She had also ordered the belt of beaten gold, the bracelets that clasped his biceps, and the jewel-studded sheath for his ceremonial dagger. And the dagger—it was even more beautiful than the one Keirith had given him, the bronze blade etched with spiraling serpents, the hilt wrapped in gold wire.

Amazing that she had procured all this finery in a day. Even more amazing that she would bother with such details. But nothing escaped her notice, including his shocked look as countless platters of uneaten food—enough to feed his village for days—were returned to the kitchens. He was relieved when she assured him that it would be distributed to the poor.

She had been just as discerning at the dawn sacrifice to Zhe. In response to her anxious inquiry, he'd managed a shaky smile as the handsome young man ascended the steps to the altar. He tried not to envision Keirith lying on the slab of stone, to remain impassive when the Zheron lifted the ceremonial dagger. But it was one thing to understand that blood strengthened and honored their god and another to watch the Zheron reach into the man's chest and raise his dripping heart skyward. Just as it was impossible to forget that Darak would have been sacrificed like this if not for the earthquake that had shaken Pilozhat.

He'd had to remind himself to look past the horrors that had befallen his family. Only then could he reluctantly acknowledge the artistry of the sacrifice: the first red rays of the sun bathing the man's body; the priest's knife darting like a minnowfly. The triumphant shouts of the crowd drowned out the bellows of the kankhs, and every face was filled with joy, with pride, with the knowledge that this nameless man had ensured Zhe's strength to carry the sun through the waning half of the year.

That's how they'll cheer when the queen presents me to her people.

My people.

It was a pity he'd have to wait half a moon for that. The queen insisted that they postpone his official recognition until she could organize a proper celebration. As if this feast wasn't grand enough.

He nodded to a hovering slave who spooned honeyed figs into a small bronze bowl. Like the man who had offered himself to Zhe, the slaves serving them were Zherosi. All looked sleek and well-fed—better fed than the folk in his village. But their presence made him uncomfortable, and he was glad to be distracted by the arrival of the dancers.

As he watched them weave a serpentine path across the tiled floor, a thought struck him. "How many of the Tree People are slaves in Zheros?"

The queen frowned, but he wasn't sure if she was displeased by his question or simply gathering her thoughts.

"It's been years since we raided the northern villages. The commanders of our fortresses try to maintain good relations with the Tree People living nearby."

"Of course. But that doesn't answer my question." He smiled to soften the reproof.

"A few hundred, perhaps." Her shrug indicated that she thought the number insignificant.

Rigat hesitated. She had agreed to proclaim him the Son of Zhe. She was considering a truce. If he pushed too hard, he risked losing her support.

"May I make a request?" Receiving a wary nod, he

asked, "As a token of your goodwill—toward me—I'd like you to free the slaves. And send them back to their homeland."

Her frown deepened. "It would take half a moon—longer—to census each estate, determine who owned slaves from the north, organize ships to—"

"Ships sail north all the time, don't they? Carrying troops and supplies to the fortresses. And surely you have enough administrators to conduct this . . . census."

Her dark eyes studied him. Then she smiled. "If it would please you, of course it will be done. Perhaps we could even include their departure in the festivities that follow your proclamation as the Son of Zhe."

Rigat seized her hand eagerly. "I could address each ship before it left. Give them food and water for the voyage. Maybe even—"

"Remind them of the beneficence of the Zherosi queen?"

Rigat laughed. "That, too." He raised her hand to his lips. "Thank you, Jholianna."

After far too little sleep, he set out the next day in search of Darak. He found him quickly enough, but it was impossible to speak with him alone. Close to a hundred men and women accompanied him now, all vying for the opportunity to walk with the Spirit-Hunter, eat with the Spirit-Hunter, do everything, it seemed, but piss with the Spirit-Hunter.

Realizing his best chance of catching Darak alone was to draw him out of camp after dark, he decided to seek out Keirith. He hadn't had a chance to talk with him since Fellgair took him to Zheros and he was eager to tell his brother everything that had happened.

He found the rebels camped on a hilltop overlooking a narrow lake. Hidden behind his mist-shield, he called Keirith and waited impatiently for him to respond to the summons. When he arrived, Rigat thought he looked tired and edgy, but perhaps that was only from the strain of fighting. Still, he was surprised when Keirith failed to hug him and just asked brusquely where he had been.

"In Zheros. Arranging a truce." He had the satisfaction

of seeing Keirith's eyes widen. "I've taken up the mantle of Son of Zhe."

"You've what?"

"Don't worry. I haven't told them you're alive. Just worked a few bits of magic and touched the queen's spirit to convince her. She's going to recognize me officially in half a moon. And has agreed to free all the children of the Oak and Holly still enslaved in Zheros. But the best thing is she's willing to consider a truce—if the rebels agree. I'm going to see Darak today. He's the only one who can convince them."

Keirith just stared at him. Rigat had expected surprise—even shock—but he'd hoped his brother would share his triumph. Merciful gods, he'd accomplished more in a sennight than the rebels had in years.

Then Keirith swallowed hard, and Rigat cursed himself for his stupidity. Any discussion of Zheros would conjure awful memories for Keirith and spark fears that he would suffer a similar fate.

"I'm sorry. I shouldn't have blurted it all out like that. But you mustn't worry. Everything's going just as I planned. Better." He peered at his brother uncertainly. "Are you all right? You look awful."

"I'm just tired."

"You've had more nightmares, haven't you?"

Keirith looked down at the grass. "It's nothing."

"When this is all over, I'll help you get rid of Xevhan. If he's there. I promise."

Keirith nodded. "You can't trust the queen. You know that."

"Oh, aye. But I *can* make sure she sends the orders for the truce. And you can start working on Temet. Get him to call off the attacks on the Zherosi now. As a measure of good faith. Just tell him you had a vision."

He thought Keirith winced, but it was hard to tell with his head bowed. The nightmares must be bad. Or maybe he was still having trouble contacting his spirit guide.

And now I've reminded him of that, too.

Unwilling to shame him by probing, Rigat just repeated, "You're sure you're all right?"

"Aye."

"And you'll talk to Temet?"

"Aye. Is there anything else? Anything you want to tell me?"

Keirith fixed him with such a piercing stare that Rigat drew back. What was the matter with him? Torn between bewilderment and impatience, he snapped, "Nay. That's all. Just . . . take care of yourself."

Keirith nodded and turned to go. Then he strode forward and flung his arms around Rigat. "Be careful. It's not a game you're playing. Your life may depend upon it. And Fa's."

"And yours and Faelia's and everyone's. I know, Keirith." Rigat eased free, nettled that his brother had so little faith in his judgment.

He opened a portal onto one of his secret places. It was just a grassy meadow watered by a small stream, but the scarlet poppies filled it with color. Unwilling to linger on his unsettling encounter with Keirith, he stretched out on the grass, hoping to snatch a little sleep before he met with Darak.

The hard earth beneath him was a far cry from the luxurious chamber he had slept in last night. The goose down pallet was so thick it was like floundering through a snowdrift. The puffy clouds that adorned the ceiling were more luminous than those floating overhead, the painted blue of the sky more brilliant than the real one.

Although Fellgair had expected him to leave the palace after the feast, he was glad now that he had stayed. What better way to demonstrate his authority than to sleep in the bedchamber of the late king?

He had reminded Fellgair of that this morning when he'd visited the temple of the God with Two Faces. For a long moment, Fellgair studied the mural that adorned one wall of his private chamber, a forest of majestic oaks in greenleafed summer splendor. Then he snapped, "Remember why you are here. And don't be seduced by soft beds and fine food. Or a woman."

Rigat scratched a midge bite, frowning. It still rankled that Fellgair should imagine him so weak—or so foolish. Of course, luxuries didn't matter. But he refused to feel guilty for enjoying them.

I'm the son of a god. And I deserve to be treated like one.

Too excited to sleep, he watched the sky fade from blue to violet to the soft gray of the gloaming. His confidence leached away with the sky's color. What if Darak didn't want to see him? What if—despite all his protestations—he was secretly relieved to be rid of him? And then there was Keirith's odd behavior. He had always been broody, but never cold. Could he be jealous of his little brother's accomplishments?

Shaking off his disquiet, Rigat summoned his power to locate Darak's camp. Except for the dozen sentries, the rebels were all asleep. He decided to wait for darkness in a stand of birches a short distance away. But moments after settling himself, he jumped to his feet and began pacing. Unable to contain his impatience, he reached out to Darak's sleeping spirit.

At first, he sensed only exhaustion. Then the stupefied confusion of sleep fled and Darak's panic slammed into him with such force that it woke an answering echo of fear in his spirit. He tamped it down, but despite the soothing energy he sent, Darak's shock hammered through him like a terrified heartbeat.

Shock, panic . . . those were reactions any man might have. But Rigat touched revulsion so deep that he was stunned. Sick at heart, he retreated, only to be inundated by Darak's memories: Morgath oozing through his spirit, whispering in his mind, taunting him with his helplessness.

Fa! It's only me. Rigat.

Instead of relief, he touched suspicion and doubt.

I didn't mean to scare you.

Even before Darak's shame flooded him, he wanted to take back the thought. He might as well be Morgath, taunting Darak for his fear.

I'm sorry. I couldn't reach you any other way. And I need to talk with you.

Darak's panic resurged. For a moment, he thought it came from the prospect of seeing him again. Then he realized the truth.

I'm fine. So's everyone else.

He hoped it was true; it had been half a moon since he'd seen Mam and Callie.

Please. I'll be waiting in the stand of birches. Across the stream and up the hill.

Gently, he withdrew from Darak's spirit, cursing himself for his missteps. First Keirith, now Darak. How was he going to convince either of them of the soundness of his plan if he made such foolish mistakes?

Even with his keen senses, he failed to hear Darak approach. Then he saw the tall figure atop the rise, black against the gray sky.

As Rigat moved out of the trees, Darak froze, then padded forward again, the long stride as easily recognizable as the silhouette. At the last moment, his steps faltered. Rigat hesitated, too. Then pride reasserted itself. He had negotiated with a queen. He refused to allow Darak to transform him into a tongue-tied child.

He took a step back just as Darak's arms came up. Quickly, he stepped into Darak's embrace, but the moment was spoiled.

"Are you well?" Darak asked.

Rigat swallowed down the lump that formed in his throat. "Aye."

"And you're certain your mam's all right? And your brothers and sister?"

Of course. It was them he was really worried about. Not me.

"They're fine. I told you."

"Is . . . is he treating you well?"

Rigat twisted away from the hand cupping the back of his neck. "It's been better than I could have dreamed."

He was acting like a child, striking out because Darak had wounded him. It was stupid to use his power to pierce the darkness and search that familiar face for a hint of genuine affection. Worse still, to find it and feel the senseless renewal of hope. He fought the urge to blurt out all the fears and doubts that plagued him, desperately wishing he could return—just for a few moments—to a time when he really had been Darak's son and the Trickster was only a god, fascinating but remote.

Instead, he told Darak about the family, then quickly turned to the subject of a truce. Darak stirred restively as he outlined his plan, but when he revealed that he was using the guise of the Son of Zhe to bring it to fruition,

Darak exclaimed, "Are you out of your mind? Have you forgotten what those people did to your brother?"

"Of course not. But Keirith wasn't the Son of Zhe."

"Neither are you!"

"Nay. But I *am* the son of the God with Two Faces. Or have you forgotten that Fellgair is worshiped in Zheros?"

"I haven't forgotten anything about Zheros! Least of all the sight of Keirith lying on an altar with his life's blood pouring out. Do you have how any idea how dangerous this is?"

"I'm not a fool."

Darak took a deep breath, clearly fighting for control. "I know you're not. But if they should discover the truth—"

"They won't. They can't. Besides, they need me. They want to believe. Even the queen."

"She might want to placate you by—"

"She's not placating me!"

"—by considering this truce. What does she have to lose? They log the forests in the winter. That gives them plenty of time to send more men north, to augment the strength of their existing garrisons, and build new fortresses along the river."

"She won't do those things," Rigat retorted with more confidence than he felt.

"She's using you."

"Nay! I'm using her. To put an end to the bloodshed and buy time to work out a permanent peace that will satisfy both the Zherosi and the Tree People."

Darak recoiled. "The Tree People?" he repeated very softly.

"It's just an expression."

"A Zherosi expression."

"What does it matter?"

"The children of the Oak and Holly are your people."

"If I am truly my father's son, the Zherosi are my people, too."

"If you're truly your father's son—"

"What? Say it." When Darak remained silent, Rigat said, "Then I will. If I'm truly my father's son, you want nothing to do with me."

"That's not—"

"I come here with the offer of a truce that could save hundreds—thousands—of lives. And you won't even consider it because I'm Fellgair's son."

"Rigat . . ."

"You think he betrayed you. Well, maybe he did. But he had his reasons. And one of them was to foster peace. And I can make that happen, although you obviously think I'm too stupid and trusting—"

"Stop putting words in my mouth!"

They were practically nose to nose, both of them breathing hard. Then Darak stepped back and let out a long sigh. "I'm just worried, is all. About you. About all that's happening. You're right—I don't know the queen. But she hasn't survived this long without being clever. And you're . . . you may be the son of a god, but you're still very young. I know you hate being reminded of that, but it's true. You're not immortal, Rigat. Your blood can stain an altar as easily as Keirith's did."

"But don't you see I have to try? As long as there's any chance for success. What were the odds that you could march into Chaos and return with Tinnean's spirit? And the Oak-Lord's? But you went all the same."

"I didn't march into Chaos. Fellgair pushed me." It was hard to read Darak's expression in the uncertain light, but the dry humor in his voice was plain enough. "As to the rest . . ." He sighed again. "You're right. I had to go. And short of killing me, there was nothing anyone could have done to stop me."

"So you'll help?"

He was silent for so long that Rigat thought he was going to refuse.

"There's a Gathering," Darak finally said. "Of several rebel bands. At the full moon."

Rigat wondered why Keirith had failed to mention it. Surely, he had to know.

"I'll talk to them, Rigat. Tell them what you've told me. But I can't tell them a truce is in our best interests when I'm not certain myself."

"But you've never supported the rebellion."

"Aye. But like it or not, I'm part of it now. And there are eighty-six young men and women who've joined it because of me."

"You have to convince them to accept a truce. You have to!"

"I'll talk to them," Darak snapped. "That's all I can promise. And scowling at me won't change my mind."

Reluctantly, Rigat smiled. "It's too dark to tell if I'm scowling."

"Aye. Well, I did live with you for thirteen years." Darak hesitated, shifting his feet. "Can you stay a while longer? Tell me what you've been doing? And . . . how your Mam is?"

Rigat knew he should return to Pilozhat, but right now, he would exchange all the feasts and soft beds and adulation in the world for the chance to sit and talk the way they used to.

"Aye. I'll stay."

Darak's hug made him catch his breath. Rigat released him reluctantly, grateful that the darkness hid his watering eyes.

Bad enough that he continued to yearn for Darak's love and approval, but even worse to accept such scraps of affection with damp-eyed gratitude. And he would always get scraps; Darak's love was reserved for the children of his blood. He had to accept that and stop longing for what he could never have.

Chapter 28

THE TOWERING THUNDERHEADS gathering over the fortress at Little Falls were as dark as Geriv's mood.

He had left Eagles Mount half a moon ago to continue his tour of inspection, taking only two members of his personal staff with him: his aide Jonaq do Mekliv and an enthusiastic Korim. Although reluctant to bring his son into the heart of rebel territory, Geriv knew he must begin treating Korim like a real officer or the boy would never win the respect of his peers. But he'd given him strict instructions to stay inside the fortresses; the situation upriver was far too unsettled for him to dash off to the neighboring villages as he was wont to do at Eagles Mount.

After a disheartening stay at Deepford, they had continued on to Little Falls, accompanied by two ships bearing troops and supplies. Geriv had quickly discovered that conditions here were even worse than at Deepford.

"The whole place stinks of fear," Jonaq muttered, brushing past Korim as he paced the parapet.

"Not surprising. With two komakhs lost in the last moon. Settle, Jonaq."

Jonaq planted his feet, but his fingers drummed an impatient tattoo against one of the logs of the palisade. "Two komakhs *presumed* lost."

"The first message was clear enough."

"And since then, there's been no word at all."

"The rebels could never take The Bluff," Geriv replied, speaking more for Korim's edification than Jonaq's. "More likely they killed the birds bearing the messages."

He had originally planned to transfer the fresh troops to The Bluff, but five days at Little Falls had convinced him to keep the men here until the second convoy arrived from Graywaters. He had helped to put down a mutiny during the first Carilian campaign. The situation at Little Falls was not that desperate, but all the ingredients were there: an isolated outpost, a string of defeats, an unseen enemy lurking nearby, and an atmosphere of smoldering tension exacerbated by bad food and monotony. Despite the lack of rebel activity in the last half-moon, the men remained holed up in the fortress, under orders from their commander to venture no farther than the river.

Geriv turned away from the compound to look out over the palisade, his frown deepening as he regarded the ship that had arrived earlier today. As bad as conditions at Little Falls were, the news it brought was worse.

Although his uncle's message was more detailed than the

queen's, both recounted the appearance of a boy claiming to be the Son of Zhe. Had the information come from more credulous sources, he would have dismissed it, but Vazh's description of the boy's powers was disturbing. Bad enough that he had invaded the queen's spirit. More shocking still, he claimed to be the foster-son of the Spirit-Hunter. And he was seeking a truce.

To agree was to admit that the rebels had them on the run. Given that encouragement, they would only attract more recruits.

He swore softly, and silently reproved himself when Korim asked, "What is it, Father? Vanel."

Geriv nodded toward the beach. "Those fires. When darkness falls, the guards will never be able to spot anyone creeping up on their position."

Jonaq spat over the palisade. "The rebels would never dare attack this fortress."

"It's that kind of assumption that's cost us dearly in the past," Geriv snapped.

"Shall I order them to extinguish the fires?" Korim asked eagerly.

"No. I'll suggest it—strongly—to the Remil. But we'll let him give the order. He's still in command, after all."

Together, they made their way down the ramp of packed earth and strode through the compound. It was easy to distinguish the fresh troops, chatting easily around their cook fires, from the silent Little Falls men. They jumped to their feet and saluted crisply enough, but their eyes watched him with mingled hope and desperation.

Observing Jonaq's grimace, he muttered, "Guard your face."

"I don't care how many komakhs they've lost," Jonaq whispered. "They should act like warriors, not whipped dogs."

The allusion was unfortunately apt. The men were either sunk in apathy or snarling at each other. According to the Remil, there had been several incidents, ranging from fist-fights to a brawl with knives. Floggings had been meted out and rations of ale cut, but clearly more drastic measures had to be taken. Soon.

He had intended to ease into the discussion during his private dinner with Remil do Fadiq, but when the man downed his fourth cup of wine, Geriv bluntly shared his concerns and asked how the Remil proposed to address them.

"I was thinking of a feast, Vanel."

Geriv took a deep breath. "We just had a feast."

"Not much of one. And that was to celebrate Midsummer." The Remil splashed more wine into his cup. "This would celebrate your continued presence at Little Falls. Unless you plan to head back to Graywaters soon?" he added hopefully.

"No."

The Remil drowned his disappointment with another gulp of wine. "I thought venison. The men would like that. And games."

"Games?"

"Footraces, archery, wrestling. That sort of thing."

He had to admit the suggestion had merit. Games would be as welcome a change from the monotony of drilling as venison would be from fish and porridge. They would also allow the men to hone their skills. A temporary stopgap, of course, but it was a start.

"An excellent idea, Remil."

"Thank you, Vanel." The man rubbed his bulbous nose, purple with broken veins, then carefully set his cup on the table. "I know what's happening. I've seen it at other outposts. Men stuck out in the middle of nowhere. Haven't seen Zheros in years. But it's worse here. Marching hither and yon looking for the rebels. Half the time finding nothing. Rest of the time, they come screaming out of the trees and then they're gone—poof! Like attacking the wind. Gets on the men's nerves. That's when the rot sets in."

"As their commanders, it's up to us to combat it." Geriv grimaced; he sounded like a sanctimonious prig. "I've seen your record. You're a good soldier."

"I'm a drunk, Vanel. That's why I was sent to this backwater. I know my troops, though. They're good men. Good fighters. But they're a long way from home and each time they go into that forest, they're scared shitless.

Begging your pardon. They need a victory to lift their spirits. But I don't even know where the gods-cursed rebels are."

"You have no way of contacting this informant you spoke of?"

"He comes and goes with one of the rebel bands. It was him who told me they were planning that ambush upriver. Near the village of some chief named Gath. I haven't heard from him since."

The Remil reached for his cup, then let his hand fall onto the table. "I just hope he's still alive. His information's been invaluable. And without it, I'm not about to send any more of my men into the forest. So they drill and pick fights with each other. And I flog them and drink. And plan games. I don't suppose you could ship us some whores? That would really lift their spirits."

Drunk or not, there were limits. He was the Vanel of the Northern Army, not a procurer.

"I wouldn't be troubling you about it, Vanel. It's just that we daren't touch the local women. And most of my boys haven't had leave since they got here. Two years is a long time between . . . well."

At his old post, Geriv had availed himself of the local pleasure house from time to time, but it had been years since he had been driven by such urges. He forgot that other men—especially young ones—were different.

"Surely, you could have made such . . . arrangements yourself."

The Remil eyed him blearily. "I haven't received any messages from Headquarters in a year. Those supplies you brought? They're the first to reach us since last autumn."

No wonder the men's uniforms were patched and worn and they were subsisting on fish and rotting millet.

"The new troops will bring this garrison up to full strength. Once reinforcements reach The Bluff, you may arrange leave for your original komakhs."

That would have to suffice; he was not about to start ferrying whores upriver.

Gods, I'd give anything for a nice, bloody battle.

"With permission, Vanel?"

"Yes?"

"Do you mean to get rid of me?"

A hesitant knock saved him from an immediate reply.

"That'll be supper," the Remil said.

At his summons, a guard in a rain-sodden cloak entered and saluted. Eyeing the brace of wood pigeons dangling from his fist, Geriv wondered if they were supposed to pluck the birds themselves.

"Your pardon for interrupting, Remil. The village chief sent these over for you."

The Remil was on his feet with astonishing quickness.

"The boy who brought them insisted we give them to you at once. So you could have them for your meal tonight, he said."

"Is the boy still here?"

"Yes, Remil. At the gate. Shall I bring him in?"

"No. Just tell him to give Birat my thanks."

As the guard saluted and withdrew, the Remil tossed the birds onto the table. Geriv watched him paw through the plump bodies, appalled. Clearly, the food situation was even more desperate than he had realized if the prospect of wood pigeon for supper excited the man so.

The Remil settled back on his haunches, his grin revealing a broken front tooth. "He's back."

He pushed aside the neck feathers of one bird. Apparently, it had been caught in a snare for the sinew bit deep into its broken neck, trapping a cluster of green leaves against the gray feathers. Only when Geriv bent closer did he realize that the leaves were carefully tied in place with a tiny strand of sinew.

"The chief knows about your informant?"

"It was Birat's idea to use him." The Remil snatched his cloak from a hook by the door. "He'll be waiting for us in the usual place."

"He won't bolt if he sees two men instead of one?"

"He trusts me. But I'll go first. You should hear for yourself what he has to say."

"Won't there be talk if we're seen leaving the fortress this late?"

"It's still light out." The Remil's grin widened. "And I can always let it slip that the Vanel insisted on nosing around the fortifications again."

The storm had left the hills a morass of mud. Geriv slogged after the Remil, reflecting grimly that anyone watching their lurching progress would suspect they were both drunk. He had to clutch at tree stumps and saplings to keep from falling on his face. By the time they approached the crest of the second hill, he was caked in mud up to his calves.

The queer half-light of the gloaming painted the land a monotonous gray, but he could make out the new growth that had sprung up since the trees had been cut. The damnable forest was relentless, always battling back no matter how ruthlessly they cleared it.

The Remil held up his hand, and Geriv halted. Peering through the gloom, he watched do Fadiq zigzag along the top of the hill then come to an abrupt halt. For a moment, Geriv thought he was conversing with a stump. Then the stump shot skyward and became a man's silhouette. After a protracted conversation—clearly, the spy was reluctant to have a third party join them—the Remil waved him forward.

Geriv instinctively veered left to keep the spy on his good side. He looked wiry but strong, with a quiver of arrows on his back, a bow slung across his chest, and a sword at his hip.

There were no introductions; the Remil simply gestured to the man to speak.

"There's to be a Gathering of several bands. At the full moon. Three days southwest of here."

The spy's information about the site was concise and detailed, from the description of the hill to the easiest trails to reach it. But he could only guess at the numbers in the other rebel bands and the likely routes they would take.

When Geriv learned that the Spirit-Hunter's son and daughter were with one group and the Spirit-Hunter himself with another, his heartbeat quickened. By the time the man finished speaking, his palms were damp.

The Remil had not exaggerated his value. The information he had given them tonight might be enough to crush the rebellion forever. If they chose to act on it.

With or without a truce, the Spirit-Hunter's foster-son

would seek vengeance if anything happened to his family. Was it worth risking his anger? Especially if he possessed even greater power than his brother?

He asked a few questions about the Spirit-Hunter and his two children, careful to keep his voice casual. The spy's answers only confirmed the idea forming in his mind.

The hill had too little cover to conceal his men, and if the rebel scouts spotted his troops, the rest would scatter. Besides, the bands were likely to straggle in over the course of a day. Even if he succeeded in ambushing the first, the others would escape.

The Spirit-Hunter and his children—they're the primary targets.

He'd send a messenger by ship to Deepford. Let them deal with the third band. Then he could deploy the forces of Little Falls against the others.

The spy jolted him from his thoughts by demanding, "So what are you going to do?"

Because Geriv needed him, he was careful to banish any trace of anger from his voice before replying. "I'm still deciding."

The spy eyed him a long moment. "You don't know me. And you've only the Remil's word that I can be trusted. But I was nearly killed when your troops attacked Gath's village. This time, I want to know the when and where ahead of time. You want the Spirit-Hunter? Just look for an old man with fingers missing on both hands. You want to target his son or daughter? They're easy, too. He looks like a Zheroso. She's got fiery red hair and a temper to match. Me—I don't stand out so much. So if you're going to attack my band, I mean to be out of the way. And seeing how useful I've been, I'd think you'd prefer that as well."

"You *have* been useful," Geriv replied. "Why? What made you turn against your people?"

"My people are in the village across the river."

"But you've lived with the rebels. Fought with them. Can you simply stand by and watch them die?"

He thought the man winced, but all he said was, "The rebellion will fail. Even with the Spirit-Hunter. Better it fail now than drag on for years." He shifted his feet restively. "It wasn't an easy choice I made two years ago. It hasn't gotten any easier since. I pray for the spirit of every comrade I've helped to kill. And I pray that this time, you'll land a blow hard enough to crush the rebellion for good. So we can mourn our dead and get on with our lives. Now where and when do you plan to attack?"

Geriv stiffened. It had been a long time since anyone had spoken to him in such a peremptory tone. That the man was a traitor made it all the more disagreeable. But again, he kept any hint of distaste from his voice.

"Battle plans are not drawn up in an instant. The Remil and I need to discuss our options. But first, I want you to tell me everything you know about the Spirit-Hunter's village."

Darkness had finally fallen when he made his way to his quarters. Pujh greeted him with a muted tirade about the benefits of a good night's sleep, but Geriv was too pleased with his night's work to admonish him.

He woke Jonaq and gave him his orders, then summoned his scribe and dictated a terse message to his uncle, begging him to convince the queen to postpone any decision regarding a truce until he had completed his inspection of the river fortifications. Vazh would suspect there was more to it than that, but it was all he dared reveal; if Rigat had the temerity to invade the queen's spirit, he would not scruple at attacking Vazh.

His scribe secured the leather cords around the tablet-box and handed it to him to seal. Geriv dripped wax onto the two knots, pressed his ring firmly into the congealing puddle, and tied on the small copper tag that indicated the message was urgent.

He prayed that his uncle could sway the queen and that, together, they would find a way to keep the reputed Son of Zhe in Pilozhat. If—gods forbid—Rigat discovered his plan, at least Vazh and the queen would be spared.

And if his wrath falls upon me, it will be worth it.

Chapter 29

DARAK SCRAMBLED UP the hill after the excited young scout. As he swerved to avoid a blackthorn, he spotted the other man through the screen of trees. He didn't know their names; in his effort to remain aloof, he'd steadfastly refused to learn the names of all the recruits. For his purposes, these two were the Chatterer and Cleft Chin.

"Almost there," the Chatterer said. "You'll see it. Plain as day. And no more than a two-day march. Or three. Depending on whether we wait for Sorig and the others. Mind that root, Spirit-Hunter. I nearly snagged my foot."

That the boy managed to keep from falling on his face was a miracle, since he insisted on glancing back every other word to ensure Darak was still behind him.

"They should have been back by now, don't you think? Sorig and the others, I mean."

"Aye."

"They've been gone a whole day. Day and a half, really."

"Aye."

"I know Sorig can take care of himself, but my cousin's with him. Iann. The tall fair-haired lad? With a bit of a squint to his left eye? Oh, gods. Don't let on that I mentioned that. I always tell him it's hardly noticeable, and he's sensitive about it, the silly gawk."

Mercifully, they had reached the summit where Cleft Chin greeted him by pointing west.

"There. What did I tell you, Spirit-Hunter? Plain as day."

To give the Chatterer his due, the hill *was* as plain as day, even to his aging eyes. Black Hill, Sorig had called it. Grass must have sprung up since last summer's fire, for the summit looked distinctly green now. No wonder Temet had chosen it for the Gathering. From that vantage point, they would be able to spy an approaching force for miles.

"So what do you think, Spirit-Hunter? Two days?"

Darak scanned the narrow valley. Although it was only early afternoon, the trail lay deep in shadow. According to Sorig, it wound west for three miles before the land leveled out.

"There's little chance of encountering a Zherosi patrol so far from Little Falls," Sorig had assured him. "But I'll take a few men and scout ahead. I'd rather be late to the Gathering than get trapped in that valley."

That was a day and a half ago.

"We can make it in two days easy," the Chatterer said. "If we start now. But if we wait for Sorig—"

"Let the Spirit-Hunter think."

Although Cleft Chin had spoken kindly, the Chatterer's face turned scarlet. He started to stammer an apology, then clamped his lips together.

As Darak studied the terrain to the north, Cleft Chin said, "Someone's coming."

Peering through the trees, Darak made out three men, running flat out through the valley. Without waiting for orders, the Chatterer plunged back down the hill to alert the others.

"Your eyes are better than mine," Darak said to Cleft Chin. "Are those Sorig's men?"

"I think it's the ones you sent out this morning. The one in front looks like Owan. The skinny, red-haired lad."

Like the Chatterer, Cleft Chin had noted his reluctance to learn the names of the recruits.

After watching a few moments longer, Darak said, "Stay here and keep watch."

Cleft Chin nodded, and Darak retreated down the slope. The others were clustered around the Chatterer, but they broke off their eager questioning as he approached.

"You," he said, pointing at the Chatterer. "Come with me. The rest of you, into the trees. No one moves until we know what's happening."

As they scattered up the sides of the hills, Darak trot-ted along the trail until it plunged into the valley. Waving the Chatterer off to his right, he strung his bow and nocked an arrow. Then he crouched behind a fallen tree and waited.

As the three men struggled up the rise, he glanced up and discovered that Cleft Chin had changed position, ma-neuvering along the ridge so he could watch both him and the valley below.

He's smart, that one.

But, of course, he was one of the older recruits. Most were as young as Sorig, but there were a dozen or so like Cleft Chin—grown men, wise in the ways of the forest—who seemed to have joined because they wanted to fight for the cause, not enjoy an adventure.

The red-haired scout had already passed when Darak rose. The other two shied like startled deer. The sudden rustling of leaves made the lad—Owan, he conceded reluctantly—skid to a halt.

"Are you being followed?"

Owan shook his head.

"Catch your breath. Then tell me what happened."

It came out in bits and pieces. As one lad paused for breath, another took up the story. But their information was clear enough. A full komakh. More than one hundred strong. Heading due south. No sign of Sorig's scouts. The column had stopped at the western entrance of the valley and sent eleven men ahead.

Clearly, despite Rigat's confidence, the orders for a truce had not reached these troops. More likely, the queen had never sent them.

"You're sure of the numbers?" he asked.

The small lad with the birthmark on his cheek nodded. "We climbed a hill. And counted as they passed through a big clearing."

"You did well. All of you."

Grins split their sweat-streaked faces at the praise.

"What should we do?" Owan asked. "Divide our force and catch them between us?"

"Better to take the high ground and shoot from there," Birthmark argued. "Once they're in the valley—"

"They're trapped," Darak said. "So why would they come into the valley?"

"They don't know we're here," Birthmark said. "They couldn't have seen us."

"And if they did," Broken Nose added, "they might think they can trap us."

"Aye," Darak conceded. "But only if they have another force behind us."

Three heads jerked east, then slowly turned back to him.

"They wouldn't venture so far from Little Falls unless they were hunting us."

Three heads bobbed in agreement.

"So. Chances are they know we're here. Or at least they know the direction we're heading. Which means someone betrayed us."

"Who?" Birthmark demanded. "We haven't ventured near a village in a sennight."

"A hunter could have seen us," Owan said. "And told his chief. If his chief sent word to the Zherosi—"

"It would take days," Birthmark argued.

"And he wouldn't know for sure that we'd continue west," Broken Nose said.

Unless the informant was one of their own. Someone who knew the location of the Gathering and the route they were taking to reach it.

Darak silenced the boys with an impatient wave. "If the Zherosi know we're here, they also know our strength. They'd never come after us with a force only a little larger than ours. There has to be another column somewhere."

Owan nodded. "Behind us, you said."

"If they were counting on us going through the valley."

"You think . . ." Broken Nose licked his lips uncertainly. "You think the column meant for us to see them? To draw us into a trap?"

"It's possible."

"What should we do, Spirit-Hunter?" Owan asked again. And again, the three faces lifted to his, eyes wide and trusting.

Chaos take me, how should I know? I'm not a warrior. Or a shaman. The Zherosi might be marching into the valley right now or they might have doubled back. The second force could be a mile away or five. They could be hidden in the hills to the north or circling up from the south or coming up behind us.

He thrust aside his frustration and gathered his thoughts. On a forced march from Little Falls, the Zherosi would have had no time to flank them, but if they had known about the route for days, they could have set up an ambush. With three or four hundred men, they could encircle the entire area. But they had never sent such a force against the rebels.

Until now, they never had an opportunity to capture Darak Spirit-Hunter.

Every moment he delayed, the net was closing.

"We move north." -

"North?" Birthmark echoed.

"If they think we might scatter, the logical direction for us to go is south. To draw them farther away from their fortress. So we'll go north."

And pray the Zherosi weren't waiting for them.

He sent some of the older recruits to scout ahead and guard their flanks. Cleft Chin and five others made up the rear guard. He remained with the main group, comprised of the newest and least experienced recruits, hoping his presence would ensure calm.

The first few miles were the worst: starting at every cracking twig, every rustle in the underbrush; struggling up steep rises and slipping, sliding down the other side; always pushing the pace, exhorting stragglers, and glancing back over his shoulder for any sign of pursuit.

The afternoon was waning when Cleft Chin caught up with them. Darak led him away from the others, who slumped to the ground, heads bowed in exhaustion.

Cleft Chin sank onto a fallen log and took a deep swig from his waterskin. "They're following us. No more than a few miles behind."

"Damn."

"They have a guide. One of our people."

Which explained how the Zherosi had been able to pick up their trail so quickly.

"How many?" Darak asked.

"About two hundred."

More than twice their number—and experienced troops, not raw recruits.

"It's either west or east, then," he said, thinking aloud. "I chose poorly last time. What would you do?"

Cleft Chin looked startled at being asked his opinion, but said, "East is safer. We know the territory. West . . ." He frowned. "No way of knowing where Temet is. Or whether another Zherosi column might be blocking the way to Black Hill. I just wish we knew what their objective was. If they're striking the other bands, too, we should head east. But if they just want you, we should go west. Try to link up with Temet before they cut us off."

Darak nodded; he'd come to the same conclusion. But he was reluctant to endanger the others if he was the target.

"What if we sent the main body east? While I go west with a small group. Five or six men. Come the gloaming, we might manage to slip past the Zherosi and get word to Temet."

"Sorig wouldn't like putting you at risk."

"Sorig isn't here."

"Do you think he was captured? Tortured to reveal our plans?"

"I don't know. I say we split up."

With obvious reluctance, Cleft Chin nodded.

"You'll lead the main body," Darak said.

"I'm staying with you."

"I need an experienced man. One who won't panic—"

"Holtik is just as experienced. The others respect him."

"I don't even know—"

"The heavy-set man. Sharpening his dagger. The others'll follow him."

"I want—"

"I'm staying, Spirit-Hunter."

Darak frowned. "Aye, so you've said. Why?"

"Sorig told me to guard your back. I thought I could do that best in the rear guard. But now . . ."

"All right. Let's tell the others."

Cleft Chin hesitated. "For what it's worth . . . I'd have gone north, too."

While Cleft Chin gathered the rest of the band, Darak considered Sorig's order again. Against his will, he recalled all the times Sorig had slipped away from the circle of villagers who had gathered to hear the great Spirit-Hunter speak.

It might only mean he was sick of listening to me. Just as his absence now might mean he's run into trouble.

Or it might mean Sorig had used those moments to pass information to someone. And if Cleft Chin was in league with him, he was more likely to put a dagger in his back than guard it.

In the end, only three others went with them, and he let Cleft Chin choose them. All were experienced hunters, young and strong, if not the best at hand-to-hand combat.

"Gods willing, we won't have to fight," Cleft Chin said. "Stamina and a knowledge of the forest will serve us better."

Bear was a huge man with beetling brows. Save for his blue eyes, the Dark One could easily be mistaken for a Zheroso. Freckles was the youngest, the fastest runner among them according to Cleft Chin—and a girl.

Her fierce eyes reminded him of Faelia, her stubborn chin of Griane. Her frown dared him to choose someone else, and he was tempted to do just that. Reluctantly, he accepted her, assuaging his doubts by reasoning that she might be safer with him than with the main group. Faelia would shudder at that kind of thinking, but the instinct to protect a woman was too ingrained to slough off now.

They quickly discovered that the Zherosi were still following them, but the forest was too dense to see whether the entire force was on their trail. They tried to disguise their path, splashing through shallow streams, leaping from rock to rock or balancing on fallen logs to avoid leaving footprints. But the effort sapped their strength and slowed them down—and speed was critical if they hoped to outrun their pursuers.

No one spoke, even during their brief stops to rest and refill their waterskins; they needed all their energy for the hunt. That was how he thought of it, only instead of being the hunters, they were the prey.

After nearly two moons tramping from village to village with Sorig, Darak prided himself on regaining much of the physical strength he'd lost during his years as chief. But the flight from the valley had left the muscles in his calves and thighs burning. After five more miles, he no longer trusted himself to sit when they stopped for rest for fear his trembling legs would refuse to support him when he tried to rise. Each rasping breath clawed at his chest, forcing him to stop at every hilltop until the ache eased.

Maker, don't let my heart fail me now. Or my legs. Just let me get these four to safety. And see my family one more time. And Tinnean.

He actually found himself smiling, imagining the Maker tapping an impatient foot while listening to the growing list of his requests.

It was the only time that day he smiled. By sunset, will-power alone was keeping him on his feet. But as the gloom under the trees deepened, his spirits rose. The Zherosi hated the forest even at midday; in the uncertain light of the gloaming, they would be even more apprehensive.

Much as he wanted to push on, he knew he lacked the energy. Shamed but infinitely grateful, he let the others take the watches while he slept.

It seemed only moments later that a hand shook him awake. It was considerably darker now, although he could still make out chinks of gray sky through the canopy of leaves. Assuring the others that he felt rested enough to move on, he forced himself to his feet.

The pace slowed as they picked their way through a wide valley pocked with boggy places from the recent rains. Swarming midges bit unprotected necks and faces, making the journey even more miserable.

They had gone less than a mile when a faint orange glow brightened the sky.

"Could it be Temet?" the Dark One whispered.

"If Sorig wouldn't allow fires," Darak replied, "neither would Temet."

"Are they the ones who were following us?" Freckles whispered. "Or another group?"

"No way of telling."

To circle north meant crossing low-lying ground with

little cover. There seemed to be no choice but to go south and try to sneak past the camp before sunrise.

The Dark One led the way, with Darak behind him. The damp mulch underfoot helped muffle the sound of their passage, as did the freshening breeze that blew from the west, carrying the scent of rain as well as woodsmoke from the Zherosi camp. Although he strained to detect any sounds, all he could hear was Cleft Chin's breath behind him, the shushing of the leaves, and a soft rustle when someone pushed a low-hanging branch out of the way.

The absence of sound from the camp nagged at him. Perhaps it was too far away; the gloaming made it hard to judge distance. But he had been a hunter too long to ignore his instincts, and they told him something was wrong.

As he skirted an overhanging ledge of rock, he reached out to tap the Dark One on the shoulder. Before he could, the Dark One came to such an abrupt halt that Darak had to pull up short to keep from walking into him. They all froze. Darak's nostrils flared as he caught the scent of urine.

A man stood on an outcropping near the top of the rise, staring skyward as he pissed. It took Darak a moment to pick out three others, barely visible among the trees; there were probably dozens more nearby.

The Zherosi had baited the trap with the fire and they had walked right into it.

The man above them groaned as he eased his bladder. One of his comrades chuckled. Fighting the urge to bolt, Darak turned his head to scan their surroundings, then swiveled with equal slowness to motion Cleft Chin back. As he did, Cleft Chin's fingers closed around his forearm. Darak staggered, scraping his head on rock. Before he could recover, Cleft Chin shoved him under the ledge.

His pack cushioned his back as he slammed against the hillside. A hand covered his mouth. A knee held him immobile. He managed to clamp his teeth on the fat of a finger, but his right arm was pinned against earth and his left against Cleft Chin's body, making it impossible to draw his dagger.

Something heavy thudded onto the ledge. He twisted his head in time to see a body land before their grotto and skid through the damp leaves. The broken shaft of an arrow protruded from the man's neck, and his penis flopped against his baggy khirta.

Darak tasted blood in his mouth. Heard shouts from above. A scream. Another body slid headfirst down the rise. There was a loud crashing in the underbrush. More shouts. Cleft Chin whispered "Don't move" as two more bodies tumbled past their hiding place. Arrows skittered off rocks and thudded into tree trunks.

And then—incredibly—laughter. And Freckles' voice calling, "You couldn't hit a bear if it was standing in front of you."

What was the girl thinking?

He craned his neck, searching for her, until a bellow of anger from above made him freeze. A Zherosi warrior pelted down the hill, ignoring a shouted command.

A second burst of laughter—off to the left this time— and another rain of arrows. More warriors staggered past, cursing as they tripped over tree roots and stones. He counted more than thirty before he heard the scream, thin and distant. A Zheroso or one of his folk?

A horn blared, and he flinched. The last time he had heard the sound was when the Zherosi led him to the sacrificial altar.

He could smell the fear-stink of his sweat, feel the faint tremor coursing through Cleft Chin's leg. At least he knew now that the man had been trying to save him. Perhaps he'd seen something on the hill or realized the others were about to bolt. If only they had kept their heads, they all might have retreated unseen. Why had Freckles turned back to taunt the Zherosi?

The horn sounded again. This time, he heard the faint blare of another. Too far away to be sure of the direction. Perhaps the Zherosi had split their forces, leaving half to guard the camp while the rest fanned out to catch them. But it was just as likely they had simply left the fires blazing while their entire force took to the woods.

Cleft Chin shifted position. Relieved of the pressure on his chest, Darak took a grateful gulp of air. They crouched together beneath the ledge until the long twilight finally yielded to darkness. He helped Cleft Chin tug the body closer, using it to shield them from the warriors straggling back up the hill. None paused to examine their fallen comrade. Gods willing, they would wait until daylight to retrieve their dead.

The forest was quiet, the scent of rain stronger. He could only pray Bear, the Dark One, and Freckles had escaped. And that the storm would come before dawn. Even if it didn't, he and Cleft Chin would have to sneak past the watchful Zherosi who showed every intention of remaining on the hill above them.

He heard a soft, wet sound and realized Cleft Chin was sucking the finger he had bitten. His fingers groped for the man's knee and closed around a muscular thigh instead. He squeezed it all the same, in thanks and apology.

He must have dozed, for he came awake to the rumble of thunder. Lightning flashed, briefly illuminating the silhouettes of trees. They waited until the drizzle became a downpour before crawling over the dead Zheroso and scuttling down the slope, guiding themselves by touch. At the bottom, they froze, listening for any sounds of pursuit, then groped their way deeper into the forest.

There were no stars to guide them. No familiar landmarks. All they knew was that the Gathering place lay somewhere to the southwest. Darak waited for another flash of lightning to take a bearing on the hill they had just fled. Then he padded off with Cleft Chin behind him.

If any Zherosi had been lurking in the woods, he would have stumbled right into them. As it was, he tripped over the body. Lightning revealed Freckles' pale face. The once-fierce eyes were open and empty; the rain made it look as if they were filled with tears.

He laid his palm against her wet cheek and whispered a prayer. Then he obeyed Cleft Chin's urgent tug on his arm and moved on.

Each time they reached high ground, they stopped, waiting for the lightning to take a new bearing. After the storm passed, stars began peeping through the breaks in the scudding clouds. As the sky lightened, they discovered the dark mound of Black Hill in the distance, rising above the gently rolling plain.

They collapsed onto the ground, soaked and shivering.

"You sleep," he told Cleft Chin. "I'll keep watch."

"I'm fine."

"Sleep."

Cleft Chin lay down beside him, but his eyes remained open. "They didn't capture you. That's the most important thing."

It took a moment for the truth to dawn. When it did, Darak wondered how he could have been such a fool.

None of them had panicked. They had deliberately distracted the Zherosi while Cleft Chin pulled him into their hiding place. They must have planned it while he slept. He could picture them, crouched on their haunches, discussing the role each should take: Bear who had the advantage of size; the Dark One, whose coloring made him harder to spot in the shadows; and Freckles, the fastest runner in the group. Tonight, she had not been able to run far or fast enough.

"Their names?"

Cleft Chin regarded him silently. Then he said, "The big man is Terias. The dark lad is Fannir. The red-haired girl—she was called Mattia."

Darak repeated their names aloud, silently adding a prayer after each. "And you?"

"My name is Kelik."

His uncle's name. His father's brother who had died before he was born. He could easily have met him tonight in the Forever Isles.

A woman—little more than a girl—had died for him. Likely, two men had as well. The gods only knew if the other recruits were alive. And Sorig and the two scouts who had gone with him.

Tonight had shown him the futility of keeping his distance. Would he mourn the loss of any of these young men and women less because he refused to learn their names? They were all part of this rebellion. Part of his pack. And as pack leader, it was up to him to know their strengths and weaknesses, to keep them strong, to fight side by side with them, and—as far as he was able—keep them safe.

"If you won't sleep, would you tell me the names of the others?"

One by one, Kelik described them—each man, each

woman—and Darak repeated their names. A formidable
task to remember them all, even for a man who had once
been a Memory-Keeper. A long litany of names, like the
one he had memorized when he went south to rescue Keirith. That had been a litany of the lost—captured, sold into
slavery, sacrificed on a foreign altar. He prayed this was a
litany of the living.

The sky was a glory of pink and purple when he repeated
their names a third time.

Three times for a charm.

Shouldering their packs, they headed south to the Gathering of rebels.

Chapter 30

FAELIA LAY BELLY-DOWN in the long grass atop
Black Hill, watching the shadows of clouds chase each
other across the rippling grass. Between the drenching
thunderstorm three nights ago and the need to stand
watches day and night, none of the scouts had gotten much
rest, but she was far too excited to sleep. Silly, really. It
might be another full day before her father arrived.

*Please, gods, let him be all right. And let him bring two
hundred recruits.*

A soft snore from her right made her glance over at
Mikal. A fly buzzed perilously near his half-open mouth.
She suppressed a giggle. The poor man had barely finished
giving his report on the fortress at Little Falls before
marching south with them. Temet had urged him to go with
the main body, rather than lead a forced march to Black
Hill, but Mikal took his status as acting second-in-command
seriously—too seriously, she sometimes thought—and he
had brushed off Temet's concern.

Spying on Little Falls always upset him, no matter how hard he tried to hide it. Bad enough to see your childhood home sitting in the shadow of a Zherosi fortress; Mikal had the added burden of knowing his tribe had helped build it.

The discovery that Zherosi ships had arrived with reinforcements only added to Mikal's gloom—and hers. If that part of Keirith's vision was true, the rest might be, too.

Which was another reason sleep eluded her. Keirith didn't seem to think Fa was in any immediate danger, but even she knew visions were difficult to interpret. She also knew her brother well enough to sense he was hiding something. When she'd pressed for details, he had reminded her that the vision might be a warning of danger, not betrayal. But his frown belied those comforting words.

"Sorig will guard your father," Temet had assured her. "And once he's with us, I'll keep a bodyguard around him at all times."

Neither of them shared their worst fear: that the traitor Keirith had Seen might be a member of their band. She hated looking at her comrades with suspicion, hated her helplessness even more. During the sleepless nights, only Temet could banish the doubts and fears that stalked her.

This was the longest they had been apart since that nightmarish flight to her village. She missed the comfort of his body, their fierce, wordless lovemaking. She had never expected to need a man so—or find one who measured up to her father.

Sometimes she wondered what it would have been like if they had met under ordinary circumstances. Would he have expected her to change from hunter to wife, to remain at home to cook and sew and bear his children? From the little he had said of his wife, that was the role she had played.

The rebellion had changed everything. Women fought alongside men. They endured the same privations and dangers, shared the same triumphs and defeats. When she allowed herself to daydream about the future, she imagined returning to her village with Temet, spending their days hunting together and their nights making love. But there were no children in that idyllic future—and certainly, no possibility of them now.

She monitored her moon times as stringently as she

quelled her fears for his safety. Only once had her moon flow come late, and although it might have been due to the stress of battle or the ever-present hunger, she had purged herself with the herbs Hircha had given her. She'd been weak enough afterward to wonder if pregnancy could possibly be worse, but once the cramping and the bleeding ceased, common sense prevailed.

This war needed all her energy. She would think about the future after the Zherosi were defeated.

Please, gods, let it be soon. So Temet and I can start a new life together.

As she rolled her neck to relieve the ache of tension, she glimpsed Eilin's auburn hair off to her left. Keirith had insisted that Temet allow him to join the scouting party—a measure of renewed trust in the boy. So far, he'd earned that trust. But she still kept an eye on him.

He reminded her so much of Keirith as a lad. He wasn't much older than Keirith had been when the Zherosi had stolen him. And he had the same coloring. But it was the haunted look that sometimes flashed across his face that reminded her most of her brother.

The rebellion did that to some. Others—like Mikal— grew hardened by the violence. Perhaps she had, too.

She tensed, caught by a flash of movement in the scrub. It was probably just an animal; there was barely enough cover for a man to approach unseen, never mind a column of Zherosi warriors. The long grass on the slope of the hill rippled in the breeze. Easy to become hypnotized by its gentle swaying, but she had hunted the moors most of her life and it was easier still to notice a swath of green where the grass jerked back and forth.

She clasped Mikal's wrist, and he woke at once. She nodded to the slope, and while he rolled over to inspect it, she turned onto her side to string her bow, hissing softly to attract the attention of the nearest sentry. The alert passed silently, until every bow was strung and every pair of eyes sought the intruders.

From the same swath of grass came the liquid purr of a wood pigeon. There were none on this grassy knoll; it was the reason they had chosen that birdcall as the signal. After a moment a man's voice called out.

As Faelia heaved herself up, Mikal's hand came down on her back, pushing her flat. "Could be a trap."

"I'm going to stand up," the hoarse voice croaked. "For mercy's sake, don't shoot."

Sorig staggered to his feet, arms extended from his sides, and stood there, swaying like the grass. "If you're there . . ." His gaze swept the hilltop. He took a step forward and fell to his knees.

Faelia pushed Mikal away. "I'm going down."

He swore, then glanced over his shoulder. "Cover us."

She charged down the hill, with Mikal behind her. Sorig's head came up as she approached, his face gaunt with exhaustion.

"Is Darak here? And the others?"

Fist pressed against her mouth, Faelia shook her head.

They helped Sorig up the hill. The others clustered around, grim-faced and anxious. In an agony of impatience, she waited for him to take a few swigs of water and plunge into his tale.

"We were scouting ahead when we spotted the komakh. On our way back, Iann slipped and twisted his ankle. I sent Liath on to warn Darak and got Iann to a hiding place where I thought he'd be safe. Then I made my way to the pass. The Zherosi marched in, but they never came out. I waited until the light started to go before I followed. There was no sign of a battle. No bodies. Nothing. So I figured Darak must have gotten the others away."

"Then they'd have been here by now," Faelia said.

"Not if they retreated east," Mikal replied. "Or swung—"

"They went north," Sorig interrupted. "At least, that's the direction the Zherosi went. There was no point in following. And I had Iann to think about."

"Where is he?" Faelia asked.

Sorig's shoulders slumped. "The young fool must have come after me. He was gone when I got back to the place I'd left him. I spent half the night searching. Finally found him near the bottom of the pass. He'd broken his neck in the fall." He rubbed his eyes with grimy fingers. "I buried him as best I could, then headed here. I'd hoped to find Darak and the others waiting for me."

Not if the Zherosi caught them.

Faelia banished the traitorous thought; if anyone could lead the recruits to safety, it was her father.

"The Zherosi knew we were there," Sorig said bitterly. "They were hunting us."

"Someone in one of the villages must have betrayed your route," Mikal said.

"Or else the traitor is one of our own." Sorig silenced the chorus of denial with a violent gesture. "I'm not saying it's true. But we can't ignore that possibility."

Faelia exchanged a quick glance with Mikal. Of the scouts at Black Hill, only they knew the details of Keirith's vision; if there was a traitor among them, Temet didn't want to warn him—or her—by allowing their suspicions to be known.

"We'd better warn Temet," Mikal said. "And tell him the Spirit-Hunter's . . . missing."

"I'll go," Faelia said.

Sorig shook his head. "Bad enough I couldn't get back to help Darak. If anything should happen to you . . ." His fingers flew in the sign to avert evil.

"I can't just sit here worrying. I'll go mad."

"She might be safer with Temet," Mikal said. "Especially if that Zherosi column is marching here."

Before Sorig could reply, a loud hiss drew their attention. "Someone's coming up the northeast slope," Eilin called softly.

They snatched up their weapons and moved swiftly to their positions. Again, Faelia heard the throb of a wood pigeon. Again, a voice called out. "Don't shoot. There are two of us."

Faelia squeezed her eyes shut and whispered a quick prayer of thanks. The next moment, she was on her feet, screaming, "Fa! We're here!"

He pushed himself to his feet, slow and ponderous as a bear. But a huge smile split his face and his arms came up as if to embrace her.

Half laughing, half crying, she plunged down the hill. He staggered backward as she threw herself into his arms. They lurched back and forth like drunkards, laughing at their clumsiness and from the sheer joy of seeing each other again. He was filthy and unshaven and tired—gods, she'd never seen him look so tired—but he was here, he was alive, he was safe.

"This is Kelik," he said, belatedly introducing his companion. "And this is my daughter, Faelia." Her father's gaze moved past her and his smile vanished. "When did Sorig arrive?"

"Just a few moments ago."

"And the others?"

"He was alone."

"Aye. Well. It would have taken them longer. They went east . . ." His voice trailed off as Mikal and Sorig clambered down the slope toward them.

Sorig pulled her father into a hard embrace. "Thank the gods," he kept saying as he thumped Fa on the back.

Anyone watching would have believed that exhaustion alone tempered the enthusiasm of Fa's greeting. But Faelia had noted the tension in his body as Sorig approached, the sudden blankness of his expression before the smile returned.

"Gods, I'm a fool," Sorig said. "You look half dead and I'm keeping you standing here. Take my arm and I'll help you up the hill."

"I can manage," her father replied.

"If he needs to lean on anyone," she quickly added, "it'll be me."

At her father's nod, Kelik followed Sorig and Mikal up the hill. As soon as they were out of earshot, she asked, "What is it, Fa? What's wrong?"

"What did Sorig say?"

In a hushed whisper, she told him.

"Is Keirith with you?"

"Nay. With the main band. They should be here by nightfall. What's troubling you?"

"I don't know. It may be nothing. I can't accuse the man without proof."

"Proof of what?"

"That Sorig betrayed us." Before she could speak, he added, "Later. They'll want to hear my story now." The gray eyes bore into hers with sudden fierceness. "If I'm right, we must be careful. And we must keep him close."

Chapter 31

"I DIDN'T EXPECT YOU BACK so soon." Jholianna motioned the Khonsel to the bench opposite hers. "Leave us," she told her hovering scribe. "We'll deal with these later."

The small walled garden was her favorite retreat. The splash of the fountain soothed her, and the stunted palms shaded the latticed pavilion from the sun's heat. Although she relished her privacy, her guards had orders to admit the Khonsel at any time.

He lowered himself onto the bench, eyeing the tablet-boxes that littered the simple wooden table between them. "Trouble?"

"Nothing out of the ordinary." As soon as her scribe collected his writing supplies and withdrew, she demanded, "Well?"

"They're being taken to their cells now."

"Loudly protesting their innocence, of course."

"Oh, they admit to meeting with the Carilians, but claim they were only trying to bring the war to an end."

She grimaced. She had no objection to secret negotiations— she had sent an envoy to Carilia three moons ago for exactly that purpose—but she could not allow a group of noblemen to take matters into their own hands.

As the Khonsel recited the names of the accused, she grimaced again. "Axhad do Vinikh? Why didn't he just come to me instead of going behind my back?"

"We'll find out soon enough. I've told the examiners I want the truth in two days' time. Before the Blessing of the Adders."

"I can't believe do Vinikh would countenance any sort of violence."

"Nor can I. But the streets will be mobbed for the procession. Which means you'll be exposed. And the boy," he added as an obvious afterthought. "Have you learned anything more about his meeting with the Spirit-Hunter?"

"Enough to know I shouldn't bring up the subject."

Although Rigat had assured her that the meeting had gone well, his manner suggested just the opposite. She'd told him that runners had been sent to all the major cities, ordering the tax collectors to conduct a new census of the Tree People. Even that news failed to pacify him. In the end, she'd had no choice but to accede to his repeated demands for a truce.

To prevent him from devising any new plans to help the Tree People—or spend her treasury's funds—she had done her best to keep him occupied during the last sennight: seeking his advice on every aspect of his recognition ceremony; inviting him to her council meetings; arranging for her Jherazo to instruct him in Zherosi protocol and her Stuavo to educate him about trade. In the evenings, she held feasts for visiting dignitaries, organized contests of strength and skill, summoned poets and singers and musicians to entertain him.

And still he'd managed to slip off to the north. To bring his half brother—Khallum, Khalli, whatever his name was—news of the truce. Or so he claimed.

"The moon of celebration has yet to begin," she concluded, "and I'm worn thin from—"

She broke off as the Khonsel's head jerked toward the fountain. At first she thought his gaze had been caught by the iridescent sheen of the hummingbird darting between the rosy fronds of fireweed. Then she noticed the brighter gleam of Rigat's hair.

As he rounded the fountain, she and the Khonsel rose. Rigat bent to kiss her hand, then returned the Khonsel's bow, precisely deep enough to convey the proper respect to one of high—but still inferior—rank. Clearly, his etiquette lessons were bearing fruit.

She studied him intently, seeking a clue to his mood. His smile had wavered when he discovered the Khonsel with her, but the two had been sparring since their first meeting.

"Welcome back, Khonsel. You're just in time for the council meeting." Rigat's gaze drifted to the collection of tablet-boxes. "Any news from the north?"

"Nothing since the Vanel's message from Deepford," Jholianna replied.

She'd had her scribe read him Geriv's report—after she had learned its contents, of course. A brief yet depressing description of conditions at the fortress and a plea for yet another shipment of grain. Rigat had been disappointed that there was no mention of the truce until she reminded him that the orders could not possibly have reached Geriv so quickly.

And—if my plan succeeds—won't reach him for another half-moon.

"I'm sure he'll send another report from Little Falls," she said.

Rigat nodded and turned to the Khonsel. "Were there any messages from your nephew awaiting you? Or did you come straight from the ship?"

The Khonsel took a deep breath. So did Jholianna, fearing another contest of wills.

"I went to my quarters. My lord. To change before my audience with the queen. There were no messages from Geriv. The last one I received was from Eagles Mount. But you know that. You had the queen's scribe read it to you. And the reply I sent."

The Khonsel had been livid when Rigat insisted on inspecting his private correspondence. His fury only increased when Jholianna assured him that she was allowing Rigat to monitor her messages to Geriv as well.

"I read *a* reply," Rigat said. "It would have been easy enough to send another while you were in Iriku."

Watching them glare at each other, she wondered again what lay behind their enmity. Rigat seemed to blame the Khonsel for what had happened to his half brother and foster-father all those years ago. Surely, he must realize that she had given the order that had sent the Spirit-Hunter to the sacrificial altar. Perhaps Rigat was simply jealous of her relationship with Vazh. Certainly Jholin had been.

Rigat's gaze shifted to her. "I'm curious." The tension in his body belied his musing tone. "Did you tell the Khonsel about the Gathering?"

"Of course." Eyeing his rising color, she added, "You never asked me to keep it a secret."

"Perhaps I should have!"

"What does it matter?" the Khonsel demanded. "Yes, the queen told me. And yes, I passed the information along to Geriv. But it's a five-day voyage to Graywaters. Another two or three upriver to Little Falls. He won't get my message until this damn Gathering is over."

"Then why bother telling him about it?"

"Because you don't withhold information like that from the commander of your army!" With an effort, the Khonsel controlled his temper. "I know you're concerned about the situation in the north. But by now, Geriv's received the queen's orders for a truce. He would never disobey them to attack the Gathering."

"Because he's a loyal servant of the queen," Rigat observed.

"That's right."

"As loyal as his uncle?"

Oddly, the Khonsel's expression froze. As Jholianna struggled to understand the undercurrents of their exchange, the Khonsel gasped and tottered backward. His stick clattered onto the bricks as his hands flailed for the arms of the bench.

Jholianna rushed over to him. His mouth worked soundlessly and his eyes bulged, wild with shock.

"Stop! You're killing him!"

The Khonsel groped for her hand and squeezed it. Then his breath exploded in a wheeze and the viselike grip relaxed. He fixed Rigat with a look of such loathing that Jholianna recoiled. Even Rigat took a quick step backward. Then he recovered his equanimity.

"I had to be sure. That he was as loyal as he claimed."

"I have never disobeyed an order from my queen," the Khonsel managed between gasps.

"I did try to be gentle."

"Damn your gentleness! No man wants another poking around inside his spirit."

Jholianna's hand clenched convulsively around the Khonsel's, silently urging calm. "Please excuse him," she begged Rigat. "He's upset."

Before her eyes, Rigat transformed from an implacable interrogator to an awkward boy. "No. He's right. I should have asked. My apologies, Khonsel. I was . . . showing off. Trying to impress you."

The taut lines of the Khonsel's face relaxed. "Well, you certainly managed to do that."

To Jholianna's astonishment, they grinned at each other. *Men. No matter their age, they're all boys competing in a pissing contest.*

With a grunt of effort, the Khonsel pushed himself to his feet. "I suggest we go to the council chamber."

Relief made it difficult for her to concentrate on the meeting. When the Zheron launched into a tedious description of the recognition ceremony, her thoughts drifted to her narrow escape.

She had sent a message to Geriv with information about Rigat's parentage and power. And later, the order to cease hostilities. She had dictated that one in front of Rigat. And still he had insisted on touching her spirit to verify that the message had been sent. Feigning shock and sorrow at his lack of trust, she had acquiesced.

Rigat's touch lasted only long enough to learn that she had given the message to the ship's captain as she'd promised. Then he retreated from her spirit, inundating her with apologies.

So eager to retreat that he failed to notice that she had neglected to affix the copper badge to the tablet-box. And still so unfamiliar with the Zherosi communication system that he would never have known to ask about it. But her simple omission ensured that some clerk at Graywaters would set the orders for the truce aside to await his commander's return instead of transferring them to another ship that would carry them upriver immediately.

The Khonsel knew nothing of her plan; loyal as he was, he was still Geriv's uncle. At the time, she had felt a twinge of guilt for deceiving him. Now she was simply relieved.

Rigat still might discover the truth if he chose to attack her spirit. But so far, he was eager to maintain her goodwill.

And strangely ambivalent about his power. So odd, the Tree People's reluctance to touch the spirits of others. Odder still for the son of a god to shrink from using his power. But that, of course, was why she had risked deceiving him in the first place. She only hoped the results would merit the risk.

If Geriv could find the site of this Gathering and destroy the rebels, it would solve their problems in the north. Geriv might protest that he had never received the order for a truce, but she doubted Rigat would care, especially if any of his family was harmed. She would console him for his terrible loss. And his wrath would be directed at Geriv.

A pity to lose him; he had served her well. But she could always appoint another Vanel. There was only one Son of Zhe.

The sound of raised voices interrupted her thoughts. Belatedly, she realized that the Stuavo was grumbling about the census of the Tree People.

"I've been inundated with complaints, Earth's Beloved. From the tax collectors, the mayors, the slave owners protesting the seizure of their property."

"They're human beings," Rigat snapped. "Not property."

"With respect, my lord, in Zheros, slaves are property. And their owners insist on being compensated for their losses."

"Then we'll compensate them," Rigat replied, casually dispersing untold sums from her already depleted treasury.

"It's not that simple," the Stuavo insisted. "Most of the women have borne children since they were brought to Zheros. Are they to be considered Tree People as well? Not to mention the fact that some of the slaves don't want to leave."

"That's ridiculous!" Rigat retorted. "The slave owners are just saying that."

"Perhaps some are. But many of the slaves have lived here since they were children. It's the only home they know and—"

"Enough!" Rigat snapped. "To question my judgment shows disrespect."

As a greasy film of sweat appeared on the Stuavo's

forehead, the Supplicant cleared her throat. "I'm sure the Stuavo intended no disrespect, my lord."

As always, the priestess seemed undaunted by the threat of Rigat's power and, alone among Jholianna's counselors, even dared to reprove him. Always politely, even diffidently, but clearly with the intent to curb him.

Jholianna's spies had informed her that Rigat often met the Supplicant during his morning stroll around the plateau. They spoke only briefly, but she doubted such encounters—despite appearances—were by chance.

Although the Supplicant denied it, Jholianna was convinced that the priestess had somehow engineered Rigat's return after their disastrous encounter in this very chamber. Clearly, something lay between them. And just as clearly, it weighed on the Supplicant's mind. She looked thin and strained these days, the teasing mockery that had enlivened so many council meetings replaced by watchful silence.

Still, her words encouraged Rigat to bestow one of his most charming smiles on the sweating Stuavo. "The heat has made me irritable. Of course, you meant no disrespect. Please present me with a report outlining the difficulties that have arisen and your suggestions for addressing them."

As the Khonsel turned the discussion back to the security measures for the recognition ceremony, Jholianna studied Rigat covertly. Hard to reconcile this confident young man with the eager one who had whisked her off to that northern forest only ten days ago. Or the contrite one who had apologized to the Khonsel for "showing off." All young men enjoyed their first taste of power, but if Rigat was this difficult to control now, what would he be like after she declared him the Son of Zhe?

At the sound of voices outside the chamber, the Khonsel broke off. A guard called out a request to enter and upon receiving it, strode into the room.

"Forgive me, Earth's Beloved. A message from Iriku."

She frowned when she saw the small bronze cylinder. The news was either very good or very bad. No one ever sent a routine report by bird.

When she saw the Alcadh's seal, she sighed impatiently. She would have to appoint a new mayor for Iriku; this one was always sending hysterical pleas for help.

"Summon my scribe."

As the guard retreated, Rigat extended his hand. "May I?"

Reluctantly, she surrendered the cylinder and watched him break the seal and extract the tiny roll of fetal calfskin.

"Could the Carilians have broken through again?" the Motixa asked.

"No," the Khonsel replied. "I just returned from Iriku. Our troops are still holding their position. But the city's unsettled. More refugees are arriving every day."

"Yes," Rigat said. "And now it seems there's been a food riot. And looting."

Jholianna was the first to break the silence. "You can . . . read the message? Without the aid of a scribe?"

Rigat nodded, peering at the strip of calfskin. "But he should read it, too. Just to make sure I'm getting it right. The Alcadh fears the whole city will go up in flames."

"The Alcadh is a fearful man," Jholianna said, still stunned by Rigat's revelation.

"That's true," Rigat agreed. "Wasn't it last summer that he was certain the yellow plague had broken out?" At her start of surprise, he added, "I was studying some of the histories the other day. That's when I began deciphering the writing. It looked like bird scratches at first. But the Biteko . . . that's his title, isn't it? The head of the library?"

She nodded.

"He was very helpful."

Jholianna smiled and silently vowed to have her helpful Biteko flayed. "I wonder that you had the time."

Rigat looked up. "What could be more important than learning about my people?"

"If the situation is as serious as the Alcadh indicates, we'll have to send troops," the Khonsel said.

The gods only knew where she would get them. Or the grain the city desperately needed. The royal treasury had been drained by the war; compensating the slave owners would further deplete it. The royal granaries were nearly empty, and the recent Carilian offensive had left a swath of ruined villages and burned fields. Without the province's harvest of barley and millet, all of Zheros would suffer this winter.

"Why don't I go to Iriku?" Rigat suggested. "I can be back in plenty of time for the recognition ceremony. It'll be just like playing eagle for—" A telltale blush flooded his face.

"Playing eagle?" she echoed.

"When I spied on Zheros," he mumbled. "Before I appeared in your throne room."

She didn't dare let him go to Iriku; it would be far too easy for him to flit off to the north again. And if he somehow discovered that she had deceived him . . .

Suddenly, she realized how to keep him in Pilozhat. Who better to interrogate the traitors? Skilled as her examiners were, men would say anything under torture. Only Rigat could uncover the truth. That's why he was so valuable— and so dangerous.

As Rigat entered his bedchamber, the dozen slaves assigned to serve him prostrated themselves.

"A bath, Nekif."

"It has already been drawn, great lord. And there is chilled water or wine—"

"Wine."

"Yes, great lord." Nekif beamed and waved one of the slaves toward the low stone table where two sweating bronze pitchers stood.

Although Nekif had served him only a sennight, he seemed to have learned all of his preferences. A bowl of honeyed figs sat on one end of the table and a basket of those plump purple grapes he liked on the other.

He had yet to learn the names of the other slaves. They all looked alike, these slender, young men who served him with bowed heads and averted eyes. The efficient Nekif usually anticipated his needs. If he required something unexpected, he had only to tell Nekif who snapped out orders to the rest.

Until yesterday, he had slept in the winter bedchamber one floor below, while a horde of artisans redecorated the summer bedchamber to Jholianna's exacting specifications. It seemed a useless expense, especially since the bath adjoined the winter bedchamber and that was the greatest luxury he could desire. But he had given in to her wishes, praising the thick rugs with their brilliant flowers of scarlet and gold, the stylized adders that slithered along the base of the walls, and the mural behind his bed that depicted Zhe soaring above a pine forest. Clearly, Jholianna's visit had provided the inspiration; the artist had painted a line of does and fawns picking their way across a stream.

He allowed the slaves to remove his jeweled belt and sandals, then held out his arms so Nekif could unwind his khirta. The old slave folded it and handed it to another who held it as if he feared it would fly away.

At first, Rigat had insisted on dressing and undressing himself, but he'd soon overcome his embarrassment. Today, he welcomed the efficient hands that stripped off his clothing, cooled him with palm fans, and proffered the cup of wine, the bowl of figs.

He was still unsettled by the day's events. He'd agreed to interrogate the conspirators; the Gathering would not conclude for days and he was tired of etiquette lessons and the endless round of feasts and entertainments. But he would have to look into these difficulties about freeing the slaves.

It had seemed like such a wonderful idea—the perfect way to help his people. He should have foreseen the possibility that after decades of exile, some would consider Zheros their home. Or at least consulted Fellgair to ensure that everything went smoothly. But he'd had so little time to speak privately with Fellgair since his return from the north. A quick meeting after the dawn sacrifice. A brief exchange of words at a council meeting.

His frustration had led him to commit two blunders today. The exchange with the Stuavo had been unpleasant, but attacking the Khonsel's spirit had been stupid—especially since he'd found no evidence of treachery. The meetings with Keirith and Darak had left him edgy and irritable, looking for conspiracies that did not exist. He couldn't give into his nerves now—not when he was so close to achieving everything he desired.

Impatiently, he drained his goblet and held it out to be refilled. In his haste to obey, the slave poured too quickly, splattering wine on Rigat's bare feet.

"Clumsy fool!" Nekif cuffed the cowering slave before

seizing a cloth and patting Rigat's feet dry. "I shall have him whipped, great lord."

"No. It was just an accident."

Nekif bowed low. "As you command, great lord."

If he had said he wanted the slave killed, Nekif would have said exactly the same thing and bowed with just as much reverence.

More, perhaps. That's how people expect a god to behave.

Eager for his bath, he hurried down the stairs to the winter bedchamber, followed by his retinue of slaves. Outside the little bathing room, he paused to allow Nekif to unwind the loincloth of soft lambskin. Another slave, given the privilege of receiving the discarded kharo, averted his eyes and held up a length of flaxcloth. After Nekif laid the kharo on it, the slave quickly bundled it up. The loincloth would be burned in a formal ceremony; after such intimate contact with the Son of Zhe's body, it was deemed too precious to wash and wear again.

Oil lamps flickered in the bathing room, but the light filtering in from the sky-well rendered them more decorative than necessary. Here, another slave waited. He draped a fleece over the back of the hipbath, then retrieved a bronze pitcher from the wall niche.

Postponing the bliss of immersing himself, Rigat allowed Nekif to rinse his body, watching the water trickle through the bronze-slatted drain. Really, the Zherosi artisans were marvels. They had even created special rooms where the rulers could relieve themselves. Perched on the wooden seat, surrounded by walls decorated with blooming flowers and lush vegetation, any man would feel like a god.

Three times, Nekif dipped the pitcher into the bath and poured the water over him. "In token of your parentage," the Zheron had explained. "Once for Zhe, once for Heart of Sky, and once for Womb of Earth."

The Zheron had invented dozens of such rituals. Rigat had one slave whose sole function was to place a special bronze bowl under the latrine seat to collect his waste, then hand it to a priestess of Womb of Earth—discreetly waiting outside—who carried it to the temple for consecration. The Motixa herself carried the consecrated shit to the fields to increase the earth's fertility.

At least that served a purpose. At home, they collected

dung to fertilize the soil and used stale urine for tanning hides and setting dyes. They just didn't make such a fuss about it.

As Nekif handed the pitcher back to the waiting slave, Rigat climbed gratefully into the cool water. He leaned forward to permit Nekif to untie the gold cord at the end of his braid. The slave's dexterous fingers loosened his hair and kneaded the back of his neck, drawing a contented groan from Rigat.

"I think you have magic in your fingers."

Nekif chuckled. "No magic, great lord. Just many years of experience."

"You served the king, didn't you?"

"For most of my life, great lord. May his spirit find eternal rest in the shaded groves of Paradise."

"And afterward?"

"The queen gave me the position of Chief Palace Slave. An immense honor. But nothing compared to the honor of serving you, great lord."

"Were you frightened? When she asked you to attend me?"

The fingers hesitated, then returned to their gentle kneading. "At first, great lord. There were so many rumors."

Rigat smiled. "That I had wings? And claws?"

"And scales." Nekif's voice was solemn. "It must sound foolish to you, great lord, but it was a relief to discover that you were so . . ."

"Ordinary?"

"Human. In appearance. And you were . . . are . . . so kind. I had not expected that."

Rigat digested this in silence. Then he felt the trembling of Nekif's fingers. Before he could speak, the old man prostrated himself on the honey-colored tiles.

"Forgive this unworthy slave, great lord. I should not be disturbing you with my chatter."

"You're not disturbing me. I hope I can always rely upon you to be honest with me—and to teach me the things I need to learn."

"Great lord, I am unworthy to teach you anything."

"You taught me that kugi are even better on the eyes than in the mouth."

Nekif's head came up. After a moment, he grinned. The

first time Nekif had placed the thin vegetable rounds over his eyes, Rigat had laughed so hard they fell into the water.

"Shall I fetch them now, great lord?"

"Please."

Nekif rose and returned with a small tray, inlaid with sparkling quartz that flashed in the light of the oil lamps. Rigat's gaze lingered on the luxuries it held: the tiny bowl with the slices of kugi; the fist-sized ball of scented soap; the washing cloth made of fetal lambskin; the bronze vial with the emulsion of whey, seaweed, and alojha juice for washing his hair; and the smaller one containing oil of sweet spike for scenting his body.

Growing up, a bath had consisted of a plunge in the lake. The Zherosi had elevated it to an art form.

"Remember why you are here."

He lay back against the fleece, frowning as he recalled Fellgair's words.

"My lord? Is something wrong?"

"No. I just . . . I thought I heard my father's voice."

The vials rattled on the tray. Nekif gazed skyward as if expecting Zhe to burst through the ceiling.

"Leave me."

"Yes, lord. At once." Nekif deposited the tray on the stool beside the bath and prostrated himself. "Shall I summon the musicians?"

"Yes. Fine."

Nekif scuttled out. Moments later, Rigat heard the trill of a flute and the gentle thrum of a lyre. The musicians must have been hovering in the corridor. As always, Nekif had anticipated his wishes. For some reason, the slave's efficiency irritated him now. As did the mural on the opposite wall with its cascading waterfall and brilliant blue pool and—of course—the ever-present adders basking on the rocks.

The flute gave a piercing shriek. The lyre fell silent. A shadow darkened the doorway of the bathing room.

"Great lord. Forgive me." Nekif swallowed hard.

"What is it?"

"The Supplicant. She begs permission to speak with you."

He was too tired for one of Fellgair's lectures, but it was

foolish to risk his ire. And lately, Fellgair was always irritable. Rigat missed the mocking humor of their early days.

Less than two moons ago. A lifetime.

He nodded to Nekif and rose. Hoping he might still enjoy a relaxing soak, he simply wrapped a length of flaxcloth around his hips. Then he took a deep breath and marched out to face his father.

The slaves and musicians had fled. Fellgair sat alone on a bench against the far wall. As his head came up, Rigat's steps faltered. For a fleeting moment, he thought he saw the features of the fox-man superimposed on those of the Supplicant. It was probably just the play of light and shadow in the chamber. But there was no mistaking the strain on Fellgair's face. Shocked, Rigat hurried over to him.

"Are you unwell?"

The deep grooves between his eyebrows and the dark circles beneath his eyes simply vanished, leaving his face its usual smooth, smiling mask.

Fellgair patted the bench. "Sit with me."

Rigat obeyed, wondering what sort of game Fellgair was playing now.

"I must leave Pilozhat."

"Leave?"

"Today."

"But the Blessing of the Adders . . . my recognition ceremony . . ."

"I hope to return by then."

"You have to be here!"

"I said I will try!" Fellgair snapped. "I can do no more than that."

Alarmed, Rigat asked, "What is it? Has something happened? Not Mam . . ."

"No. I saw her three days ago. And Darak." A smile lightened Fellgair's face. "He was trudging toward the Gathering spot with his recruits trailing after him like sheep. Faelia's waiting for him there. And Keirith should arrive soon with the rest of Temet's band."

"You saw them all?" Relief gave way to renewed anxiety; it was almost as if Fellgair was bidding them farewell, too. "Did you speak with them?"

The smile fled. "After our last meeting, I didn't think they would welcome me."

"But if they're all right . . . I don't understand. Why do you have to leave now?"

Fellgair hesitated, staring at the tiles. "There's something I must do. Something that cannot be postponed any longer."

"What could be more important—?"

"This need not affect our plans. But I wanted you to know that it might be impossible for me to return as quickly as I desire. And to urge you once more to remember why you are here."

"How can I forget when you're always reminding me?"

"Please. Just listen to me. This one last time."

"Last time?" Rigat echoed, his anger abruptly vanishing.

"Before I go."

Fellgair's dismissive wave drew Rigat's gaze. The red polish on his nails was gone. Perhaps he had simply tired of it, but Rigat's uneasiness increased.

"Something's wrong. I know it. When you touched my spirit during the council meeting, it felt . . . different. And now—"

"Now I'm simply tired. Even gods get tired."

Did they? Fellgair was the only god he had ever met, and he never seemed tired. At least, he hadn't until now.

"Please. Tell me what's wrong. Maybe I can help."

Fellgair leaned forward. "Then you do care about me. A little."

"Well, I . . . of course. You're my father."

"That is no guarantee of filial devotion."

The dry tone sounded so much like the old Fellgair that Rigat smiled with relief.

Fellgair smiled, too, but his expression quickly became grave. "The best way you can help is to let nothing distract you from your plan for peace."

"I won't."

Fellgair seized his hand. "Promise me, Rigat."

The nails bit into his flesh, but the intensity of Fellgair's gaze bothered him more. "I promise. For now."

"Then I'll say good-bye. For now."

At the doorway, Fellgair hesitated. "I should have

waited. To take you with me. If I could have given you a
few more years with Darak and Griane . . ." He frowned
and shook his head impatiently. "It doesn't matter now.
You've accomplished so much, so quickly. More than I
dared to hope. I'm proud of you, my son."

Before Rigat could reply, Fellgair turned abruptly and
strode out.

Jholianna had just finished dressing for dinner when one of
her attendants rushed in to whisper that the Khonsel was
waiting in her private reception chamber. She hurried down
the winding stairs, fighting to control her anxiety.

The Khonsel bowed but refused her invitation to sit.
"I've just received a message from Geriv. Requesting that
you postpone the truce until after the dark of the moon.
When he will have finished his inspection of the river fortifications and be better able to advise you."

Before she could stop herself, she blurted, "He's already
received my orders?"

"No. Or hadn't when he sent this message. It was dated
six days ago. From Little Falls."

The captain must have kept the slaves at the oars day
and night to reach Pilozhat so quickly. That nonsense about
inspecting fortifications was clearly a precaution in case the
message was intercepted. Geriv must be planning something. But what? The Gathering would begin on the morrow. If he planned to attack the rebels then, why did he
require another half-moon to notify them of his success—
or failure?

The Khonsel's expression provided no hints. Even if he
knew what Geriv intended, he would refuse to tell her in
order to protect her from Rigat.

"The interrogations will keep Rigat busy until the Blessing of the Adders," she said. "But once the Gathering con-
cludes, he'll want to go north immediately. We can't
allow that."

"Why not suggest that he visit the estates of the slave
owners? To speed the census along and talk to the slaves
himself."

"It would be too easy for him to open a portal to the Spirit-Hunter. We need to keep him close."

The Khonsel frowned thoughtfully. "I'll come up with something, Earth's Beloved. But we should not discuss this again."

She nodded; it had been a risk to reveal as much as he had. But there were always risks in ruling an empire—especially in the shadow of the Son of Zhe.

As the Khonsel rose, she voiced the fear that was always with her these days. "If Rigat discovers the truth . . ."

"He won't."

"If he touches your spirit again . . ."

He won't." The Khonsel smiled grimly and patted the sheath of his dagger. "I'm a warrior, Earth's Beloved. So is my nephew. If it comes to that, we both know how to die well."

Chapter 32

G ERIV WIPED THE SWEAT from his eyes and examined the site again.

By now, Jonaq would have returned to Little Falls—with or without the Spirit-Hunter. Hoping for a message, Geriv had waited as long as he dared, but he couldn't jeopardize the second part of his plan by waiting to learn the outcome of the first.

Jonaq had argued against a two-pronged attack. Argued even more passionately against leaving only a token force at Little Falls. But he didn't understand that securing the Spirit-Hunter—one way or another—warranted any risk.

Geriv had taken the precautions he could. Three days ago, he had marched his troops out of the fortress at dawn and sailed ten miles downriver before beaching the ships.

Following the crude map drawn by the spy, they had
marched south. Geriv had led the scouting party himself,
discarding one site after another until reaching this one.

He had archers in the woods to pick off any rebel scouts.
More on the rise on which he stood. And the rest of his
men arrayed around the site, ready to close in once the
rebels reached the stream. More than two hundred men
against a band less than half its size.

If the spy's information was correct. If he was wrong, if
he had deliberately misled them . . .

"You can't trust him," Jonaq had insisted.

"I don't."

"At least let the Remil lead the troops. Don't risk
yourself."

"Only if I lead the attack do I demonstrate its importance to the men."

"Then let me stay with you."

"I need you to lead the attack on the Spirit-Hunter's
band."

He had kept his voice patient, preferring to reward Jonaq's loyalty rather than reprimand him for his doubts. He
always encouraged his aides to offer their opinions, but on
this matter, his mind was made up.

He had been equally adamant in his refusal to allow
Korim to accompany him. The boy had pleaded and whee-
dled until Geriv finally lost his temper.

"If you're so eager to be blooded, practice your sword
work. And if you want to be treated like a real officer,
learn to obey orders."

Korim's head had snapped back as if he had struck him.
Then he had thumped his chest with his fist and stalked
out of the room.

I should have reasoned with him. Explained myself better.

*I shouldn't have to explain myself. When he accepted the
rank of skalel, he accepted the duties that came with it—first
and foremost, obedience to his commander.*

They had ruined him, his grandmother and mother.
Stuffed him full of poetry and music and all the gentle
graces. Even after a year, the boy still had no conception
of the dangers in this land. Of the hard life a warrior led.
Or the hard choices a commander had to make.

A shiver racked his body, and he scowled. The one thing

he hadn't anticipated was this damnable fever. It had begun two days ago and worsened on the march south. At first, he had stoically endured the pervasive aches and the alternating bouts of chills and sweats. But this morning, he had barely managed to keep down his breakfast.

He turned to study the two skalekhs lined up to receive their final orders. He had insisted on seasoned warriors who could be counted on to keep their heads during the heat of battle. The Remil had selected the men himself, and they seemed to warrant do Fadiq's confidence. Their faces held the barely-suppressed excitement every warrior felt before a battle, but there was none of the greasy sweat or nervous shifting of eyes and feet that betrayed fear or doubt.

Conscious of their gazes, he straightened his aching shoulders.

"You all have descriptions of the targets. They are your only objective. It's possible that one—or both—may have gone ahead to scout the site for this Gathering. We won't know that until the rebels arrive. If you don't. see your target, you may draw your swords and engage the enemy at will. Otherwise, you are to use your clubs. I want them alive. Is that understood?"

He waited for every head to nod before turning to the officer who had been given the most important responsibility. He was older than the others, his lean face pocked with plague scars.

"The man possesses the power to attack another's spirit. He must be secured quickly and rendered unconscious."

The Skalel thumped his chest with his fist. "I understand, Vanel. I will not fail you."

Geriv dismissed them and studied the site a final time. Then he crouched behind a tree to wait.

Keirith trotted beside Pedar, trying in vain to shake off his gloomy thoughts.

He had dutifully told Temet about the truce he had "Seen," and was relieved that Temet had seemed as skeptical as he was. He feared the Zherosi were only using Rigat, but his brother had returned three days later to assure him that the queen had ordered a cessation of hostilities until the next full moon.

Keirith's relief was fleeting; yesterday, he'd had a true vision that seemed to contradict Rigat's promise of peace.

It began with a chaotic battle, somewhere in a forest. He was in the center of the fighting, yet neither his friends nor his enemies seemed to notice him. It was as if an invisible shield surrounded him. As he cried out to his comrades, his gaze was drawn to a rocky slope. Two boulders stared down at him. The ledge beneath cracked open in a crooked grin, and Xevhan's laughter roared out.

He had shared the vision with Temet, dismayed that he could recall so few details of the terrain. At the outset of today's journey, every boulder made his heart thud, but as the afternoon wore on, weariness took the edge off his anxiety.

Despite the coolness of the forest, sweat soaked the band of flaxcloth inside his leather helmet. Under the padded leather armor, taken off a dead Zheroso, his tunic clung to his body. He let out a sigh of relief as the pace slowed, then started when he heard a yelp from Pedar.

"If it's not the midges, it's the deerflies." Pedar rubbed his neck and scrutinized him sourly. "They don't seem to find you very appetizing."

"I guess they don't like the taste of Zherosi."

"Well, that's hardly fair," Pedar replied. "If the bastards are going to steal our land, at least they should be plagued by our bugs." His scowl turned to a smile when he saw Selima approaching. "Why are we stopping?"

"There's a stream up ahead. Temet's letting us rest and refill our waterskins." She grinned as Pedar warded off another deerfly. "Getting eaten, are you?"

"Devoured."

"Poor babe."

She nipped the swelling lump on his neck, and Pedar gave an exaggerated shiver of delight. "It's much nicer when you do it."

"I should hope so."

Keirith cleared his throat. "All right, all right," he said, doing his best to imitate Temet's most fatherly tone. "There'll be plenty of time for that later."

Selima laughed and punched his arm, easily dodging his

return blow. "Cocky, but slow. I like that in a man." With a grin for both of them, she strode off.

"Keep your hands off my woman," Pedar cautioned.

"As if I could catch her."

Pedar laughed, then spun around with a curse, waving madly at the persistent deerfly.

Temet walked over, a rare grin lightening his features. "Since you're feeling so frisky, Pedar, why don't you pass the word to those in the rear that we'll rest here?"

Pedar's head drooped, then jerked up. Howling, he slapped at his neck, but the deerfly was already buzzing away in triumph. "That one was your fault," he said, glaring at Temet. Muttering dire threats, he stomped off, head darting from side to side in search of other attackers.

"When will we reach the Gathering?" Keirith asked.

"Sunset."

When he failed to suppress a groan, Temet slapped his back. "You'll feel better after you've had some water." As they walked toward the stream, he added, "I just wish we had time to bathe. I stink."

"We all stink."

"Aye. But I'd hate to see Faelia wrinkle her nose when she gets a whiff of me."

"You could smell like a stoat and it wouldn't put Faelia off."

Temet's expression softened as he contemplated their reunion. Then he noticed Keirith's amused look and frowned. "Well. She's an affectionate woman."

Laughing at that understatement, Keirith knelt beside the stream. He drank deeply and refilled his waterskin, then pulled off his helmet and plunged his head into the water.

Gods, it was good. It was all he could do to keep from ripping off his clothes and jumping in. He sat back on his haunches and shook his wet hair off his face, savoring the cool trickles running down his neck. Minnows darted through the shallows, flashing silver in the shafts of sunlight. He watched them, smiling, until Temet's fingers dug into his arm. Caught by his frozen expression, Keirith followed the direction of his gaze.

Two boulders, halfway up the slope. Beneath them, a slanting ledge of rock bisected by a long, uneven fissure.

His eyes met Temet's. For a moment, they both crouched there, bound together in shared recognition and horror. Then Temet leaped up and shouted, "Ambush!"

Like a flock of deadly birds, arrows flew between the trees, cleaving flesh and saplings alike. He heard Temet shouting, but his voice was soon lost amid the screams. Then Keirith spotted him, fair hair streaming behind him as he ran. Too late, he remembered he had left his helmet and shield beside the stream and spun back, only to retreat as dozens of Zherosi poured down the slope.

He stumbled past one body, leaped over another. Glimpsed Pedar and Selima rallying a group to them. As he veered toward them, a spear thudded into a sapling. He shied away and collided with Temet.

"Get behind me!" Temet yelled, flinging up his shield.

Four Zherosi darted toward them from the right. Three more moved in from the left. Back to back, he and Temet met the charge.

He slashed at an unprotected throat, then spun and hacked at a club-wielding arm. Both men danced out of range.

Wet hair slapped his cheek, blinding him. He flung it back, then quickly ducked under the sweep of a club. Still in a crouch, he thrust up with his sword to rip open the man's leg.

A scream of pain. The sweet smell of blood. A surge of triumph as his enemy staggered away. A wave of despair as another stepped forward to fill the gap.

Slash and pivot. Duck and thrust. Just as Temet had taught him. Just as he had practiced dozens, hundreds of times.

He was no longer a warrior, hardly even a man, just a cornered animal, fighting for its life. Around him, dozens of others must be doing the same. He could hear the shrieks of pain, the clang of swords, but they seemed far away. Only these enemies, these weapons were real.

Hacking at the sword thrusting toward Temet's throat. Beating aside the club arcing toward Temet's head. Desperately bracing for an attack, only to watch his enemies backing away.

Why won't they fight me?

He heard the crack of shattered wood. Temet's savage howl. Another crack. Then Temet slammed into him.

Something slimy and warm spattered against the back of his neck, but he was fighting for balance on the blood-slick grass and could only pray Temet wasn't badly wounded. He regained his footing before the Zherosi could press their advantage. They shifted their feet, clubs at the ready, watching him, waiting for his next move. Did they know about his part in the ambushes? Is that why they wanted him alive?

He took a step back and stumbled over something soft. A hoarse cry escaped him when he glanced down.

Shards of bone protruded from the bloody pulp of Temet's jaw. Shattered teeth filled the gaping hole of his mouth. Above the smear of flesh that had once been his nose, the blue eyes stared up at him, glazed and unseeing.

Keirith turned in a slow circle, eyeing the warriors closing in around him. Between their bodies, he glimpsed his comrades, fleeing into the woods, up the rise, across the stream, zigzagging left and right in a helpless attempt to evade their pursuers.

He flexed his fingers, adjusting his grip on the sweat-slick leather of his sword hilt. If he attacked the spirit of one man, he might distract him long enough to break through to freedom. But which one?

The older one. With the pockmarks. He must be the commander.

He was still drawing on his power when the man shouted, "Now!" With a snarl of defiance, Keirith charged.

Chapter 33

DARAK LOOKED UP from sharpening his dagger to watch Faelia. Ignoring Sorig's order to stay low, she paced the perimeter of Black Hill. Each time she reached the north face, she paused to gaze into the distance before continuing her relentless circuit.

After listening to his report, Sorig had sent two men to intercept Temet. By nightfall, they were all gazing north, hope warring with concern. Shortly after dawn, Holtik had arrived with the rest of the recruits, but their relief leached away when midday came and went with no sign of Temet's band.

Eyeing the track Faelia's feet had beaten through the grass, Darak rose and strode over to Sorig. "We can't just sit here and wait."

"I know!" Sorig snapped. Then he sighed. "Sorry."

Darak shook his head, still watching his daughter. "We're all on edge."

"I'll send out two more scouts."

"I'm going with them."

"You're not going anywhere."

Darak dragged his gaze from Faelia. "You mean to stop me?"

"I won't put you in danger."

"Good gods, man, there's danger all around us."

For a long moment, Sorig just stared at the ground. Then his head came up. "There's not going to be a Gathering, is there?"

When Darak shook his head, a visible shudder racked Sorig's thin frame.

All his life he had relied on instinct, but lately, he had made so many mistakes—misjudging Kelik, misinterpreting the actions of the three who had sacrificed their lives for him. Instinct told him Sorig was no traitor, but perhaps he wanted to believe that because he liked the lad. They had endured long marches and scanty rations. Slept huddled together for warmth when drenching thunderstorms left the dead branches too soaked to start a fire. Traveled for miles to reach a village, only to walk away without a single recruit. Yet Sorig's confidence never waned. Now, he looked as uncertain as a raw recruit.

"If we wait for two more scouts to return," Darak said, "it might be another day—maybe longer—before we know anything. We should all go. Now."

Sorig's gaze swept the exhausted men and women enjoying their first real sleep in days. Then he nodded, reassuming the burden of command with a visible effort.

As Darak walked away to retrieve his pack, he heard footsteps behind him.

"You think it's me, don't you?" Sorig asked. "The spy." When Darak hesitated, he added, "I've seen you watching me. At first, I thought you blamed me. Because I'd failed you—and the others—as a commander. But that didn't seem like you. Then I thought about it some more. I arrive alone. No one to prove my story is true."

Sorig's voice was flat and unemotional, but his body was strung tight as a bowstring.

"My gut tells me you're not the traitor," Darak said. "I'd stake my life on it. But not the life of my daughter. Or my son. If I'm wrong, I can only hope to make amends for my doubts."

"And I hope to prove myself to you. One day."

They discovered the two scouts first. Their bodies had been dragged off the trail and hastily covered with leaves, now scattered by the carrion eaters. A few of the recruits lurched away, white-faced and retching; the rest helped dig shallow graves and cover them with stones.

Darak knew the men deserved a proper burial; knew,

too, that before the day was over they would probably have many more graves to dig. But the delay only fed his concern for Keirith.

Fear is the enemy.

A mile later, they found Selima sprawled unconscious on the trail. A bandage smeared with dirt and blood bound her right arm and a blood-soaked wad of flaxcloth had been shoved under her tunic and strapped against her shoulder. Faelia peeled away the bandage, revealing the clumsy stitches. Why would the Zherosi tend her wounds and then leave her behind?

"Temet might have sent her ahead," Faelia said as she cleaned Selima's wounds. "To warn us. She might have run into the same patrol the scouts did."

Darak nodded, unwilling to destroy his daughter's hopes. He had promised Griane that he would bring their children home. If Fellgair were here, he would have pointed out that he had never promised to bring them home alive.

Control the fear.

His gaze returned to the small doeskin bag around Selima's throat. Some of the women who had found refuge in his village arrived with bags of charms that had belonged to their dead husbands, but he could not recall any of the women in Temet's band ever wearing them.

"Is that hers?" he asked Faelia.

"Nay." The roll of nettle-cloth slipped from her shaking fingers. She bit her upper lip, looking so much like her mother that Darak's heart clenched. "Pedar's, perhaps. He was—is—Selima's man."

Kelik and Mikal trotted forward with a stretcher, hastily fashioned from borrowed mantles lashed to two dead branches with spare bowstrings and lengths of rope. As they bent to lift Selima, Darak said, "Wait."

Gently, he raised her head and slipped the bag free. The soft doeskin was warm from her body. He fumbled with the drawstrings, silently cursing his maimed fingers.

"Would you recognize them?" Faelia asked.

"I don't know. But I have to look."

One doeskin bag looked much like another; he doubted he could tell Callie's from Keirith's. But he might recognize the charms inside. Only the boy who collected them was supposed to touch them; for another to do so would diminish their power. But he had no choice.

Faelia's hands were the steady ones this time. Big hands like his, but freckled like her mother's. Strong enough to pull a bowstring back to her ear, yet nimble enough to tie a lure on a fishing line—or wriggle into the mouth of a bag of charms.

She handed the bag back to him. With two bold sweeps of her hands, she cleared away the leaves and twigs at his feet, leaving a patch of bare earth. Darak framed a silent prayer to the Maker. Then he upended the bag.

An eagle's feather. A round, red stone. A quickthorn twig. A strand of hardened lakeweed, faded to a pale yellow-green. Any boy might have collected them. Then his gaze fell on the polished stone, its green-black surface spattered with red.

"I taught Malaq to seek a vision without relying on qiij. He used this stone with red splotches on it. Like freckles. A bloodstone, he called it."

Before he died, the Zherosi Pajhit had given Keirith that freckled stone. A gift to the boy who had become a second son to him.

Control yourself.

He lowered the fist pressed against his chest. Made himself open his eyes and look into his daughter's. Forced his mouth to speak the words.

"They're Keirith's."

As they hurried along the trail, he told himself Keirith might still be alive, that the bag might have been sent as proof of a capture rather than a kill. But as he crested a rise, the sickly sweet stench of decay hit him like a physical blow.

Bodies sprawled on the slope, cut down in a futile attempt to flee. Others clogged the little stream. Through the screen of trees, he made out still more, covering the forest floor as far as he could see.

Faelia broke first, pushing past Sorig to race downhill. Mikal covered his eyes with his hand, then squared his shoulders and walked back to where the others waited.

Darak heard him cautioning the recruits to cover their mouths and noses. As if wool or doeskin could possibly blot out the stench.

His legs carried him down the slope. His eyes scanned the bodies, passing over those with fair hair, those who were too tall, too big-boned. His mind cautioned him that some faces might be tanned from long days in the sun, while others—buried under a heap of bodies—would be darkened by putrefaction. But try as he might to hold himself aloof from the horror, his senses cataloged it all.

The croaking of the crows and ravens that ascended in a black cloud as they approached. The obscene buzzing of the flies that swarmed in iridescent waves over the corpses. The shit-slimed leaves and the metallic scent of blood and piss. Men's bellies swollen like pregnant women's. Tunics ripped open, spilling flyblown guts onto the leaves. Shattered skulls, leaking clods of partially devoured brains. Empty eye sockets staring skyward out of blood-caked faces.

Relentless as death, he moved among the corpses, bending close to inspect faces destroyed by swords and clubs and scavengers; pushing back the sleeve of a severed arm in search of the familiar tattoo; letting out his breath when he failed to discover it; continuing the hunt, fingertips tingling from their brush against cold flesh.

Distantly, he was aware of the living who stalked the battlefield with him: the grunt of effort as a body was rolled over; the inarticulate sound of protest when another friend was recognized; vomit spattering against leaves; the stomach-churning stink that followed; choked sobs from those who allowed themselves to weep. He wondered that his senses could remain so sharp when everything seemed utterly unreal—a nightmare, more vivid than most, from which he must surely wake.

Faelia's cry pierced the fog that enveloped him. Fear pounced, sending his heart into a wild tattoo.

She was on her knees, clawing through bodies. As he raced toward her, she flung her head back, her mouth opening in a silent scream.

Please gods, don't let it be Keirith. Don't let it be my boy.

His steps slowed. Even matted with blood and dirt, he recognized Temet's distinctive yellow hair.

His face had been crushed by a club, his body hacked by

swords. His head lolled, connected to his neck by a few strands of muscle and the blood-encrusted column of his spinal cord. Gently, Faelia lifted his head and cradled it in her lap. She rocked back and forth, eyes squeezed shut, teeth clenched in a rictus of grief.

He stared at Temet's ruined face, recalling the expression it had worn during their first meeting in the Zherosi slave compound—dreamy with the drugs the guards had fed him, but also with memories.

"I was the fastest runner in my village. Won every race at the Gatherings. Swift as the wind, I was. Swift as the wind."

Darak knelt and wrapped his arms around his daughter, swaying with her in the silent rhythm of grief and loss. But his eyes scanned the bodies around them, seeking his boy's face.

"Darak."

He looked up to find Kelik looming over him.

"Selima's awake. We can't make much sense of what she's saying, but she keeps repeating your name."

Darak hesitated, torn between the urge to comfort his daughter and the need to find out what Selima knew.

"Go. I'll stay with her."

Still, he hesitated. In the wildness of grief, Faelia might do anything.

Even as the thought crossed his mind, she drew her dagger. Darak rose into a crouch, ready to seize her arm if she turned the blade on herself, but Faelia simply cut off a lock of Temet's hair.

"Faelia."

Sorig looked as if he had aged years since he had descended the rise.

"Faelia. I need you."

He had to repeat her name again before her head turned. She stared up at him, her eyes glazed and unseeing.

"We have to bury them."

Darak opened his mouth to object. Then he saw his daughter's gaze sharpen.

"We'll need to dig pits. And gather rocks. I need you to take charge."

After a long moment, she sheathed her dagger. Opened her belt pouch. Tucked the lock of hair inside. With the same dreamlike slowness, she bent and kissed Temet's ruined mouth. Then she got to her feet and walked away. Without a word, Kelik followed her.

"It helps," Sorig said. "To do . . . something." His gaze lingered on Temet. Darak knew better than to touch him; even the smallest gesture of sympathy would break him, and Sorig needed all his strength now.

Together, they made their way across the stream and up the rise. Mikal crouched beside Selima, dribbling water between her cracked lips. Darak squatted down and squeezed her hand, only to have it yanked from his grasp with surprising strength. She groped at the neck of her tunic until Darak pulled Keirith's bag of charms from his belt pouch.

"Alive . . ." she whispered.

His breath wheezed out in a shuddering sigh of relief.

"The Zherosi commander . . . he took Keirith to Little Falls. He gave me his bag of charms. As proof. And said to find you . . . to tell you . . ."

Her eyes closed, and he resisted the urge to shake her. Then they flew open again.

" 'Your son is my prisoner. I will free him if you surrender yourself at Little Falls by the half-moon. If you do not arrive by then, your son will die.' "

He was aware that Selima was still speaking, but all he could hear were those awful words, echoing over and over in his head: " . . . *your son will die.*"

Selima's fingernails bit into his palm. "I was to tell you his name. The commander's. Vanel do Khat."

He shook his head; the name meant nothing.

"Vanel is a rank," Mikal said. "The supreme commander of the Zherosi forces in the north. But I don't recognize the name. He must have assumed command recently."

"He's the nephew of an old acquaintance of yours," Selima said. "Those were his exact words. 'An old acquaintance.' A man named . . ." She paused, searching for the words. "Khonsel . . . oh, gods, what was it?"

"Do Havi," Darak replied. "Khonsel Vazh do Havi."

The man who had helped them escape to honor a promise to a dead friend.

"The Vanel. Did he have a patch over one eye?"

Selima nodded.

Geriv. He could barely remember the face, but the name was imprinted on his memory. Like that of the Khonsel, he had repeated it in his prayers for fourteen years.

A harsh bark of laughter escaped him. The others stared at him, no doubt wondering if shock had weakened his mind.

A pity he had sworn never to speak to Fellgair again. Only the Trickster would appreciate the irony.

Chapter 34

DULL PAIN RADIATING DOWN the back of his head. The creak of branches in the wind. The splash of water.

Keirith tried to open his eyes, but they seemed to be glued shut. So was his mouth.

He could hear the drone of men's voices, but the words were muffled by the rhythmic pounding of a drum. Then a man called, "Raise oars." In Zherosi.

Only then did he realize that the creaking he heard was the sound of oars, and the gentle rocking was the motion of a ship. He thrashed in helpless terror, only to freeze at the nauseating pain that stabbed his right shoulder.

Footsteps on wood.

They've found me—the Big One, Gap-Tooth, Greasy Hair.

Hands seized his head.

Not again. Dear gods, not again!

Ignoring the pain, he fought them, but his hands and feet were bound, and there were so many of them—seizing his limbs, raising his head, fumbling with the gag and yanking it down. He screamed in terror and frustration. Someone slapped him. A deep voice ordered him to drink.

He pressed his lips together, shaking his head wildly. A hand seized a fistful of hair and yanked his head back. Fingers pinched his nose closed until he was forced to open his mouth to steal a breath. He choked on the sweet liquid, spat it out, but there was no escaping the unseen hands that yanked his head back again, shoved a cup against his teeth, and forced him to swallow.

Sticky dregs dribbled down his chin. A fingernail scratched his cheek as the gag was pulled back over his mouth. The footsteps receded. And he slid back into darkness.

As Geriv collapsed onto the cushions in his pavilion, he heard do Fadiq's startled exclamation and footsteps thudding across the deck.

He closed his burning eyes against the early morning sunlight and coughed, despising his weakness. He heard the Remil grunt. Felt the cushions sag as the man knelt beside him. Fingers tugged at the straps of his helmet. A hand slid behind his neck and lifted his head. Geriv wheezed a sigh of relief as do Fadiq slid his helmet off.

A callused palm brushed his forehead with unexpected gentleness. "Good gods, man, you're burning up!"

The Remil called for water. Unbuckled the straps securing his armor. Slipped a cushion under his aching neck.

"Drink."

Geriv sipped the lukewarm water gratefully, then sank back on the cushions, spent. "Watch him," he managed. "Kheridh."

The Remil asked something, but a racking chill prevented him from replying.

Something warm and heavy covered him. Wool. A cloak. The Remil's urgent voice receded. And he slid into darkness.

Keirith woke to another nauseating stab of pain in his shoulder. He seemed to be lurching through the air. Something hard dug into his belly—a man's shoulder. Something cool and wet splattered against his cheek—rain. The scent

of woodsmoke and animal dung. Through the haze of fear
and pain, he tried to pick out other details that might tell
him where he was, but it was all he could do to keep from
vomiting into the gag.

A grunt. The crackle of something—rushes? bracken?—
as he was lowered to the ground.

He kicked weakly with his bound feet until a boot caught
him in the ribs, stealing his breath and the little strength
he possessed.

Soft fur beneath his cheek. The clink of metal. The dull
thump of a mallet pounding wood. And then the hands
again, yanking down the gag. Before he could ask where
he was, the cup was pressed against his lips.

"Drink."

He drank, even though he knew it had to be drugged,
knew that was why he kept drifting into oblivion and waking with a furred tongue and dulled senses. He could remember attacking the pockmarked man. An explosion of
pain in his shoulder that shattered his burgeoning power.
A blow to the head. And then nothing until the ship.
How long had he been on it? What had happened to
the others?

"There's a waterskin. By your left arm. And a bowl to
piss in."

The same deep voice that had commanded him to drink.

"Your shoulder is out of joint. Our physician will set it.
Remain still or you'll injure it again. Nod if you understand."

Keirith nodded.

"If you refuse food or drink, you'll be beaten. If you
attempt to remove the gag or the blindfold, you'll be
beaten. If you speak without permission, you'll be beaten."

*I'm in the slave compound at Pilozhat. In a moment, the
Slave Master will begin reciting the litany of punishments.*

"Do you understand?"

He nodded.

The rushes crackled. The labored breathing grew louder.
Beneath the odor of stale sweat, Keirith caught a whiff of
some spicy scent. Hands fumbled for his wrist and shoved
his sleeve up. He could almost feel the intensity of the man's
gaze as he scrutinized the snake tattooed on his forearm.

"Do not try to use your power, Kheridh."

The man's breath warmed his ear. It took all his control to keep from flinching.

"If you do, I will kill you."

The crunch of rushes. Raindrops pattering dully on the thatch, echoing the frantic beat of his heart. And then the soft slide toward calm, as oblivion, soothing as the drugged brew, came to claim him once more.

Faces swam in and out of Geriv's vision: Korim's, frightened; the physician's, puckered in a frown; Jonaq's, scowling.

Had he asked Jonaq about the Spirit-Hunter? He was certain he'd seen his aide waiting on the shore, but he couldn't remember talking with him. Nor could he remember how he had gotten to his quarters. Just stumbling along the stone pathway that suddenly lurched toward him.

Another face swam into view. The Remil. His loud voice made Geriv wince. He was pathetically grateful that the physician replied in a low murmur.

"Tick fever . . . aches . . . nausea . . . confusion . . . high fever . . ."

He tried to ask about the Spirit-Hunter, but managed only a hoarse croak.

Cold fingers clasped his. Korim's.

"Chill phase . . . flushing phase . . ."

"Jonaq . . ." he mumbled. "The Spirit-Hunter . . ."

"He escaped us. Forgive me, Vanel."

Even through the fever haze, he heard the shame in Jonaq's voice. Geriv shook his head, trying to reassure him; the ensuing wave of nausea forced him to lie still.

A damp cloth wiping his face. A wooden cup pressed against his mouth.

The bitterness of the tea made him gag. As his body heaved, someone—Korim?—tried to steady him, but he barely managed to turn his head to keep from vomiting on himself.

"Crisis . . . three to five days . . . possible relapse . . ."

He didn't have three to five days. The Spirit-Hunter was

coming. And he wasn't the kind of man to surrender without a fight.

And then there was Kheridh. Had he given orders that there must be two guards watching him at all times? Even drugged and gagged and blindfolded, he might be able to summon his power and steal a guard's body. And then he could walk out of the fortress a free man. And destroy everything.

He had to be strong. He had to be ready. This fever would not defeat him. Nor would the Spirit-Hunter and his son.

"Father?"

He flinched at the sound of Korim's voice so close to his ear.

"Tell me how I can help. Tell me what I can do."

"Just . . . stay . . . away . . ."

Korim recoiled. Tears filled his eyes as he leaped up from the bed.

Geriv tried to summon the strength to call him back, to correct the terrible misunderstanding, to assure his son that he had only meant for him to stay away from Kheridh. But Korim was already pushing past the others, fleeing the room that began to spin and darken as black dots swarmed his vision and engulfed him.

He ate when they pressed a bowl of porridge to his mouth. He pissed when they shoved another bowl against his thighs. When he had to move his bowels, they held him while he squatted, helpless and humiliated, but too weak to object.

No one questioned him about the rebel forces or the part he had played in the ambushes. No one questioned him about his power. They seemed content to keep him prisoner—and that frightened him more than anything.

What were they waiting for?

The truth came to Keirith in one of his few lucid moments. If Deep Voice knew his name, he must know who his father was. The Zherosi wanted Darak Spirit-Hunter, and they were using him as bait.

He tried to keep from swallowing the dream-brew, but the healer pried open his mouth after he drank. He tried to contact Natha, but the honeyed brew subverted every attempt. In desperation, he sought Rigat. If he could touch his brother's spirit, he could tell him the truce was just a trick, urge him to force the Zherosi queen to free him or—failing that—find Fa and warn him to stay away. But he didn't possess Rigat's gift of tracking a person's unique energy and he had never thought to ask him how he did it.

His father would come. The Zherosi would kill him. And there was nothing he could do to stop it.

Chapter 35

IN THE VILLAGE, Midsummer came and went. Griane listened to Callie recite the ancient legend, chanted as Gortin and Barasa opened the way to the First Forest, and waited for their return at sunset to celebrate the Holly-Lord's defeat of the Oak-Lord and the turning of the year.

She helped three new babes enter the world and eased the passage of three old folk as they left it. She gathered bracken and meadowsweet for strewing, dock and sunstar for treating rashes, comfrey and yarrow to make ointments for scrapes and bruises. In the evenings, she spun yarn for the weavers and mentally prepared her list of the lichens and plants she would need to gather for mordants and dyes.

She eyed the golden barley and prayed for a good harvest. She eyed Ennit, guarding the flock, and prayed that time would ease his grief. She eyed the hills to the south, mantled in purple heather, and prayed that her husband and children were safe.

Hircha moved back into her hut. Young Lorthan moved into Ennit's. Callie presented his bride-gifts to Ennit and Lisula, who gladly gave permission for him to marry Ela at the Fall Balancing.

And Madig grew stronger.

By Midsummer, he was able to close his fist around the ball of grain Colla had made for him. By the full moon, he took his first wobbling steps around the fire pit. When he emerged from his hut, the whole village cheered. Red-faced and sweating, he lurched to the next hut and back, dragging his right foot and leaning heavily on the crutch Othak had so thoughtfully crafted.

Othak spent part of every day with Madig. He accompanied him on his walks. Told him all the goings-on in the village. Sat beside him when Griane came to check on her patient's progress.

At the end of each visit, Othak took her aside to ask how soon Madig's speech would return. She invariably shrugged and told him she simply didn't know. He invariably sighed and told him he would pray. His voice conveyed only concern. His smile conveyed only hope. But those pale eyes remained as cold as frozen ice on the lake.

After yet another polite exchange, Griane stormed home and hurled her healing bag across the hut. "Othak's enjoying himself."

"Aye," Hircha replied, patiently gathering up the supplies that had spilled out. "But if he had any proof, he'd have come out with it."

"He's just waiting for Madig to accuse Rigat."

Callie squeezed her hand. "As long as Madig's speech is garbled—"

"It's getting clearer every day," Griane interrupted. "When I told him he was as stubborn as a bullock, he said, 'So are you.' "

"What he said," Hircha corrected, "was 'Oh ah oo.' "

"If I can understand him, so can Othak! If he's not hanging around Madig, he's hovering over poor Gortin. And don't tell me he's just concerned about Gortin's health," she added, glaring at Callie.

"Oh, he's concerned," Callie replied. "Like a raven's concerned about a dying rabbit."

Hircha gaped at him. "I've lived with you half my life. And I swear that's the first time I've heard you speak ill of anyone."

"Well, I'm sick of it, too! To hear Othak talk, Nemek's death was part of some plot so I could become Memory-Keeper."

"He dared say that?" Griane demanded.

"He never comes out and says anything directly. But it's there. In those sidelong glances. Or the thoughtful pauses. Or that wondering shake of his head." Callie stroked his chin with his thumb. "Such a tragedy," he said, mimicking Othak's nasal voice. "To lose our beloved Memory-Keeper. Who would have thought it possible?"

"Anyone who got within three paces of him and smelled the wounds." Griane silently asked Nemek's forgiveness before turning to Hircha. "Have *you* heard anything?"

"When has anyone ever gossiped to me? I'm surprised Othak said as much to Callie."

"He didn't," Callie replied. "Ela overheard him talking with Rothisar and some of the other hunters. And Sion came to me the other day."

"Sion?" Griane echoed. It was a rare day that Sion spoke three sentences in a row, never mind initiating a conversation.

"He said he'd heard Othak talking about all of us. Rigat and Keirith, mostly. But you and Hircha, too."

Slowly, it all came out, and what it amounted to was a subtle campaign to plant suspicion in people's minds. Whose families had suffered most in the Zherosi attack? Those whose deaths benefited their family: Nemek, the Memory-Keeper; Seg, Rigat's keenest rival. Who could see that a wound went untreated or knew which herbs could be fatal if administered improperly?

"And Conn?" Hircha asked. "Did Othak mention how I benefited from my husband's death?" When Callie hesitated, her lips twisted in a bitter smile. "Of course. Because I secretly wanted Keirith and could only get him if Conn was out of the way. Nay, it's really quite clever. If you overlook the fact that Keirith and I had fourteen years to make up our minds."

She took a deep breath, clearly fighting for calm. Then

she fixed them with a gaze as cold as Othak's. "We have to do something. Before he turns the whole tribe against us."

Griane nodded. "I'll talk with Gortin now. While Othak's still with Madig."

Moments later, she was standing outside Gortin's hut, softly calling his name. But it was Othak who appeared in the doorway—as if he had guessed her intentions.

"The Tree-Father is resting before the council meeting," he informed her.

"Perhaps he could spare me a moment first."

Before Othak could speak, she heard Gortin's voice, bidding her to enter. Suppressing a triumphant smile, she sidled past Othak.

Although fresh bracken had been strewn on the dirt, the hut smelled old and musty. As she approached Gortin, she realized the odor came from him. Bits of food clung to his robe. The gods only knew when it had been washed last. Or when Gortin had bathed.

She crossed to the doorway and flung back the hide. "You need fresh air, Tree-Father. And a bigger fire to add some light and cheer."

Ignoring Gortin's protests, she crouched beside the fire pit and added a bundle of twigs to the glowing peat bricks. The fire blazed into life, revealing Othak's disapproving frown.

"I can see to the Tree-Father's needs."

"Apparently not," she snapped.

The bowls near the fire pit were crusted with yesterday's porridge, while the pot . . . dear gods, she wasn't sure if the dark sludge in the bottom was burned porridge or stew. She fetched another pot and set some water to boil. If she accomplished nothing else, at least poor Gortin would have clean dishes.

"Don't fuss," Gortin urged. "Unmarried men are apt to be untidy."

She smacked his hand lightly with the heather scrub brush, ignoring Othak's indignant sniff. "Either I do it or I send a girl to see to things."

Gortin and Othak looked equally horrified; likely, she was the only female who had ventured into their hut in years.

She made a whirlwind of herself, hoping to drive Othak away, but he just watched her with his arms folded across his chest.

"Really, Griane," Gortin chided, "if this is why you came to see me—"

"I was hoping you'd visit Catha," she lied. "The babe's ailing. Nothing serious," she added quickly, "but your presence might ease Catha's mind. You know how she's been."

After losing Nemek and young Nionik, Catha clung to her remaining children. She barely let poor Arun out of her sight, and when her newborn broke out in suppurating pustules, she had fallen into hysterics, even after Griane assured her it was only a milk-rash.

Gortin sighed. "Forgive me, my dear, but I'm feeling so weak . . . and with the council meeting to attend . . ." He sighed again, then brightened. "Othak, perhaps you would go."

"Of course, Tree-Father. After I help you to the longhut."

"Mother Griane will help me. You go along."

Othak fixed her with his pale gaze. Then he returned Gortin's smile. "Yes, Tree-Father."

After Othak ducked outside, Gortin watched the doorway for several moments. Then he said, "Sit down, Griane. And tell me what you didn't want Othak to hear." He smiled at her start of surprise. "I may be dying, Griane, but I still know when you're worried."

"You're not dying."

"The Midsummer battle of the Oak and the Holly was the last I'll ever witness. And we both know it. But I'm not afraid. It'll be a relief to shed this tired old body and fly to the Forever Isles. I only wish I could live long enough to see our land free again. And . . ."

Impulsively, she squeezed his hand. "What, Tree-Father?"

His rheumy gaze lingered on the doorway. "I wish I could be certain Othak is the best man to follow me."

"Who else is there?"

Gortin shook his head in gentle reproof.

"Keirith," she whispered.

"Rigat has great power, but he is too young, too

impulsive. And I think his life-path takes him on another journey." He waited for her to nod before adding, "It should have been Keirith. He was born to lead our people. Just as Darak was. And Tinnean. And you, Griane. What an extraordinary family. Faelia, a leader in this rebellion. Callie, our Memory-Keeper. Truly, the gods have chosen you for great things."

"I wish the gods would leave us alone."

Once, Gortin would have chided her. Now, he simply patted her hand. "Those the gods choose for the greatest tasks are always given the hardest paths."

"It's one thing to hear about it in a tale and another when you're the one stumbling along the path."

"You're worried about Darak and the children."

"Of course I'm worried! Rigat promised to . . . to bring me word from time to time, but it's been nearly a moon since I've seen him. And even longer since Darak . . ." Emotion choked her voice, and she swallowed hard.

"What can I do?" Gortin asked quietly.

This time, she was the one to glance at the doorway.

"Those silly rumors about Rigat being responsible for Madig's condition?" Gortin shook his head. "I've already assured people they couldn't be true."

"Othak is the one spreading the rumors. And not only about Rigat."

By the time she finished repeating what Callie had told her, Gortin was trembling. "He was always frightened," he whispered. "As a child. Afraid to stand up to his father. Afraid to embrace his power. And jealous. So terribly jealous of Keirith's gift. As I was."

"You conquered your jealousy. Othak's has festered."

"I had hoped . . . once Keirith was cast out . . ." Gortin shook his head. Then he straightened, a glimmer of the old strength shining on his face. "You've only confirmed my doubts about Othak's ability to lead the tribe after I'm gone. When Keirith returns, I'll announce that he will be my successor."

"Even if Keirith agreed, the tribe—"

"I am still Tree-Father. The tribe will accept my choice. We need a strong man to lead us. One with a clear gift of vision. And one who puts the needs of his people first."

As he struggled to rise, Griane took his arm and handed him his blackthorn staff. Gortin caressed the wood, worn smooth by the generations of Tree-Fathers who had gripped this symbol of their authority. The hand clutching her arm trembled, but Gortin's expression was both determined and serene.

"After the council meeting, I'll speak with Othak about these rumors. And seek the gods' wisdom on how I should break the news to him about my choice of successor."

She guided him to the longhut, aware of the curious glances from those who had grown used to seeing Othak at his side. Every step of the way, Gortin talked, his voice carefully raised to be heard by all: praising her treatment of Madig; dismissing the rumors that linked Rigat to his seizure; commending Rigat for his part in the rebellion; and assuring her that her husband and children would soon return.

"What a happy day that will be. For the entire tribe. We'll need Darak and Keirith to guide us in the days to come."

By the time they reached the longhut, he was shaking with exhaustion, but his smile was triumphant. "Did you see how they stopped and listened?" he whispered, excited as a child. "In all my time as Tree-Father, I've never gotten so much attention. If Struath were here, he would scold me for pride."

"If Struath were here, he'd scold you for stealing attention from him."

Gortin pursed his lips, then burst out laughing, drawing astonished looks from the elders filing into the longhut.

"You're in a cheerful mood today," Trath muttered.

"I'm enjoying the sting of Mother Griane's words. They remind me how good life is."

Trath snorted. "If it's all the same, Mother Griane, I enjoy life just fine without the sting of your words."

"Aye, Alder-Chief." She lowered her gaze demurely, and Trath snorted again.

Her amusement faded as she walked toward her hut. She had desperately wanted to ask Gortin to find Rigat, but she doubted he had the strength to seek a vision. Still, if she'd managed to thwart Othak, her visit was successful.

She returned to her hut and told Hircha what Gortin intended, then repeated the story when Callie returned from the council meeting. And after they all retired to their pallets, she vowed to go to the boulder on the morrow and offer another sacrifice to the Oak and the Holly, beseeching them to bring Darak and the children home safely.

The scream jolted her awake. It took her a moment to recognize Othak's voice. Even before she made out the words, she knew what had happened.

Torchlight flickered in the darkness, illuminating men hurrying through the village. Women peeped from doorways, their faces tight with fear. A cluster of people had already gathered at the priests' hut by the time she reached it. Lisula's sorrowful expression told her she was too late.

Gortin was sprawled in the dirt. Othak crouched beside him, weeping. As she bent down, he screamed, "You did this!"

Shocked, she drew back.

"Don't be a fool," Trath said. "Griane's been in her hut all night."

"She asked him to seek a vision! And it killed him!"

"That's not true," Griane protested.

But Gortin had seen how anxious she was. And he was kindhearted enough to attempt to help. Seeking a vision might have exhausted him, but Griane had been a healer for more than thirty years and she knew it had not killed him.

As she bent to examine Gortin, Othak shoved her.

"That's enough!" Trath seized Othak's arm and yanked him to his feet. "Stop acting like a hysterical woman. You're Tree-Father now." He peered around the circle of onlookers. "Sion. Rothisar. Carry Gortin inside."

They laid Gortin on the furs. Keeping a cautious eye on Othak, Griane knelt beside him. She pressed her fingers to his wrist and drew back with a startled exclamation.

"He's cold. Why didn't you summon me at once?"

"I did!" Othak protested. "As soon as I found him."

"What was he doing outside?"

"I don't know. Perhaps he was going to your hut. To tell you what he had Seen."

"He could have sent you."

"I was asleep!" Othak's gaze darted around the circle of frowning faces. "I meant to sit with him. I did. But I . . . I failed him. And when I woke . . ." His voice trailed off on a sob.

"Instead of placing the blame on Mother Griane," Lisula said, "you'd do better to shoulder it yourself. If you had called her immediately—"

"It doesn't matter," Griane interrupted. "Nothing will bring him back now."

She folded Gortin's hands over his chest. There were no signs of suffocation or any indication of a struggle. There was a lump on the side of his head, but that could have been the result of his fall. There was nothing—nothing—to indicate Othak was responsible.

Numbly, she stroked the thin gray hair. Soon, Gortin's spirit would reach the Forever Isles, where—if the gods were kind—Struath would be waiting to welcome him. At any rate, he was free now. Free of his tired body and failing memory. Free of the loneliness that had haunted him since Struath's death. Free of Othak's hovering presence and tainted, jealous nature.

She would never be able to prove that Othak had killed Gortin. To accuse him would only create more dissension in the tribe, as would her claim that Gortin had wanted Keirith to become Tree-Father.

As she made her way back to her hut, she paused to gaze up at the moon. Perhaps it was only her imagination that made her see a half-smile on Gheala's face, a narrowed eye that seemed to wink at her, mocking her impotence.

"Oh, Rigat," she whispered. "Hurry home. I need you."

Chapter 36

R IGAT LEANED ON THE LOW wall of his balcony in a vain attempt to glimpse the temple of Zhe. All he could see was the milling crowd, little more than a seething black fog in the uncertain light.

The eager ones had begun arriving days ago to witness the dawn ceremony that would proclaim him the Son of Zhe. By yesterday afternoon, there were so many people on the plateau, Womb of Earth was groaning.

Or so Nekif assured him. For the last two days, he'd been trapped in the bowels of the palace, interrogating the thirteen noblemen accused of conspiring with Carilia.

The interrogations had been easy enough, although the drain on his power was noticeable. This morning, he'd been so tired that Nekif had to shake him in order to rouse him—and then prostrated himself, babbling apologies for touching the Son of Zhe without permission.

More disturbing was discovering that the noblemen had met several times with their Carilian counterparts, and exchanged some clumsily coded messages about pressuring their rulers to end the war. Three of the men had gone so far as to suggest more drastic measures—including inciting a mutiny among the troops in the east. In the end, they had shied away from such outright acts of treason. And in every spirit, he had touched a genuine love for the queen and for Zheros.

Although both Jholianna and the Khonsel made it clear that they considered the men guilty of treason, he continued to waver. "If they're guilty of anything," he'd told her, "it's being foolish enough to believe they could bring the war to an end."

He could still remember her eyes, dark with pity—for him, not the prisoners.

"They're playing on your kind heart. And the fact that you're still a stranger here. I've lived many centuries, Rigat. And I've learned the importance of ruling with a firm hand."

"And is there no place for mercy?"

"Yes. But it must be used sparingly. The world interprets mercy as weakness."

Reluctantly, he recalled the times he had played When I Become Chief. He had decided to cast Elasoth's daughters out of the tribe simply because their father had voted against Keirith. Yet now he was acting squeamish about punishing men who had conspired against their queen.

He'd never really imagined that his game could become so serious, that he might really control whether people lived or died. But now he did. The accused men would all receive trials, but the verdict was as certain as sunrise—unless he intervened. Saving them from execution might demonstrate how merciful the Son of Zhe was, but it was just as likely to prove that he was a softhearted boy, easily manipulated by others.

With Fellgair still absent, he had no one to turn to for advice. In the end, he won Jholianna's grudging consent to postpone the sentencing until after the moon of celebration. That would give him time to consider his choices—and give Fellgair time to return to Pilozhat.

Impatiently, he adjusted the golden serpent that circled his neck and traced the dimples in the hammered gold scales of his breastplate. For the third time, he smoothed his hair. Jholianna had insisted on braiding it herself, alternating between marveling at its softness and scolding him as she combed out the tangles. Just as his mam used to.

What would she think if she saw me now?

He had dreamed of her last night, standing in the center of the village, gazing up at the moon. Her eyes were closed, but he could see her lips moving so he guessed she was praying. He heard a voice calling him—too deep to be hers. And then he woke to find Nekif shaking him.

I'll go see her on the morrow. Just for a little while. I'll be back before Jholianna even notices I'm gone.

Hearing footsteps on the tiled floor, he whirled around. "Well?" he demanded as Nekif prostrated himself.

"Forgive me, great lord. But the Supplicant was not at her temple."

He ordered Nekif out of his chamber and began pacing, anger warring with concern. This was the most important day of his life. Fellgair should be here to witness it. Surely, nothing could have happened to him. He was a god, after all, not some puny mortal.

Refusing to let disappointment taint the day, he summoned his power. Although it was still sluggish from the interrogations, he easily opened a tiny sliver of a portal behind the temple. The first shafts of sunlight spilled through the serpentine pillars onto the altar, revealing the bloody carcass of a white ram, a special sacrifice to honor the Son of Zhe.

Rigat winced and looked away; one day, he would be able to see a sacrifice on that altar without imagining his brother lying there.

Torchlight danced across the bronze armor of the guards surrounding the temple. Clusters of scarlet and gold at the front of the crowd allowed him to identify the priests of Zhe and Heart of Sky. He spotted the half-shaven heads of the servants of the God with Two Faces, but had to squint before he made out the priestesses of Womb of Earth in their brown robes.

The kankhs blared, and the ground-fog of people seethed, only to fall still a moment later when the drums began. In contrast to the slow, measured tattoo, Rigat's heart raced. His power shuddered through him, flashing brighter with each drumbeat. The muscles in his legs trembled, and he had to fight the urge to leap through the portal to relieve the growing tension in his body.

Just when he thought the procession would never arrive, he saw Jholianna marching between the two lines of guards flanking the walkway from the palace. Like him, she was bedecked with jewelry, from the thin gold chain woven through her elaborate braids to the gem-studded one around her throat, and the bracelets encircling her arms.

"The common folk expect to see us dripping with jewelry," she had told him. "Especially on an occasion like this."

Rigat was certainly dripping; although the sun had barely risen, his power alone kept the sweat from running in streams down his body. He hated to use it for such a mundane purpose, but the Son of Zhe couldn't sweat like a slave.

If her jewelry seemed excessive, her gown was stunningly simple, the sheath binding her breasts the color of the first green leaves of spring, the flounces on her skirt the deeper greens of a Midsummer forest. She looked as a slender as a sapling, reminding him of the ancient legend of the rowan that had pulled up its roots and become the world's first woman.

Her simple elegance made the Zheron's finery look slightly ridiculous. Red, gold, and black feathers sprouted from the band of bronze that circled his forehead. More cascaded over his shoulders in a feathered cloak. By contrast, the Pajhit's shimmering cloak of pink and rose and ruddy red lent the little priest a rare dignity.

Rigat eagerly peered at the tall priestess walking beside the Motixa, and swallowed his disappointment when he realized it was not Fellgair. The common folk probably wouldn't even realize that it was not their Supplicant, for the Acolyte's half-shaven head and robe were identical to hers. A garland of honeysuckle crowned her head, while the Motixa wore one of bitterheart. In her brown robe, the plump Motixa was doomed to look dowdy, yet her innate grace and serene expression enhanced the aura of maternal compassion that shone from her.

Slowly, they mounted the steps and took their places, Jholianna directly in front of the altar, the priests and priestesses one step below, flanking her. The kankh blared again and the drums ceased.

It was almost time.

"By these signs shall you know him," the Zheron intoned. "His power shall burn bright as Heart of Sky at Midsummer. His footsteps shall make Womb of Earth tremble."

"Speechless, he shall understand the language of the adder," Jholianna proclaimed. "And wingless, soar through the sky like the eagle."

"No pageantry shall attend his arrival. No poet shall sing

his name. No mortal woman shall know his body. No mortal man shall call him son."

By now, all the assembled priests and priestesses were reciting the ancient words. And when the crowd joined them—hundreds of voices filling the air—a delicious shiver shook Rigat.

"Hail the Son of Zhe, the fire-haired god made flesh. Welcome him with reverence and with dread, for with him comes the new age."

As one, the queen and her chief priests turned to face the altar.

Rigat allowed the tension to build until it seemed the air itself would scream for release. Then he ripped open the portal and stepped into the rosy shaft of sunlight beside Jholianna.

Every person in the crowd drew breath in a collective gasp. The shocked silence that followed made him glance nervously at Jholianna, who gave him a reassuring nod. As if to affirm her confidence, the silence was shattered by a deafening roar of acclamation.

It went on and on, as wild and unstoppable as flames consuming dry wood. His power surged, feeding on the crowd's excitement, and he trembled with the effort to contain it.

Jholianna's gleaming eyes mirrored his intoxication. A flush stained her cheeks. Her lips parted. When her tongue flicked out to wet them, he realized he was licking his as well. He quickly tamped down the lust and the power until the thundering of his blood ebbed.

Jholianna dropped gracefully to her knees and prostrated herself before him. Like grain bowing before the wind, every man, woman, and child on the plateau followed suit.

"The prophecy is fulfilled!" Rigat cried. "The fire-haired god is made flesh. Rise, my people! Rise and look upon the face of Zhe's beloved son."

They rose. They cheered. They shrieked in delight as the priests of Zhe showered him with red petals. Shrieked again as he descended the steps, unaware that his careful movements were prompted by the fear that he would trip over his long scarlet khirta.

Hand in hand, he and Jholianna walked down the pathway. Children gawked. Old folk wept. Women trilled the high, ululating cry that the Zherosi used to express triumph or defiance or exaltation. Hundreds of voices became one continuous chant: "Rigat! Rigat! RIGAT!"

An old man stepped forward. Immediately, a guard blocked his path, but lowered his spear at Rigat's signal. As Rigat reached for the outstretched hand, the old man's fingertips moved higher, then hesitated.

Rigat took the trembling fingers and guided them to his hair. With a start, the old man pulled his hand back and stared at his palm in shock.

"It doesn't burn!" he cried. And laughed, showing toothless gums.

Rigat laughed with him, and a roar—louder than any of the others—split the air.

He zigzagged down the path, clasping hands, laying his palm atop the heads of children, blessing them as he had seen Fellgair do. Glancing over his shoulder, he saw people crawling forward to kiss the stones his sandals had touched.

Only when he neared the eastern wall of the palace did the uproar ebb. The priests of Zhe spread out in a red-robed circle around the pit Rigat had first glimpsed during his vision quest. This time, there were no terrified shouts, no guards brandishing spears to drive him off, only a respectful silence as he stepped to the edge.

The pit was larger than the longhut in his village. Brush and grasses littered the bottom. Piles of rocks created shady nooks for the adders. Water glimmered darkly in a shallow bronze bowl and spilled over the sides to trickle down a tiny causeway of pebbles.

A few adders had left their nests to bask in the first rays of sunlight. The female was easy to identify, her body swollen and fat. The ceremony he had witnessed through the portal had blessed their mating. Now, he offered his father's greetings to his beloved children and blessed the safe delivery of their young.

Another roar greeted his pronouncement. He was turning away from the pit to acknowledge it when a flicker of movement caught his eye.

Two of the basking males slithered back between the rocks. The female raised her head. A tongue flicked out, scenting the air. Red-brown eyes gazed up into his.

It was only a trick of the light that made that unblinking

gaze seem malevolent, only his overwrought nerves that conjured the wave of revulsion that rippled through her swollen body. She uncoiled with slow, deliberate grace and glided after her brothers, repudiating the false Son of Zhe and his empty blessing.

He shot a wild glance at the Zheron, but he was nodding and smiling like all the others.

Jholianna's fingertips brushed his arm. "Rigat?"

He forced himself to smile. To raise his hands and accept the acclamation of the crowd. To ignore the dryness of his mouth and the weight of the gold breastplate that suddenly seemed heavy enough to crush him. And to dismiss as imagination Faelia's voice, as sibilant as an adder's, whispering, "You are not our father's son."

The disturbing voice continued to echo in his mind as he visited the other temples. The Motixa placed a crown of bitterheart on his head. The Pajhit slipped thick gold bracelets over his wrists. The Acolyte offered him a sip of honeyed wine. When he raised his hands to accept the goblet, his bracelets clattered like chains.

The priests and nobles paraded after them into the central courtyard where the litter awaited. It had been specially constructed for the triumphal procession through the city. He clambered onto the thick red cushions, while Jholianna settled herself—with infinitely more grace—on the mound of gold ones.

Instead of the usual curtains, the litter's sides were open to permit spectators to see them. Four serpentine posts, painted red, reared up from each corner. Gauzy red fabric, studded with precious gems, had been draped over the top, but it did little to keep out the merciless sun. Even the six slaves who carried their litter were red. As the paint on their bodies began to drip in the heat, they seemed to be oozing blood.

Jholianna sighed. "Perhaps the people will think it's symbolic. The blood of Womb of Earth, spilling forth as she gave birth to Zhe. Or the tears of Heart of Sky who wishes he could spend a day reclining in a litter."

"The dawn of a new age," Rigat said, "when flesh melts in the heat."

"And slaves sweat wine."

"Voiceless, he shall curse the salty vintage, and wineless, fall on his face like a drunkard."

Their shared laughter dispelled his lingering disquiet.

The kankhs offered the obligatory salute. Slaves grasped the gilded wooden poles of the litter and raised them carefully to their shoulders. With Jholianna's bodyguard surrounding them, they marched toward the main gate, followed by the council members and a horde of priests and priestesses. Today, all would walk behind the litter; nothing must distract from the glory of the Son of Zhe and his queen.

The procession passed through a smaller courtyard whose soaring columns always reminded him of a grove of trees. Too soon, the grove was behind them and there was only the crowd of people lining the walkway, waving frantically behind the screen of guards.

At the edge of the plateau, Jholianna wrapped one arm around the nearest post and braced her feet against the front of the litter. Moments later, Rigat understood why. He clung to a post with both hands as they lurched down the steps, his crown of bitterheart hanging precariously from one ear.

The procession soon faded into a blur of sweating faces and incessant noise. People hung out of windows and clogged the cobbled streets, all screaming his name, all craning for a glimpse of the Son of Zhe. By the time they reached the harbor, Rigat's jaw ached from smiling, his arm ached from waving, and his ribs ached where the breastplate stabbed him each time he shifted position.

"I'll be black and blue by the time this is over," he grumbled.

"We must bear our discomfort with smiles," Jholianna replied, tucking an errant braid into place.

"Next time, you wear the breastplate. Then we'll see if you're smiling at the end of the day."

Her laugh drew another wave of cheers from the crowd.

"All that's left now are the presentations," she reminded him. "Then we can return to the palace and enjoy the luxury of a long soak before the feast."

Jholianna's plan had called for them to make stops throughout the city to receive the guild masters, but the

Khonsel had refused to allow it, claiming his forces were inadequate to provide security in a dozen plazas. Even when Rigat reminded him that his interrogations had revealed no conspiracies to harm him or the queen, the stubborn old man remained adamant.

"What's the point of having the procession if the guild masters can't present their gifts to me personally?" Rigat demanded.

"The Son of Zhe must meet his people," Jholianna agreed. "And I must be by his side when he does."

The Khonsel reluctantly compromised by allowing a single presentation. This pleased no one, especially the guild masters, who resented having to share their moment of glory.

Rigat let out a sigh of relief as they entered the Plaza of Justice. It was just as crowded, but he felt less trapped here than in the narrow streets.

It's the Khonsel's fault. His fears have infected me.

The procession came to a halt in front of a raised dais, shaded—of course—by a scarlet canopy. As the litter scraped cobblestones, he scrambled off the cushions, hoping those watching would interpret his awkwardness as godlike exuberance.

The cheers continued unabated as the council members followed them up the steps. The Khonsel, Rigat noted, placed himself closest to the queen. His narrow-eyed gaze moved ceaselessly, scanning the crowd, observing the disposition of the guards around the dais and atop the roofs. For a moment, their eyes met and held. Then the Khonsel's gaze moved on.

Suddenly, all the elaborate security measures made sense. Ever since his arrival, the Khonsel had challenged him. This was just another test.

Rigat nearly laughed in relief. It was all a game, just as Fellgair had always claimed. Now that he understood that, it was easy to smile when Jholianna presented him, to offer a pretty speech about the dawning of a new age, to accept the jubilant acclamation.

It was harder to maintain his smile during the interminable presentations that followed. After the windy welcome of Pilozhat's Alcadh, he blessed a bag of gold serpents specially minted by the Merchants Guild, a vat reeking of urine for the Tanners Guild, and a motley collection of nets and hooks presented by the Fishers Guild. He consecrated a flower-bedecked loom for the Weavers Guild, and a flower-bedecked bullock hauled forward by the beefy-looking master of the Fleshers Guild.

He praised the artistry of leatherworkers and potters, barrel makers and alewives. He patted the heads of the wide-eyed children apprenticed to the Musicians Guild. He accepted armlets and rings, casks of ale and crates of wine, haunches of meat and bolts of precious lilmia, and—from the whiskery old crone who headed the Bakers Guild—a loaf of bread ostensibly made in his image.

"She must be a seer as well as a baker," Jholianna whispered as the old woman backed away. "The loaf's burned, too." She ran her forefinger lightly down his sun-reddened arm.

"It's wonderful," Rigat assured her. "All of it."

"You look tired."

"And you look as fresh and crisp as a new leaf."

Her breast brushed his arm as she leaned against him. "I feel about as fresh as yesterday's lettuce."

"I shall eat nothing else at the feast tonight," Rigat vowed.

"Yesterday's lettuce? Or . . . ?" Her eyebrows soared suggestively and she laughed at his embarrassment. "And in your honor, I shall eat nothing but boiled langhosti. For surely your skin will be the same color as their shells before this day is over."

He was soon grateful for his sunburn. It hid his blush when the beautiful young men and women of the Prostitutes Guild began to dance. Even a few of the stern-faced guards gawked at their sinuous gyrations. But all too soon it was over, leaving Rigat even more aware of the late afternoon heat.

It rose in waves above the crowd, making the buildings on the far side of the plaza swim before his eyes. He could scarcely draw breath, and when he did, the dry air seared his lungs. His power staved off the worst of its effects, but his poor people had to be suffering. As for the guards in their bronze helmets and breastplates, it was a miracle they hadn't collapsed.

Finally, the last representative rose from his ritual

prostration. He was younger than the other guild masters, his thickly muscled arms testifying to his profession as a smith. Across his palms lay a dagger, its hilt and sheath encrusted with precious gems.

The head of Jholianna's bodyguard stepped forward to receive the gift; no one with a weapon—even a sheathed one—was permitted to approach the Son of Zhe.

The guild master smiled as the guard approached. He was still smiling when he knocked him aside with one hard shove of his shoulder.

It happened with dreamlike slowness, but it must have taken only a few heartbeats. The guard staggering. The Khonsel's shout. The naked dagger in the man's hand as he vaulted up the steps. A tiny red gem on the hilt, gleaming like a drop of blood. Jholianna's fingernails scoring his forearm as she stumbled backward. The man's defiant shout—"Carilia!"—as he hurtled toward them, dagger upraised.

Rigat's power roared out of him, but it was too unfocused to stop the dagger from descending. The best he could do was push, as he had once pushed Seg.

The assassin reeled and lost his footing. A guard lunged. The guild master's body went rigid, impaled on the point of the sword. Then the rest of the bodyguard fell on him, swords slashing.

Rigat whirled around and found Jholianna sprawled on the dais. He knelt beside her and pulled her into the shelter of his arm.

"I'm not hurt," she managed.

He heard shouts and screams, but could see little; a forest of legs and a wall of bronze-armored backs surrounded them.

"Is the queen safe?" The Khonsel's voice, closer now and urgent with fear. "And the Son of Zhe?"

Even in the midst of his confusion and fear, Rigat noted that the Son of Zhe's safety was an afterthought.

"Let the Khonsel through," he ordered the guards. But they were already backing away.

Disregarding his bad leg, the Khonsel fell to his knees and seized the queen's hand. "Earth's Beloved. Are you injured?"

She shook her head, but the Khonsel seized her shoulders, twisting her from side to side before pulling her forward to inspect her back. Then he remembered himself and fell back on his haunches.

"Earth's Beloved. Forgive me. I—"

Jholianna pressed her fingertips to his mouth. The intimacy of the gesture startled the Khonsel as well as Rigat. "I'm well, old friend. Just bruised."

"We must get you both back to the palace."

With a trembling hand, she pushed a lock of hair off her face. "First, we must show the people that we are safe."

"Earth's Beloved, the man might have an accomplice."

Someone shoved past the barrier of guards and knelt beside them. The head of the bodyguard, Rigat realized.

"Earth's Beloved, I formally request permission to end my life."

The Khonsel muttered a filthy oath and struggled to his feet. "You don't deserve such an honor. I'll disembowel you myself and have your corpse flung on the midden for the dogs."

Jholianna held out her hand so Rigat could help her to her feet. "Punishment can be meted out later. Now we must calm the people."

The Khonsel scowled and barked out orders. A huge roar went up as they walked to the edge of the dais. Jholianna acknowledged it with an upraised hand and a brilliant smile, but her gaze remained fixed on the corpse of the assassin still sprawled on the lowest step.

"Was it you? Who stopped him?"

"I didn't do much. I didn't have time. All I could do was push him away."

"That was enough."

When Rigat put his arm around her waist, he could feel the tremors coursing through her. For just a moment, she leaned against him. Then she shrugged free and lifted her hands, commanding silence.

"People of Pilozhat!" Her voice shook. She took a deep breath and then another before whispering, "Help me."

This time, she allowed his arm to remain around her. He nodded to her, all the while scanning the crowd for another assassin, but there was no movement in the plaza, no sound at all save for the thin wail of a babe somewhere. He drew on his power again to ensure that his voice would reach those at the back of the crowd.

"People of Pilozhat! Our queen is safe. And the Carilian assassin who attacked her is dead. Truly, the gods are smiling upon Zheros. This is why my father sent me. To protect our queen. To prevent attacks like this from ever happening again. And to bring a victorious end to the war that has sapped our strength for too many years."

He paused only long enough to acknowledge the frenzied cheers with a wave. Then, surrounded by the guards, he led Jholianna down the steps, carefully skirting the corpse. As he handed her into the litter, he slipped on the blood-slick cobblestones and had to seize one of the litter's posts to keep from falling.

Something brushed his cheek, soft as Jholianna's hair. But when he looked up, he found her gaze fixed on a clump of feathers on the cushion beside her. Bemused, he wondered how they had gotten in the litter. When his mind finally registered what his eyes were seeing, his bowels clenched.

Before he could pull the arrow free, he heard the Khonsel shouting and the frenzied slap of leather-shod feet. Someone shoved him into the litter. He sprawled across the cushions, but when he tried to sit up, a hand thrust him down again.

"The Avokhat's house! Quickly!"

As the litter lurched forward, he twisted his head and discovered the Khonsel's stark face a handsbreadth from his own. The late afternoon sunlight penetrating the gauzy awning cast a rosy glow on his cheeks, as if he were blushing.

Screams erupted as the guards beat a way through the terrified spectators with the flats of their swords. The litter rocked wildly. A violent tug on his khirta kept him from sliding out.

"Jholianna!" He had to shout to make himself heard. "Are you hurt?"

"I can't . . . breathe. Khonsel . . . please . . ."

The Khonsel shifted his weight, and her breath eased out in a shaky sigh. Rigat wriggled one hand free to give her arm a comforting squeeze and was rewarded by a wan smile.

There was a brief moment of shade as they passed under a stone archway. Then renewed heat as the litter bearers entered a courtyard. The splash of water from an unseen fountain made Rigat realize he desperately needed to empty his bladder. Only because he'd had no opportunity to do so all day, he told himself. Not because he was afraid.

Even before the litter came to rest, the Khonsel slid out and bent to lift Jholianna. Ignoring her weak protestations, he gathered her in his arms and limped off, surrounded by guards.

"My lord." The anxious face of a young guard loomed before him. "Inside. Quickly."

The guard extended his hand. Rigat reached for it and froze, staring at his palm.

"Sweet Zhe! Were you hit? My lord, are you hurt?"

Still staring numbly at the smears of blood, Rigat shook his head. "I don't . . . no. I . . ."

Without waiting for permission, the guards yanked him out of the litter with as much ceremony as fleshers hauling a haunch of meat from a cart.

"Shields up!"

Fingers bit into his arms as they marched him toward the dark entranceway of the house.

The interior was dim and blessedly cool, but filled with frantic activity. As Rigat obediently submitted to the hands tugging him this way and that, searching for a wound, the Khonsel barked orders to post guards on the roof and the entranceways. A dozen raced to obey. Others were already slamming wooden shutters across windows.

An elderly man—probably the judge who owned the house—watched the activity with helpless amazement. His wife snapped at the slaves to light torches to alleviate the gloom. Both fell to their knees when they saw him.

"Please," Rigat murmured. "Rise."

Only then did he spy Jholianna, slumped on a bench against the far wall. The Khonsel sat beside her, his face bent close to her blood-smeared arm. When Rigat spotted the shallow cut near her shoulder, the wave of relief left him giddy; he could heal that in moments.

"We've sent for a physician," the Avokhat's wife said. "But it might take him some time. The crowds . . ."

A richly dressed girl—the Avokhat's daughter?—hurried toward the Khonsel, a bronze basin clutched in her hands. The Khonsel plucked the cloth from her arm, dampened it, and dabbed gently at Jholianna's wound.

She bore it without flinching. Indeed, she seemed scarcely aware of the chaos around her. Her head rested against the wall, seeming to sprout incongruously from the dark center of a painted sunflower. Her eyes were half-closed, but they fluttered open when the Khonsel suddenly leaned forward and seized her chin.

Rigat heard a gasp behind him and the shuffling of feet. A guard hurried forward, gripping the black shaft of the arrow between his thumb and forefinger as if he feared it would come to life. Rigat clamped his lips together to prevent a burst of nervous laughter from escaping. Then he noticed the man's expression.

Although he could still hear the slaves' bare feet slapping against the tiles and a guard racing up a flight of stairs, everyone around him was frozen, every pair of eyes riveted on the arrow. And every face wore the same expression of horror as the guard's.

The Khonsel was the first to recover. He unsheathed his dagger and sawed a long strip of fabric from his khirta. But instead of bandaging Jholianna's wound, he tied the fabric higher on her arm.

"What are you doing?" Rigat protested.

"It's poison," the Khonsel snarled. Jholianna's arm jerked as he knotted the fabric. "The Carilians always paint the shafts of poisoned arrows black. So they don't mistake them."

He'd assumed she was just suffering from the shock of the attack. Only now did he notice her waxy complexion and drooping eyelids. Her chest rose and fell in quick pants as she sucked at the air like a fish out of water. Spittle oozed out of the corner of her gaping mouth. The Avokhat's wife slipped onto the bench beside her and gently wiped it away.

"We can't wait for a physician," the Khonsel said. "Fetch the Motixa. Or the Pajhit."

Rigat had half turned to obey before he realized that the Khonsel was speaking to a guard.

"We must prepare her to Shed." Even as he snapped out the orders, the Khonsel's hands were moving, one gripping Jholianna's wrist, the other lifting his dagger. He made two small incisions above her wound. Jholianna's body jerked in protest, but he ignored her to suck at the cuts. He reared up and spat, spraying blood onto the yellow tiles. Three more times, he repeated the ritual, then sat back, rubbing his lips with his fist.

"Can you save her? Or at least keep her alive until she can Shed?"

They were all watching him, just as before their eyes had been riveted on the arrow. Rigat tried to form words, but it was all happening too quickly.

"Rigat!" the Khonsel shouted.

"I . . . I don't know. I've never healed someone who's been poisoned. But I'll try."

The Avokhat's daughter eased back. Her hands shook so badly that water sloshed over the side of the basin, wetting his khirta and dripping down his leg.

"I'll need to touch her. It. The wound."

The Khonsel slid off the bench, allowing him to sit. Jholianna's hand felt limp and boneless, but her flesh was warm and her pulse thudded rapidly under his thumb.

A hand descended on his shoulder. "They use different poisons." The Khonsel's voice was calm, but his hand trembled, and that terrified Rigat. "Usually a combination. Yew berries. Helmet-flower. Snake venom. I don't know if that helps . . ."

Rigat nodded automatically. If only his mam were here. Or Fellgair.

Gods, give me the strength. Show me what to do.

Silently, he cursed himself for wasting his power on cooling his body and drying his sweat, especially when it was already weakened by the interrogations. He closed his eyes, thrusting aside the useless regrets, desperately trying to steady himself. Dimly, he was aware of the Khonsel muttering orders. A woman's muffled weeping. A man's soft prayers. And the hoarse, uneven rasp of Jholianna's breath.

When he placed his right palm over the wound, heat

seared him. Not the ordinary heat of injured flesh, but sharp, penetrating pain as if dozens of bees were stinging him.

The poison.

He fought the urge to snatch his hand away and flung his power into the wound. Jholianna's hand ripped free of his grasp. He opened his eyes to find her writhing in the arms of the Avokhat's wife, one hand clawing at the vial of qiij at her throat. With an oath, the Khonsel stumbled to the other side of the bench, shoved the woman aside, and used his weight to pin Jholianna against the wall.

"We must give her the qiij now! While she can still swallow."

As the Avokhat's wife fumbled with the stopper of the vial, the Khonsel pulled Jholianna into his arms and held her head back. She reared up, choking on the qiij, but he clapped his hand over her mouth until she swallowed.

Rigat squeezed his eyes shut again. Jholianna's terror screamed inside his spirit, but he could not afford to squander his power on calming her.

Despite the sting of the poison, it was as amorphous as fog. Deadly and elusive in the tidal race of her blood, every heartbeat sent it coursing through her body.

He made his power into a spear, hurling a pure current of energy through Jholianna's blood. Tiny black dots blossomed and exploded as he cleaved the miasma. But in his wake, the poison coalesced again, oozing through the chinks in the barriers he erected to dam it up.

He poured more of his power into her, fighting both the poison and the certainty that it would swallow up the healing energy, even as it was devouring Jholianna's life. He heard the wild drumbeat of her heart, then realized the sound came from outside his body.

Jholianna's heels, he realized. Pounding on the tiles.

"She can't breathe!" a woman shouted.

Abandoning the effort to hold back the poison, he sent his power surging toward her lungs. They were as flaccid as empty waterskins. He surrounded them with his power, squeezing them as the smith's apprentice pumped the bellows in the royal armory. Slowly and rhythmically, the boy had worked, and although fear urged him to hurry, Rigat did the same.

He was so focused on helping Jholianna breathe that he sensed the upwelling of her power too late. The energy crashed into him with such force that he lost connection with his body. He could no longer feel the bench against his thighs or the smoothness of Jholianna's flesh. A dense cloud veiled his vision. He could still hear voices, but they faded as his hearing deserted him along with his other senses.

Shock coursed through him when he realized that she was trying to cast out his spirit. For a heartbeat, he hung suspended, clinging to his body by a fragile thread. But if Jholianna's instinct to survive was strong, so was his.

Terror and desperation fueled his faltering power. It roared up from the core of his being, hotter and wilder than he had ever known it, spinning strength into the thread of his existence, seizing his drifting spirit and hurtling it back into his body.

Before his power, Jholianna's wilted. Neither qiij nor her instinct for survival could match it. He was ablaze with the power, gloriously alive, spirit and body alike inundated by sensations. And all so vivid, so beautiful. To feel the grain of the wooden bench through his khirta. To hear the slap of sandals on cobblestones and the anxious murmur of a guard in the courtyard. To smell the scent of fresh-baked bread from the kitchens and the oil that perfumed the Avokhat's hair and the fear-stink of the Khonsel's sweat. To be supremely alive, supremely powerful.

This was what it meant to be a god.

Light flared behind his closed eyelids—red light and orange and a fiery white. Hundreds of bursts of light that filled his senses and shimmered with the luminescence of the Northern Dancers, until his entire being seemed infused with their radiance.

A tiny red star exploded, blinding him with its brilliance. As it flickered and died, another exploded, and another and another. The dance was still beautiful, but it was dying now, the blaze ebbing to a dull red glow. A wave of sadness engulfed him, and with it, an overwhelming lassitude. Only then did he realize that it was not only the dance that was dying, but his power.

Panic destroyed the last vestiges of his exultation. His power shuddered in response to the sudden jolt of fear, and it horrified him to feel how weak it had become. Lost in the glory of the dance, he had continued to expend it recklessly when he should have been conserving it for Jholianna's sake—and his.

Her death would cripple Zheros and destroy any hope for peace in the north. The Zherosi would turn on him. For how could the true Son of Zhe fail to save their queen?

The connection between their spirits faded. Her terror leached away, replaced by anguish. And then it, too, receded, until all he could feel was her hopeless acceptance of death.

No! Jholianna, don't give up. Come into me. I'll protect you.

Without any power, Darak had sheltered Keirith's spirit. Surely, he could do the same for Jholianna until a Host could be found.

The Khonsel was shouting something, but Rigat ignored the intrusive voice, focusing all his energy on the link between his spirit and hers. She had drifted so far away in those wasted moments of self-congratulation. How could he have been so careless?

He drew what strength he could from the wooden bench beneath him, from the incense-scented air, from the meager light of the oil lamps, and the sweat rolling down his face. And then he opened himself and drew her fragile spirit closer.

He felt a moment of resistance as she clung to the body that she knew.

Let go, Jholianna. Just let go and trust me.

It happened so quickly it caught them both by surprise. There was a moment of shared recognition and relief. Then his limbs began to flail.

He landed hard on the tiles, writhing helplessly. He fought down his panic, trying to soothe her, to control her without terrifying her, to overcome centuries of Shedding that told her she must gain possession of this new body and cast out the alien spirit that still shared it. In the end, all he could do was retreat and throw up a barrier to shield them from each other.

His body went limp. Somewhere, a woman moaned. "Oh, sweet Womb of Earth, we've lost them both."

He managed to wheeze out a denial, and a hand seized his. He opened his eyes. Felt Jholianna's terror piercing the shield. And saw the Motixa's tear-streaked face looking down at him.

"In me. She is . . . in . . . me."

The damp brown eyes widened, then squeezed shut as she whispered a prayer.

"What did he say?" The Khonsel's voice, thick with phlegm and fear.

"The queen's spirit is safe. The Son of Zhe is sheltering it."

"Hurry," Rigat whispered.

"Yes. Yes." The Motixa squeezed his hand again. "She must have a new Host. Now. If their spirits remain in his body too long they will bleed together."

Another flash of terror from Jholianna. He tried to send soothing energy, but maintaining the shield required all his strength. He could not even muster the will to keep his eyes open.

"Where is the Host?" the Motixa demanded.

"Fetch a slave," the Khonsel replied. "Any woman. Quickly!"

"No."

Rigat didn't recognize the woman's voice. It was shaking, though.

"It's not fitting for a slave to Host the spirit of our queen. I will do it."

He opened his eyes and found everyone staring at the Avokhat's daughter. Her face was strained and the flounces of her skirt trembled, but she returned the Khonsel's gaze steadily. Her mother and father were weeping, but they seemed unsurprised. Clearly, they must have come to this decision while he was fighting to save Jholianna.

The Khonsel's knees thudded on the tiles. He seized the girl's hand and kissed it.

"My lady. Your sacrifice will be honored and your memory revered as long as the sun rises and sets on Zheros."

She swallowed hard and nodded.

How old was she? Fifteen? Sixteen? And in a few moments, she would die. It happened every year, of course, hundreds vying for the privilege of serving as the queen's

Host. But knowing the rite existed was far different than witnessing a girl's death.

Rigat watched the Motixa drain her vial of qiij. And then he closed his eyes.

The Avokhat's daughter had probably awakened early, eager to witness the ceremony in the Plaza of Justice. Perhaps she had stood in one of the upper story windows, craning for a glimpse of the Son of Zhe and the queen, observing the parade of guild masters with the same impatience he had felt.

Tonight, she might have accompanied her parents to the palace—so excited, so honored that her father's position had won them a coveted invitation to the feast. Perhaps her dark eyes would have lingered on a young man—the son of a nobleman or a prosperous merchant. After the feast, they might have slipped away from the stifling hall to stroll the moonlit grounds and breathe in the scent of night-blooming flowers. Hidden by the darkness, she might even have permitted him to steal a kiss.

And in time, a match would have been made and a wedding planned. Tears would have been shed then, too—happy tears celebrating a daughter's marriage instead of honoring her death.

The Motixa was murmuring something. Telling him that she was going to touch his spirit, reminding him to prepare the queen, assuring him that he need do nothing himself, that she and the queen had done this many times. He lowered the barrier slightly, just enough to convey the information to Jholianna. Before he retreated behind it again, a wave of joyful anticipation reached him.

"She's ready," he whispered.

During the formal Shedding, the Host was given qiij to ease her spirit on its journey. This girl would have to manage without it. Nor could he help her; his power was as dull as the embers of the dying stars. He prayed that the Motixa was skillful and gentle. Eager to root herself in a new body, he doubted whether Jholianna would be.

His eyes fluttered open. He turned his head, searching for the Avokhat's daughter. She was sitting on the bench with the Khonsel, staring down at the lifeless body of her queen. Someone had straightened Jholianna's gown and draped a shawl over her face.

"Your name. Please."

Her head came up. Her eyes were bright with unshed tears, but she managed a trembling smile. There was a tiny gap between her front teeth, Rigat noticed.

"Miriala, my lord."

"Miriala." The name emerged on a sigh. "Gods keep you, Miriala."

The Motixa's touch was light and assured. One moment, Jholianna's spirit was waiting expectantly, and the next it was gone.

He heard a gasp. The shuffle of feet. The rustle of a gown. The Khonsel urgently repeating, "Earth's Beloved? Earth's Beloved?"

As Rigat drifted into unconsciousness, he heard the Motixa's joyful cry. And amid the relieved babble of prayers that followed, the soft, unceasing sound of a mother weeping for her lost child.

PART THREE

Like the oak,
A good father shelters his children from the storm.
Unlike the oak,
A good father ensures that his shadow
Never blocks the sun.

—Tribal proverb

Chapter 37

HIS ANKLES WERE CHAINED to some kind of stake. When his bare toes touched wood, Keirith realized they had removed his shoes. It seemed such an unnecessary precaution that he laughed. Barefoot or shod, where was he going to run? The chain was shorter than his forearm. His ankles were bound together. He was blindfolded and gagged, drugged and guarded.

Trust the Zherosi to be thorough.

His head no longer hurt when he turned it, and the pain in his shoulder had subsided to a dull ache. The Zherosi healer still forced the dream-brew on him several times a day, but he had longer periods of clarity upon waking.

He used that time to lie on his furs, pretending to sleep, while calling on his senses to help him discover anything that might be useful. There were always two guards with him; he could detect the differences in their breathing. Occasionally, he heard the tramp of marching feet, voices shouting orders, the bellow of a bullock. The stink of woodsmoke pervaded the camp, but he failed to catch the briny scent of the sea. He must be in one of the fortresses along the river.

He wasn't sure whether to be relieved or alarmed that the deep-voiced man did not return. But one morning—two days after arriving? Three?—he heard someone enter the hut and caught a whiff of that familiar spicy scent.

The guards shifted on the rushes. Fists thumped against leather. There was a whispered discussion. Then a guard protested, "But the Vanel gave no orders—"

He abruptly fell silent. Keirith heard more whispering and the crackle of rushes as someone approached.

"My name is Jarel," a voice said in the tribal tongue. "I am the grandson of the Holly-Chief from the neighboring village. He sent me to make sure you are being treated well."

Which Holly-Chief? Which village?

"Are you thirsty? Would you like some water?"

He nodded, desperately trying to gather his thoughts. The voice held just a trace of an accent, a guttural swallowing of the consonants. Where had he heard it before?

"Can you lift your head?"

Urkiat. He'd had a similar accent. Dear gods, had the Zherosi taken him that far south? Surely, he couldn't have been on the ship that long.

Something brushed his fingertips—the smooth texture of a deer's bladder. A hand patted his shoulder. Gentle fingers fumbled with the gag.

"Don't touch him!" a guard shouted.

Water splashed his chest and belly. Someone shoved him. A heated conversation ensued, with Jarel protesting that he was only offering the prisoner some water, and the guards insisting that he keep his distance. Jarel's grasp of the Zherosi tongue was flawless. His village must have been cooperating with them for years. Which meant he was as likely to be a spy as a friend.

Rough hands dragged the gag from his mouth. With a final warning, the guards retreated.

"I am sorry," Jarel said. "They are nervous."

His speech was strangely formal. But perhaps he was nervous, too. Keirith could smell his sweat—and that spicy scent. Why did he smell like the deep-voiced man? Unless he was a Zheroso, pretending to be a friend to lure him into damning revelations.

Jarel expressed concern about the rope burns on his wrists and ankles. He seemed shocked to learn he had been given only porridge to eat and promised to do his best to alleviate his discomfort—as if he were an honored guest instead of a prisoner.

"Thank you," Keirith said. "You're very kind."

Another commotion at the doorway prevented him from saying more. An unfamiliar voice bellowed, "Zhe's coils, what are you doing in here?"

There was a flurry of movement. Whispering voices growing fainter as the footsteps retreated. A sigh from one of the guards. A mutter from the other. The crackle of rushes as one approached. The overwhelming stink of fear-sweat as the man yanked the gag over his mouth.

Keirith waited, tense and alert. When he heard someone enter, he wondered if Jarel had gotten his way. Then he recognized the musty scent of herbs and knew the healer had come to drug him again.

When he woke and heard Jarel's voice outside the hut, relief swamped him. He had feared that the Bellower would keep him away, but clearly Jarel was important enough to overrule him. Whether he was a Zherosi officer or the chief's grandson, Keirith was certain he was young; when he was nervous, his voice broke like a boy on the cusp of manhood.

He caught the aroma of roast mutton as soon as Jarel entered the hut. His hands shook so badly, he feared he would drop the wooden plate. He tore into the meat and licked the juice from his fingers; it took an effort of will to keep from licking the plate as well.

At first, they talked of unimportant things, like the prospects for the harvest. Then Jarel asked a tentative question about his childhood. Soon they were sharing stories about hunting, Jarel confiding that he preferred playing his flute, Keirith admitting he puked the first time he made a kill. What was the harm in telling him that? But he had to be careful. He was still muzzy-headed from the drug and it would be too easy to let damaging information slip.

When Jarel learned that Keirith had been a fisherman before joining the rebellion, he exclaimed, "But I, too, am a fisherman! Trout, salmon. Trout, most of all. They are clever."

Those were the words of someone who fished for pleasure rather than to put food in the mouths of his family. Yet another indication the boy was a Zheroso.

"Salmon are fierce, though," Keirith replied. "And

strong. Swimming upriver from the sea. You have to admire that."

"You admire strength more than cleverness?" Jarel sounded disappointed.

"I don't know. When I was a boy, perhaps. I was never fierce or strong."

"But you cast out the spirit of a Zherosi priest. That took strength. And fierceness."

"That was different. I was fighting for my life. And my father's."

He waited for Jarel to inundate him with questions about Fa. Instead he fell silent.

"I guess everyone's nervous," Keirith said. "The Zherosi and your folk. Waiting for my father. That's why I'm here, isn't it? The Zherosi want to exchange me for him."

After a brief pause, Jarel said, "They do. I am sorry. I did not want to upset you by talking about it. Or your father."

"I don't mind talking about my father. People are always curious about him."

Even with that encouragement, Jarel merely asked, "Was it hard? Having such a great man as your father?"

"Sometimes. I always felt like I was in his shadow."

Jarel sighed. "It is the same for me."

He sounded gloomy, but there was something else in his voice—resentment?

"You're young," Keirith said, then wondered if he had revealed too much. "I can tell by your voice. It gets easier when you're older. When I was a boy, I had my share of arguments with my father, but now we're—"

Unexpected emotion choked him.

We're part of each other. We know each other's thoughts, each other's feelings. He'll be coming soon. Hoping to rescue me. If he can't, he'll offer his life for mine. That's the kind of man he is. And I parted from him with the coldest of farewells, because I was too hurt and too angry to forgive him for keeping Mam's secret.

That's the kind of son I am.

"Are you all right?"

A hand brushed his shoulder, but he turned his face away. With a whispered apology, Jarel left.

He knew what he had to do. And he knew he had little time. If the Zherosi had brought him to Little Falls, it would take Fa only three or four days to reach it from the Gathering site.

He lay motionless on the furs, waiting for the effects of the dream-brew to ebb, for his mind to grow clear, for his quarry to return. And when he did, Keirith had a smile in place to greet him.

"I was afraid you weren't coming back."

"I wanted to say again that I was sorry. For upsetting you. Please forgive me."

"There's nothing to forgive."

"I was clumsy. And stupid."

"Nay, you're kind. The only person who's been kind to me here." A shaky breath. A determined squaring of the shoulders. A soft, reluctant confession: "I've always felt so alone. Never more so than now."

"I understand."

"I know you do. I felt that—right from the start."

Their conversation was halting, but each time an awkward silence fell, Keirith shifted to another topic, offering stories about his youth that encouraged Jarel to respond in kind. They talked about their first clumsy attempts to fish, laughing at each other's tales of tangled lines and lost lures. They shared the dreams they had as boys. Keirith even spoke of his time in Pilozhat, careful to praise the beauty of the sea, the majesty of the palace, the kindness of the Pajhit.

When the healer came and tried to give him the dream-brew, Jarel sent him away with an authority that dispelled Keirith's lingering doubts about whether he was a Zheroso.

Without the brew to hinder him, he felt renewed strength in his limbs, renewed clarity in his thoughts. He laughed at the boy's jokes. Sympathized over the death of his mother. Praised him for defying the Zherosi healer. And as the words flowed effortlessly from his mouth, his stomach roiled with the sickening knowledge that he had to cast out this gentle, lonely spirit.

If the Zherosi captured Fa, they would either keep him

a prisoner forever or kill him. He had to suppress the reluctant sympathy he felt for this boy and use his body to escape.

He pulled energy from the earth beneath him, from the breeze drifting in through the open doorway. He let his awareness drift beyond his little prison to the river that flowed past the fortress and the sun that beat down upon it. He called on Natha to guide him, the Maker to protect him, and the powers of earth and air, water and fire to fill him.

Fear for his father sparked the power. Visions of his slain tree-brothers fueled it. Memories of his kidnapping and rape, his captivity and murder . . . he called on all of them to feed the smoldering fire.

Driven by the fierce tattoo of his heart, the power surged up from his belly and down through his limbs, leaving his toes and fingertips tingling. It thundered through flesh and bone and blood, drowning out the boy's soft words. It seared his mind and his spirit, white-hot and inexorable. It sang inside him, as sweet as the dream-brew, but a hundred times more potent.

And he loved it.

He was the lightning strike that consumed a forest, the torrent that swept away everything in its path, the battle cry that called down death and destruction on his enemies. Let them bind his hands and feet. Let them blindfold his eyes and stop up his mouth. When the power raged through him, he was invincible.

Take him, the power sang. He is weak.

Use him, the power urged. He is foolish.

Kill him, the power demanded. He is helpless. As helpless as you were on that ship.

Poised for the strike, the song faltered.

Take him.

In the distance, he heard a man shouting.

Kill him. Now!

"I'm sorry. I must go. It's my . . . it's the Vanel."

He could feel the song dying—and with it, his power.

You are weak.

Gasping, he fell back on the furs.

You are foolish.

Uncontrollable shivers racked his body.

You are helpless.

Limp and drained, he could only lie there and listen to the boy hurrying away.

You have killed your father.

Chapter 38

"UNBELIEVABLE!"

Afraid that his shaking legs would betray him, Geriv leaned against the wall.

For three days, he had drifted in and out of consciousness, racked by fever and chills. This morning, he had recovered enough to take a few sips of the horrible nettle broth that the physician insisted would restore his strength. He had been eager to see Korim—he remembered something about a misunderstanding that he needed to clear up—but relief that the Spirit-Hunter had not yet arrived drove the matter from his mind. As did the messages that had arrived during his illness.

His satisfaction at learning that the Deepford force had annihilated the third band of rebels had leached away as his scribe read the message from Vazh. It contained belated information about the Gathering and the disturbing news that Rigat would be declared Son of Zhe at the Blessing of the Adders.

Despite his best intentions, he had slept through the afternoon. When he awoke, he summoned Pujh to dress him, ignoring the trembling of his limbs and the slave's protestations. He could not rest easy until he assured himself that all security measures were in place before the Spirit-Hunter reached the fortress. A few steps from his quarters, the physician descended upon him, but instead of chiding him for leaving his bed as Geriv expected, he launched into a tirade about Korim visiting the prisoner.

"What were you thinking?" he demanded, glaring at Korim and do Fadiq.

"I was trying to help," Korim replied, his voice as sullen as his face. "It was a good plan."

"It was reckless. And foolish. And in direct defiance of my orders."

"Begging your pardon," the Remil said, "but your orders were to keep two guards on the prisoner at all times. And to use extreme caution around him. And we did. He was still getting the drugs."

"And he thought I was from the village."

"Did it ever occur to you that he was only pretending?" Geriv asked, appalled by his son's gullibility. "That he was trying to wheedle information from you? Or allay your fears so he could attack you?"

"That's . . . it wasn't like that. We just talked. About all sorts of things. The games we played as boys, and fishing, and—"

"Fishing!"

"I was trying to draw him out!"

"You talk as if he were your friend."

"At least he listened to me! Which is more than you do."

Geriv bit back a retort and turned to do Fadiq. "You may go."

The Remil saluted stiffly, then hesitated. "Permission to speak, Vanel."

"What?"

"When I discovered what Skalel do Khat was up to, I was hesitant. But even if the prisoner guessed he wasn't from the village, we figured a man on drugs might let things slip. And he did. Small things, of course, but the Skalel was making progress. In the end, it was my decision. If anyone is to be punished, it should be me."

"And you will be. Now leave us."

As the Remil saluted again and left, Korim said, "The guards were there all the time. If Kheridh had tried anything—"

"You would not have known until it was too late. I was there when he cast out the Zheron's spirit. No one—not even his own father—realized what had happened."

For the first time, his words seemed to reach Korim. His son swallowed hard. "That's why you gave the orders. I thought . . . I assumed you just wanted to . . . tighten discipline."

Good gods, a commander didn't order a prisoner drugged and bound and guarded at all times simply to "tighten discipline."

"And if he had cast out your spirit," Geriv continued in the same deliberate tone, "I would have had to choose whether to kill him or stand beside him—the man who had stolen my son's body—and exchange him for the Spirit-Hunter."

By the time he finished speaking, Korim was staring at him with undisguised horror. He wanted to touch the boy, as much to reassure himself as Korim. He needed to touch him, to know that he was truly safe, to quell the lingering terror that still clenched his bowels when he imagined what might have happened.

"Yes," Korim said, his voice strangely calm. "I understand now."

Geriv cleared his throat. His hand came up to grasp his son's shoulder.

"It would have been horrible for you. To lose the chance to capture the Spirit-Hunter."

Geriv's hand froze.

"Which would you have chosen, Father? To kill me or exchange me?"

His hand slowly fell to his side. "I . . . that's not . . . the situation will not arise. You are never going inside that hut again."

"Of course not. It might jeopardize your plans."

Was this what Korim thought of him? That he was so cold, so unfeeling that he would consider the death of his son a mere disruption of his plans? More likely, the boy was choosing to misunderstand, lashing out because he was ashamed of his foolhardy actions.

Fear gave way to anger and the desire to strike back, to hurt his son as he had been hurt. "You will never go to

Kheridh's hut," he repeated. "I'm sending you back to Pilozhat."

Korim's body trembled with suppressed emotion. "You won't allow me to fight. You object when I use my gift for languages to interrogate a prisoner. So what would you have me do?"

Goaded beyond endurance, Geriv shouted, "Do as you please! Play your flute. Compose a poem. Better still, pack! You leave on the morrow."

He stalked over to the window and waited until he heard the door slam. Then he punched the logs in impotent fury.

Why had he imagined he could turn Korim into a warrior? Or forge a genuine relationship with him? He should have realized long ago that it was too late for that.

Chapter 39

HIDDEN BY THE TALL GRASS on the hilltop, Darak gazed across the river. Even in the uncertain light of the gloaming, he could still make out the palisade of sharpened logs that surrounded the Zherosi compound.

All day, he had watched slaves filling buckets of water at the river, warriors ferrying haunches of meat from the village, craftsmen mending a sail and replacing oars on one of the warships. Everyone who left the fortress had to endure an inspection before the guards readmitted them. Not once had a villager passed through those massive wooden gates, nor had a single coracle ventured onto the river.

The Zherosi were taking no chances that someone could slip into the fortress.

Darak let his head droop onto his folded arms. They had pushed themselves hard, making the three-day journey to

Little Falls in two. Even the young men were exhausted; after keeping watch with him throughout the day, Sorig had finally drifted off to sleep beside him.

After they had arrived last night, Kelik had suggested firing the ships beached on the far shore. But even if such a diversion distracted the Zherosi long enough for a few of them to climb over the walls, what were the odds that they could find Keirith, kill his guards—for surely, the cautious Geriv had men guarding him—and escape?

"Slim," Sorig had admitted. "Impossible," Mikal had claimed.

Geriv's deadline was still three days away, but they were no closer to devising a plan to free Keirith than they had been when they headed north.

At least Faelia was safe. He had insisted that she take the bulk of the recruits home. Even if their numbers had been greater, freeing Keirith would require stealth, not force. And if a spy had given the Zherosi the site of the Gathering and the routes they were taking to reach it, he might easily have revealed the location of their village as well.

She had grudgingly accepted his logic, but insisted that he send Sorig or Mikal to warn the village. Finally, Darak had folded his fingers around her fist.

"I cannot help Keirith if I'm worrying about you. I'm asking you to do this. Because you love me and because we must make Temet's death—all those deaths—count. Take them home, Faelia. Please."

He might have shielded his daughter from harm, but his son was still caged. The knowledge sickened him, as did the mutilation of the land around Little Falls. Although Sorig had described what had happened at Eagles Mount, this was Darak's first glimpse of the devastation wrought by the Zherosi. All along the river, the forest had been reduced to rotting stumps. A few brave saplings clung to the hillsides, but the Zherosi would soon chop those down for firewood.

Too late, he realized Temet had been right to resist. But Temet was dead. And most of his warriors. No one knew if Nial's band had escaped the carnage. Although he had urged Faelia to keep the fight alive, her band was too small and inexperienced to rout the Zherosi from one fortress, never mind drive them back to the sea.

So many lives lost. He would not add Keirith's to that list.

For the first time in his life, he wished he possessed magic so that he could contact Rigat. It might be days before he ventured north to learn the results of the Gathering. By then, it would be too late. No matter what inducements the queen offered, Rigat would never remain in Pilozhat if he knew that the Zherosi had massacred the rebels and imprisoned his brother.

But the Trickster had to know. Which meant he was deliberately hiding the truth from Rigat.

Darak's hands clenched into fists.

I will not ask for his help. I will never speak his name again.

Reluctantly, he shook Sorig awake. As much as he longed to stay near Keirith, it would be full dark soon and it was three miles to the forest. Although he doubted the Zherosi would look for them there, someone from the village might stumble upon them. They had already moved camp twice, choosing spots that were far from the trails and streams where the hunters stalked game.

The gloaming gave way to darkness long before they reached the forest. Weaving between the stumps of trees, stumbling over unseen roots and rocks, Darak cursed himself for tarrying so long. Yet he was grateful for the clouds that hid Gheala from view; at least, he was spared the sight of her dwindling body and the visible reminder of how little time remained to devise a plan that would save him and Keirith.

Suddenly, Sorig drew up short. Darak gripped the hilt of his sword, peering into the darkness for an enemy. Instead, he spotted a faint green glow off to their left. Another blossomed a few paces in front of them. Frozen, Darak watched the hills flare with the luminescent glow of foxfire.

Only once—during his vision quest—had he ever seen the eerie green light that radiated from the bark of rotting trees. Legends claimed they were the spirits of dead trees, unwilling or unable to leave the shell that had held them. Generations ago, someone had named it foxfire. A hunter, perhaps, reminded of a fox's eyes, gleaming in the light of his campfire.

He had never thought to see so much foxfire in one place, but neither had he imagined that the Zherosi would come to his land and chop down whole forests of his tree-brothers. Recalling the Watchers who guarded the grove of the One Tree, he wondered if these tree-spirits had chosen to remain behind, offering a mute protest to the destruction.

As they picked their way around the stumps, he whispered a prayer. Perhaps his Tree-Brothers heard—or perhaps they sensed that the men who walked among them were not the ones who had murdered them. But he still let out his breath in relief when they reached the forest.

Sorig paused at the edge of the trees and glanced back. "It's beautiful, isn't it? Until you remember what caused it."

It was so dark under the trees that Darak smelled the others before he entered the tiny clearing. He heard a few muted greetings and the shuffle of bodies as the men made a place for them to sit. He had brought only ten with him, mostly the older, more experienced hunters. But only those without wives or children.

"Is everything all right?" Kelik whispered. "We were worried."

"I'm sorry. I didn't mean to stay so long."

"Eat something. There are still a few suetcakes. And the last of the dried trout."

"Stop fussing. You're worse than my wife." But he patted Kelik's knee and gratefully accepted the hard sliver of fish pressed into his hand. "Did you find out anything?" he asked, raising his voice just a little so the others could hear.

"Nothing that can help." Mikal's voice, ragged with exhaustion. "The Zherosi have stockpiled provisions. And water. No one will be leaving the fortress after tonight."

Although Mikal had wanted to take Sorig with him, Darak had suggested Kelik instead. Mikal had grumbled, claiming people didn't know Kelik, but Sorig had accepted the decision in silence. Even if Mikal didn't suspect the reason for his choice, Sorig did. Both men had had the opportunity to betray them. For all he knew, the cousins might be working together. Darak didn't want either of them venturing near the village unless someone he trusted went with them.

"They're sending a ship downriver," Kelik said. "You must have seen them outfitting it."

"Aye. But I can't believe Geriv will transfer any troops. Not this close to the deadline."

"Just some of their sick and wounded," Kelik replied. "And his son."

"His son?" Darak echoed as Mikal growled, "That's just a rumor."

"Aye," Kelik said. "But rumor has it they had some sort of quarrel and the Vanel's shipping the boy off."

"Who told you?" Darak demanded.

"Mikal's father," Kelik replied. "Birat overheard some of the warriors talking when they came to pick up provisions."

"Is Geriv sending an escort with the boy? Other than the sick and wounded?"

"I don't know, Darak. I'm sorry."

"Likely, they'd send at least a skalekh," Sorig said. "If you're thinking of snatching the boy when he embarks—"

"Nay. But they use their ships to carry dispatches. Geriv will want to send messages about his victory. Instructions for the fortifications downriver. They might stop at Deepford. Maybe even spend the night."

"Maybe," Sorig replied. "But they'll have the current with them. And the wind, unless it changes. If they left at dawn, they might be able to make Eagles Mount in a day."

"What does it matter when they leave?" Mikal asked. "Or where they spend the night?"

"Because it might give us a little more time," Darak replied.

"Time for what?"

"To set a trap for the Vanel's son."

Chapter 40

THE FIRST TIME, RIGAT WOKE in darkness, dimly aware of the smoky scent of incense and the drone of chanting. Flickering torchlight danced on the ceiling, creating the illusion that the painted clouds were drifting across the brilliant blue sky.

A long face loomed above him, blocking out the clouds. The thin mouth curved in a satisfied smile. As the face vanished, a voice proclaimed, "He wakes! The Son of Zhe wakes!" Joyous cries greeted this announcement, but Rigat was already drifting into sleep.

The second time he woke, the face was back, this time at a safer distance. From the man's questions, he realized this must be Jholianna's physician. He tapped Rigat's chest briskly and fingered the five pulses of health, all the while murmuring, "Good . . . very good." Rigat was even more comforted by the power—faint but discernible—that simmered inside him.

As the physician backed away from his bed, others clustered around: the Pajhit squeaking out his relief, the Zheron intoning a prayer, the Stuavo tracing a spiral across his chest, and the Motixa with tears shining in her eyes. Even the Khonsel looked relieved.

Jholianna's face was not among those peering down at him. Nor was Fellgair's.

"The queen?" Rigat asked.

"She's well, my lord." For the first time, the Khonsel didn't hesitate before speaking his title.

Before he could ask about the Supplicant, the Zheron said, "We've declared a day of thanksgiving on the morrow, my lord."

"You *will* be strong enough to attend?" the Stuavo asked anxiously.

Rigat nodded, wondering how he could endure a day of ceremonies when he still felt as weak as a newborn lamb.

As if sensing his thoughts, the Khonsel said, "Just a brief appearance in the throne room."

The Zheron frowned. "And at the temple of Zhe."

"Out of the question."

"But they should offer sacrifices—"

"I won't permit either of them to leave the palace," the Khonsel insisted. "Not until we've apprehended the conspirators."

As the argument escalated, the physician said, "The Son of Zhe is not to be disturbed with these matters now. He needs his rest." And with that, he shooed the council members out as if they were a pack of fretful children.

The third time he woke, Rigat was immediately aware that he was ravenous. The physician declared this an excellent sign, but would only allow him a bowl of clear soup and a piece of flatbread.

"You haven't eaten in two days, my lord. It would be unwise—"

"Two days?"

The Gathering would be concluding soon. Maybe it already had; even with the truce, he doubted the rebels would remain in one place more than a few days.

". . . but after the ceremony," the physician was saying, "perhaps a nice millet gruel."

The prospect of a bath was far more inviting. He was pleased that he managed to sit up without Nekif's assistance, but puzzled by a twinge in his right wrist. Frowning, he examined the flaxcloth bandage.

"Just a shallow cut," the physician assured him. "At first I was afraid you'd been injured in the attack. Then I saw the scar and realized it was an old wound. Perhaps the drain on your power allowed it to reopen? Well, no matter. I stitched it close again. In a day or two, you'll hardly notice it."

Rigat nodded automatically, but instead of the physician's voice, he heard Fellgair's: *"You're not a god. The healing will fade. That's why I sealed your wound."*

"Has the Supplicant returned yet?" he asked Nekif.

"Surely not, great lord. The Acolyte would have relayed your command to her as soon as she—"

"Send someone to the temple to make sure."

"At once, great lord."

He might not be a god, but Fellgair was. So why would his father's healing fade?

Brief as it was, the ceremony of thanksgiving left him limp and exhausted—and gave him something else to worry about besides Fellgair.

Although he knew perfectly well what Jholianna would look like, it was still a shock to see Miriala walking toward him. None of the other courtiers seem bothered by Jholianna's new body, but of course, they had all witnessed dozens of Sheddings.

Had Darak reacted with this shock, this . . . revulsion . . . when he'd first seen Xevhan walking toward him and known it was Keirith? And what must Mam have felt? Expecting to celebrate the return of her son and greeting instead a tawny-skinned stranger?

He regretted the impulse that had made him ask Miriala's name. Everyone knew names had power. Knowing hers forged a closer link between them and made it even harder to accept Jholianna's usurpation of an innocent girl's body.

Jholianna avoided his gaze as she thanked him for saving her life. He avoided hers as he apologized for any suffering he might have caused her. As soon as the ceremony was over, they both hurried back to their chambers.

As disturbing as Jholianna's appearance was, he was more worried about what she might have discovered while their spirits dwelled together in his body. He hoped she'd been too frightened to learn anything. Certainly, he'd had no time to probe her spirit; he'd needed all his concentration to maintain his shield and keep her from seizing control of his body.

Keirith and Darak never talked about the time their spirits had been linked. Each time he pressed, a look would pass between them—a dark intimacy silently acknowledged and accepted. Ultimately, that experience—as terrifying as it must have been—had brought them closer. But they had been bound together by love, not duty or circumstance. The moments of enforced intimacy that he and Jholianna had shared now seemed to divide them more effectively than any shield.

Lying uselessly in bed only fueled his concerns about Fellgair, about his relationship with Jholianna, about the progress of the Gathering, and the investigation into the attempted assassination. Although Nekif dutifully reported everything that had happened while he was unconscious, Rigat needed a more reliable source of information. Postponing the inevitable confrontation with Jholianna, he summoned Vazh do Havi.

The Khonsel's limp was more pronounced, his face tight with pain and exhaustion. Wondering when he had last slept, Rigat waved him to the bench next to his.

Ignoring the gesture, the Khonsel bowed. "I would like to offer my apologies, my lord. For failing to protect you. And my thanks for saving the queen."

I didn't save her. If I had, Miriala would still be alive.

But he was unwilling to discuss Miriala with the Khonsel. Instead he said, "I owe you an apology, too. For insisting on the presentation in the plaza. Please. Sit." As the Khonsel slumped onto the bench, Rigat asked, "Have your investigations uncovered anything? I'm told the archer was dead when you found him. And that he was a Carilian."

"Might be a Carilian," the Khonsel corrected. "Anyone can paint an arrow black. Or gain access to poison. But it's probable, yes. I've had his likeness drawn and sent to the commanders in the east. Perhaps one of their prisoners can identify him."

"And his coconspirator? The man with the dagger?"

"The head of the Smiths Guild, not an imposter. Lived in Pilozhat all his life. Mother's people are from Iriku, though. Might be a connection there. I've brought in his family and associates for questioning, but still haven't discovered a link between him and the second assassin."

"Hold off further interrogations. When I'm stronger, I'll

examine them." The gods only knew how many innocents had already suffered. At least he could spare them further torture.

"There are more than fifty people—"

"I will examine them, Khonsel."

"The queen's orders—"

"And I'll deal with the queen."

The Khonsel bowed his head.

"You don't suspect the noblemen in this plot, I hope? I would have discovered their involvement when I interrogated them."

"Unless they were unwitting dupes of the real conspirators."

Rigat conceded that possibility with a reluctant nod. "I'm certain those men would never knowingly countenance an attack on the queen."

The Khonsel stared down at the tiles. "My lord, the queen might not have been the target."

As many times as he had gone over the events, that thought had never occurred to him. Stupid to assume that because he was the son of a god he was immune to attack.

"I could be wrong. It might have been some madman with a personal grudge against the queen. But a planned conspiracy by the Carilians?" The Khonsel shook his head. "Killing the queen would only harden resistance to any peace overtures."

"While killing me . . ."

The Khonsel shifted uncomfortably. "Your death might be taken as a sign. That the gods had turned against Zheros."

"Yes. I see." He was pleased that his voice sounded so calm.

"That would benefit Carilia, of course. But Lilmia, too. They're both jealous of our power. The whole damn world is jealous of our power. Which makes it hard to figure out who was behind this. Anyone can buy an assassin. All it takes is money and connections."

Rigat leaned back against the wall, staring up at the garish sunset that adorned one corner of the ceiling. "Even in Zheros, there are those who would benefit from my death. The slave owners, for instance, who oppose my plan to return the Tree People to their homeland. Or the families of the noblemen."

"The slave owners will be compensated for their losses. As for the noblemen's families, they should be grateful you used your power instead of torture."

"Someone who doubts my claim to be the Son of Zhe."

"It's . . . possible. Yes."

Rigat idly smoothed his khirta. "Someone who opposes the truce."

The Khonsel stiffened.

"Someone with money and connections. Like you."

The flush began at the base of the Khonsel's bull neck and rose up to stain his cheeks a dusky red. With a grunt, he shoved himself to his feet. "Are you accusing me of planning the assassination?"

"Did you?"

"You think I'd trust an assassin to make that shot? With the queen a handsbreadth away?" The Khonsel hawked a gob of phlegm onto the tiles. "If I wanted you dead, I could have taken you out after the interrogations. Or any time these last two days when you were too weak to piss without slaves holding you up. I'd have plunged this dagger into your heart and damned the consequences!"

Rigat folded his hands to hide their trembling. "So many lost opportunities."

The color slowly faded from the Khonsel's face. "Burn me. You're too cool by half." But there was grudging admiration in his voice.

"Once again, I apologize, Khonsel. These days, it's easy to see conspiracies everywhere."

The man's outrage seemed genuine enough, but when his power recovered, he would touch the Khonsel's spirit. Just to be sure. For now, he would maintain his vigilance—and choose new guards to replace the ones the Khonsel had posted outside his chamber.

The confrontation spurred him to visit Jholianna. If he was the target of the attempted assassination, he could not permit their relationship to unravel.

Like Fellgair's healing.

Could Fellgair's powers really be failing? Or was this some kind of twisted test?

First Jholianna. Then Fellgair.

The corridor between their apartments bristled with guards. Outside the doorway of her bedchamber, one stepped forward to block his path.

"Forgive me, great lord. But we have orders to announce everyone."

"Announce me, then. And be quick."

Before he could, Jholianna appeared in the doorway. "Fool," she said, glaring at the guard. "Those orders do not apply to the Son of Zhe. He is to be admitted at any time." As the guard retreated, inundating them both with apologies, she added, "Please. Come in."

Rigat strode into the chamber, shaking his head. "I suppose the Khonsel gave that order?"

"The Khonsel wanted every visitor searched. I pointed out that the Son of Zhe was unlikely to hide a dagger in his khirta when he could simply cast out my spirit."

Jholianna grimaced. So did Rigat.

"Let's go out on the balcony," she suggested. "It's cooler there. A little. And more private."

They made stilted conversation about the weather, the moon of celebration, anything to avoid talking about The Shedding. Finally, they lapsed into silence, both gripping the wall of the balcony and staring at Kelazhat's brooding silhouette.

Jholianna cleared her throat. "Thank you again. For preserving my spirit."

"I wish I'd been stronger. You would have suffered less."

And Miriala would still be alive.

"You mustn't blame yourself."

"Who else?"

"I thought . . . perhaps . . . you blamed me."

"No. At least . . . no."

"But you cannot bear to look at me."

"A weakness we seem to share," he snapped, then quickly murmured an apology.

"When I fought you . . . I didn't mean . . ." Her hand

stirred, then settled back on the stone. "It shames me to remember."

"There's no shame in fearing death."

"But there is shame in facing it so poorly. That girl . . ."

"Miriala. Her name was Miriala."

He felt more than saw her turn toward him. "You do blame me." When he remained silent, she added, "You regret her death."

"Of course I regret her death! And I blame myself for it. And you for asking me to conduct the interrogations, and the assassin who shot you, and the Khonsel for failing to protect you, and Miriala's parents who stood back and let her die, and—gods forgive me—Miriala, too. For going to her death like a sheep to the slaughter. I know that The Shedding is a holy rite. But I can't help thinking of the hundreds of girls who have died. All because you couldn't bear a child. And refused to grow old."

Her breath hissed in. "You think I instituted the rite out of vanity?"

"No. Because you were terrified of dying. The same reason you tried to cast my spirit out of my body."

"My death would have left the empire in chaos!"

"Chaos is a part of life. Chaos and order."

"You talk like one of the Tree People."

"I *am* one of the Tree People!" In a calmer voice, he added, "And my father is a Zherosi god. And I've tried so hard to make sense of that. To understand the Zherosi as well as the children of the Oak and Holly. To do what's best . . ."

To his horror, his voice broke. He gripped the stone hard as he fought for control.

"This power I possess . . . I try to use it responsibly. To heal people. To make things better. I don't always succeed. Even the son of a god makes mistakes. Or . . . falls short. And when I do, I hope you'll believe it's not for want of trying. Everything . . . it's all happening so fast. Three moons ago, I didn't even know who my real father was. And now—" He caught himself before he blurted out something damaging. "It's been a sennight since we've spoken. Sometimes, I think he's forgotten me."

As soon as the words emerged, he wanted to take them

back. Gods, he was pathetic. Whining about his father. Next, he'd be confessing how much he missed his mam.

He stalked away, only to freeze as her hand gripped his forearm. Instead of the slender, tapering fingers he had always admired, these were short and blunt-nailed, the cuticles red and raw where Miriala must have gnawed them.

It was strange to look down to meet Jholianna's gaze. Did she mind being shorter now? Did she consider the cheekbones too high, the mouth too wide? Or resent the tiny gap between her front teeth? Oddly, the small imperfections increased her vulnerability and made her—in his eyes, at least—more beautiful.

"We're both tired," she said. "And our nerves are frayed from all that's happened."

There were gold flecks in her dark eyes—or perhaps that was just the reflection of the torchlight.

"I wish I could ease your mind. Give you the comfort you need. You and I . . . we're joined now. In a way no one else could understand."

Darak could. And Keirith. But he banished that thought. They were far away and could not comfort him, either.

She stepped back, regarding him gravely. "I've been thinking about this for some time, but after . . . after The Shedding, I became certain. I want you to accept the crown of Zheros and rule beside me."

Shocked, he could only stare at her.

"Please don't be offended. I know it's only an earthly honor. Hardly fitting for the son of a god. But you've done so much for Zheros. For me. If I had died . . ."

He tried to speak, but she pressed her fingertips to his mouth. He breathed in the scent of the cream she used and tried to ignore the unfamiliar calluses.

"If I had died, you are the only one who could have saved the empire. The only one my people would trust."

Gently, he took her hand from his lips. "Would they? Would you? As you say, I'm one of the Tree People. And I don't always understand your customs."

"A moon ago, we didn't even know one another. And look what we've accomplished. Time is our ally, Rigat." She squeezed his hand. "You don't have to answer now. Just . . . think about it?"

The new hesitancy in her voice endeared her to him in a way that her flirting never had. But how could he accept the crown? She'd been right to describe him as a stranger here. There was still so much he needed to learn. And he'd made so many mistakes—bungling that initial confrontation with her, rushing forward with his plan to free the slaves, dismissing the danger of assassination as a game of wills with the Khonsel. Never mind the fact that his foolish squandering of power had nearly cost Zheros its queen.

Jholianna's fingers tightened on his. Seeing her anxious expression, he fumbled for a way to reassure her.

"There's only one drawback to your plan. If I become king, the Zheron will invent a hundred new rituals for everyone to perform."

Jholianna's smile was the first genuine one he had seen since the assassination attempt. "And a title. Jholin was called Sky's Light, but you'll need another. Wingless Eagle?"

Rigat glanced at his freckled arms. "Supreme Langhosto," he suggested and was rewarded by her laughter.

They shared a light supper, and as they talked of the future, his anxiety dissipated. But as soon as he returned to his chamber, he sent Nekif to the temple of the God with Two Faces. Again, Nekif returned alone, regretfully informing him that the Supplicant was not there.

Rigat touched the power smoldering inside him, each day a little stronger. Surely strong enough to search for Fellgair. He had to talk with him—about Jholianna's offer of the crown, about the assassination attempt, about the puzzle of his unraveled healing. Even if it meant delaying his return to the north one more day.

Chapter 41

SORIG HAD GIVEN DARAK the information he
needed—and with it, his first real hope of rescuing
Keirith.

"Just ten miles downriver," he'd whispered, pounding
Darak's knee in his excitement. "I passed it on my way to
Little Falls. I remember because it reminded me of the
channel between Stag's Leap and Eagles Mount."

Mikal had suggested stealing coracles from the village,
but Darak feared that might give away their intentions.
And navigating the river in the dark would be dangerous
for hunters who had never handled the tiny boats before.
In the end, they marched the ten miles, arriving at the
narrows just after dawn to begin their feverish preparations.
By midmorning, they were ready.

As ready as they could be. Crouched behind a boulder
on the northern shore, Darak now saw only the flaws in
the plan that had so excited him.

They had chopped down pine spars to leverage boulders
into the channel, but most simply piled up along the base
of the southern hill. Those that had reached the water disappeared
into the depths. With its shallow draft, the warship
could skim right over them and escape unscathed.

But even the most accomplished steersman would need
steady hands and steadier nerves to navigate between the
rocks that dotted the channel. Their best hope—their only
hope—was to drive the ship onto them. And pray that the
steersman panicked when the flaming arrows descended on
his ship.

Darak had cautioned all his men to direct their fire away

from the pavilion where Sorig swore the Vanel's son would be seated. But if the boy became restless, wanted to stretch his legs or simply chat with the captain . . .

He shook his head, trying to dismiss his gloomy thoughts. "Darak?"

He glanced over his shoulder and found Mikal watching him.

"Anything wrong?" Mikal asked.

"Nay. Just . . . thinking it through. Again."

"We've done everything we can."

But was it enough?

Fear is the enemy.

He glanced upriver, reassured by the sight of Kelik calmly inspecting his arrows. To him, Darak had entrusted the critical task of killing the steersman. Even if Kelik missed his shot, the steersman would surely guide the ship away from Sorig's archers, bringing it close to the jagged rocks near the northern shore—and to the men waiting nearby. All they had to do was snatch the boy when the ship foundered and kill any of the surviving warriors.

If the ship foundered. If Geriv sent a dozen warriors instead of a hundred. If the boy didn't drown. Or crack his skull.

Control the fear.

He examined the southern hill, relieved that the brisk easterly breeze carried away any telltale threads of smoke. At least they had been able to use deadwood for the archers' fire; given their limited supply of pitch, they had no choice but to tap the pines for their sticky sap.

Recalling the sight of the men hacking at the trees with daggers and axes, Darak winced. He had sprinkled water on the roots of the injured trees and sliced open his forearm to make a blood offering for the three pines they had chopped down. He prayed that his tree-brothers understood his need and accepted his sacrifice.

His gaze snapped to a pale smear moving among the greens and browns and grays. A hand waving back and forth.

The ship had been sighted.

He took a deep breath and began his preparations: stringing his bow, settling his quiver more firmly in the

crack between two rocks, choosing an arrow. As he drew
it from the quiver, it slipped from his shaking fingers and
clattered onto the pebbles. Cursing softly, he retrieved it.

Control yourself.

He wiped his hands on his thighs, remembering too late
that his breeches were even damper than his palms. Mikal,
their strongest swimmer, had barely managed to fight his
way across the river. Even clinging to the rope Mikal carried across, Darak's muscles were aching by the time he
reached the northern shore. But he took comfort in knowing that the Zherosi would have to fight that relentless current under fire.

He peered around the boulder and discovered the ship
closing fast, square sail bellying in the breeze. In spite of
his anxiety, he marveled at the way the sleek vessel
skimmed over the water. Recalling the sickening rise and
fall of the currachs he had sailed in when he had begun his
search for Keirith all those years ago, his stomach lurched.
Then lurched again when he contemplated what failure
today meant.

He heard a faint shout and tensed before realizing the
captain was simply calling out an order. As the ship veered
south, the captain's hand came up, waving the ship north
again.

*I have to take him out. Without the captain, the steersman
will be sailing blind.*

He flexed his fingers, relaxing his grip on the bow. Tried
to ignore the fierce tattoo of his heart. Told himself this
was just another hunt.

Please, Maker. Let this work.

A low rumble made him jerk his head to the right. Freed
from their imprisoning ropes, the pine spars caromed down
the slope of the southern hill.

Shouts erupted onboard. Men leaped up, gazes riveted
on the spars. But the captain—damn him—might have been
carved from stone, left arm outthrust as he guided the ship
through the channel.

As the spars rolled harmlessly into the shallows, a fiery
star arced down from the hill, trailing smoke behind it. A
group of warriors rushed to the railing as the arrow cleaved
the water in front of the ship and died.

Please, gods.

Two more arrows etched fiery paths across the sky. A tiny orange flame blossomed on the sail, then another.

Darak drew his bowstring back to his ear, took aim on the broad chest of the captain, and let fly. The outthrust arm jerked up as the arrow struck the man's shoulder. Cursing, Darak drew another arrow and loosed it, baring his teeth in a ferocious grin as it struck home. The captain staggered back, the hand that had pointed the way now clutching the shaft of the arrow. Moments later, the ship veered away from the southern hill.

Slaves clambered up the mast, beating at the flames with cloths. Others hurled buckets of water at the sail in a futile attempt to quench the resinous fire. Darak ignored them, picking out a man with a bronze helmet, another in leather armor. He heard Mikal laugh as a warrior toppled over the side. Laugh again as another sagged against the railing.

Flaming shreds of sail drifted onto the deck. Slaves howled as they beat at their naked necks and shoulders. Warriors stamped on the fiery wisps, only to scream like the slaves as sparks shot upward, feeding on their flax-cloth khirtas.

Beneath the awning of the pavilion, he caught a flash of movement. A slender figure racing toward the steps to the main deck, only to be yanked back by a brown hand.

Relief turned to dismay as he realized the steersman was correcting his course. The ship skimmed toward the center of the channel, narrowly avoiding the rocks that would have ripped it open.

"Take him out!" he screamed.

If Kelik heard, he gave no indication. He pivoted slowly, tracking the passing ship with his arrow. Then his hands moved in such a blur of motion that Darak never knew how many arrows he released.

As the ship glided toward his hiding place, he glimpsed the steersman slumped across his giant oar, but his gaze was held by the gap between the vessel and the closest rocks. Thirty paces? Twenty? The ship could easily slip past them, unscathed.

An arrow clattered against the boulder, and he flinched.

Fifteen paces.

A wall of wood filled his vision.

Ten.
It's going to escape.
Five.
Keirith . . .

He closed his eyes. And heard a low groan that crescendoed into a horrifying shriek of rending wood.

He had always hated the Zherosi ships. Giants hewn from the dead bodies of countless tree-brothers. Monstrous beings that had carried his son and countless others to slavery or death. But as he watched the rocks rip open its side and water pour into the jagged wound, he couldn't help recalling his first impression: a sleek, graceful bird flying over the water rather than cleaving a path through it.

And now it was dying, timbers splintered, mast leaning drunkenly toward the shore, tattered sail flapping desperately. Lurching from rock to rock in its death throes.

The screams of men jolted him from his thoughts. Flailing limbs churned the river white as men fought to keep afloat. A few clung to planks and other pieces of wreckage as the current swept them downriver. A line of slaves bobbed past and vanished under the water; gods, they must have roped the rowers together. Corpses floated past as well, hair streaming around them like seaweed. Others were wedged between rocks or sprawled atop them, limbs splayed in the abandonment of death.

Mikal and his men splashed into the river, methodically dispatching the warriors crawling onto the shore and floundering in the shallows. Realizing they needed no help to complete their grisly task, Darak's gaze sought the pavilion.

A slender figure clung to the railing. Clad only in a loincloth, it had to be a slave. But where was the boy?

Kelik was already loping up the shore. Darak paused to snatch up his coil of rope before racing after him. He slowed to scan the dead and dying, praying that none of the beardless young faces belonged to the Vanel's son.

With the coiled rope slung across his chest, he braced himself for the shock of the cold water and waded into the shallows. Fighting the current was useless; he and Kelik would have to ride it downriver to reach the wreck and—please, gods—the boy.

His heart raced when he spied a figure clinging to a

boulder. It could be any Zheroso, of course, but this one was staring up at the slave still dangling from the railing of the pavilion. Kelik had spied him as well, and was fighting his way toward him. He was within arm's reach when the river swept him past and slammed him into a rock. He slid under the water, then came back up, scrabbling for a handhold.

Praying he was unhurt, Darak took a deep breath and gave himself to the river.

The force of the water knocked him off his feet. When he surfaced again, he saw the boy lift one arm to gesture to the slave. Without both hands gripping the rock, he began sliding into the water. Desperately, he tried to claw his way back to safety, but each time he managed to pull himself up, the river tugged him down.

Gods, give me strength.

His hands slapped against rock. He flung an arm around it, gasping for breath. Then he launched himself toward another rock. Another pause to gather his strength. Another leap toward a safe handhold. Crawling through the water rather than swimming, but each lunge brought him closer.

He shook his wet hair out of his eyes, gauging the distance. Then he hurled himself through the water, pulling hard for the boulder. The current lifted him, and he flailed helplessly. Then the river flung him against the boy.

He caught a brief glimpse of wide brown eyes as the boy slipped. Flinging one arm around the boulder, Darak grabbed for him. His fingers brushed a slippery braid. Before it could slide through his fingers, he twisted the braid around his wrist, hauled the boy out of the water, and braced him against the boulder.

For a moment, he could only hang there, breathless and panting. The water pounded his back as fiercely as the boy's heartbeat thudded against his chest.

He was even younger than Darak had expected. No older than Rigat. Handsome enough in a girlish way with those dark, feathery lashes and finely sculpted cheekbones. Blood oozed from a scrape on his forehead, but he had no other visible wounds. A chain of braided bronze circled the slender neck. A small medallion dangled from it, bright against the brown of his tunic. An amulet, perhaps. Or just something he found pretty.

Pretty was the word for him. Pretty and soft. Not a warrior, that much was certain. Skinny as he was, this boy had never wanted for food or clothing, never shivered in the cold or sweated on a forced march. And likely the only men he had seen die were those sacrificed on an altar.

Until today.

He wondered if he should rouse him, make certain he was Geriv's son. But his strength was waning, and he wasn't sure he could drag an unwilling captive to shore. Realizing he would never manage to rope them together, he simply tightened his grip on the long braid and slipped into the water.

An anguished cry made him glance back to discover the slave screeching something in Zherosi. Still screeching, he dropped into the water and bobbed up, coughing.

Darak lost sight of him after that; he had enough to do to hang onto the boy without worrying about his slave, too. He gave up any attempt to steer them toward the shore and simply fought to keep their heads above water.

His body slammed painfully against a rock and for a moment, he lost his grip. He flung an arm around the boy's neck, praying he didn't choke him to death as their bodies plunged downriver.

He went under once and emerged, sputtering. Glimpsed Kelik's face for an instant as they tumbled past him. Slammed into something soft and recoiled with a startled yelp when he found himself staring into the wide, unseeing eyes of a dead Zheroso. Felt pebbles beneath his feet and breathed a shaky sigh of relief. Chest heaving, he crawled through the shallows, dragging the boy behind him, and collapsed.

Belatedly, he realized he should take away the boy's sword. His shaking fingers fumbled with the belt. Finally, he simply drew it from the sheath.

He raised his arm to toss it aside when he heard the splashing. Groaning, he rolled into a crouch, but it was only Kelik, tugging the protesting slave by the wrist. Despite his age, the slave seemed far less exhausted than Kelik who simply sank onto the pebbles while the old man threw himself on his master, weeping and babbling.

Kelik nodded toward the boy. "That's the Vanel's son?"

"After all that, he better be."

Darak's tired smile faded as he looked past Kelik and saw Mikal striding toward a cowering slave, sword upraised.

"Stop!"

He pushed himself to his feet and staggered down the beach. Mikal's scowl deepened when he saw the naked blade in his hand.

"You'd kill me to save them?" He spat. "They're all Zherosi."

The slaves were roped together, ankle to ankle. Two clung to each other, whimpering. The others simply stared up at Mikal, too terrified to even try and loosen their bonds.

Darak tossed the sword to the ground. "There's been enough killing for one day. And these are slaves, not warriors. They've never done us harm."

"They row the ships. Make the food." Mikal jerked his head at the old man who was pressing his lips to the boy's hand. "Care for their fallen masters."

"I won't slaughter unarmed men."

"They'd kill you given half the chance."

"With what?" Darak demanded. "Their bare hands? Cut them loose." When Mikal hesitated, he shouted, "Cut them loose!" His gaze swept the five men flanking Mikal. "Do any of you speak Zherosi?"

"Some," Radirom replied.

"Then translate for me." Darak gestured to Mikal who had sheathed his sword in favor of a dagger. "This man is going to cut your bonds. After that, you're free to go. Tell them."

If they understood Radirom's stumbling Zherosi, they were too terrified by Mikal's dagger to give any indication.

"Maker, give me patience."

Darak knelt before one of the slaves who recoiled, shaking his head and weeping. He patted the man's knee, murmuring the kind of nonsense a mother would use to soothe a fretful babe. Careful to keep his gestures slow, he mimed cutting the rope, then waved them away, pointing downriver. The slave just stared at his mutilated hands with horrified fascination.

"If you will permit me," a soft voice said in the tribal tongue, "I will translate."

He glanced over his shoulder and found the boy sitting

up. Quelling his shock at his fluency with the tribal tongue, Darak stammered, "Aye. Thank you."

The old slave extended his hands to help his master to his feet, but the boy shook his head. Cautiously, he pushed himself to his knees, then rose, swaying slightly. He took a moment to steady himself, then walked forward. In the same soft voice, he addressed the slaves, then glanced up at Darak as if awaiting further instructions.

"Tell them there's a village. Five miles downriver. Or they can wait here for the ship from Little Falls."

The boy frowned. "There is no other ship leaving Little Falls."

"There will be. Once we send word to your father."

The boy went very still. His gaze darted to Darak's hands, then back to his face.

"Of course. The Spirit-Hunter."

Slowly, he drew himself up. Then he bowed. It should have made him ridiculous—a skinny boy in a dripping khirta, bowing as if he stood in the great palace of Pilozhat. But it took courage to face defeat with such dignity, and Darak had to admire him.

"I am Skalel Korim do Khat, aide to the Vanel of the Northern Army." A visible shudder, quickly suppressed. "And your prisoner."

Chapter 42

FAELIA STARED UP AT THE TWINS and felt neither joy at reaching home nor satisfaction at leading her band to safety. When Selima squeezed her shoulder and whispered, "You did it," she simply stared at her.

Eighty men and women had begun the journey with her;

less than half remained. Eilin had been one of the first to leave. He had begged Fa to let him go to Little Falls to rescue Keirith, but of course, Fa had refused to take such an inexperienced fighter. Perhaps he'd lost heart after that. Or feared that without Keirith's presence to steady him, his courage would fail him.

At least Eilin had told her he was going home. Most of the others simply slipped away during the night. Every morning, she woke to discover their ranks had thinned. Every evening, she watched the moon rise, her hopes dwindling along with Gheala's body. And every night, she saw Temet's ruined face and mutilated body in her dreams.

Losing him had been a crushing blow, but somehow, abandoning her father was worse. In joining Temet, she had chosen a life where danger stalked them every day. Her mind had always known that death could separate them; her heart simply refused to dwell on it.

But when Fa sent her away, something inside of her had died. Although she had managed to hold back her tears when they parted, she had clung to him like a frightened child. Then she'd stumbled away without daring to look back.

Why hadn't she paused—just for a moment—to catch a final glimpse of him? Why had she thrown away that opportunity to study his expression and posture, to imprint them on her mind and heart forever? How could she leave, knowing she would never see him again?

Even the great Darak Spirit-Hunter would not be able to free his son from that fortress. And once he surrendered the Vanel would either execute him or ship him to Zheros, where there was no possibility of escape or rescue.

To be shut away behind stone walls. Never to feel the wind on his face or snow melting on his tongue. Never to see the sun or the forest or his family. Better a speedy execution than such a living death.

"Keep this fight alive," Fa had said. But even if a miracle occurred and he succeeded in freeing Keirith, what then? More useless attacks on the Zherosi? More ceaseless wandering through the wilderness, seeking new recruits, other rebel bands? Temet had tried and failed. Rigat's truce was a sham. And she was crawling home like a whipped dog.

As the sentinels blew two long blasts on their horns to signal the arrival of strangers, she squared her shoulders and started toward the gap in the hills. In the dying rays of the sun, the sprawling clumps of heather on the slopes of The Twins looked like dozens of small fires. Once, she might have gloried in the sight. Today, she felt only dread.

Her mam's face would be lit with hope as she watched them arrive. She would scan the faces, looking for Fa and Keirith. And as hope slowly died, her gaze would settle at last on the traitorous daughter who had lured them away.

Griane recognized Faelia's bright hair first. It took longer to discover that Darak and Keirith were not with her. When she saw Faelia's grim expression, her hand sought Callie's.

"They're alive," Faelia said by way of greeting.

"But where—?"

"Later, Mam. After I get these people settled. Selima— you'd best go to Mam's hut and have her take a look at you."

It was Selima who told them about the massacre. Numb, Griane sat by the fire pit and allowed Hircha to inspect the woman's wounds.

Keirith, a captive of the Zherosi. Darak, determined to rescue him. It was as if time had spiraled backward and the nightmare was beginning again.

"But why did you come here?" Hircha asked. "Instead of staying with Darak and the others?"

"Darak's decision." Selima flexed her shoulder carefully. "It would have taken more men than we had to free Keirith by force. And Darak feared the Zherosi commander would send troops here. There's a history between them."

Hircha's hands froze on the roll of nettle-cloth. "What's his name?"

"Do Khat. Geriv do Khat. A one-eyed man." Selima studied Hircha a moment before adding, "You know him, too."

"Aye."

"That's right. I'd forgotten you were there."

"I was there."

As soon as Hircha helped her ease into a fresh tunic, Selima headed for the doorway. As she reached for the deerskin, she paused. "Faelia . . . she thinks you blame her, Griane."

"But she wasn't even with Keirith when—"

"Not that. For taking him and Darak away in the first place."

Griane shook her head wearily.

"Then tell her that," Selima said. "And make her believe you. She's hurting."

"Thank you," Griane replied stiffly. "I'm aware of that."

Selima grimaced. "Sorry. I'm not . . . I'm used to giving orders. Or taking them. When you don't know if you'll be alive on the morrow, you don't waste breath on niceties. I meant well."

"Thank you," Griane repeated with more warmth. "It's kind of you to look out for her."

"She's a good woman. And a good fighter. Losing her man . . ." Selima stared up at the thatch and swallowed hard. Then she turned abruptly and left.

Moments later, Callie slipped into the hut.

"You heard?" Griane asked.

He nodded. She had never seen him look so grim. For a moment, they all sat in gloomy silence. Then Hircha asked, "And where was Rigat during all this?"

Bad enough that Othak continued to circulate his malicious lies. For a member of her family to doubt Rigat was unbearable.

"Are you accusing him, too?"

"Nay. But why didn't he warn them?"

"Because he's not omnipotent! He doesn't see everything that happens like . . ."

"Fellgair," Callie finished. "Do you think this is his doing?"

His way of punishing us. Of punishing me.

"I don't know."

Somehow, she had to find a way to get word to Rigat. Only he could help Darak and Keirith now. But first, there was her daughter to think about. For once, she would put Faelia first.

While Callie headed to Trath's hut to pass along the information Selima had given them, she and Hircha made their way to the cave. Mirili had already gathered spare bedding and food. Griane was relieved to discover that the most serious problems were blisters, exhaustion, and hunger. The recruits seemed appallingly young—most of them only a few years older than Rigat. As she spread ointment on scrapes and bandaged blistered feet, she intercepted more than a few wide-eyed looks.

"You're Griane the Healer?" a red-haired boy whispered. "From the tale?"

He looked so crestfallen that she laughed. "I was younger then."

The heavy-set man sitting beside him cuffed the boy lightly. "That was thirty years ago. Even Darak Spirit-Hunter and Griane the Healer can't make time stand still. He was well when we saw him last," he added.

"Thank you." She took a moment to control her voice. "You're married, too, I take it."

The boy gaped. The man simply said, "My wife died. Last winter."

"How did you know?" the boy blurted. "That he had a wife?"

"A married man would think to give another man's wife news of him."

Her explanation deflated the boy further. Clearly, he had imagined that Griane the Healer possessed the power to see into men's minds as well as ease the aches of their bodies.

"My name is Holtik," the man said. "This one—with his mouth hanging open—is Owan."

"You are welcome to our village," she replied automatically. "I wish we could offer you a more comfortable place to stay."

Holtik shrugged. "We've been sleeping in the open. A cave's a luxury."

She hesitated. Although she had just met the man, she liked his broad, honest face and his innate sensitivity.

"There's a bound to be a council meeting soon. To discuss what steps should be taken in case the Zherosi march on the village. I think you should be there."

He frowned. "Faelia and Selima—they're the leaders."

"Aye. But some men listen better to the words of another man."

"Your elders must all be unmarried, then. Else they'd have learned better." A brief, wistful smile lit his face. "But I'll mention it to Selima."

Although she hungered for more news of Darak, Griane rose and made her way over to her daughter.

"Walk with me."

"I need to—"

"You need to walk with me."

Reluctantly, Faelia followed her toward the lake. Griane waited, hoping she would speak. When Faelia remained silent, she reached up and grasped her shoulders.

"This wasn't your fault."

Faelia wrenched free. "I knew he didn't want to fight. And I tricked him into joining us. And now—"

"Now, he's going after your brother. You think you could have stopped him? Or stopped the Zherosi from capturing Keirith? Stop blaming yourself. Trust me, it will only make you more miserable."

Griane pulled her into her arms. Faelia stood there, tense and unmoving. Then her daughter's arms locked around her.

The last time she could remember holding her like this was the day the Zherosi attacked Eagles Mount. Not once in the intervening years had Faelia sought the comfort of her mother's arms. Perhaps it had taken Temet's death to forge this bond, one that only women could understand and share: to be left behind by the men they loved.

At least Darak and Keirith were still alive. And she refused to stand by helplessly while they met their fate.

Lisula had helped her find Keirith all those years ago. Perhaps she could help her find Rigat now. Her magic had required moon blood and Griane's had long since ceased to flow, but if it would help Darak and Keirith, she would surrender every drop in her body.

And if Lisula's magic failed, she would have to ask for Fellgair's help—and pay any price he demanded.

Chapter 43

THE DAY HAD BEGUN BADLY with his stilted farewell to his son. Korim had saluted him before marching up the boarding plank. Although Geriv remained on the shore until the ship disappeared beyond the bend in the river, Korim never looked back. Or if he did, he never acknowledged his father's wave.

He spent the rest of the day tramping about the fortress: doubling the men guarding the ships and patrolling the parapet; posting additional guards around Kheridh's hut; inspecting the disposition of provisions; meeting with his officers to ensure that each understood the importance of the next few days. By late afternoon, he was exhausted, but satisfied that he had taken every conceivable precaution to ensure that the Spirit-Hunter could never breach his walls and that Kheridh could never escape them.

He was less sanguine about his relationship with his son. He had tried to ease matters this morning, even asked Korim to remain at Headquarters until he returned so that they would have an opportunity to "reevaluate the future." Korim had simply nodded and replied, "Yes, Vanel."

From beginning to end, he had handled the matter poorly. As a commander, he rarely allowed his emotions to rule him; as a father, it seemed to happen with increasing frequency.

What infuriated him the most was that he felt as if he were in the wrong. Dear gods, it was Korim who had endangered himself—endangered everyone in the fortress—with that foolish escapade. Interrogating the prisoner, indeed. Showing off, more likely.

He still hadn't decided what to do about Remil do Fadiq. His lack of judgment was even more appalling than Korim's. Perhaps he should send for do Nizhi. He'd held things together at Eagles Mount well enough. Why not offer him a promotion and let him take charge here? And ship do Fadiq off to one of the smaller posts downriver.

He'd decide after the Spirit-Hunter surrendered. Until then, he needed his mind to be free of all distractions. Including the unfortunate situation with his son.

After a joyless supper with Jonaq, he returned to his quarters. As the slave assigned to serve him fumbled with his sword belt, he regretted the impulse that had made him send Pujh downriver. Whether or not Pujh's presence provided any comfort for Korim, his absence certainly ensured more discomfort for him.

"Never mind. I'll do it myself. Leave me."

Wearily, he hung his sword belt on the wooden hook and sat on his pallet to remove his sandals. He was still reaching for the laces when he heard the hysterical cry.

He leaped to his feet and grabbed his sword belt. His fingers froze as he belatedly recognized the voice.

Without knocking, Remil do Fadiq flung open the door and stepped aside. Jonaq followed, supporting a weeping Pujh.

"What happened? Did the ship founder? Is Korim all right?"

Unable to make sense of Pujh's babbling, Geriv turned to the Remil who simply held out his hand. Dangling from his clenched fingers was Korim's amulet.

Geriv took it, pleased that his hand was so steady, that he could listen so calmly to Pujh's faltering account of the ambush. Then Pujh cried, "He said to tell you . . . he made me memorize it . . ." The old man choked on a sob. "He said, 'Your ship is destroyed. Your warriors are dead. Your son is my prisoner. I will exchange him for mine on the morrow at sunrise. At the narrows. Ten miles downriver. Beach your ship on the southern shore. You may bring ten men across the river as . . . as an escort. I will be waiting for you.' It was the Spirit-Hunter, master!"

Geriv nodded, transfixed by the amulet in his palm. He

wondered if the Spirit-Hunter had chosen the site deliberately; before marching south to ambush the rebels, Geriv had beached his ship at that very spot.

He carefully laid Korim's amulet on the table. Then he walked to the window and gripped the frame until his fingers ached. To have come so close to success and have it snatched away. And all because of his son's foolhardy behavior.

No. Because I sent him away with only a skalekh to guard him.

What would happen if he refused to hand over Kheridh? The Spirit-Hunter must realize that killing Korim would only result in Kheridh's death as well.

Stalemate.

"Vanel?" the Remil asked. "What are your orders?"

He tried to think, to analyze the situation as a commander would, but he kept seeing his son's stark face as he reprimanded him, hearing his own voice, cruel and sarcastic, as he suggested that Korim pack.

The Spirit-Hunter would have men watching the narrows. And probably upriver as well. Could they make a forced march at night and surprise them? Likely, they would just melt into the forest, taking Korim with them. And if by some miracle they did find them, it would be too easy for his son to be killed in a night battle—by the Spirit-Hunter's men or his.

Geriv's gaze swept the compound, the palisades, the half-moon that hung over the southern hills, seeking inspiration, seeking some way out.

"I'm sorry, Vanel." The Remil's voice sounded resigned. "I think he's beaten us."

Slowly, Geriv straightened and walked back to Pujh. The slave fell to his knees.

"Forgive me, Master Geriv. I failed you. And our boy."

He helped Pujh to his feet and patted him awkwardly on the shoulder. When the old man flung his arms around him and burst into a fresh storm of tears, he merely patted the heaving shoulders again until the sobs abated.

Then he gently freed himself and said, "Now, Pujh. I need you to tell me exactly what happened. Every detail, no matter how small. Everything about the terrain where the exchange is to take place. And everything you can re-call about the Spirit-Hunter."

Darak leaned against a pine, staring down at the silver stripe of moonlight bisecting the river. Kelik and Mikal should have been back by now. Even if the old slave slowed them down, they would have reached Little Falls before sunset. The night was half gone and there was still no sign of them.

Perhaps they'd waited until dark to set the old man free. That would have been smart. Give Geriv less time to come up with a plan. He should have thought of it himself. Then he wouldn't be standing here, worrying.

He didn't expect Geriv to attempt a night rescue; it was in both their interests to go through with the prisoner ex-change. But he had posted sentries in the forest and at the base of the hill. He and Sorig watched the river from the summit. If Geriv came, they'd know.

The ambush had gone better than he could have hoped. He hadn't counted on the slaves, though. They were too terrified of the forest to head downriver to the village. In the end, he'd had to tie them up again; if they were fright-ened by an owl or a bat and went rushing off into the forest, his men might kill them, mistaking them for Geriv's warriors in the dark.

It was probably for the best; there was no way of know-ing what sort of reception they would find at the village. A few of the Zherosi might have made it there, but he doubted they would be in much shape to lead a counter-attack.

In spite of his exhaustion, sleep eluded him. The waiting gnawed at his nerves almost as much as the fixed and pene-trating gaze of the boy behind him.

Pine needles crunched, and he tensed, only to relax again as he realized the boy was only shifting position. He had refused to give his oath that he would not run away, so Darak had bound him to a tree. The boy had submitted without a struggle. When Darak assured him that he would not be harmed, he'd turned his head away with the same disdain he had shown in refusing his offers of food and water. Later, though, the dark eyes had turned back to him, filled with such resentment that Darak considered blind-folding him. Instead, he had simply turned his back. But he could still feel that gaze burning into him.

What did the boy expect? That he would feel ashamed of capturing him? It was absurd. Yet as the night wore on, his elation at the success of his plan faded, replaced by the very shame he found so ridiculous. He would have pre-ferred not to use a mere boy as a pawn, but Geriv had left him no choice.

The pine needles rustled again, and he glanced over his shoulder. Although he was standing only ten paces away, the boy was little more than a dark shape under the trees. He was turning back to study the river when he heard the soft groan. Reluctantly, he walked over to investigate.

"Are you cold?"

It was a warm night, but the Zherosi were notoriously thin-skinned.

"If you're cold, I'll fetch my mantle."

The rustling was continuous now as if, despite his best efforts, the boy could not control his trembling. But he still refused to speak.

Nearly blind in the darkness, he checked the ropes. The ones binding his wrists were tight, but the flesh around them didn't feel swollen. And although those that encircled his arms and chest were also secure, Darak was certain they could not be causing the boy's discomfort. Perhaps his arse was simply sore from sitting so long.

"If you're in pain, you need to tell me."

When this statement failed to elicit any response, Darak sighed. As he straightened, the boy made a hoarse sound, then cleared his throat.

"I need to . . . relieve myself."

It could be a ploy, but the boy's squirming made it unlikely.

"All right. I'll untie you. Don't do anything stupid like trying to run away. Likely, you'd just tumble down the hill and break your neck."

It would be easier to saw through the rope with his dag-ger, but they had no more to bind him again. His fingertips were burning by the time he managed to loosen the knots. He left the rope around the boy's wrists; even with his hands bound, he should be able to take a piss.

He pulled the boy to his feet and gripped his arm to keep him from dashing off. The precaution proved unnecessary; his legs were so wobbly he could barely walk. As Darak led him behind the tree, the boy lurched in the opposite direction. Uncertain what he was up to, Darak let him lead. A reluctant smile tugged at his lips when he realized his prisoner clearly intended to piss on the tree he had been leaning against.

Well, that's one way of showing contempt for your enemy.

He kept his grip on the skinny arm as the boy tugged at his khirta. From his grunts, he was making little progress. And from the way he danced from one foot to the other, it was anyone's guess whether he would manage to loosen it before he pissed himself.

Darak let the dance go on for a few moments before pushing the boy's hands aside. He fumbled with the heavy folds of cloth, hindered by the darkness and his unfamiliarity with the khirta's draping. He finally found the section that passed between the boy's legs, but it was firmly tucked under his belt.

"Bel's blazing ballocks," he muttered. "How does the damn thing—?"

"Just pull the cloth aside. So I can reach my kharo."

"What's a—?"

"My loincloth!"

Sweet Maker, there's a loincloth, too. He'll never make it.

He grabbed the bulky fold and pulled. The boy yelped. Darak muttered an apology, but haste and embarrassment only made his fingers clumsier. He was sweating by the time he managed to yank the cloth loose.

The boy wrenched free and twisted to the side. After a few more moments of frenzied dancing, Darak heard a heartfelt groan and the gush of liquid pelting the pine needles.

It went on and on and on. He wouldn't have thought a man could have that much piss inside him, never mind this skinny boy. The stubborn young idiot's bladder must have been near to bursting.

The stream subsided to erratic spurts and finally to silence. The boy sighed. So did Darak, aware of both the sympathetic twinges in his bladder and the peculiar intimacy of the moment.

As the boy tugged and squirmed and adjusted himself, he asked, "Can you manage? Or do you need me to—?"

"I can manage. Thank you."

Darak was so intent on the boy's progress that he was unaware of Sorig's approach until he heard him whisper, "Everything all right?"

They both started. The similarities of their reactions disturbed Darak; the last thing he wanted was to feel any sort of connection to this boy. After reassuring Sorig, he seized the skinny arm with more force than necessary, led the boy back to the tree, and tied him up again.

He tested the ropes and heard a soft grunt of pain. Angry with himself, he wasted more time loosening the bonds a bit before crouching in front of the boy.

"Do you want water?"

"Nay."

"Something to eat?"

"I am not hungry."

The rumble of his belly belied that statement, but Darak refused to shame him by mentioning it.

He knew he should walk away; the boy clearly hated his company. But he couldn't help recalling Keirith's stories of his first days in Zheros: the fear of not knowing what his captors intended, the need to guard himself every moment lest he betray that fear or reveal a damning piece of information that could result in his death.

"Try and get some rest. And don't worry. You'll be back at Little Falls before midmorning."

When no response was forthcoming, he rose.

"He will not come."

The boy's voice was flat, utterly devoid of emotion.

Darak slowly sank back down. "Why not?"

"Because Kheridh is more valuable than I am."

Again, a calm statement of fact.

"Aye. Well. From a warrior's perspective, perhaps. But he's a father, too."

"You do not know him."

"Nay. But I've met him. When I was a captive in Zheros."

"I know."

"He . . . watched over Keirith."

"Why?"

The boy sounded startled. Of course, Geriv would never have revealed his part in their escape. And despite everything, Darak was reluctant to do so now. Not to protect Geriv, but to shield this boy. He shook his head, impatient with himself, but still chose his words with care.

"Malaq—the Pajhit—befriended Keirith and feared for his life. So he asked Khonsel do Havi to protect him. The Khonsel had your father shadow Keirith. To make sure he came to no harm. For that, I have remembered him—all of them—in my prayers."

"You . . . prayed for my father?"

"Aye. It's ironic. Given all that's happened. I can't remember him well—save for the eye patch, of course. He struck me as a good fighter. Stern but not cruel. Or stupid. He'll make the exchange. It may gall him, but he'll do it."

After a long moment, the boy said, "Kheridh talked about you."

"You've seen him? He's all right?"

In the silence that followed, his heart nearly failed him. Finally, the boy said, "His shoulder was injured. In the ambush. But he is . . . well." Another interminable pause before he added, "They were drugging him."

One part of his mind noted that the boy had said "they" not "we." But he was too relieved to know that Keirith was all right to pursue that. It took him a moment to understand why they would drug him, but of course, Geriv had been there when Keirith cast out the Zheron's spirit. But why Keirith would talk to this boy—the son of his captor— mystified him.

"He was blindfolded," the boy explained in response to his question. "I pretended to be from the village. To fool him into giving away information. But I was the fool," he concluded bitterly.

"It was worth trying." The words surprised him as much as his desire to shield the boy had. "You speak our language well. Very well. There's the accent, of course, but—"

"Accent?"

"More guttural. Like the tribe folk of the south. But with the drugs dulling his senses, Keirith probably didn't notice."

"We did not even talk of the rebellion. Not really. Only . . . everyday things. Growing up. Fishing. Our fathers." The boy cleared his throat. "You must love him very much. To follow him to Zheros all those years ago. And to risk your life for him now."

Reluctant to discuss his feelings, Darak mumbled an affirmative.

"That is the difference, you see. My father does not love me. Especially now when I have ruined his plans."

"Aye. Well. A father can get angry with his children and still love them. I've raised my voice—and my hand—to all of mine at one time or another. And your father—"

"My father cannot abide me."

His voice shook a little, but it was as calm as ever.

"I am . . . a disappointing to him. Disappointing? This is the right word?"

"Disappointment."

"Thank you. Disappointment. That is why he will not exchange Kheridh for me."

"I think you're wrong. I pray you are."

"And if I am not? What will happen at dawn?"

"You've nothing to fear," Darak assured him. "Even if I were the kind of man who would kill a boy, what would I gain? Your father would kill Keirith, and then we'd both lose our sons."

"This is true. But my father knows this about you. That you are not a killer. That you love your son. So he can wait. And gamble that, in the end, you will back down."

He had considered that possibility, but had managed to convince himself that no man would risk his son's life. Confronted by the calm certainty in the boy's voice, Darak couldn't help feeling that, although the boy was his prisoner, he was the one who was trapped.

Chapter 44

THE GUARDS SHOOK HIM AWAKE. They handed him his bowl of porridge. When they put on his shoes, Keirith knew something unusual was happening. But only when they led him out of the hut did he realize the appointed day had arrived—for his freedom or his death.

Blindfolded, he shambled forward, stumbling over uneven paving stones and gulping great lungfuls of air; even tainted by woodsmoke, it was sweet after the stale air in the hut.

He knew he should be afraid. Instead, he felt oddly calm—like that final dawn in Pilozhat when he had led the adders to the temple of Zhe. Every sensation seemed magnified: the rub of his breeches against his thighs, the grip of the guards' fingers on his arms, even the trembling of his leg muscles after days of inactivity.

Wavering orange light filtered through the blindfold. Men moved around him, speaking in hushed voices. From behind came the tramp of leather-shod feet on stone. In front, a soft command to open the gate. Keirith heard grunts from the straining men and the protesting creak of wood. Then he felt earth beneath his feet instead of stone.

As earth gave way to pebbles, he realized the sound of the rapids had grown louder. They were leading him to the river.

"Step up," a voice ordered.

Wooden planking. The sound of flapping cloth. Why were they taking him back aboard the ship?

He stumbled as he stepped onto the deck, drawing muttered curses from his guards. They tightened their grip on his arms and led him forward.

"Sit."

A column of wood at his back. Ropes pulled tight across his chest. Pebbles scraping the hull. And the gentle rocking as the ship floated free.

He strained to hear something that might tell him where they were heading, but there was only the flap of the sail and the slap of water against the hull and the occasional creak of the timbers. No light penetrated the blindfold. No sun warmed his body. Why would they risk a night voyage? Something must have happened. Could Fa have been captured? Or—gods forbid—killed? But why would they be hustling him away in darkness?

He tensed as footsteps thudded on the planks. Flinched as fingers tugged at his blindfold and gag. After so many days in darkness, the torchlight blinded him. He turned his head away, eyes watering.

A shadow blocked the light. When he looked up, he could only make out a dark silhouette, framed by the too-brilliant glare of the torches. Then he caught a whiff of the familiar spicy scent. Expecting a hulking body to match the deep voice, he was surprised that the figure looked as short and wiry as an ordinary Zheroso.

He raised his bound wrists and wiped his eyes with the back of his hand. Slowly, the man came into focus: a helmet with three eagles' feathers; a black patch over his left eye; a stern mouth.

His gaze dropped to the scarlet tunic, then jerked back to the man's face. It was older, of course. Seamed by years of squinting into the sun. But it was clearly the same man— the shadow who had followed him in Pilozhat, the obedient warrior who had led Fa to freedom, the trusted aide to Khonsel Vazh do Havi who had advised his uncle to kill them.

All he could do was gape, aware that Geriv was speaking, but unable to focus on the words.

"Do you understand?"

"I . . . no . . . I'm sorry, but—"

"Your father has captured my son. We're exchanging you for him."

"Your son? Was that . . . is his name Jarel?"

"My son's name is Korim."

For a long moment, Geriv studied him, frowning. Then
he bent down so abruptly that Keirith recoiled.

"Korim stopped the drugs. You could have taken his
body. Why didn't you?"

*Because I remembered Xevhan's scream. And mine when
they raped me. And the horror of being utterly helpless. And
even with my father's life at stake, I hesitated.*

Keirith looked away. "Because I'm weak."

When Sorig raced down the beach shouting, "The ship is
coming!" Darak murmured a shaky prayer of thanks. In
his relief, he pounded the boy on the back so hard he
staggered.

"See? I told you he'd come."

The boy nodded and quickly averted his face, but Darak
had already seen the tears glistening in his eyes. To give
him time to recover, he scanned the spot he had chosen
for the prisoner exchange.

Hoping to allay Geriv's fears of an ambush, he'd selected
a site near the beach with little cover. But he'd been careful
to position his men within bowshot, hidden behind boulders, lying in the long grass, standing behind trees.

Kelik and Mikal were among them, thank the gods.
They'd reached the narrows late in the night to report the
safe arrival of Pujh at Little Falls. So far, everything was
going according to plan. And every moment brought his
boy closer.

But he couldn't help worrying. About Keirith. About
Geriv's intentions. And about last night's dream.

Griane had been bending over him, urging him to wake
up, reminding him that he would have plenty of time to
sleep after he was dead but in the meantime, he had far
too many things to do. The sun was behind her, turning
the spiky ends of her hair to fire.

Although he was still asleep in his dream, he had asked,
"What did you do to your hair?"

"What do you think?" she had snapped. "I cut it off and
left it along the trail to mark the way for you."

"Well, that was silly. I know the way home."

His dream-self awakened then and reached for her, but she melted into a shaft of sunlight like some otherworldly spirit.

The dream still haunted him—and the terrifying feeling that he would never see her again.

"Spirit-Hunter? Are you all right?"

"Aye. Just thinking about . . . things."

"Forgive me. Of course. I should have realized . . ." A deep flush stained the boy's cheeks. "I am stupid."

Darak shook his head. He was so hard on himself. Just like Keirith.

Ever since he had conceived the idea of the ambush, Darak had been careful to think of him only as "the boy," seeking the same distance he once had with his recruits. Now his mind reluctantly formed the name: Korim.

"They'll be here soon," he said. "Remember what I told you. Everyone will be watching us. My men and your father's. If things grow heated, they'll get nervous. And nervous men make mistakes. So it's up to us to stay calm. To set an example."

Korim nodded solemnly.

"Does your father speak the tribal tongue?"

"Aye." Korim hesitated, then added, "But not very well."

"Then I'd like you to translate. If you would. So there are no misunderstandings."

He waited for Korim to nod again before walking down to the water. The ship was heading to the southern shore as he'd directed. He paced nervously, watching its progress, then forced himself to stop when he saw Korim watching him.

"The waiting," he said. "That's the hardest part." Then wondered why he was confiding in the boy.

"You are not . . . I expected you to be different. The stories . . ."

"Men make up the stories. And they like stories with heroes. If we'd had more time, I'd have told you what really happened on that quest."

"Not that. I thought you would be . . . hard. Cruel. And then I met Kheridh . . . and you . . . and . . ." He shrugged helplessly.

"Aye. Well. I can be hard, but I hope I'm not cruel. Mostly, I'm just a man. A husband. A father."

Korim nodded, watching him with those big doe eyes. Darak had never expected a Zherosi boy to stare at him with the same wide-eyed awe as the lads in the villages.

Not awe, he realized. Yearning.

What kind of life had he led that made him so hungry for kindness that he'd accept it from the man who had captured him?

"Don't worry. Everything'll be fine."

He wasn't sure if he meant the prisoner exchange or the unhappy lad's future.

Chapter 45

WHEN RIGAT SAW THE FIGURE silhouetted in the doorway, he imagined it was Fellgair. Then reason overcame desire, and he recognized Nekif.

"Great lord, I packed the supplies you requested. Dried fruit and meat. They are there—next to your chest of clothes. With the waterskin. And I took the liberty of bringing a bowl of honeyed figs. It's not wise to begin a journey on an empty stomach."

"Thank you, Nekif."

"Shall I help you dress? Or would you prefer to bathe first?"

"I've no time to bathe."

He had already wasted an entire day trying to trace Fellgair's energy: in Zheros, in the north, in all the places they had visited during their first days together, including the First Forest. There was only one place left to look.

Chaos.

He tried and failed to suppress a shudder. But if Darak—
a man with no magic—could survive Chaos, so could the
Trickster's son.

Splashing cool water on his face helped clear his mind.
Bolting a few of the figs assuaged his hunger. He only
wished he could replenish his power so easily, but he was
afraid to postpone his mission any longer.

"No, not a khirta," he said, as Nekif held out a fresh one.
"I want my old tunic and breeches today. And my shoes."

He waited impatiently as Nekif padded back to the
carved wooden chest and rummaged through it; no doubt
his old clothes were buried under all the Zherosi finery.
Nekif finally uncovered them and hurried toward him, the
breeches slung over his arm and the tunic held at arm's
length. Although the doeskin had been brushed and
cleaned, the old man's nose wrinkled.

Rigat snatched the tunic away. "You object to my choice
of clothing?"

The grimace vanished. "Of course not, great lord."

"These are the clothes of my mother's people. And as
such, as worthy to be worn by the Son of Zhe as any
golden breastplate."

Nekif fell to his knees and prostrated himself. "Please
forgive this miserable slave. I deserve to be beaten for my
impertinence and driven from your presence."

"And if you ever show such disrespect again, you will
be. Now hand me my breeches."

The tunic was too tight through the shoulders, the
breeches straining at the thighs, but after making such a
fuss, he couldn't very well take them off.

"After I've left, you may tell the queen I've gone north.
I should return in a day or two."

"Yes, great lord."

He dismissed Nekif and dug through the chest to retrieve
his leather belt and bag of charms. It comforted him to feel
the familiar weight of his dagger against his thigh and the
small doeskin bag rising and falling with every breath. And
perhaps it would bring him luck to emulate Darak who had
entered Chaos armed only with the flint of his dagger, the
power of his charms, and the strength of his will.

He slipped his arms through the leather straps of the

courier's satchel and settled it on his back. Then he slung the waterskin over his shoulder. He was as ready as he would ever be—if he could open a portal.

He could not follow Fellgair's energy trail between the worlds. Since the landscape of Chaos was always changing, there was no point in picturing any of the things Darak had described. But if the Trickster's nature combined elements of order and chaos, surely his son's must, too.

He focused his mind, trying to tap into the part of his power that drew its strength from the Unmaker. He had often felt it raging uncontrolled through his body, yet now it eluded him.

Frustration made his power leap. And suddenly, he understood.

Analyzing his power with his mind was fruitless. Only when his emotions ruled him did the chaotic aspect of his power burn brightest.

He called on his darkest memories: his terror when Madig nocked the arrow in his bow; the lust that Jholianna aroused in him; the shock of discovering his true identity and the desolation of believing his mam had wanted to kill him; the desperate desire to please both his fathers; and the angry helplessness of being deserted by Fellgair.

With each memory, the power flared. And when it raged through him, hot as a fire through dry brush, he ripped his dagger from its sheath and scored his wrist. Blood bound him to Fellgair as well as magic. It would take both to find his father.

Picturing Fellgair's face, he raised the blood-spattered dagger and slashed open the veil between the worlds.

Greenish-yellow light seeped through the slit. Gingerly, he pulled on one side and peeped through. A stunted, dead tree loomed before him. A few paces away, a boulder reared out of the ground, its black surface incongruously smooth and glossy, as if it had been polished. The sky was the color of an old bruise, the sickly ocher stained here and there by purple blotches that might be clouds.

"I am the Trickster's son. Welcome me or not."

The portal oozed around his shoulders. Before his power could dissipate, he shoved through and sealed the portal behind him.

Immediately, his heart began to race, and he had to gasp for air. Was Chaos trying to destroy him? Then why was his power surging as wildly as his heart?

He staggered forward, clutching at a limb of the dead tree for support. Shimmering black dots rose before his eyes, as if ants were swarming over the ground. A sharp pain stabbed his side with every breath, but he forced himself to breathe slowly and deeply until the pain ebbed and his vision cleared.

Shaking but relieved, he stepped back from the tree, only to be pulled up short. Assuming the sleeve of his tunic was snagged, he reached up. Then froze.

A cluster of dark twigs curled like claws over his wounded wrist. Thick red slime oozed out between them, solidifying as it spread until the claws appeared to be webbed and bloody. Fat globules dripped onto his fingers, sticky as sap but impossibly warm.

As he recoiled, the branch above dipped, weighted down by another cluster of twigs groping for his left wrist. He yanked it out of reach and tore at the imprisoning claws, but the twigs were as resilient as flesh. He grabbed one in his fist and bent it back until it snapped.

The tree shrieked. Not the harsh sound of splintering wood but an agonized scream that echoed through his body and spirit alike. Before he had time to recover, a shudder raced through the branch that still gripped him. Then the other branches began to sway as if rocked by gusts of wind. But there was no wind, not the faintest breeze.

A branch bent low to pluck at the leather thong of his bag of charms. Another snagged the strap of his satchel. He slipped his arm free, but it claimed his waterskin, dangling it just out of reach as if mocking him.

He didn't dare try to retrieve it. He had to keep moving, wriggling and twisting to avoid the grasping branches. Frantically, he grabbed another claw and snapped it off. A spray of bloody sap splashed warmly against his cheek. He broke off another claw and another after that, wincing at each all-too-human shriek.

Cursing, sweating, constantly dancing away from the treacherous branches, he finally broke away, only to be tugged back as a relentless claw seized the strap of his satchel again. He wriggled free, abandoning his supply of food as he had his water. In his haste to escape, he stumbled and went down hard. Heels digging into the loose soil, he scuttled backward like a crab.

The branches of the tree were still moving, but now they flapped with perfect precision like so many featherless wings. The roots pulled free and curled under the trunk. With a final screech, the thing rose into the air and flew off.

He had learned the tale at Darak's knee. How could he have forgotten that Chaos was a place of illusion?

He was still staring at the tree-bird when the black boulder heaved up, spewing sand. Too stunned to move, he watched it grow larger—first, the size of a hut in his village, then a small hill, then as tall as Kelazhat. All in absolute silence.

Yellow flowers sprouted on the gleaming black slopes and grew to the size of trees. Giant sunflowers, he realized, swallowing hard when dozens of eyes blinked open in the dark centers.

Water gushed out of the ground, forming a perfectly circular pool at the base of the mountain. A column of water rose out of it, bluer than the sea at Pilozhat, sparkling silver and gold as if lit by the light of moon and sun alike. The column rose higher and higher until it crested at the mountain's summit, flashing rainbow-colored shards skyward. The most beautiful waterfall he had ever seen—cascading up the mountainside.

His power raced, as frantic as his heartbeat, as rapid as the continuing shifts in the landscape. Squat brown bushes reared out of the ground near the pool, sprouted eight spindly legs, and skittered away like giant spiders. The sandy soil leached away, forming a sinkhole. Before he scuttled back, he glimpsed the black void that filled it.

As if in sympathy, the sky darkened, illuminated only by a curtain of light that shimmered like the Northern Dancers. Only these Dancers were the same sickly greenish yellow that the sky had been moments earlier.

Something flew past his face, hissing, and he batted it away. Something pattered onto the earth—the earth that was now as hard as stone and as black as the mountain. Although the tiny pellets of hail clattered against the polished surface, they felt as soft as milkweed fluff when they brushed against his hands.

Lightning zigzagged across the ground, opening gaping fissures that closed a moment later. Waves rolled and crested in the sky, shattering the curtain of light. When the ground began rolling as well, Rigat flung himself flat, clutching at the thick stalks of grass that shot up around him. They were as insubstantial as water. Helpless, he was carried up into the air on the wave. Then it crested, hurling him down, drowning him in green.

His stomach heaved and he vomited, tasting bile and honey, spewing bits of undigested figs onto the ground. The figs sprouted like mushrooms, caps whirling, and spun into the air.

"You're not real!"

He shut his eyes, but that only made the earth's undulations more sickening. He retched again, fighting to control his body, his mind, and the power that blazed through him. Was it feeding on the unpredictable energy of Chaos—or was Chaos feeding on him?

"My father told me that the spirits in Chaos were drawn to me," Darak had explained. "Because I was alive. They wanted to get close to that life force."

If the presence of Darak's life force had been enough to attract the spirits of Chaos, his power must be even more alluring. Panting with the effort, he tried to tamp it down.

The ground heaved again and went still, plunging him facedown in something cold. He pushed himself up on his elbows and discovered that he was lying at the edge of an ice-scummed pond. Insects swarmed above it, iridescent bodies gleaming as they darted between shafts of murky light. Their monotonous whine maddened him. And his reaction only made the sound louder.

Control. According to Darak, that was the key to surviving Chaos. Only by controlling every emotion—fear, wonder, desire—could you keep the illusions at bay. If Darak had done so through the force of his will, so could he.

He closed his eyes again, trying to calm his breathing and bank the fires of his power. Then something slimy crawled over his hand, shattering his concentration.

"Stop!" he screamed.

The slug's tiny tentacles waved. He smashed the thing with his fist, only to watch the flattened blob separate into two pieces, then four, each sprouting a dark tentacled head and a glistening blue body.

Don't look at it. Don't give it power.

On hands and knees, he edged back from the pool, but couldn't help staring with sick fascination as the slugs continued to multiply and grow. There were dozens of them now, the original ones nearly as long as his forearm, the newborns barely the length of his little finger.

As one, they turned to him. Their mouths gaped open, revealing saliva-slick fangs.

"Stop!" But the scream emerged only as a hoarse whisper.

His breath caught on a sob, and he suppressed it ruthlessly. But still they grew, trailing viscous slime as they slid toward him.

"Stop."

It took Rigat a moment to realize that the voice came from behind him. And another to recognize it. He froze, afraid to look, afraid that this, too, would be an illusion.

A pair of black-clawed feet strode over the slugs, which dissipated like mist. Rigat's gaze traveled up the red-furred legs to the broad chest and finally to the familiar golden eyes.

"Are you real?" he whispered.

"Very much so."

Strong arms enfolded him, rocking him like a babe. Rigat clung to them, grateful and ashamed. Then Fellgair grabbed his shoulders and held him at arm's length.

"What are you doing here?"

Rigat swiped at his nose. "I came to rescue you."

As Fellgair's gaze swept over him, Rigat realized how ridiculous that statement must sound, especially coming from a trembling boy with snot running down his chin. At the same moment, they both began to laugh.

Relief at seeing Fellgair again left him giddy and weak. Without his father's hands steadying him, he would probably collapse. Or dissipate as the slugs had. From slavering beasts to misty nothings in a single heartbeat.

His laughter grew louder, edged with hysteria. Fellgair's fingers tightened on his shoulders. With a hiccuping gurgle,

Rigat clamped his lips together, controlling the hysteria and the flare of power that had accompanied it.

"That's better."

"It's true, then? That my power is stronger here?"

Fellgair released him and leaned back on his hands. With a start, Rigat realized that the ever-shifting landscape had solidified into a featureless plain of browning grass. If not for the bruised sky, they might be sitting somewhere in Zheros.

"Stronger? Possibly. But certainly more difficult to control."

"How did you find me?"

Fellgair frowned. "I felt your energy the moment you entered Chaos. Didn't you feel mine?"

"I . . . I'm not sure. Everything happened so fast."

"Blood calls to blood here. Surely Darak must have told you."

He remembered now how Darak claimed his father had sensed his presence. And just as Reinek had tracked down his son, so had Fellgair.

"And speaking of blood . . ." Fellgair nodded at Rigat's wrist.

"I used my blood to help open the portal."

Fellgair held out his hand, and Rigat obediently offered his wrist. Instead of sealing the wound, Fellgair used his claws to rip a strip of doeskin from his tunic.

"How did you discover I was here?" Fellgair asked as he wrapped the doeskin around his wrist.

"I looked everywhere else I could think of. This was the only place left."

Fellgair nodded without looking up.

"Why did you come here?" Rigat asked.

Fellgair knotted the bandage and examined his handiwork.

"It was because of me, wasn't it?"

"It's not important."

"It *is* important. I needed you. After you left . . ."

Finally, the golden eyes met his. "Has something happened? Is Griane in danger?"

"Mam?" Rigat shook his head, confused. "Why would you think that?"

"I thought I heard her call me. Perhaps I was wrong.

Even for a god, it's hard to distinguish reality from illusion here. Or desire. Did you see her when you went north?"

As he fumbled for an answer, Fellgair seized his arm, fingers biting deep into the flesh. "You did go back? After the Gathering?"

"There wasn't time!"

He blurted out everything that had happened in Fellgair's absence: the interrogations, the attempted assassination, The Shedding. "Jholianna offered me the crown," he added, hating the sulky tone of his voice, but unable to disguise it.

Fellgair stared out over the grasslands. Then he sighed. "I'm sorry I wasn't there."

"I'm sorry, too." Rigat's voice shook, and he swallowed hard.

"You should have called me," Fellgair said. "I would have come. No matter the cost."

"The cost?"

"Do you know who was behind the assassination attempt?"

"Not for sure. I even wondered if the Khonsel was involved. What cost?"

"He would never use a poisoned arrow. Too much risk of hitting the queen."

"That's what he said. What cost, Fellgair?"

"In a moment. I'm thinking." Fellgair rose and paced restlessly, flattening a trail in the tall grass. "It's likely that attack was genuine. The man with the dagger, though . . ."

"I thought it was just to distract us. From the real assassin."

"That's possible. But it's also possible the two attacks were unrelated." Abruptly, Fellgair stopped pacing. "You're certain the orders for a truce were sent?"

"I told you that before you left."

"And Geriv received them?" When Rigat hesitated, Fellgair's gaze sharpened. "Did Geriv acknowledge receipt of his orders?"

"I . . . he must have. I didn't ask. So much happened, I just assumed—"

"Yes. You did."

Stung, Rigat snapped, "What does that have to do with the other assassin?"

"Perhaps nothing. Perhaps a great deal."

"Stop talking in riddles."

"If the orders were delayed—if Geriv never received them—he would have free rein to continuing pursuing the rebels. Which you might have discovered if you had met Darak. What better way to keep you in Pilozhat than to stage an assassination?"

Rigat's bowels clenched. He shook his head, unwilling to meet Fellgair's gaze.

"It's only one possibility," Fellgair said. "But he took the initiative once before. After the earthquake."

"The Khonsel, you mean?"

"The king was dead. The queen weak from Shedding. The city in ruins. Who took control? Who knew Keirith's spirit had survived? Who arranged for Keirith and Darak to escape?"

Bile surged up from Rigat's belly, choking him. He bent over, retching dryly, and felt Fellgair's hands steadying him once again.

"I may be wrong," Fellgair said. "But if your mother called me . . . she would never do that unless . . ."

"Unless something awful had happened."

"Or was going to happen," Fellgair corrected firmly. "Which means you may still have time to prevent it."

Rigat got to his feet. "Then let's go. Now."

Fellgair hesitated.

"You can leave, can't you? A moment ago, you said—"

"Yes. I can leave."

"But there's a cost."

"There's always a cost. No matter what one chooses. The trick is to weigh all the costs before making the choice." Fellgair stared off into the distance, his expression almost wistful. Suddenly, he smiled. "You're right, Rigat. It's time for us to leave. But I think I should go to Pilozhat. To keep an eye on things there while you're in the north."

It could not be that easy. Fellgair would never have left Pilozhat unless the Unmaker had summoned him. And if he were free to leave, he would have done so when he thought he heard Mam call.

Before he could speak, Fellgair ripped open a portal and pulled him through. Bemused by the forest of green-leafed oaks, he wondered if Fellgair had decided to come north

with him after all. Then he realized the trees were painted
on the wall and that they were standing in Fellgair's opu-
lent private chamber in the temple of the God with Two
Faces.

He was suddenly aware that he was exhausted. His power
still smoldered within him, easy to control now but notice-
ably weaker.

"It's a good thing we left when we did. If I'd stayed
much longer . . ."

His observation died, unspoken, as he turned to Fellgair.

Ruddy fur shifted to black hair, claws to fingernails.
Before the transformation was complete, the Supplicant
melted back into the fox-man. Breasts grew and shrank.
Fur sprouted on flesh and vanished, the changes happening
so quickly that Fellgair's shape became little more than
a blur.

"Dear gods . . ." he whispered.

Fellgair's face froze in a grimace. The Supplicant emerged,
but her form continued to waver before Rigat's horrified
eyes.

"What's happening?"

Fellgair staggered toward a thick pile of cushions and
collapsed. As Rigat hurried toward him, Fellgair waved him
away. "The portal," he wheezed. "Close it. Quickly."

It took Rigat two tries before he managed it. Then he
fell on his knees next to his father.

"What is it? What can I do?"

He lifted his hand to brush back the long hair covering
Fellgair's face, then recoiled as white hair sprouted among
the lustrous black.

Fellgair lifted his head. Deep lines scored his forehead
and seamed the corners of his eyes. Slowly, they vanished,
and with them the white streaking his hair, but flecks of
gold still gleamed in the dark eyes.

"It's the Unmaker," Rigat whispered. "He's doing this
to you."

Fellgair pushed himself up on the cushions and held out
his left hand, frowning when he noted its tremor. He stared
fixedly at his hand. The tremor ceased. One by one, fingernails sprouted. Five perfect ovals. Only then did Fellgair
lower his hand to his lap.

"I think I'll forgo the paint for now."

"Fellgair . . ."

"Yes. This is my father's doing. We have been . . . somewhat at odds lately."

"Because of me."

"He summoned me to Chaos the morning after you were conceived and threatened to hold me there forever to prevent any further . . . interference. But my mother—the Maker—interceded for me. And for Griane."

"For Mam?"

"The Maker accepts the need for death, but she also understands a mother's love for her child. In the end, though, I think the Unmaker was simply eager to see what disorder you might bring to the world. I was permitted to leave, but only if I promised never to contact you. At first, I kept my distance, but after you discovered the truth . . ." Fellgair shrugged helplessly. "You are my son."

"And that's why he summoned you a sennight ago?"

"He summoned me the morning after your vision quest. I chose to ignore him."

Rigat's mouth dropped open. How did anyone—even a god—ignore the Lord of Chaos?

"He retaliated by draining my power. Just a little at a time. Much crueler, really, than simply destroying me."

Suddenly, it all made sense: the fluctuations in Fellgair's energy, the unexplained weariness, the unraveled healing.

"But you went to him in the end," Rigat pointed out.

"Because he threatened to kill you if I didn't." A brief, mirthless smile. "Not all fathers are as forgiving as Darak. He gave me a choice. If I remained in Chaos until you reached the end of your life, he would permit me to return to the world with my powers—those I still possessed—intact. If I left before that . . ."

"But if the Maker helped you once, surely—"

"No." Fellgair's voice was very quiet. "Not this time."

"Then we'll beat the Unmaker at his own game. I'll give you some of my power and—"

"No! Yours is weak enough already."

"It's strong enough to get me to the north and back. Besides—"

"No, Rigat. You must leave. Now."

Rigat hesitated, concern for Fellgair warring with fear for his family's safety.

"Please. Go to your mother. Talk to Darak. Make sure all is well. And when you come back, we'll see about beating the Unmaker at his own game."

As Rigat reluctantly rose, Fellgair seized his hand. "I made my choice when I created you and I've never regretted that decision. If you need me, call. I'll come—if I can."

Chapter 46

GERIV AUTOMATICALLY SCANNED the terrain, confident that the Spirit-Hunter had men hidden behind every boulder and tree in sight. But his gaze kept returning to the tall figure standing motionless in the grass.

Damn the man. Ever since their first meeting, Geriv had been unnerved by him. Not merely his physical presence, but that odd combination of power and vulnerability. One moment, tenderly cradling the dead body of the mute in his arms and the next, condemning the Zheron to an eternity in the Abyss in a voice so cold and inexorable that it still sent shivers down Geriv's spine to recall it. And then, the naked anguish when he believed his son's spirit was lost.

A muffled grunt made his head whip around. "Help him up!" he snapped to the guards. "And take off the blindfold."

They hauled Kheridh back to his feet—again. Hard to believe he had possessed the power to cast out the Zheron's spirit. Even harder to make sense of his strange confession. "I'm weak," he'd admitted. Yet the Spirit-Hunter had risked everything to save him.

He waited impatiently while the guards untied the blindfold. For a moment, Kheridh just stood there, dazed. Then his wandering gaze fixed on his father and his face came alive, the combination of joy and yearning as naked as the Spirit-Hunter's anguish all those years ago.

Did Korim watch his approach with so much yearning? With half that joy?

As they neared the little rise, the Spirit-Hunter moved behind Korim, cleverly shielding himself with the boy's body. Geriv countered by signaling his archers to nock arrows and fan out behind him. The Spirit-Hunter simply rested both hands on Korim's shoulders and waited.

It was clear he was not restraining Korim. Nor did Korim seem to resent the gesture. Incredibly, as the Spirit-Hunter leaned down to whisper something, Korim smiled. As if the man were his protector instead of his captor.

Rage flooded him. Fury at the Spirit-Hunter who had apparently won Korim's affection in a single night when he had striven in vain to do so for years. And even greater fury at his son—for being so easily beguiled and for destroying his plans to capture this man and crush the rebellion for good.

Damn Korim and his soft heart. And damn the Spirit-Hunter for playing on it.

With the small part of his mind that remained dispassionate, he noted his labored breathing, his racing heartbeat, the surge of bloodlust that filled his mouth with saliva. At that moment, he wanted nothing more than to cut the Spirit-Hunter down and be done with this.

In the end, the commander triumphed. His breathing slowed. His heartbeat calmed. He spat to clear his mouth and continued down the beach, only to draw up short as Kheridh cried out.

Geriv whirled around and found him staring up at the two hills that guarded the narrows.

"What? What do you see?"

"Nothing. The hills. They reminded me of . . . but it's nothing."

"Then stop this nonsense! Before you get us all killed."

As the first red rays of the rising sun spilled through the trees, he seized Kheridh's arm and marched him toward the Spirit-Hunter.

"Vanel do Khat," his father called.

"Spirit-Hunter."

Nearly three moons since he'd heard his father's voice. Keirith wished he could see his face more clearly, but the shadows of the trees lay across him. Although only a few dozen paces separated them, Geriv had cautiously ordered the rest of his warriors to remain behind, out of range of any archers that might be hidden around the meeting place.

"The Spirit-Hunter has asked me to translate for him. To avoid misunderstandings."

Korim's features were equally shadowed, but Keirith recognized the voice at once. Saw, too, the way Geriv tensed. But his expression remained wooden. If he was happy to see his son or relieved that he was unhurt, no one would ever know.

"Are you all right, son?" his father called.

Without waiting for Korim's translation, Geriv demanded, "What did he say?"

Keirith swallowed hard. "He asked if I was all right."

"Answer him."

"I'm fine, Fa. And you?"

"Tired. And worried about you, of course. But otherwise, I'm holding up."

Keirith translated for Geriv's benefit and waited for him to ask after Korim. But Geriv simply called out, "Let's get on with this."

Keirith heard the murmur of his father's voice. Then Korim said, "The Spirit-Hunter is anxious to avoid bloodshed. He gives his oath that none of his men will attack yours."

"My men are easy targets. His are hidden. Let them show themselves."

After Korim translated, Fa hesitated for a moment, then called out the order. One by one, figures appeared, arrows nocked. Keirith's breath hissed in when a man rose behind Fa, then eased out in a shaky sigh of relief when he recognized Mikal.

"And the rest?" Geriv demanded.

"There are no others," Korim replied.

Ten men. Fa had done it all with just ten men. Seeing Geriv's look of shock and the flush that crept up his neck, Keirith struggled to hide his pride lest he antagonize the man further.

"The Spirit-Hunter suggests that both sides lay down their bows. To ensure there are no . . . accidents."

Geriv cursed softly, then nodded. As both commanders shouted the order, their warriors reluctantly placed their bows on the ground.

"Send Korim over to me. And I will release Kheridh."

Whatever Fa said in response to Korim's translation made the boy smile—and provoked another soft curse from Geriv.

"The Spirit-Hunter prefers that both prisoners are released at the same time."

Geriv's fingers tightened on his arm. "Your oath," he muttered, all the while keeping his gaze fixed on Fa and Korim. "On your father's life. That you will not use your power."

Keirith stared at him in disbelief. Why would he use his power? This was a straightforward exchange of prisoners. Was Geriv planning some trick? Or was he just nervous?

"And if I refuse?"

"I'll order my archers to cut him down where he stands."

"And risk killing Korim?"

Geriv's expression hardened. "Your oath."

"If you give me yours that my father leaves with me."

Before Geriv could answer, Fa called out, "Keirith? What's wrong?"

Keirith glanced at his father. His vision swam. He blinked hard and realized it was not his vision, but some disturbance in the air next to Fa. He raised his bound wrists to shade his eyes, still uncertain if what he was seeing was real. Then Fa's head jerked toward the odd rippling. He took a step back, pulling Korim with him.

Geriv's fingers dug deeper into his bicep. "What's happening?"

The air split open. Keirith could have sworn he heard his mam and Callie, but when the figure stepped forward into the sunlight, the voices ceased.

"Geriv do Khat. I am the Son of Zhe, the Promised One

of prophecy. In the name of the winged serpent who is my
father, I command you to release Keirith at once."

Keirith heard the nervous muttering of the Zherosi archers. Saw one of Fa's men reach for his bow. Quickly, he
shouted, "Don't shoot! It's my brother Rigat!"

"Kelik! Hold!" his father cried. Geriv's head snapped
around and he shouted the same order to his men.

Gods, why couldn't Rigat have come a sennight ago?
Why now when his presence only fueled the tension?

"Rigat, please. Just go!"

Rigat gaped at him. Then he shouted, "Release my
brother! Now!"

The hand gripping Keirith's arm began to tremble.
Slowly, the fingers uncurled. Geriv stared at his hand as if
it were some foreign object attached to his wrist.

"Keirith—come to me."

The urge to obey was irresistible—as if Rigat were pulling him forward, just as he had compelled Geriv to release
his grip. He took a step. Geriv's hand came up as if to
yank him back and hung there, trembling violently, before
it slowly fell to his side.

He took another step, and another. Son of a god or not,
he would knock his little brother on his arse later. His
penchant for drama had come close to ruining everything.

Something moved in the shadows behind Fa. Mikal, he
realized. Ducking behind a boulder. And reemerging with
his bow.

Keirith's footsteps slowed, stopped. Too late, he realized
what was going to happen, what *was* happening.

Mikal raising the bow. The man named Kelik snatching
up his. Shouts all around, a garbled chorus of Zherosi and
the tribal tongue. The voices oddly distant, as if they came
from miles away. Another voice—his voice—screaming,
"Fa!" But only in his mind, his lips uselessly shaping the
word.

His feet, stumbling over a stone. His hands, flung out to
catch himself as he fell.

Rigat's eyes, as piercing and blue as the sky. His red
braid swinging wildly as he turned toward Mikal.

His father's hand, planted against Korim's back, shoving
him to the ground. His other hand, reaching for Rigat, pull-

ing him close, shielding him with his body, never realizing that he was the one who needed protection.

Fa's arms, flung out as if to embrace him. Fa's mouth, opening as if to call his name. But his eyes, oh, gods, his eyes . . .

Gray braids masked his face as he spun around. The arrow quivered in his broad back. Rigat screamed, as high and shrill as the wood pigeon.

Natha hissed in his ear. Feathers brushed his cheek. His father staggered as the second arrow hit his shoulder. Rigat caught him as he fell, and both of them toppled to the ground.

Arrows flew overhead, all hissing with Natha's voice. The earth trembled with the impact of men's feet.

A cacophony of shouts. His father's face twisting in agony. Rigat's hand grasping his. Rigat's voice ordering him to hold on, hold on tight.

Fa's features blurred. And the world vanished.

Chapter 47

THEY SAT IN ANXIOUS SILENCE, hope warring with fear as they waited for Rigat's return.

Griane had just begun ladling Hircha's porridge when the shoe sprouted from the air. The bowl slipped from her fingers and shattered on the stones of the fire pit. She heard Callie whisper, "Merciful Maker," but she could only stare at the disembodied shoe.

A leg appeared, clad in worn doeskin. And then Rigat had stepped into the hut and asked her if everything was all right. Moments later, he was gone. Now they could only wait—and pray.

Suddenly, the wall of the hut melted into a shaft of sunlight. Keirith crouched in it, gazing wildly around him. His body sagged with relief when he saw them. As he staggered to his feet, she glimpsed the two figures behind him.

"Help me!" Rigat cried.

Callie was the first to recover, rushing forward to help Keirith pull Darak into the hut. She could hear shouts and glimpsed the frightened face of a boy staring at her. Then Rigat stepped through the portal, and it snapped shut behind him.

"Callie," Keirith whispered. "Pull the doeskin across the doorway."

Darak sprawled on his right side, his head resting in Keirith's lap. One arrow had gone through the meaty part of his left shoulder. The other was embedded in his back. Worse than the blood drenching his tunic or the terrible pallor of his face was the liquid gurgle of his breath and the bloody froth that stained his lips.

His lung is punctured, the healer analyzed.

He's going to die, the woman screamed.

Nay. I won't allow it.

As if he had heard her, his eyes fluttered open. Incredibly, he smiled. He spat out a mouthful of blood and whispered, "I told you I'd bring him home."

He choked, his body heaving helplessly as he spewed thick gouts of blood over Keirith's thighs.

"Sit him up!" she cried. "Hircha—"

But Hircha was already shoving the healing bag into her arms. Callie and Keirith tried to drag Darak to a sitting position, but the shaft of the arrow in his shoulder prevented Keirith from getting a good grip.

"Snap it off!" she ordered.

She didn't remember jumping to her feet. One moment, she was sitting beside the fire pit and the next, crouching beside him. His gaze held hers, his lips framing a word.

"Faelia arrived yesterday," she assured him. "With the others. She's hunting."

His head lolled, and he choked again. Keirith grabbed a fistful of hair and yanked his head up, averting his face as blood sprayed him.

Hircha flung a mantle down on the rushes behind Darak. Griane crawled over to it and dumped out the contents of her healing bag.

Darak had often spoken of that moment right before a kill when he was both hunter and observer. It was the same with a healer. Part of her agonized over him—her husband, her lover, the father of her children. Yet her hands quickly laid out her tools: the daggers, the nettle-cloth bandages, the needles and sinew, the two-pronged bone hook she called the "ram's horns" that she would need to remove the arrowhead. Her voice spoke in the confident tone she had learned from Mother Netal, urging Keirith and Callie to hold Darak still, asking Hircha for bowls of water and fresh yarrow compresses. And her mind pictured the incisions she would make even before she picked up the narrow-bladed dagger.

"Do something!" Keirith demanded.

Her head snapped up. But he was looking at Rigat.

"You're the son of a god! Save him!"

She had been so intent on saving him herself that it hadn't even occurred to her.

Rigat's gaze met hers. For one terrifying moment, she thought he would refuse. Then he nodded.

Rigat watched his mother slice open the back of Darak's tunic and break off the shaft of the arrow. He knew this was what a healer did, knew that she had helped dozens—hundreds—of wounded men. But how could her hand be so steady as she cut into the flesh of the man she loved? How could her voice be so calm as she instructed Hircha to put deadwood on the fire so she would have more light? How could she do anything but weep as Darak vomited up his life's blood?

He had seen men die. Seen some writhing in agony as they were carried into the longhut, and others, white-faced with shock from their wounds. When he was only a child, he had watched his mother set Callie's broken arm, bandage a gash on Faelia's leg, minister to the dozens of minor injuries they all incurred. The threat of illness and injury and starvation had always hung over them. But until today, the specter of death had never entered their home.

He had always been prepared for Darak's heart to fail him, for him to go to sleep one night and never wake up. A clean, peaceful death. Not this. Darak Spirit-Hunter simply couldn't die like this.

Perhaps that was why he had stood by until Keirith's voice jolted him. Or perhaps he was still too dazed by what had happened. How could everything go so wrong so quickly?

Geriv would pay. And that man—Mikal. And Jholianna and the Khonsel if they had known about Geriv's plan. By the time he was finished, they would all be on their knees.

"Rigat!"

Keirith's voice, once again jolting him from his thoughts. Why did his brother keep staring at him as if he were the enemy? And why—when he had come to save them—had Keirith pleaded with him to leave?

He forced himself to smile at his mam, but she was bent over Darak. "Brace him," she said, shooting quick glances at Keirith and Callie. She gripped the handle of the ram's horns and pulled. Darak slumped against Keirith. Unable to look at him, Rigat kept his eyes on his mam: her face screwed up in a grimace as she tugged, her body rocking backward as the arrowhead jerked free, her quick, fierce smile as she stared at her bloody prize.

As he eased past Hircha, his mam pressed·a damp wad of yarrow leaves against the wound and murmured, "Hurry."

"Take them off," Rigat said. "I need to put my hands on him."

He closed his eyes so he wouldn't have to look at the wound, but beneath the warm slipperiness of the blood, he could feel the torn flaps of flesh where the arrow had penetrated Darak's back and the deep incisions his mam had made while probing for the arrowhead. This was what it was to be human—to have your flesh ripped open by an enemy's weapon, to bleed and suffer while a healer fought to keep you alive.

His power absolved him of such a fate. It separated him from everyone in the hut, from everyone in the world. His power was stronger than a dozen healers. His power was life.

It crackled through his body, eager as ever to do his bidding. But he had called on it so often in the last sennight: to save Jholianna, to search for Fellgair, to enter Chaos. Was there enough left?

He had to control its impatience or the initial shock might kill Darak. Today, he needed the gently flowing stream, not the raging fire.

He couldn't risk touching Darak's spirit; he knew too well how he would react to that invasion. Instead, he let the power fill him, let it pass from his tingling palms into Darak's torn flesh. Tiny bumps rose under his fingertips, and Darak shivered. As the wash of calm flowed through him, his breathing eased and his frantic pulse steadied.

The power spiraled deeper, tunneling like a vole along the path the arrow had taken, past severed arteries and veins and muscles that waved like fronds of lakeweed. A river of blood pulsed through the tunnel, thick and red and relentless, driven by the inexorable beat of Darak's heart. It was like swimming upstream against a strong current, but his power was stronger still, cleaving through the river toward the fiery glow at the end of the tunnel.

Darak's body heaved. Above the murmur of frightened voices, he heard blood splattering on the bracken. Relentlessly, he shut out the sensations, but a shiver rippled down his spine.

He could see it now, the wound like a narrow crevice in a rock. The lung looked like a flaccid waterskin—just like Jholianna's. The crevice glowed a malevolent red. He had to call on more of his power to reach it, struggling against the fierce current of blood that seemed determined to drive him back.

Another shiver coursed through his body as he reached the crevice and discovered what looked like a red lake inside a cavern. The cavern shuddered with every breath Darak took. Tiny waves moved across the lake as blood slopped through the crevice, leaking into Darak's lung, drowning him.

Panicked, he wondered if he should have sealed the walls of the tunnel to stop the flow of blood. Should he go back and start again? Or seal the crevice first? But if he left the lake of blood inside, Darak would continue choking on it.

He fought back his panic and directed his power at the

crevice, but the damage was so much more extensive than the gash Fellgair had sliced across his wrist, as impossible to contain as the poison that had coursed through Jholianna.

He pulled deeper on his gift, felt the jolt of renewed power surging through his body, surging into Darak's, no longer a gentle stream but a molten river of fire. He was the Trickster's son, the most powerful mortal in the world. He could suck dry a lake of blood and dam up a punctured lung and hold back the raging current that wanted to steal Darak's life.

He poured his power into Darak. His wounded body devoured it greedily and demanded more, insatiable in its hunger, desperate to absorb the life-giving energy.

Fellgair. Help me.

From a great distance, he heard a dull roar like waves beating against the shore. Nay, not waves. A drum. Thudding like the footsteps of a giant striding through the forest.

The drumbeat pounded into him and through him, throbbing through his chest, his head, his fingertips. A second drum answered the first, growing stronger with every beat. As if another giant stalked the first, guided by the call of the drum.

More, it demanded.

Numbness crept through him, and the same rapturous tingling he experienced when he climaxed. But this sensation was keener, sharper. A hundred needles piercing his spirit as Othak's had pierced his flesh to create the antler tattoo.

More.

When he saw the curtain of light, he panicked, knowing his power was failing. He swayed, both hands on Darak's back to support himself, his cheek resting against the curve of Darak's neck.

The light flared red and orange and white, a wild dance driven by the pounding of the drums.

My heart. My heart and Darak's.

The exploding stars blinded him. His breath came in feeble gasps. Numbness stole sensation from his limbs. He had to clutch Darak's shoulders to keep from collapsing.

More.

He wanted to weep, to cry out that he had so little left

to give. And if he gave it—if he sacrificed all his power—
what then? Darak might live a year. Or his heart might fail
him on the morrow.

And he would have sacrificed everything: the ability to
heal even the smallest injury, the worship of the Zherosi,
the admiration of his queen, and the years of life—a hundred? a thousand?—that were his birthright.

No one could ask so much of him. Not even Darak. His
body might demand more, but Darak knew the life of one
man was less important than the greater good. And what
could be more vital to the world than the preservation of
his foster-son's power?

The drumbeats faded. The flickering dance froze. He saw
Fellgair lift his head, golden eyes watching him. Was he
here? In the hut? Nay, it was only his imagination, a vision
brought on by his weakness. How else could he feel the
breeze in the First Forest die? And the green leaves of the
Oak and the Holly cease their soft rustling?

The rhythmic pulses of the three spirits inside the One
Tree fell silent. Even the eternal thrum of the World Tree
hesitated. It was like that moment before dawn, when the
world held its breath, waiting.

Behind his closed eyelids, Rigat sensed a burst of light.
Bracken crunched behind him. He heard a gasp. And Faelia's voice, demanding to know what was happening, what
was wrong with Fa, what was *he* doing here, what was he
doing to Fa?

Rigat yanked his hands away.

His head drooped, but he was too tired to raise it, too
tired to explain. His body felt drained and limp, but deep
inside, the tiny kernel of power glowed. It would be days
before he dared draw on it again, but it was there. It was
safe. It was his.

He heard voices, but the words flowed over him in a
meaningless stream. Then a hand grasped his shoulder.

"Why did you stop?" Keirith demanded.

The buzz of conversation died. He could feel them watching him, waiting. Like Fellgair and the Tree-Lords and the
World Tree.

"Rigat! He's still bleeding."

His head snapped up. "I couldn't do any more!"

Keirith's face looked like a skull, but the fear on his mam's was worse.

"I'm sorry," he whispered as his gaze slid away from her.

He heard her ordering Keirith and Callie to lay Darak on his pallet. Asking Hircha for more compresses. Silencing Faelia's protests with a sharp, "Not now! Help me with your father."

Amid the flurry of movement, he could only remain on his knees, staring down at the blood-soaked bracken. Then he felt breath against his cheek.

"Will he live?" Keirith whispered.

"For now."

Keirith's fingers dug into his arm. "How long?"

"I don't know. He needed so much . . ."

Keirith drew back his hand as if he had touched something dirty. "You stopped."

Only once before had he heard such coldness in his brother's voice—in the moments before the rockslide when Keirith had passed judgment on the Zherosi.

"If you hadn't interfered, Geriv would have exchanged me for Korim, and everything would have been fine. Now— when Fa really needs you—you'd rather save your power than him."

His mam's eyes squeezed shut. Before he could explain, Faelia strode toward him and yanked him to his feet. "You have this . . . this gift. And you won't use it?"

"I did! I tried!"

"Not hard enough," Keirith said.

"I didn't have enough power. And even if I did, the healing wouldn't last. It never lasts. You don't understand. Any of you. You have no idea—"

Faelia spat in his face. Rigat reared back, but she seized his tunic with one hand and backhanded him across the mouth with the other. His legs buckled and he fell to his knees.

"You could have saved him."

Her kick took him in the belly. He gasped and toppled over. His power was too weak to stop her assault or even open a portal and escape. All he could do was curl into a protective ball.

Pain exploded in his side as she kicked him again.

"Stop!" his mam cried.

But Faelia was mindless in her fury, kicking him and screaming curses. "What kind of a son are you?"

I am the Trickster's son.

The blows suddenly ceased, and he dared to look up. Callie had pinioned Faelia's arms, but she continued to struggle and curse.

"Faelia."

She went still at the sound of Darak's voice.

"Stop."

Too weak to sit up, Darak stared back at him from his pallet. All his life, Rigat had felt those gray eyes on him, studying him with mingled suspicion and love. Now, he found only sadness.

"I'm sorry," he whispered.

"It's not your fault."

And somehow that was worse than Faelia's curses or Keirith's accusations or his mam's misery. Darak knew he could have saved him—not forever, not without another infusion of power—but he could have given him another sennight, another moon, another year. Darak knew—and still his father forgave him.

He had to crawl to the doorway of the hut, dig his fingertips into the chinks between the stones to pull himself upright. He stood there, swaying with the effort to keep his feet, unwilling to look back and find those sad eyes watching him.

He shoved the doeskin aside and stumbled into the sunlight, only to be confronted by a knot of villagers, drawn by Faelia's screams. Some faces held confusion, others concern; a few simply looked startled to see him. As he staggered away, another face swam into view, mouth working in inarticulate rage.

"Ree gahh!"

Madig pounded the earth with his stick, all the while shouting and clutching Othak's arm. Othak's empty eye socket proclaimed him Tree-Father—dear gods, when had Gortin died?—and his fingers flew in the sign to avert evil. All around him, Rigat saw other hands doing the same.

"With his own voice, Madig condemns him!" Othak shouted. "Here is the man who attacked him. The man who used his unholy power to try and kill him. And now he's tried to murder his own father."

Voices muttered his name. Mouths twisted with revulsion. He glanced around wildly, fixing those nearest him with the most threatening stare he could muster. They all retreated. Weak as he was, he could still make them fear him.

He backed toward the entrance of the hill fort, but they followed.

"His own sister cursed him!" Othak shouted. "She knew what he was."

A woman screamed, "Murderer!"

"Traitor!"

"Abomination!"

Rigat turned and ran. An agonizing burst of pain ripped through his head, sending him reeling into the wall of a hut. Something thudded against the thatch. He looked up as a rock tumbled to the ground. For a moment, he simply stared at it, too shocked to move. His people were stoning him. Stoning *him*. Then another rock grazed his arm, and he spun away.

He could hear them behind him, howling like wolves. A rock smacked into a wall. Another thudded against his back. He drew on his power—just a little, just enough for a final burst of strength that carried him out of the hill fort.

He skidded down the slope. Tripped over something and staggered. Gasped as his knee came down hard on a rock.

His fall drew louder howls from the mob. He dared a glimpse behind him and saw Rothisar nocking an arrow in his bowstring. Trath's arm came up to knock the bow aside. Keirith and Callie surged through the crowd, shoving people out of the way, ripping rocks from fingers, using elbows and fists to ward them off.

Rigat pushed himself to his feet. Pain lanced through his left knee, his head, his side, but fear drove him on.

He reached the lake and veered east around the shore. His lungs felt like they were on fire. A sharp stitch of pain stabbed his side with every breath, along with the duller throb where Faelia had kicked him.

He clawed his way up the hill and paused, panting like a winded deer. They were clustered near the lake, still screaming, still shaking their fists. He didn't wait to observe more. He had to keep running. Far enough for them to give up the chase. And then find a place to hide. Somewhere safe where he could recover his strength and his power.

The Trickster's son. Stoned like a mad dog.

A sob tore at his throat. He swallowed it down. They would not make him weep. Neither those miserable villagers nor his sister. He was stronger than all of them.

He was the Trickster's son.

He fell into a shambling trot. Then he walked, one leaden step after the next. When he glimpsed the stand of alders, he lurched toward them. And when his legs finally gave out, he crawled down the slope and fell belly-down by the little stream, lapping up water like an animal.

When he raised his head, he found Fellgair crouching beside him. Even through the haze of exhaustion and pain and simmering rage, Rigat was shocked to see how haggard he looked. The Unmaker was exacting a brutal retribution from his son.

But even that realization could not prevent him from whispering, "I called you. But you didn't come."

"By the time I managed to open a portal . . ." With a great effort, Fellgair straightened his slumping shoulders. "You must consider what you will do next."

The words surprised a harsh bark of laughter from him. " 'Next?' There is no 'next.' "

"There is still the hope of peace. If you intercede for your people."

"My people stoned me. My sister cursed me. Spat on me."

"One village, Rigat. There are many others—"

"Don't you understand? It's over! I wanted an end to the fighting and I got it. The Zherosi have won. The rebels are dead. And Darak—" His voice broke. "Can you save him?"

"No."

Hearing genuine grief in Fellgair's voice was frightening, but rage consumed the fear. "Are you afraid of what the Lord of Chaos will do? Or doesn't it suit you to save Darak? Because you're still angry about the things he said."

"No."

"Then do something! Go to the Summerlands. Bring Mam the healing plants. And the water. She'll know how to use them. Just do that much."

"I can't."

"Then open a portal for me and I'll go. I don't have the strength to do it myself."

"I can't! I cannot go to the Summerlands. I cannot open a portal for you to go to the Summerlands. The way is . . . barred to me."

The Unmaker's doing. It had to be. To punish Fellgair, but also Fellgair's son.

"There's still time to set things right," Fellgair was saying. "If you put aside your pride and your anger—even your concern about Darak—and think about the greater good."

That was why he had refused to give up his power. But that was before his own people had turned on him. And if those who had known him for years always believed the worst of him, how would he convince strangers to trust him?

The rebellion was broken. No more men and women would sacrifice their lives for a doomed cause. Perhaps that was the greater good. Perhaps, from the very beginning, this was how it was meant to end.

He was so tired. Tired of trying to do the right thing and failing. Tired of always being on his guard, of putting on an act for others, of bearing the weight of responsibility thrust upon him by Fellgair and Jholianna. All he wanted to do was go home and lay his head in his mam's lap and have her stroke his hair and tell him everything would be all right, that he was not evil, that he had done everything he could.

Everything within reason.

But would she say that? Or would she look at him with loathing because he had failed to save her first love? Would she choose Darak, just as she had chosen him over Keirith all those years ago?

"There's always a cost," Fellgair had said. "No matter what one chooses."

He had chosen Fellgair. Because he had helped one father, he had no power to save the other. And now he

could never go home. They would only drive him out—or
kill him.

He heard their shrill voices again, saw their faces, twisted
with fear and hatred and eagerness for his blood. Then he
recalled the voices that had chanted his name in Pilozhat,
the wonder and joy of the people in that mountain village
after he had healed the little boy.

"I don't know what the greater good means anymore."

"Rigat—"

"Just leave me alone."

He closed his eyes. He heard the sound of Fellgair's retreating footsteps. And then he let exhaustion carry him
into dreamless sleep.

Chapter 48

T HE RIVER GLISTENED in the early morning sunlight. From a nearby tree, a blackbird warbled. The
freshening breeze caressed Geriv's face. Bitterly, he reflected that it was going to be a beautiful day.

"The bodies are laid out for your inspection, Vanel."

Geriv nodded to the Remil and strode back with him.
He still couldn't believe the Spirit-Hunter had planned to
rescue Kheridh with only ten men. Once his warship had
crossed the river, he'd sent men to scour the area, but they
found no sign of a larger force—only a few slaves tied
to trees.

At the far end of the row, the spy crouched beside one
of the bodies. Riddled with arrows, like the others. Probably only a few years older than Korim, who stared at the
corpses, sickened.

"A pity you didn't kill him," Geriv remarked to the spy.

Korim looked up. "No man could have killed the Son of Zhe."

"I was talking about the Spirit-Hunter."

Korim's head jerked toward the spy. "You . . . you shot Darak? Deliberately? But why would you—?"

"Because our anonymous friend wants to end this rebellion," Geriv replied. "That's what you said, wasn't it? The night we met at Little Falls?"

The spy ignored him, his gaze fixed on his dead comrade.

"What better way to do that than by depriving the rebellion of its leader?"

Still, the spy remained silent, as oblivious to their presence as he was to his wounds. The broken shaft of an arrow protruded from his right arm. Another was embedded in his left shoulder. Blood soaked the sleeves of his tunic and dripped onto the grass at his feet.

Geriv glanced curiously at the dead man whose long face bore a slight resemblance to the spy's. "A kinsman?"

"My cousin. Sorig." He whispered the name as if it were a prayer. Gently, he closed the staring eyes. "Will you take them to Little Falls? So they can have a proper funeral?"

"I have my own dead to attend to. If Birat wants their bodies, he can send men to collect them." He turned to the Remil. "I'm going north. On the morrow. With three komakhs. Get the troops ready when we return to the fortress. You'll remain in command there until I return."

"North?" Korim asked. "Why?"

"I intend to command the assault on the Spirit-Hunter's village."

"Darak's lung-shot," the spy said. "He's probably dead already."

"I'll believe that when I see his body."

He started toward the river, only to be brought up short when Korim seized his arm. "Why are you doing this?"

"Because it's likely that boy—Rigat—took them back to their village. If the Spirit-Hunter is dead, the other members of his family will make excellent hostages."

"But . . . the Son of Zhe . . ."

"I take my orders from the queen, not some scruffy boy who claims to be the Son of Zhe."

"Why can't you just leave them alone?"

Geriv jerked his arm free. "You don't allow your enemies to escape if it's in your power to stop them."

And he would stop them—both the Spirit-Hunter and
his accursed son—even if it cost him his command and his
life. Damn Vazh. He should have killed them both when
he had the chance.

Staring down into his son's shocked face, he chose his
words with care. "Kheridh tricked you. The Spirit-Hunter
captured you. There was nothing you could have done to
prevent that," he added quickly. "Or to escape. But it
doesn't change the fact that they humiliated you."

Korim winced. When Geriv laid his hand on his son's
shoulder, Korim's head came up, his eyes wide and
uncertain.

"You may return to Headquarters if you wish. But I
hope you'll come with me. The only way to regain the
respect of your fellow officers—to regain any measure of
self-respect—is to go after these men and crush them. Once
and for all."

After a long moment, Korim nodded.

Chapter 49

AFTER THEY DROVE RIGAT from the village,
Othak demanded explanations, but Griane barred him
from the hut, shouting that she had a wounded man to
attend to. It was Darak who insisted the council of elders
be allowed to enter, Darak who told them how Rigat had
rescued him and Keirith, Darak who explained that his
youngest son possessed the shaman's gift of traveling between worlds and the healer's gift of mending torn flesh.
Still bleeding from the wounds in his back and shoulder,

still weak from the loss of blood, he left no room for argument or doubt. And when his voice failed him, Keirith took up the story, telling them that Rigat had used his gift to inform the rebels about Zherosi troop movements, that Rigat had given them so many victories. Even Faelia admitted she might have misjudged him.

If there were whispers in the village after that, Griane ignored them. She spent all her time with Darak, watching every movement, monitoring every grimace of pain. It was not enough to be in the same hut with him. She had to touch him, even if it was only her knee brushing his hip or her hand resting on his arm.

She fed him. Bathed him. Changed his bandages. Guided his hand when he had to relieve himself. And studied his body as she had not since they were first married, tracing the groove of his backbone, the whorl of dark hair above the cleft of his buttocks, the tiny mole on the back of his right leg.

After three days, he insisted on getting dressed. With Callie and Keirith supporting him, he tottered about the village. He sought out the young men and women he had recruited, addressing each by name and thanking them for their loyalty. Rebel and villager alike clustered around him, hands thrust out to pat his arm or clasp his hand—as if he were some kind of magic talisman.

When she shared that observation with Darak, he smiled. "Nay. Just their chief."

And weak as he was, he insisted on resuming those responsibilities. He met with the council, warning them that the Zherosi commander would likely pursue them. He gave orders to step up the training of the young men and women, to send some of the boys south to collect pine resin for making pitch, to send his recruits to more distant hills to keep watch, to develop a warning system using flaming arrows to alert the village of the approach of the Zherosi army, to stockpile food and water—and to make plans to evacuate.

"We have a sennight—or less—to prepare. When the signal comes, we must send the women and children into the hills. And my family. If I'm fit to travel, I'll go with them. Otherwise, I'll surrender. Gods willing, the Zherosi will be satisfied with that and leave the rest of you in peace."

The children protested that they would never leave him. He silenced them with a weary shake of his head. Griane insisted that if there was fighting, the tribe would need their healer.

"If there's fighting," Darak replied, "there'll be no one left alive to heal."

When Lisula and Ennit came to visit, she assured them he was growing stronger every day. When Callie whispered that he looked so pale, she patted his hand and told him that was only to be expected. When Keirith blamed himself for failing to recognize the truth of his vision, she overrode his choked voice and sternly told him it was not his fault—and reminded him that such talk would only upset his father.

She showed a smiling face to the world and told herself that Rigat's magic and her skill had saved him. When she could no longer smile, she snatched up her withy basket and told them she needed to gather yarrow and other healing plants in the hills. No one reminded her that Hircha could do that. And when she returned, no one ever commented that her basket was still empty and her eyes red-rimmed from weeping.

On one such escape, Faelia followed her and bluntly demanded to know the truth about Rigat. In a few stark sentences, Griane told her. Expecting shock or denunciations, Faelia simply nodded. But her voice was hard when she asked, "If he's the Trickster's son, how can we ever trust him?"

"Because he's my son as well. And he loves us."

But he hadn't loved Darak enough to save him.

She never voiced that bitter thought, but saw it reflected on Faelia's face, on the faces of all her children. They defended Rigat to the rest of the tribe, but in the privacy of their hut, no one spoke of him except Darak. Alone among them, he seemed to accept Rigat's choice.

For five days, she watched and prayed and tried to banish her fears. Perhaps Rigat had healed him. Perhaps the magic would last. Perhaps Darak's body was strong enough to recover without it.

On the sixth day, the two of them were sitting with Ennit and Lisula, reminiscing about the early days of their marriages. Inevitably, Ennit brought up her unrestrained response to Darak's lovemaking. Every time he told the story, his yowls became louder and more ridiculous, but this time, he made her sound positively demented. Lisula and Darak laughed. Griane punched Ennit's arm.

Then Darak choked.

Ennit and Lisula abruptly fell silent. Griane froze, caught by the stark fear in Darak's eyes.

The coughing fit passed. The tension in his body eased. He slowly lowered his hand from his mouth and stared at the blood staining his palm. Very carefully, he wiped his hand on his breeches and drew his sleeve across his mouth. Then he smiled.

"Aye. Well. It shut Ennit up, didn't it?"

She just stared at him, stricken.

He took her hand and squeezed it gently. "I've been thinking about visiting Tinnean and Cuillon. Perhaps they know what the Zherosi are up to. It couldn't hurt to ask. Would you mind very much if Lisula opened the way for me on the morrow?"

Twice before, he had left her—once to seek Keirith in Zheros, and later, to join the rebellion. The first time, he had not asked her permission. The second time, he had sought her counsel and advice, and she had agreed that, for the sake of his tribe and his family, he must go.

Now, he wanted to leave her again. Only for a single day. Only from sunrise to sunset. She knew why he wanted to go—and why he wanted to go now. And she also knew that if she refused, he would stay.

He had seen the way she hovered over him, understood her need to touch him, to stay close. He knew that she would worry every moment that he was gone. Knew, too, how the crossing would drain him. He knew exactly what he was asking and what it would cost them both.

One day. Out of all the days and nights they had shared, it seemed such a little thing. Out of those that remained to them—ten? twenty?—the thought of being without him for even a moment was too terrible to contemplate.

She tasted blood and realized she had bitten through her lip. She swallowed down the blood and with it, the fear that threatened to choke her. Then she cleared her throat and said, "I'll hold supper until you return."

For five days, Jholianna waited. She tried to lose herself in the myriad details of running an empire, but her mind was consumed by Rigat's absence.

She questioned Nekif again in a vain attempt to glean some new information. She sought out the Supplicant, only to discover that the priestess had vanished yet again. She consulted the Khonsel, who admitted that he, too, feared something must have happened in the north. She even took qiij and sought the wisdom of the gods, but the gods, as always, remained silent.

On the sixth day, she met with her council and reminded them to have patience and trust the Son of Zhe. The Pajhit whined. The Zheron intoned prophecy. The Stuavo speculated about the effect on commerce. It was all she could do to keep from screaming.

Instead, she dismissed them abruptly and spent the rest of the morning reviewing the latest reports from Iriku and the dismal results of the Khonsel's investigation.

There had been other attempts on her life during her long reign, but always, the Khonsel's efficient network of spies had discovered the conspirators before she was in danger. For days, he had tirelessly questioned the guards, the members of the Smiths Guild, and dozens of merchants and military officials who might have reason to complain about the handling of the war. And still he was no closer to finding those behind the attempted assassination.

It was little comfort to speculate that Rigat had been the target; the loss of the Son of Zhe would have been disastrous. She could only pray that the Carilians had fostered the plot; if it was her own people, the gods only knew how far the treason had spread.

When the midafternoon sezhta arrived, she bathed and retired to her bed, a damp cloth draped across her forehead to relieve her headache. Instead of drowsing through the heat of the day, she stared up at the starry night sky that adorned the ceiling, and sought the same patience she had reprimanded her counselors for lacking.

A shadow darkened the doorway of the balcony. She reared up, her heart pounding when she saw the figure through the gauzy draperies. After a long moment, Rigat stepped inside.

His hair hung loose and wild about his shoulders. His clothes were filthy and torn. He looked like an unruly boy who had been playing in the dirt, but his face seemed to have aged years since she had last seen him.

He watched her, body rigid with tension, fists clenched at his sides. But again his face belied his appearance for his eyes seemed to plead with her. For understanding? For forgiveness? Or simply to welcome him?

As she watched, his expression hardened. She flinched, awaiting the inevitable attack on her spirit. Instead, he strode forward to loom over her like a vengeful god.

"Did you send the orders for the truce?"

"You were there. You saw me—"

"Did you send other orders, countermanding those?"

"No. No!"

"Did Geriv receive them?"

"Of course. He must have. Please. Tell me what—"

"Did you know about the ambush?"

"In the Plaza of Justice?"

"In the north!"

"When?"

"And the prisoner exchange?"

"What prisoners? What are you—?"

"Geriv captured my brother. He meant to exchange him for Darak. But I prevented it. Did you know?"

She shook her head wildly, hands raised to ward off a blow.

"And the assassination attempt. Was that your idea?"

Anger swamped the fear, giving her courage. "You know what that day was like for me. Better than anyone. And you think I could have planned it?"

"Not the poisoned arrow. But the man with the dagger. You could have come up with that. Or the Khonsel. To keep me here. To keep me from discovering Geriv's plan."

"I didn't know the plan!" she screamed.

Lady Alikia rushed into the chamber and drew up short. "Great lord . . . my lady . . ."

"Leave us," Rigat commanded. When Lady Alikia hesitated, he roared, "Leave us!"

Rigat stalked to the balcony and remained there, his back

to her. As she watched his heaving shoulders, Jholianna fought for calm. She had to think. To make sense of Rigat's accusations. To find a way to placate him.

Geriv would have to die. She only regretted that he had failed to kill the Spirit-Hunter first. And the Khonsel? Had he known about the prisoner exchange? If he had, he—like Geriv—had concealed it from her.

Which left the assassination attempt. The Khonsel had promised to find some way of keeping Rigat busy. He would not have risked poison, but that clumsy attack with a dagger?

Yes, he could have planned that, counting on the subsequent hysteria—and endless interrogations—to keep Rigat in Pilozhat. Little knowing that a real assassin would find an even better way of preventing Rigat from leaving.

He would have known better than to forewarn her. Ignorance was her only protection.

Brave, loyal Vazh do Havi. Like Geriv, he had risked everything—and lost. But she might still win. Despite everything, Rigat had come back to her.

She whispered his name and saw him flinch. Very slowly, he turned.

When she held out her arms, he stumbled toward her and fell on his knees beside the bed. She cradled his head in her lap, stroking his hair, gently plucking out twigs and leaves. She discovered a lump on the back of his head, a yellowing bruise on his wrist. Scratches and scrapes discolored the hands clutching her thighs.

She heard a sound—desperate, choking—and realized he was weeping.

He began to speak, his head still burrowed in her lap, his fingers twisting the folds of her sleeping robe. It was hard to make sense of what he was saying; he leaped from events in his childhood to those that had happened in the last few days. Sometimes, the words were muffled, sometimes far too clear, a wild outpouring of abasement and blame and rage.

He told her how he had refused to make the ultimate sacrifice to heal the Spirit-Hunter. How he had tried—and failed—to reach some place called the Summerlands. How they had driven him from his village with stones and curses.

Only then did she understand why he had not invaded

her spirit. He was terrified that he might learn something that would prove that she, too, had betrayed him. His family had turned against him. His people had reviled him. She was all he had. Now—finally—he belonged to her.

Her sense of triumph was overshadowed by horror. To stone the son of a god. Even if they had acted in ignorance, it was unforgivable. They were barbarians, animals, unworthy of him.

As his broken sobbing continued, the horror receded, replaced by pity and an uncomfortable sense of kinship. How many times had Jholin knelt at her feet like this? Mourning the death of another friend, hating the necessity of their endless existence or—during those last years—wild with fury over some slight, real or imagined.

And now, this boy-god. Seeking her strength, her comfort. Recognizing—perhaps unconsciously—that despite their differences, they were very much alike. Unique beings, both of them. Wielding more power than any other rulers in the known world. Fated to live far longer than ordinary mortals.

She stared down at the flame-colored hair splayed across her knees, the freckled hands still gripping her thighs. The long fingers looked like claws, ruthless and predatory. Yet—endlessly twisting the folds of her robe—so helpless.

He would always be this strange amalgam of god and man, predator and prey, implacable destroyer and amusing companion. She would never feel entirely safe with him or be able to control him as she had Jholin. But he needed her now. And she needed him. So she stroked his head and offered the same soothing phrases that had always comforted Jholin: you mustn't worry, I'm here, I will never leave you, everything will be all right.

His head jerked up, his face swollen and damp. "It won't be all right! It will never be all right. Everything is ruined."

"No, my dear. You can make it right. *We* will make it right."

The tear-filled eyes blazed with sudden fury. "You made me stay."

It took all her control not to recoil. "I'm sorry. I didn't know. You're right, it was my fault. Please forgive me."

Quick as it had come, the fury disappeared. "No. It was my fault. It was all my fault."

"You did everything you could. You're grieving for your foster-father now, but even if you'd sacrificed all your power, you couldn't have saved him. If anyone is to blame, it's that priest. But he cannot touch you here. In Zheros, you're safe and loved and worshiped."

His expression hardened. "Not by the Vanel. He defied me."

"And he'll be punished. I will—"

"And the Khonsel. I'll punish him, too. I'll punish everyone who betrayed me."

"But later. You're tired. And heartsick. You should rest. Or are you hungry? I could—"

He shook his head.

"A bath, then. And afterward, we'll talk again."

She bent down, intending to press a gentle kiss to his forehead. His hand seized the back of her neck. He pulled her closer and clamped his mouth on hers.

She froze, uncertain whether to respond. She had teased him, enjoying his blushes, wondering how far she should take it. Now that the moment had come, she could only register the bruising desperation of the kiss—the rough, unskilled fumbling of an unhappy boy.

As suddenly as he had grabbed her, he pushed her away and staggered to his feet. "I can't."

"It's all right." Clearly, his mind was too caught up in the events of the last few days to allow him to enjoy the pleasures of the body.

"The prophecy."

Puzzled, she just stared at him.

"The Son of Zhe. He must be a . . . a virgin."

The blush rose up from his throat. His arousal strained against the tight breeches.

Her mind whispered that there was no better way to bind him to her. Her body responded with an unforeseen eagerness. It had been fourteen years since Jholin's death. Even before, he had only been capable in the first moon after The Shedding; the qiij that fueled his ardor inevitably stole it.

To lie with the son of a god. To feel the power that had invaded her spirit penetrating her body.

Warmth flooded her loins. Her nipples hardened under the sheer robe. His gaze dropped to her breasts. Immediately, he looked away, but his breath quickened.

Jholianna chose her words with care. "The prophecy states that 'no mortal woman shall know his body.' Well, I've lived for five centuries. Can any mortal woman claim that?"

He licked his lips and swallowed hard.

"And while it implies that the Son of Zhe must be a virgin when he first appears, it certainly doesn't demand that he remain one."

"But the priests . . ."

"We rule Zheros. Not the priests."

Again, she held out her arms. Awkward but eager, he came to her.

Chapter 50

IT WAS STILL DARK when they left the hill fort. Callie and Keirith pleaded with Darak to let them carry him, but he insisted he would walk.

Stubborn as a rock, Griane thought, and silently vowed not to weep.

He leaned heavily on his sons as he walked slowly down the slope. She followed behind, trailed by Lisula, Faelia, and Hircha. When they reached the stream, he leaned against an alder, his good arm draped over Keirith's shoulder. Lines of strain creased his face, but he managed a smile as they waited for dawn.

She had lain awake most of the night, curled on her side, one hand resting on his hip, reassured by the sound of his breathing, the warmth of his body. She must have dozed as dawn approached, for she came awake, instantly aware that his breathing had changed, that he was awake, watching her as she had watched him, although the hut was too dark to see his expression.

His hand brushed back her hair. His thumb slid along her cheekbone, then moved lower to follow her jaw to her lips. She leaned close to kiss him, breathing in his breath, savoring the gentleness of the chapped lips. Their foreheads touched. His hand continued its slow path down her neck, over the curve of her shoulder and down her arm. Their fingers played together, her thumb tracing the puckered scar on his palm, his winding a serpentine path around her swollen knuckles. Then his hand slipped away, moving over her hip to cup her bottom and pull her close.

She felt him rouse to her and pulled back in surprise.

"Are you strong enough?" she whispered.

"Nay. But a man can dream."

They had laughed together, a mere exhalation of breath, and continued touching and stroking and kissing until it was time to dress.

As the sky continued to lighten, the children moved closer.

"Are you sure you don't want to wait until you're stronger?" Faelia asked again.

"The crossing is easy, child. Don't worry."

"We'll be waiting right here," Callie assured him. "When you come back."

"I know."

"Callie and I can carry you to the One Tree," Keirith said.

"I'll manage. Stop fussing, all of you."

"It's nearly time," Lisula said. And softly began the chant.

There were to be no lingering farewells; Darak had made that clear. But as dawn crept closer, Griane struggled to obey his wish. She wanted to wrap her arms around him and pretend that she could heal the hurts of his body. She wanted to bury her face against that broad chest and breathe in the smell of him, feel his bones and flesh under her fingers, trace the lines on his face and the curve of his mouth. She wanted to beg him to stay.

The soft gray eyes settled on her. "I'll be home at sunset. Try not to worry."

That made her scowl, and her scowl made him smile.

"I don't want you sitting here all day."

"And I don't want you to go. So we'll both be disappointed."

His smile became a grin. It quickly vanished. He raised her chin with his thumb and kissed her softly on the mouth.

"You are my heart," he whispered.

She gripped the sleeves of his tunic and pulled him close. His heart thudded beneath her cheek and she could feel hers pounding with equal fierceness.

"It's time," Lisula said.

Griane's fingers clenched. She forced herself to open them, to lower her arms, to take a step back. To let him go.

Lisula wrapped her arm around his waist. The top of her head barely reached his shoulder. They tottered forward, the big man and the little priestess.

Their figures wavered, half in and half out of this world. Swaying in the effort to keep his feet, Darak glanced over his shoulder. He raised his hand and smiled. Then Lisula stepped back, and he was gone.

For a moment, Darak stood there, their faces still imprinted on his mind: Hircha, solemn and still; Callie, smiling despite the tears in his eyes; Faelia, scowling fiercely to hide her emotions; Keirith, looking so terribly bereft.

And Griane. His girl. Standing straight as a spear. White hair pulled back in a tight braid, but always those few wisps escaping around her face. Her eyes, the blue that lived at the heart of a flame. Her mouth, curved in a smile, but her upper lip caught between her teeth.

What had he ever done to deserve such a woman? Or such children?

His legs were shaking badly. The walk to the stream had taken more of a toll than he had expected. But he was damned if he was going to be carried.

Reeling like a drunkard, he staggered toward the One Tree and clung to the pale trunk. Blood clogged his throat, and he turned his head away to spit. He winced when he saw the thick, gleaming clots staining the dry leaves. Then he shrugged. He had offered a blood sacrifice before that long-ago Midwinter quest. If this one was less elegant, he knew Tinnean and Cuillon wouldn't mind.

He took a few careful steps back so he could study the One Tree. Despite the gloom, the green leaves of the Holly seemed brighter than those of the Oak. But, of course, the Oak-Lord's spirit would be resting in the Summerlands now, gaining strength after his defeat at Midsummer, awaiting the Fall Balancing when it would return.

The effort of staring up made him dizzy. So he tottered forward again to rest his palms and forehead against the trunk.

Are you there, Tinnean? Can you see me? Will you give me a sign—just this once?

But as always, there was only the rustle of leaves.

He took off the mantle Griane had insisted that he bring, grimacing as the movement pulled at wounded muscles and flesh.

"I don't want you taking a chill," she had told him before they left the hut.

"It's summer!"

"Summer chills are the worst. And what if there's a storm?"

"It's not going to rain."

"Well, your old arse will be a lot more comfortable with a mantle underneath it than a pile of leaves."

And she called him stubborn.

Smiling, he folded the mantle and laid it between the two large roots that had once been his brother's feet. Then he slowly lowered himself to the ground. His hands automatically reached out to stroke the roots on either side of him. The bark was smooth, as if the wood had been polished. Only someone who knew the tale would realize that the knobs under his thumbs had once been the joints of a man's toes.

He leaned against the tree, wincing. His mantle would have served him better behind his back, but he was reluctant to have even that much of a barrier between him and the tree. In the end, he simply adjusted his position so that the trunk didn't press against his wounds.

Death held no horrors for him, although he didn't relish the process of dying. What gnawed at him were all the things left undone. There might still be scattered pockets of resistance, but who could unite the tribes? Darak Spirit-Hunter's name might be invoked—a symbol to inspire hope and determination—but who among the rebels possessed Temet's vision and determination?

Sorig, perhaps. But in his heart, he knew all the men at the prisoner exchange were dead. Only after Keirith described his vision had Darak realized that Mikal was the traitor, that it was his arrow that had struck him in the back. He hoped Sorig had gone to his death without knowing that—and vowed to apologize for his doubts when they met in the Forever Isles.

He said a prayer for Sorig and Kelik and the others. As for Mikal, the Zherosi might have spared him if they had recognized him in time. He would never know. Just as he would never understand why he had betrayed his friends.

He took a deep breath and let it out slowly. Once, he had held the fate of the world in his hands. Not anymore. But he still had some say in the fate of his tribe. He had done what he could to prepare them for the Zherosi. Trath would be a good chief, but he was old. So was Lisula. And Gortin's gentle leadership would be sorely missed. But his first priority must be his family. Keeping them safe. Assuaging their fears. Concealing his pain for as long as he could.

He grimaced. It was not the death he would have chosen, but what man ever got to choose the manner of his death? Still, he had some time left—days, certainly, maybe even half a moon—and he intended to make the most of them. There was some benefit in knowing your death was imminent. It gave you time to say the things that must be said, to hold your wife in your arms, to assure your children of your love.

He hoped Rigat knew that he understood his choice. Now, it was up to him to ensure that the rest of the family did. Especially Faelia and Keirith.

He rested his head against the trunk, allowing the forest to calm him. It was good to sit with Tinnean and Cuillon, to watch the first shafts of sunlight penetrate the dense canopy, to hear the purr of the wood pigeons and the scolding chatter of a squirrel and the soft rustle of small creatures scurrying through the leaves.

And the smells . . . dear gods, how he loved them. Decaying leaf mold and summer-warm earth, the mustiness of wild mushrooms and the faint sweetness of the fading quickthorn blossoms. Despite his fears for his people, his concern for his family, and his grief that he would leave them so soon, he felt the familiar peace steal over him and whispered a prayer of thanks to the Maker for the gift of this day.

As the morning grew warmer, he drifted between sleep and wakefulness, content to doze and dream, knowing the Watchers would guard him. Sometimes he talked to Tinnean and Cuillon, recalling the day he had taught Tinnean to swim, the night he and Cuillon had made their pact to find their lost brothers. Smiling when he pictured Tinnean's excitement the first time he had seen the Northern Dancers, and Cuillon's as he explored his strange, new body.

There had been many times that he'd wished for an ordinary life. Now—despite everything—he would not trade places with any man. He had called the Holly-Lord friend. Heard the song of the World Tree. Felt the Forest-Lord's gentle touch.

And he had known the Trickster.

These last years, it seemed Fellgair had given him far more pain than joy. Only now could he admit that the Trickster had meted them out in equal measure. If he had lain with Griane, he had given them Rigat. If he had forced him to open his spirit, that experience had helped him save Keirith. And if Fellgair had not shoved him through that portal to Chaos, he would never have found Tinnean or the Oak-Lord. Or his father. Or Wolf, lost to him for so many years after his vision quest.

What happened to a man's vision mate when he died? Would Wolf simply vanish into the mists of the First Forest? Or would she come with him to the Forever Isles?

He called her name softly, then repeated it twice more. And saw movement in the underbrush.

At first, he thought it was Fellgair, but the man who emerged was smaller, with gray hair at his temples and a strange garment of mottled fur covering his body. Then Darak saw the golden eyes and realized that his first impression had been correct.

Fellgair's mouth curved in the familiar mocking smile. A

deprecating wave of his hand encompassed the changes in his appearance. "The Lord of Chaos is displeased with me. Because of my interference."

"And he waited until now to punish you?" Darak blurted.

Fellgair laughed. After a moment, Darak did, too. Then he choked.

Blood gushed from his mouth, terrifying him. He doubled over, the cough tearing at his chest and his wounded back until his whole body was awash with pain.

Gods, not yet. Please, not yet.

Fellgair's hands gripped his arms, steadying him. Slowly, the coughing eased. He spat to clear his mouth, grimacing at the blood-slimed leaves between his feet. Then he slumped against the tree, crying out as his back hit the trunk. Fellgair had to help him shift position. He closed his eyes, trying to steady his breath and the frantic beating of his heart, but the small bird inside his chest refused to cease its fluttering.

Fellgair squeezed his hand gently, and the bird's wings stilled. He opened his eyes to discover thick streaks of gray marring Fellgair's russet hair.

"You're losing your power," he managed.

"Yes. But I still have enough to ease your pain. And to give you more time—if you wish."

More than anything in the world, he wanted that. Another sennight, another moon. Every day was precious to him now. But could he steal that time if it meant draining Fellgair's power?

Who would watch over Rigat then? And Griane? With Geriv surely marching to the hill fort and Rigat desperately trying to maintain the guise of the Son of Zhe, his family and his tribe—perhaps all the children of the Oak and Holly—needed Fellgair's help more than he did.

Another sennight. Another moon. No matter how much time Fellgair gave him, it would never be enough.

"Thank you," he said. "But nay."

Fellgair nodded, accepting his choice.

"If you would . . . I know I don't have to ask, but . . . Griane . . . and Rigat . . ."

"Of course, I'll look after them. That's the one benefit I

can find in this . . . disconcerting change my father has forced upon me. I can interfere with impunity now."

"You always interfered with impunity."

"And you were always exceedingly rude."

"Plainspoken."

"And proud."

"I humbled myself to you often enough."

"And were always the better for it afterward." Fellgair smiled. "We sound like a quarrelsome old married couple."

"Gods forbid." But Darak smiled, too.

Fellgair's gaze slid away. "Shall I stay with you? Or would you prefer—"

"Stay. Please. But I don't have the strength for talking."

Fellgair's hand cupped the back of his neck. "Close your eyes, then. And rest a bit."

His mam's gesture, his mam's words. To ease him when he was broody. Of course, Fellgair would remember.

He must have rested for a long while. When he opened his eyes, the shadows in the grove were much longer, but Fellgair still sat beside him.

"It'll soon be time for me to go," Darak said.

"Yes."

"I wish . . ."

"What?"

"I wish I could have seen Wolf. Just once more."

Fellgair smiled and nodded toward the underbrush.

At first, Darak saw only the shadows beneath the trees. And then he saw her, a shadow among the shadows.

Her steps were as uncertain as his when he had approached the One Tree, her muzzle as white as Griane's hair. Twice, her legs gave out. Tears filled his eyes as he watched her fight her way to her feet again. When she finally reached him, she collapsed beside him and rested her muzzle on his thigh.

His hand shook as he stroked her head. After a long moment, she raised it. A milky film clouded her golden eyes, but her tail thumped the familiar greeting.

"Little Brother."

"Wolf."

"It is good to see you."

"And good . . . so very good . . . to see you."

The cloudy eyes regarded Fellgair. "He seems familiar.
But I do not think I have ever seen him before."

"He's . . . an old friend."

"He looks at me as if he can see me."

"I *can* see you," Fellgair said.

"That is strange. I thought only my brother could." Her
head flopped down on his thigh again. "It took so long to
reach you. I was afraid . . ."

She whined softly. He managed to raise his hand, to
scratch behind the tattered left ear, and was rewarded by
another feeble thump of her tail.

"I smell blood, Little Brother. Are you hurt?"

"A fight between packs. It's over now."

"And your pack drove them off?"

"Nay, Wolf. They drove mine off."

A soft growl rumbled in her throat. "And your mate?
And your pups?"

"They're safe. Our . . . our den is well-hidden."

"That is good." Her tongue flicked out to lick his hand,
and he smiled to feel the warm, wet roughness.

Can you hear me? If I only think the words?

Her ears pricked up as if he had spoken aloud. *<I do
hear you. But this has never happened before.>*

Strange to hear her voice inside him, to know that they
were touching spirit to spirit, and to feel relief instead of
the usual terror.

<Not so strange, Little Brother. We are pack.>

Aye, Wolf. Now and always.

<I do not like this weakness in my legs and body.>

*We're getting old. And I don't like it much either. Espe-
cially since I don't feel old inside.*

<Inside, you are still a pup.>

*The same pup squatting in a thicket, afraid to move when
you howled my name.*

*<But strong. Very strong. I could feel you calling to me
from far away.>*

I called to you?

*<Of course, Little Brother. That is how I knew we were
pack. That is how I knew you were mine.>*

Her face blurred before him. If the gods had given him
a good woman and loving children, they had also been generous in their choice of vision mate.

<I wish we could hunt together. Just one last time.>

It's enough to see you. And talk. I was talking to my brother. Before you came. But he couldn't hear me.

He tried to touch the root, but he was so tired. He closed his eyes and let his head fall back against the trunk.

He felt Wolf raise her head. His hand slid down the coarse fur of her shoulder. Her wet nose nudged it atop the root.

So smooth, the bark. Smooth as polished wood. And supple as flesh.

His eyes flew open, his mind finally registering what his fingers were telling him. But the root looked unchanged. It must have been his imagination. Or another fever-dream. Still, he struggled to sit up, gasping with the effort.

Something touched his shoulders. Warmth seeped through his tunic. The warmth of real flesh, the pressure of real fingers, gently stilling his feeble movements. Fellgair, of course.

Energy flooded his spirit, an outpouring of joy and love so fierce that he knew it was Tinnean. And when the second stream filled him, far more powerful and more ancient than the first, he realized Cuillon was with him, too.

For thirty years, he had longed for this moment. Now that it had arrived, all he could do was weep in helpless gratitude.

He could feel the rhythmic pulsing of their spirits, a slow counterpoint to the pounding of his heart. And the other pulse he had first heard during that dream-journey through Chaos.

The steady vibration filled him. It soothed the torn flesh and the tortured lungs. It stilled the trembling muscles and the palsied shaking of his hands. With unhurried patience, it flowed through bone and blood and spirit.

The World Tree sang. The song echoed through the One Tree, through Tinnean and Cuillon, through his body and Wolf's, through the silent Watchers and the giant trees. The grove resounded with the song, the First Forest rang with it. Every tree knew the song, every creature that crawled upon the earth or swam in the rivers or soared through the air.

Even the small bird in his chest seemed to recognize the song. It beat its wings wildly, eager to fly with its brothers and know the freedom of the skies. He fought to hold it, to keep it close.

If he had the strength, he might have laughed. The quest to find Tinnean had taught him that his need for control was his greatest strength and his greatest weakness. Yet all his life he had battled with it. To protect himself, to protect the people he loved.

As a boy, he had been afraid he would lose his father's respect. As a young man, he had been afraid he would lose his brother. But ultimately, he had been afraid that if he relinquished his carefully maintained control, he would lose himself.

Time and time again, he had learned the impossibility of controlling either events or the people he loved. He had learned that he could give up control and not only remain whole, but become stronger. Yet he'd sat here today, fretting over the fate of a rebellion he could never lead, the fate of a world he would soon depart.

Perhaps that's what it meant to be human. Or perhaps that was simply his nature. Stubborn as a rock.

Wind and water wore away the strongest rock, chipping away the edges, reshaping it. But unlike a rock, a man could accept the changes or resist them.

He liked Fellgair's metaphor of the web of life better. Certainly, his life had been woven and rewoven hundreds of times, threads ripped away, new ones spun. And now all that was left was a slender strand, trembling under the frantic wings of that small bird.

Struath would say that life was a battle of opposites. Gortin would remind him that despite the battle, balance was always restored. Fellgair would smile and say something cryptic. And Griane . . .

He bit back a cry of pain. The song of the World Tree flowed through his spirit. Tinnean and Cuillon waited with inhuman patience for his choice, their love—as eternal as the song—filling his spirit.

Oh, Griane . . .

Her eyes, the blue that burned at the heart of a flame.

Fellgair's, golden as honey, dark as that portal to Chaos.

Rigat's face, alight with triumph when he brought down the stag.

Keirith's, filled with exhaustion and a newfound peace when he brought little Hua back from the shadowlands.

Faelia, whooping with excitement when she snared her first rabbit.

Callie, lisping the tribal legends at his knee.

Tinnean's voice in the grove during their final moments together: "This isn't good-bye. Not really. I'll always be here."

His mam's hand cupping the back of his neck, her voice urging him to rest a bit.

His father's arms outstretched to catch him as he took his first step.

With a sigh of acceptance, Darak released the small bird and gasped as it soared skyward. Brilliant light flooded his vision. As if the Northern Dancers had suddenly lit up the sky. But it was still daylight so it must be the sun—the most glorious sunset he had ever witnessed.

It danced inside of him, filling the emptiness left behind by the lost bird, bathing his spirit with warmth, bathing the grove in luminous golden light. The circled trees took up the dance, limbs swaying as if they shared his ecstasy.

Something tugged at his breeches. Through the haze of light, he saw Wolf. She bounded away, then raced back. Her yellow eyes gleamed. Her body wriggled with pleasure. She nipped at his breeches again, then bounded toward the light of the setting sun.

He eased away from the tree, astonished to feel no pain in his back or shoulder or chest, no pain in his knees as he scrambled to his feet, no pain at all—only the enveloping warmth of the sunset.

He turned back to whisper his farewell to Tinnean and Cuillon and Fellgair. The tree was lost in the wash of golden light, but Fellgair was still there, a faint shadow amid the light's glory. Darak lifted his hand, uncertain if Fellgair could see him. He thought the shadow moved, but he couldn't be sure. The light was blinding now. He could no longer see Wolf either, although he could still hear her yipping excitedly, urging him to run with her.

As he hesitated, he caught a flash of blue amid the gold.

Speedwell. Hundreds of them. Springing out of the earth, sprouting around his feet, vanishing into the light.

Once before, Tinnean had offered him this living pathway of heart-shaped leaves and bright blue flowers. The last time, the path had connected him to the One Tree. This time, it led him toward the sun.

He thought of Griane and the children. Felt a fleeting stab of regret for their grief. But the light called to him and the song urged him on.

Darak walked along the path of speedwell, then broke into a trot. A dark shadow streaked across the light as Wolf bounded toward him. Side by side, they ran, hunting the sunset.

Three hundred people crowded the throne room of the palace. Three hundred people stared up at the dais where the Son of Zhe blazed as brilliant as the sunset in his scarlet khirta and golden breastplate.

Jholianna smiled as she lifted the crown from the jewel-encrusted platter. A circlet of gold, beginning and ending with the head of an adder devouring its tapering tail. As the priests chanted a blessing, she slowly ascended the steps of the dais and bowed three times before circling behind him. He felt cool metal against his brow as she proclaimed him king and Promised One.

The kankhs bellowed. The crowd roared. Despite the haste in planning the coronation, everything had been perfect.

Out of the corner of his eye, he saw someone walking toward him. He wondered who would dare approach at this moment, then glimpsed the red and brown robe of the Supplicant beneath the hooded cloak.

Fellgair leaned close. The glow of torchlight illuminated a lock of black hair, a scruffy white beard, and a single tear glistening on his cheek.

"Darak is dead."

As the Trickster bowed his head and slowly walked away, the cheering crowd blurred, replaced with an image of Darak. Not the helpless man convulsing in pain, but the father who had tried to love him, the hunter who had shared the excitement of the kill.

"You and I . . . we're children of the forest. It's in our blood and our bones and our spirits. It's the home we always long for, the dream we always seek."

Rigat blinked hard, banishing the memories and the moisture that filled his eyes. Then he raised his hands and accepted the thunderous ovation of his people.

PART FOUR

Broken arrows in the glade.
Scattered bones beneath the trees.
Like autumn leaves, my people fall.
Like autumn leaves, my people die.
Yet I dare to dream of spring.

—Lament of the Hunted

Chapter 51

"WE HAVE CARRIED DEATH out of the village," Othak proclaimed.

Dully, Keirith repeated the ritual response with the rest of the tribe. "Let it not return to us soon."

The first rays of the sun slanted across the Death Hut, shedding the false glow of life on his father's face.

"A blessing," Lisula said. "A blessing from Bel on the spirit of our chief and the tribe he loved."

Good words. Kind words. And mostly true. His father might not have liked every person gathered here today, but he *had* loved his tribe. He had left his home and his family to protect it, spent his final days trying to ensure its safety.

And how did his people repay him? With a rite conducted in haste, their fearful gazes straying south in search of the Zherosi army marching toward them.

The signal had come during last night's vigil, sparking a panic in the village. When the tribe gathered at dawn, they discovered that most of his father's recruits had slipped away during the night. Now, instead of lingering on the hilltop to honor their chief, men were herding their women and children down the hill, grasping the elbows of old folk to hurry them along.

No word would be sent to other tribes to let them know of his passing. No representatives would arrive to honor the man who had carried the spirit of the Oak-Lord out of Chaos. There would not even be a feast to share memories of the Spirit-Hunter, the chief, the man.

Lying in the Death Hut, his father looked much as he had when they had found him: his mantle draped around his shoulders, his hands folded across his chest, his expression peaceful. Keirith had been too dazed with grief to think about it then, too shocked to even marvel that he was standing before the One Tree. But now he wondered if his father had seen the Dark Hunter approaching and willingly surrendered his spirit—or if someone had found Fa before they had.

He wouldn't save Fa, but he'd take the time to lay out his body.

He wasn't sure if he meant Rigat or Fellgair.

Contrary to tradition, his mam had insisted on washing Fa's body. Those were the only words she spoke after that first strangled cry when he and Callie returned with Fa in their arms. Just "Darak!"—a prayer, a plea, a desperate cry of hope, quickly shattered.

Hircha had shooed them from the hut, leaving Mam alone with Fa. Neither Faelia nor Callie would permit Othak to enter. And when Othak reminded them that it was customary to cut off a finger to inter in the cairn, Faelia retorted that Fa had few of enough of them left and he would take all of them to the Forever Isles.

They lingered helplessly by the doorway. Callie wept in Ela's arms. Hircha crouched in the dirt, her face stark. Faelia paced back and forth, angry tears streaming down her face. When Mam finally flung back the doeskin, she seemed composed, but then—as now—Keirith could feel her anguish buffeting his spirit.

Tears still eluded him. It was all he could do to breathe. A fist had clenched his heart when his father failed to answer Lisula's summons and it refused to relinquish its relentless grip. He was almost grateful. If the fist relaxed—even for a moment—he was afraid he would shatter.

Behind him, Trath cleared his throat. "Griane . . ."

His mam nodded, but didn't move.

"Give them a moment," Lisula said.

"Fine. But you must leave the village before the Zherosi get close."

"We will," Keirith assured him.

Hircha's eyes burned into him. "We'll stay hidden in the hills. And we won't do anything foolish like sneaking back to surrender ourselves."

How had she known? He had told no one about his plan.

Although the elders had demanded that his family leave, they had allowed the other men to decide whether to stay in the hill fort or flee. When every man chose to remain, Trath selected ten to protect the women and children who would hide in the hills until the Zherosi departed. Faelia and Keirith had argued against the plan, reminding Trath that the hill fort could never withstand a siege. But Trath was convinced that once the Zherosi discovered Darak dead and his family gone, they would leave. So Keirith had agreed to go—and silently vowed to slip back to the village later.

"I'm putting everyone in danger," Keirith said. "If I surrender—"

"You think that will satisfy them?" Faelia demanded.

"Fa's dead! Geriv will be furious at losing him, but he might settle for me."

"Aye, Darak's dead," Hircha agreed. "He died trying to rescue you."

Keirith recoiled. No one in his family had ever made the accusation directly, but he knew they were all thinking it.

"And this is how you repay him?" Hircha's expression was as cold as her voice. "By throwing your life away?"

"I'm not—"

"Nay." His mam's voice was quiet but firm. "I won't have it. I want your oath, Keirith. On your father's spirit. That you will not surrender."

The fist inside him tightened its grip.

His mam seized his wrist and pressed his palm against his father's hand. He flinched at the touch of the cold flesh, but she forced his splayed fingers down.

"Your oath. On his body. On his spirit. And on the love you bear him."

"I swear." He grated the words out between chattering teeth, then jerked his hand free.

Hircha broke the silence. "Trath's right. We should go." She rested her hand lightly atop Fa's, then turned away and limped down the slope.

One by one, the others made their farewells, Trath first, then Lisula and Ennit and Ela. Callie bent and kissed Fa's forehead. Faelia laid her palm against his cheek. Then Keirith was left on the hilltop with his mother.

Still staring down at Fa, she said, "If you mean to die, make it count, Keirith. As your father did."

"It's Rigat, isn't it?" He tried and failed to keep the bitterness from his voice. "You want me to live for him."

"I want you to live for yourself! That's all I've ever wanted for you. But if you can't—or won't—then aye, consider Rigat. You and I are the only ones with any influence over him now. I don't think even Fellgair can control him. Not after what happened in the village."

"He let Fa die! But you still love him."

"He's my child, Keirith. Just as you are."

Nay, not as he was. She would always love Rigat more.

"If it had been me—"

"You would have given up your power and your life to save your father. I know."

But he hadn't been willing to kill to save him.

"I had a chance," he whispered. "To cast out a boy's spirit. To take his body. But I couldn't. If I had been stronger—"

"You're confusing strength with ruthlessness. You were never a killer. Perhaps because you could sense the pain of others. So you hate inflicting it yourself."

Recalling the pain he had inflicted on her in the days following Fellgair's revelations, he whispered, "Forgive me."

"For what?" His mam seemed genuinely puzzled.

"Everything."

Her arms went around him, gripping him hard. He clung to her, surprised by her smallness, the delicacy of the bones beneath his fingers. He had never thought of her as either small or delicate, perceiving instead the power of her personality, the strength of her spirit.

As she pulled away, she drew back her hand and slapped him.

The unexpected blow made him stumble backward. With a muttered curse, she flew at him, punching his chest, his arms. He retreated before her fury, hands raised to block the wild blows. Finally, she stopped, breathing hard.

"Well?" she demanded. "Do you feel better now?"

"Nay!"

"That's a pity. I hoped I could knock the foolishness out

of you. I should have started years ago. Now you're too big. And too quick."

He had to smile. So did she. The fist inside him relaxed its grip just a little.

With infinite tenderness, his mother smoothed the three eagle feathers braided in Fa's hair. Then she bent over the low stone wall and kissed him softly on the mouth. As she straightened, she stroked Fa's bag of charms and suddenly stiffened.

"Dear gods. His fingers. The ones Morgath took."

Keirith's breath caught. He had never suspected that Fa had carried them in his bag of charms all these years.

"Take the bag," he said. "Else the Zherosi might."

Gently, he raised his father's head so she could slide the leather thong free. As her fingers closed protectively around the small bag, Keirith found himself squeezing his bag of charms. Before leaving the hut for the rite, Mam had cut a lock of Fa's hair for each of them. His now rested among his other charms, the most precious of all.

"Later," Mam whispered. "There will be time to cry later."

Keirith swallowed hard and kissed his father farewell. Together, he and his mother started down the hill. Neither of them looked back.

Chapter 52

NAKED, RIGAT PADDED TO the balcony of his bedchamber and stared north, watching the sky brighten.

By now, they would have carried Darak's body to the Death Hut. It should have been Gortin leading the rite; he hated to think of Othak intoning the ancient words and opening the way for Darak's spirit to fly to the Forever Isles. Keirith would retreat into guilt and despair. Callie would weep. Faelia would scream and wail with the other women, but his mam's grief would be too deep to display to the world.

Her face rose before him, the lines around her mouth carved deeper by Darak's death, her teeth digging into her upper lip to keep any cry from escaping. Had Darak known he would never return from the First Forest? Nay, he would not have left her, not even to see Tinnean one last time. And she would never have been able to let him go. They all must have believed they would have a few more days together.

Fellgair had realized the truth. And although he could not save Darak, he had chosen to spend those last moments with him, to witness his death instead of his son's coronation.

Lucky Darak. In the end, everyone chose him.

Behind him, bare feet pattered on the tiles. A moment later, Jholianna's arms twined around his waist.

"Come back to bed," she whispered.

A lock of hair fell over his shoulder as she kissed his neck. Her bare breasts pressed against his back and her pubic hair tickled his buttocks. The sensations aroused him, as did the memory of their lovemaking. But despite the promise of pleasure, he pushed away the hand slipping down his belly.

She stepped around him and studied his face. "You're going back."

"Yes. But first I have to pay a call on the Khonsel."

She looked away, her long hair masking her expression. "He has served me well."

"I know."

He dressed in a simple khirta and sandals and left her.

The corridors in the north wing of the palace were still quiet; the guests at his coronation had only sought their beds a short while ago. But in the west wing, he passed slaves bearing platters of food and guards returning to their quarters after the night watch. Scribes slipped in and out of the chambers on either side of the windowless corridor.

All prostrated themselves when they saw him. Some of the faces were curious, most fearful.

If they knew my mission, they would fear me even more.

He had to ask a groveling slave the way to the Khonsel's chamber. When he reached it, he was surprised to discover that it was an ordinary workroom. The Khonsel stood with his back to the doorway while a scribe, seated on a low stool, scribbled furiously. Apparently, the Khonsel had not yet been to bed; he was still dressed in the formal khirta he had worn at the coronation feast. But now a sword hung at his hip.

When the scribe saw him, he fell to his knees, knocking over his box of writing supplies in his haste to prostrate himself.

The Khonsel glanced over his shoulder, then turned and bowed formally. "Good morning, Promised One. Please. Come in." He gazed down at the trembling scribe. "It's finished? Then you may go."

The scribe handed a tablet-box to the Khonsel. Then he gathered up the rest of his supplies and scurried out of the chamber.

The Khonsel seated himself at the simple wooden table. A clay pitcher rested on one corner, with two cups beside it. Clearly, he had anticipated this visit.

Instead of offering him a drink, the Khonsel pulled a gold ring from his finger and pressed it into the wax. After peering at the impression, he closed the tablet-box and began tying the leather cords.

"Darak is dead."

The Khonsel's fingers fell still. He looked up, frowning. "I'm sorry."

"Are you?"

"For the sake of my country, no. But he was your foster-father. And you loved him. His death must pain you."

"Yet you planned it. You and your nephew."

The Khonsel picked up a stick of wax from a small clay dish at his elbow and held it to the flame of an oil lamp. As he watched the melting wax drip onto the knots, he said, "No. Geriv was careful not to apprise me of his plans."

"But you suspected. And arranged that sham attack by the smith to keep me here."

The Khonsel regarded him for so long that Rigat wondered if Fellgair's suspicions were misplaced. Then he said, "When did you figure it out?"

"It doesn't matter. Your deception cost Darak his life."

"And now mine will be forfeit as well."

"Yes."

The Khonsel nodded, unperturbed. But, of course, he must have been expecting it.

"The queen didn't know," the Khonsel said. "About Geriv's plan. Or the false assassin."

Rigat hid his relief with a disinterested shrug. "I've been trying to decide if I should tell her that you lied about Keirith's death. And arranged for him and Darak to escape Pilozhat."

For the first time, he caught a glimmer of emotion on the man's face. "I would prefer that you didn't. But I don't suppose my feelings count for much."

"No."

"And the manner of my death? Will I have any say in that?"

Rigat hesitated. As Jholianna had noted, the Khonsel had served her well. And if not for him, Darak and Keirith would have died in Zheros.

"Do you have a specific request?"

"Let me die by my own hand."

He had never seen a man take his life. Would the Khonsel be able to do it? Or would his courage fail him?

Rigat folded his arms and nodded.

"Thank you, my lord." The Khonsel pressed his ring into the blobs of wax, sealing the knots of the tablet-box. "Instructions regarding my estate."

"Are you wealthy?"

The Khonsel laughed. "Hardly. But I have property in Pilozhat. And slaves. None of them Tree People. Are you really the Son of Zhe?"

"No. I'm the son of the God with Two Faces."

His eyes widened, but he recovered quickly. "Well, that explains a lot." He hesitated a moment before adding, "I suppose there's no point in asking you to spare Geriv."

"No."

The Khonsel's mouth tightened. With a brisk nod, he

rose and walked across the room to pluck a scarlet cloak from a hook. After settling it across his shoulders, he picked up the pitcher and poured wine into both cups.

"The last of the Carilian late harvest. Would you join me?"

Ballocks the size of boulders, Rigat had said at their first meeting. Despite the man's treachery, he had to admire his courage.

He downed the wine quickly. The Khonsel sipped his, his mouth curving in an appreciative smile.

"The Carilians might copulate with dogs, but they do know how to make wine."

He raised the cup in salute and drained the contents. Then he picked up a dagger—Rigat hadn't even noticed it on the table—and walked into the adjoining chamber, motioning for him to follow.

This room was as simple as the other. A sleeping shelf with a pillow at one end and a neatly folded coverlet at the other. A threadbare rug. A stool in one corner. And in the small window niche, a vase containing a spray of red flowers.

"Bitterheart," the Khonsel said, noting the direction of his gaze. "Malaq's favorite. And especially appropriate today."

He sat on the sleeping shelf, adjusting his sword so that he was comfortable. His thumb stroked the worn leather on the hilt of his dagger. Then he gripped it firmly and held the blade under the left side of his throat.

"Good luck, Rigat. I think you'll need it."

Before he could frame a suitable reply, the Khonsel plunged the dagger into his neck. Blood fountained from the wound, spraying the whitewashed wall. His mouth twisting in a grimace, the Khonsel dragged the blade across his throat.

His body slumped sideways. The dagger clattered onto the tiles. Unmoving, unmoved, Rigat watched the body convulse once, the eyes glaze, the relentless gouts of blood slow as the heart faltered. The choked gurgling subsided, until the only sound in the little chamber was the droning buzz of a fly.

Rigat stared down at the body; it seemed so much smaller without that fierce spirit inhabiting it. He had expected to feel triumph or satisfaction or perhaps revulsion at witnessing his death throes, at seeing all that blood, as scarlet as the bitterheart. Instead, he felt nothing. Nothing at all.

He opened the portal atop a hill just south of the village. Coracles dotted the river. Children trotted from the shore with bulging waterskins. Women moved among the golden barley, rooting up weeds. On the ridge to the east, the black forms of carrion birds perched on the roofless walls of the Death Hut.

Rigat scanned the fortress on the opposite shore where Keirith had been imprisoned. Then he headed toward the Death Hut.

He had gone to the site of the hostage exchange first. Finding all of the bodies gone, he had come here, hoping for information—and retribution.

As he crested the hill, the sweet-rotten stench of decay hit him. Crows ascended with protesting squawks; clearly, they had been feasting for days. And animals as well. Empty eye sockets stared skyward. Tunics and breeches had been ripped open by sharp beaks and fangs and claws. Partially gnawed entrails spilled out of bellies; in some places, bone showed through the torn flesh.

He managed to identify the man—Sorig?—who had recruited volunteers with Darak. The others were nameless strangers. But he said prayers for each of them, hoping their spirits had reached the Forever Isles. They were loyal. They had died trying to defend Darak.

None of the ravaged faces belonged to the traitor Mikal. With a grim smile, Rigat walked down the hill to the village.

Although he had changed into his breeches and tunic, people stared openly as he passed; a few mothers pulled their children close. After the recent battle downriver, the presence of any stranger might trouble them, but the Zherosi might have circulated a report about the red-haired boy who had disrupted the hostage exchange. If so, he'd have to be cautious.

He approached a group of old women, who left off their mending and gossiping when they saw him. In answer to his inquiry, one pointed the way to the chief's hut. He thanked her politely and continued on his way.

Outside the hut, he paused to identify himself as a friend of Mikal's and requested permission to enter. When a man's voice answered, he ducked inside, hesitating by the doorway until his eyes adjusted to the gloom.

Birat peered up at him suspiciously. "Callum, you said your name was? Mikal never mentioned you."

"I'm one of the new recruits." He allowed emotion to choke his voice. "I managed to escape. After the battle."

"You were there? You saw what happened?"

His expression remained suspicious rather than grief-stricken. Had he plotted Darak's death with his son? Or was he ignorant of Mikal's treachery?

Rigat bowed his head and whispered, "I . . . gods forgive me, I ran. That's why I came here. To beg Mikal's forgiveness and try to make amends for my cowardice."

Birat spat into the fire pit. The peat sizzled briefly. "Don't apologize for being smart. Or lucky. These days, it's the only way to survive. Look what happened to the others. And the Spirit-Hunter." He spat again. "Mikal spouted some nonsense about him vanishing during the battle. Him and his son. And some red-haired lad claiming to be . . ." His eyes narrowed.

". . . the son of some god. Aye. Came out of thin air. If I hadn't seen it with my own eyes, I'd never have believed it. I couldn't make sense of half of what he said. All I know is right after that, the arrows started flying."

"And so did you." Birat chuckled. "No wonder the Vanel all but had fire coming out his nose. Watching the Spirit-Hunter slip through his fingers like that." His expression clouded. "Still . . . that sort of magic . . . it gives a man the shivers. The Vanel should have just let them go."

"He didn't?"

"Marched out the very next day. Off to attack the Spirit-Hunter's village. Never thought he was such a headstrong fool, but when a man's pride is touched . . ." He shrugged.

"Were there any other survivors? I . . . I couldn't bear to go to the Death Hut."

"Only Mikal. He's gone to the healer. His shoulder's troubling him. But he should be back soon. So you can beg his forgiveness."

Ignoring the malicious smile, Rigat shook his head. "If you don't mind . . . I'd rather get this over with now."

"Suit yourself. Mother Eminna's hut is across the way. If you get lost, just ask."

Rigat bowed and quickly ducked out of the hut. Tempted as he was to kill the spiteful old man, he needed to conserve his power for more important tasks.

He entered the hut without announcing himself. The healer glanced over her shoulder, frowning at his rudeness, but Rigat ignored her, his gaze focused on his prey. Even in the dim light, he could see Mikal's eyes widen with recognition. He was still fumbling for his dagger when Rigat invaded his spirit.

He touched fear and helpless rage, but beneath those emotions lurked another. Without bothering to analyze it, he concentrated his power into a tight ball of fury and hurled it deep into the traitor's spirit.

The silent scream echoed inside him long after Mikal's spirit drifted away. Into Chaos, he hoped. The man had betrayed Darak in life; he didn't deserve to join him after death.

While the healer bent over the body, frantically searching for a pulse, he opened a portal onto a moor where he could rest and allow his power to recover. It must be strong when he came face-to-face with the Vanel.

He lay back in the long grass and closed his eyes. He had felt nothing at the Khonsel's death, but Mikal's warmed him as surely as the late summer sun. His pleasure waned when he identified the other emotion he had touched before he cast out the traitor's spirit. In his last moment of existence, Mikal had felt relief.

Chapter 53

STANDING AT THE FOOT OF THE HILL, carefully out of range of the defenders' arrows, Geriv surveyed the earthwork fortress. Thin curls of smoke rose from the unseen huts. Here and there, he glimpsed heads peering over the walls. A well-trodden path led to an entrance so narrow it would admit only one man at a time; the defenders had blocked it with a breast-high heap of rubble.

A waste of labor. The spy had sworn the village had no spring inside the walls and fewer than fifty men and boys of fighting age. They were ill-equipped to withstand either an assault or a siege.

Geriv was prepared for both. His men had rations for another half-moon, easily supplemented by fish from the lake and the sheep grazing on the hillsides. The bullocks he had requisitioned had proved invaluable in dragging the pine spars across the moors. But before he wasted time with a siege or men in an assault, he would try another tactic.

"Tell them we wish to parley."

"Yes, Vanel," Korim replied.

Those two words had comprised the bulk of his son's conversation since the prisoner exchange. He seemed neither resentful nor sullen, just strangely withdrawn. Geriv had included him in his meetings with the other officers, attempted to address the problems that lay between them—done everything but plead with his son to talk with him—before abandoning the effort.

Still, he found himself admiring Korim's stiff back and firm stride as he marched halfway up the path to the hill fort. Disdaining a shield, he stood slender and erect—easy prey to an overeager archer—and relayed the request.

After a brief delay, two men clambered over the rocks and started down the hill. Waving Jonaq back, Geriv walked forward to take his place at Korim's side.

The robed man was obviously the head priest and, judging by the scars around his left eye, recently elevated to the position. Geriv's stomach lurched when he saw the three eagle feathers tied to the older man's braid. He reminded himself that this might only be the acting chief, appointed while the Spirit-Hunter recovered, but his gaze drifted to the Death Hut atop the western hill.

He waited impatiently for the ritual introductions to conclude. Even with an army of three hundred men surrounding his village, the chief insisted on reciting the interminable list of his ancestors, as if this were a social call. At least he was a better actor than the priest whose shaking voice and sweat-sheened forehead betrayed his fear.

As soon as the preliminaries were concluded, he asked the question that had been burning in his mind for the last eight days. "Where is the Spirit-Hunter?"

The chief jerked his head toward the Death Hut.

Disappointment rose like bile in Geriv's throat. "When?"

"Yesterday."

If not for the bullocks slowing his progress and the morning spent felling trees for battering rams and scaling ladders, he might have been in time.

"And Kheridh?"

After he gleaned that the Spirit-Hunter's son had fled with his family, he lost interest in the long reply and concentrated on controlling his face and his breathing.

"They've sent all the women and children away," Korim said. "The chief hopes your army will retire and leave his people in peace. He says there are no rebels in the village. And claims that—with the exception of the Spirit-Hunter and his son and daughter—no member of his tribe has ever fought with the rebels and only once—when their village was attacked—have they taken up arms against us."

Of course he would say that. Perhaps it was even true. But according to the spy, the village had provided a safe haven for the rebels.

"I wish to see the Spirit-Hunter's body. You will accompany me."

Without waiting for Korim's translation, he retraced his steps, squinting against the glare of the westering sun. In silence, they marched up the hill to the Death Hut.

Sweat poured off him as he climbed. He wanted to believe it was merely exertion, but he knew better.

"There is a danger of relapse," the physician had warned him before he left Little Falls. "And a forced march will only increase that danger. Please, Vanel. Be reasonable. Your health is more important than chasing after a few miserable rebels."

He had ignored that advice, enduring long marches when his body screamed for rest, and the fever and chills that denied him the healing respite of sleep. And all for nothing. He had lost the chance to face his enemy one more time, to look into those gray eyes and find an acknowledgment of defeat.

Crows rose up with a loud flapping of wings. As they neared the low-walled structure, Korim checked suddenly. Geriv just studied the body laid out on the shelf of stones.

The gray eyes were gone, of course—the first prize sought by the birds. Strips of ragged flesh hung from the exposed cheekbones. Yet the maimed hands, folded atop that broad chest, retained an echo of strength, and the three eagle feathers, now hanging askew, held a certain sad dignity.

If such a man had died in Zheros, his body would have been anointed with sweet oils and dressed in a khirta of softest lilmia. His arms would have been banded in gold, his feet shod in sandals studded with precious gems. The greatest poets in the empire would recite the tales of his achievements. The greatest architect would construct his tomb. All commerce would cease during the three days of mourning. Women would tear their garments, men would rub ashes onto their faces. Warriors would carry his body through the streets. Thousands of mourners would follow them to the tomb, where murals depicted his great deeds and the smoky scent of incense sweetened the air. And after his spirit flew through the tiny roof hole to the green shores of Paradise, his body would rest forever in the cool darkness.

Instead, Darak Spirit-Hunter—the greatest man of his people—was left to the scavengers.

At best, he would become a martyred hero. At worst, an avenging spirit. Every spear hurtling out of the shadows would be flung by the Spirit-Hunter's unseen hand. Every accident that befell a logging party, every unexplained blight on Zherosi livestock, every ship that foundered at sea and every warrior who sickened with the Freshening cough would be proof of his enduring power. The cynics would use him for their own purposes and the superstitious would whisper his name with awe.

He could march every member of the Spirit-Hunter's tribe through every village in the north. Have them proclaim that they had carried his body to the Death Hut. Have them point to the head impaled on a spear and shout, "This is all that remains of Darak Spirit-Hunter." And those who did not claim it was a lie would raise their voices in horror at the desecration. As if leaving it for the birds and animals to devour wasn't desecration enough.

Barbarous people. He would never understand them.

He turned abruptly and found the chief's gaze fixed on Korim. His son's head was bowed, his hands gripped tightly together. Then his head came up. His lips moved, whispering words too soft to hear. But there was no mistaking the spiral he sketched in the air—the symbol of the coiled adder and the traditional Zherosi blessing.

"Korim," he grated.

Ignoring him, Korim turned and bowed to the chief. "He was a great man." He spoke slowly so Geriv had no difficulty following the words. "I am sorry that he is dead."

The priest stiffened, but the chief returned the bow, his expression thoughtful. With a supreme effort of will, Geriv bit back a curse and stalked down the hill.

The words thudded into his brain with every footstep. When he reached the end of his days, would his son tell strangers what a great man he had been? Would he stand beside his bier with bowed head and stricken expression? Geriv doubted he would feel anything except—perhaps—relief.

The fact that he bore part of the blame for their disastrous relationship only fueled his fury. But what should he

have done? Given up his career? Chosen to forgo the rank
and privileges he had fought for his entire life? He had a
province to subdue. Thousands of men who depended upon
him. Korim should have understood that. He should have
tried harder to bridge the gap between them, instead of
misinterpreting every gesture, disdaining every overture.

"I have no time for this!"

Only when he heard Korim's polite "Vanel?" did he realize he had spoken aloud.

Jonaq hurried toward him. "What are your orders,
Vanel?"

He could see the eagerness in Jonaq's eyes, in the eyes
of all his officers, and knew every man arrayed around the
hill fort shared it. For days, they had dreamed of avenging
the defeats they had suffered at the hands of these barbarians, of abandoning the monotony of drilling for the exhilaration of battle. Like him, they yearned for it the way some
men lusted for women, every sense heightened, every nerve
thrilling to the jarring impact of sword cleaving flesh, the
hoarse scream of a wounded foe, the salty spray of blood
anointing their lips.

Saliva filled his mouth and he swallowed it down, but the
blood lust still churned in his belly, and the palm resting
on the hilt of his sword was damp with sweat. He resisted
the urge to wipe it on his khirta as he turned to the chief.

"You claim Kheridh and his family have fled. You will
have no objection if my men search the village to confirm
that."

After Korim translated, the chief hesitated, narrowed
eyes searching his face. But all he would find there was the
ill-concealed impatience of a commander who wished to
complete this thankless mission and return to the comfort
of his headquarters.

"Search if you like," the chief said. "You won't find
them. But afterward, your army will leave?"

"You have my oath. How large is the village?"

"We have twenty-six huts." Cannily, he avoided giving
away the number of defenders.

Geriv shrugged. "Then fifty men should suffice."

"I'd think twenty-six should suffice."

Geriv kept his smile gentle and his voice condescending.

"Let us compromise on forty. You must have double that number of defenders. My men are the ones at risk."

"With an army at their backs?"

"That's my offer. Either accept it or prepare for our attack."

The chief's gaze lingered on the battering rams and scaling ladders lying at the base of the slope, then drifted across the formations of warriors that surrounded the hill fort—as if a forest had sprung out of the barren ground. He spat, then gave a grudging nod.

Eyeing the gob of phlegm a finger's breadth from his sandaled foot, Geriv said, "The priest will stay. A token of your goodwill."

A nice touch, he thought. Besides, it couldn't hurt to leave one man alive to attest to the Spirit-Hunter's death and the terrible cost of incurring the enmity of their conquerors.

Invisible behind his mist-shield, Rigat listened and watched. He had rushed to the prisoner exchange to save Darak and Keirith, only to have his brother accuse him of ruining everything. This time, he would study the situation before deciding what to do.

His gaze lingered on Othak. Hard to believe that shrinking figure could have incited the whole village to turn on him. Harder still to believe that the gods could be so kind as to deliver two prizes into his hands.

As Trath started up the hill, the Vanel motioned a hawk-faced young man aside; even Rigat had to strain to catch the words.

". . . but wait until all your men are inside. Deploy them so the huts shield them from the archers. You'll be outnumbered, Jonaq. But you have surprise in your favor and far better training than that rabble. As soon as you give the signal, we'll storm the fortress."

Rigat studied the Vanel with renewed interest. He knew Geriv was proud; he had discovered that when he'd touched the man's spirit during the prisoner exchange. But he was clever, too. He had not broken his oath, merely sworn to take his army away after searching the village. Trath had simply assumed that he meant to leave them alive.

Rigat already knew his family was not inside the hill fort. As soon as he'd opened the portal, he had used his power to search for them. Now, he confirmed that Ennit and Lisula were absent as well. Likely, Trath had sent all the old folk away, along with the women and children.

Only a few moons ago, he had played When I Become Chief. Now it was no longer a game. If he wished, he could stop the slaughter. Just step through the portal and give the order. Would the defenders fall on their knees in gratitude? Offer him—finally—the respect he was due? More likely, they would believe the Vanel had kept his word and left them in peace. They would never know—or believe— that they owed their salvation to him.

Although sunlight still flooded the valley, a wave of cold engulfed him. His reluctant gaze drifted to the Death Hut. He knew what Darak would do. Knew, too, that the rest of his family would expect him to save his people. But none of the men inside had raised their voices to protest Othak's accusations. If they hadn't hurled stones, they had allowed others to do so. Why should he protect them now?

"You gave your word!"

For a moment, Rigat thought the boy was accusing him. Then he realized he was speaking to his father.

"I said my army would leave after we conducted the search. And it will."

"That's trickery."

"That's war! Did you expect me to waste time with a siege? Sacrifice half my troops on an assault?"

"They've done nothing to deserve this."

"They sheltered rebels. Rebels who repeatedly attacked the forces of Zheros." As the boy continued to protest, he said, "Enough, Skalel! I've given my orders."

"Then I respectfully request permission to accompany Jonaq."

"Permission denied."

"Please, Father. I beg you not to do this."

The Vanel eyed his son coldly. "If you cannot remain silent, I will have you escorted from the field."

During the prisoner exchange, he'd had little time to observe the boy. Korim, that was his name. Clearly, he was better suited to be a priest than a warrior. He had probably dreamed that the Zherosi and the children of the Oak and Holly could live together in harmony. As Rigat had once dreamed. But he was wiser now, and after today, Korim would be, too.

Rigat watched Jonaq lead his men up the slope. Contrary to what the boy thought, the men inside the hill fort deserved their fate. They had humiliated the Trickster's son. They had cursed him and hurled rocks at his head. If they had caught him, they would have ripped him apart with their hands. Let them save themselves if they could.

The last man scrambled over the barrier of rocks. From the Death Hut came the hoarse jeers of the crows. They were drowned out by a shouted command in Zherosi and answering shouts in the tribal tongue. And then the screams.

The Vanel brought his sword down. A kankh blew. With well-ordered precision, the Zherosi warriors ringing the hill fort trotted up the slope with scaling ladders, shields upraised to protect them from arrows. The shields proved unnecessary; the defenders were too busy fighting the warriors already inside the fort to notice those planting ladders against its walls.

Belatedly, a few arrows arced over the earthworks, a few spears thrust wildly at the new wave of attackers. One ladder swayed and toppled, but warriors continued to scramble up the others and leap onto the ramparts.

Rigat found himself praying to the Maker, silently exhorting the defenders. Then the shouting ebbed and the clang of metal became sporadic, and he stopped.

A profound silence hung over the hill fort. It was broken by a triumphant cry and voices shouting the Vanel's name. The troops took up the cry. In moments, the entire valley rang with the man's name. The Vanel accepted the acclamation with the same detachment he had manifested during the battle, but a shudder racked his son's skinny body. Rigat was surprised to discover a similar shudder coursing through his, a continuous tremor that made his legs shake.

The kankh sounded again. The few surviving warriors

straggled down the slope. The Vanel's expression brightened when he saw Jonaq. Blood ran freely from the wounds in his arms, but he was smiling.

As the Vanel congratulated him and gave orders to slaughter the sheep for a celebratory feast, Rigat's gaze returned to the hill fort. They were dead—all of them. Slaughtered as surely as the sheep would be. Rothisar who had always sneered at him, Madig who had been the first to turn on him, old Trath who used scowls and cuffs to disguise an embarrassingly good heart.

He was old. He would have died soon anyway.

They would all die, he realized. The women, the children, the old folk. How would they survive without the hunters and fishermen who lay dead inside the hill fort? Without the sheep that gave them wool and milk and meat? Come the winter, they would starve. Why hadn't he thought of that?

Not my family. I'll take care of them. Even Faelia.

"And on the morrow," the Vanel was saying, "I'll lead two komakhs back to Little Falls. You take the third and hunt for the remaining villagers."

Jonaq saluted smartly. "Yes, Vanel."

"I want the Spirit-Hunter's family alive."

"And the others? The women and older children would be useful as slaves."

"Kill the men and boys. Take only the strongest women. As for the rest, either kill them or leave them to starve. It makes no difference to me."

Jonaq jerked his head toward Othak. "What about him?"

Othak seemed to have succumbed to shock, standing numbly between the two guards who gripped his arms. As the Vanel's cold gaze raked him, he gave a soft whimper.

Rigat forced himself to concentrate, to master his trembling legs, to remember why he was here.

He stepped out of the portal, directly in front of the Vanel. Jonaq stumbled backward, one hand groping for the hilt of his sword. Korim gasped. The Vanel went rigid. The other officers were still snapping orders to subordinates, calling for healers, and organizing litters to carry the wounded down from the hill fort.

"You know who I am," Rigat said.

"I know who you claim to be."

With the same detachment the Vanel had shown during the battle, Rigat sent his power lancing through the man's spirit, driving him to his knees.

Now do you know who I am?

He waited for the Vanel's silent assent.

Call off your aide.

The Vanel held up a hand, but it took several attempts before he managed to gasp, "Jonaq! Sheathe your sword."

With obvious reluctance, the younger man obeyed. Only then did Rigat withdraw from the Vanel's spirit. By now, the other officers had noticed his presence. Noticed, too, that their commander was on his knees.

"I am Rigat. The Son of Zhe and newly-crowned king of Zheros."

Ignoring the shocked murmurs and incredulous stares, he turned to Othak. The priest shrank back, but his face held the same malevolence Rigat remembered.

"It's the day of judgment, Othak."

"Only gods have the right to judge men," Othak declared, his voice surprisingly strong despite its tremor.

"I *am* the son of a god. In Zheros, he takes the form of a winged serpent. Here, he's called the Trickster."

Othak's eye widened. "You're a liar! A liar and an abomination!"

The simmering power leaped. Rigat smiled and unleashed it.

Othak screamed as it hurtled into his spirit. Wrenching free of the guards, he took two tottering steps before collapsing. With brutal efficiency, Rigat crushed the pitiful barriers Othak erected, driving hard and fast into the hidden places where all his secrets lurked.

He touched Othak's lingering fear of his brutish father and the helpless terror of cowering in their hut, trying in vain to ward off the leather belt, the upraised first. He touched the shame of failing so many of his early tests as Gortin's apprentice, and his envy of Keirith, doubly blessed with a natural gift and his father's love. Keirith who had everything he lacked until the gods finally smiled upon Othak and cast his competitor out of the tribe.

He touched the pride that blossomed when he became

Tree-Brother, and the satisfaction of having better, stronger men defer to him. The hunger for women, never satisfied, as each tentative advance was met by rejection—until the tribe fled Eagles Mount for a new village, where no one remembered the shrinking boy with the watchful eyes and the bruised face.

He saw the dark-haired girl, barely thirteen, who was impressed by Othak's title and flattered by his attention. The frustrating summer of awkward kisses and inept fumbling. The evening he could bear it no longer and took her, one hand covering her mouth to muffle her screams. And all the other evenings when he discovered the pleasure—hotter and sweeter than lust—of watching someone cower before him, and the unexpected joy of enforcing his will with his leather belt, his upraised fist.

He touched the ever-present fear of a Zherosi attack and the dread that he might prove to be a coward in battle. He touched the shock of that first meeting with Keirith after so many years, the bitter humiliation of knowing Gortin still favored him, and the growing frustration that the old man would never, ever die and he would always remain in his miserable shadow.

The excitement of planning the murder. The terror that he would be discovered. The suspicion that Mother Griane knew, but could say nothing, for he knew her secret—that her adored youngest son had used his power to render Madig an idiot.

The delicious agony of the knife plucking out his eye. The triumph of finally becoming Tree-Father. And the incomparable satisfaction of driving out Keirith's brother while the family of the great Darak Spirit-Hunter stood by, helpless.

Rigat touched every secret, shameful place in that quailing spirit and watched its owner writhe on the ground at his feet, as helpless as his family had been. Abruptly, he withdrew from Othak's spirit, soiled by the contact.

"He calls the Son of Zhe an abomination," he declared for the benefit of those watching. "For that alone, he deserves to die. But his spirit has been tainted by a lifetime of crimes against his people."

Murder. Rape. Envy. Lust. He listed them all, speaking

in the tribal tongue so Othak would understand, trusting to Korim's frantic translation to carry his words to the Zherosi.

"You spread lies about me. About my mother. And because you suspected Gortin wanted to name my brother Tree-Father, you killed him."

Othak screamed a denial. Rigat ignored it.

"You hoarded the herbs my mother gave Gortin. The ones to help him sleep. So you could blame her if anyone questioned his death. I saw it when I touched your spirit, Othak. I saw everything."

"Please . . ."

"I know what you are. I know what you've done. Now is the time of reckoning."

He pointed his forefinger at the ground and slashed it through the air. The long grass parted. The earth cracked open, spraying clods of dirt onto Othak's shoes. Rigat closed his hands into fists and pulled. The grass rolled back as neatly as if he had turned down the sheet on his bed in Pilozhat. But it was not earth that filled the fissure, but a dense thicket of vines and thorn bushes, barely visible through the sickly ocher haze of Chaos.

"Merciful gods," someone whispered. "What is that?"

"That," Rigat replied in Zherosi, "is the Abyss."

As one, they stumbled back. The Vanel halted after one step and sharply ordered his men to stand fast. Their bodies trembled with the desire to escape, but they obeyed, fingers sketching frantic signs of protection.

Othak scuttled away, but at Rigat's command, the guards seized his arms and dragged him to the edge of the fissure.

A sudden movement within the tangled foliage drew everyone's gaze. A single vine slid free. Its tiny brown leaves rustled as it snaked between the finger-length thorns and shriveled berries that studded the branch of the thorn bush. With mesmerizing slowness, it slithered from one branch to another, climbing skyward as if seeking the light of the true sun.

The leading end of the vine reared up. All along its length, yellow dots appeared on the leaves, shimmering like tiny stars. In perfect unison, the stars winked out, then reappeared.

Behind Rigat, a man gasped. "Blessed Womb of Earth, protect me. They're eyes."

Under the intent gazes of those tiny yellow eyes, a shriveled berry near the end of a branch swelled into a round, purple mass. A slender filament snaked out, and then another, quivering like an insect's antennae. The branch sagged under the weight of the expanding berry, but still it grew, until the center of the fruit split open with a wet slurp.

Othak screamed. Screamed again when five hand-sized petals peeled back from the core. Tiny spikes lined the perimeter of the petals, miniature fangs enclosing a gaping red mouth. The filaments waved liked beckoning arms, the knobby protrusions on their ends like upraised fists. The petals twisted, following the vine that rose out of the fissure to turn its yellow-eyed gaze on Othak.

The smell of urine filled the air. With supreme satisfaction, Rigat watched the stain spread down the front of Othak's robe.

"Do you admit your crimes?"

"Aye! I'm sorry. For everything."

"Will you beg for your life?"

"Aye! Please!"

Rigat walked slowly around the portal and signaled the guards to release their prisoner. Othak pressed his forehead against Rigat's foot, begging for mercy, gasping out incoherent pleas, promising to perform any penance, to do anything Rigat wanted.

Rigat bent down to rest his palm against the lowered head. Othak raised his tear-streaked face. Snot leaked from his nose and he snuffled hopefully.

"You may perform your penance in Chaos."

Confused by his gentle tone, Othak just stared at him. Rigat waited until horrified understanding dawned. Then he called on his power and shoved Othak into the fissure.

It was as easy as pushing Seg.

He allowed himself a moment to savor Othak's scream, to watch the vine ensnare his flailing limbs, and the five hungry mouths close around his arms and legs and head. Then he snapped the portal shut.

The air was thick and charged with the remnants of the portal's energy, thicker still with the stink of fear. They were all staring at him, some with terror, others with loathing.

The Vanel's hand dropped to the hilt of his sword. Rigat let his power brush the man's spirit.

Attack me and your son will follow the priest.

The Vanel's fingers clenched convulsively. Then he let his hand fall.

"Now, Vanel," Rigat said. "It's your turn."

Too late, he realized he'd misjudged the boy. With a strangled cry, Korim unsheathed his sword and lunged at him. Only the Vanel's hand, whipping out at the last moment to seize his forearm, stopped the thrust.

"Hold him!" he snapped at the guards who had restrained Othak. "And you," he ordered two others, "restrain Skalel do Mekliv. Forgive me, Jonaq, but you're as hot-headed as Korim and I refuse to sacrifice either of you."

"What has he ever done to deserve this?" Korim shouted, struggling uselessly.

"He held my brother hostage. He used him to try and capture my foster-father, who is dead because of him. He murdered every man in that hill fort."

"That was . . . we are at war!"

"A moment ago, you accused your father of trickery. Now you defend him?"

"Against you, yes. How can you call yourself the Son of Zhe and kill my father who has spent his whole life defending Zheros?"

"Korim. Stop." The Vanel sounded weary. "You won't change his mind. And you'll only bring his anger down on you."

"I don't care!"

"But I do. Please. If you . . . if you honor me as your father, you will obey me."

Tears welled up in the boy's eyes. He blinked furiously to keep them from spilling over.

"So." The Vanel gazed back at him steadily. "You intend to cast my spirit into the Abyss as well?"

Rigat allowed the silence to stretch for a few moments, but there was no change in the Vanel's expression. A hard man. A warrior like his uncle. And like his uncle, he, too, had served the empire well. Even the plan to use Keirith as bait to capture Darak was a sound one.

"No," he said at last. "I'll allow you to take your own life. That's more fitting for a warrior. Your uncle died well. I hope you will, too."

The Vanel's eye closed briefly. Then he nodded. "My uncle was always a brave man. I look forward to meeting him in Paradise."

"Please." Korim's voice was softer now but just as emphatic, the brown eyes clear and hard. "We've all seen your power. We know how implacable you can be. Now show us you can also be merciful. That you recognize the value of a commander who has fought with bravery and honor all his life. That you can overlook your personal grudge because he targeted your family. I've met Kheridh. And Darak. Do you think they would demand my father's death?"

"No," Rigat replied. "But they're better men than I am."

"Do you want me to beg as the priest did?" He fell on his knees in the dirt. "Then I beg you. Please. Don't do this."

For the first time since he had stopped Korim from attacking, the Vanel looked at his son. Rigat could find little resemblance between them, Korim's face so young, almost girlish, Geriv's hard and angular, lined by years of exposure to the elements and the burdens of command. The one, pleading yet defiant, and the other twisted with grief and regret and a longing so naked and hungry that Rigat caught his breath.

"I cannot give you the gift of your father's life. Instead, I give you the gift of his love."

Confused, Korim glanced up at his father. Immediately, the mask fell back into place. But for just a moment, the boy glimpsed the truth—perhaps for the first time in his life—and the tears he had fought so hard to control poured unheeded down his beardless cheeks.

"Korim." The Vanel cleared his throat. "Don't."

Korim swallowed hard and swiped at his cheeks with his fists like a little child. The Vanel pulled his son to his feet. Then he freed his hand and stepped back, studying his son's face.

"I have not . . . we were . . . ill-suited, you and I. But that was my fault, not yours."

Korim shook his head vehemently, drawing a weary smile

from his father. The Vanel opened his mouth as if to speak again, and closed it. Awkwardly, he embraced his son, but when Korim continued to cling to him, he gently but firmly pulled away.

He removed his helmet and cloak and handed them to Jonaq. With steady fingers, he unbuckled the leather straps at his sides. Korim helped him pull the bronze armor over his head, then stood there, cradling it in his arms. Finally, he unsheathed his sword. Turning west, he raised it in salute. It took Rigat a moment to realize he was staring up at the Death Hut.

The Vanel faced him and bowed. "With your permission, I will address my troops."

"Very well."

Rigat smiled when he began reciting the prophecy. A noble gesture and a fitting tribute to the enemy who had defeated him. But as the Vanel continued speaking, his smile faded.

"He will kill without mercy. He will strike down all who offend him. No mortal woman shall call him beloved. No mortal man shall call him friend."

It was in his power to silence the man, but to do so would seem petty and childish. Better to let him finish and have done with this.

The Vanel knelt in the dirt and grasped the hilt of his sword with both hands, carefully placing the tip beneath his breastbone. "Hail the Son of Zhe, the fire-haired god made flesh. Tremble before him and greet him with dread. For with him comes only death."

With a muttered oath, Rigat stepped forward. The Vanel drove the sword home, his smile a rictus of agony. The weight of his body forced the blade so deep that the tip protruded through the back of his tunic. Without a sound, he slowly toppled to the ground.

Rigat quelled the desire to kick the supine body, to obliterate the grimace that still twisted the mouth. He stepped back, gauging the reactions of those around him. All the fight seemed to have left the boy, but the other one—Jonaq—was breathing hard. He could sense the wariness of the other officers, hear the faint growl that circulated from man to man as they gazed from their fallen commander to the one who had ordered his death.

A delicious shiver of fear rippled through him. Othak had used words to turn the tribe against him. The Vanel had attempted to do the same. But if they could use words as weapons, so could he. And with his power, he could ensure that every man—from those clustered around him to the warriors by the lakeshore to those still arrayed on the hillsides—could hear.

"Listen, my warriors, to the words of Rigat, Son of Zhe and King of Zheros. Geriv do Khat is dead. He was a brave man, but he challenged my authority. He paid for that mistake with his life. As will any man who defies me. But I honor this man's bravery and his lifetime of service to our empire, and command you to do the same. Hail, Geriv do Khat!"

A ragged cheer echoed his. He let his gaze drift across the ranks of men, bringing the force of his personality and the strength of his power to bear on all those assembled. The cheer grew louder. Sword hilts thumped against shields, spears pounded the ground, until the valley thundered with the ovation. Only Korim remained silent, staring at him with undisguised hatred.

Rigat held up his hands and waited for the cheering to die. "Let those who did the killing have first choice of the spoils. Salvage any foodstuffs. Slaughter the sheep and chop up the scaling ladders to build a fire. Tonight, we feast!"

This time, it was his name on the lips of the troops, his name that echoed through the valley. The officers clustered around the Vanel's body cheered the loudest, their white-rimmed eyes and stark faces belying their enthusiastic bellows. Full bellies and the promise of loot might win the support of the common warriors, but they had the added incentive of that glimpse into the horrors of the Abyss.

Was it really so easy to control men? The promise of rewards, the threat of punishment? He should have grasped it much sooner. After all, balance was the essence of the tribal religion.

As the officers dispersed to carry out his orders, Jonaq lingered. "My lord? If I may speak to you?"

Rigat waved his permission, inwardly smiling at the transition from the Vanel's ravening wolf to the Son of Zhe's eager and obedient hound.

"What of the others? From the village. Shall we pursue them as ordered?"

Rigat hesitated. His family wouldn't welcome him so soon after Darak's death. But if they were forced to flee from the Zherosi, they would have time to recognize their danger, to realize that he was the only person who could save them.

He couldn't take them to Zheros, but he could find some other place where they would be safe. Perhaps he would whisk all the survivors away. Perhaps—as the boy had said—it was time to show how merciful he could be, even to those who had hurled rocks at him.

A sennight or two. Perhaps a moon. By then, his family would realize just how much they needed him.

"Pursue them," he instructed Jonaq. "But do not engage them. And under no circumstances allow any member of my family to be harmed."

"Just . . . pursue them? But not capture them?"

Rigat nodded, enjoying Jonaq's confusion. He had no intention of taking the man into his confidence. The incomprehensible orders would add to the Son of Zhe's mystery and provide a good test of Jonaq's loyalty. If the man balked, he would find another to command.

"And if they attack us, my lord?"

"A band of women, children, and old folk? Not very likely. But if they do, you may defend yourselves. So long as none of my family is harmed. I want that clearly understood."

Jonaq's mouth worked. He glanced skyward as if seeking inspiration—or courage—then thumped his chest with his fist. "Yes, my lord."

Suppressing a smile, Rigat flung a companionable arm around Jonaq's shoulders and felt him flinch. "I'll make it easy for you."

Gently, he entered Jonaq's spirit. His arm tightened around his shoulder, holding him immobile while he silently calmed the instinctive rush of terror. Then he pictured each member of his family in turn. As an afterthought, he added Lisula and Ennit and Ela. He could hardly allow his mother's best friends and his brother's intended to be killed by accident. Nedia would have to take care of herself; she should have welcomed his advances and spurned Seg's.

He withdrew from Jonaq's spirit, pleased at his fearful expression. "Get one of the mapmakers to make sketches so all your men will be able to recognize them."

"Yes, my lord." Jonaq hesitated, then added, "Forgive me, my lord. I still don't understand why—"

"You don't have to understand. You merely have to obey."

Chapter 54

FROM HER VANTAGE POINT atop the hill, Faelia watched the Zherosi army breaking camp.

For a day and a night, she and Holtik had hidden here. They were too far away to see much, but when the parley began, she had recognized the Vanel's scarlet cloak and Othak's robe. The third man had to be Trath and the other looked to be one of the Vanel's junior officers.

She had held her breath as the four men walked to the Death Hut. When they returned without apparent incident, she began to hope. She even exchanged a brief smile with Holtik. It vanished when the small party of Zherosi followed Trath into the hill fort. Dear gods, what was the old man thinking—letting them inside their defenses? Her fears were confirmed when the horn blared and the rest of the Vanel's warriors charged up the slope.

After a long while, she became aware of the dull pain radiating through her fingers and discovered that she had gouged ten deep furrows in the earth. She was still staring at them when she realized that an odd silence had fallen over the valley.

A figure moved away from the cluster of Zherosi officers. She caught her breath when she spied the red hair. Rigat might have arrived too late to save those in the hill fort, but he could still avenge their deaths.

Impossible that a boy's voice could carry so far. But of course, he wasn't just a boy; he was the Trickster's son.

When she heard him claim responsibility for the Vanel's death, she smiled, wishing she had witnessed it. When the troops looted the village and slaughtered the remainder of the flock, she told herself that Rigat was simply assuaging their blood lust. When she watched the battering rams destroy the walls, and flames engulf the fields of barley, and black smoke stain the sky above the village in which she had spent half her life, she convinced herself that only such drastic measures would keep the Zherosi from falling upon those who had fled.

She had clung to that belief throughout the night. But now, as she watched one komakh break away from the main body of the army and turn east, hope died.

A stonechat called from a nearby clump of gorse, its sharp clack eerily reminiscent of the pebbles that had clattered down the hills during the rockslide. Rigat had defended his people that day; now he encouraged the Zherosi to annihilate them.

Holtik tugged on her arm. "Faelia, we have to go. We have to warn the others."

Fa had almost persuaded her to trust Rigat. She should have known better. He could never be trusted. He was the Trickster's son.

It was midmorning before they reached the encampment. The cold fury at Rigat's betrayal leached all emotion from her voice as she told them about the massacre. Shame as well as caution kept her from revealing Rigat's presence at the hill fort. She would have to tell her family, but they had already been tainted by his actions and she had to protect them from the tribe's enmity.

The women's anguished cries turned shrill when they learned the Zherosi were pursuing them. In the same flat voice, Faelia gave orders to abandon the sheep Ennit had refused to leave behind, to fill their waterskins at the stream, and to gather the few supplies they had brought to sustain them until the Zherosi marched away.

"You'll command the rear guard," she told Selima. "Choose ten men . . ." She looked around and grimaced. "Choose ten of the older boys to go with you." As she turned toward her family, she saw Donncha pushing through the crowd.

"They want you!" she screeched, pointing a trembling forefinger at Keirith. "That's why the raiders came. Why they killed our men and burned our homes. Why don't you give yourself up and save the rest of us?"

When some of the other women took up the cry, Faelia unsheathed her sword. At her nod, Selima and Holtik took up positions on either side of Keirith who was trying in vain to be heard above the commotion.

Lisula stepped in front of Donncha and slapped her. The contentious voices broke off in a collective gasp.

"Don't be a fool, Donncha. If Darak's life didn't satisfy them, do you think Keirith's will? Or should we give them all of Darak's family? And these young men and women who have risked their lives fighting the Zherosi?"

Shaking with emotion, Lisula turned in a slow circle, fixing her fierce gaze on the faces around her. "You know what the Zherosi are capable of. They'll slaughter the children and the old folk. Rape the women and girls. And if any are alive after that, they'll rope them together like beasts and ship them to Zheros to spend the rest of their lives as slaves."

Only the muffled sobbing of a woman and the wail of a babe broke the silence.

Lisula's grim expression softened. "If we turn on each other, the Zherosi have truly conquered us. Our strength lies in remaining together. Our strength lies there." She flung out her hand, pointing south. "When our ancestors came to this land, they found shelter and sustenance in the forest. That is our home. And it's the one place the Zherosi fear. The forest is our past—and our hope for the future."

For Faelia, the flight south was a dreamlike amalgam of the one from Gath's village and that long-ago journey from Eagles Mount. Once again, young Braden, who had helped her herd the villagers toward the pass, darted back and forth along the line, exhorting stragglers, shifting bundles of food and clothing, and making the younger children laugh by pretending it was all a strange game of hide-and-go-seek. And once again, they were accompanied by sheep.

"I'm not leaving them for the gods-cursed Zherosi," Ennit insisted. "We've only food for a few days and we'll have no time to hunt."

She didn't waste breath arguing, but insisted that if the sheep wandered or slowed them down, they would have to be abandoned.

"You worry about the Zherosi. I'll see to my sheep."

And with Lorthan's help, he did, driving the stupid beasts south as relentlessly as she drove the human members of their band.

Late in the afternoon, they spied the first scraggly pines. A few of the women wept. The older children echoed Braden's cheer. The little ones had long since stopped laughing, but even they managed to stifle their whimpers.

"Just a few more miles and we'll be in the forest," Faelia told them.

"And then can we go home?"

It was Blathi, Madig's younger daughter. Before Faelia could reply, Colla took her sister's hand. "We're going to have a new home now."

Colla had lost her mother when the Zherosi attacked her village. Now, both her brother and father were dead and her second home was destroyed. Little wonder her face looked as pinched as an old woman's.

I probably looked the same after I killed that raider all those years ago.

Faelia led them deep into the safety of the forest before giving the order to make camp beside a small stream. She sent Braden and Holtik ahead to scout. To Mirili and Lisula, she gave the responsibility of rationing their food supplies. She considered sending the older boys and girls out with slings and snares, but since they didn't dare light a fire, she let them rest and conserve their strength for the morrow.

Finally, she turned her attention to the boy that Selima had sent from the rear guard. Quelling her impatience at his endless description of the day's march, she finally learned that the Zherosi were more than five miles behind them and had also made camp. She loaded him with six bulging waterskins and even managed a smile when he thanked her effusively for the extra food; no wonder Fa had nicknamed him the Chatterer.

"I'm that hungry I could eat grass," Rendaron assured her. "I tell you, the sheep are the lucky ones. Or were. Not much grass to be had in the forest, is there? I don't suppose you mean to butcher any of them tonight? Nay, of course not. Still, what I wouldn't give for a nice bit of mutton. But we're tough. We'll make the Spirit-Hunter proud."

His face turned bright red. "I . . . forgive me . . . I didn't mean to remind you of your loss. Not that you'd forget. It's just . . . I can't believe he's really gone. He was the greatest man I've ever known. The greatest! Not much of a talker, but . . . well . . . you know. Sorry. Gods."

She leaped into the pause, thanking him for his report and asking him to convey her thanks to Selima for sending someone with such an eye for detail. Selima would detect the sarcasm; Rendaron simply puffed up like a blackcock in the mating season.

Faelia's smile faded as she wandered through the camp in search of her family. She found them sitting a little apart from the others with Lisula, Ennit, and their girls. She accepted a broken nutcake gratefully, but quickly became aware of Keirith's silence. She knew him well enough to realize he was still brooding over Donncha's remarks. Knew, too, that nothing she could say would ease him. Instead, she told them about Rigat.

Keirith's head came up, shock and disbelief warring on his face. Callie offered half a dozen possible explanations. Ennit made her go over and over what she had seen until she wanted to throttle him. Finally, they fell silent, all of them staring at her mother who had said nothing throughout the soft but heated discussion.

Mam glanced around the circle of faces. "Callie's right. There must be an explanation."

Faelia clenched her teeth to bite back a retort. Her mother had always defended Rigat. She had coddled him as a babe. Excused his bad behavior as a child, claiming he was too young to know better. Even now, she refused to see him for what he was—an abomination.

She took the first watch; tired as she was, her mind was too restless for sleep. Twice before she had been forced into the role of leader, once after the flight from Gath's village and again after the ambush near Black Hill. Both times, she had led her people home. Now she was leading them into the unknown, like her father during the quest through the First Forest.

Oddly, the thought comforted her. She was her father's daughter, after all, and the forest was a second home to her. But nearly a hundred lives depended upon her, and she longed for Temet's strength and Fa's wisdom.

Staring up through a break in the pine boughs, she found the Archer. She had always thought of it as Fa's constellation, for both were hunters. And no matter the season, the Archer was always present in the night sky, just as her father had always been the most powerful, enduring presence in her life.

Now he was gone. Yet the Archer maintained his nightly vigil and on the morrow Bel would still rise in the east. After all Fa had done, surely the world should note his passing. A star should fall from the sky. A storm should sweep across the land. Winds should howl their grief.

She could imagine what her father would make of such thoughts: "Aye. Well. A shower of brogac would be nice. Then the world could get drunk in my honor."

Her chuckle turned into a hiccuping sob. She pressed her knuckles against her mouth to stifle it. Later, she would allow herself the luxury of grief. When her family was safe. When the Zherosi had been defeated. When Rigat had been stopped.

The scratchy chorus of night insects ebbed and flowed as she made her way back to camp. Picking her way between the sleeping figures, she heard the whimper of a child, the restless moans of a dreaming woman, the harsh ratchet of snoring men. She shook Callie awake and reminded him to pass along her instructions to the next watch. Then she lay down beside Keirith and closed her eyes.

She never knew what awakened her. Perhaps she had spent enough time with the rebels that the mere crunch of pine needles was enough to disturb her sleep. As she rolled over, two shadowy figures sat up. In silence, Hircha and Mam watched Keirith slip away from camp.

"I alerted the sentries," Faelia whispered. "They'll stop him, Mam."

"He's not going to the Zherosi."

"After what Donncha said—"

"He gave his oath."

They watched him weaving in and out among the trees, little more than a moving shadow in the darkness. When he reached the top of the slope, he simply stood there, barely visible in the light of Gheala's newborn crescent.

"What's he doing?" Faelia whispered.

"Seeking a vision, perhaps," her mother replied. "Or escaping from his dreams."

As Faelia rose, Hircha's hand snagged her wrist. "If you want to help, keep him busy. And away from Donncha and the other malcontents. Let him scout with Holtik. Put him on sentry duty at night. Perhaps he'll be too tired to worry—or dream."

Faelia hesitated, then decided to speak her mind. "There's another way to keep his worries at bay. But you're the only one who can offer him that."

Hircha's fingers tightened on her wrist. "Stay out of it, Faelia."

She returned to her wolfskins and stared up at the Archer until Keirith returned. Her fingers fumbled for his in the darkness and she felt him start, then relax.

Death, she understood. Privation and struggle. The blood-pounding excitement of battle and sex, the bone-deep ache of grief. She would never understand Keirith's complicated relationship with Hircha, any more than she could understand the strange magic he possessed or the demons that haunted his dreams. All she could do was try and protect him from the dangers of this world: the women who accused him of cowardice, the Zherosi who sought his blood—and Rigat, the greatest threat of all.

Chapter 55

JHOLIANNA WELCOMED RIGAT BACK to Zheros with a feast and an invitation to her bedchamber. He left the feast after the fish course, but remained with her all night.

She thought she had seen all his faces: the man-god wild with rage when his wishes were flouted; the wide-eyed newcomer laughing with pleasure over each new experience; the weeping child; the blushing adolescent; the grim-faced avenger. But the dispassionate young man who spent the entire night discussing affairs of state was a stranger.

His questions were thoughtful, his suggestions intelligent. He volunteered to help bring the war in Carilia to an end. Offered his assistance with the upcoming trade negotiations with Lilmia. Weighed the merits of executing the noblemen who had conspired against her versus the benefits of leniency. Promised to visit the estates of the slave owners and ensure that all the Tree People who wished to remain in Zheros were allowed to do so. But he shied away from discussing the northern provinces, save to urge her to appoint a new Vanel who would continue Geriv do Khat's practice of buying the loyalty of wavering chiefs with grain.

"Why change an effective policy just because the commander who devised it is dead?"

He showed the same lack of emotion when he learned that she was planning a state funeral for Vazh do Havi.

"People will expect you to honor him. Just don't expect me to be there when you do."

"And your family?" she asked, daring his displeasure.

"I'll deal with them in my own way."

She knew enough not to pursue the subject.

After that, she rarely saw him during the day, although he usually returned to her in the evening. Only then, as he boasted about his successes in Carilia, did she catch a glimpse of the eager boy who had taken her to that northern forest. But mostly, he was restless and edgy, prowling about her bedchamber like a caged beast.

When he was in Pilozhat, Nekif brought her daily reports of Rigat crying out in his sleep, Rigat kicking a slave for failing to chill his berry juice properly. When he was in Carilia, birds brought messages from the Vanel of the Eastern Army that mixed extravagant praise for the Son of Zhe's tactics with carefully neutral descriptions of similar bouts of temper.

She burned the messages and displayed unfeigned delight each time Rigat returned to her with the account of his latest triumph. At this rate, the Carilians would be subdued before the second harvest. Later, alone in her bed, she wondered if these proud recitations of his accomplishments repeated a pattern begun long ago with his mother. Although she would sometimes catch Rigat watching her with his old fascination, he failed to respond to her tentative overtures. She accepted the change in their relationship with equanimity; if it ensured a victory in Carilia, she could play the surrogate mother as easily as she had played the lover.

She appointed a new Vanel for the north and a new Khonsel to oversee security. The Vanel of the Eastern Army reported that the assassin had finally been identified—the son of a Carilian nobleman who had lost both his father and brother in the war. Although her spies were still trying to learn if the man had acted alone, the announcement helped dissipate the tension that had pervaded the court since the attempted assassination.

Commerce boomed in the wake of the victories in Carilia. She missed the brusque efficiency and common sense of Vazh do Havi. And the mocking humor of the Supplicant; no one seemed to know where she was. But Jholianna reminded herself that neither was as vital to the empire as the Son of Zhe.

On the evening before negotiations with Lilmia were to begin, Rigat presented her with a small leather bag. Smiling, she watched him tug open the drawstrings. When he opened his lightly clenched fist, three tiny white balls, whiskered in wood ash, rolled across the polished stone of the table. In disbelief, she stared at the fortune that came to rest against the sweating bronze pitcher.

"Seems like a lot of fuss about worms," he said.

The small island nation of Lilmia had one export, the precious fabric of the same name, and its ruler guarded her monopoly with such diligence that Jholianna's spies had been unable to steal a single cocoon in which the insects bred. Each year, she was tempted to cancel the shipment, and each year, she relented, knowing it would only increase the hunger for the fabric and create an illegal market for it in Zheros. So she sat through the haggling, a fixed smile on her face, and tried to charm the ambassador into a few meager concessions.

"How did you do it?"

"How do you think? I stole them. Gods, it was hot inside that hut. I don't know how the children could breathe. They use children to tend the cocoons, did you know that? You should have seen their faces when I appeared."

The mask vanished as he grinned. Then the frowning stranger returned. "I couldn't manage to snatch a dewberry bush. When the moths hatch, we'll have nothing for them to feed on. But maybe the sight of these will encourage the Lilmian ambassador to be generous."

She leaped up and raced around the table to embrace him. When he stiffened, she let her arms fall. But as she stepped back, he seized her hand. She had only a moment to glimpse his desperate eyes and twisted mouth before he pushed her down on the rug.

Rough fingers fumbled with her gown and spread her thighs. His face averted, he took her with frantic haste. Then he rolled off her, adjusted his khirta, and hurried out.

She removed her crumpled gown and walked slowly down the stairs to her bathing room. As she drizzled a few drops of sweet spike oil into a bowl of water, she considered whether to go after him. By the time she had cleaned and dried herself, she had decided to risk his anger.

Lady Alikia was waiting, a nightdress over one arm and a boar bristle brush in her hand. "He went to his bedchamber," she whispered as she eased the tangles from Jholianna's hair.

Jholianna nodded and raised her arms to allow Lady Alikia to slip the nightdress over her head. Disdaining slippers or robe, she padded barefoot down the corridor, past guards who discreetly averted their faces.

She hesitated in the doorway of his apartments. Then she saw him through the draperies, a dark silhouette against the deepening blue of the evening sky.

He straightened when he heard her footsteps, but continued staring north. His body was rigid with tension, his fingers curved like claws over the top of the stone wall.

Careful not to touch him, she asked, "Why don't you go to her?"

His quick intake of breath betrayed his surprise. "I'm not ready yet."

"But you watch her. You watch all of them."

After a long hesitation, he nodded.

"She's your mother. And you love her. Do you think I resent that?"

"No."

"Then what? If I've offended you—"

"No. It's just . . . I can't keep both of you in my mind."

"I don't understand."

"When I see her, all I want is to go to her. To go home. Back. And when I'm with you . . ." His hands clenched into fists. "I thought it would help if I stayed away. From both of you. If I . . . if you and I didn't . . ." He took a deep breath. "I want you both. But I can't have that. And I can't choose."

She risked touching him then. A fine tremor coursed through his arm, steady as the purr of a cat. "I'm not greedy. I can share your love. But if you're happier apart from me . . ."

For the first time, he faced her. "What do you get from me? Not Zheros. You. I know it's not . . . the lovemaking isn't . . ."

Again, the boy resurfaced, red-faced and stammering. She found herself recalling those first few moons with Jholin—almost as young, certainly as impatient—then resolutely pushed all thoughts of him away.

"Did you open a portal the first time you tried? Or understand the language of birds? Lovemaking is a skill like any other. It takes practice. And patience. My experience is limited, but I'm told young men are notoriously lacking in patience. Although I believe they generally enjoy the practice."

That surprised a smile from him. Encouraged, she took his hand. "Be patient, Rigat. In time, you'll have everything you desire."

"And what do you desire?"

"You."

"And a child?"

She caught her breath. "That . . . that's not possible."

"I'm the son of a god. Who knows what's possible?"

He led her to the bed where he proved he could be both patient and tender. And when he brought his power to their lovemaking, he gave her greater pleasure than she had ever known. But when she woke near dawn, he was standing on the balcony again, his body quivering with tension as he stared north.

She knew then that she would never truly possess him as long as his mother lived.

Chapter 56

BOUND BY HIS OATH to his mother, Keirith made no attempt to escape, but each day, the weight of the accusing stares grew heavier. Scouting with Holtik allowed him to avoid them during the day. Sentry duty at night postponed sleep, which brought twisted dreams of blood-drenched battles and Xevhan's insidious whispers about his cowardice.

His father's death, the slaughter in the village—it all

seemed as unreal as this endless flight to nowhere. They had hoped the Zherosi would abandon the hunt once they reached the forest, but they knew from Selima's runners that the komakh was still pursuing them. Never closer than a mile behind the rear guard, never farther than three, the Zherosi seemed content to trail them without closing in for the kill.

After a sennight, Faelia risked calling a day of rest. While the boys and girls gathered deadwood for a fire, Callie helped Ennit slaughter three of the ewes. The novelty of full bellies helped eased the tension in camp. When Holtik and Braden returned the next morning from carrying food to the rear guard, they reported that the Zherosi had never stirred from their camp.

"They must have seen our smoke," Faelia said. "Gods, they're close enough to have smelled the meat. What are they doing?"

"Why don't we find out?" Keirith suggested. "All warriors grumble about orders. If we can get close enough—"

"They post sentries at night. Selima's seen them."

"But not many." Keirith had heard that report, too. "And they won't expect us to try and infiltrate. I could slip past them—"

"Nay. We'll stay here. Another day. And see what happens."

For a day they sat in their camp while the Zherosi remained in theirs. After that, Faelia reluctantly agreed to send him and Holtik to find out what Selima knew.

When they reached her camp at midday, Selima greeted him with a fierce hug. "I hope you brought more mutton."

Keirith smiled and shoved the bag into her arms. "And here I thought you were just happy to see me."

"I am. I'm surrounded by children."

The recruits protested with noisy good humor, clearly used to Selima's chaffing. Although she was probably Faelia's age, that still gave her ten years over the most senior member of her band. To compensate, they were all attempting to grow beards; the scraggly fluff on their cheeks made them look like a flock of fledglings.

"They're a pretty worthless lot," Selima continued with a heavy sigh. "I don't know what Darak was thinking."

Her breath hissed in. Keirith interrupted her stammered

apology to remark that his father had always been fond of children, and the awkward moment passed.

Over a shared meal of cold mutton, it soon became clear that they were as mystified by the Zherosi tactics as Faelia.

"When we move, they move," Selima said. "When we stop, they stop. I've let them come within bowshot, Keirith! But they just stand there, waiting for us to shoot first."

"Do you?"

"Once—over their heads. I wish Faelia would let me kill a few. Maybe that would drive them off."

"Or bring them down on us."

"Aye. But still . . ." Selima spat. "Better a real fight than this. It makes no sense."

The red-haired lad named Owan spat, too. "The Spirit-Hunter always said the Zherosi plan everything. So there must be a reason."

Keirith kept his suspicions to himself, determined to broach them first to his family.

As talk turned to other subjects, his father's name came up again and again. Tentative until they gauged his reaction, the fledglings were soon vying to offer anecdotes about the Spirit-Hunter.

"It was like he could smell danger on the wind."

"And his eyes—they could see right through you."

"Remember when he spoke in the village? His voice made my ballocks quiver."

"Your ballocks are always quivering!"

"He patted me on the shoulder."

A respectful silence greeted Owan's words. The boys' faces grew dreamy as if each imagined himself the recipient of that approving pat.

"That day we came back from scouting. Me, Lendon, and Cradaig." Owan nodded to the boys flanking him.

It was a simple story of panicked boys reporting the approach of a Zherosi war party, but the hushed voices of the three who took turns telling it and the faces of those listening changed it into something almost magical.

If Owan lived to start a family, he would tell the tale to his grandchildren. By then, the approving pat would have become a hug and the decision to head north an example of the Spirit-Hunter's godlike wisdom. That was the way with tales, always changing and growing, no matter what the Memory-Keepers recited. And that was why his father had insisted on deflating the myth when he told the tale of his quest to the children of Eagles Mount, emphasizing his fear instead of his bravery, his doubts rather than his certainty of success.

"They need to know there's no shame in being afraid," Fa once told him. "It's how you meet the fear that counts. If they grow up thinking only great men can accomplish great things, they'll never dare anything for fear of failing."

The Memory-Keeper lived on in Callie, the hunter and warrior in Faelia. But what part of Fa lived on in him?

The boys fell silent. A sigh eased around the circle. Even Selima's face was soft with recollection. But it was Holtik who said, "You knew him best, Keirith. Would you share a story about him?"

Keirith's gaze moved across the eager, expectant faces. With the Zherosi so close, they didn't need to hear about the man who had screamed when Morgath hacked off his fingers. A tale from Keirith's youth would only remind them of families they might never see again. But perhaps he could give these boys a tale from Fa's youth, one that might give them a source of strength in the coming days.

He cleared his throat and began to speak of his father's vision quest. How he had expected to find a wildcat or a fox when he went into the forest, for they were solitary creatures as he was. How he waited three days and nights, crouched in a thicket, fighting hunger and thirst and the fear that came with every snapping twig and rustle in the underbrush. He described his father's surprise at hearing the she-wolf call his name, and later, the realization that she had come to remind him that he was not alone, but a member of a pack. And he spoke of the comfort and wisdom that his vision mate had offered—on the treeless moors, on the plains of Zheros, even in Chaos.

The boys' silence made him fear he had failed them. Then Lendon looked up. Absently stroking the birthmark on his cheek, he said, "I found a bear on my vision quest. Some of the other boys laughed. Because I was small for my age." His defiant look dared any of them to comment.

"But our Tree-Father said it was because my spirit was fierce."

Owan elbowed him in the ribs. "And because you'd eat anything."

Keirith listened to their bantering, their shared memories of vision quests and hunts and the villages they had left behind. And for the first time in moons, he felt at peace. Talking about Fa had eased his grief, and realizing he had banished the boys' fears—if only for a little while—gave him a greater sense of accomplishment than his visions ever had. The same quiet joy he had first experienced after healing Hua.

When they left Selima's camp near sunset, Keirith carried that joy with him. It shattered when they arrived to find the main camp in turmoil. His mam drew him away from the knot of wailing women and told him Donncha was dead.

"Dead? How?"

"I don't know. She took a nap this afternoon and never woke up."

A shrill cry made them turn. Catha was clutching her babe to her breast, but one hand came up to point at him. "It was your doing! Donncha spoke against you and you killed her."

"Keirith wasn't even in camp!" Callie exclaimed.

"Donncha was old," Ennit added. "For days, she's been complaining about her shortness of breath. Likely, her heart gave out. You should be glad she was granted a peaceful death instead of accusing Keirith of murder."

"Who knows what he can do with his magic?" Catha insisted. "He cast out the spirit of a Zherosi priest, didn't he? And now he's done the same to poor Donncha."

"That is not so!"

Duba's voice shocked them all into silence. Even after Keirith helped reclaim her broken spirit, she seldom spoke to anyone save Alada and their orphans. In all his life, he had never heard her voice raised in anger.

"What do you know of Keirith's magic?" Duba demanded. "I felt him—searching for me through the emptiness that filled my spirit after my boy died. I know his power. The light he carries inside of him. And the darkness, too."

As he had done during his other spirit-healings, he had opened himself to Duba, sharing his pain and fears to ease hers. But hearing her speak of that connection made him feel naked before the tribe.

"We all have our dark places. Our secrets. I've touched Keirith's. And I know he did not do this. Now stop upsetting the children, Catha, and help us gather stones for a cairn."

Catha's face crumpled. Arun awkwardly patted his mother's shoulder and led her away. Slowly, the others dispersed, the priestesses to prepare Donncha's body, the women and children to gather stones.

His mother touched Duba's arm and murmured something. Duba smiled and shook her head. When Keirith thanked her, she patted his cheek, as if he were one of her orphans. Then she and Alada herded their little ones away, smoothing hair and wiping tear-streaked cheeks.

His mother stared after her. She looked old and tired, but under his scrutiny, she straightened, thrusting out her pointed chin with the same stubborn defiance that had helped her survive starving winters and illness and death. He had never seen her weep for Fa, but sometimes he caught her clutching the bag of charms she wore about her neck. Her hand came up now, fingers closing convulsively around the doeskin.

"Mam . . ."

"Not here."

He followed her along the stream until they were out of earshot. For a long moment, she stared at the water trickling over the stones. Without looking at him, she asked, "Do you think Rigat killed her?"

He could not bring himself to speak the truth. "I don't know."

"He's settling old scores, isn't he?"

"I think so."

His mother astonished him by smiling. "Then he hasn't turned against us. He's still trying to protect his family."

And if we speak against him? How long before he turns on us?

But how could he say that when his mam's face was alight with hope?

Instead, he asked, "And the Zherosi? They could have

caught us—killed us—days ago. He must have told them
not to. But if that's true, why bother sending them after
us?"

"A test, perhaps. Of our loyalty. Our love."

"Love shouldn't require a test."

"But it's tested every day. In little ways, mostly. But also
in the hard choices we make."

He nodded, uncomfortably reminded of the choice the
Trickster had forced upon her, but he couldn't help asking,
"And Fa's death? Was that a test, too?"

Again, her hand closed around the bag of charms.
"Darak was the center of my world—and yours. If we can
forgive Rigat for that, surely we can forgive him anything."

"Killing an old woman whose only crime was to speak
aloud what others thought?"

Her gaze slid away from his.

Abandoning his resolve, he demanded, "Where does it
end, Mam? Will Catha be next? Or Faelia?"

"He would never harm his sister!" When he was silent,
she said, "Nay, Keirith. I won't believe that." But doubt
shadowed her expression.

"There are limits to love, Mam."

Her fingers worried the bag of charms, but once again,
her chin came up. "Then we must find him, Keirith. And
reclaim him. Before we reach those limits. Or Rigat does."

The tribe moved east as soon as the cairn was built. "It
will only remind them of Donncha's accusations," Faelia
told him. But she also confided that she wanted to find a
more defensible site. "If Mam's right—if Rigat's testing
us—he'll soon tire of this game. When he does, we must
be ready."

None of the sites satisfied her, but after three days on
the move, the children were so exhausted that they had to
call a halt. Ennit slaughtered two more sheep while the
men hunted and the boys and girls fished and set snares.
They smoked most of the meat and fish; Faelia insisted
they have food that would last if they had to flee.

During the day, Keirith supervised the fishing with Dirna,

but every day at sunset, he slipped away from camp, seeking stillness and solitude—and Natha. Where once he had struggled to obtain a vision, they had come with disturbing regularity since he had fled the village. Three times, Natha had shown him the eagle chicks. Now, instead of the elder killing the younger, they battled each other with bloodstained beaks and claws.

Only once had he Seen something else. In that vision, he stood on a barren hill, watching a line of people walk one by one over the edge of a cliff. A woman raised her hand in farewell. Although he could not see her face, her belly was big with child. Suddenly, he found himself in a cave, staring down at his sleeping parents. His mother's face was peaceful, but his father's was turned away. Fa looked oddly small, as if age had shrunk him. When he walked toward them, the vision abruptly ended.

He hoped the image of the people vanishing over the cliff was a metaphor for the flight of his tribe rather than an omen of its annihilation. He could make little sense of the part about Mam and Fa. Still, if they could never lie together again, perhaps it meant he and Rigat would never battle.

"Foolish boy," Natha chided him. "The message is clear to a hatchling. You simply refuse to accept it."

"But how can I accept it if it means Rigat's death or mine?"

"You are confusing the message with the outcome."

"Can I change the outcome?"

"Is the future fixed?"

It was like the years had rolled back and he was once again Gortin's apprentice. Only it was Natha answering questions with questions, and scolding him for his impatience.

He envied Callie who could comfort the tribe with the ancient story of their people's flight north. And his mam and Hircha who soothed their bruises and scrapes with poultices. His visions offered only the promise of death.

The promise was fulfilled on their fourth evening in the new camp. The shouts shattered his trance and sent him racing downstream. His steps slowed when he discovered the entire tribe clustered together on the bank. The women

backed away to let him pass; the fear in their eyes sickened him.

Mam and Hircha crouched on either side of a woman.
Even before he saw her face, he knew it was Catha.

Dirna sidled up to him. In a few moons, she had lost her
father, her uncle Nemek, her cousin Nionik, and Adinn,
the man she'd hoped to marry. Now her aunt was dead as
well. Although her face was stricken, her voice trembled
only a little as she whispered, "She was washing the baby's
clouts. We saw her slip and hit her head. By the time we
reached her . . ."

Catha's wet hair straggled across the grass like strands
of lakeweed. His mam smoothed it and brushed her palm
across Catha's face, closing the shocked, staring eyes. Although no voices were raised in accusation, everyone had
to be thinking the same thing: Catha had spoken against
him, and now she—like Donncha—was dead.

They buried her that night and broke camp at dawn.
Wila nursed Catha's babe with hers. Mirili told Keirith she
knew it was not his fault, that Catha's behavior had become
increasingly erratic since the deaths of Nemek and young
Nionik. A few people speculated that Catha had killed herself, but Keirith knew that was impossible. Little Ailsa was
less than two moons old. Catha would never have left her
motherless.

He helped the others set up camp before heading upstream, uncertain if he wanted to seek another vision or
simply escape the brooding tension. The splashing water
soothed him and the trunk of the tree-brother at his back
lent him strength. Pine boughs whispered in the breeze and
sunlight danced across the water, playful as a child. This
was the kind of magic his father had loved, the ordinary
magic of the forest that he'd worshiped as reverently as the
gods who had created it.

He let himself drift, his senses mesmerized by the slap
of water against rock, the hiss of foam dissolving in the
shallows, the ever-changing play of colors as the water
passed from light to shadow: sparking gold and silver, darkening to a dull greenish gray, foaming white over the rocks.

His smile faded as the foam coalesced into shapes. Un-
gainly wings sprayed water droplets as they flapped. Sharp

beaks sprouted. Two feathered heads twisted toward him. Two pairs of eyes stared back at him.

The blue-eyed chick chuckled. "How's it going to end this time, Keirith?"

He stared back, too shocked to reply.

<Well?>

This time the voice spoke inside him.

<Will you kill me? Or will I kill you?>

He whispered Rigat's name and felt another chuckle resonate in his spirit. Beneath it, the power smoldered, stronger than ever. If Rigat choose to turn it against him, the power would destroy him. Just as it was consuming Rigat.

<Nay, brother. I control the power, not the other way round.>

The teasing voice carried echoes of Fellgair's mockery, but beneath the confidence, Keirith sensed a throb of loneliness. Immediately, the sensation vanished and with it, Rigat's presence.

"Nay! Don't go!" He staggered to his feet, whirling around in search of his brother.

Rigat leaned against the trunk of a pine. His face was thin and bronzed from exposure to the sun. It was as if all the softness had been burned away, and with it, the boy who had teased him for his inability to walk quietly through the underbrush, who had eagerly proposed that he play eagle and spy on the Zherosi, who had dreamed that, together, they could change the world.

His brother's glance wandered from the stream to the sky—everywhere except in his direction. Yet Keirith was certain Rigat was studying him covertly, gauging his reactions. How many times had Rigat invaded his spirit without his knowledge? Often enough to know about the vision of the eagle chicks.

He suppressed the flash of anger, along with the questions he wanted to ask: about Donncha and Catha, the attack on the hill fort, the Zherosi's senseless pursuit. And Fa.

It would always lie between them, tainting their relationship. Keirith knew his father would be the first to urge him to find a way to salvage the love they had once shared.

Knew, too, that any sort of confrontation would drive Rigat away. But he couldn't help blurting, "Why wouldn't you save him?"

Pine needles rustled as Rigat swung his foot in a slow arc. "You don't understand. I couldn't save him. The healing doesn't last. Not when the wound is mortal. It always needs more. And if I had no more to give . . ."

Rigat could have given them more time with Fa, but that might simply have prolonged his suffering—a day or two of health before the inevitable decline began. Fa had always recalled his father's slow march toward death with horror. Keirith could never have forced him to endure that—even if it meant losing him sooner.

He thrust aside the memory of his father's face, twisted in agony, to recall his mother's, desperate and hopeful as she urged him to reclaim his brother.

"Come back to us," he said.

Rigat started, but quickly converted his reaction into a shrug. "Why?"

"You don't belong with them."

"They worship me."

"But they don't love you."

Rigat studied the dark furrow his foot had carved in the earth. "And you do?"

"Aye."

For the first time, his brother met his gaze. The bloodshot blue eyes searched his face. For all he knew, the power searched his spirit as well, intent on uncovering any doubts.

"Come back to us," he repeated. "We're your family. Your tribe."

Rigat's fingers clenched in his khirta. "They hate me. Not you and Mam. Or Callie. But the rest of them. Even Faelia."

"Nay."

"They drove me from the village."

"They were frightened."

"They wanted to believe Othak's lies!" Rigat slammed his fist into the trunk of the pine. A tiny shower of dead needles drifted onto his head and shoulders. "Just like they wanted to believe Donncha's lies. And Catha's."

Keirith closed his eyes. Although Faelia had not seen

Othak after the massacre, Keirith had always suspected that Rigat had killed him. Given Othak's role in driving Rigat from the village—and Mam's suspicions about his involvement in Gortin's death—Keirith found it difficult to blame Rigat for that. But Donncha was an old woman with a vicious tongue, and Catha, just a frightened young mother. Rigat had deliberately snuffed out their lives. How could he forgive that? How could he encourage this vengeful boy to return to them when any slight—however small—might bring down his wrath?

He didn't know the limits of love, but his mam still believed Rigat could be reclaimed. And for her sake, he had to try.

Keirith opened his eyes to find Rigat watching him. Immediately, his brother's gaze slid away and he began shaking pine needles from the folds of his khirta.

"Give up the power," Keirith urged him. "Before it destroys you. Give it up and come back to us."

Three times for a charm. But was any charm powerful enough to influence the son of a god? Or avert the death his visions foretold?

"I'll stand by you," Keirith promised.

Rigat's head came up. For a long moment, his brother studied him. "Will you? I wonder."

With a flick of his forefinger, Rigat opened a portal and was gone.

Chapter 57

RIGAT SANK DOWN AGAINST THE boulder where Darak had crouched the morning of their hunt—the last completely happy day he could remember. As exciting as the kill had been, it was Darak's pride in him and the triumph they had shared that had made the day so joyful.

Would he still be proud now? Or as horrified as Keirith?

The song of the stream sounded like the babble of a fretful child; the breeze in the pines, an ominous whisper. He told himself that his unsettling encounter with Keirith had tainted his perception. But he hadn't imagined the dark emotions that shadowed his brother's spirit: horror at the deaths of Donncha and Catha; fear and envy of a power so much greater than his; and the anguish of losing Darak, still as raw as a fresh wound, an insurmountable barrier to any reconciliation.

Yet beneath it all, reluctant and barely acknowledged, he had touched love.

"Come back to us."

But only if he gave up his power. The power Keirith claimed would destroy him.

When he'd learned that the Unmaker was draining Fellgair's power, he had feared his would dissipate as well. If anything, it felt stronger. He could always feel it now, flickering inside of him. As he called upon it, the tension in his body drained away, replaced by the same joy, the same comfort he had once found in this place. How could that be bad? His spirit might be weary and his nerves frayed, but that was a small price to pay for all that he had accomplished.

Why couldn't his brother understand that he had killed Donncha to protect him? He'd even arranged Catha's death to look like an accident to prevent anyone from blaming Keirith.

It had been a mistake to seek him out. Keirith had always been ambivalent about his own gift, and his too-tender conscience made it impossible for him to understand that power must sometimes be used to punish the guilty as well as protect the innocent.

He had hoped this last half-moon would show his family how much they needed him, would help them understand why he couldn't save Darak. But only his mam had remained steadfast.

He would go to her. Let her love soothe him like his power. But first, he would go to the Summerlands and fetch those healing plants for her. After Darak's healing, he had been too weak to open a portal. Now it would be easy.

The pines in front of him blurred, as if tears distorted his vision. Then their trunks became distinct again. Frowning, he raised his hand and tried again. The air felt impossibly thick; it was like moving his finger through water. Yet his power surged eagerly in response to his summons.

He fixed the Summerlands in his mind. Pictured the waterfall cascading over the ledges. The long shadows of the oaks stretching across the pool. The vibrant green of the grass and the sparkle of quartz in the rocks.

A third time, the portal refused to open.

"I cannot go to the Summerlands," Fellgair had said. "The way is barred to me."

Clearly, the way was barred to him as well.

Despite the warmth of the afternoon, Rigat shivered. Then he shook his head impatiently. If he couldn't open a portal directly into the Summerlands, he would find another way there.

It was nearly sunset before he managed to carve a gateway into the First Forest. Shaken by his difficulty in opening the portal, he peered at the grove.

In the slanting rays of red-gold light, the One Tree seemed to glow. Shadowy Watchers darted between the trees. Birds sang a final chorus to the fading glory of the day. And in the midst of the dead leaves that carpeted the grove, a brilliant blue path of flowers stretched west from the One Tree to his feet.

Speedwell. Of course. Tinnean had offered Darak that sign when they parted all those years ago. He must have done so again, allowing Darak to go to his death knowing his brother still remembered and loved him.

Would Keirith offer such proof of his love if I were dying?

As he blinked back tears, he noticed a mound of leaves nestled among the roots of the One Tree. Had Darak sat there during his final day of life? It seemed such a lonely death—a world away from his family, with only the trees and the Watchers as witnesses. And Fellgair.

He abandoned me to go to Darak. Just like he's abandoned me now.

The pathetic little nest drew him, but the path of speedwell blocked his way. Reluctant to crush the flowers, he stepped carefully through the portal and closed it behind him.

The light in the grove faded. The birds fell silent. Even the Watchers hesitated. Although the sky was still the same deep blue, it was as if twilight had suddenly fallen.

Despite his uneasiness, he refused to be thwarted now. Dead leaves crunched as he stepped off the path. He turned to inspect the damage and caught his breath.

Two black shapes marred the blue, as if the weight of his sandals had not only crushed the speedwell, but scorched it beyond recognition. As he watched, the devastation crept slowly toward the One Tree. The brilliant blue of the flowers faded. The heart-shaped leaves trailed limply on the ground. When the dying path reached Darak's nest, the leaves erupted in a tiny whirlwind, swirling like those he had made dance so many years ago.

As he hurried toward it, the Watchers streamed out of the trees to surround the One Tree. The dance subsided, scattering leaves over the exposed roots, but the Watchers only grew more frantic.

A dark form leaped at him, then retreated as he stumbled aside. To his shock, more rushed at him. Spectral limbs buffeted him like gusts of wind. Waves of cold assailed him as the Watchers passed into him and through him, trailing fear and malevolence in their wake.

Anger flared and with it, his power. He hurled it at an approaching Watcher, which dissipated like the slugs in Chaos. His grim satisfaction turned to panic as the others renewed their attack. He staggered away from them and tripped over a root. Flinging out his hand, he touched bark.

The Watchers froze. Beneath his palm, the Tree-Lords' thrumming energy raced as wildly as his heartbeat. The song of the World Tree faltered. Then Rigat felt Tinnean's energy swell and pressed both hands against the trunk. Tinnean would tell them he had not come here with any evil intent, that he had simply defended himself against an unprovoked attack.

The song of the World Tree throbbed inside him, relentless as death, slow as rot eating through heartwood, the energy of the world that moved with the unhurried patience of the ages. It crawled over his body, scouring skin, gnawing through bone. It penetrated his spirit, illuminating the dark places, scorching them with pitiless fire.

The World Tree screamed.

From the Tree-Lords and Tinnean came answering screams. From the Watchers and the trees in the grove came a circle of relentless, unforgiving cries. Birds erupted from branches. Animals crashed through the underbrush, maddened. The scream of the World Tree lanced through Rigat, through the First Forest, through every being created by the Maker since the world's first dawning, a howl of anguish and despair that sent him staggering backward.

In the sudden silence, the Watchers melted back into the trees. The birds returned to their roosts. But the scream echoed inside of Rigat, thudding like a second heartbeat.

"You should not have come here."

Fellgair's voice sounded weary. Rigat had not seen him since the coronation. Nor had he sought him out, secretly fearing his displeasure at the choices he had made, the lives he had taken. Now, he wanted to run to him and let his father shield him from the horror of the Tree-Lords and the revulsion of the World Tree.

Instead, he took a moment to steady his breathing and arrange his features into some semblance of calm. Then he turned.

"Dear gods . . ."

Patches of pale flesh peeked out between the matted clumps of fur on Fellgair's shrunken body. Scraggly locks of white hair clung to the balding head. A fretwork of lines marred his face. But the golden eyes were the same.

"They fear you," Fellgair said. "And what you're becoming."

Hiding his terror, Rigat demanded, "And what is that?"

"A creature of Chaos."

"You're the one who said I had to make choices! And I have. Hard choices. With little enough help from you. And what about all the good I've done? I'm bringing the war in Carilia to an end. I won trading concessions from Lilmia. Good gods, I even carved irrigation canals through Zheros to keep the crops watered. I'm bringing order, not chaos."

"And what of the children of the Oak and Holly?"

"I freed them from slavery, didn't I? A ship is on its way north now, carrying them home. Some of them. Those who wanted to go."

"But what kind of life awaits them?"

"A better life than they had in Zheros!"

"And your dream of peace?"

Rigat winced. "Peace requires sacrifice."

"Is that what Darak was? And Vazh? And Geriv? And—"

"That's not fair!" His voice broke. "I'm not a monster."

"No. Of course not." Fellgair sighed. "I'm sorry, Rigat. I've failed you."

"You gave me life and power and the skill to use it. Thanks to you, I'm changing the world."

"Yes. Thanks to me." For a long moment, Fellgair simply stared at the roots of the One Tree. Then he roused himself. "So. What will you do next?"

"I want . . . I'm going to see my mother."

He sounded like a small, scared child, but the encounter with the World Tree had shaken him badly. And Fellgair's words only undermined his confidence further.

"I'm glad. Listen to her counsel, Rigat. She's far wiser than I am." Fellgair laid his palm against the trunk of the One Tree and recoiled. "We don't belong here."

"That will change," Rigat replied with more assurance than he felt. "In time."

And he could change as well. He would prove that to his family—to the whole tribe—by calling off the hunt.

He summoned his power, eager to leave the One Tree behind. Then he hesitated. "Can I stop it? What's happening to you?"

"It's too late for me. But you still have time to change your path."

Rigat glanced at the dead speedwell and shuddered.

The portal opened easily, as if the First Forest was eager to be rid of him.

Chapter 58

IN GRIANE'S DREAM, Rigat stood knee-deep among pink spikes of foxtails, his hair blazing in the sunlight.
<Come to me, Mam. Please come.>

She knew it was the glade Faelia had discovered while she was hunting. Knew, too, the trail that would take her there. Yet when she awoke, she quelled the urge to rush away from camp and joined Mother Narthi and Hircha at the fire pit. They spent the morning melting the beeswax the older children had gathered and mixing in handfuls of knitbone leaves to make an ointment for the burns and scrapes and rashes incurred almost daily.

Their work was frequently interrupted as folk sought help for ailments ranging from moon flow cramping to morning sickness to the joint-ill. With their dwindling supply of barley reserved for nursing mothers and toddlers, it seemed half the tribe was costive.

"Our bowels trouble us more than the Zherosi," Hircha muttered as she brewed up another decoction of dandelion root and dock.

Blessing Hircha for giving her an excuse to leave camp, Griane wiped her hands on her skirt. "I'll see if I can find some more." It was the wrong season for harvesting the roots, but her supplies would run out long before the Fall Balancing.

"I'll go," Hircha replied.

"I'm not an invalid, girl. I'll just follow the stream east for a bit. See if I find a patch of open ground. You see to these folk. Get Colla to help."

Madig's daughter had a gift with plants, perhaps from nursing her father. In the moons after the raid, the girl had shadowed Griane so persistently that she began instructing her in treating simple ailments. Although Colla was still too young to become her apprentice, she valued the girl's help and knew the work offered a distraction from grief.

No one asked where she was going; the tribe was used to the sight of her scouring the woods with her doeskin bag slung across her chest. She paused beside the stream to fill her waterskin. As soon as she was out of sight, she veered south toward the glade, only to draw up short when she saw Callie and Ela.

Their guilty expressions made her smile. Everyone knew when the two slipped away and had entered a quiet conspiracy to give the lovers some privacy. Since Faelia had warned Callie that it was too dangerous to leave camp after dark, they confined their lovemaking to the daylight, oblivious of the fond looks and knowing smiles that followed them as they casually wandered into the trees.

Griane wondered if Ela had confided her secret to Callie. She had suspected for some time, even before Ela came to her to request a brew to ease her unsettled stomach. She wished now that she had shared her suspicions with Darak; the knowledge that his line would continue would have brightened his last days. But mostly, she was happy that Callie and Ela had found joy during this dark time.

Callie cleared his throat. "What are you gathering today, Mam?"

Since they had seen the direction she was heading, she replied, "Foxtails. There's a glade south of camp."

"You know Faelia doesn't like people wandering off alone."

"I'm not wandering. And it's only a short walk. I'll be back soon."

Still frowning, Callie nodded. She patted his cheek, then carefully plucked a leaf from his hair. Ela blushed. Callie's frown became an abashed smile. She kissed them both and walked on.

Excitement and trepidation built with every step. Keirith had told her about his meeting with Rigat. It was a measure of his trust in Hircha that he had included her in the conversation as well. Keirith had viewed the meeting as a test and believed he had failed it. Today's meeting would be another test; how well she met it would determine whether she could convince Rigat to return to them.

An empire worshiped him now. A queen bowed before him. Rigat had been unwilling to sacrifice his power for Darak. Would he give it up for her?

Perhaps it was too much to expect. Perhaps she should only ask him to call off their pursuers. Even those who had refused to listen to Donncha and Catha were whispering now, wondering how much longer they would have to run.

"People are frightened," Lisula had said only yesterday. "And Faelia's refusal to speak with them only makes it worse. Talk to her, Griane."

Faelia was a good fighter and wise in the ways of the forest, but she knew little about leading a tribe. Temet had a cause to unite his band. Darak had his stature as the Spirit-Hunter and a lifetime of leadership. If the two men had chafed at the interminable meetings of their councils, they had understood the necessity of involving their people in the important decisions facing them.

Griane had tried to convince Faelia to do the same. "If they feel they have a say in their future, they'll follow you more willingly."

"When have women ever had a say in their future?" Faelia had demanded.

The same resentment she had been nursing since childhood. Women were not allowed to hunt or find a vision mate. Unless they chose the path of healer or priestess, they could only hope to become wives and mothers. Faelia had defied those rules. But too often, she belittled the opinions of women who had chosen a more traditional life-path. And her attitude only made them more reluctant to follow her.

Griane dispensed common sense and calming words along with her poultices and infusions, but her nerves were frayed by the conflicting demands of healer and mother, and even more by the dissension among her children over Rigat. Although she continued to champion him, the deaths of Donncha and Catha had shocked her. If he intended to kill every person who spoke against his family—or him— there would be no end to the bloodshed. Added to those worries was the daily struggle to survive and the fear of what the future might hold. And beneath it all, the ever-present pain of losing Darak.

Her hand came up to caress his bag of charms. Through the worn doeskin, she traced the knobs and grooves of his finger bones. She had never opened the bag to look at them, but had memorized their contours.

As a child, she had paid little attention to his hands, save for the time he had smacked her bottom for filling his shoes with porridge. And the day he had ripped the belt out of her uncle Dugan's grasp. Darak held out his hand afterward, but she refused to take it; she was nine years old, after all, not a baby. But she still remembered the warmth of his palm on her back as he guided her to his hut, how he talked with her at supper without the annoying condescension of so many adults, and later, tucked her under the wolfskins with Tinnean and awkwardly tweaked a braid by way of wishing her good night.

She had studied his hands many times after she had grown to love him. Even after Morgath's dagger had done its damage, the strength remained and traces of the beauty they had once possessed. He'd always blushed when she called them beautiful. The blush only deepened as her fingers glided over his skin, massaging the knotted scar on his palm, tracing the calluses on his thumb and the fat pad of flesh at its base.

Her breath caught, and she had to lean against the trunk of a pine. That was the danger of memories; even the sweetest ones could transform the ache of loss into a sharp stab of grief. Especially the sweetest ones.

But the pain reminded her that she was alive. After the

first shock of Darak's death, the days had passed in a muffled haze. Her mind meticulously cataloged the hurts she must heal, her hands sorted herbs and brewed decoctions, but her spirit seemed to have left with Darak's. Gradually, it had returned, and with it, the will to keep her tribe strong and her family intact.

She continued walking, drawing strength from Darak's fingers clutched in hers. She would need all her strength—and his—for this meeting with Rigat.

The dappled sunlight among the trees gave way to the brightness of the glade. Accustomed to the muted colors of the forest, the brilliant pink of the foxtails startled her eyes. A skilled healer could use the leaves to regulate the heartbeat, but in the wrong hands, they could be deadly. Even she had feared to use them to help Darak, preferring to rely on the weaker brew of broom and quickthorn.

Perhaps if I had, he would be alive today.

She shook off the thought and slowly knelt among the colorful spikes. Years of healing were too ingrained to ignore the bounty before her.

She gathered a few handfuls of leaves, wrinkling her nose at their unpleasant odor, and paused to flex her fingers. Heat infused her swollen joints and the dull ache ebbed. She stared skyward before she realized that the sun could never have effected the healing. Shading her eyes, she scanned the trees.

Rigat stood at the edge of the glade, a being of sunlight and shadow like his father. Then he stepped forward, a tentative smile on his face, and he became her little boy again.

Too long since she had felt the softness of his hair against her cheek and the strong bones of his shoulders beneath her hands. Longer still since she had felt the smooth flesh of his back. In her dream, he had been dressed in his old tunic and breeches, but he wore Zherosi garb today. She tried to hide her displeasure as she stepped back to look at him.

The red-gold hair on his chest shocked her. More shocking was his haggard face. Even Keirith's warning failed to prepare her. His eyes were bloodshot and pouched. Deep grooves bracketed his mouth, and the bones stood out like ridges above his hollowed cheeks. She stifled a cry and pulled him back into her arms, wishing she could protect him from the burdens that had turned him from a boy into this tired, old man.

"It's all right, Mam," he whispered, his breath warm against her cheek. "Everything will be all right now."

Reluctantly, she drew back. "Talk to me."

She sat with him among the foxtails, his hand clasped between hers. No longer a boy's hand, but a man's, just as the triumphs he recited were a man's. Only two moons ago, his face had been alight as he described each obstacle overcome, each new piece of knowledge gained. He seemed to take little joy in his successes now. Perhaps even magic grew stale.

He mentioned the queen, but only in passing and always with a sidelong glance as if gauging her reaction. Of Donncha and Catha, of the men at the hill fort, he said nothing.

When his voice finally ran down, he began plucking blades of grass. She waited for him to look at her, but his head remained bowed.

"You've told me much about Zheros. What about this land?" His hand moved between hers, and she tightened her grip. "The children of the Oak and Holly are your people as well."

"If you're just going to blame me—"

"Have I blamed you? For anything?"

"But you have doubts."

"Of course, I have doubts! Donncha is dead. And Catha. And most of the men of my tribe. Our tribe."

"And Darak."

"And Darak."

He waited, obviously hoping she would say that he couldn't have saved Darak. But she refused to assuage his guilt. She had to be ruthless, using any weapon to win her boy back.

"You look awful," she said.

The abrupt change of subject made him start. "I'm just tired."

"No wonder. Dashing around the empire. What does the queen say about that?"

The flush started at the base of his throat and rose up

into his cheeks. She knew that they ruled together, but were they also lovers? Distaste vied with admiration for the woman's cunning. What better way to bind the adolescent man-god to her than sharing her bed as well as her throne?

"She tells me to be patient," Rigat finally said.

"Well, at least she has common sense as well as beauty."

"How do you know she's beautiful?"

"She changes bodies every year. What woman in her right mind would choose an ugly one?"

The familiar grin made her ache. It vanished as quickly as it had appeared. "I haven't forgotten my . . . homeland. But first, I need to consolidate my power in Zheros."

"Ballocks."

He gaped at her. No one in Zheros would dare speak to him that way, of course. But she had wiped his bottom and washed his dirty clouts. No matter how much power he possessed, she refused to be awed by him.

"To hear you tell it, everyone in Zheros jumps if you so much as sneeze. If your power is not consolidated now, when will it be?"

He yanked his hand free and leaped to his feet. "I can't do everything!"

"Then do nothing."

"What?"

"Stop winning the war in Carilia. Stop winning trade concessions from . . . that place with the worms. Just let the world muddle along by itself."

"I can't."

"Why? Why?" she repeated, her voice fierce. "Because you want them to need you? To admire you? To fear you?"

He stalked away, leaving a trail of crushed foxtails in his wake.

Once, she had been enough for him, but no longer. Much as he loved her, he loved the power—and all that it brought him—more. It had seduced him. Just as it had seduced Morgath.

Nay. Never like that.

But even as she denied the possibility, she realized something else. "That's why you sent the Zherosi after us, isn't it? So you could swoop in and rescue us. Oh, Rigat . . ."

He whirled around to confront her again. "And where would you have been if I hadn't rescued you from Donncha? And Catha?"

"I survived Morgath and the First Forest. Keirith lived through that ordeal in Zheros. Faelia's a veteran of a dozen battles. We didn't need to be rescued from two frightened women. And whatever their faults, Donncha and Catha didn't deserve to die."

He was breathing hard, his body poised for flight. As she struggled to rise, he hesitated, then strode forward and held out his hands to pull her to her feet.

She clung to them and deliberately softened her voice. "You've lost sight of your vision of peace."

"It was hopeless, Mam. From the beginning."

"Maybe so. But vengeance is an abuse of your gift. You know I love you," she added as he opened his mouth to argue. "I'd give my life for you. But I won't stand by and watch you—"

"Destroy myself? That's what Keirith thinks."

"Lose yourself."

He stared down at their clasped hands. "Maybe I'm already lost."

"If I believed that, I wouldn't have come today."

His hands clenched convulsively around hers. "Do you know why I came? Other than to see you again, I mean?" His head came up, his eyes shining. "To tell you that I would call off the Zherosi."

She pulled him into her arms and held him tight. "Oh, Rigat, I'm so glad. So proud of you."

He pulled away, his face eager and excited. "You're right. It was stupid. I don't have to prove myself to the tribe. Or anybody. Least of all, you."

"I'll tell them today. As soon as I get back to camp. Everyone will be so relieved. So happy to go home."

Then she remembered what they would find there: the ruins of their homes, the corpses of the slain. She thrust the images aside, unwilling to let anything spoil this moment.

"And then we'll go away together," Rigat said.

She smiled, imagining him opening portals to give her glimpses of unknown places just as Fellgair had done that day in the Summerlands when they had created Rigat.

"You can come with me to Zheros. Or I'll find another

place. Wherever you like. I'll take care of you. I'll keep you safe."

Griane's smile faded. "You mean . . . leave the tribe?"

"It's the only way we can be together, Mam. Don't you see? I can't come back. No matter what Keirith says."

"But the tribe needs me."

"So do I!" He scowled. "You did it before. For Keirith."

"Keirith was cast out! How could we let him leave the village alone?"

"But you'll let me leave. You'll let me go on alone."

"It's not the same."

"You said you'd give your life for me."

It was no longer her child standing before her but his father, bargaining over the price of opening a portal to Chaos. She had misinterpreted Fellgair's demands, but Rigat's were clear: to give up her family, her friends, her home. Would he allow her to see her other children? Or would she spend the rest of her life as his prisoner? Cherished and protected, but jealously guarded against anyone with a claim on her affection.

If she refused, he might rescind his offer to call off the Zherosi. Hurt and angered by her rejection, he might abandon the children of the Oak and Holly altogether. She had to prevent that. Later—perhaps—she could reason with him.

"All right, Rigat. I'll go with you."

For the first time in her life, she had to force herself to return his embrace. As she stepped back, he seemed to sense her reluctance.

"I want you to do something for me," she said.

His expression grew wary. "What?"

"I want you to promise that you'll do everything in your power to protect your people and your tree-brothers."

"You're bargaining with me?" he demanded. "As if I were Fellgair?"

She wanted to point out that he was forcing her to choose between him and her other children, just as Fellgair had forced her to choose between Darak and Keirith. Instead, she kept her voice gentle.

"I'm willing to give up everyone I love for you. Can't I ask this favor in return?"

"I need you more than they do."

"There are more important things in the world than what you need! Or what I need." She took a deep breath, willing herself to be calm, to be persuasive. "The Zherosi are swallowing us up. Already, chiefs sacrifice their tree-brothers for a few sacks of grain. How long before they make sacrifices in Zherosi temples? Our way of life will die, Rigat. Who knows, even our gods may die."

Her last words startled a reaction from him, but instead of shock or surprise, Rigat looked stricken. Only for a moment, though. Then he shrugged and kicked a foxtail spike. Pink flowers tumbled into the grass.

"Will you give me your promise? Will you help your people?"

When Rigat stiffened, she feared she had pushed too hard. Then she realized he was looking past her.

"You might as well come out," Rigat called. "I know you're there."

Among the trees, a figure moved. Sunlight flashed off the bright hair.

"Oh, gods," Griane whispered.

Faelia stepped out of the shadows, an arrow nocked in her bowstring.

"I should have known," Rigat whispered. "It was all a trick."

"Nay!"

She reached for him, but he backed away, his mouth twisting in an ugly scowl.

"First Keirith would try to convince me to give up my power. Then you'd promise anything if I'd use it for the tribe. And if that failed—"

"That's not true!" Finding only scorn on her son's face, Griane turned to her daughter. "Faelia. Lower your bow."

Faelia simply moved to her left, seeking a clear shot. Immediately, Griane countered, shielding Rigat with her body.

"He is your brother!"

Rigat eased away. "Go on, Faelia. You've been wanting to do this since the day I was born."

"Stop it! Both of you!" Again, Griane stepped between them. "Faelia, don't be stupid. His power is greater than any arrow."

"Take your shot. I won't even use my power until you release. I call that fair."

She took a step toward her daughter, hands outstretched in supplication, and tried to keep the panic from her voice. "Please, Faelia. Lower your bow and we'll talk."

She heard the swish of grass behind her. Watched Faelia's bow move to the right. Saw her daughter's strong hands drawing back the bowstring, her wide mouth curving in a smile.

Griane whirled around and flung herself at Rigat, stumbling in her haste. His head snapped toward her. His hands came up to steady her. His mouth curved in a reassuring smile, her little boy's smile that promised he would always protect her. Then he suddenly spun away and staggered backward.

They both stared in disbelief at the arrow piercing his arm. Griane shouted at Faelia, who was already nocking another in her bowstring. When she turned back to Rigat, her little boy had vanished. In his place, stood the implacable man-god who killed all who opposed him.

"Rigat! Nay!"

His lips curled in a feral snarl. She never saw him snatch the arrow out of the air. One moment, it was flashing toward him and the next, he was clutching it in his fist. She was still reaching for his arm when he spun the arrow around and hurled it at Faelia.

How long does it take an arrow to cut down your child? Two heartbeats? Three? Long enough to burn the image of her in your mind forever. The long legs slightly apart to steady her stance. Left arm outstretched, fingers gripping the bow. Right elbow high, just as her father had taught her. The bright hair, so like Rigat's, unruly wisps escaping from her braid to caress her sunburned cheeks.

And then the picture shatters. The mouth opens in a silent scream. The arrow falls harmlessly into the grass. The bow that had never failed her slips from nerveless fingers. Her head dips as she gazes down at the arrow in her chest. The long braid slides over her shoulder. And the hands that had crafted the arrow and the bow, that had wielded both so expertly against animals and men alike, those strong hands reach up to grip the shaft, only to fall, as weak and helpless as the legs that buckle beneath her.

All this Griane saw as she ran across the glade, screaming her daughter's name, trampling foxtails underfoot along with the hope that Faelia would live, that she was young and strong, she had her whole life before her, she could not die, not like this, it should be me, why couldn't it have been me?

She wanted to believe Faelia felt her mother's hands struggling to lift her, that she heard her mother's voice repeating her name, the only word Griane could manage, a prayer and a promise and a testament to a love too often unspoken. She wanted to believe the wide blue eyes recognized her. That the slack mouth curved in a smile. That the final exhalation of breath was Faelia whispering, "Mam."

And when she could no longer pretend, she closed the staring eyes and gripped the limp fingers and rocked her daughter in her arms, praying that Darak would find their girl and guide her spirit to the Forever Isles.

When she finally raised her head, dark clouds shadowed the glade. Rigat was gone. She opened her mouth to call his name and closed it again.

She eased Faelia onto the ground and pushed herself to her feet. Slowly, she walked back across the glade to retrieve her waterskin and healer's bag. Then she returned to her daughter.

She broke the shaft of the arrow, but it had penetrated Faelia's breastbone and she could not pull the arrowhead free. Instead, she dampened a scrap of nettle-cloth and gently washed the dirt from her daughter's face and hands. She turned Faelia's head so she could untie the thong binding her braid. With her fingers, she combed the pine needles and grass and fragments of birch leaves from her hair, then carefully braided it again.

She brushed the dirt from her breeches. Straightened the sprawling legs. Folded her hands around the broken shaft of the arrow. There were not enough stones for a cairn, but she gathered what she could and laid them around her daughter's body. She kissed her on the forehead, on the mouth, and on both cheeks. Then she drew her dagger and cut off a lock of the fiery hair.

After intoning the prayer to free her spirit, Griane hesitated, uncertain whether she had the strength for what she meant to do. Then she lifted Faelia's right hand and laid it atop a stone.

She spread the fingers wide. She picked up her dagger once more. Slowly, carefully she cut through the flesh and sinew and bone of her daughter's forefinger.

She had to pause then, until the dizziness passed. Then she washed the finger, wrapped it in a strip of nettle-cloth, and placed it in her bag of charms.

Someday, perhaps, they would find a new home and erect a cairn. Until then, she would carry the bones of her loved ones next to her heart.

Chapter 59

"SHE SHOULD HAVE BEEN BACK by now," Callie said.

Hircha paced back and forth along the stream bank. Her limp was more noticeable than usual, a testament to her anxiety as well as the hard days of travel. "It's my fault. I shouldn't have let her go alone."

"It's no one's fault," Keirith said. He gazed at the lowering sky and frowned. "Which way did she go?"

"Upstream," Hircha replied at the same time that Callie said, "South."

Hircha drew up short. "She told me she was going upstream. To look for dandelion and dock."

"But she was heading south when Ela and I met her. To gather foxtails." Callie shook his head. "Why would she lie?"

Before Keirith could reply, he spied Holtik striding toward them with Owan at his side. Holtik's expression was grave and Owan was so breathless that some of the women turned to look after them.

"What is it?" Keirith asked.

As Owan struggled for breath, Holtik said, "The Zherosi have broken camp. They're heading this way."

Callie was the first to recover. "Why now?" he asked.

"Rigat," Keirith replied. "It must be. I saw him yesterday. We parted on good enough terms, but something must have happened afterward."

"Dear gods," Hircha whispered. "Faelia's hunting. You don't suppose the two of them met and—"

"You saw him?" Callie echoed.

"I'm sorry," Keirith said, wincing at Callie's expression. "I wanted to tell you, but—"

"There's no time for this," Holtik interrupted. "We have to move. Now!"

"Griane's missing," Hircha snapped. "And so is Faelia."

"Then Keirith must lead," Holtik replied. "You've more experience fighting the Zherosi than any of us."

Faelia had spoken often of the need to find a defensible site and discussed strategies to hold off their pursuers. But it was hard to think about making a stand when they needed all their energy simply to survive. Now that the day had come, they were no better prepared than they had been when they first began their flight.

They were all watching him, waiting for his command. Had his father felt this instinctive panic when his tribe turned to him for wisdom? Or was he so used to leading them that he could meet every crisis calmly?

Nay, even Fa would be scared. But he'd hide it. And so must I.

"How close are they?" he asked Owan.

"Three miles. Selima will hold them off as long as she can." Owan swallowed hard, clearly wondering how many of his friends would be dead before sunset.

Keirith turned to Holtik. "You've done the most scouting. What's the best position?"

"The bald spot. But that's a full day's journey southeast."

Again, Keirith eyed the sky. Rain would make it harder for the Zherosi to trail them, but it would slow his folk down as well. And Selima's band—no matter how skillful or lucky—could not hold off the Zherosi indefinitely.

Finally, he said, "We'd better make for the notch instead. At least it's high ground. If we have to, we can make a stand there."

Holtik would have to lead. He had to find his mother. Faelia would be able to survive on her own, but if Mam was hurt . . .

Don't think about that now.

Drawn by Owan's arrival, people had begun drifting toward them. He wished he had his father's gift for inspiring confidence or Callie's gift for words. Then he recalled how the simple tale of Fa's vision quest had eased Selima's fledglings. That was what was needed now—not the exhortations of a chief or the poetry of a Memory-Keeper but simple words, spoken with conviction.

As he waited for the rest of the tribe to gather, he sought his allies: Lisula and Ennit, Mirili and Mother Narthi, Alada and Duba. The strong ones who could be counted on to keep the others from panicking. His gaze rested on Owan, who hid his fear behind a grimace; on Holtik, who had become a loyal friend in the short time they had known each other; on Callie whom he had failed to take into his confidence but who rewarded him now with a quick nod of support.

Always, the family had tried to shield "little Callie," the youngest, the sweetest, the one who deserved to be free of the doubts and fears that plagued the rest of them. But Callum was a man. He had proven himself in battle and in the everyday disputes that arose among the tribe. As Keirith nodded back, he resolved never to exclude his brother again.

His gaze rested longest on Hircha. Her face was very pale, her lips pressed together in a thin line, but her eyes glittered. Hard and blue as the sky in Pilozhat he had thought them when he first saw her, and so they were now. But he had also seen them filled with wicked merriment when she teased Fa, had seen them grow soft and thoughtful when she smiled at Conn. Her sharp tongue could be merciless, but she rarely used it to wound, only to jolt others—especially him—out of a spiral of blame and guilt. If her temper was less volatile than Faelia's, she was just as brave. If she rarely indulged in displays of affection, she was as fierce as his mam in protecting her family.

Conn had been his best friend. His father had been the center of his world. Since losing them, he had felt adrift and alone. But here was Hircha, with her hard mouth and her glittering eyes. The girl who had shared adversity with him in Zheros. The friend who had always told him the truth, however painful. The woman who knew his dark places and helped him look at them without flinching.

As he continued staring at her, her brows drew together in a quizzical frown. Then her mouth curved in a smile so unexpectedly sweet that his body and spirit seemed infused with its warmth.

With a profound effort, Keirith steadied his breathing. The tribe was waiting. The Zherosi were closing in. His mam and Faelia were missing. And Rigat . . . only the gods knew what had happened to turn him against them.

He took a deep breath. "The Zherosi are marching this way." There were a few gasps, but most of his folk just nodded grimly. "They're still several miles off, but we must assume they mean to attack. We need to break camp now and head east. Holtik knows the route."

"Braden took a group of boys and girls into the forest," Mirili said. "To gather deadwood and set snares."

"Ennit, sound the ram's horn." Even the little ones knew to race back to camp when they heard it. And only the hunters and scouts ventured farther afield.

And Mam. Gods, why did you have to leave today? Was it Rigat? Did he contact you, too?

"Pack quickly. Leave the fires burning. It'll make it harder for them to guess when we left. We must move fast, but I want an orderly retreat, not a rout." He paused, seeking some words to strengthen and inspire them. "We've survived the Zherosi before. We'll do it again. Let's go."

Hardly inspirational, but they sent the tribe hurrying away with resolve on their faces instead of panic.

"Callie, choose a few of the older boys to make up a rear guard. Owan, tell Selima to harry the Zherosi for a few miles, then follow us to the notch. You can see it from any hilltop. Try and reach us before nightfall. If you can't, make camp and head for the bald spot on the morrow."

As Owan sprinted off, Keirith heard the protesting bleat of sheep. He whirled around to find Arun and Lorthan tying their belts around the necks of the two ewes. Ennit had already leashed Dugan; the ram's tongue lolled, and he surveyed his captor with baleful eyes.

"Ennit!" he shouted, striding toward them. "Leave the damn sheep!"

"These are my best breeders."

"Good gods, man, we're running for our lives! We can't drag sheep with us."

Keirith felt a light touch on his arm and turned to find Lisula gazing up at him. "He'd risk his life for those sheep, but he won't risk the tribe. If they slow us down, he'll abandon them."

Hearing smothered laughter, he glanced over his shoulder. "Ennit's just following a precedent," Hircha said. "After all, we left Eagles Mount with three sheep."

He had to laugh. Callie joined in, then Lisula. Ennit's affronted expression only fed their hilarity. It was absurd, yet oddly comforting to share laughter at such a moment.

"Let's use our sheep, then," Keirith said. "Ennit, can you drive them along the stream for a mile or two while the Holtik leads the way to the notch?"

A slow smile blossomed on Ennit's face. "Draw the Zherosi off, you mean. Aye. My sheep'll do it. With a little help from me and Lorthan."

"You'll be able to find us later?" Lisula asked.

Ennit's smile became a scowl. "I'm no hunter, but I can still follow a trail left by a horde of women and children."

"Let's just hope the Zherosi can't," Keirith said.

"They couldn't find their arses with both hands." Ennit slapped Dugan's broad rump and the ram let out a nasal bleat of indignation.

Keirith's laughter abruptly died as the white-haired figure emerged from the trees. The droop of her shoulders and her slow stride told Keirith she was exhausted, but it was his mother's face that stopped him in mid-stride. Her expression was as remote as a dream-walker's or a shaman's, her body moving through this world, but her spirit still ensnared by the visions of the other.

She stopped, blinking as if uncertain she recognized those clustering around her. Callie raised his hand to touch her, but at Keirith's gesture, he let it fall.

"Mam?" Although he spoke softly, she started at the sound of his voice. "It's Keirith, Mam."

She scanned his face and nodded.

"Are you hurt?"

She shook her head.

"Can you tell us what happened?"

Her hand groped for Fa's bag of charms. Her eyes closed. When they opened again, the glazed expression was gone, replaced by grief so stark that Keirith shivered.

"Faelia is dead. Rigat killed her."

Chapter 60

THROUGHOUT THAT LONG AFTERNOON, her words echoed in Keirith's mind, as relentless as the hurried tramp of feet. And like the rain seeping into the earth, his hope of salvaging Rigat leached away.

He had no time to learn more than the bare facts before he took command of the rear guard. There were so few boys of fighting age and no women with sufficient training that he took only Callie, Braden, and Takinel, another of the orphans from Gath's village. He prayed Ennit's ruse would work, that the rain would obliterate their tracks, that the children would be strong enough for the journey.

They clawed their way up steep hills, slipping and sliding on the wet pine needles. Sidestepped down treacherous slopes, clinging to tree trunks and boulders and fallen logs, knowing one misstep might bring the disaster of a twisted ankle, a wrenched knee. At the top of every rise, Keirith scanned the terrain behind them, searching for movement among the trees, but the dense forest and driving rain made it impossible to spy their pursuers.

By the time they reached the notch, the rain had subsided to a drizzle. The women spread skins on the ground and huddled together, mantles shielding the children from the freshening breeze. The little ones clung to their mothers, too tired to cry, too tired even to eat.

At twilight, Ennit and Lorthan stumbled into their makeshift camp, still dragging the sheep behind them. When darkness fell without any sign of Selima and her recruits, he prayed that they had simply made camp for the night and would catch up with them on the morrow.

He and Callie chose to take the second watch so they could spend some time with their mother first. As they walked toward her, Hircha blocked their path.

"She hasn't said a word. Not to me. Not to anyone. I've never seen her like this, Keirith. Even after Darak died."

Because she hasn't just lost her daughter, Keirith thought, but her son as well.

At least they had seen Fa's body. Faelia's death was unreal. He kept expecting her to appear out of the gloom and roll her eyes when he told her they had all believed she was dead. Only his mam's tight mouth and staring eyes confirmed the truth.

He crouched on one side of her, Callie on the other. He was reluctant to touch her; she still had the look of a shaman lost in a vision. Or Duba, dream-walking through the long years after she had lost her son.

It was that image that made him clasp her unresisting hand. "I don't know what to say, Mam. Or what to do. But I'm here. We're all here. Please. Don't . . . go away."

His voice broke on the final words, the voice of a scared little boy, caught up in events he could not control.

He had meant to comfort her, to lend her his strength. But she was the one to pull his head down to her shoulder. Her strong hands held him, her voice murmured his name softly. And his murmured in counterpoint: "Mam. Mam. Mam."

In his dream, Faelia screamed when the arrowhead cleaved her breastbone. Even when she stopped clawing at the shaft of the arrow, even after she fell to the ground, even after she was dead, the scream just went on and on and on. Only then did he realize it was his mam clawing at the arrow, his mam falling to her knees, his mam's scream tearing the air, tearing his spirit, tearing him apart.

Rigat jolted awake, his cry echoing off stone walls as cold and unforgiving as his mother's face. But her strong hands cradled him against her body, her lips pressed gentle kisses to his wet cheeks, her voice murmured his name softly. And his offered a broken, sobbing counterpoint: "Mam. Mam. Mam."

Then he saw the waterfall of black hair and the dark eyes, wary as a doe's in the flickering torchlight. He pushed her away, wincing at the pain in his arm and the memories it evoked. "I want the Supplicant! Where's the Supplicant?"

"She's not in Pilozhat. Remember? You sent Nekif to the temple before you went to sleep."

"She might have come back."

"Her servants would have given her your message. She would have come to you at once."

Rigat fell back on the fleeces. "No. He's abandoned me. Like everyone else."

Her silence confirmed what he had always known: that she would leave him, too. In the end, they would all leave, and he would be alone.

"I'm here. I'll never abandon you."

The patter of bare feet. Her voice, whispering to a slave. Her hand, touching his bare shoulder.

"Drink this."

The metal of the goblet, as cool as the fingers stroking his neck. The brew, as sweet as her voice urging him to sleep. Sweeter still, the peace that filled him, deep and dreamless as death.

Selima and her recruits were still missing when Keirith roused the tribe at dawn. Fear sharpened senses dulled by lack of sleep. His mind sifted plans and tactics. His body responded automatically to obstacles: ducking under low-hanging limbs, dodging a thorn bush sprawling across the trail. A small part of him even noted the fresh-washed beauty of the forest: water droplets sparkling in the shafts of sunlight, the crispness of the morning air, the leaves of the birches edged in gold. Like his folk, summer was fleeing.

At every hilltop, he glanced back. Each time he caught the flash of metal among the trees, his bowels clenched. Callie's eyes reflected his fear, but neither of them gave voice to it.

When the tribe stopped beside a stream, swollen with last night's rain, he gulped down a few swallows of the cool water and refilled his waterskin. Then he was on his feet again. Rest brought only the renewed consciousness of aching muscles, the reminder that the Zherosi were coming closer with every heartbeat. Better to seek out Holtik and discuss the next leg of the journey, to walk among his tribe mates offering reassurance to the adults and praise for the children's resilience.

Just a little longer. Just a little farther. Look, you can see the bald spot through the break in the trees. By sunset, we'll be there. By sunset, we'll be safe. Then he recalled Temet's assurances before the ambush, and fear strained his smile.

They followed the stream southeast, marching single file along the narrow bank. Keirith eyed the thickening clouds and prayed for rain to hide their tracks. The brief downpour only soaked their clothes and left them more miserable.

Each time the tribe paused to rest, he and Callie trudged up a hill with Holtik. From the notch, the bald spot had been little more than a pale blob amid the dark greens of the pines. As they grew nearer, they could make out more details.

"It looks like a head," Callie said. "See? The trees on the summit are hair, standing on end. Those two dark spots are eyes. And that part in the middle that juts out? That's the nose."

"You'll have to tell the children," Holtik said. "It'll make for a good tale."

Keirith forced a smile, staring at the lower half of the face where the jaw had melted away. A shattered face, too reminiscent of Temet's, crushed by a Zherosi club.

His unease grew as they neared the base of the hill. To

the east, it plunged straight down to the stream. But it was the rockslide on the north face that brought him up short. Uprooted pines littered the slope, but it was the same boulder-strewn desolation he had seen in his vision.

He choked back the bile that filled his mouth, fighting the overwhelming urge to flee. Leaving Holtik to lead the main body west around the rockslide, he and Callie trotted ahead.

The site was virtually impregnable. The stream curved around the hill, guarding its eastern and southern flanks. Although the boulders and fallen trees on the north face provided shelter for attackers, the loose scree of pebbles made the footing treacherous. The only place to mount an assault was the western slope.

Together, they scrambled up it. Hard enough for two grown men to claw their way over the rocks near the summit; they would have to rope the younger children together. The scrub pines atop the hill offered little protection from the wind, but after the exertion of the climb, they welcomed the gusts of cool air.

The tribe was easy to spot, moving slowly around the base of the hill, but if the Zherosi were nearby, they were well hidden in the forest. Keirith paused long enough to wave to Holtik before following Callie through the tumble of boulders near the summit.

The dark spots that had looked like eyes were really two small grottos, carved out by the rockslide. Under the "nose," they found the shadowy entrance of a cave.

Keirith checked so violently that Callie had to grab his outflung arm to steady him. He closed his eyes, but still he saw the image of his parents from the vision.

"What is it?" Callie asked.

"Just dizzy. I'm fine now."

But he let his brother go inside the cave first.

They had to duck to keep from scraping their heads against the low ceiling. The overhanging jut of the nose blocked most of the wind, but the interior was so gloomy, Keirith had to explore it with fingertips skimming the rock. Although fairly shallow, the cave was wide; it might be large enough to shelter the tribe, but they would be crammed shoulder to shoulder.

At first, he thought the dark shapes were a trick of the

uncertain light or the uneven surface of the rock. But closer to the entrance, he was able to make out images: the triangular shape of tall pines with drooping boughs; small stick figures bearing bows; antlered stags; and a massive humanlike shape that might be a bear standing erect.

"There are some on this wall, too." Callie's voice echoed eerily. "The legends say The People paddled up the river. But I suppose others could have fled overland." He leaned close, peering at a group of stick figures. "I wish we had a torch."

They left off their explorations and stood under the shelf of rock, staring north.

"We might have lost them," Callie said. "The rain might have washed away our tracks."

"Aye. Maybe."

"Even if they pass this place, they might never discover we're here."

"But if they do, we're trapped."

With adequate food and water, they could hold off the Zherosi indefinitely. But their food supplies were limited. And the only source of water was the stream far below. The Zherosi wouldn't risk an assault. Not when they could wait and starve them out.

Callie rubbed his eyes. "It seemed like a good site from a distance. But if you think we should move on . . ."

In a halting voice, Keirith described his visions: their parents lying asleep in a cave; the battle between the eagle chicks; the line of people disappearing over the edge of the cliff.

"You're sure it was Mam and Fa?"

"I'm pretty sure it was Mam. But I couldn't see his face. He looked . . . old. And fragile. I thought . . . maybe . . . it was Fa's spirit, comforting her."

"And the other woman? The one who was pregnant?"

"She had a mantle over her head, so I couldn't see her, either. But she was near her time—her belly was huge. And none of the women are that close to birthing. So either that part of the vision happens much later or it's a symbol. That life will go on."

"Aye." Callie cleared his throat. "The thing is . . . Ela's with child."

For a moment, Keirith could only gape at him. Then he

pulled Callie into his arms and hugged him hard. He wasn't sure whether to offer congratulations or sympathy. To be carrying a new life at such a time. What a joy and a burden for them both.

His happiness faded when Callie asked, "The eagle chicks? You and Rigat?"

"It has to be."

Callie sighed. "I'm not a shaman. But it seems you were meant to come here."

"Or I'm being warned to stay away."

"If this is the place where you're supposed to confront Rigat . . ." Callie shook his head in frustration. "Gods, Keirith, I don't know. If he's the one controlling the Zherosi, then the only way we'll escape them is to convince Rigat to change his mind. Or . . . or kill him."

A faint shout spared Keirith from answering. Hurrying out of the cave, they found Holtik scrambling across the rocks. One look at his face told Keirith the news was bad.

"It's Owan," Holtik said.

He gave them the gist of Owan's information as they made their way down the hill. The crowd parted as they approached. Although the women's faces were strained, everyone was calm. Even the children waited in hushed silence.

Mam and Hircha were bandaging Owan's wounded arm. His tunic and breeches were torn, his hair matted with dirt and leaves, but his listless expression worried Keirith more; it reminded him too vividly of Eilin's after his first battle.

He crouched beside the boy and rested his hand on the bony shoulder.

Owan took a trembling breath. "Selima . . . she said she'll delay them. If she can. But there's only the three of them left. Selima, Cradaig, and Rendaron."

His face crumpled, and Keirith tightened his grip.

"They know," Owan finally managed. "That we planned to meet here. They captured Lendon. We heard him. Screaming."

Lendon. The small lad who had found a bear for his vision mate. Because his spirit was fierce.

Keirith had no words of comfort to offer, no assurances

that the boys' sacrifice had been worthwhile. He could only rest his forehead against Owan's matted hair and share his grief.

But only for a moment. There was no time to mourn these dead boys, no time to use his power to ease Owan's pain. They had to prepare. And although his stomach churned at the implications, he knew he had to lead his people onto that barren hilltop to make their final stand against the Zherosi—and Rigat.

From his vantage point atop a plateau in western Carilia, Rigat surveyed the battlefield far below. The warriors dispatching the wounded and looting the dead looked more like ants than men. Industrious little ants swarming through the grass.

The late afternoon sun painted the grasslands gold. Bronze helmets winked at the sun. A shallow red stream meandered across the plain; at dawn, it had been brown.

"A great victory, Promised One." The Batal's voice oozed satisfaction. "The Carilians have no choice but to sue for peace. And with the terms we'll offer, it'll be ten generations before they recover."

Hundreds of little ants swarming through the grass. Hundreds of others lying in the grass. Some ants would feast. Some would be a feast for the crows and ravens circling patiently overhead. The aftermath of battle was always the same, whether it involved warriors on a wind-swept plain or a brother and sister in a sun-dappled glade of foxtails.

By now, the birds will have taken her eyes.

"My officers and I would be honored if you'd join us tonight to celebrate."

The others will be feasting on her flesh. Gnawing her bones.

"Nothing like the food you'd get in Pilozhat, of course."

Weasels. Mice. Foxes.

"But victory lends flavor to the humblest fare."

Maggots.

He staggered toward the tent they had erected for him

and found Nekif waiting outside. He was glad that Jholianna had insisted he take the old slave with him this time. Nekif would know what to do.

The heat inside the tent was stifling, but he made no move to stop Nekif from lowering the flap. Better to sweat than allow the Batal to see him sprawled on the red and gold cushions, shaking like a frightened child.

Why had he thought coming to Carilia would distract him? He should have known that witnessing today's slaughter could only conjure memories of her.

He flexed his arm. The wound still throbbed. Jholianna's physician had removed the arrowhead, but he couldn't allow the man to stitch him up as if he were an ordinary mortal. He'd healed the wound himself, eliciting gasps of wonder. Within days, it began leaking blood. Now, he began every morning by resealing the gash.

Nekif crouched beside him, a goblet in one hand and a tiny packet in the other. At Rigat's nod, the old slave laid the goblet carefully on the rug and unwrapped the flax-cloth. The powder looked like green dust; only the scent—faint and bitter—proved that it had once been a living plant. Just as the dead ants on the battlefield had once been men.

She had meant to kill him. He had only defended himself. It was her fault, not his, that it had ended this way.

Nekif stirred the mixture and held out the goblet. Rigat took it with both hands, but Nekif still had to wrap his fingers around the goblet to steady it. The honey failed to disguise the bitter taste of the herbs. That was probably a good thing. If oblivion were too sweet, no one would want to return.

As he lay back, he heard Nekif slip outside; he would prevent anyone from entering until the effects of the drug wore off. He was drifting into the welcoming darkness when hands gripped his shoulders. Rigat frowned, wondering that Nekif had the temerity to shake him. And to call him by his name instead of his title.

He opened his eyes and stared blearily up at the slave. Strange that Nekif should be wearing a moth-eaten pelt around his shoulders. And that his eyes kept changing color—from their usual soft brown to gold. As gold as the honey in the brew. He was speaking in an urgent whisper. Something about going back. But there was no going back. Not anymore.

Rigat closed his eyes. When he woke, he would have to punish Nekif. A pity. But disobedience always had to be punished and obedience rewarded. Only then could balance be maintained.

Chapter 61

SQUINTING INTO THE GLARE of the rising sun, Keirith watched the Zherosi filling their waterskins at the stream. Now and then, one would glance up at the hilltop, but they seemed blithely confident that no arrows could reach them.

With a whisper of rustling grass, Holtik slid to the ground beside him. He observed the scene in silence, then noted, "They're within bowshot."

"Not until we've heard their terms."

"Terms?"

"There may be room to negotiate."

"With what? Your life?"

"Let's just hear what they have to say."

"Don't make the same mistake Trath did. He was foolish enough to trust them and every man in the hill fort paid for it."

"You think I've forgotten?"

Holtik blew out his breath. "Nay. Sorry. I'm grumpy this morning. Killing a few Zherosi would have brightened my spirits." He rolled onto his elbow and scratched his crotch. "Might as well light a fire. Braden snared three rabbits this morning. That's half a mouthful apiece."

"Good gods, where?"

Holtik jerked his head over his shoulder. "Here. On the summit. Now all the boys are mad to set snares."

"Braden can take Arun and Takinel. They're responsible. But for mercy's sake, tell them to stay under cover."

Holtik nodded and slipped away.

All night, the tribe had huddled in the cave, while sentries kept watch on the hilltop. They had lit no fires, conversed only in whispers, all of them praying the Zherosi would pass them by. But as darkness fell, Keirith had seen their campfires, twinkling like fireflies among the trees to the west.

They had prepared as best they could. The children had gathered stones for their slings. The women and girls filled every waterskin, pot, and cup at the stream. The men had chopped up fallen trees for firewood.

It was a miracle they had accomplished so much in the short time they had. Even more miraculous than getting the children up the hill had been hauling the damn sheep. Keirith had been tempted to tell Ennit to leave them, but they both knew the tribe would need the meat.

So Ennit, Lorthan, and Braden coaxed, tugged, and prodded the protesting sheep up to the summit. It had cost Ennit a sprained ankle and the boys a good number of bruises, but they had done it. Once there, the sheep settled down to graze in the tall grass that sprouted among the scrub pines. They would eat better than the rest of the tribe.

Keirith knew their fate depended less on prayer and preparation than on Rigat. Perhaps his brother regretted Faelia's murder. Perhaps he would relent and sweep in to save them. That had been his plan once. Although he had no way to contact him, Keirith was certain Rigat would come—and that they would fight.

Oddly, he felt little fear. That was the comfort of knowing at least part of the future; it left you free to worry about more immediate concerns.

The sound of approaching footsteps made his head jerk up. He relaxed when he saw Callie scuttling through the scrub pines.

"What's happened?" he asked as his brother flung himself to the ground.

"Two Zherosi. At the edge of the rockfall. I think they want to parley."

Keirith had little hope of securing any terms other than surrender, but at least he could take the measure of the officers who led the enemy force.

"Do you want Holtik to go with you?" Callie asked.

"I'd rather have you. If you'll come."

Callie cuffed him. "Of course, I'll come. Idiot. I just didn't want to ask."

It took forever to pick their way across the loose pebbles. Twice, Keirith skidded, but he managed to reach the bottom without disgracing himself before his enemies.

The hawk-faced commander looked familiar; he must have been with Geriv at Little Falls. Keirith's mind had been too muddled by the drugs and the prospect of the prisoner exchange to pay much attention. But when he turned his gaze on the slim young officer standing next to him, he drew up short.

"What is it?" Callie whispered.

"The young one. It's the Vanel's son. Korim."

"The one Fa captured? Gods."

He had never imagined Korim would be among those pursuing them. From the stories they had exchanged, he knew the boy had little stomach for battle. Perhaps Geriv's death had changed that.

The commander surveyed them both with a grimace of distaste. "I am Jonaq do Mekliv, acting Komal. You've already met Skalel do Khat."

A dark flush stained Korim's beardless cheeks, but his expression remained wooden.

"I am Keirith, son of—"

"I know who you are."

"And this is my brother, Callum. As he does not speak your language, I would prefer to conduct these negotiations in the tribal tongue." He bowed to Korim. "If you'll translate."

Before Korim could respond, the Komal said, "The negotiations, as you call them, will be brief. You can tell him what he needs to know."

Keirith shrugged and translated for Callie, who whispered, "We won't get any concessions from him. Arrogant bastard."

"What terms are you offering?" Keirith asked.

"Terms?" The Komal laughed. "Surrender. And you and your family will be spared."

"And the rest of our tribe?"

"They're unimportant."

"Not to me. If we surrender, do I have your word that no harm will come to them?"

"For that, you must apply to the Son of Zhe. His moods are . . . changeable."

"And if we refuse to surrender?"

The Komal gestured brusquely. Three warriors emerged from the trees, spears held aloft.

Sickened, Keirith stared at the severed heads: Rendaron, the one Fa had nicknamed the Chatterer; Cradaig, who had shared with Owan and Lendon the thrill of reporting the planned ambush to the Spirit-Hunter; and Selima, her cracked lips still curled in a grimace of defiance.

"The others are rotting somewhere in the forest. And those with you will rot as well—unless you surrender. I'm a patient man. I can wait until you starve."

"But the Son of Zhe is not patient," Keirith replied, and had the brief satisfaction of watching the Komal's smile vanish. "And it will be many days before we starve."

"But far fewer until thirst drives you mad."

Keirith just shrugged. Let the man wonder if there was a spring hidden among the rocks.

"You have my terms. What is your answer?"

"I have your terms, but not your oath that my people will be spared."

The Komal hesitated. Then he smiled. "Very well. My oath, then. Your people will leave this place unharmed."

The massacre at the hill fort was too fresh in Keirith's memory to take comfort in those words. Komal do Mekliv would keep his oath. But once the tribe left its stronghold, he would slaughter everyone.

Keirith searched Korim's face, but he could read nothing in his dark eyes. "And will you give me your oath that my people will be safe?"

For the first time, Korim met his gaze. "I give you my oath that they will leave the hill unharmed," he said, his voice as cold as his expression.

The deliberate repetition of the Komal's phrasing could be a warning not to trust him. More likely, Korim had repudiated the tentative friendship that had sprung up between them at Little Falls. And why not? Keirith had deceived him, Fa had captured him, and Rigat had ordered his father's death.

He considered casting out the Komal's spirit and ordering the Zherosi to march away, but immediately rejected the idea. The Zherosi knew the power he possessed. He would never be able to fool them for long. His hesitation in replying to the offer had already made the Komal's eyes narrow in suspicion.

"I'll bring your ultimatum to the tribe. And I ask permission to take the heads of our dead comrades with us so that we may give them the proper rites."

"The heads remain atop our spears. But I'll leave them here. Where your people can see them."

As the Komal stalked off, Korim hesitated. Then he bowed and followed his commander.

When Keirith told Callie of the Komal's decision to display the heads, Callie spat. Then he marched toward the warriors, still standing at attention with their grisly prizes. Seeing the men tense, Keirith called out, "We only wish to say a prayer for our dead."

Only a shaman could open the way for their spirits to fly to the Forever Isles, but Keirith repeated the words, staring from one pair of empty eyes to the next.

"I'll tell the tale," Callie whispered. "And I promise your sacrifice was not in vain."

As they made their way up the hill, Keirith told Callie about the ultimatum and the Komal's oath.

Callie spat again. "They'll cut us down as soon as we're in the open."

"Save your spit. We have thirsty days ahead of us."

"Could we provoke him? Force an attack?"

"Only a madman would storm that hill."

They continued toward the summit in gloomy silence. Then Callie blurted out, "Do you think Rigat gave the order? To kill everyone except us?"

"I don't know."

But the Komal would never risk the wrath of the Son of

Zhe. Either Rigat had tacitly approved the slaughter or he had simply shrugged off the loss of the rest of the tribe.

"He might be testing us," Callie said. "The way he did before."

"Do you really believe that?"

"Nay." Callie turned back to stare at the severed heads. "There must be something we can do. It can't . . . it just can't end this way."

But this wasn't one of the tales Callie told. In those, the hero always triumphed against the malevolent forces arrayed against him. Even a tale of defeat, like the diaspora of The People, became a tale of redemption and rebirth in the mouths of the Memory-Keepers.

Who would be left alive to tell their tale? Or that of Selima and her brave boys? The Memory-Keepers would recite the legend of the Spirit-Hunter's epic quest, but the true story of his life would be lost, and with it, the story of the man—the real man—and his determination to preserve his family, his tribe, his way of life.

"Keirith?"

Callie's voice jolted him from his thoughts.

"There's something I've been meaning to ask you. Ela and I want to marry. Now."

Keirith nodded; only the gods knew if any of them would be alive at the Fall Balancing.

"We want you to perform the rite. You and Barasa."

"But . . . I'm not a Tree-Father. I can't—"

"You're the closest thing we have. You were Gortin's apprentice. And you performed the rite of manhood with me when I returned from my vision quest."

Would it even be a real marriage without a Tree-Father to officiate? Looking into Callie's pleading face, Keirith decided it didn't matter. "We can do it today."

"Not today! Ela would kill me. She'll want to fix her hair and brush her tunic. Make herself pretty."

Mam would have stood before the tribe barefoot and dressed in a ripped tunic in order to marry Fa. And Hircha . . .

She never paid any attention to her appearance. But she had looked beautiful the day she married Conn, that moon-gold hair flowing down her back like a waterfall, her seren-

ity and stillness such a contrast to Conn who kept rolling
his shoulders as if his tunic had grown suddenly tight, his
face alternately anxious and beaming.

"On the morrow, then," he said to Callie. "That'll give
us all time to prepare."

As he ducked into the cave, his mood darkened again.
No tale should end with severed heads and starving children. Or with a child dying unborn in its mother's womb.
There had to be a way out. If Rigat refused to help them,
perhaps Natha could.

Chapter 62

AS CALLIE AND ELA TOOK their places, Griane
could not help contrasting this wedding with hers. Instead of standing under the open sky in the center of their
village, the tribe huddled in the cave, while sentries kept
watch on the summit. Instead of a daylong feast, they
would share a few sips of lukewarm water, a few mouthfuls of roast mutton. And instead of dancing around a
bonfire at night, the children would whimper in their sleep
while the adults talked in muted voices about surviving
another day.

Yet Callie and Ela gazed at each other as if this hurried
ceremony were the perfect culmination of their love. Their
expressions dreamy, they listened to Keirith and Barasa
reciting the ancient words, oblivious to their kinfolk's filthy
clothes and strained smiles—and to the threat that hung
over them all.

In Keirith's dark eyes, Griane found an acknowledgment
of that reality. In his smile, the desire to forget it. And in
his voice, deeper than usual and soft with meaning, she

heard the lilt of a Memory-Keeper, rather than the grave cadences of a Tree-Father.

Can you see us, Darak? Do you know how happy our Callie is?

She wanted to believe he was watching, that Faelia stood beside him in the Forever Isles, Temet's arm around her waist, celebrating the rite they had never shared in life.

The sudden stab of grief brought the memory of her last glimpse of Faelia. Some claimed the dead looked like they were sleeping, but even from across the glade, she would have known Faelia's spirit had left her body. She had spent too many nights listening to her daughter thrashing on her pallet, grunting, muttering, sighing. Ever restless, her Faelia. Except in death.

Even if they had been home, Darak's absence would have made tonight's celebration bittersweet. Faelia's death was too recent, the wound too raw to feel joy. But for Callie's sake, she tried to put grief aside, along with thoughts of what Rigat had done—was doing—to them.

Keirith and Barasa enclosed the couple's clasped hands in theirs. The smile Keirith offered Callie was so full of love that it made her ache.

"What vows do you make to each other?" Keirith asked.

"I give you the love of my heart," Callie said, "the comfort of my body, and the protection of my sword-arm."

Ela swallowed hard at that reminder of the Zherosi. "I give you the love of my heart, the guidance of my wisdom, and the promise of the new life that grows in my body."

They both smiled at the intake of breath that greeted her final words. Griane knew every woman was eying Ela's belly, hidden under her shapeless tunic, trying to guess how far along she was.

What kind of future awaited their child? A life of slavery in a Zherosi field? Death in its mother's womb before it even beheld the world?

Don't think about the future. Or the morrow. Just think about this day, this moment.

Nedia knelt beside her sister and sprinkled a fistful of dirt over the two pairs of bare feet. "May the body of the earth goddess be ever strong beneath your feet."

Keirith breathed four times into the couple's faces. "May the breath of the wind gods blow lightly upon your heads."

Lisula eased sunwise through the narrow space around the couple, a flaming torch held aloft. "May Bel's fire always warm your days."

Barasa dipped her finger into a bowl of water and anointed their lips. "May Lacha's water always quench your thirst."

Griane stepped forward, the needle-sharp dagger resting across her uplifted palms. Keirith stared at the dagger for a long moment before grasping it. His left hand came up to stroke the fleshy mound at the base of his right thumb where he still bore the scar from his blood vow with Conn.

His gaze moved past her. The intensity of his expression made Griane catch her breath. Perhaps he heard, for he gave her a quick smile and turned back to Callie and Ela.

Griane glanced over her shoulder. Hircha's cheeks were flushed, but that could be due to the press of bodies in the cave. And many women's eyes were bright with unshed tears, remembering their bride-days, their lost husbands. But Hircha was watching Keirith.

Dear gods. Has it finally happened? After all these years?

"You're supposed to be staring at the bride," Hircha whispered.

Keirith made the small cut at Callie's wrist, then Ela's. While Nedia wiped the dagger clean, he and Barasa bound the couple's hands together with a strip of doeskin.

"Hand to hand they are bound," they recited. "Blood mingles with blood. Life joins with life."

Barasa unwrapped the doeskin. Nedia stepped forward to bandage Ela's wrist with nettle-cloth, while Keirith did the same for Callie. Then Barasa accepted a small stone cup from Lisula. Instead of elderberry wine, the couple would seal their union with water.

"As the Oak and the Holly grow from one root, so Callum and Ela are forever joined."

She raised the cup first to Callie's lips and then to Ela's. After the ceremonial sip, they faced each other, their eyes wide and serious as Keirith intoned the final blessing.

"What was two is now one. One blood. One body. One life. Callum and Ela, may your days together be long and fruitful, and may you meet once more in the Forever Isles."

A woman's choked sob was quickly drowned out by the shout of acclamation: "Blessed be!"

Please, Maker, bless them with many days together. Bless all our children with a future.

Callie cupped Ela's face between his hands and kissed her gently. The tribe cheered. Ennit hobbled forward to congratulate the couple. Hircha crumbled a fragment of nutcake over their heads to ensure that they would never know hunger.

Keirith hung back. When Griane touched him lightly on the shoulder, he muttered, "It cannot end like this." And she knew he was not thinking of the marriage rite, but of the Zherosi, waiting patiently for them to starve to death or surrender.

Soon after, he left the celebration. Griane slipped away, too, snatching up her healing bag from her meager pile of belongings. She chose a spot nearby that was shielded from the cave by a pile of boulders.

Her fingers fumbled inside her healing bag until they found the smallest of her clay jars. Ardal's mantle, they called the plant, for the drooping purple sepals resembled a cloaked head. But it was the poison in the root that had inspired some healer long ago to name it after the god who hunted the spirits of the dying.

A few grains could kill a rabbit within moments. A single drop of the root's juice on a wounded finger produced numbness throughout the entire body.

It would be easy to mix the powdered root with water. There was certainly enough for the children—probably for the entire tribe. A quicker death than starvation. And more merciful than a Zherosi blade.

"A healer's job is to relieve pain," Mother Netal had told her, "and save lives. But when there's no hope of saving a life, you must ease the person's suffering and—if necessary—offer a quick death instead of a lingering one."

She had done it before. But it was one thing to grant a peaceful death to men with their bellies ripped open by Zherosi blades and another to raise a cup of death to the mouth of an innocent child.

She returned the jar to her healing bag and called Rigat's name, hoping that somehow he could hear her, that he would return and end this. Three times, she called Fellgair's. She watched the blue of the sky deepen and Gheala's waning crescent rise above the trees. Then she rose and returned to the celebration.

She kept a smile on her face, but inside, felt only a numb weariness. Like his son, Fellgair had deserted them.

Keirith rose and stretched; short as he was, even he could not stand upright. To ease the crowding in the cave, the older boys slept in the grottos when they weren't on sentry duty. This one was too small for a fire pit—barely large enough to accommodate more than four or five people—but at least you had room to stretch out your legs, something only the children managed in the cave.

Tonight, Callie and Ela would share the other grotto, and the rare privilege of privacy. He had peeked inside when he left the celebration. The boys had built a fire there. The women had spread wolfskins beside the fire pit and scattered daisies across them. The sight of the flowers had made his throat tighten with love for his brother and for those who had tried to create a beautiful bower out of a gloomy hole.

This grotto was less cheerful. A broken pine spar partially blocked the entrance. The men had chopped off some of its boughs to use as bedding. Stones were piled near the entrance where a slinger could quickly snatch them up.

He had settled himself atop the boughs and closed his eyes, seeking stillness and emptiness—and Natha. As always, it was a comfort simply to reach his spirit guide and hear that familiar voice, affectionate and scolding. Less comforting was the concern in Natha's voice before he vanished.

"Be careful, hatchling. And remember that I am with you. Always."

Keirith paused by the entrance of the grotto to fix the details of the vision in his mind. Instead of disappearing over the side of the cliff, the line of people seemed to melt, vanishing like mist before the rising sun. And for the first time, neither eagle chick won the contest; the vision ended abruptly in the middle of the battle. He wanted to believe these small changes were good omens, but Gortin had always cautioned him about allowing his personal desires to influence his interpretation.

Skittering pebbles disturbed his thoughts. A ragged skirt appeared in the grotto's entrance, then a spill of blond hair as Hircha peered inside. "Callie's been asking for you."

Instead of stepping aside to let him leave, she scrambled over the pine spar and motioned him deeper into the grotto.

"What is it?" he asked. "Has something happened?"

"It's your mam. Nay, she's fine. But she left the celebration, too. And I was worried so I followed her." Hircha hesitated. "I heard her calling Rigat."

Keirith's bowels clenched. "He's here?"

"Nay. But I thought you should know."

"It would be better if he stayed away."

He sank down on the pine boughs. After a moment's hesitation, he pulled Hircha down beside him and described his visions.

"Have you told Griane?" she asked when he fell silent.

"It would kill her to imagine her sons battling. And the other . . ." He shuddered. Where once he had believed his mother was sleeping, now he feared that he had Seen her death.

"I've been thinking," he said. "About Rigat. How much he's changed since he began pretending he was the Son of Zhe. And I couldn't help wondering—"

"If you should have become the Son of Zhe when you had the chance?"

"I was never powerful enough to convince them of that. But the Khonsel gave me the opportunity to stay in Pilozhat. To pretend to be Xevhan."

"You never told me that."

"It was Malaq's dream to find a way for our people to live together. Perhaps as the Zheron, I could have made it come true."

"If the son of a god failed, how could you have succeeded? Nay, Keirith. You made the right choice. You could never have spent your whole life pretending to be someone else."

"Sometimes, I feel that's all I've ever done. I hid my gift as a child. I was meant to be a shaman, but somehow turned into a rebel. Today, I pretended to be a Tree-Father to make my brother happy. And now . . ."

Hircha butted him with her shoulder. "Now, you're sitting in a hole in the rock, feeling sorry for yourself."

Keirith butted her back. "Now, I'm sitting in a hole in the rock, feeling sorry for myself and wondering what's going to happen to all of us. We've only got water for a few more days. Sooner or later—"

"Stop. Just for today. And come celebrate with Callie and Ela."

She rose and pulled him to his feet. When he clung to her hand, her eyebrows drew together in a puzzled frown.

"Was it hard for you?" he blurted. "Watching the wedding? And remembering yours?"

She stared at the darkening blue of the sky beyond the grotto as if the answer lay there. "It was hard. I miss Conn. I loved him. In my way. But I never should have married him. Maybe if we'd had more time . . . I don't know."

"Xevhan casts a long shadow."

"Aye. But only because we've let him. Fourteen years is too long, Keirith. It's time we both came into the sunlight."

As they stepped out of the grotto, Hircha said, "There's something else. Griane called Fellgair's name, too. She waited a long while. But he didn't come."

"You're surprised?"

"I can't believe he'd abandon her. That he'd let her die here without trying to help."

"I can," Keirith said, his voice bitter. "For all we know, this is what he intended all along."

Chapter 63

IN HER DREAM, DARAK PACED on a sun-drenched beach. Tiny waves creamed the pebbles, leaving them glistening like precious gems.

Suddenly, he stopped and turned. A great smile blossomed on a face no longer lined with age, but smooth and young again. His hands came up, reaching for her—a young man's hands, whole and strong as they had been before Morgath's dagger did its damage.

She raced toward him, but he was already turning away, striding now through a shimmering sea of grass. He seemed to glow in the brilliant sunlight, while she remained shrouded in shadow—as if a cloud hovered over her, although there were none marring the vibrant blue of the sky. Now and then, Darak glanced over his shoulder and waved her on, but no matter how fast she ran, she could never catch him.

As he crested a little rise, she cried, "Wait!" But he just kept walking. And when she reached the top, he was gone.

She fell to her knees beneath one of the crab apples that dotted the hill. Two eyes blinked open in the knotty trunk. A blossom slid past one eye and caught on the groove of its mouth.

"I love you, Mam," the tree whispered. "More than anything in the world."

She looked up as more blossoms drifted downward. That's when she saw the other trees—rowan, apple, quickthorn—weeping white-petaled tears for her.

Griane awoke to Hircha's voice murmuring her name, Lisula's hands shaking her gently.

"You were calling Darak's name," Lisula whispered.

"I was chasing after him in the dream, but I couldn't catch him." She grimaced. "Soon enough, I will. Likely, we'll all reach the Forever Isles in—" Her breath caught. "Not the Forever Isles. The trees were in the Summerlands."

Lisula and Hircha exchanged glances, no doubt fearing she'd lost her mind. With an effort, Griane kept her voice low so she would not disturb those sleeping nearby.

"We've always had the answer. But none of us saw it. The First Forest, Lisula! You and Barasa can open the way for the whole tribe. And we could stay there until it's safe. You *can* open the way?" she added as Lisula frowned.

"I did think of it, Griane. When we first arrived here. But I was afraid to raise people's hopes. I've never had to hold the way open for so many. And the power fades so quickly. Perhaps on the hilltop. With our tree-brothers to help. But without Gortin . . ." She glanced over her shoulder. "Barasa's gift isn't very strong."

"We have to try! Even if it has to be done in stages. Half at sunset, the rest at dawn."

"Not at sunset," Hircha said. "There's too little cover on the hilltop. And if the Zherosi see us disappearing—"

"At dawn, then. On the morrow. Will you try, Lisula?"

"I'll talk with Barasa and Nedia now."

"And later—"

Griane broke off, watching Holtik picking his way toward them. Hircha made a space for him to crouch beside her, but Holtik just bent down and whispered, "Would you come with me, Mother Griane?"

She must have looked frightened, for he quickly added, "I don't think it's trouble. But . . ." He glanced around at the women and children just beginning to stir. "Please."

She allowed him to take her hand to lead her up the slope, but once out of earshot, she impatiently tugged free. "Tell me."

Holtik scratched his head. Opened his mouth. Closed it again.

"Bel's blazing ballocks! Just—"

"There's an old man. At the summit. Asking for you."

"An old . . . a stranger?"

"Aye."

"But . . . how did he get past the sentries?"

Holtik shrugged helplessly. "I'd just left my post. And there he was. Sitting with his back up against a pine tree. And when I went up to him, he asked if I would fetch you." Holtik cleared his throat. "He's naked."

A naked old man. Sitting on the summit. Asking for her. Griane was tempted to pinch herself to make sure she wasn't still dreaming.

"Well, mostly naked," Holtik corrected. "He has a scrap of red-and-brown cloth around his . . . private parts. And this . . . it might have been a tunic. Once. Made of fox fur, it looks like. But all that's left of it—Mother Griane! Wait!"

But she was already scrambling away, heedless of the shower of pebbles that cascaded down the hill in her wake. A rough hand seized her elbow and Holtik grated, "Killing yourself won't help matters."

Acknowledging the sense of his words with a brusque nod, she accepted his hand. When they reached the top, she spotted Keirith among the small knot of boys in the stand of pines. His stunned expression made her steps falter. As the boys made way for her, she understood the reason for Keirith's shock.

The long nose was the same. And the golden eyes. Otherwise, she would never have recognized the wizened creature slumped against the pine. Wisps of thin white hair framed the wrinkled face. A few patches of fur still clung to his shoulders, but his body was so thin she could see the outlines of his ribs.

"Hello, Griane. It's good to see you."

The voice that had once sent shivers of pleasure down her spine was little more than a whisper. She fell to her knees beside him, unable to stifle a cry.

Blue veins branched like twigs across the back of the hand that patted hers. Cracked yellow fingernails had replaced the black claws.

"Give him a mantle, one of you. Can't you see he's shivering?" Her voice was sharp with fear, but she prayed the others would mistake it for impatience. "Holtik, fetch Callie. Braden, send Hircha to me."

"You know him?" Braden blurted.

To reveal that this was their Trickster-God would terrify them and shame Fellgair. "He's . . . an old friend. Don't just stand there," she snapped as they continued to gape. "Go on. And not a word of this to anyone."

Even Holtik fled before her glare. She turned back to find Fellgair smiling. "What a queen you would have made."

"There are enough queens in this world." She picked up the mantle one of them had dropped and draped it around him. "Can you make it partway down the hill? Keirith and I will help you. There's a grotto where you can—"

"I'm fine. Don't fuss."

"You're not fine!"

Her voice broke. When Fellgair patted her hand again, it took all her control to keep from weeping. She had argued with him, cursed him, hated him for the pain he had brought her family. But he had brought her as much joy as pain. And he had given her the child of her heart.

"What's happened to you?"

"I'm being punished."

"The Maker would never do this."

"No. But the Unmaker would."

"Because of Rigat?" Keirith demanded. "Why should the Unmaker care? What's a little more chaos in the world?"

"It's not the chaos he resents, but my interference. He seemed to feel I was usurping his powers. So he's stripping away my immortality. Little by little."

"I remember now," Griane said. "When I met you by the stream. After Rigat disappeared. You looked . . . different. That's when it started, didn't it?"

"More or less. But I didn't come here to discuss that."

"I know. You came because I called."

"Did you?" The beetling white brows rose.

"You . . . you didn't hear me?" Griane asked.

"My powers are . . . diminished. As you can see. I can no longer maintain any shape but this one." His long nose wrinkled. "Nor can I read minds or hear the voices of those who call upon me."

"Then how did you find me?"

"I can still feel Rigat's energy. Although even that skill

is fading. I followed it. And opened a portal. After that, I walked. An army is very easy to trail." His rueful smile vanished. "The place that held Rigat's energy . . . it was a glade of foxtails." He squeezed her hand gently. "I'm so sorry, my dear."

Griane nodded, unable to speak. It was Keirith who said, "Rigat killed her."

The golden eyes widened, then squeezed shut as Fellgair leaned his head against the trunk of the pine.

"Did you see that in your web of possibilities?" Keirith demanded, his voice savage.

"Yes," Fellgair whispered. "But I hoped . . ."

"He allowed the Zherosi to slaughter our kinfolk. Then he set them on us. He cast out the spirits of two women and killed his own sister."

Fellgair opened his eyes. "Then, perhaps, it's too late."

His gaze sharpened. Glancing over her shoulder, Griane spied Hircha and Callie hurrying toward them.

"The beautiful Hircha," Fellgair said as they drew up short. "We met in Pilozhat. Of course, I was beautiful then, too. And you must be Callum." A wistful smile curved Fellgair's mouth. "You're so like your uncle Tinnean."

Callie smiled uncertainly. Hircha looked wary.

"It's the Trickster," Keirith said. "What's left of him."

"That's enough!" Griane cried.

"Should I be solicitous? After what he's done to my family? To the world?"

"You should be respectful. He's still the god of our people, the god who helped your father rescue Tinnean and the Oak-Lord."

Keirith had the grace to look abashed, but his voice was still defiant when he asked, "You said it was too late. To reclaim Rigat or save us?"

"I said it might be too late. To do either."

Callie knelt beside Fellgair. In his face, Griane saw the wonder of coming face-to-face with the god of legend—and pity for what the god had become.

"Because what Rigat has set in motion cannot be wiped away. The balance has shifted. The world has changed. The old ways are dying." Callie's head drooped. "Even the old gods are dying."

"But gods can't die," Hircha protested.

"They can," Fellgair said. "Oh, not the way I'll die—like an ordinary mortal." Again, his nose wrinkled in distaste. "The others will simply . . . fade away."

Griane seized his hand. "Not Cuillon. Not the Oak-Lord."

"Perhaps not—if there are still people who worship them. But I think even they will change. There's always change. Order and chaos vie for power. And that struggle changes the world and every living creature in it—gods and men alike. In time, another Trickster will emerge. Where would the world be without one?" Fellgair sniffed. "Even if he's only a pale shadow of what I once was."

"Then there's no hope," Keirith said. "For us or for the world."

Hircha squeezed his shoulder. "There's always hope."

As she explained their plan to cross into the First Forest, Griane watched her boys. Callie's face reflected his excitement; Keirith's showed only his doubts.

"Can it work?" Callie asked.

They all turned to Fellgair. Even now, wasted and frail as he was, they still looked to the Trickster for answers.

"Yes. I think so. I'll help Lisula hold the portal open."

Callie smiled. Hircha looked relieved. Only Keirith continued to look doubtful. Perhaps, he, too, heard the false note in Fellgair's confident voice.

"But right now, I'd like to speak with Griane. I doubt we'll have time later."

Callie rose and bowed. Hircha backed away. But Keirith bent over Fellgair and thrust his face close. "If you hurt her, I'll kill you."

Griane's protest faded as Fellgair said, "I owe you an apology."

Keirith's face went blank with surprise.

"For what I said the last time we met. It was not my secret to reveal. And doing so was . . . malicious. If I had been myself . . . but I was already changing. Prey to the more unpleasant human emotions. And Darak . . . Darak wounded me. So I lashed out." His lips pursed as if he had tasted something sour. "Quite unforgivable."

"Aye. It was."

Fellgair just smiled. "Callum's like Tinnean. And you're like Darak. He was just as fierce when he was young. Fierce, proud, stubborn. And lonely and bitter, too."

Keirith flinched.

"It took Griane to mellow him." Fellgair's gaze drifted past Keirith. "You really must find a good woman. Like your father did."

For a moment, Keirith was taken aback. Then he scowled. "Haven't you interfered enough?" He stalked away, striding past Hircha without a glance.

"Love among the ashes," Fellgair mused. "How romantic."

"Is it love?" Griane wondered aloud. "I'm not sure."

"Give them time."

"They've had years."

"I keep forgetting that a year is a long time for a mortal. To me, their first meeting in Pilozhat happened only a moment ago. And my first meeting with you and Darak, a moment before that. I was with him. At the end."

"Darak?"

He leaned forward, his face anxious. "If I could have saved him, Griane . . ."

"I know."

"His vision mate was there, too. They . . . left . . . together."

Tears blurred her vision and spilled over. Fellgair wiped her cheek and raised his forefinger to his lips. After a moment, he sighed. "They used to be so delicious. Now they simply taste like tears. Forgive me, my dear. I always seem to make you cry."

"Nay. I'm glad you told me. Glad he wasn't alone."

"How could he be alone in the grove of the One Tree? With Tinnean and Cuillon?"

"Did Tinnean speak to him? Before the end?"

Fellgair frowned. "You didn't see? When Lisula opened the way?"

She shook her head; they'd all been too shocked to see anything but Darak.

"Whether or not he spoke to Darak in words, Tinnean sent him a path of speedwell. Darak knew his brother was with him, Griane. Bidding him farewell."

And now Fellgair had come to bid her farewell. It seemed impossible that she would never see him again. That he would die. They had met only a few times in the course of her life, but even during the long absences, he was always there. As much a part of her world as the air she breathed and the earth under her feet. And later, of course, she had Rigat to remind her.

"What will happen to him?" Then she remembered that Fellgair could no longer read her thoughts and added, "Rigat."

"That's why I shooed the children away. I wanted to see you, of course. But I came to talk about our son."

"Is he . . . how is he?"

"I saw him only once. After . . . after Faelia. He was . . . sleeping. I found him in Carilia. He'd gone there to end the war."

Fellgair's tone told her that Rigat had not gone to seek a truce, but to use his power to destroy his enemy. Again.

"You're the only one with any hope of controlling him, Griane. The only one who may still be able to stop him from doing more harm."

"I love you, Mam. More than anything in the world."

"I've tried to talk to him, to convince him—"

"It's too late for talk."

"What are you saying? That I should lure him here and stand aside while the tribe kills him?"

"It needn't come to that. Without his power, Rigat is as mortal as any other man. He could not continue to play the Son of Zhe. Or control the fate of nations." Fellgair hesitated. "But only if his power was drained. Completely."

"You said you'd give your life for me."

And suddenly, she understood what Fellgair refused to say outright. It was as obvious a solution as the tribe fleeing to the First Forest. And just as necessary.

Darak had offered himself on that tree in Chaos. This was her sacrifice. And if it could protect the children of the Oak and Holly, the life of one old woman was a small price to pay.

"Can you take me to him?"

"I'm not certain he's still in Carilia. And my power is

ebbing. Bringing you through portals with me while I search for him will only drain it faster. I'm sorry, Griane. It must be here."

"The grotto, then. Before nightfall. The men sleep there and—"

"Give me until sunset. I'll bring him to you then. I swear it."

"And if he refuses to come?"

"He'll come. He will always come for you."

She had Ardal's mantle. But she needed a method that was slower, if just as sure. After a moment's hesitation, Griane drew her dagger, surprised by the steadiness of her hand. Aye, a dagger would be best.

Something warm and wet splashed on her hand. She blinked hard to clear her vision. But when she looked up, she realized it was the Trickster who was weeping.

The day passed in a sort of haze. Griane heard herself speaking to people in what sounded like a normal voice. She watched her hands wrap a fresh bandage around Owan's arm with their usual skill. But a part of her was already sitting in the grotto, waiting for Rigat.

There could be no farewells, of course. Nothing to suggest that this day was different from any other. All she could do was share time with those she loved.

As she inspected Ennit's ankle, she reminisced with him and Lisula about happier times. She admired Mirili's granddaughter and spoke of the joys and tribulations of raising children. She thanked Holtik for his loyalty to the tribe and his friendship with Keirith.

It was harder to be with her family. She hoped they would understand her choice. More than anything, she hoped they would forgive Rigat for forcing her to it.

With Callie, she shared memories of Darak's first experience with fatherhood. With Hircha, she tried to speak only of practical matters such as conserving their supply of herbs, but inevitably, she ended up talking about Keirith.

"I've never pried. You know that. But if you love him— or believe you could . . ."

"How can I even think of that?" Hircha demanded in a fierce whisper. "With everything that's happening?"

"How can you not?" Griane countered.

Hircha shoved a hank of hair out of her face. "I don't know what I want, Griane. I just know I don't want to hurt him by making promises I can't keep."

"Then don't make promises. Just . . . be with him. Share his worries. Don't let him retreat into himself."

The afternoon was waning before she managed to get Keirith alone. He was lying belly-down at the western edge of the hilltop, watching the smoke of the Zherosi campfires. Expecting him to pelt her with questions about Fellgair's appearance, his brooding silence disturbed her. In the end, she asked that he try and forgive the Trickster.

"You saw him, Keirith. He's going to die. Soon."

"He had enough power to open a portal."

"And the effort left him too weak to stand! Blame him for telling you of my choice. Blame him for creating Rigat. But don't become so bitter that you forget the good he's done. He saved me from Morgath. He helped Darak survive Chaos. And he gave Darak the means to save you in Pilozhat. Can't you see that?"

"I See far more than I want to!"

It was the way his face froze after he blurted out the words that made Griane seize his arm. "What? What have you Seen?"

He shook his head, but she clung to him even when he tried to rise. Finally, he slumped beside her again. "I Saw you. Lying in the cave. Asleep. I thought the man with you was Fa. But when I saw Fellgair today . . ."

Griane went very still. "We were sleeping?"

Although Keirith nodded, he refused to look at her. She knew then that he had Seen her death—and Fellgair's.

"You should have told me."

"How could I?" he whispered. "I wasn't even sure myself."

"What else have you Seen?"

He shook his head.

"Keirith . . ."

"I've Seen your death! Isn't that enough? Oh, gods, Mam. I'm sorry. I—"

"Hush. It doesn't matter. And if your vision was true, it sounds like a peaceful death."

His fingers clamped around her wrist. "It may not happen. It may happen years from now. There's no way of knowing."

"Aye. Visions are chancy. At least, that's what Gortin always said. Well, chancy or not, I've got too much to do to worry about dying."

She managed a rueful grin and was relieved when Keirith smiled, too. But she left him after that, afraid she would say too much.

She found Hircha in the cave, bandaging Arun's finger and scolding him for being so careless with his dagger. Impatiently, Griane waited for her to send the boy away, then leaned down to whisper, "I must talk with you. Alone."

They made their way to the grotto Callie and Ela had shared. The daisies had been placed in a small clay flask. They were wilted now; water was too precious to waste on flowers. The shriveled petals on the wolfskins reminded Griane of the weeping trees of the Summerlands.

She thrust the memory aside and pulled Hircha down beside her. "Has Keirith spoken of a vision about Rigat?" When Hircha hesitated, she grabbed her shoulders. "I know he's Seen my death. I don't care about that. But if he's Seen anything to do with Rigat, you must tell me."

She listened with growing horror to Hircha's description of the battle between the two eagle chicks, a battle in which the female eagle was present but aloof. Did that mean she would already be dead when her boys fought? Or that she was helpless to stop them?

"Why didn't he tell me? Why didn't *you* tell me?"

Hircha mumbled something about protecting her, and Griane bit back a rebuke. "Hircha, listen to me. There's very little time."

She told Hircha her plan and watched the color drain from her face.

"There has to be another way!"

Griane just shook her head.

"And if he refuses to give up his power?"

"Rigat loves me."

"He's changed, Griane."

"Not that much. But he'll need time for the healing. You must keep Keirith away from the grotto, Hircha. By any means in your power."

The blush rose and faded on Hircha's cheeks. "I tried to seduce him once. At Xevhan's behest. Did you know that?"

"I'm not . . . I only meant . . ."

"I know what you meant. So do you. Let's not fool ourselves. If I . . . distract him . . . he'll realize the truth soon enough. And he'll never forgive me for deceiving him."

"It's his life, Hircha! If they confront each other while Rigat still possesses his power, Keirith will die. You're the only one who can prevent that."

Hircha rose. "Don't worry. I'll play my part. Just as I did the last time. But you might have allowed me to volunteer my services. I would have, you know. No matter the cost to me. That would have been . . . kinder."

Griane's cry stopped Hircha at the entrance to the grotto. "Don't go! Not like this. I was wrong to suggest . . . what I did. I've always been too plainspoken. And now, I'm . . . I'm frightened for my boys. But I can't part with you like this, knowing I may never speak with you again."

Griane held out her arms, and Hircha stumbled into them. She hushed her flood of apologies and held her until the trembling ceased. Then she wiped Hircha's damp cheeks and sent her off with a final kiss.

She glanced around the grotto and found the tools she would need. Patiently, she twirled the firestick until a spark caught in the tinder. Breathed life into the smoking nest. Fed the fire with dead twigs and branches until she was certain it would provide enough light for Rigat to work by. Belatedly, she realized he might not even require the light, but the fire cheered her.

She murmured a prayer to the Maker. Another to Fellgair. Then she drew her dagger and waited for sunset.

Chapter 64

FROM THE BALCONY OF HIS bedchamber, Rigat watched the purple shadows crawl up the western face of Kelazhat. Darak had always considered sunrise the magical time, because it heralded the beginning of a new day. Rigat preferred sunset. It heralded Nekif's arrival with the brew that brought darkness and escape.

Nekif had cried during the whipping, although Rigat had given him only six strokes with the rod, enough to demonstrate the Promised One's displeasure without leaving any lasting scars. Since then, he had been very gentle with him, but the old slave always trembled in his presence.

Behind him, sandals pattered softly against tile, then abruptly ceased.

"You're not dressed yet," Jholianna said.

He turned. The dusky rose artfully applied to her cheeks deepened under his scrutiny.

"You're very beautiful."

His words seemed to startle her. He must remember to compliment her more often.

"The feast will begin soon," she reminded him.

"The feast. Yes."

He would have to postpone the pleasure of oblivion. The Carilians had surrendered. The war was over. He had brought the news yesterday and accepted the frenzied acclaim of the court. Messages had been sent by bird, by runner, by ship. The empire would resound with praise and prayers for the Son of Zhe, the Promised One, the fire-haired god made flesh.

"Tremble before him and greet him with dread. For with him comes only death."

A discerning man, Geriv. Except in the case of the noblemen. True, three were executed—the ones who had considered inciting a mutiny—but thanks to him, the others had lost only their fortunes and estates.

"You *are* coming? To the feast?"

"Of course."

He would make a passionate speech that would move the drunken courtiers to tears. He would smile during the songs composed in his honor. He would even listen to the Zheron recite the prophecy without wincing. He knew his role as well any player in the acting troupe that would perform tonight.

"Shall I send Nekif to help you dress?"

"Yes. Thank you." But he turned back to gaze north once more.

"Are you all right?"

"Just tired. Give me a few moments. Then send Nekif in."

Despite the obvious dismissal, Jholianna continued to hover behind him. Slowly, he turned. His expression must have alarmed her, for she shrank back.

Schooling his voice to patience, he asked, "Was there something else?"

"I was thinking . . ." A tentative smile. A light brush of fingertips against his forearm. "Now that the war is over, perhaps we should go to the summer palace. In the mountains. It's quiet there. Restful. The change would do us both good."

As if a change of scenery would banish the nightmares. As if the mountains would do anything but remind him of the steep, forested hills of his homeland. But he nodded. A small concession to ease her anxiety.

"You've accomplished so much since you came to Zheros. More than I dared dream."

The words seemed familiar. Then he remembered that Fellgair had said much the same thing before he went to Chaos. Before everything went wrong.

"Remember those accomplishments, my dear. And try not to dwell on the past. On what cannot be changed. That way lies despair."

Or madness. Or the slow slide into oblivion afforded by the drugs. Perhaps Jholin had been wise, after all.

"Give yourself time. And try to be kind to yourself."
She raised his hand to her lips. "And remember, I am always here."

Always here. Always watching. Like a fox in the grass.

As her footsteps retreated, he chastised himself. Jholianna was only trying to be kind, to offer him the wisdom of her experience. She would offer whatever he needed—wisdom, passion, solace, drugs. Anything to keep him beside her, to harness his power for Zheros. But at least she was loyal. Unlike the others. The Khonsel and Geriv. Faelia and Keirith. Mam.

He was turning to go inside when he caught a flicker of movement in the corner of the balcony. The air rippled and subsided. Rippled again. For just a moment, he glimpsed a figure. Then the air shattered, and he stumbled backward.

An old man swayed between the roiling columns of air. The bulky woolen mantle draped around his hips only accentuated the frailty of his body. It took Rigat a moment to recognize Fellgair, another to recover from the shock of his father's continuing deterioration.

Rigat summoned his power to hold the portal open. Fellgair took a single uncertain step. Then his legs buckled.

Rigat caught him as he fell. Fellgair's mouth opened, but all that emerged was a wheezing gasp. He squeezed his father's hand—the fingers like dry twigs between his—and let his power seep into him.

Fellgair's body sucked it up as greedily as Darak's. Flesh fattened the hollows between his ribs. Color returned to the ashen face. But he shook his head, his eyes so desperate that Rigat broke off the healing. Only then did the straining body relax in his arms.

"Why didn't you come to me sooner? I told you I would help."

"I did." A reedy voice, barely recognizable. "You were too drugged to listen."

It was possible. He needed the drugs every night to keep the nightmares at bay. But he recalled one time in Carilia. Golden eyes staring into his. A voice calling his name. He'd assumed the drugs had twisted his perception. So he had blamed Nekif. And beaten him.

Guilt made his voice brusque. "Well, I'm not drugged

now. What do you want? And if you're just going to lecture me—"

"Your mother is dying."

Rigat recoiled. "If this is one of your tricks—"

"Don't be a fool, boy! Griane is dying! Use your power if you don't believe me. Search for her energy. But hurry. Please! There's not much time."

The raw terror on the Trickster's face swayed him. And when Rigat focused his power on his mother and felt the uncertain flicker of her energy, the same terror engulfed him.

The sky blazed with color—gold, rose, purple. It reminded Keirith of the spectacular sunsets he had seen in Zheros. He was still admiring it when he heard the rustle of grass. Glancing over his shoulder, he saw Hircha trotting toward him.

"I brought your supper," she said, sliding to the ground beside him.

"You didn't have to do that. Holtik will take the watch as soon as it's dark."

She handed him a tiny doeskin bundle. "The last of the mutton."

"That's for the children. We all agreed."

"The women decided the men needed the meat more. You're skin and bones, all of you."

He unwrapped the bundle and rolled onto his side, chewing the tough meat slowly. Hircha lay beside him, gazing west.

"It's like a gift," he said. "A final, beautiful sunset before we cross into the First Forest."

"Do you think it will work?"

"It has to."

"Even with Fellgair's help, we may not get everyone through."

Keirith grimaced; talking about Fellgair spoiled the beauty of the sunset.

"Why do you hate him so much?"

"Why does everyone keep defending him? You. Mam."

"Griane cares about him. And I . . . I care about Griane."

"I wished he'd stayed away. Why can't he just let her go?"

"Because he loves her. Just as he loved Darak."

"He has a strange way of showing his love."

Still gazing out over the forest, Hircha said, "So do you."

For a moment, he could only stare at her. Then he cleared his throat, feeling as awkward and uncertain as he had that afternoon on the beach in Zheros when she had tried to seduce him. And the morning three years later when they had kissed for the second time.

It had taken him days to work up the courage. When he had seen her walking toward the lake, he'd clutched his fishing line so tightly his nails dug into his palms. He must have looked desperate—or terrified; her smile of greeting changed into an anxious frown. Before he lost his nerve, he dropped the line and grabbed her shoulders. He could still remember her waterskins bumping against his legs, the painful click of their teeth—and then, her hands pushing him away.

A hot flush of shame suffused him at the memory. And then another—hotter still but not of shame—as her tongue flicked out to moisten her lips. He waited for her to look at him, to give him some sign, but she kept staring at the forest.

Then she licked her lips again. "Everyone in the cave . . . they're packing and talking and telling the children stories about the First Forest."

Confused by the sudden shift in the conversation, he mumbled, "Are they?"

"The children can't wait to see the One Tree. But the adults are thinking about what might go wrong. Wondering if this is our last night together."

"It won't be," he said with more confidence than he felt.

Hircha nodded, clearly unconvinced.

"You said yourself there was hope."

"Like a child reciting a charm. Say it often enough and maybe the bad things will go away. But they never do."

For the first time, she looked at him. He was taken aback by her fierce expression.

"Well, if something goes wrong, don't expect me to say ood-bye. I lost my birth family. My husband. And one by ne, I'm losing my second family. First Darak. Then Faelia. And now—" She broke off. "I can't lose you, too."

Before he could offer any meaningless reassurance, she ushed him back on the grass. His arms automatically went round her, but his mind registered the bruising intensity f her kiss, the rigidity of her body. He told himself it was only her need to make up for so many lost years. His body ched with the same need. It urged him to forget that they ould be seen by anyone on the hilltop, to accept their wkward groping as an indication of passion long sup- ressed, to ignore the gnawing doubt that there was some- hing wrong about this moment.

He tore his mouth away from hers to whisper, "Hircha. Wait."

She silenced him with more kisses and shoved his tunic up. The shock of her cool fingers sliding over his flesh jolted im into momentary forgetfulness, but when she fumbled with the drawstrings of his breeches, his hands captured ers.

"Not here. Later. In one of the grottos."

"Nay!"

The fear in her voice doused his passion. "Why not?" He grabbed her arms, holding her away from him so he ould look up into her face. "Why not, Hircha?"

"I want you now."

"We've waited this long . . ."

Strands of hair brushed his cheeks as she shook her head. Her fear stabbed his spirit, as real as the scream of the wood pigeon all those years ago, as visceral as the screams of dying men.

He pulled her into his arms and stroked her hair. One part of him marveled that this was happening; another con- inued to seek explanations. She could have come to him anytime since they had arrived at the hill. Why today? Es- pecially since they had a plan that could—would— guarantee the tribe's survival.

It must have something to do with Fellgair's visit. He would not have come simply to bid Mam farewell. They were planning something. And Hircha knew about it and was determined to keep it from him.

Rigat. It had to be. Rigat was coming to see Mam. And
Hircha had decided to seduce him rather than risk having
his vision come true.

He thrust her away and shook her hard. "When is he
coming?"

No mistaking the terror in her eyes or the desperate way
she clutched at him. When he broke free, she grabbed his
ankle. He fell hard, bruising his hip. She fought him as
fiercely as she had kissed him, but he finally managed to
push her off.

"Please, Keirith! You have to wait!"

"For what?"

Her gaze shifted past him and her eyes widened. Keirith
staggered to his feet and spun around, groping for his dagger. Then he froze.

"You must wait," Fellgair said, "for Rigat to choose."

Chapter 65

BLOOD. EVERYWHERE. Soaking her skirt. Staining
the wolfskins. Snaking into the crevices in the rock.
Pooling in the deep gashes in her wrists. The metallic stink
of it filling the tiny cave. The brilliant streams of it glistening in the firelight.

"Nay . . ."

He had expected an arrow wound, a sword slash, broken
bones from a fall. Anything but this.

He had driven her from her home. Hunted her like an
animal. Killed her only daughter. And now, trapped on this
barren hill, she had chosen to kill herself rather than surrender to the Zherosi.

Rigat knelt beside his mother. So white, her face. And
her hand, so cold beneath the warm coating of blood.

"Nay."

He dug his fingertips into her neck. Flattened his palm between her breasts. Pressed his face against hers, searching in vain for a pulse, a heartbeat, a faint exhalation of breath.

She couldn't be dead. She was Griane the Healer. She was his mam.

"Nay!"

Three times. Three times for a charm.

The power surged on an upwelling of terror and defiance. Her body convulsed, shocked by the onslaught, but her heart refused to answer his summons.

He reached into her spirit. For a terrifying moment, he felt nothing. Then he found a wisp of energy, as fragile as a single strand of a spiderweb.

Clinging to their tenuous connection, he gave her more power, but the thread of her spirit drifted farther away, seeking the longed-for release from pain and the brilliant sunlight of the Forever Isles. Seeking Darak, her first love.

"Don't leave me, Mam!"

Hers was the face that was always before him, the voice that he always heard—sharp or sweet, chastising or praising—when he considered his actions. Long before he had recognized his power, he knew her face, her voice, her touch. And before that, a tiny creature in her womb, they had been one body, one blood, one being that was also two. Like the magical tree of the First Forest.

His power flooded her spirit, a summons, a plea, a desperate cry. The gossamer strand of her spirit shivered as new threads sprouted, twisting together into a pulsing braid of life, an umbilical cord that linked them as surely as that first one in her womb.

His power roared into her heart. Again, her body convulsed, but this time, he felt a feeble flutter beneath his hands. Like the wings of a tiny bird. Like Darak's heart.

He seized the hands that had cradled him as a babe and reached out to catch him when he took his first tottering steps. The hands that had braided his hair and sewn his clothes and bandaged his scrapes. That had tickled him and made him laugh and, once or twice, smacked his bottom before pulling him close for the hug that always followed a scolding.

If he could force open the gates of Chaos to find his

father, he could defeat the Dark Hunter Ardal to save his mother.

His power spiraled into the ruined flesh of her wrists. He thrust aside terror to draw on patience, on skill, on determination. On love.

He was the spider repairing her web, the salmon that battled upstream to spawn. The fox that outsmarted his prey and the wolf that outran his. He was the relentless heat of Heart of Sky and the eternal strength of Halam, the earth goddess. He was the gentle rain of The Changing One of the Clouds and the thundering force of Lacha's waterfalls. He was Fellgair the Trickster who had defied the Lord of Chaos, and Griane the Healer who had brought the Spirit-Hunter back from death.

He began to stitch together the lacerated veins and arteries, to weave the severed strands of sinew, to patch the tough bands of ligaments. His hands grew hot. Beads of sweat ran down his cheeks like tears.

Light flared behind his closed eyelids, the same dazzling explosions of red and orange and fiery white he remembered from healing Jholianna and Darak. But there were so many more this time, as if thousands of tiny suns were exploding along with all the stars in the night sky.

Something soft against his cheek, something tickling his mouth. The swell of his mother's breast, a strand of his mother's hair. He couldn't remember slumping against her. He hadn't the strength to pull himself upright. He could only lie there, breathing in her scent as he used to when he crept under her wolfskins at night.

He could no longer feel her hands, only the cool stickiness of the blood under his fingertips, under his knees. The blood that had drained from her body.

A sob rose up in his throat. He could repair the wounds. He could jolt her heart into life again. But without blood, she would still die.

Why had he tried to repair this poor, empty shell? There was only one way to save her.

Come into me, Mam.

The smallest flicker of response.

Come into my body.

The smallest spark of awareness.

I'll keep you alive.

The way Darak had saved Keirith.

The way he had sustained Jholianna.

Until he could find a Host for her. A new body, young and strong and whole. She would never have to endure the pain of aging. She would never have to fear injury or illness or death. And they would remain together forever, their love uniting them, their lives spanning centuries.

Hurry, Mam! Come into me.

Three times for a charm.

He flung aside every barrier and opened wide the gateway to his spirit. Waited for her to abandon her ruined body and follow the energy that linked her spirit to his. Braced himself for the initial tumult of their joining, ready this time as he had not been when Jholianna's spirit crashed into his.

Ready.

Eager.

Joyful.

But her spirit held back, unable to surrender its hold on her body. Gently, he urged her closer, only to feel her recoil.

Don't be afraid.

And then he realized the truth. She wasn't afraid. Nor was she unable to break free of her body. She refused to.

How could she reject that hope—her only hope? How could she choose death instead of life? How could she choose death instead of him?

He enveloped her spirit with his power, determined to pull her spirit into his, only to sense the cord between them—the cord he had created with love—begin to fray.

The sob tore free of his throat in a howl of despair. He would not lose her. If she could not endure life in a stranger's body, he could not face centuries of existence without her.

Blood pounded through his face, his chest, his fingertips. His blood, calling to hers.

He summoned it from soaked doeskin and wet fur. Called it from crevices in the rock. Stirred it from congealing puddles around the fire pit.

He couldn't retrieve all of it. He didn't need to. Just

enough to feed her body, to win her time to create more herself.

Two streams of blood flowing over the cold fingers and into the gaping wounds at her wrists. Two streams of life spiraling through her veins, up her arms, into her chest, reaching for her heart and embracing it. Two hearts, beating like drums, his thudding with renewed hope, hers sending the sacrificial blood pulsing through her body, filling it with life.

Spilling through the unsealed wounds at her wrists.

"Please . . ."

Her life was still draining away, her spirit tied to her body only by his determined grasp, her heart beating only through his will. His power was as sluggish as the streams he sought to dam, as faint as his mam's heartbeat.

He poured himself into her. The will that had brought an empire to its knees. The power that had dazzled the greatest ruler in the world. The love that had filled him, nurtured him, sustained him through every moment of his existence.

The dying stars shimmered like fireflies in the darkness. Who could have imagined that death could be so beautiful?

The light faded from the brilliant reds and oranges of a sunset in Zheros to the softer roses and pinks of the north. He had forgotten how pretty sunsets were here. How the lingering twilight turned the sky the muted blue-gray of a dove's wing before finally surrendering to the darkness.

A star exploded and died. Another blinked out. But the two drums beat a tattoo as slow and stately as those that had accompanied him into the throne room on the day he had been proclaimed king. His mam's heart and his. Beating together as if they were one being.

A single star still hovered in the sky. White as his mam's hair. Pulsing bravely in the darkness. The last flickering ember of his power.

He had to preserve it. Just that one tiny star. Until he could find someone to stitch her wounds and stop the relentless flow of blood. Until he could grow strong enough to offer another infusion of power.

Desperately, he reached for the star, but it drifted deeper into the vast, black sky.

Come back.

The star winked, daring him to catch it.

Please. Don't leave me.

He could feel its light pulsing inside him, the indescribable sensation that had been as much a part of him as his mam's love. And then the star winked again, and there was only darkness.

The twin drumbeats stopped. The brush of his mam's spirit disappeared. There was only the soft sound of her breathing, the slow rise and fall of her chest. Ordinary sensations like the spiky fur of the wolfskins against his bare legs and the hard solidity of the rock underneath, the warmth of the fire and the dull crack as a branch shifted and fell.

Rigat opened his eyes. Embers blazed up from the fire pit only to flicker and die like the stars of his power. The flames danced, but he could only hear the crackle of dead branches. The fire's song—soaring and frenzied in its wildest moods, cheerful and warm when it was banked to embers—that was lost to him now. As was his innate understanding of the birdsong he heard outside the cave, reduced to a discordant chorus of cheeps and trills and squawks.

Empty.

Hollow.

Ordinary.

With an effort, he raised his head and stared into his mam's still face. He could endure the loss of the stream's song and the fire's. The ability to open a portal between worlds with a mere flick of his finger. To understand the language of animals. Even the unquestioned power he had enjoyed in Zheros. But how long before the flush of color on her face faded to the corpselike pallor he had seen when he'd first entered the grotto? How long before his healing unraveled like a poorly woven mantle?

Rigat lowered his head onto her shoulder and sobbed.

It was all for nothing, like his futile attempt to forge a lasting peace. He had squandered his gift and doomed her to the same lingering death Darak had suffered.

Outside, he heard the dull clatter of pebbles. They must have discovered his presence. And now, they were coming for him. They would kill him. Or drive him away. Certainly, they would never let him to stay with his mam.

Somehow he managed to push himself up. He reached

for the bloodstained dagger, then let his hand fall. Better
to let them kill him. At least that way, he and his mam
could be together.

A figure darkened the entrance of the grotto. Once, he
would have known the identity of the man simply by sensing his energy. Now, he had to wait for him to duck inside.

Of course, it was Keirith. He had Seen how it was supposed to end.

But he had expected Keirith to come alone. Instead, Hircha pushed past, clutching Mam's healing bag to her chest.
Then Rigat noticed the hunched figure hovering behind
Keirith and realized that his first instinct had been correct:
it was another of Fellgair's tricks and they had all been
part of it—even his mam.

A tear slid into the corner of his mouth. It merely tasted
salty. But he could still recall the tears he had tasted the
day he had discovered he was the Trickster's son. And he
knew that whatever his mam had done, she had acted out
of love.

A great weight settled upon him. Once, his power would
have enabled him to shrug it off. But if that was lost, he
still had enough willpower to stagger to his feet.

He knew what he had to do. For once, the path was clear.

Chapter 66

THE GROTTO REEKED of blood: soaking Mam's
clothes, staining Rigat's hands, dripping down his
brother's legs. More shocking still was Rigat's smile.

"A clever plan, Keirith. Your idea or Fellgair's?"

"It was hers," Hircha shot back. She was holding Mam's
wrist, fumbling for a pulse. She settled back on her

haunches, her expression dazed. "She's alive. I didn't think . . . with all the blood . . . but she's still alive."

Something—someone—brushed past him. Fellgair, he realized, as he watched the Trickster kneel beside Hircha. And then Rigat said something about "a family reunion."

He was leaning against the wall of the grotto, grimacing as he wiped his bloodstained palms on his khirta. He looked up long enough to say, "Pull yourself together. You've seen sacrifices before."

All Keirith could do was shake his head—just as he had when Fellgair told him what Mam intended. The Trickster's face had been so sad, his voice so gentle, even kind—like a father patiently explaining something to a child too young to understand.

When he had finally willed his body to move, it was like wading through the sea, every step slow and awkward. And suddenly—the way the world abruptly shifted in a vision— he was running, stumbling on the uneven ground, slipping on loose pebbles, careening from boulder to boulder, unable to pray, barely able to think. The only thing that kept going through his head was "Nay." Just that one word.

He repeated it now, his voice as thick and choked as if he were strangling. An errant thought struck him—Fa telling him what it was like right before he loosed an arrow at a deer, of being in the moment, but standing apart, observing everything from a distance. And so it was now, his body shaking, but his mind cataloging random observations: the firelight dancing across his mam's still face; the frenzied blur of Hircha's hands upending Mam's healing bag and digging through the contents; Fellgair's eyes, watching him, watching Rigat; and Rigat, still leaning against the wall of the grotto, looking impossibly bored. Despite the graceful slouch and the impatient sigh, the folds of his brother's khirta shook.

Not bored. Barely able to stand.

"So now what?" Rigat asked. "We fight to the death? Play out your vision of the two eagle chicks?"

Before he could answer, Fellgair asked, "Did you use all your power?"

Rigat's laugh made Keirith wince. "Wouldn't you like to know?"

"Yes," Fellgair replied. "I would. That's what she wanted. That's why she was willing to sacrifice her life."

"And that's why you pretended to be so weak when you came to fetch me. You wanted to be sure you could reduce me to an ordinary mortal."

"I wanted what Griane wanted. To stop you and Keirith from fulfilling that vision. To save the world that she loved. To save you from yourself."

"By robbing me of the one thing that makes me myself?" Keirith finally shook off the enveloping numbness. "You're more than just your power."

"*Just* my power?" Rigat shook his head. "You've never understood. My power is everything."

"If that were true, you wouldn't have saved her."

"I didn't."

Keirith shot a glance at his mother. Hircha was kneeling beside her, needle darting like a minnowfly as she stitched one wrist.

"Oh, she'll live. For a day or two. But she's lost too much blood. Without another infusion of power, the healing will fade. Just as Darak's did. So you can kill me and save the world. But if you do, Mam will die." Rigat grinned. "Quite a choice, isn't it? The world or Mam. Which will it be, Keirith?"

"He's lying," Fellgair said.

"I love her." For a moment, genuine emotion tore at Rigat's voice. "Would I squander my gift knowing that would doom her?"

"Then go," Keirith said. "Take Mam and go."

Rigat's face went blank.

Fellgair began speaking in a low, urgent voice, but Keirith cut him off with an impatient gesture, still watching Rigat. His brother's head drooped. A trembling hand covered his face.

"I don't know whether you have power or not," Keirith said. "But I won't risk Mam's life to find out. Open a portal. Go to Zheros. Go anywhere. Just keep her alive."

"That's not what she wanted," Fellgair persisted.

"She didn't want me to kill my brother, either!"

Rigat slowly straightened. "A noble gesture," he said softly.

"I just want—"

"Gods, you make me sick."

Keirith's head snapped back as if Rigat had struck him.

"You have a gift, Keirith. Puny compared to mine, but still a gift. You might have been great if you had been willing to use it. If—just once—you'd actually done something other than fly with your damn eagle. I'm half your age and look at all I've done."

"Like killing your sister?" Keirith demanded, and had the savage pleasure of seeing Rigat wince.

"Like ending wars."

"And abandoning your people."

"Didn't you just tell me to walk away? But you would say that. It's what you've always done. Walked away. Given up. Your power. Your position in the tribe. Hircha."

"Leave Hircha out of this."

"Don't tell me you finally convinced the chilly widow to open her legs?"

"That's enough!" Keirith shouted.

"Nay, I didn't think so. Well, thank the gods, I won't die a virgin. Too bad we won't have more time together. I could share some of what I've learned from my queen."

Keirith bit back a retort. Why was Rigat deliberately goading him? Why didn't he just leave?

"I won't fight you, Rigat. Though that's what you seem to want."

"You wouldn't like to test your power against mine? Just once? The odds are as even now as they'll ever be. Or perhaps, you'd prefer a more old-fashioned test."

Rigat lurched forward, fists clenched. Hircha cried out. So did Fellgair. But their voices were drowned out by another.

<Take him. End this.>

Xevhan's voice whispered inside Keirith, as soft and seductive as a lover's.

<You're the strong one now. Prove it.>

He didn't have to prove anything. All he had to do was let Rigat walk away.

<Coward.>

He was keeping his mam safe. Honoring her last wish.

<Her last wish was to stop Rigat. She was willing to die to accomplish that. Will you fail her as you failed your father?>

He would not fight Rigat. He would not kill his brother.

<But you have to. You've Seen this battle.>

That didn't mean it was inevitable.

<But it is. It has been. From the moment he was conceived.>

I won't condemn my mam to death!

<She condemned you first.>

Nay.

<She chose Darak.>

It's not the same.

<Then let him go. Watch him grow strong. Watch him cut down every tree in this land. Hunt down every person in this tribe. He's already killed your father. And your sister. Let him go. And watch him destroy everyone and everything you've ever loved.>

Keirith clutched his head, as if that would shut off the insidious voice. Instead, others crowded his mind.

Mam's voice, gently scolding. *"You were never a killer. Perhaps because you could sense the pain of others."*

Fa's voice outside Hua's hut: *"You're a healer. Like your mam. Only you heal spirits. That's your gift. And you must use it."*

Rigat's voice, so young, so eager: *"I think we're like Fa and Tinnean. It took both of them to save the world."* And a more somber Rigat: *"If someone has power, there must be a reason."*

The soft voice assured him there was a reason, the same reason he had survived his ordeal in Pilozhat: to kill Rigat. He was the only one who could. And this was the only chance he would ever have.

The air in the grotto seethed with unseen energy. The rocks vibrated with it. As if Rigat were calling on the remnants of his power, preparing to strike him down.

And all the while, the seductive litany continued, a ceaseless whisper that ebbed and flowed inside Keirith's spirit, now hissing like foam on a beach, now crashing against him like a mountainous wave, taunting him, beating him down, urging him to yield.

<You must kill him.>

Half his life, spent in thrall to that voice.

"Why do you cling to him?"

Rigat was his brother. To destroy him was to destroy part of himself.

"Until you understand, he will never leave you."

Keirith's breath caught. He staggered backward and slammed into the wall of the grotto. Natha had known. His spirit guide had tried to show him the truth. But he had been too frightened to face it.

Not Xevhan's voice. It had never been Xevhan's voice. That was simply the name he had given to the shadowy parts of his spirit where the lingering shame of rape lurked, the doubts about his gift, the fears about his manhood. The hidden places he had tried to ignore until they emerged in nightmares. The dark places he had never wanted to acknowledge.

Far easier to believe it was Xevhan who ruled that side of him, a foreign taint that stained his spirit. But they were all part of him—the dark places and the light, the fear and the courage, the cruelty and the mercy.

Foolish hatchling, Natha had called him. And so he was if he could look into the spirits of others, but fail to see the truth inside his own.

Rigat stood a few paces away, studying him intently. The dancing flames cast harsh light on one half of his face. The other was bathed in the soft glow of twilight that spilled through the entrance of the grotto. His hands were fisted at his sides, but to Keirith, it felt as if they were clenched around his heart.

His brother's face was as ravaged as Fellgair's, his body shaking with exhaustion. He was little more than a boy, but he was as old and ruined as the god who had fathered him.

Keirith eased along the wall of the grotto. He could feel the energy spiking, that same unsettling shift in earth and air that he had felt moments before the wood pigeon screamed. He had to escape before he was drawn into the death struggle he had foreseen.

A wave of revulsion twisted Rigat's face. "Dear gods," his brother cried, "what do I have to do?"

Rigat walked toward him, one slow step at a time. "Shall I describe how Faelia's spirit screamed before she died? Or the way Conn made love to Hircha? Or how our mother would always choose me over you? Just as she chose Darak all those years ago?"

"You can't make me fight."

"Not even if I told you that Darak's last words were

about me? That with his last breath, he whispered my name? In the end, even *he* chose me."

Rigat was so close Keirith could see the sweat on his forehead, the lines of strain that bracketed his mouth. But his brother's eyes were veiled, fixed on something else.

Rigat's right hand darted out, pinning him against the wall. His left fumbled at Keirith's hip. But only when he looked down and saw Rigat's fingers clenched around the hilt of his dagger did he realize what his brother had been staring at.

He grasped the skinny wrist. Braced to combat a thrust to his midsection, he was unprepared when Rigat's arm jerked him away from the wall. Locked together, they both staggered. Keirith regained his footing first, staring transfixed at the dagger between their bodies, the lethal tip pointed not at his belly, but at Rigat's.

The blue eyes—so like their mam's—met his, fierce and bright and shining with unshed tears. The ravaged face—so like his father's—tightened as he forced the point closer.

Keirith planted his feet and threw his weight backward. Rigat's breath caught on a sob, but he swung his forearm around their locked hands to give him added leverage. It was terrible and inhuman, the strength of those thin arms and the determination on that straining face.

He had Seen this battle again and again, but he had never imagined that he would be fighting to save his brother.

She was drifting, insubstantial as a cloud. Not like the first time. She had been flying then. Soaring skyward into peace and freedom. She'd heard Darak's voice, faint but clear. And Rigat's, pleading with her.

The voices she heard now seemed familiar, too. But they were quarreling. Childishly, she had assumed that people never quarreled in the Forever Isles, that they spent their days frolicking on the sunlit shores. But people were people, after all. And spirits—whether or not they had bodies—probably didn't change much after death.

The voices grew louder. Men's voices and a woman's,

querulous and shrill. Her disappointment grew; instead of Darak, she was apparently fated to meet some sharp-tongued stranger.

The quarreling voices shredded her pleasant cloud. Or perhaps it was the sharp thing that kept stabbing her wrist. Briefly, she fought, seeking the delicious weightlessness and peace. But her will was as insubstantial as the cloud she had once been, and reluctantly, she surrendered to the voices and allowed them to carry her earthward.

Her body felt weighted down now, as if trapped under dozens of woolen mantles. Yet they offered as little warmth as the sun, although she could sense it flickering somewhere in the darkness.

Disappointment gave way to despair. Had the Maker denied her entrance to the Forever Isles? Was it the uncertain light of Chaos she saw behind her closed eyelids? And the voices those of the doomed spirits imprisoned there?

Griane opened her eyes. She saw neither the brilliant blue sky of the Forever Isles nor the ocher-colored light that Darak claimed filled the sky of Chaos. There was only rock. It was rather pretty—filled with sparkling bits of orange and white that winked at her—but rock, all the same.

Something soft and spiky beneath her hands. Something cold and wet in her lap. And a woman's voice shouting, "Let me go!" so close that Griane flinched.

Slowly, she turned her head. Hircha was struggling in Fellgair's restraining arms. Griane blinked, uncertain if she was dreaming. But when she opened her eyes again, Hircha still fought and cursed, and Fellgair still strained to hold her.

She turned her head away. Firelight dazzled her eyes. Above it—beyond it—two men shuffled back and forth, clumsy as bears.

A moan formed in her throat as the truth slowly dawned. Keirith and Rigat, her firstborn son and her youngest, locked in a death struggle.

Helpless tears leaked down her cheeks at the enormity of her failure. Why had she imagined that she could save the world? She should have thought only of saving her children. She should have waited for Rigat and left with him and used whatever influence she possessed to work on him later.

She had thought the greatest sacrifice she could offer was her life. Now she would pay a far higher price—the life of one or both of her sons.

Her lips framed the word "Stop," but only a whistle of breath emerged from her mouth. She turned her head toward Fellgair, willing her hand to seize his bare ankle. All she managed to do was flex her fingers.

A muffled grunt made her turn her head again to see Keirith pinned against the wall of the grotto. She could hear his hoarse gasps as he struggled with Rigat. But he was going to lose. Even drained from the healing, Rigat was stronger.

A soft whimper escaped her. She had abandoned Keirith once. She had promised the Maker her life for his. She could not watch him die now, nor allow him to shoulder the guilt of killing his brother.

That was her responsibility. To strike down Rigat before Keirith could. To destroy him just as she had tried to do before he was born. To kill the child of her heart.

Her gaze fell on the bloodstained dagger next to Fellgair's grimy heel. She took a deep breath, then another, and dug her fingers into the fur. With terrible slowness, her hand crawled across the wolfskin. Her fingertips brushed rock, then crawled forward again to curl around the hilt of her dagger.

The worn leather thongs were as familiar as the tiny imperfections on the narrow flint blade. This dagger had made the incisions in Darak's back. It had taken Faelia's finger. It had sliced open her wrists. Not as pretty as a Zherosi blade, but just as keen when making a sacrifice.

Maker, help me.

They were only a dozen paces away. And her will had always been strong.

Griane rolled onto her side. She heard Hircha's shocked cry. Fellgair's voice, calling her name. But she ignored them, gathering the strength she needed to reach her sons.

Something brushed her shoulder. A hand covered hers. She turned her head. Golden eyes filled her vision, huge in that wasted face.

"Are you sure?" Fellgair asked.

She nodded.

"Then I'll do it."

She shook her head. The grotto tilted. Black dots swarmed before her eyes, obscuring Fellgair's face. She clutched at the dagger, but it was already gone.

Hircha's arms, helping her to sit. Hircha's tears, warm and wet against her neck. She wanted to look away, to blot out Fellgair's figure walking toward her boys, but if she could not perform the deed herself, at least she could witness it.

Oh, Rigat.

Rigat slammed Keirith against the wall of the grotto. Keirith's legs buckled, and he slid slowly to the ground.

"Nay," she heard him gasp. "I won't let you do it."

Rigat tensed. Then Fellgair called his name and he whirled around.

He stared at the dagger in his father's upraised hand and the tension drained from his body. His head turned. His eyes met hers. She tried to shout, "I love you." Perhaps he heard her whisper, for a smile of pure joy lit his tired face.

My dearest child.

Fellgair held out his arms as if to embrace their boy, the flint blade of her dagger as black as a Midwinter night.

Forgive me.

Still smiling, Rigat threw himself into his father's arms, flung himself onto his mother's dagger. His body went rigid, his eyes suddenly wide. But it was Keirith who screamed, an animal howl of grief and rage that echoed through the grotto and through Griane's spirit.

He charged Fellgair and battered him with his fists. Fellgair staggered, but made no attempt to ward off the blows. Only as Rigat slid from Fellgair's arms did Keirith abandon his assault. He caught his brother, dark head bowed over the bright one.

"Please," Griane whispered. "Please."

"Keirith!" Hircha cried. "Keirith, bring him here! Your mam . . ."

Keirith lifted Rigat, swaying with the effort. When Fellgair tottered toward him, he snarled at him to keep away. But even if he had wanted to bear his burden alone, he was not strong enough. It took both of them to ease her boy into her waiting arms.

As she brushed the tangled hair from his face, his mouth twisted in a grimace of pain. "It hurts, Mam."

"I know, love. But not for long. Hircha will give you something."

"Callie . . ."

"Hircha will bring him, too."

Fellgair and Keirith supported her so that Hircha could slide free. As she ran from the grotto, shouting Callie's name, someone slipped behind her, cushioning her back from the hard stones. It must be Fellgair, for Keirith crouched beside Rigat and took his hand.

Rigat looked up at him. "Don't be mad, Keir."

Keirith's eyes squeezed shut, but he opened them immediately and shook his head.

Rigat's gaze drifted to Fellgair. "Thank you. I didn't . . ." The spasm of pain that silenced him rippled through his body into Griane's. After it subsided, he fell back in her arms, his breath coming in short, hoarse pants. "I didn't want it . . . to be Keirith."

An unearthly moan escaped Keirith, abruptly cut off as another spasm seized Rigat. Griane closed her eyes, unable to watch his agonized face. She felt Keirith's arms, straining to hold Rigat until the convulsion passed.

She heard the splash of water. Felt someone touch her arm. Griane opened her eyes to find Hircha emptying the contents of the tiny jar into a cup. Callie stood behind her, his face as white as Rigat's. Griane took the cup from Hircha. Fellgair steadied her hand as she held it to Rigat's lips.

"I'm sorry," Rigat whispered.

"I know, love. Hush, now."

His teeth rattled against the stone, but he swallowed obediently.

As his head lolled back against her shoulder, she whispered, "Help me. Help me turn him." She did not want the cold rocks of the grotto's ceiling to be the last thing her boy saw.

Callie helped Keirith roll Rigat onto his side. Griane lay back in Fellgair's arms, her face close to her son's. His mouth moved, but already the numbness would be setting in, making speech impossible.

A few grains could kill a rabbit within moments.

"I love you," she whispered. She kissed his mouth. Her lips tingled. Before Ardal's mantle could numb them, she whispered, "Sleep, my beautiful boy."

She breathed in his breath, his eyelashes brushing hers. The fire crackled once and was silent. Outside the grotto, she heard the liquid trill of a wren. The sacred bird of the Holly-Lord, offering a final glorious salute to the dying light of day. But her boy could not hear it.

In a trembling voice, Keirith began reciting the ancient words that would open the way to the Forever Isles. Griane's mind formed other words, equally ancient: *I seek but cannot find you. I call but receive no answer. Oh, beloved, beloved. Would I had died for you.*

Chapter 67

KEIRITH NEVER KNEW how long he sat there with Rigat's cold hand gripped in his. At some point, he noticed that the fire had died to mere embers. Glancing at the entrance of the grotto, he discovered it was dark outside.

Hircha leaned over and whispered something to his mam. She nodded, without taking her gaze from Rigat's face. But as Hircha slipped out of the grotto, his mother reached over and laid her hand atop his.

When Hircha returned, she brought Lisula, Nedia, and Ela. She must have already told them what had happened, for their expressions were dazed rather than horrified. Ela threw herself into Callie's arms and burst into tears, but the priestesses simply sat down beside his mam. Lisula winced, though, when she saw the blood staining the mantle Callie had draped over Rigat's body.

"There are things that need to be done," Lisula said. "For Rigat and for Griane. My daughters and Hircha will help me. When we're finished, Hircha will fetch you. So you can sit with them for the rest of the night."

It took Keirith a moment to realize he had been dismissed. His mam gave him a weak smile. When Callie bent down to kiss her forehead, her hand came up to touch his cheek. Fear shredded Keirith's haze of grief when he noticed the fresh blood staining the bandage around her wrist.

He followed Fellgair out of the grotto and leaned against a boulder, sucking in great gulps of the cool night air. Callie draped one arm around his shoulder. Gratefully, Keirith leaned against him. After all the years of protecting Callie, now he was the one who needed his younger brother's strength.

In silence, they watched Hircha and Ela trot past them and return carrying two bundles. In silence, they watched them slip back into the grotto. Gheala rose over the trees and the Archer took his place among the stars and still they stood there, unable—unwilling—to speak.

Finally, the question seared on Keirith's mind burst free. "Why?" he demanded in a fierce whisper. "I would have let him go. I didn't want to fight him."

"Without his power?" Fellgair replied. "Without the means to save his mother?"

"He could have started over. I would have helped him. He had his whole life ahead of him!"

"Yes. I know."

The dull grief in Fellgair's voice reminded Keirith that the Trickster was suffering, too. Hard enough for a god to sacrifice his son. Now that he was becoming mortal, grief and guilt must be flooding his spirit. And how much more terrifying those emotions must be for someone who had never felt them before. Even Keirith had to pity him.

After a moment's hesitation, Callie rested his hand on Fellgair's shoulder. "It was his choice. How could he live with himself after Faelia? And without Mam . . ." His voice shook. "How long does she have?"

"Better to ask a healer than a fallen god," Fellgair replied, "but . . . not long, I think. He didn't finish the healing."

Callie sank down on a boulder, his head bowed.

"I can sustain her for a little while. But I must save some of my power to help Lisula hold the portal open for you."

Callie's head came up. "You're not coming with us?"

"The Zherosi must know the Son of Zhe is dead. They must . . . see the body. And carry the news to Pilozhat."

The crunch of pebbles alerted them to another presence. Hircha's hair gleamed as golden-white as Gheala's crescent. "You can come back now."

As she continued walking past them, Keirith cried, "Where are you going?"

"Griane wants Ennit."

The women had washed Rigat's body and folded his hands across the jagged wound in his chest. They had dressed Mam in clean clothes and combed her hair. Her head rested on Lisula's belly. They must have changed the wolfskins, Keirith noted dully as he sat beside her; the fur was unstained.

Her gaze drifted around the grotto until she found Fellgair who hung back near the entrance. "Sit," she whispered. "Beside Keirith."

Fellgair hesitated. Their eyes met. Keirith considered all the pain the Trickster had caused his family. Remembered the mocking voice of the Supplicant, the taunts of the foxman. He didn't know if the rare moments of tenderness outweighed all that Fellgair had done, only that he had to let go of the bitterness before it stained his spirit forever.

He shifted to his right, allowing Fellgair to sit at Mam's shoulder.

"I'm feeling . . . a little weak," she whispered. "Can you help me?"

Fellgair nodded.

"Just a little. You must save your power. For the crossing. But there are things I need to say and—"

"Hush, you foolish girl."

His mam smiled. Her eyes closed as Fellgair took her hand. A faint flush appeared on her sunken cheeks. Then Fellgair sagged against him. Automatically, Keirith's arms went around the frail body.

Fellgair's eyes fluttered open. "Forgive me. I'm all right."

But the pouches beneath his eyes were dark as bruises

now. The last clumps of fur had vanished. And the honey-colored eyes had faded to a dull yellowish-brown.

"That bad?" Fellgair whispered, the ghost of a smile curving his mouth.

"Nay," Keirith managed as he helped him sit up. "You're fine."

Fellgair's laugh was a mere exhalation of breath. "And I thought Darak was a bad liar."

The shifting shadows drew Keirith's gaze to the entrance of the grotto. Ennit hobbled past Hircha, tears oozing down his lined cheeks. He drew up short, staring at Rigat. Then he glared across the fire pit.

"I'm not saying good-bye, woman. You hear me?"

"The Zherosi can probably hear you," Lisula said. "Hush and sit."

There was barely room for them all to crowd around the fire pit. Ela sat across Callie's lap, while Hircha carefully lifted Rigat's head onto hers.

"You are the people I love most in this world," his mam said. "But I've never been one for sloppy sentiment and I won't start now."

Her voice was stronger, the result of Fellgair's infusion of power. But Keirith suspected her will was just as strong. She had things to say and she knew she had little time.

His mother was dying. Fading as he watched. The rational part of him was resigned to that and determined to do whatever he could to make her last days peaceful and happy. That was the part that reminded him that she was probably glad to go, eager to see Fa again and—please, gods—Rigat and Faelia. But the child in him just wanted to cling to her and beg her not to leave.

"I'm not sure how long I have. If I don't live long enough to see our village again, I want you to—Ela, stop that weeping, you're as bad as your father—I want you to take my body to the Death Hut and lay it beside Darak's."

"Griane . . ." Fellgair began.

"Wait."

Ennit's eyebrows rose as the Trickster meekly subsided.

"Lisula, take Darak's bag of charms. His finger bones are in it. And Faelia's and Rigat's."

Keirith exchanged a shocked glance with Callie. The

priestesses had folded Rigat's hands to hide the missing forefinger. But Faelia . . . dear gods, his mam must have cut it off herself. He could not imagine the courage that must have taken.

"Lay Darak's bones and mine in the cairn," she continued calmly. "And the children's."

"Griane . . ."

She frowned at the second interruption, but even she must have noticed the urgency in the Trickster's voice.

"Forgive me, my dear. But I'm not sure your people should return to the village."

Stunned silence greeted his words.

"I had hoped that, without Rigat's power to guide them, the Zherosi would cease gobbling up your land. That they would content themselves with what they already possessed. But now . . ." Fellgair's gaze drifted to Rigat's body, then returned to Mam's face. "If they make a martyr of him, the north becomes a holy land. This hill, a shrine to their fallen god. And they will seek vengeance against those who killed him."

Yet the Trickster had helped Rigat die. The god who had played games with their lives—with the lives of thousands, millions—had opened his arms without hesitation and given his son the death he so desperately desired. Had he known then what the consequences might be? Or had he simply wanted to grant Rigat's wish—like an ordinary father?

"Then it was all for nothing," Hircha said bitterly.

Callie shook his head. "I won't believe that. There has to be a reason. There has to be hope."

"I want to believe that, too," Fellgair replied. "But I fear for your people. I've seen many futures, but in most, the Zherosi cut down the forests. Build settlements. Marry the girls of the tribes. In only a few generations, there might be none left to worship the Oak and the Holly."

"But there would always be priests to hold the rites," Lisula said. "And Memory-Keepers to tell the tales."

"The tales—yes. Those will survive. But that's all they'll be—wonderful stories. About a hunter named Darak. A healer named Griane. A boy named Tinnean."

Fellgair's voice held only an echo of its former beauty, but it still sent a shiver through Keirith.

"You must keep the tales alive, Callum. In the First Forest."

"You mean . . . stay there?" Callie asked. "Forever?"

"How would we survive?" Ennit demanded.

"Darak did. Griane did."

"You gave them fire," Lisula pointed out.

"Do you think the Tree-Lords would do less? Cuillon would break limbs from his body to feed the fire that would warm you. The Oak-Lord would offer his to give you bows and spears. And the tree-folk of the Summerlands would do the same for the sons of Griane."

"So great a sacrifice," Nedia murmured.

"Your people have offered countless sacrifices to the gods," Fellgair reminded her. "For your people to survive, the gods must make sacrifices, too."

"That's really why you're staying behind, isn't it?" Callie asked. "To sacrifice yourself."

"I've already told you why I'm staying," Fellgair replied with a touch of his old asperity. "I have little time left. When I lose the last remnants of my power, I will die." A shudder rippled through his thin shoulders. Then he gave a hollow chuckle. "But tell the tale that way if you like. It will make me sound so much nobler."

Keirith was suddenly aware that his mam had not spoken since Fellgair's announcement. The flush had fled her cheeks and she looked terribly frail, but her expression was as determined as ever.

"Fellgair is right. I'd hoped . . ." She shook her head. "It doesn't matter. On the morrow—before dawn—I want to be carried up to the hilltop so I can watch you go."

It took a moment for the import of her words to reach him. His cry of protest was immediately joined by others, but his mam simply waited for their voices to fall silent.

"I won't argue. I haven't the patience—or the time—for that."

"But we can't just leave you here alone!" Hircha cried.

"I won't be alone." Her gaze drifted to Rigat before settling on Fellgair. He seemed unsurprised by her choice.

Resentment blazed, hot and fierce, at the prospect of Fellgair sharing Mam's final moments of life, but when the Trickster's mud-colored eyes fastened on him, it leached away. Whatever Fellgair had done—to him, to Mam, to Fa—it didn't matter any longer.

But the thought of leaving her behind was unbearable.

"Callie," she said, "give me your dagger." Her hand rose, only to fall back onto her lap. With an impatient sigh, she said, "You'll have to do it."

Uncertainly, Callie glanced at the blade in his hand. "Do what?"

"Cut off a lock of my hair."

Callie rose onto his knees and carefully sliced off a small strand.

"Winter is cruel in the First Forest—even with the gods' help. The tribe must go to the Summerlands. And you must lead the way, Callie. You know the tale by heart. Go to the mouth of the great river and call Rowan. I know . . . I'm sure she'll hear you. And she'll take you in."

Callie's fingers clenched around the lock of white hair. "Mam . . ."

"Promise."

He took a shuddering breath and nodded.

"That strand is for you. Cut two more, please. For Keirith and Hircha." As Callie obeyed, she mused, "I did this in the First Forest. To mark the trail for Darak. That was the first thing he said when he woke up. 'What happened to your hair?' I could have killed him."

Keirith's hand shook as he accepted the lock of hair. He knotted it once and placed it in his bag of charms with Fa's.

"He kept it, you know. That circlet of hair. In his bag of charms." Suddenly, her hand darted out to squeeze Callie's knee. "You must take his bag. Show the hair to Rowan. She'll remember. I gave her one just like it."

"Aye, Mam."

Reassured, she sank back again. Even that small effort had drained her.

"Lisula. Ennit. Girls. Go back to the others. Tell them what has happened. And help them prepare for the crossing."

"And you?" Lisula asked.

"I'll just rest a bit. So I'll have strength for the morrow."

But it was already the morrow. Too soon, dawn would arrive. And then they would be parted forever.

All night, they sat with her, watching the slow rise and fall of her chest. She drifted in and out of sleep, sometimes waking long enough to talk with them. Always of the past—of the happy times. Mostly, she seemed content to listen, offering an occasional nod or smile.

Hircha changed the bandages on her wrists. Keirith and Callie added wood to the fire. Each time Mam stirred, they all tensed, only to relax when she drifted off again.

Fellgair spoke only once. Staring at Rigat's body, he whispered, "He was born in a cave, too."

Dully, Keirith reflected that the Maker—and perhaps even the Unmaker—must appreciate the symmetry. Order and chaos fought, but in the end, balance was restored. And so it was with his brother, a creature of light and dark, order and chaos, god and man. All his life, Rigat had struggled to find that balance. Perhaps in death he had.

Their sporadic conversation waned along with the night, until only the crackle of burning wood and the soft sound of their breathing disturbed the stillness. Keirith stared into the fire, awash in memories. Images formed before his dazzled eyes: the widespread wings of an eagle, the sinuous shape of an adder. A small shadow swallowed up by the longer one of the man who walked before him. A bronze blade slicing open the blue expanse of the sky. The frenzied splashing of fish in a pool. A stag, crafted from the water's foam. Malaq's freckled bloodstone. Rigat's freckled face. And the pregnant woman from his vision, waving farewell.

He pulled himself from his reverie to stare around their little circle. There was Callie, who had always known his life-path and would fulfill it in the First Forest. Rigat, who had tried—and failed—to fulfill his. Hircha, who would become healer to the tribe. Fellgair, who had shaped the destinies of millions. And his all-too-human mam, the only woman in the world who had walked the fields and forests of the Summerlands, who had shared a life with the hero who helped save the world, and created a son with the god who was becoming a man.

His twisting life-path had brought him to this grotto. What lay beyond it? A future with Hircha, perhaps. But whether as friends or lovers, he couldn't guess. Tree-Father to the tribe? Once that thought would have filled him with joy; now, he felt strangely empty.

He would see many wonders in the First Forest. He would have the opportunity to help his people weather the difficult days ahead and recover from the suffering they had endured. He had insisted that Rigat could start over, yet here he was, hanging back. Had the losses of this world left him immune to the wonder of the other? Or was he destined by his nature—or fate—to be forever dissatisfied?

Impatiently, he rose, startling Hircha and Callie. He muttered something about going outside to clear his head, but the crisp air did little more than chill him.

The orange glow of the fire faded. Turning, he discovered Fellgair at the entrance of the grotto, hands splayed on the rock to support him. As he shuffled forward, Keirith flung an arm around his waist and carefully eased him onto a boulder.

"Can I get you something? Water? Or—?"

"No. Listen. I know you hate the idea of leaving your mother with me."

"Nay. I mean . . . it's different now. Everything's . . . changed." His voice sounded forlorn, like a child crying for a lost toy—or an old man, longing for the happy, half-remembered past.

Fellgair seized his hand, startling him. "Stop looking back, Keirith. Stop clinging to the boy who died in Pilozhat. Or the wounded young man who lived on in the body of a stranger. Rigat's words tonight were cruel, but they were mostly true. You've always been reluctant to use your gift. In Pilozhat, circumstances forced you to act. But in your own land, you seemed content to . . . drift. I'm not blaming you," Fellgair quickly added. "When choices bring pain— to you or to others—it's easier to avoid making them. But you must seize your life, Keirith. As shaman or rebel, healer or chief. You must weave the pattern yourself."

Fellgair paused, gasping for breath. But when Keirith bent over him, the Trickster pushed him back. "Forgive me if I'm interfering. An old habit. Or if I appear to be playing the role of father. I'm ill-equipped to do so. But I love your parents. And I want their son to be happy. As mine never was."

"Just . . . happy?"

Fellgair reared back, peering at him in the darkness. "Isn't that enough?"

"I don't know. Fa wasn't seeking happiness when he joined the rebellion. Nor was Rigat when he declared himself the Son of Zhe. Now that they're gone, it seems selfish to seek happiness when they were willing to die for the causes they believed in."

"Darak never believed in the rebellion."

"He believed in his family. In keeping us safe. That was always his cause. No matter what the tales say, he went into the First Forest to save Tinnean, not the Oak-Lord."

Fellgair sighed. "And lived to raise a family of zealots. You. Faelia. Rigat. Even Callum, with his fervent devotion to the old tales. The world is changing, Keirith. Gods are dying. Tell your own tale."

Keirith went very still. The image of the pregnant woman flashed through his mind. The intent faces of Selima's fledglings as they listened to the story of Fa's vision quest. And the trembling smiles of those whose spirits he had healed with his power—Hua and Eilin, Duba and Luimi, Idrian and Nuala.

He bowed to the Trickster. "Thank you. I understand now."

Chapter 68

IT WAS STILL DARK when Holtik and Braden came to the grotto, packs strapped to their backs. They carried others that they handed to Callie and Hircha and finally, to him. Keirith hesitated, then slipped his arms through the ropes. Then he strapped on his sword belt.

As Holtik turned to go, Keirith stopped him. "Thank

you. For everything. I wish—" But he couldn't tell Holtik what he wished. He could only add, "You're a good friend."

Callie gathered Mam in his arms. The Trickster managed a few tottering steps before he collapsed. Ignoring his protests, Keirith picked him up; he was as light and spindly as a lamb.

When they reached the hilltop, he made out the shadowy forms of the rest of the tribe, huddled in the small stand of pines. Carefully, he set Fellgair down beside Mam and eased through the crowd, seeking Lisula. He heard the fretful wail of a babe, quickly hushed. A man's low murmur. And the nasal bleat of Young Dugan.

His head jerked toward the pale blur of fleece. Cursing under his breath, he hurried toward it.

Ennit's head came up as he approached. "He's coming with us," he whispered, nodding to the struggling ram. "Him and Blossom."

"Blossom?"

"My ewe."

"Ennit . . ."

"If we're meant to stay forever, I'm taking my flock with me. They made it this far. They deserve to come."

They would be lucky to get the tribe across, never mind the damn sheep. But he had more important battles to fight.

Now that the time had come, his choice weighed heavily upon him. His carefully prepared words fled as he walked toward Callie and Hircha, still sitting at the edge of the trees with his mam and Fellgair.

He eased the pack off his back, crouched next to his mother, and took her hand. "There's not much time. So I'll be quick. I'm not going with the tribe. Nay, let me finish! Fa and Rigat and Faelia . . . hundreds of men and women . . . they sacrificed their lives for this land."

"And you mean to do the same?" Hircha demanded.

"Listen to—"

"You'll never get past their camp."

"One man. Alone. Who looks like a Zheroso in the dark? Of course I can."

"If you're doing this," his mam began in a reedy

whisper, "because you don't want to leave me . . . or because you believe you're somehow unfit . . ."

"I'm doing this because I want my life to mean something. Fa called me a healer of spirits. Maybe I got that from you, Mam. But I always wondered what part of Fa lived in me. I think I've finally discovered that."

He took a deep breath. "In the days to come, our people are going to need my power to heal. But they also need to hear the tales. Not just the ones about Darak Spirit-Hunter and Griane the Healer, but Fellgair's tale and Rigat's. And Temet's and Faelia's. Tales of our vision quests and our rites. Simple tales about the way we live, the truths we believe in. Those are the stories I want to tell. I'll go village to village, like Fa did when he was looking for recruits."

Hircha shook her head. "Who will listen to what a Zheroso has to say? Even if you manage to convince them that you're Darak's son, you'll only revive the old accusations that got you cast out of the tribe."

"Hua will listen. And Eilin. I might even be able to find Idrian and Nuala. They all know me. And trust me. They'll tell their tribes who I am. What I do. And we'll find others. Tree-Fathers and Grain-Mothers who can help heal the spirits of the wounded. Memory-Keepers who can help preserve the tales and teach them to others. There may only be a few in the beginning. But isn't that how Temet started? And Fa? In time, there will be more. And if the gods are kind, we'll keep our ways—and our truths—alive."

"But we need you, too," Callie protested. "As our Tree-Father. Our chief."

"Holtik will be a better chief. And young Arun already has the makings of a shaman. Please, Callie. Try and understand. More than anything in the world, I want to come with you. But someone must do this."

"Then it should be me. I'm the Memory-Keeper."

"And a husband. Soon to be a father. And you're the heart of the tribe. Without you, they'll be lost."

"And without you, I'll be lost!" Callie cried.

"No," Fellgair said. "You've always known your path. Keirith has finally found his. And today is not a farewell. As long as there's a Grain-Mother or a Tree-Father to open the gateway, you will find each other."

Keirith rose and opened his arms to his brother. "Please help me," he whispered. "I can't do this without you."

He felt Callie nod, although his shoulders continued to shake. Then his brother straightened. Callused fingers cupped his cheeks. Chapped lips pressed lightly against his.

"We'll find each other," Callie promised. "In the grove of the First Forest or the Summerlands or the Forever Isles."

Keirith heard the crowd stirring and reluctantly released his brother. When he saw Ennit hobbling forward, leaning on Lisula, he knew it was time.

Ennit bent to hug Mam. "Tell Darak I love him. And that Lisula and I will join you soon."

Lisula whispered something that made Mam smile. Then she straightened. "Lord Trickster. Are you ready?"

"As ready as I'll ever be, my dear."

"You don't have to move. I'll open the gateway near you. And remain on this side with Nedia, while Barasa leads the way. Is there anything I should know? Or do?"

"Just make sure they move quickly."

"They will." She crossed her hands over her heart and bowed. "Bless you, Lord Trickster. We will always remember you in our prayers." Her gaze met Mam's once more. Then she and Ennit walked slowly back to the tribe.

Hircha's fingers dug into his arm. "You're sure?"

"Aye." Keirith brushed the untidy hair off her face. For a moment, they simply stared at each other. "No farewells," he whispered. "You and I . . . our lives were bound together back in Pilozhat. And they always will be. No matter where we are."

He leaned forward to kiss her, but Hircha pushed him away. "No farewells."

Her coldness shocked him. This could be the last time they ever saw each other. But she just stood there, staring off at the forest as if he had ceased to exist.

Numbly, he watched Callie kiss their mam and carefully slip Fa's bag of charms free. Callie lifted her hand and pressed her palm against the bag of charms. Then he straightened, swiping at his cheeks.

"The gods go with you," Keirith whispered.

"And you." Blindly, Callie reached for Ela. She took his hand and led him toward the others.

Deep blue rimmed the eastern horizon as the three priestesses filed sunwise around the stand of trees. Their soft chants ebbed and flowed as they walked past Keirith, as soothing as the cool morning air. But his body was trembling with fear and anticipation.

Please, gods. Let it work.

Hand in hand, the rest of the tribe followed the priestesses, circling the trees like stately dancers. Everything they possessed was strapped to their backs or slung across their chests so their hands would be free to grip those next in line. In the uncertain light, they looked like creatures from another world, bows and spears jutting above the men's heads like horns, bundles creating large humps on their backs. The smaller children clung like leeches to the men and women who carried them. The older ones stumbled along, still half-asleep, guided silently by the adults.

Lisula and Nedia dropped out of the long line to flank Barasa. Lisula's lips moved. Behind her, the sky shuddered as a dark sliver pierced the blue. She nodded to Barasa. With Wila's hand clasped in hers, the Grain-Mother stepped forward and vanished.

One by one, they followed. It was like watching the history of his people—of his life—pass before him. Three generations of the children of the Oak and Holly. People who had sprung from a dozen different tribes. Some he had known since childhood, others he had only come to know in the last moon. All bound together by determination and courage and dedication to their gods.

Holtik, straight and fearless. Mother Narthi, white hair blazing in the gloom. Mirili, with her granddaughter slung in a makeshift sling across her chest. Dirna, with little Luimi clinging to her hand. Duba and Alada, leading the rest of their orphans. Owan, leaning on Takinel's shoulder.

Although they could not raise their hands, they all paused as they neared the front of the line to cast a farewell glance at his mam, little realizing they were bidding him good-bye as well. But when the time came to enter the portal, none hesitated; they had all witnessed their Grain-Mother and Tree-Father crossing into the First Forest. Even the ewe trotted blithely beside Lorthan.

Keirith stood beside his mam, his hand upraised, his vision blurring. Then he heard a grunt and glanced down.

Fellgair's eyes were closed, his forehead creased in concentration. A bead of sweat trickled down his face. Keirith glanced back at the dwindling line and saw Ennit draw up short. Fearing Dugan had balked, he raced forward, but after a few steps, he, too, checked his stride.

The air in front of Ennit roiled, as if a whirlpool had opened between the sky and the ground.

"Don't stop," Keirith whispered. "Fellgair's holding the way open."

Ennit nodded and tugged on Dugan's lead. The ram let out a loud bleat. Cursing, Keirith added his strength to Ennit's, but Dugan refused to budge. Finally, he circled behind the ram and pushed. Another pair of hands appeared on the wide rump.

He looked up into Callie's straining face. His brother suddenly grinned. "Add this to your tale."

They both froze at the blast of a Zherosi kankh.

"Poke him with a stick," Keirith said, then raced for the west rim of the hill.

Hircha was already crouched among the rocks. Even before she pulled him down beside her, he could hear the shouting.

Sentries raced along the tree line. They were too far away for Keirith to make out their words, but there was no mistaking the upraised swords, pointing at the hilltop.

He glanced over his shoulder. He could make out the two priestesses silhouetted against the rosy sky, but surely from the base of the hill, they would be indistinguishable from the pines.

Another kankh blasted the early morning stillness. Shadows moved among the trees. A cluster of helmeted figures emerged to scan the hilltop.

Dugan let out a bellow nearly as loud as the kankhs. Every head jerked toward the sound. One of the men drew a sword and shouted something. Within moments, a line of warriors marched out of the trees.

"Ennit and his gods-cursed sheep!" Abandoning any attempt to remain hidden, Keirith tugged Hircha to her feet. Together, they ran back to the tribe.

Ennit was on the ground, clinging to Dugan's lead with Ela. The last of the women cautiously circled them and vanished through the portal. The air was swirling madly—

foaming like water over rocks—but even as Keirith watched, the portal shrank until the taller boys had to duck to enter.

"Leave him!" Keirith shouted at Ennit. "The Zherosi are coming!"

Ennit's grip slackened at the same moment that Callie thumped Dugan on the rump with a branch. With an outraged bleat, the ram leaped over Ennit's legs and bolted through the portal.

"Hurry!" Keirith shouted to Ela.

"Not without Callie!"

"I'll be right behind you," he assured her. "Go! The portal won't hold much longer."

Nedia's chanting was ragged with effort; even Lisula was clutching the trunk of a tree for support. Still, Ennit hesitated. "What about Griane? If the Zherosi find her—"

"Keirith will protect her," Hircha said. "And Fellgair. For mercy's sake, Ennit, go!"

Keirith squeezed Ennit's shoulder and helped him to his feet. Braden ducked through the portal. Ela waved frantically and followed. Ennit whispered, "Maker keep you safe," and vanished.

"Go, Callie," Hircha said. "Quickly."

"What about you?"

"I'm staying."

A kankh blared, louder than before, and an answering roar rose from the Zherosi.

"Don't be a fool!" Keirith shouted.

"I'm staying!"

She wrenched free of Callie and pushed him through the portal. Keirith caught a last glimpse of his white face as he disappeared.

Nedia swayed. Keirith shoved her toward Hircha. "Help her through! I'm going for Mam."

He raced to his mother, but when he bent to lift her, she frowned. "What are you doing?"

"Taking you to the portal. I won't leave you to the Zherosi."

"What can they do to me?"

"Kill you!"

"I'm dying, Keirith. Let me be."

He pulled her arm around his neck. Her left hand flailed helplessly. "I can't leave him."

Fellgair's breath came in short, hoarse gasps. Only a faint trace of gold remained in the muddy depths of his eyes. His mouth moved, but Keirith couldn't make out the words.

"Get Lisula through," his mam whispered. "Before it's too late."

"Mam . . ."

"Please."

He straightened, only to see the portal flicker uncertainly.

It wasn't supposed to be this way. His mam deserved a peaceful death. Lisula deserved to be with Ennit and her family. And Hircha . . .

Please, Maker.

He didn't know if he was praying that Hircha would go or that Fellgair would find a hidden reserve of power or simply for it all to be over.

As he hurried toward Lisula, a concussive blast of air sent her reeling. The sky split open. Through the jagged rent, Keirith glimpsed Ennit's terrified face. Ennit thrust his hand through the gap and shouted Lisula's name. She dragged herself to her knees, reaching for him.

The gap began to close, as if some divine hand was weaving the sky together again.

"Help me!" Keirith shouted to Hircha.

They shoved Lisula hard, and she tumbled through the portal. Ennit caught her and pulled her into his arms. Her head came up. She opened her mouth to speak. And then there was only blue sky before him.

Keirith sank onto his knees. He looked up into Hircha's eyes, bluer even than the sky.

"Why?" he asked.

"Don't be a fool."

From the hillside came a shouted command to straighten the line. Dear gods, they were close.

Fellgair lay slumped across his mam's lap. For one terrifying moment, Keirith thought he was dead. Then he heard the weak pants and let out a sigh of relief. He knelt beside them and took his mother's hand.

"Go," she whispered.

"I can't just leave you."

"You must."

"I'll carry you to the grotto."

"There's no time. Keirith. Please."

He could hear the sharp crack of stones ricocheting off boulders, a man shouting for the archers to move up. Still, he clung to his mam's hand. He told himself to remember everything: her swollen knuckles, hard as pebbles; her upper lip caught between her teeth; her clear, steady gaze, as fierce as the will that commanded her failing body.

"Mam . . ."

"I know. I love you, too."

He raised her hand and kissed the palm, breathing in the faint scent of herbs, the scent that had always meant home and safety and Mam. And then he recalled the words his father had spoken that final day before they had left the village.

"Just tell her that you love her. You do, you know. And sometimes, a man needs to say those words. Especially if he doesn't know when he'll get the chance again."

He squeezed her hand gently. "I love you, Mam. I always have. And I always will."

Her eyes filled as she smiled. A tear slipped down her cheek. He brushed it away and laid her hand atop Fellgair's. Then he staggered to his feet and lurched off.

Hircha steadied him, eased his pack onto his back, took his hand. When they reached the stony path that led down the northern face of the hill, he paused to look back.

The first rays of sunlight bathed the two still figures in a rosy glow. Birds welcomed the dawn with a burst of song, only to be drowned out by the voices of the Zherosi.

Not yet. Give them a peaceful death, Maker.

Hircha tugged his hand, and he stumbled after her, following the path she chose, leaning against boulders when she paused, crouching when she pulled him down.

"Look."

Peering between two boulders, he saw a disorderly line of warriors struggling up the northern slope.

"The empty grotto," Hircha whispered. "There's nowhere else."

Ignoring the pebbles that dug cruelly into their hands and knees, they crawled forward. His leather sheath thud-

ded dully against the stones. Behind him, he could hear
Hircha's hoarse breathing and the occasional skitter of
loose pebbles. He dared another glance at the warriors, but
they needed all their concentration to keep their footing
on the shifting stones.

He had to squirm out of his pack in order to belly under
the pine spar. Hircha shoved her bundle toward him, then
clawed her way over the pebbles. He tossed the packs aside
and pulled her into the grotto.

They sat there, panting. Then he seized the pine boughs
that the men had used as bedding and laid them near the
spar, carefully placing them to hide the deep cuts made by
the axes. In the full light of day, the ruse would fool no
one, but while the sun was still low, the Zherosi might
simply see the broken branches and never notice the grotto
hidden behind them.

He motioned Hircha against the wall of the cave. She
ripped the leather thong from her disordered hair. Gripping
it between her teeth, she calmly wove a tight braid and tied
it with the thong. Then she drew her dagger and gave him
a fierce nod.

Together, they waited.

The rough bark of the pine scraped her back, but she was
too tired to move. Too tired even to squeeze the hand
beneath hers.

A racking breath shuddered through Fellgair and into
her.

"Soon," Griane whispered.

The voices of the Zherosi were much louder now. Such
an ugly, guttural language. As if they were all choking on
the words. Or perhaps that was Fellgair.

"Awful. Being human."

"And beautiful. I wish you had known that part."

"It was enough . . . to know you."

The newly risen sun slanted across them, but it held no
warmth. Even Fellgair's body, sprawled across hers, failed
to drive away the chill.

"Forgive . . ."

"Aye. Rest."

Another racking breath shuddered through them. She couldn't tell if it was his or hers.

Where did fallen gods go when they died? Did they cross the rainbow bridge into the silver branches of the World Tree? Or—being human—did their spirits fly to the sunlit shores of the Forever Isles? Or tumble into Chaos? Surely, the Maker would forgive Fellgair's interference in the affairs of this world and would secure a safe place for him in the next.

But what of Rigat?

Please, Maker. I know he made mistakes. Many mistakes. He killed men—and women. He didn't always use his power wisely. But he was so young. And he did try to build a better world for your people. Remember that—and forgive him.

Fellgair's body heaved. Huge, terrified eyes stared up into hers.

"Don't be afraid. I'll be with you."

He whispered her name. And then Darak's. His eyes widened, as if in surprise. For a heartbeat, golden fire flared in their muddy depths. Then a deep sigh eased free and the frail, tortured body relaxed.

A tear oozed down Griane's cheek and splashed on the still face. The Trickster was gone. And the world had changed forever.

"In time, another Trickster will emerge. Where would the world be without one?"

But for her, there would only be one. The Trickster who had teased her in the First Forest. The fox-man who had lain with her in the Summerlands. The god who had become a man and had shared—if only for a short while—the beauty and the pain and the fear of being human.

The voices of the Zherosi were becoming fainter. Perhaps they had decided to leave. She hoped so. She would like to die knowing Keirith and Hircha were safe.

Keirith loved her. She had always known that, of course. But it eased her to recall his words, to know that he had forgiven her for the choice she had made so long ago.

The ground rumbled as it had the evening Rigat caused the rockslide. But her boy was gone, so it must only be a storm approaching. The sun was still shining, though. Its light grew more brilliant with every heartbeat. Before her watering eyes, the stunted pines blurred into a smear of green and brown, mingling with the translucent blue of the sky.

Once again, she was flying. Flying into the sun. Dizzy with the giddy exhilaration of it. Insubstantial as a cloud.

Was this what Keirith had felt when he had flown with his eagle so many years ago? No wonder he had mourned when he was forbidden to fly again. And how foolish they had all been to imagine that such a glorious experience could ever be evil.

I must tell Gortin when I see him.

But of course, he would have realized it already.

In the distance, she heard voices, but they were too far away to make out the words. Warmth enveloped her like a loving embrace, banishing the pervasive cold. The tang of pine filled the air. And the sweet aroma of honeysuckle.

A shadow blocked the sun, and she frowned. Then the shadow moved.

His face—impossibly young—filled her vision. His voice—caught between a laugh and a sob—spoke her name. His hands—whole and strong and perfect again—reached down to cup her cheeks.

Darak smiled. And Griane knew she had come home at last.

Chapter 69

KEIRITH HEARD SOMEONE shout that he had found a cave. Another shout—much closer—and then shocked cries as the Zherosi discovered Rigat's body. A voice rose above the clamor, ordering four men to carry the Son of Zhe down the hill.

Sandals crunched against pebbles. The light from the entrance faded and swelled as figures slipped past their hiding place. Like clouds drifting past the sun, Keirith thought, and wondered how that fanciful idea could occur to him at such a moment.

A voice shouted, "Wait! I think there's something here!"

To his left, the pine boughs rustled. He flattened himself against the wall, ignoring the rocks that dug painfully into his back. As more light filtered into the grotto, his fingers tightened on the hilt of his sword.

"Another cave!" the same voice said. "It looks empty, but—"

"Stand back. I'll go in first."

Keirith closed his eyes. Why—of all the Zherosi—did it have to be this one who discovered them, this one he'd have to kill first? He wondered if Fellgair had seen this confrontation in his web of possibilities, and wished the Trickster could have told him the likely outcome.

He opened his eyes, preparing himself. Impatient hands ripped away the last of the pine boughs. The light suddenly dimmed.

He's standing in the entrance.

The tip of a bronze blade appeared in the gloom, belly-high. A sandaled foot took a cautious step forward, then hesitated.

Korim thrust his head inside. Still blinded by early morning sunlight, he blinked uncertainly and peered around.

Perhaps he caught the gleam of Hircha's fair hair or smelled their sweat. Suddenly, he whipped around, sword drawn back for a killing slash. Framed in the light, Keirith saw recognition widen the dark eyes.

He had never sensed that moment before dawn. Never felt the fear or the hope or the tremulous anticipation when the world hovered between night and day. Staring back at Korim, he finally understood what his father had tried so hard to describe.

"Skalel?"

The sword point wavered, then steadied. Korim's mouth tightened. Keirith tensed, ready to parry the blow.

For a few days, their lives had touched, a boy and a man out of place among their people. They had shared memories of their childhoods as well as their doubts and fears.

Like him, Korim had lived his life in his father's shadow.
And like him, Korim must still be grappling with his father's death, trying to find his place in a world that had
suddenly shifted under his feet. But for all they had in
common, Korim was still a child of Zheros while he was a
child of the Oak and Holly.

Only five paces separated them, but the gulf that yawned
between them was immeasurable.

"Skalel!"

The dark eyes continued to watch him as Korim straightened. "Just some discarded bundles of clothing. Nothing to
interest us. Tell the Komal."

A fist thumped against leather. The crunch of pebbles
slowly faded. Outside, voices still shouted and cursed—in
consternation, in wonder, in anger—but in the grotto, it
was utterly silent.

*How do you thank someone for giving you your life? For
giving you hope?*

Keirith bowed, as formally as if he stood in the throne
room of Pilozhat. Korim returned the bow, just as formally.
Then he ducked out of the grotto and walked away.

They waited, straining to hear the occasional shout and the
tramp of marching feet, gauging the passage of time by the
light outside. When a kankh blared three times, Keirith
counted to one hundred, then crawled to the entrance of
the grotto. He lay there, watching the column of Zherosi
march north along the stream. When the last figure disappeared into the trees, he whispered a brief prayer of thanks
and held out his hand to Hircha.

As they crested the hilltop, they were momentarily
blinded by the sun's brilliance. Then they saw the two figures by the pine.

Fellgair lay across her lap, his face upturned to the sun,
his eyes wide and empty. Mam slumped sideways, one hand
outflung as if reaching for something. Her face was peaceful, though. The half-open mouth might have been caught
in a gasp or a laugh. He wanted to believe it was a laugh,
a joyous laugh when she found Fa waiting for her.

They carried them to the grotto where Rigat had died and laid them side by side on the wolfskins. Keirith repeated the prayer of opening, although he hoped their spirits had already flown to the Forever Isles. Then they simply stood in silence.

"How do you begin a new life?" he wondered.

"One step at a time, I guess."

They shouldered their packs and slowly descended the hill. The heaviness of grief lay upon them. Uncertainty lay ahead. And the half-formed idea that had kept him from following his tribe to the First Forest seemed like a boy's romantic notion.

But romantic or not, impossible or not, the idea still kindled a flame within him. And when he recalled Korim, bowing to him in the grotto, the flame burned brighter. Malaq had dreamed of peace between their people. So had Rigat. And even the Trickster. Neither the god nor his son had been strong enough to realize that dream, but if there were enough men like Korim and Malaq, perhaps it was still possible.

Until then, he would walk the land, healing the spirits of the wounded and telling the tales of their people. And Hircha would walk beside him.

"Keirith."

He looked up from filling his waterskin, following Hircha's pointing finger.

Far above them, an eagle soared. Three times, it circled the hilltop. Then, with a graceful flap of its majestic wings, it flew west.

They watched it until it was little more than a black dot against the cloudless sky. Then their eyes met in wordless communion and they rose.

They turned their backs on the barren hill and followed the eagle. West to Eilin's village. To Idrian's and Nuala's. West to the distant sea—and Hua.

Only the gods knew how long their journey would take. Or if his dream would ever be realized. But the breeze at his back urged him onward and the soft mulch of pine needles eased every step. The stream gurgled encouragement and the birds sang of new beginnings. Warmed by Bel's sunlight and Hircha's smile, it seemed to Keirith that the world teemed with life and possibilities and hope.

Violette Malan

The Novels of Dhulyn and Parno

THE SLEEPING GOD

978-0-7564-0484-0

new in trade paperback:
THE SOLDIER KING

978-0-7564-0516-8

Raves for Violette Malan:

"Believable characters and graceful
storytelling."
—*Library Journal*

"Fantasy fans should brace themselves:
the world is about to discover Violette Malan."
—*The Barnes & Noble Review*

To Order Call: 1-800-788-6262

www.dawbooks.com

DAW 58

Sherwood Smith

Inda

"A powerful beginning to a very promising series by a writer who is making her bid to be a major fantasist. By the time I finished, I was so captured by this book that it lingered for days afterward. I had lived inside these characters, inside this world, and I was unwilling to let go of it. That, I think, is the mark of a major work of fiction...you owe it to yourself to read *Inda*." -Orson Scott Card

INDA
978-0-7564-0422-2

THE FOX
978-0-7564-0483-3

KING'S SHIELD
978-0-7564-0500-7

And arriving in hardcover August 2009...

TREASON'S SHORE
978-0-7564-0573-1

To Order Call: 1-800-788-6262
www.dawbooks.com

MICHELLE WEST
The House War

"Fans will be delighted with this return to the vivid and detailed universe of the *Sacred Hunt* and the *Sun Sword* series.... In a richly woven world, and with a cast of characters that range from traumatized street kids to the wealthy heads of highest houses in Averalaan, West pulls no punches as she hooks readers in with her bold and descriptive narrative." —*Quill & Quire*

THE HIDDEN CITY   0-7564-0470-3

and don't miss ***The Sun Sword***
THE BROKEN CROWN   0-88677-740-1
THE UNCROWNED KING   0-88677-801-9
THE SHINING COURT   0-88677-837-8
SEA OF SORROWS   0-88677-978-8
THE RIVEN SHIELD   0-7564-0146-7
THE SUN SWORD   0-7564-0170-2

and ***The Sacred Hunt***
HUNTER'S OATH   0-88677-681-7
HUNTER'S DEATH   0-88677-706-7

To Order Call: 1-800-788-6262
www.dawbooks.com

DAW 41

Tanya Huff

The Finest in Fantasy

To Order Call: 1-800-788-6262
www.dawbooks.com

KATE ELLIOTT
Crown of Stars

"An entirely captivating affair"—*Publishers Weekly*

In a world where bloody conflicts rage and sorcery holds sway both human and other-than-human forces vie for supremacy. In this land, Alain, a young man seeking the destiny promised him by the Lady of Battles, and Liath, a young woman gifted with a power that can alter history, are swept up in a world-shaking conflict for the survival of humanity.

KING'S DRAGON	0-88677-771-2
PRINCE OF DOGS	0-88677-816-6
THE BURNING STONE	0-88677-815-8
CHILD OF FLAME	0-88677-892-1
THE GATHERING STORM	0-7564-0132-1
IN THE RUINS	0-7564-0268-9
CROWN OF STARS	0-7564-0326-X

To Order Call: 1-800-788-6262
www.dawbooks.com

SHADOWPLAY

The Second Volume of *Shadowmarch*

Tad Williams

978-0-7564-0471-0

And don't miss:
SHADOWMARCH Volume One: 978-0-7564-0359-1

To Order Call: 1-800-788-6262
www.dawbooks.com